# The House of Mirth & The Age of Innocence

# The House of Mirth
# &
# The Age of Innocence

by Edith Wharton



This book is a product of its time and does not reflect the same values as it would if it were written today. Parents might wish to discuss with their children how views on race have changed before allowing them to read this classic work.



Wilder Publications, LLC.
PO Box 3005
Radford VA 24143-3005

ISBN 10: 1-61720-086-7
ISBN 13: 978-1-61720-086-1

# The House of Mirth

# Book 1
## Chapter 1

Selden paused in surprise. In the afternoon rush of the Grand Central Station his eyes had been refreshed by the sight of Miss Lily Bart.

It was a Monday in early September, and he was returning to his work from a hurried dip into the country; but what was Miss Bart doing in town at that season? If she had appeared to be catching a train, he might have inferred that he had come on her in the act of transition between one and another of the country-houses which disputed her presence after the close of the Newport season; but her desultory air perplexed him. She stood apart from the crowd, letting it drift by her to the platform or the street, and wearing an air of irresolution which might, as he surmised, be the mask of a very definite purpose. It struck him at once that she was waiting for some one, but he hardly knew why the idea arrested him. There was nothing new about Lily Bart, yet he could never see her without a faint movement of interest: it was characteristic of her that she always roused speculation, that her simplest acts seemed the result of far-reaching intentions.

An impulse of curiosity made him turn out of his direct line to the door, and stroll past her. He knew that if she did not wish to be seen she would contrive to elude him; and it amused him to think of putting her skill to the test.

"Mr. Selden—what good luck!"

She came forward smiling, eager almost, in her resolve to intercept him. One or two persons, in brushing past them, lingered to look; for Miss Bart was a figure to arrest even the suburban traveller rushing to his last train.

Selden had never seen her more radiant. Her vivid head, relieved against the dull tints of the crowd, made her more conspicuous than in a ball-room, and under her dark hat and veil she regained the girlish smoothness, the purity of tint, that she was beginning to lose after eleven years of late hours and indefatigable dancing. Was it really eleven years, Selden found himself wondering, and had she indeed reached the nine-and-twentieth birthday with which her rivals credited her?

"What luck!" she repeated. "How nice of you to come to my rescue!"

He responded joyfully that to do so was his mission in life, and asked what form the rescue was to take.

"Oh, almost any—even to sitting on a bench and talking to me. One sits out a cotillion—why not sit out a train? It isn't a bit hotter here than in Mrs. Van Osburgh's conservatory—and some of the women are not a bit uglier." She broke off, laughing, to explain that she had come up to town from Tuxedo, on her way to the Gus Trenors' at Bellomont, and had missed the three-fifteen train to Rhinebeck. "And there isn't another till half-past five." She consulted the little jewelled watch among her laces. "Just two hours to wait. And I don't know what to do with myself. My maid came up this morning to do some shopping for me, and was to go on to Bellomont at one o'clock, and my aunt's house is closed, and I don't know a soul in town." She glanced plaintively about the station. "It IS hotter than Mrs. Van Osburgh's, after all. If you can spare the time, do take me somewhere for a breath of air."

He declared himself entirely at her disposal: the adventure struck him as diverting. As a spectator, he had always enjoyed Lily Bart; and his course lay so far out of her orbit that it amused him to be drawn for a moment into the sudden intimacy which her proposal implied.

"Shall we go over to Sherry's for a cup of tea?"

She smiled assentingly, and then made a slight grimace.

"So many people come up to town on a Monday—one is sure to meet a lot of bores. I'm as old as the hills, of course, and it ought not to make any difference; but if *I'm* old enough, you're not," she objected gaily. "I'm dying for tea—but isn't there a quieter place?"

He answered her smile, which rested on him vividly. Her discretions interested him almost as much as her imprudences: he was so sure that both were part of the same carefully-elaborated plan. In judging Miss Bart, he had always made use of the "argument from design."

"The resources of New York are rather meagre," he said; "but I'll find a hansom first, and then we'll invent something." He led her through the throng of returning holiday-makers, past sallow-faced girls in preposterous hats, and flat-chested women struggling with paper bundles and palm-leaf fans. Was it possible that she belonged to the same race? The dinginess, the crudity of this average section of womanhood made him feel how highly specialized she was.

A rapid shower had cooled the air, and clouds still hung refreshingly over the moist street.

"How delicious! Let us walk a little," she said as they emerged from the station.

They turned into Madison Avenue and began to stroll northward. As she moved beside him, with her long light step, Selden was conscious of taking a luxurious pleasure in her nearness: in the modelling of her little ear, the crisp upward wave of her hair—was it ever so slightly brightened by art?—and the thick planting of her straight black lashes. Everything about her was at once vigorous and exquisite, at once strong and fine. He had a confused sense that she must have cost a great deal to make, that a great many dull and ugly people must, in some mysterious way, have been sacrificed to produce her. He was aware that the qualities distinguishing her from the herd of her sex were chiefly external: as though a fine glaze of beauty and fastidiousness had been applied to vulgar clay. Yet the analogy left him unsatisfied, for a coarse texture will not take a high finish; and was it not possible that the material was fine, but that circumstance had fashioned it into a futile shape?

As he reached this point in his speculations the sun came out, and her lifted parasol cut off his enjoyment. A moment or two later she paused with a sigh.

"Oh, dear, I'm so hot and thirsty—and what a hideous place New York is!" She looked despairingly up and down the dreary thoroughfare. "Other cities put on their best clothes in summer, but New York seems to sit in its shirtsleeves." Her eyes wandered down one of the side-streets. "Someone has had the humanity to plant a few trees over there. Let us go into the shade."

"I am glad my street meets with your approval," said Selden as they turned the corner.

"Your street? Do you live here?"

She glanced with interest along the new brick and limestone house-fronts, fantastically varied in obedience to the American craving for novelty, but fresh and inviting with their awnings and flower-boxes.

"Ah, yes—to be sure: *The Benedick*. What a nice-looking building! I don't think I've ever seen it before." She looked across at the flat-house with its marble porch and pseudo-Georgian facade. "Which are your windows? Those with the awnings down?"

"On the top floor—yes."

"And that nice little balcony is yours? How cool it looks up there!"

He paused a moment. "Come up and see," he suggested. "I can give you a cup of tea in no time—and you won't meet any bores."

Her colour deepened—she still had the art of blushing at the right time—but she took the suggestion as lightly as it was made.

"Why not? It's too tempting—I'll take the risk," she declared.

"Oh, I'm not dangerous," he said in the same key. In truth, he had never liked her as well as at that moment. He knew she had accepted without afterthought: he could never be a factor in her calculations, and there was a surprise, a refreshment almost, in the spontaneity of her consent.

On the threshold he paused a moment, feeling for his latchkey.

"There's no one here; but I have a servant who is supposed to come in the mornings, and it's just possible he may have put out the tea-things and provided some cake."

He ushered her into a slip of a hall hung with old prints. She noticed the letters and notes heaped on the table among his gloves and sticks; then she found herself in a small library, dark but cheerful, with its walls of books, a pleasantly faded Turkey rug, a littered desk and, as he had foretold, a tea-tray on a low table near the window. A breeze had sprung up, swaying inward the muslin curtains, and bringing a fresh scent of mignonette and petunias from the flower-box on the balcony.

Lily sank with a sigh into one of the shabby leather chairs.

"How delicious to have a place like this all to one's self! What a miserable thing it is to be a woman." She leaned back in a luxury of discontent.

Selden was rummaging in a cupboard for the cake.

"Even women," he said, "have been known to enjoy the privileges of a flat."

"Oh, governesses—or widows. But not girls—not poor, miserable, marriageable girls!"

"I even know a girl who lives in a flat."

She sat up in surprise. "You do?"

"I do," he assured her, emerging from the cupboard with the sought-for cake.

"Oh, I know—you mean Gerty Farish." She smiled a little unkindly. "But I said *marriageable*—and besides, she has a horrid little place, and no maid, and such queer things to eat. Her cook does the washing and the food tastes of soap. I should hate that, you know."

"You shouldn't dine with her on wash-days," said Selden, cutting the cake.

They both laughed, and he knelt by the table to light the lamp under the kettle, while she measured out the tea into a little tea-pot of green glaze. As he watched her hand, polished as a bit of old ivory, with its slender pink nails, and the sapphire bracelet slipping over her wrist, he was struck with the irony of suggesting to her such a life as his cousin Gertrude Farish had chosen. She was so evidently the victim of the civilization which had produced her, that the links of her bracelet seemed like manacles chaining her to her fate.

She seemed to read his thought. "It was horrid of me to say that of Gerty," she said with charming compunction. "I forgot she was your cousin. But we're so different, you know: she likes being good, and I like being happy. And besides, she is free and I am not. If I were, I daresay I could manage to be happy even in her flat. It must be pure bliss to arrange the furniture just as one likes, and give all the horrors to the ash-man. If I could only do over my aunt's drawing-room I know I should be a better woman."

"Is it so very bad?" he asked sympathetically.

She smiled at him across the tea-pot which she was holding up to be filled.

"That shows how seldom you come there. Why don't you come oftener?"

"When I do come, it's not to look at Mrs. Peniston's furniture."

"Nonsense," she said. "You don't come at all—and yet we get on so well when we meet."

"Perhaps that's the reason," he answered promptly. "I'm afraid I haven't any cream, you know—shall you mind a slice of lemon instead?"

"I shall like it better." She waited while he cut the lemon and dropped a thin disk into her cup. "But that is not the reason," she insisted.

"The reason for what?"

"For your never coming." She leaned forward with a shade of perplexity in her charming eyes. "I wish I knew—I wish I could make you out. Of course I know there are men who don't like me—one can tell that at a glance. And there are others who are afraid of me: they think I want to marry them." She smiled up at him frankly. "But I don't think you dislike me—and you can't possibly think I want to marry you."

"No—I absolve you of that," he agreed.

"Well, then—?"

He had carried his cup to the fireplace, and stood leaning against the chimney-piece and looking down on her with an air of indolent amusement. The provocation in her eyes increased his amusement—he had not supposed she would waste her powder on such small game; but perhaps she was only keeping her hand in; or perhaps a girl of her type had no conversation but of the personal kind. At any rate, she was amazingly pretty, and he had asked her to tea and must live up to his obligations.

"Well, then," he said with a plunge, "perhaps *that's* the reason."

"What?"

"The fact that you don't want to marry me. Perhaps I don't regard it as such a strong inducement to go and see you." He felt a slight shiver down his spine as he ventured this, but her laugh reassured him.

"Dear Mr. Selden, that wasn't worthy of you. It's stupid of you to make love to me, and it isn't like you to be stupid." She leaned back, sipping her tea with an air so enchantingly judicial that, if they had been in her aunt's drawing-room, he might almost have tried to disprove her deduction.

"Don't you see," she continued, "that there are men enough to say pleasant things to me, and that what I want is a friend who won't be afraid to say disagreeable ones when I need them? Sometimes I have fancied you might be that friend—I don't know why, except that you are neither a prig nor a bounder, and that I shouldn't have to pretend with you or be on my guard against you." Her voice had dropped to a note of seriousness, and she sat gazing up at him with the troubled gravity of a child.

"You don't know how much I need such a friend," she said. "My aunt is full of copy-book axioms, but they were all meant to apply to conduct in the early fifties. I always feel that to live up to them would include wearing book-muslin with gigot sleeves. And the other women—my best friends—well, they use me or abuse me; but they don't care a straw what happens to me. I've been about too long—people are getting tired of me; they are beginning to say I ought to marry."

There was a moment's pause, during which Selden meditated one or two replies calculated to add a momentary zest to the situation; but he rejected them in favour of the simple question: "Well, why don't you?"

She coloured and laughed. "Ah, I see you *are* a friend after all, and that is one of the disagreeable things I was asking for."

"It wasn't meant to be disagreeable," he returned amicably. "Isn't marriage your vocation? Isn't it what you're all brought up for?"

She sighed. "I suppose so. What else is there?"

"Exactly. And so why not take the plunge and have it over?"

She shrugged her shoulders. "You speak as if I ought to marry the first man who came along."

"I didn't mean to imply that you are as hard put to it as that. But there must be some one with the requisite qualifications."

She shook her head wearily. "I threw away one or two good chances when I first came out—I suppose every girl does; and you know I am horribly poor—and very expensive. I must have a great deal of money."

Selden had turned to reach for a cigarette-box on the mantelpiece. "What's become of Dillworth?" he asked.

"Oh, his mother was frightened—she was afraid I should have all the family jewels reset. And she wanted me to promise that I wouldn't do over the drawing-room."

"The very thing you are marrying for!"

"Exactly. So she packed him off to India."

"Hard luck—but you can do better than Dillworth."

He offered the box, and she took out three or four cigarettes, putting one between her lips and slipping the others into a little gold case attached to her long pearl chain.

"Have I time? Just a whiff, then." She leaned forward, holding the tip of her cigarette to his. As she did so, he noted, with a purely impersonal enjoyment, how evenly the black lashes were set in her smooth white lids, and how the purplish shade beneath them melted into the pure pallour of the cheek.

She began to saunter about the room, examining the bookshelves between the puffs of her cigarette-smoke. Some of the volumes had the ripe tints of good tooling and old morocco, and her eyes lingered on them caressingly, not with the appreciation of the expert, but with the pleasure in agreeable tones and textures that was one of her inmost susceptibilities. Suddenly her expression changed from desultory enjoyment to active conjecture, and she turned to Selden with a question.

"You collect, don't you—you know about first editions and things?"

"As much as a man may who has no money to spend. Now and then I pick up something in the rubbish heap; and I go and look on at the big sales."

She had again addressed herself to the shelves, but her eyes now swept them inattentively, and he saw that she was preoccupied with a new idea.

"And Americana—do you collect Americana?"

Selden stared and laughed.

"No, that's rather out of my line. I'm not really a collector, you see; I simply like to have good editions of the books I am fond of."

She made a slight grimace. "And Americana are horribly dull, I suppose?"

"I should fancy so—except to the historian. But your real collector values a thing for its rarity. I don't suppose the buyers of Americana sit up reading them all night—old Jefferson Gryce certainly didn't."

She was listening with keen attention. "And yet they fetch fabulous prices, don't they? It seems so odd to want to pay a lot for an ugly badly-printed book that one is never going to read! And I suppose most of the owners of Americana are not historians either?"

"No; very few of the historians can afford to buy them. They have to use those in the public libraries or in private collections. It seems to be the mere rarity that attracts the average collector."

He had seated himself on an arm of the chair near which she was standing, and she continued to question him, asking which were the rarest volumes, whether the Jefferson Gryce collection was really considered the finest in the world, and what was the largest price ever fetched by a single volume.

It was so pleasant to sit there looking up at her, as she lifted now one book and then another from the shelves, fluttering the pages between her fingers, while her drooping profile was outlined against the warm background of old bindings, that he talked on without pausing to wonder at her sudden interest in so unsuggestive a subject. But he could never be long with her without trying to find a reason for what she was doing, and as she replaced his first edition of La Bruyere and turned away from the bookcases, he began to ask himself what she had been driving at. Her next question was not of a nature to enlighten him. She paused before him with a smile which seemed at once designed to admit him to her familiarity, and to remind him of the restrictions it imposed.

"Don't you ever mind," she asked suddenly, "not being rich enough to buy all the books you want?"

He followed her glance about the room, with its worn furniture and shabby walls.

"Don't I just? Do you take me for a saint on a pillar?"

"And having to work—do you mind that?"

"Oh, the work itself is not so bad—I'm rather fond of the law."

"No; but the being tied down: the routine—don't you ever want to get away, to see new places and people?"

"Horribly—especially when I see all my friends rushing to the steamer."

She drew a sympathetic breath. "But do you mind enough—to marry to get out of it?"

Selden broke into a laugh. "God forbid!" he declared.

She rose with a sigh, tossing her cigarette into the grate.

"Ah, there's the difference—a girl must, a man may if he chooses." She surveyed him critically. "Your coat's a little shabby—but who cares? It doesn't keep people from asking you to dine. If I were shabby no one would have me: a woman is asked out as much for her clothes as for herself. The clothes are the background, the frame, if you like: they don't make success, but they are a part of it. Who wants a dingy woman? We are expected to be pretty and well-dressed till we drop—and if we can't keep it up alone, we have to go into partnership."

Selden glanced at her with amusement: it was impossible, even with her lovely eyes imploring him, to take a sentimental view of her case.

"Ah, well, there must be plenty of capital on the look-out for such an investment. Perhaps you'll meet your fate tonight at the Trenors'."

She returned his look interrogatively.

"I thought you might be going there—oh, not in that capacity! But there are to be a lot of your set—Gwen Van Osburgh, the Wetheralls, Lady Cressida Raith—and the George Dorsets."

She paused a moment before the last name, and shot a query through her lashes; but he remained imperturbable.

"Mrs. Trenor asked me; but I can't get away till the end of the week; and those big parties bore me."

"Ah, so they do me," she exclaimed.

"Then why go?"

"It's part of the business—you forget! And besides, if I didn't, I should be playing bezique with my aunt at Richfield Springs."

"That's almost as bad as marrying Dillworth," he agreed, and they both laughed for pure pleasure in their sudden intimacy.

She glanced at the clock.

"Dear me! I must be off. It's after five."

She paused before the mantelpiece, studying herself in the mirror while she adjusted her veil. The attitude revealed the long slope of her slender sides, which gave a kind of wild-wood grace to her outline—as though she were a captured dryad subdued to the conventions of the drawing-room; and Selden reflected that it was the same streak of sylvan freedom in her nature that lent such savour to her artificiality.

He followed her across the room to the entrance-hall; but on the threshold she held out her hand with a gesture of leave-taking.

"It's been delightful; and now you will have to return my visit."

"But don't you want me to see you to the station?"

"No; good bye here, please."

She let her hand lie in his a moment, smiling up at him adorably.

"Good bye, then—and good luck at Bellomont!" he said, opening the door for her.

On the landing she paused to look about her. There were a thousand chances to one against her meeting anybody, but one could never tell, and she always paid for her rare indiscretions by a violent reaction of prudence. There was no one in sight, however, but a char-woman who was scrubbing the stairs. Her own stout person and its surrounding implements took up so much room that Lily, to pass her, had to gather up her skirts and brush against the wall. As she did so, the woman paused in her work and looked up curiously, resting her clenched red fists on the wet cloth she had just drawn from her pail. She had a broad sallow face, slightly pitted with small-pox, and thin straw-coloured hair through which her scalp shone unpleasantly.

"I beg your pardon," said Lily, intending by her politeness to convey a criticism of the other's manner.

The woman, without answering, pushed her pail aside, and continued to stare as Miss Bart swept by with a murmur of silken linings. Lily felt herself flushing under the look. What did the creature suppose? Could one never do the simplest, the most harmless thing, without subjecting one's self to some odious conjecture? Half way down the next flight, she smiled to think that a char-woman's stare should so perturb her. The poor thing was probably dazzled by such an unwonted apparition. But *were* such apparitions unwonted on Selden's stairs? Miss Bart was not familiar with the moral code of bachelors' flat-houses, and her colour rose again as it occurred to her that the woman's persistent gaze implied a groping among past associations. But she put aside the thought with a smile at her own fears, and hastened downward, wondering if she should find a cab short of Fifth Avenue.

Under the Georgian porch she paused again, scanning the street for a hansom. None was in sight, but as she reached the sidewalk she ran against a small glossy-looking man with a gardenia in his coat, who raised his hat with a surprised exclamation.

"Miss Bart? Well—of all people! This IS luck," he declared; and she caught a twinkle of amused curiosity between his screwed-up lids.

"Oh, Mr. Rosedale—how are you?" she said, perceiving that the irrepressible annoyance on her face was reflected in the sudden intimacy of his smile.

Mr. Rosedale stood scanning her with interest and approval. He was a plump rosy man of the blond Jewish type, with smart London clothes fitting him like upholstery, and small sidelong eyes which gave him the air of appraising people as if they were bric-a-brac. He glanced up interrogatively at the porch of the Benedick.

"Been up to town for a little shopping, I suppose?" he said, in a tone which had the familiarity of a touch.

Miss Bart shrank from it slightly, and then flung herself into precipitate explanations.

"Yes—I came up to see my dress-maker. I am just on my way to catch the train to the Trenors'."

"Ah—your dress-maker; just so," he said blandly. "I didn't know there were any dress-makers in the Benedick."

"The Benedick?" She looked gently puzzled. "Is that the name of this building?"

"Yes, that's the name: I believe it's an old word for bachelor, isn't it? I happen to own the building—that's the way I know." His smile deepened as he added with increasing assurance: "But you must let me take you to the station. The Trenors are at Bellomont, of course? You've barely time to catch the five-forty. The dress-maker kept you waiting, I suppose."

Lily stiffened under the pleasantry.

"Oh, thanks," she stammered; and at that moment her eye caught a hansom drifting down Madison Avenue, and she hailed it with a desperate gesture.

"You're very kind; but I couldn't think of troubling you," she said, extending her hand to Mr. Rosedale; and heedless of his protestations, she sprang into the rescuing vehicle, and called out a breathless order to the driver.

# Chapter 2

In the hansom she leaned back with a sigh. Why must a girl pay so dearly for her least escape from routine? Why could one never do a natural thing without having to screen it behind a structure of artifice? She had yielded to a passing impulse in going to Lawrence Selden's rooms, and it was so seldom that she could allow herself the luxury of an impulse! This one, at any rate, was going to cost her rather more than she could afford. She was vexed to see that, in spite of so many years of vigilance, she had blundered twice within five minutes. That stupid story about her dress-maker was bad enough—it would have been so simple to tell Rosedale that she had been taking tea with Selden! The mere statement of the fact would have rendered it innocuous. But, after having let herself be surprised in a falsehood, it was doubly stupid to snub the witness of her discomfiture. If she had had the presence of mind to let Rosedale drive her to the station, the concession might have purchased his silence. He had his race's accuracy in the appraisal of values, and to be seen walking down the platform at the crowded afternoon hour in the company of Miss Lily Bart would have been money in his pocket, as he might himself have phrased it. He knew, of course, that there would be a large house-party at Bellomont, and the possibility of being taken for one of Mrs. Trenor's guests was doubtless included in his calculations. Mr. Rosedale was still at a stage in his social ascent when it was of importance to produce such impressions.

The provoking part was that Lily knew all this—knew how easy it would have been to silence him on the spot, and how difficult it might be to do so afterward. Mr. Simon Rosedale was a man who made it his business to know everything about every one, whose idea of showing himself to be at home in society was to display an inconvenient familiarity with the habits of those with whom he wished to be thought intimate. Lily was sure that within twenty-four hours the story of her visiting her dress-maker at the Benedick would be in active circulation among Mr. Rosedale's acquaintances. The worst of it was that she had always snubbed and ignored him. On his first appearance—when her improvident cousin, Jack Stepney, had obtained for him (in return for favours too easily guessed) a card to one of the vast impersonal Van Osburgh "crushes"—Rosedale, with that mixture of artistic sensibility and business astuteness which characterizes his race, had instantly gravitated toward Miss Bart. She understood his motives, for her own course was guided by as nice calculations. Training and experience had taught her to be hospitable to newcomers, since the most unpromising might be useful later on, and there were plenty of available *oubliettes* to swallow them if they were not. But some intuitive repugnance, getting the better of years of social discipline, had made her push Mr. Rosedale into his *oubliette* without a trial. He had left behind only the ripple of amusement which his speedy despatch had caused among her friends; and though later (to shift the metaphor) he reappeared lower down the stream, it was only in fleeting glimpses, with long submergences between.

Hitherto Lily had been undisturbed by scruples. In her little set Mr. Rosedale had been pronounced "impossible," and Jack Stepney roundly snubbed for his attempt to pay his debts in dinner invitations. Even Mrs. Trenor, whose taste for variety had led her into some hazardous experiments, resisted Jack's attempts to disguise Mr. Rosedale as a novelty, and declared that he was the same little Jew who had been served up and rejected at the social board a dozen times within her memory; and while Judy Trenor was obdurate there was small chance of Mr. Rosedale's penetrating beyond the outer limbo of the Van Osburgh crushes. Jack gave up the contest with a laughing "You'll see," and, sticking manfully to his guns, showed himself with Rosedale at the fashionable restaurants, in company with the personally vivid if socially obscure ladies who are available for such purposes. But the attempt had hitherto been vain, and as Rosedale undoubtedly paid for the dinners, the laugh remained with his debtor.

Mr. Rosedale, it will be seen, was thus far not a factor to be feared—unless one put one's self in his power. And this was precisely what Miss Bart had done. Her clumsy fib had let him see that she had something to conceal; and she was sure he had a score to settle with her. Something in his smile told her he had not forgotten. She turned from the thought with a little shiver, but it hung on her all the way to the station, and dogged her down the platform with the persistency of Mr. Rosedale himself.

She had just time to take her seat before the train started; but having arranged herself in her corner with the instinctive feeling for effect which never forsook her, she glanced about in the hope of seeing some other member of the Trenors' party. She wanted to get away from herself, and conversation was the only means of escape that she knew.

Her search was rewarded by the discovery of a very blond young man with a soft reddish beard, who, at the other end of the carriage, appeared to be dissembling himself behind an unfolded newspaper. Lily's eye brightened, and a faint smile relaxed the drawn lines of her mouth. She had known that Mr. Percy Gryce was to be at Bellomont, but she had not counted on the luck of having him to herself in the train; and the fact banished all perturbing thoughts of Mr. Rosedale. Perhaps, after all, the day was to end more favourably than it had begun.

She began to cut the pages of a novel, tranquilly studying her prey through downcast lashes while she organized a method of attack. Something in his attitude of conscious absorption told her that he was aware of her presence: no one had ever been quite so engrossed in an evening paper! She guessed that he was too shy to come up to her, and that she would have to devise some means of approach which should not appear to be an advance on her part. It amused her to think that any one as rich as Mr. Percy Gryce should be shy; but she was gifted with treasures of indulgence for such idiosyncrasies, and besides, his timidity might serve her purpose better than too much assurance. She had the art of giving self-confidence to the embarrassed, but she was not equally sure of being able to embarrass the self-confident.

She waited till the train had emerged from the tunnel and was racing between the ragged edges of the northern suburbs. Then, as it lowered its speed near Yonkers, she rose from her seat and drifted slowly down the carriage. As she passed Mr. Gryce, the train gave a lurch, and he was aware of a slender hand gripping the back of his chair. He rose with a start, his ingenuous face looking as though it had been dipped in crimson: even the reddish tint in his beard seemed to deepen. The train swayed again, almost flinging Miss Bart into his arms.

She steadied herself with a laugh and drew back; but he was enveloped in the scent of her dress, and his shoulder had felt her fugitive touch.

"Oh, Mr. Gryce, is it you? I'm so sorry—I was trying to find the porter and get some tea."

She held out her hand as the train resumed its level rush, and they stood exchanging a few words in the aisle. Yes—he was going to Bellomont. He had heard she was to be of the party—he blushed again as he admitted it. And was he to be there for a whole week? How delightful!

But at this point one or two belated passengers from the last station forced their way into the carriage, and Lily had to retreat to her seat.

"The chair next to mine is empty—do take it," she said over her shoulder; and Mr. Gryce, with considerable embarrassment, succeeded in effecting an exchange which enabled him to transport himself and his bags to her side.

"Ah—and here is the porter, and perhaps we can have some tea."

She signalled to that official, and in a moment, with the ease that seemed to attend the fulfilment of all her wishes, a little table had been set up between the seats, and she had helped Mr. Gryce to bestow his encumbering properties beneath it.

When the tea came he watched her in silent fascination while her hands flitted above the tray, looking miraculously fine and slender in contrast to the coarse china and lumpy bread. It seemed wonderful to him that any one should perform with such careless ease the difficult task of making tea in public in a lurching train. He would never have dared to order it for himself, lest he should attract the notice of his fellow-passengers; but, secure in the shelter of her conspicuousness, he sipped the inky draught with a delicious sense of exhilaration.

Lily, with the flavour of Selden's caravan tea on her lips, had no great fancy to drown it in the railway brew which seemed such nectar to her companion; but, rightly judging that one of the charms of tea is the fact of drinking it together, she proceeded to give the last touch to Mr. Gryce's enjoyment by smiling at him across her lifted cup.

"Is it quite right—I haven't made it too strong?" she asked solicitously; and he replied with conviction that he had never tasted better tea.

"I daresay it is true," she reflected; and her imagination was fired by the thought that Mr. Gryce, who might have sounded the depths of the most complex self-indulgence, was perhaps actually taking his first journey alone with a pretty woman.

It struck her as providential that she should be the instrument of his initiation. Some girls would not have known how to manage him. They would have over-emphasized the novelty of the adventure, trying to make him feel in it the zest of an escapade. But Lily's methods were more delicate. She remembered that her cousin Jack Stepney had once defined Mr. Gryce as the young man who had promised his mother never to go out in the rain without his overshoes; and acting on this hint, she resolved to impart a gently domestic air to the scene, in the hope that her companion, instead of feeling that he was doing something reckless or unusual, would merely be led to dwell on the advantage of always having a companion to make one's tea in the train.

But in spite of her efforts, conversation flagged after the tray had been removed, and she was driven to take a fresh measurement of Mr.

Gryce's limitations. It was not, after all, opportunity but imagination that he lacked: he had a mental palate which would never learn to distinguish between railway tea and nectar. There was, however, one topic she could rely on: one spring that she had only to touch to set his simple machinery in motion. She had refrained from touching it because it was a last resource, and she had relied on other arts to stimulate other sensations; but as a settled look of dulness began to creep over his candid features, she saw that extreme measures were necessary.

"And how," she said, leaning forward, "are you getting on with your Americana?"

His eye became a degree less opaque: it was as though an incipient film had been removed from it, and she felt the pride of a skilful operator.

"I've got a few new things," he said, suffused with pleasure, but lowering his voice as though he feared his fellow-passengers might be in league to despoil him.

She returned a sympathetic enquiry, and gradually he was drawn on to talk of his latest purchases. It was the one subject which enabled him to forget himself, or allowed him, rather, to remember himself without constraint, because he was at home in it, and could assert a superiority that there were few to dispute. Hardly any of his acquaintances cared for Americana, or knew anything about them; and the consciousness of this ignorance threw Mr. Gryce's knowledge into agreeable relief. The only difficulty was to introduce the topic and to keep it to the front; most people showed no desire to have their ignorance dispelled, and Mr. Gryce was like a merchant whose warehouses are crammed with an unmarketable commodity.

But Miss Bart, it appeared, really did want to know about Americana; and moreover, she was already sufficiently informed to make the task of farther instruction as easy as it was agreeable. She questioned him intelligently, she heard him submissively; and, prepared for the look of lassitude which usually crept over his listeners' faces grew eloquent under her receptive gaze. The "points" she had had the presence of mind to glean from Selden, in anticipation of this very contingency, were serving her to such good purpose that she began to think her visit to him had been the luckiest incident of the day. She had once more shown her talent for profiting by the unexpected, and dangerous theories as to the advisability of yielding to impulse were germinating under the surface of smiling attention which she continued to present to her companion.

Mr. Gryce's sensations, if less definite, were equally agreeable. He felt the confused titillation with which the lower organisms welcome the gratification of their needs, and all his senses floundered in a vague well-being, through which Miss Bart's personality was dimly but pleasantly perceptible.

Mr. Gryce's interest in Americana had not originated with himself: it was impossible to think of him as evolving any taste of his own. An uncle had left him a collection already noted among bibliophiles; the existence of the collection was the only fact that had ever shed glory on the name of Gryce, and the nephew took as much pride in his inheritance as though it had been his own work. Indeed, he gradually came to regard it as such, and to feel a sense of personal complacency when he chanced on any reference to the Gryce Americana. Anxious as he was to avoid personal notice, he took, in the printed mention of his name, a pleasure so exquisite and excessive that it seemed a compensation for his shrinking from publicity.

To enjoy the sensation as often as possible, he subscribed to all the reviews dealing with book-collecting in general, and American history in particular, and as allusions to his library abounded in the pages of these journals, which formed his only reading, he came to regard himself figuring prominently in the public eye, and to enjoy the the interest which would be excited if the persons he met in r sat among in travelling, were suddenly to be told that he essor of the Gryce Americana.

Most timidities have such secret compensations, and Miss Bart was discerning enough to know that the inner vanity is generally in proportion to the outer self-depreciation. With a more confident person she would not have dared to dwell so long on one topic, or to show such exaggerated interest in it; but she had rightly guessed that Mr. Gryce's egoism was a thirsty soil, requiring constant nurture from without. Miss Bart had the gift of following an undercurrent of thought while she appeared to be sailing on the surface of conversation; and in this case her mental excursion took the form of a rapid survey of Mr. Percy Gryce's future as combined with her own. The Gryces were from Albany, and but lately introduced to the metropolis, where the mother and son had come, after old Jefferson Gryce's death, to take possession of his house in Madison Avenue—an appalling house, all brown stone without and black walnut within, with the Gryce library in a fire-proof annex that looked like a mausoleum. Lily, however, knew all about them: young Mr. Gryce's arrival had fluttered the maternal breasts of New York, and when a girl has no mother to palpitate for her she must needs be on the alert for herself. Lily, therefore, had not only contrived to put herself in the young man's way, but had made the acquaintance of Mrs. Gryce, a monumental woman with the voice of a pulpit orator and a mind preoccupied with the iniquities of her servants, who came sometimes to sit with Mrs. Peniston and learn from that lady how she managed to prevent the kitchen-maid's smuggling groceries out of the house. Mrs. Gryce had a kind of impersonal benevolence: cases of individual need she regarded with suspicion, but she subscribed to Institutions when their annual reports showed an impressive surplus. Her domestic duties were manifold, for they extended from furtive inspections of the servants' bedrooms to unannounced descents to the cellar; but she had never allowed herself many pleasures. Once, however, she had had a special edition of the Sarum Rule printed in rubric and presented to every clergyman in the diocese; and the gilt album in which their letters of thanks were pasted formed the chief ornament of her drawing-room table.

Percy had been brought up in the principles which so excellent a woman was sure to inculcate. Every form of prudence and suspicion had been grafted on a nature originally reluctant and cautious, with the result that it would have seemed hardly needful for Mrs. Gryce to extract his promise about the overshoes, so little likely was he to hazard himself abroad in the rain. After attaining his majority, and coming into the fortune which the late Mr. Gryce had made out of a patent device for excluding fresh air from hotels, the young man continued to live with his mother in Albany; but on Jefferson Gryce's death, when another large property passed into her son's hands, Mrs. Gryce thought that what she called his "interests" demanded his presence in New York. She accordingly installed herself in the Madison Avenue house, and Percy, whose sense of duty was not inferior to his mother's, spent all his week days in the handsome Broad Street office where a batch of pale men on small salaries had grown grey in the management of the Gryce estate, and where he was initiated with becoming reverence into every detail of the art of accumulation.

As far as Lily could learn, this had hitherto been Mr. Gryce's only occupation, and she might have been pardoned for thinking it not too hard a task to interest a young man who had been kept on such low diet. At any rate, she felt herself so completely in command of the situation that she yielded to a sense of security in which all fear of Mr. Rosedale, and of the difficulties on which that fear was contingent, vanished beyond the edge of thought.

The stopping of the train at Garrisons would not have distracted her from these thoughts, had she not caught a sudden look of distress in her companion's eye. His seat faced toward the door, and she guessed that he had been perturbed by the approach of an acquaintance; a fact confirmed by the turning of heads and general sense of commotion which her own entrance into a railway-carriage was apt to produce.

She knew the symptoms at once, and was not surprised to be hailed by the high notes of a pretty woman, who entered the train accompanied by a maid, a bull-terrier, and a footman staggering under a load of bags and dressing-cases.

"Oh, Lily—are you going to Bellomont? Then you can't let me have your seat, I suppose? But I *must* have a seat in this carriage—porter, you must find me a place at once. Can't some one be put somewhere else? I want to be with my friends. Oh, how do you do, Mr. Gryce? Do please make him understand that I must have a seat next to you and Lily."

Mrs. George Dorset, regardless of the mild efforts of a traveller with a carpet-bag, who was doing his best to make room for her by getting out of the train, stood in the middle of the aisle, diffusing about her that general sense of exasperation which a pretty woman on her travels not infrequently creates.

She was smaller and thinner than Lily Bart, with a restless pliability of pose, as if she could have been crumpled up and run through a ring, like the sinuous draperies she affected. Her small pale face seemed the mere setting of a pair of dark exaggerated eyes, of which the visionary gaze contrasted curiously with her self-assertive tone and gestures; so that, as one of her friends observed, she was like a disembodied spirit who took up a great deal of room.

Having finally discovered that the seat adjoining Miss Bart's was at her disposal, she possessed herself of it with a farther displacement of her surroundings, explaining meanwhile that she had come across from Mount Kisco in her motor-car that morning, and had been kicking her heels for an hour at Garrisons, without even the alleviation of a cigarette, her brute of a husband having neglected to replenish her case before they parted that morning.

"And at this hour of the day I don't suppose you've a single one left, have you, Lily?" she plaintively concluded.

Miss Bart caught the startled glance of Mr. Percy Gryce, whose own lips were never defiled by tobacco.

"What an absurd question, Bertha!" she exclaimed, blushing at the thought of the store she had laid in at Lawrence Selden's.

"Why, don't you smoke? Since when have you given it up? What—you never— And you don't either, Mr. Gryce? Ah, of course—how stupid of me—I understand."

And Mrs. Dorset leaned back against her travelling cushions with a smile which made Lily wish there had been no vacant seat beside her own.

# Chapter 3

Bridge at Bellomont usually lasted till the small hours; and when Lily went to bed that night she had played too long for her own good.

Feeling no desire for the self-communion which awaited her in her room, she lingered on the broad stairway, looking down into the hall below, where the last card-players were grouped about the tray of tall glasses and silver-collared decanters which the butler had just placed on a low table near the fire.

The hall was arcaded, with a gallery supported on columns of pale yellow marble. Tall clumps of flowering plants were grouped against a background of dark foliage in the angles of the walls. On the crimson carpet a deer-hound and two or three spaniels dozed luxuriously before the fire, and the light from the great central lantern overhead shed a brightness on the women's hair and struck sparks from their jewels as they moved.

There were moments when such scenes delighted Lily, when they gratified her sense of beauty and her craving for the external finish of life; there were others when they gave a sharper edge to the meagreness of her own opportunities. This was one of the moments when the sense of contrast was uppermost, and she turned away impatiently as Mrs. George Dorset, glittering in serpentine spangles, drew Percy Gryce in her wake to a confidential nook beneath the gallery.

It was not that Miss Bart was afraid of losing her newly-acquired hold over Mr. Gryce. Mrs. Dorset might startle or dazzle him, but she had neither the skill nor the patience to effect his capture. She was too self-engrossed to penetrate the recesses of his shyness, and besides, why should she care to give herself the trouble? At most it might amuse her to make sport of his simplicity for an evening—after that he would be merely a burden to her, and knowing this, she was far too experienced to encourage him. But the mere thought of that other woman, who could take a man up and toss him aside as she willed, without having to regard him as a possible factor in her plans, filled Lily Bart with envy. She had been bored all the afternoon by Percy Gryce—the mere thought seemed to waken an echo of his droning voice—but she could not ignore him on the morrow, she must follow up her success, must submit to more boredom, must be ready with fresh compliances and adaptabilities, and all on the bare chance that he might ultimately decide to do her the honour of boring her for life.

It was a hateful fate—but how escape from it? What choice had she? To be herself, or a Gerty Farish. As she entered her bedroom, with its softly-shaded lights, her lace dressing-gown lying across the silken bedspread, her little embroidered slippers before the fire, a vase of carnations filling the air with perfume, and the last novels and magazines lying uncut on a table beside the reading-lamp, she had a vision of Miss Farish's cramped flat, with its cheap conveniences and hideous wall-papers. No; she was not made for mean and shabby surroundings, for the squalid compromises of poverty. Her whole being dilated in an atmosphere of luxury; it was the background she required, the only climate she could breathe in. But the luxury of others was not what she wanted. A few years ago it had sufficed her: she had taken her daily meed of pleasure without caring who provided it. Now she was beginning to chafe at the obligations it imposed, to feel herself a mere pensioner on the splendour which had once seemed to belong to her. There were even moments when she was conscious of having to pay her way.

For a long time she had refused to play bridge. She knew she could not afford it, and she was afraid of acquiring so expensive a taste. She had seen the danger exemplified in more than one of her associates—in young Ned Silverton, for instance, the charming fair boy now seated in abject rapture at the elbow of Mrs. Fisher, a striking divorcee with eyes and gowns as emphatic as the head-lines of her "case." Lily could remember when young Silverton had stumbled into their circle, with the air of a strayed Arcadian who has published chamung [Updater's note: charming?] sonnets in his college journal. Since then he had developed a taste for Mrs. Fisher and bridge, and the latter at least had involved him in expenses from which he had been more than once rescued by harassed maiden sisters, who treasured the sonnets, and went without sugar in their tea to keep their darling afloat. Ned's case was familiar to Lily: she had seen his charming eyes—which had a good deal more poetry in them than the sonnets—change from surprise to amusement, and from amusement to anxiety, as he passed under the spell of the terrible god of chance; and she was afraid of discovering the same symptoms in her own case.

For in the last year she had found that her hostesses expected her to take a place at the card-table. It was one of the taxes she had to pay for their prolonged hospitality, and for the dresses and trinkets which occasionally replenished her insufficient wardrobe. And since she had played regularly the passion had grown on her. Once or twice of late she had won a large sum, and instead of keeping it against future losses, had spent it in dress or jewelry; and the desire to atone for this imprudence, combined with the increasing exhilaration of the game, drove her to risk higher stakes at each fresh venture. She tried to excuse herself on the plea that, in the Trenor set, if one played at all one must either play high or be set down as priggish or stingy; but she knew that the gambling passion was upon her, and that in her present surroundings there was small hope of resisting it.

Tonight the luck had been persistently bad, and the little gold purse which hung among her trinkets was almost empty when she returned to her room. She unlocked the wardrobe, and taking out her jewel-case, looked under the tray for the roll of bills from which she had replenished the purse before going down to dinner. Only twenty dollars were left: the discovery was so startling that for a moment she fancied she must have been robbed. Then she took paper and pencil, and seating herself at the writing-table, tried to reckon up what she had spent during the day. Her head was throbbing with fatigue, and she had to go over the figures again and again; but at last it became clear to her that she had lost three hundred dollars at cards. She took out her cheque-book to see if her balance was larger than she remembered, but found she had erred in the other direction. Then she returned to her calculations; but figure as she would, she could not conjure back the vanished three hundred dollars. It was the sum she had set aside to pacify her dress-maker—unless she should decide to use it as a sop to the jeweller. At any rate, she had so many uses for it that its very insufficiency had caused her to play high in the hope of doubling it. But of course she had lost—she who needed every penny, while Bertha Dorset, whose husband showered money on her, must have pocketed at least five hundred, and Judy Trenor, who could have afforded to lose a thousand a night, had left the table clutching such a heap of bills that she had been unable to shake hands with her guests when they bade her good night.

A world in which such things could be seemed a miserable place to Lily Bart; but then she had never been able to understand the laws of a universe which was so ready to leave her out of its calculations.

She began to undress without ringing for her maid, whom she had sent to bed. She had been long enough in bondage to other people's pleasure to be considerate of those who depended on hers, and in her bitter moods it sometimes struck her that she and her maid were in the same position, except that the latter received her wages more regularly.

As she sat before the mirror brushing her hair, her face looked hollow and pale, and she was frightened by two little lines near her mouth, faint flaws in the smooth curve of the cheek.

"Oh, I must stop worrying!" she exclaimed. "Unless it's the electric light—" she reflected, springing up from her seat and lighting the candles on the dressing-table.

She turned out the wall-lights, and peered at herself between the candle-flames. The white oval of her face swam out waveringly from a background of shadows, the uncertain light blurring it like a haze; but the two lines about the mouth remained.

Lily rose and undressed in haste.

"It is only because I am tired and have such odious things to think about," she kept repeating; and it seemed an added injustice that petty cares should leave a trace on the beauty which was her only defence against them.

But the odious things were there, and remained with her. She returned wearily to the thought of Percy Gryce, as a wayfarer picks up a heavy load and toils on after a brief rest. She was almost sure she had "landed" him: a few days' work and she would win her reward. But the reward itself seemed unpalatable just then: she could get no zest from the thought of victory. It would be a rest from worry, no more—and how little that would have seemed to her a few years earlier! Her ambitions had shrunk gradually in the desiccating air of failure. But why had she failed? Was it her own fault or that of destiny?

She remembered how her mother, after they had lost their money, used to say to her with a kind of fierce vindictiveness: "But you'll get it all back—you'll get it all back, with your face." . . . The remembrance roused a whole train of association, and she lay in the darkness reconstructing the past out of which her present had grown.

A house in which no one ever dined at home unless there was "company"; a door-bell perpetually ringing; a hall-table showered with square envelopes which were opened in haste, and oblong envelopes which were allowed to gather dust in the depths of a bronze jar; a series of French and English maids giving warning amid a chaos of hurriedly-ransacked wardrobes and dress-closets; an equally changing dynasty of nurses and footmen; quarrels in the pantry, the kitchen and the drawing-room; precipitate trips to Europe, and returns with gorged trunks and days of interminable unpacking; semi-annual discussions as to where the summer should be spent, grey interludes of economy and brilliant reactions of expense—such was the setting of Lily Bart's first memories.

Ruling the turbulent element called home was the vigorous and determined figure of a mother still young enough to dance her ball-dresses to rags, while the hazy outline of a neutral-tinted father filled an intermediate space between the butler and the man who came to wind the clocks. Even to the eyes of infancy, Mrs. Hudson Bart had appeared young; but Lily could not recall the time when her father had not been bald and slightly stooping, with streaks of grey in his hair, and a tired walk. It was a shock to her to learn afterward that he was but two years older than her mother.

Lily seldom saw her father by daylight. All day he was "down town"; and in winter it was long after nightfall when she heard his fagged step on the stairs and his hand on the school-room door. He would kiss her in silence, and ask one or two questions of the nurse or the governess; then Mrs. Bart's maid would come to remind him that he was dining out, and he would hurry away with a nod to Lily. In summer, when he joined them for a Sunday at Newport or Southampton, he was even more effaced and silent than in winter. It seemed to tire him to rest, and he would sit for hours staring at the sea-line from a quiet corner of the verandah, while the clatter of his wife's existence went on unheeded a few feet off. Generally, however, Mrs. Bart and Lily went to Europe for the summer, and before the steamer was half way over Mr. Bart had dipped below the horizon. Sometimes his daughter heard him denounced for having neglected to forward Mrs. Bart's remittances; but for the most part he was never mentioned or thought of till his patient stooping figure presented itself on the New York dock as a buffer between the magnitude of his wife's luggage and the restrictions of the American custom-house.

In this desultory yet agitated fashion life went on through Lily's teens: a zig-zag broken course down which the family craft glided on a rapid current of amusement, tugged at by the underflow of a perpetual need—the need of more money. Lily could not recall the time when there had been money enough, and in some vague way her father seemed always to blame for the deficiency. It could certainly not be the fault of Mrs. Bart, who was spoken of by her friends as a "wonderful manager." Mrs. Bart was famous for the unlimited effect she produced on limited means; and to the lady and her acquaintances there was something heroic in living as though one were much richer than one's bank-book denoted.

Lily was naturally proud of her mother's aptitude in this line: she had been brought up in the faith that, whatever it cost, one must have a good cook, and be what Mrs. Bart called "decently dressed." Mrs. Bart's worst reproach to her husband was to ask him if he expected her to "live like a pig"; and his replying in the negative was always regarded as a justification for cabling to Paris for an extra dress or two, and telephoning to the jeweller that he might, after all, send home the turquoise bracelet which Mrs. Bart had looked at that morning.

Lily knew people who "lived like pigs," and their appearance and surroundings justified her mother's repugnance to that form of existence. They were mostly cousins, who inhabited dingy houses with engravings from Cole's Voyage of Life on the drawing-room walls, and slatternly parlour-maids who said "I'll go and see" to visitors calling at an hour when all right-minded persons are conventionally if not actually out. The disgusting part of it was that many of these cousins were rich, so that Lily imbibed the idea that if people lived like pigs it was from choice, and through the lack of any proper standard of conduct. This gave her a sense of reflected superiority, and she did not need Mrs. Bart's comments on the family frumps and misers to foster her naturally lively taste for splendour.

Lily was nineteen when circumstances caused her to revise her view of the universe.

The previous year she had made a dazzling debut fringed by a heavy thunder-cloud of bills. The light of the debut still lingered on the horizon, but the cloud had thickened; and suddenly it broke. The suddenness added to the horror; and there were still times when Lily relived with painful vividness every detail of the day on which the blow fell. She and her mother had been seated at the luncheon-table, over the *chaufroix* and cold salmon of the previous night's dinner: it was one of Mrs. Bart's few economies to consume in private the expensive remnants of her hospitality. Lily was feeling the pleasant languor which is youth's penalty for dancing till dawn; but her mother, in spite of a few lines about the mouth, and under the yellow waves on her temples, was as alert, determined and high in colour as if she had risen from an untroubled sleep.

In the centre of the table, between the melting *marrons glaces* and candied cherries, a pyramid of American Beauties lifted their vigorous stems; they held their heads as high as Mrs. Bart, but their rose-colour had turned to a dissipated purple, and Lily's sense of fitness was disturbed by their reappearance on the luncheon-table.

"I really think, mother," she said reproachfully, "we might afford a few fresh flowers for luncheon. Just some jonquils or lilies-of-the-valley—"

Mrs. Bart stared. Her own fastidiousness had its eye fixed on the world, and she did not care how the luncheon-table looked when there was no one present at it but the family. But she smiled at her daughter's innocence.

"Lilies-of-the-valley," she said calmly, "cost two dollars a dozen at this season."

Lily was not impressed. She knew very little of the value of money.

"It would not take more than six dozen to fill that bowl," she argued.

"Six dozen what?" asked her father's voice in the doorway.

The two women looked up in surprise; though it was a Saturday, the sight of Mr. Bart at luncheon was an unwonted one. But neither his wife nor his daughter was sufficiently interested to ask an explanation.

Mr. Bart dropped into a chair, and sat gazing absently at the fragment of jellied salmon which the butler had placed before him.

"I was only saying," Lily began, "that I hate to see faded flowers at luncheon; and mother says a bunch of lilies-of-the-valley would not cost more than twelve dollars. Mayn't I tell the florist to send a few every day?"

She leaned confidently toward her father: he seldom refused her anything, and Mrs. Bart had taught her to plead with him when her own entreaties failed.

Mr. Bart sat motionless, his gaze still fixed on the salmon, and his lower jaw dropped; he looked even paler than usual, and his thin hair lay in untidy streaks on his forehead. Suddenly he looked at his daughter and laughed. The laugh was so strange that Lily coloured under it: she disliked being ridiculed, and her father seemed to see something ridiculous in the request. Perhaps he thought it foolish that she should trouble him about such a trifle.

"Twelve dollars—twelve dollars a day for flowers? Oh, certainly, my dear—give him an order for twelve hundred." He continued to laugh.

Mrs. Bart gave him a quick glance.

"You needn't wait, Poleworth—I will ring for you," she said to the butler.

The butler withdrew with an air of silent disapproval, leaving the remains of the *chaufroix* on the sideboard.

"What is the matter, Hudson? Are you ill?" said Mrs. Bart severely.

She had no tolerance for scenes which were not of her own making, and it was odious to her that her husband should make a show of himself before the servants.

"Are you ill?" she repeated.

"Ill?— No, I'm ruined," he said.

Lily made a frightened sound, and Mrs. Bart rose to her feet.

"Ruined—?" she cried; but controlling herself instantly, she turned a calm face to Lily.

"Shut the pantry door," she said.

Lily obeyed, and when she turned back into the room her father was sitting with both elbows on the table, the plate of salmon between them, and his head bowed on his hands.

Mrs. Bart stood over him with a white face which made her hair unnaturally yellow. She looked at Lily as the latter approached: her look was terrible, but her voice was modulated to a ghastly cheerfulness.

"Your father is not well—he doesn't know what he is saying. It is nothing—but you had better go upstairs; and don't talk to the servants," she added.

Lily obeyed; she always obeyed when her mother spoke in that voice. She had not been deceived by Mrs. Bart's words: she knew at once that they were ruined. In the dark hours which followed, that awful fact overshadowed even her father's slow and difficult dying. To his wife he no longer counted: he had become extinct when he ceased to fulfil his purpose, and she sat at his side with the provisional air of a traveller who waits for a belated train to start. Lily's feelings were softer: she pitied him in a frightened ineffectual way. But the fact that he was for the most part unconscious, and that his attention, when she stole into the room, drifted away from her after a moment, made him even more of a stranger than in the nursery days when he had never come home till after dark. She seemed always to have seen him through a blur—first of sleepiness, then of distance and indifference—and now the fog had thickened till he was almost indistinguishable. If she could have performed any little services for him, or have exchanged with him a few of those affecting words which an extensive perusal of fiction had led her to connect with such occasions, the filial instinct might have stirred in her; but her pity, finding no active expression, remained in a state of spectatorship, overshadowed by her mother's grim unflagging resentment. Every look and act of Mrs. Bart's seemed to say: "You are sorry for him now—but you will feel differently when you see what he has done to us."

It was a relief to Lily when her father died.

Then a long winter set in. There was a little money left, but to Mrs. Bart it seemed worse than nothing—the mere mockery of what she was entitled to. What was the use of living if one had to live like a pig? She sank into a kind of furious apathy, a state of inert anger against fate. Her faculty for "managing" deserted her, or she no longer took sufficient pride in it to exert it. It was well enough to "manage" when by so doing one could keep one's own carriage; but when one's best contrivance did not conceal the fact that one had to go on foot, the effort was no longer worth making.

Lily and her mother wandered from place to place, now paying long visits to relations whose house-keeping Mrs. Bart criticized, and who deplored the fact that she let Lily breakfast in bed when the girl had no prospects before her, and now vegetating in cheap continental refuges, where Mrs. Bart held herself fiercely aloof from the frugal tea-tables of her companions in misfortune. She was especially careful to avoid her old friends and the scenes of her former successes. To be poor seemed to her such a confession of failure that it amounted to disgrace; and she detected a note of condescension in the friendliest advances.

Only one thought consoled her, and that was the contemplation of Lily's beauty. She studied it with a kind of passion, as though it were some weapon she had slowly fashioned for her vengeance. It was the last asset in their fortunes, the nucleus around which their life was to be rebuilt. She watched it jealously, as though it were her own property and Lily its mere custodian; and she tried to instil into the latter a sense of the responsibility that such a charge involved. She followed in imagination the career of other beauties, pointing out to her daughter what might be achieved through such a gift, and dwelling on the awful warning of those who, in spite of it, had failed to get what they wanted: to Mrs. Bart, only stupidity could explain the lamentable denouement of some of her examples. She was not above the inconsistency of charging fate, rather than herself, with her own misfortunes; but she inveighed so acrimoniously against love-matches that Lily would have fancied her own marriage had been of that nature, had not Mrs. Bart frequently assured her that she had been "talked into it"—by whom, she never made clear.

Lily was duly impressed by the magnitude of her opportunities. The dinginess of her present life threw into enchanting relief the existence to which she felt herself entitled. To a less illuminated intelligence Mrs. Bart's counsels might have been dangerous; but Lily understood that beauty is only the raw material of conquest, and that to convert it into success other arts are required. She knew that to betray any sense of superiority was a subtler form of the stupidity her mother denounced, and it did not take her long to learn that a beauty needs more tact than the possessor of an average set of features.

Her ambitions were not as crude as Mrs. Bart's. It had been among that lady's grievances that her husband—in the early days, before he was too tired—had wasted his evenings in what she vaguely described as "reading poetry"; and among the effects packed off to auction after his death were a score or two of dingy volumes which had struggled for existence among the boots and medicine bottles of his dressing-room shelves. There was in Lily a vein of sentiment, perhaps transmitted from this source, which gave an idealizing touch to her most prosaic purposes. She liked to think of her beauty as a power for good, as giving her the opportunity to attain a position where she should make her influence felt in the vague diffusion of refinement and good taste. She was fond of pictures and flowers, and of sentimental fiction, and she could not help thinking that the possession of such tastes ennobled her desire for worldly advantages. She would not indeed have cared to marry a man who was merely rich: she was secretly ashamed of her mother's crude passion for money. Lily's preference would have been for an English nobleman with political ambitions and vast estates; or, for second choice, an Italian prince with a castle in the Apennines and an hereditary office in the Vatican. Lost causes had a romantic charm for her, and she liked to picture herself as standing aloof from the vulgar press of the Quirinal, and sacrificing her pleasure to the claims of an immemorial tradition. . . .

How long ago and how far off it all seemed! Those ambitions were hardly more futile and childish than the earlier ones which had centred about the possession of a French jointed doll with real hair. Was it only ten years since she had wavered in imagination between the English earl and the Italian prince? Relentlessly her mind travelled on over the dreary interval. . . .

After two years of hungry roaming Mrs. Bart had died—died of a deep disgust. She had hated dinginess, and it was her fate to be dingy. Her visions of a brilliant marriage for Lily had faded after the first year.

"People can't marry you if they don't see you—and how can they see you in these holes where we're stuck?" That was the burden of her lament; and her last adjuration to her daughter was to escape from dinginess if she could.

"Don't let it creep up on you and drag you down. Fight your way out of it somehow—you're young and can do it," she insisted.

She had died during one of their brief visits to New York, and there Lily at once became the centre of a family council composed of the wealthy relatives whom she had been taught to despise for living like pigs. It may be that they had an inkling of the sentiments in which she had been brought up, for none of them manifested a very lively desire for her company; indeed, the question threatened to remain unsolved till Mrs. Peniston with a sigh announced: "I'll try her for a year."

Every one was surprised, but one and all concealed their surprise, lest Mrs. Peniston should be alarmed by it into reconsidering her decision.

Mrs. Peniston was Mr. Bart's widowed sister, and if she was by no means the richest of the family group, its other members nevertheless abounded in reasons why she was clearly destined by Providence to assume the charge of Lily. In the first place she was alone, and it would be charming for her to have a young companion. Then she sometimes travelled, and Lily's familiarity with foreign customs—deplored as a misfortune by her more conservative relatives—would at least enable her to act as a kind of courier. But as a matter of fact Mrs. Peniston had not been affected by these considerations. She had taken the girl simply because no one else would have her, and because she had the kind of moral *mauvaise honte* which makes the public display of selfishness difficult, though it does not interfere with its private indulgence. It would have been impossible for Mrs. Peniston to be heroic on a desert island, but with the eyes of her little world upon her she took a certain pleasure in her act.

She reaped the reward to which disinterestedness is entitled, and found an agreeable companion in her niece. She had expected to find Lily headstrong, critical and "foreign"—for even Mrs. Peniston, though she occasionally went abroad, had the family dread of foreignness—but the girl showed a pliancy, which, to a more penetrating mind than her aunt's, might have been less reassuring than the open selfishness of youth. Misfortune had made Lily supple instead of hardening her, and a pliable substance is less easy to break than a stiff one.

Mrs. Peniston, however, did not suffer from her niece's adaptability. Lily had no intention of taking advantage of her aunt's good nature. She was in truth grateful for the refuge offered her: Mrs. Peniston's opulent interior was at least not externally dingy. But dinginess is a quality which assumes all manner of disguises; and Lily soon found that it was as latent in the expensive routine of her aunt's life as in the makeshift existence of a continental pension.

Mrs. Peniston was one of the episodical persons who form the padding of life. It was impossible to believe that she had herself ever been a focus of activities. The most vivid thing about her was the fact that her grandmother had been a Van Alstyne. This connection with the well-fed and industrious stock of early New York revealed itself in the glacial neatness of Mrs. Peniston's drawing-room and in the excellence of her cuisine. She belonged to the class of old New Yorkers who have always lived well, dressed expensively, and done little else; and to these inherited obligations Mrs. Peniston faithfully conformed. She had always been a looker-on at life, and her mind resembled one of those little mirrors which her Dutch ancestors were accustomed to affix to their upper windows, so that from the depths of an impenetrable domesticity they might see what was happening in the street.

Mrs. Peniston was the owner of a country-place in New Jersey, but she had never lived there since her husband's death—a remote event, which appeared to dwell in her memory chiefly as a dividing point in the personal reminiscences that formed the staple of her conversation.

She was a woman who remembered dates with intensity, and could tell at a moment's notice whether the drawing-room curtains had been renewed before or after Mr. Peniston's last illness.

Mrs. Peniston thought the country lonely and trees damp, and cherished a vague fear of meeting a bull. To guard against such contingencies she frequented the more populous watering-places, where she installed herself impersonally in a hired house and looked on at life through the matting screen of her verandah. In the care of such a guardian, it soon became clear to Lily that she was to enjoy only the material advantages of good food and expensive clothing; and, though far from underrating these, she would gladly have exchanged them for what Mrs. Bart had taught her to regard as opportunities. She sighed to think what her mother's fierce energies would have accomplished, had they been coupled with Mrs. Peniston's resources. Lily had abundant energy of her own, but it was restricted by the necessity of adapting herself to her aunt's habits. She saw that at all costs she must keep Mrs. Peniston's favour till, as Mrs. Bart would have phrased it, she could stand on her own legs. Lily had no mind for the vagabond life of the poor relation, and to adapt herself to Mrs. Peniston she had, to some degree, to assume that lady's passive attitude. She had fancied at first that it would be easy to draw her aunt into the whirl of her own activities, but there was a static force in Mrs. Peniston against which her niece's efforts spent themselves in vain. To attempt to bring her into active relation with life was like tugging at a piece of furniture which has been screwed to the floor. She did not, indeed, expect Lily to remain equally immovable: she had all the American guardian's indulgence for the volatility of youth.

She had indulgence also for certain other habits of her niece's. It seemed to her natural that Lily should spend all her money on dress, and she supplemented the girl's scanty income by occasional "handsome presents" meant to be applied to the same purpose. Lily, who was intensely practical, would have preferred a fixed allowance; but Mrs. Peniston liked the periodical recurrence of gratitude evoked by unexpected cheques, and was perhaps shrewd enough to perceive that such a method of giving kept alive in her niece a salutary sense of dependence.

Beyond this, Mrs. Peniston had not felt called upon to do anything for her charge: she had simply stood aside and let her take the field. Lily had taken it, at first with the confidence of assured possessorship, then with gradually narrowing demands, till now she found herself actually struggling for a foothold on the broad space which had once seemed her own for the asking. How it happened she did not yet know. Sometimes she thought it was because Mrs. Peniston had been too passive, and again she feared it was because she herself had not been passive enough. Had she shown an undue eagerness for victory? Had she lacked patience, pliancy and dissimulation? Whether she charged herself with these faults or absolved herself from them, made no difference in the sum-total of her failure. Younger and plainer girls had been married off by dozens, and she was nine-and-twenty, and still Miss Bart.

She was beginning to have fits of angry rebellion against fate, when she longed to drop out of the race and make an independent life for herself. But what manner of life would it be? She had barely enough money to pay her dress-makers' bills and her gambling debts; and none of the desultory interests which she dignified with the name of tastes was pronounced enough to enable her to live contentedly in obscurity. Ah, no—she was too intelligent not to be honest with herself. She knew that she hated dinginess as much as her mother had hated it, and to her last breath she meant to fight against it, dragging herself up again and again above its flood till she gained the bright pinnacles of success which presented such a slippery surface to her clutch.

# Chapter 4

The next morning, on her breakfast tray, Miss Bart found a note from her hostess.

"Dearest Lily," it ran, "if it is not too much of a bore to be down by ten, will you come to my sitting-room to help me with some tiresome things?"

Lily tossed aside the note and subsided on her pillows with a sigh. It WAS a bore to be down by ten—an hour regarded at Bellomont as vaguely synchronous with sunrise—and she knew too well the nature of the tiresome things in question. Miss Pragg, the secretary, had been called away, and there would be notes and dinner-cards to write, lost addresses to hunt up, and other social drudgery to perform. It was understood that Miss Bart should fill the gap in such emergencies, and she usually recognized the obligation without a murmur.

Today, however, it renewed the sense of servitude which the previous night's review of her cheque-book had produced. Everything in her surroundings ministered to feelings of ease and amenity. The windows stood open to the sparkling freshness of the September morning, and between the yellow boughs she caught a perspective of hedges and parterres leading by degrees of lessening formality to the free undulations of the park. Her maid had kindled a little fire on the hearth, and it contended cheerfully with the sunlight which slanted across the moss-green carpet and caressed the curved sides of an old marquetry desk. Near the bed stood a table holding her breakfast tray, with its harmonious porcelain and silver, a handful of violets in a slender glass, and the morning paper folded beneath her letters. There was nothing new to Lily in these tokens of a studied luxury; but, though they formed a part of her atmosphere, she never lost her sensitiveness to their charm. Mere display left her with a sense of superior distinction; but she felt an affinity to all the subtler manifestations of wealth.

Mrs. Trenor's summons, however, suddenly recalled her state of dependence, and she rose and dressed in a mood of irritability that she was usually too prudent to indulge. She knew that such emotions leave lines on the face as well as in the character, and she had meant to take warning by the little creases which her midnight survey had revealed.

The matter-of-course tone of Mrs. Trenor's greeting deepened her irritation. If one did drag one's self out of bed at such an hour, and come down fresh and radiant to the monotony of note-writing, some special recognition of the sacrifice seemed fitting. But Mrs. Trenor's tone showed no consciousness of the fact.

"Oh, Lily, that's nice of you," she merely sighed across the chaos of letters, bills and other domestic documents which gave an incongruously commercial touch to the slender elegance of her writing-table.

"There are such lots of horrors this morning," she added, clearing a space in the centre of the confusion and rising to yield her seat to Miss Bart.

Mrs. Trenor was a tall fair woman, whose height just saved her from redundancy. Her rosy blondness had survived some forty years of futile activity without showing much trace of ill-usage except in a diminished play of feature. It was difficult to define her beyond saying that she seemed to exist only as a hostess, not so much from any exaggerated instinct of hospitality as because she could not sustain life except in a crowd. The collective nature of her interests exempted her from the ordinary rivalries of her sex, and she knew no more personal emotion than that of hatred for the woman who presumed to give bigger dinners or have more amusing house-parties than herself. As her social talents, backed by Mr. Trenor's bank-account, almost always assured her ultimate triumph in such competitions, success had developed in her an unscrupulous good nature toward the rest of her sex, and in Miss Bart's utilitarian classification of her friends, Mrs. Trenor ranked as the woman who was least likely to "go back" on her.

"It was simply inhuman of Pragg to go off now," Mrs. Trenor declared, as her friend seated herself at the desk. "She says her sister is going to have a baby—as if that were anything to having a house-party! I'm sure I shall get most horribly mixed up and there will be some awful rows. When I was down at Tuxedo I asked a lot of people for next week, and I've mislaid the list and can't remember who is coming. And this week is going to be a horrid failure too—and Gwen Van Osburgh will go back and tell her mother how bored people were. I did mean to ask the Wetheralls—that was a blunder of Gus's. They disapprove of Carry Fisher, you know. As if one could help having Carry Fisher! It *was* foolish of her to get that second divorce—Carry always overdoes things—but she said the only way to get a penny out of Fisher was to divorce him and make him pay alimony. And poor Carry has to consider every dollar. It's really absurd of Alice Wetherall to make such a fuss about meeting her, when one thinks of what society is coming to. Some one said the other day that there was a divorce and a case of appendicitis in every family one knows. Besides, Carry is the only person who can keep Gus in a good humour when we have bores in the house. Have you noticed that *all* the husbands like her? All, I mean, except her own. It's rather clever of her to have made a specialty of devoting herself to dull people—the field is such a large one, and she has it practically to herself. She finds compensations, no doubt—I know she borrows money of Gus—but then I'd *pay* her to keep him in a good humour, so I can't complain, after all."

Mrs. Trenor paused to enjoy the spectacle of Miss Bart's efforts to unravel her tangled correspondence.

"But it is only the Wetheralls and Carry," she resumed, with a fresh note of lament. "The truth is, I'm awfully disappointed in Lady Cressida Raith."

"Disappointed? Had you known her before?"

"Mercy, no—never saw her till yesterday. Lady Skiddaw sent her over with letters to the Van Osburghs, and I heard that Maria Van Osburgh was asking a big party to meet her this week, so I thought it would be fun to get her away, and Jack Stepney, who knew her in India, managed it for me. Maria was furious, and actually had the impudence to make Gwen invite herself here, so that they shouldn't be *quite* out of it—if I'd known what Lady Cressida was like, they could have had her and welcome! But I thought any friend of the Skiddaws' was sure to be amusing. You remember what fun Lady Skiddaw was? There were times when I simply had to send the girls out of the room. Besides, Lady Cressida is the Duchess of Beltshire's sister, and I naturally supposed she was the same sort; but you never can tell in those English families. They are so big that there's room for all kinds, and it turns out that Lady Cressida is the moral one—married a clergy-man and does missionary work in the East End. Think of my taking such a lot of trouble about a clergyman's wife, who wears Indian jewelry and botanizes! She made Gus take her all through the glass-houses yesterday, and bothered him to death by asking him the names of the plants. Fancy treating Gus as if he were the gardener!"

Mrs. Trenor brought this out in a *crescendo* of indignation.

"Oh, well, perhaps Lady Cressida will reconcile the Wetheralls to meeting Carry Fisher," said Miss Bart pacifically.

"I'm sure I hope so! But she is boring all the men horribly, and if she takes to distributing tracts, as I hear she does, it will be too depressing. The worst of it is that she would have been so useful at the right time. You know we have to have the Bishop once a year, and she would have given just the right tone to things. I always have horrid luck about the Bishop's visits," added Mrs. Trenor, whose present misery was being fed by a rapidly rising tide of reminiscence; "last year, when he came, Gus forgot all about his being here, and brought home the Ned Wintons and the Farleys—five divorces and six sets of children between them!"

"When is Lady Cressida going?" Lily enquired.

Mrs. Trenor cast up her eyes in despair. "My dear, if one only knew! I was in such a hurry to get her away from Maria that I actually forgot to name a date, and Gus says she told some one she meant to stop here all winter."

"To stop here? In this house?"

"Don't be silly—in America. But if no one else asks her—you know they *never* go to hotels."

"Perhaps Gus only said it to frighten you."

"No—I heard her tell Bertha Dorset that she had six months to put in while her husband was taking the cure in the Engadine. You should have seen Bertha look vacant! But it's no joke, you know—if she stays here all the autumn she'll spoil everything, and Maria Van Osburgh will simply exult."

At this affecting vision Mrs. Trenor's voice trembled with self-pity.

"Oh, Judy—as if any one were ever bored at Bellomont!" Miss Bart tactfully protested. "You know perfectly well that, if Mrs. Van Osburgh were to get all the right people and leave you with all the wrong ones, you'd manage to make things go off, and she wouldn't."

Such an assurance would usually have restored Mrs. Trenor's complacency; but on this occasion it did not chase the cloud from her brow.

"It isn't only Lady Cressida," she lamented. "Everything has gone wrong this week. I can see that Bertha Dorset is furious with me."

"Furious with you? Why?"

"Because I told her that Lawrence Selden was coming; but he wouldn't, after all, and she's quite unreasonable enough to think it's my fault."

Miss Bart put down her pen and sat absently gazing at the note she had begun.

"I thought that was all over," she said.

"So it is, on his side. And of course Bertha has been idle since. But I fancy she's out of a job just at present—and some one gave me a hint that I had better ask Lawrence. Well, I *did* ask him—but I couldn't make him come; and now I suppose she'll take it out of me by being perfectly nasty to every one else."

"Oh, she may take it out of *him* by being perfectly charming—to some one else."

Mrs. Trenor shook her head dolefully. "She knows he wouldn't mind. And who else is there? Alice Wetherall won't let Lucius out of her sight. Ned Silverton can't take his eyes off Carry Fisher—poor boy! Gus is bored by Bertha, Jack Stepney knows her too well—and—well, to be sure, there's Percy Gryce!"

She sat up smiling at the thought.

Miss Bart's countenance did not reflect the smile.

"Oh, she and Mr. Gryce would not be likely to hit it off."

"You mean that she'd shock him and he'd bore her? Well, that's not such a bad beginning, you know. But I hope she won't take it into her head to be nice to him, for I asked him here on purpose for you."

Lily laughed. "*Merci du compliment*! I should certainly have no show against Bertha."

"Do you think I am uncomplimentary? I'm not really, you know. Every one knows you're a thousand times handsomer and cleverer than Bertha; but then you're not nasty. And for always getting what she wants in the long run, commend me to a nasty woman."

Miss Bart stared in affected reproval. "I thought you were so fond of Bertha."

"Oh, I am—it's much safer to be fond of dangerous people. But she IS dangerous—and if I ever saw her up to mischief it's now. I can tell by poor George's manner. That man is a perfect barometer—he always knows when Bertha is going to—"

"To fall?" Miss Bart suggested.

"Don't be shocking! You know he believes in her still. And of course I don't say there's any real harm in Bertha. Only she delights in making people miserable, and especially poor George."

"Well, he seems cut out for the part—I don't wonder she likes more cheerful companionship."

"Oh, George is not as dismal as you think. If Bertha did worry him he would be quite different. Or if she'd leave him alone, and let him arrange his life as he pleases. But she doesn't dare lose her hold of him on account of the money, and so when *he* isn't jealous she pretends to be."

Miss Bart went on writing in silence, and her hostess sat following her train of thought with frowning intensity.

"Do you know," she exclaimed after a long pause, "I believe I'll call up Lawrence on the telephone and tell him he simply *must* come?"

"Oh, don't," said Lily, with a quick suffusion of colour. The blush surprised her almost as much as it did her hostess, who, though not commonly observant of facial changes, sat staring at her with puzzled eyes.

"Good gracious, Lily, how handsome you are! Why? Do you dislike him so much?"

"Not at all; I like him. But if you are actuated by the benevolent intention of protecting me from Bertha—I don't think I need your protection."

Mrs. Trenor sat up with an exclamation. "Lily!—*Percy*? Do you mean to say you've actually done it?"

Miss Bart smiled. "I only mean to say that Mr. Gryce and I are getting to be very good friends."

"H'm—I see." Mrs. Trenor fixed a rapt eye upon her. "You know they say he has eight hundred thousand a year—and spends nothing, except on some rubbishy old books. And his mother has heart-disease and will leave him a lot more. *Oh, Lily, do go slowly*," her friend adjured her.

Miss Bart continued to smile without annoyance. "I shouldn't, for instance," she remarked, "be in any haste to tell him that he had a lot of rubbishy old books."

"No, of course not; I know you're wonderful about getting up people's subjects. But he's horribly shy, and easily shocked, and—and—"

"Why don't you say it, Judy? I have the reputation of being on the hunt for a rich husband?"

"Oh, I don't mean that; he wouldn't believe it of you—at first," said Mrs. Trenor, with candid shrewdness. "But you know things are rather lively here at times—I must give Jack and Gus a hint—and if he thought you were what his mother would call fast—oh, well, you know what I mean. Don't wear your scarlet *crepe-de-chine* for dinner, and don't smoke if you can help it, Lily dear!"

Lily pushed aside her finished work with a dry smile. "You're very kind, Judy: I'll lock up my cigarettes and wear that last year's dress you sent me this morning. And if you are really interested in my career, perhaps you'll be kind enough not to ask me to play bridge again this evening."

"Bridge? Does he mind bridge, too? Oh, Lily, what an awful life you'll lead! But of course I won't—why didn't you give me a hint last night? There's nothing I wouldn't do, you poor duck, to see you happy!"

And Mrs. Trenor, glowing with her sex's eagerness to smooth the course of true love, enveloped Lily in a long embrace.

"You're quite sure," she added solicitously, as the latter extricated herself, "that you wouldn't like me to telephone for Lawrence Selden?"

"Quite sure," said Lily.

The next three days demonstrated to her own complete satisfaction Miss Bart's ability to manage her affairs without extraneous aid.

As she sat, on the Saturday afternoon, on the terrace at Bellomont, she smiled at Mrs. Trenor's fear that she might go too fast. If such a warning had ever been needful, the years had taught her a salutary lesson, and she flattered herself that she now knew how to adapt her pace to the object of pursuit. In the case of Mr. Gryce she had found it well to flutter ahead, losing herself elusively and luring him on from depth to depth of unconscious intimacy. The surrounding atmosphere was propitious to this scheme of courtship. Mrs. Trenor, true to her word, had shown no signs of expecting Lily at the bridge-table, and had even hinted to the other card-players that they were to betray no surprise at her unwonted defection. In consequence of this hint, Lily found herself the centre of that feminine solicitude which envelops a young woman in the mating season. A solitude was tacitly created for her in the crowded existence of Bellomont, and her friends could not have shown a greater readiness for self-effacement had her wooing been adorned with all the attributes of romance. In Lily's set this conduct implied a sympathetic comprehension of her motives, and Mr. Gryce rose in her esteem as she saw the consideration he inspired.

The terrace at Bellomont on a September afternoon was a spot propitious to sentimental musings, and as Miss Bart stood leaning against the balustrade above the sunken garden, at a little distance from the animated group about the tea-table, she might have been lost in the mazes of an inarticulate happiness. In reality, her thoughts were finding definite utterance in the tranquil recapitulation of the blessings in store for her. From where she stood she could see them embodied in the form of Mr. Gryce, who, in a light overcoat and muffler, sat somewhat nervously on the edge of his chair, while Carry Fisher, with all the energy of eye and gesture with which nature and art had combined to endow her, pressed on him the duty of taking part in the task of municipal reform.

Mrs. Fisher's latest hobby was municipal reform. It had been preceded by an equal zeal for socialism, which had in turn replaced an energetic advocacy of Christian Science. Mrs. Fisher was small, fiery and dramatic; and her hands and eyes were admirable instruments in the service of whatever causes he happened to espouse. She had, however, the fault common to enthusiasts of ignoring any slackness of response on the part of her hearers, and Lily was amused by her unconsciousness of the resistance displayed in every angle of Mr. Gryce's attitude. Lily herself knew that his mind was divided between the dread of catching cold if he remained out of doors too long at that hour, and the fear that, if he retreated to the house, Mrs. Fisher might follow him up with a paper to be signed. Mr. Gryce had a constitutional dislike to what he called "committing himself," and tenderly as he cherished his health, he evidently concluded that it was safer to stay out of reach of pen and ink till chance released him from Mrs. Fisher's toils. Meanwhile he cast agonized glances in the direction of Miss Bart, whose only response was to sink into an attitude of more graceful abstraction. She had learned the value of contrast in throwing her charms into relief, and was fully aware of the extent to which Mrs. Fisher's volubility was enhancing her own repose.

She was roused from her musings by the approach of her cousin Jack Stepney who, at Gwen Van Osburgh's side, was returning across the garden from the tennis court.

The couple in question were engaged in the same kind of romance in which Lily figured, and the latter felt a certain annoyance in contemplating what seemed to her a caricature of her own situation. Miss Van Osburgh was a large girl with flat surfaces and no high lights: Jack Stepney had once said of her that she was as reliable as roast mutton. His own taste was in the line of less solid and more highly-seasoned diet; but hunger makes any fare palatable, and there had been times when Mr. Stepney had been reduced to a crust.

Lily considered with interest the expression of their faces: the girl's turned toward her companion's like an empty plate held up to be filled, while the man lounging at her side already betrayed the encroaching boredom which would presently crack the thin veneer of his smile.

"How impatient men are!" Lily reflected. "All Jack has to do to get everything he wants is to keep quiet and let that girl marry him; whereas I have to calculate and contrive, and retreat and advance, as if I were going through an intricate dance, where one misstep would throw me hopelessly out of time."

As they drew nearer she was whimsically struck by a kind of family likeness between Miss Van Osburgh and Percy Gryce. There was no resemblance of feature. Gryce was handsome in a didactic way—he looked like a clever pupil's drawing from a plaster-cast—while Gwen's countenance had no more modelling than a face painted on a toy balloon. But the deeper affinity was unmistakable: the two had the same prejudices and ideals, and the same quality of making other standards non-existent by ignoring them. This attribute was common to most of Lily's set: they had a force of negation which eliminated everything beyond their own range of perception. Gryce and Miss Van Osburgh were, in short, made for each other by every law of moral and physical correspondence—"Yet they wouldn't look at each other," Lily mused, "they never do. Each of them wants a creature of a different race, of Jack's race and mine, with all sorts of intuitions, sensations and perceptions that they don't even guess the existence of. And they always get what they want."

She stood talking with her cousin and Miss Van Osburgh, till a slight cloud on the latter's brow advised her that even cousinly amenities were subject to suspicion, and Miss Bart, mindful of the necessity of not exciting enmities at this crucial point of her career, dropped aside while the happy couple proceeded toward the tea-table.

Seating herself on the upper step of the terrace, Lily leaned her head against the honeysuckles wreathing the balustrade. The fragrance of the late blossoms seemed an emanation of the tranquil scene, a landscape tutored to the last degree of rural elegance. In the foreground glowed the warm tints of the gardens. Beyond the lawn, with its pyramidal pale-gold maples and velvety firs, sloped pastures dotted with cattle; and through a long glade the river widened like a lake under the silver light of September. Lily did not want to join the circle about the tea-table. They represented the future she had chosen, and she was content with it, but in no haste to anticipate its joys. The certainty that she could marry Percy Gryce when she pleased had lifted a heavy load from her mind, and her money troubles were too recent for their removal not to leave a sense of relief which a less discerning intelligence might have taken for happiness. Her vulgar cares were at an end. She would be able to arrange her life as she pleased, to soar into that empyrean of security where creditors cannot penetrate. She would have smarter gowns than Judy Trenor, and far, far more jewels than

Bertha Dorset. She would be free forever from the shifts, the expedients, the humiliations of the relatively poor. Instead of having to flatter, she would be flattered; instead of being grateful, she would receive thanks. There were old scores she could pay off as well as old benefits she could return. And she had no doubts as to the extent of her power. She knew that Mr. Gryce was of the small chary type most inaccessible to impulses and emotions. He had the kind of character in which prudence is a vice, and good advice the most dangerous nourishment. But Lily had known the species before: she was aware that such a guarded nature must find one huge outlet of egoism, and she determined to be to him what his Americana had hitherto been: the one possession in which he took sufficient pride to spend money on it. She knew that this generosity to self is one of the forms of meanness, and she resolved so to identify herself with her husband's vanity that to gratify her wishes would be to him the most exquisite form of self-indulgence. The system might at first necessitate a resort to some of the very shifts and expedients from which she intended it should free her; but she felt sure that in a short time she would be able to play the game in her own way. How should she have distrusted her powers? Her beauty itself was not the mere ephemeral possession it might have been in the hands of inexperience: her skill in enhancing it, the care she took of it, the use she made of it, seemed to give it a kind of permanence. She felt she could trust it to carry her through to the end.

And the end, on the whole, was worthwhile. Life was not the mockery she had thought it three days ago. There was room for her, after all, in this crowded selfish world of pleasure whence, so short a time since, her poverty had seemed to exclude her. These people whom she had ridiculed and yet envied were glad to make a place for her in the charmed circle about which all her desires revolved. They were not as brutal and self-engrossed as she had fancied—or rather, since it would no longer be necessary to flatter and humour them, that side of their nature became less conspicuous. Society is a revolving body which is apt to be judged according to its place in each man's heaven; and at present it was turning its illuminated face to Lily.

In the rosy glow it diffused her companions seemed full of amiable qualities. She liked their elegance, their lightness, their lack of emphasis: even the self-assurance which at times was so like obtuseness now seemed the natural sign of social ascendency. They were lords of the only world she cared for, and they were ready to admit her to their ranks and let her lord it with them. Already she felt within her a stealing allegiance to their standards, an acceptance of their limitations, a disbelief in the things they did not believe in, a contemptuous pity for the people who were not able to live as they lived.

The early sunset was slanting across the park. Through the boughs of the long avenue beyond the gardens she caught the flash of wheels, and divined that more visitors were approaching. There was a movement behind her, a scattering of steps and voices: it was evident that the party about the tea-table was breaking up. Presently she heard a tread behind her on the terrace. She supposed that Mr. Gryce had at last found means to escape from his predicament, and she smiled at the significance of his coming to join her instead of beating an instant retreat to the fire-side.

She turned to give him the welcome which such gallantry deserved; but her greeting wavered into a blush of wonder, for the man who had approached her was Lawrence Selden.

"You see I came after all," he said; but before she had time to answer, Mrs. Dorset, breaking away from a lifeless colloquy with her host, had stepped between them with a little gesture of appropriation.

# Chapter 5

The observance of Sunday at Bellomont was chiefly marked by the punctual appearance of the smart omnibus destined to convey the household to the little church at the gates. Whether any one got into the omnibus or not was a matter of secondary importance, since by standing there it not only bore witness to the orthodox intentions of the family, but made Mrs. Trenor feel, when she finally heard it drive away, that she had somehow vicariously made use of it.

It was Mrs. Trenor's theory that her daughters actually did go to church every Sunday; but their French governess's convictions calling her to the rival fane, and the fatigues of the week keeping their mother in her room till luncheon, there was seldom any one present to verify the fact. Now and then, in a spasmodic burst of virtue—when the house had been too uproarious over night—Gus Trenor forced his genial bulk into a tight frock-coat and routed his daughters from their slumbers; but habitually, as Lily explained to Mr. Gryce, this parental duty was forgotten till the church bells were ringing across the park, and the omnibus had driven away empty.

Lily had hinted to Mr. Gryce that this neglect of religious observances was repugnant to her early traditions, and that during her visits to Bellomont she regularly accompanied Muriel and Hilda to church. This tallied with the assurance, also confidentially imparted, that, never having played bridge before, she had been "dragged into it" on the night of her arrival, and had lost an appalling amount of money in consequence of her ignorance of the game and of the rules of betting. Mr. Gryce was undoubtedly enjoying Bellomont. He liked the ease and glitter of the life, and the lustre conferred on him by being a member of this group of rich and conspicuous people. But he thought it a very materialistic society; there were times when he was frightened by the talk of the men and the looks of the ladies, and he was glad to find that

Miss Bart, for all her ease and self-possession, was not at home in so ambiguous an atmosphere. For this reason he had been especially pleased to learn that she would, as usual, attend the young Trenors to church on Sunday morning; and as he paced the gravel sweep before the door, his light overcoat on his arm and his prayer-book in one carefully-gloved hand, he reflected agreeably on the strength of character which kept her true to her early training in surroundings so subversive to religious principles.

For a long time Mr. Gryce and the omnibus had the gravel sweep to themselves; but, far from regretting this deplorable indifference on the part of the other guests, he found himself nourishing the hope that Miss Bart might be unaccompanied. The precious minutes were flying, however; the big chestnuts pawed the ground and flecked their impatient sides with foam; the coachman seemed to be slowly petrifying on the box, and the groom on the doorstep; and still the lady did not come. Suddenly, however, there was a sound of voices and a rustle of skirts in the doorway, and Mr. Gryce, restoring his watch to his pocket, turned with a nervous start; but it was only to find himself handing Mrs. Wetherall into the carriage.

The Wetheralls always went to church. They belonged to the vast group of human automata who go through life without neglecting to perform a single one of the gestures executed by the surrounding puppets. It is true that the Bellomont puppets did not go to church; but others equally important did—and Mr. and Mrs. Wetherall's circle was so large that God was included in their visiting-list. They appeared, therefore, punctual and resigned, with the air of people bound for a dull "At Home," and after them Hilda and Muriel straggled, yawning and pinning each other's veils and ribbons as they came. They had promised Lily to go to church with her, they declared, and Lily was such a dear old duck that they didn't mind doing it to please her, though they couldn't fancy what had put the idea in her head, and though for their own part they would much rather have played lawn tennis with Jack and Gwen, if she hadn't told them she was coming. The Misses Trenor were followed by Lady Cressida Raith, a weather-beaten person in Liberty silk and ethnological trinkets, who, on seeing the omnibus, expressed her surprise that they were not to walk across the park; but at Mrs. Wetherall's horrified protest that the church was a mile away, her ladyship, after a glance at the height of the other's heels, acquiesced in the necessity of driving, and poor Mr. Gryce found himself rolling off between four ladies for whose spiritual welfare he felt not the least concern.

It might have afforded him some consolation could he have known that Miss Bart had really meant to go to church. She had even risen earlier than usual in the execution of her purpose. She had an idea that the sight of her in a grey gown of devotional cut, with her famous lashes drooped above a prayer-book, would put the finishing touch to Mr. Gryce's subjugation, and render inevitable a certain incident which she had resolved should form a part of the walk they were to take together after luncheon. Her intentions in short had never been more definite; but poor Lily, for all the hard glaze of her exterior, was inwardly as malleable as wax. Her faculty for adapting herself, for entering into other people's feelings, if it served her now and then in small contingencies, hampered her in the decisive moments of life. She was like a water-plant in the flux of the tides, and today the whole current of her mood was carrying her toward Lawrence Selden. Why had he come? Was it to see herself or Bertha Dorset? It was the last question which, at that moment, should have engaged her. She might better have contented herself with thinking that he had simply responded to the despairing summons of his hostess, anxious to interpose him between herself and the ill-humour of Mrs. Dorset. But Lily had not rested till she learned from Mrs. Trenor that Selden had come of his own accord. "He didn't even wire me—he just happened to find the trap at the station. Perhaps it's not over with Bertha after all," Mrs. Trenor musingly concluded; and went away to arrange her dinner-cards accordingly.

Perhaps it was not, Lily reflected; but it should be soon, unless she had lost her cunning. If Selden had come at Mrs. Dorset's call, it was at her own that he would stay. So much the previous evening had told her. Mrs. Trenor, true to her simple principle of making her married friends happy, had placed Selden and Mrs. Dorset next to each other at dinner; but, in obedience to the time-honoured traditions of the match-maker, she had separated Lily and Mr. Gryce, sending in the former with George Dorset, while Mr. Gryce was coupled with Gwen Van Osburgh.

George Dorset's talk did not interfere with the range of his neighbour's thoughts. He was a mournful dyspeptic, intent on finding out the deleterious ingredients of every dish and diverted from this care only by the sound of his wife's voice. On this occasion, however, Mrs. Dorset took no part in the general conversation. She sat talking in low murmurs with Selden, and turning a contemptuous and denuded shoulder toward her host, who, far from resenting his exclusion, plunged into the excesses of the *menu* with the joyous irresponsibility of a free man. To Mr. Dorset, however, his wife's attitude was a subject of such evident concern that, when he was not scraping the sauce from his fish, or scooping the moist bread-crumbs from the interior of his roll, he sat straining his thin neck for a glimpse of her between the lights.

Mrs. Trenor, as it chanced, had placed the husband and wife on opposite sides of the table, and Lily was therefore able to observe Mrs. Dorset also, and by carrying her glance a few feet farther, to set up a rapid comparison between Lawrence Selden and Mr. Gryce. It was that comparison which was her undoing. Why else had she suddenly grown interested in Selden? She had known him for eight years or more: ever since her return to America he had formed a part of her background. She had always been glad to sit next to him at dinner, had found him more agreeable than most men, and had vaguely wished that he possessed the other qualities needful to fix her attention; but till now she had been too busy with her own affairs to regard him as more than one of the pleasant accessories of life. Miss Bart was a keen reader of her own heart, and she saw that her sudden preoccupation with Selden was due to the fact that his presence shed a new light on her surroundings. Not that he was notably brilliant or exceptional; in his own profession he was surpassed by more than one man who had bored Lily through many a weary dinner. It was rather that he had preserved a certain social detachment, a happy air of viewing the show objectively, of having points of contact outside the great gilt cage in which they were all huddled for the mob to gape at. How alluring the world outside the cage appeared to Lily, as she heard its door clang on her! In reality, as she knew, the door never clanged: it stood always open; but most of the captives were like flies in a bottle, and having once flown in, could never regain their freedom. It was Selden's distinction that he had never forgotten the way out.

That was the secret of his way of readjusting her vision. Lily, turning her eyes from him, found herself scanning her little world through his retina: it was as though the pink lamps had been shut off and the dusty daylight let in. She looked down the long table, studying its occupants one by one, from Gus Trenor, with his heavy carnivorous head sunk between his shoulders, as he preyed on a jellied plover, to his wife, at the opposite end of the long bank of orchids, suggestive, with her glaring good-looks, of a jeweller's window lit by electricity. And between the two, what a long stretch of vacuity! How dreary and trivial these people were! Lily reviewed them with a scornful impatience: Carry Fisher, with her shoulders, her eyes, her divorces, her general air of embodying a "spicy paragraph"; young Silverton, who had meant to live on proof-reading and write an epic, and who now lived on his friends and had become critical of truffles; Alice Wetherall, an animated visiting-list, whose most fervid convictions turned on the wording of invitations and the engraving of dinner-cards; Wetherall, with his perpetual nervous nod of acquiescence, his air of agreeing with people before he knew what they were saying; Jack Stepney, with his confident smile and anxious eyes, half way between the sheriff and an heiress; Gwen Van Osburgh, with all the guileless confidence of a young girl who has always been told that there is no one richer than her father.

Lily smiled at her classification of her friends. How different they had seemed to her a few hours ago! Then they had symbolized what she was gaining, now they stood for what she was giving up. That very afternoon they had seemed full of brilliant qualities; now she saw that they were merely dull in a loud way. Under the glitter of their opportunities she saw the poverty of their achievement. It was not that she wanted them to be more disinterested; but she would have liked them to be more picturesque. And she had a shamed recollection of the way in which, a few hours since, she had felt the centripetal force of their standards. She closed her eyes an instant, and the vacuous routine of the life she had chosen stretched before her like a long white road without dip or turning: it was true she was to roll over it in a carriage instead of trudging it on foot, but sometimes the pedestrian enjoys the diversion of a short cut which is denied to those on wheels.

She was roused by a chuckle which Mr. Dorset seemed to eject from the depths of his lean throat.

"I say, do look at her," he exclaimed, turning to Miss Bart with lugubrious merriment—"I beg your pardon, but do just look at my wife making a fool of that poor devil over there! One would really suppose she was gone on him—and it's all the other way round, I assure you."

Thus adjured, Lily turned her eyes on the spectacle which was affording Mr. Dorset such legitimate mirth. It certainly appeared, as he said, that Mrs. Dorset was the more active participant in the scene: her neighbour seemed to receive her advances with a temperate zest which did not distract him from his dinner. The sight restored Lily's good humour, and knowing the peculiar disguise which Mr. Dorset's marital fears assumed, she asked gaily: "Aren't you horribly jealous of her?"

Dorset greeted the sally with delight. "Oh, abominably—you've just hit it—keeps me awake at night. The doctors tell me that's what has knocked my digestion out—being so infernally jealous of her.—I can't eat a mouthful of this stuff, you know," he added suddenly, pushing back his plate with a clouded countenance; and Lily, unfailingly adaptable, accorded her radiant attention to his prolonged denunciation of other people's cooks, with a supplementary tirade on the toxic qualities of melted butter.

It was not often that he found so ready an ear; and, being a man as well as a dyspeptic, it may be that as he poured his grievances into it he was not insensible to its rosy symmetry. At any rate he engaged Lily so long that the sweets were being handed when she caught a phrase on her other side, where Miss Corby, the comic woman of the company, was bantering Jack Stepney on his approaching engagement. Miss Corby's role was jocularity: she always entered the conversation with a handspring.

"And of course you'll have Sim Rosedale as best man!" Lily heard her fling out as the climax of her prognostications; and Stepney responded, as if struck: "Jove, that's an idea. What a thumping present I'd get out of him!"

*Sim Rosedale*! The name, made more odious by its diminutive, obtruded itself on Lily's thoughts like a leer. It stood for one of the many hated possibilities hovering on the edge of life. If she did not marry Percy Gryce, the day might come when she would have to be civil to such men as Rosedale. *If she did not marry him?* But she meant to marry him—she was sure of him and sure of herself. She drew back with a shiver from the pleasant paths in which her thoughts had been straying, and set her feet once more in the middle of the long white road.... When she went upstairs that night she found that the late post had brought her a fresh batch of bills. Mrs. Peniston, who was a conscientious woman, had forwarded them all to Bellomont.

Miss Bart, accordingly, rose the next morning with the most earnest conviction that it was her duty to go to church. She tore herself betimes from the lingering enjoyment of her breakfast-tray, rang to have her grey gown laid out, and despatched her maid to borrow a prayer-book from Mrs. Trenor.

But her course was too purely reasonable not to contain the germs of rebellion. No sooner were her preparations made than they roused a smothered sense of resistance. A small spark was enough to kindle Lily's imagination, and the sight of the grey dress and the borrowed prayer-book flashed a long light down the years. She would have to go to church with Percy Gryce every Sunday. They would have a front pew in the most expensive church in New York, and his name would figure handsomely in the list of parish charities. In a few years, when he grew stouter, he would be made a warden. Once in the winter the rector would come to dine, and her husband would beg her to go over the list and see that no *divorcees* were included, except those who had showed signs of penitence by being re-married to the very wealthy. There was nothing especially arduous in this round of religious obligations; but it stood for a fraction of that great bulk of boredom which loomed across her path. And who could consent to be bored on such a morning? Lily had slept well, and her bath had filled her with a pleasant glow, which was becomingly reflected in the clear curve of her cheek. No lines were visible this morning, or else the glass was at a happier angle.

And the day was the accomplice of her mood: it was a day for impulse and truancy. The light air seemed full of powdered gold; below the dewy bloom of the lawns the woodlands blushed and smouldered, and the hills across the river swam in molten blue. Every drop of blood in Lily's veins invited her to happiness.

The sound of wheels roused her from these musings, and leaning behind her shutters she saw the omnibus take up its freight. She was too late, then—but the fact did not alarm her. A glimpse of Mr. Gryce's crestfallen face even suggested that she had done wisely in absenting herself, since the disappointment he so candidly betrayed would surely whet his appetite for the afternoon walk. That walk she did not mean to miss; one glance at the bills on her writing-table was enough to recall its necessity. But meanwhile she had the morning to herself, and could muse pleasantly on the disposal of its hours. She was familiar enough with the habits of Bellomont to know that she was likely to have a free field till luncheon. She had seen the Wetheralls, the Trenor girls and Lady Cressida packed safely into the omnibus; Judy Trenor was sure to be having her hair shampooed; Carry Fisher had doubtless carried off her host for a drive; Ned Silverton was probably smoking the cigarette of young despair in his bedroom; and Kate Corby was certain to be playing tennis with Jack Stepney and Miss Van Osburgh. Of the ladies, this left only Mrs. Dorset unaccounted for, and Mrs. Dorset never came down till luncheon: her doctors, she averred, had forbidden her to expose herself to the crude air of the morning.

To the remaining members of the party Lily gave no special thought; wherever they were, they were not likely to interfere with her plans. These, for the moment, took the shape of assuming a dress somewhat more rustic and summerlike in style than the garment she had first selected, and rustling downstairs, sunshade in hand, with the disengaged air of a lady in quest of exercise. The great hall was empty but for the knot of dogs by the fire, who, taking in at a glance the outdoor aspect of Miss Bart, were upon her at once with lavish offers of companionship. She put aside the ramming paws which conveyed these offers, and assuring the joyous volunteers that she might presently have a use for their company, sauntered on through the empty drawing-room to the library at the end of the house. The library was almost the only surviving portion of the old manor-house of Bellomont: a long spacious room, revealing the traditions of the mother-country in its classically-cased doors, the Dutch tiles of the chimney, and the elaborate hob-grate with its shining brass urns. A few family portraits of lantern-jawed gentlemen in tie-wigs, and ladies with large head-dresses and small bodies, hung between the shelves lined with pleasantly-shabby books: books mostly contemporaneous with the ancestors in question, and to which the subsequent Trenors had made no perceptible additions. The library at Bellomont was in fact never used for reading, though it had a certain popularity as a smoking-room or a quiet retreat for flirtation. It had occurred to Lily, however, that it might on this occasion have been resorted to by the only member of the party in the least likely to put it to its original use. She advanced noiselessly over the dense old rug scattered with easy-chairs, and before she reached the middle of the room she saw that she had not been mistaken. Lawrence Selden was in fact seated at its farther end; but though a book lay on his knee, his attention was not engaged with it, but directed to a lady whose lace-clad figure, as she leaned back in an adjoining chair, detached itself with exaggerated slimness against the dusky leather upholstery.

Lily paused as she caught sight of the group; for a moment she seemed about to withdraw, but thinking better of this, she announced her approach by a slight shake of her skirts which made the couple raise their heads, Mrs. Dorset with a look of frank displeasure, and Selden with his usual quiet smile. The sight of his composure had a disturbing effect on Lily; but to be disturbed was in her case to make a more brilliant effort at self-possession.

"Dear me, am I late?" she asked, putting a hand in his as he advanced to greet her.

"Late for what?" enquired Mrs. Dorset tartly. "Not for luncheon, certainly—but perhaps you had an earlier engagement?"

"Yes, I had," said Lily confidingly.

"Really? Perhaps I am in the way, then? But Mr. Selden is entirely at your disposal." Mrs. Dorset was pale with temper, and her antagonist felt a certain pleasure in prolonging her distress.

"Oh, dear, no—do stay," she said good-humouredly. "I don't in the least want to drive you away."

"You're awfully good, dear, but I never interfere with Mr. Selden's engagements."

The remark was uttered with a little air of proprietorship not lost on its object, who concealed a faint blush of annoyance by stooping to pick up the book he had dropped at Lily's approach. The latter's eyes widened charmingly and she broke into a light laugh.

"But I have no engagement with Mr. Selden! My engagement was to go to church; and I'm afraid the omnibus has started without me. *Has* it started, do you know?"

She turned to Selden, who replied that he had heard it drive away some time since.

"Ah, then I shall have to walk; I promised Hilda and Muriel to go to church with them. It's too late to walk there, you say? Well, I shall have the credit of trying, at any rate—and the advantage of escaping part of the service. I'm not so sorry for myself, after all!"

And with a bright nod to the couple on whom she had intruded, Miss Bart strolled through the glass doors and carried her rustling grace down the long perspective of the garden walk.

She was taking her way churchward, but at no very quick pace; a fact not lost on one of her observers, who stood in the doorway looking after her with an air of puzzled amusement. The truth is that she was conscious of a somewhat keen shock of disappointment. All her plans for the day had been built on the assumption that it was to see her that Selden had come to Bellomont. She had expected, when she came downstairs, to find him on the watch for her; and she had found him, instead, in a situation which might well denote that he had been on the watch for another lady. Was it possible, after all, that he had come for Bertha Dorset? The latter had acted on the assumption to the extent of appearing at an hour when she never showed herself to ordinary mortals, and Lily, for the moment, saw no way of putting her in the wrong. It did not occur to her that Selden might have been actuated merely by the desire to spend a Sunday out of town: women never learn to dispense with the sentimental motive in their judgments of men. But Lily was not easily disconcerted; competition put her on her mettle, and she reflected that Selden's coming, if it did not declare him to be still in Mrs. Dorset's toils, showed him to be so completely free from them that he was not afraid of her proximity.

These thoughts so engaged her that she fell into a gait hardly likely to carry her to church before the sermon, and at length, having passed from the gardens to the wood-path beyond, so far forgot her intention as to sink into a rustic seat at a bend of the walk. The spot was charming, and Lily was not insensible to the charm, or to the fact that her presence enhanced it; but she was not accustomed to taste the joys of solitude except in company, and the combination of a handsome girl and a romantic scene struck her as too good to be wasted. No one, however, appeared to profit by the opportunity; and after a half hour of fruitless waiting she rose and wandered on. She felt a stealing sense of fatigue as she walked; the sparkle had died out of her, and the taste of life was stale on her lips. She hardly knew what she had been seeking, or why the failure to find it had so blotted the light from her sky: she was only aware of a vague sense of failure, of an inner isolation deeper than the loneliness about her.

Her footsteps flagged, and she stood gazing listlessly ahead, digging the ferny edge of the path with the tip of her sunshade. As she did so a step sounded behind her, and she saw Selden at her side.

"How fast you walk!" he remarked. "I thought I should never catch up with you."

She answered gaily: "You must be quite breathless! I've been sitting under that tree for an hour."

"Waiting for me, I hope?" he rejoined; and she said with a vague laugh:

"Well—waiting to see if you would come."

"I seize the distinction, but I don't mind it, since doing the one involved doing the other. But weren't you sure that I should come?"

"If I waited long enough—but you see I had only a limited time to give to the experiment."

"Why limited? Limited by luncheon?"

"No; by my other engagement."

"Your engagement to go to church with Muriel and Hilda?"

"No; but to come home from church with another person."

"Ah, I see; I might have known you were fully provided with alternatives. And is the other person coming home this way?"

Lily laughed again. "That's just what I don't know; and to find out, it is my business to get to church before the service is over."

"Exactly; and it is my business to prevent your doing so; in which case the other person, piqued by your absence, will form the desperate resolve of driving back in the omnibus."

Lily received this with fresh appreciation; his nonsense was like the bubbling of her inner mood. "Is that what you would do in such an emergency?" she enquired.

Selden looked at her with solemnity. "I am here to prove to you," he cried, "what I am capable of doing in an emergency!"

"Walking a mile in an hour—you must own that the omnibus would be quicker!"

"Ah—but will he find you in the end? That's the only test of success."

They looked at each other with the same luxury of enjoyment that they had felt in exchanging absurdities over his tea-table; but suddenly Lily's face changed, and she said: "Well, if it is, he has succeeded."

Selden, following her glance, perceived a party of people advancing toward them from the farther bend of the path. Lady Cressida had evidently insisted on walking home, and the rest of the church-goers had thought it their duty to accompany her. Lily's companion looked rapidly from one to the other of the two men of the party; Wetherall walking respectfully at Lady Cressida's side with his little sidelong look of nervous attention, and Percy Gryce bringing up the rear with Mrs. Wetherall and the Trenors.

"Ah—now I see why you were getting up your Americana!" Selden exclaimed with a note of the freest admiration but the blush with which the sally was received checked whatever amplifications he had meant to give it.

That Lily Bart should object to being bantered about her suitors, or even about her means of attracting them, was so new to Selden that he had a momentary flash of surprise, which lit up a number of possibilities; but she rose gallantly to the defence of her confusion, by saying, as its object approached: "That was why I was waiting for you—to thank you for having given me so many points!"

"Ah, you can hardly do justice to the subject in such a short time," said Selden, as the Trenor girls caught sight of Miss Bart; and while she signalled a response to their boisterous greeting, he added quickly: "Won't you devote your afternoon to it? You know I must be off tomorrow morning. We'll take a walk, and you can thank me at your leisure."

# Chapter 6

The afternoon was perfect. A deeper stillness possessed the air, and the glitter of the American autumn was tempered by a haze which diffused the brightness without dulling it.

In the woody hollows of the park there was already a faint chill; but as the ground rose the air grew lighter, and ascending the long slopes beyond the high-road, Lily and her companion reached a zone of lingering summer. The path wound across a meadow with scattered trees; then it dipped into a lane plumed with asters and purpling sprays of bramble, whence, through the light quiver of ash-leaves, the country unrolled itself in pastoral distances.

Higher up, the lane showed thickening tufts of fern and of the creeping glossy verdure of shaded slopes; trees began to overhang it, and the shade deepened to the checkered dusk of a beech-grove. The boles of the trees stood well apart, with only a light feathering of undergrowth; the path wound along the edge of the wood, now and then looking out on a sunlit pasture or on an orchard spangled with fruit.

Lily had no real intimacy with nature, but she had a passion for the appropriate and could be keenly sensitive to a scene which was the fitting background of her own sensations. The landscape outspread below her seemed an enlargement of her present mood, and she found something of herself in its calmness, its breadth, its long free reaches. On the nearer slopes the sugar-maples wavered like pyres of light; lower down was a massing of grey orchards, and here and there the lingering green of an oak-grove. Two or three red farm-houses dozed under the apple-trees, and the white wooden spire of a village church showed beyond the shoulder of the hill; while far below, in a haze of dust, the high-road ran between the fields.

"Let us sit here," Selden suggested, as they reached an open ledge of rock above which the beeches rose steeply between mossy boulders.

Lily dropped down on the rock, glowing with her long climb. She sat quiet, her lips parted by the stress of the ascent, her eyes wandering peacefully over the broken ranges of the landscape. Selden stretched himself on the grass at her feet, tilting his hat against the level sun-rays, and clasping his hands behind his head, which rested against the side of the rock. He had no wish to make her talk; her quick-breathing silence seemed a part of the general hush and harmony of things. In his own mind there was only a lazy sense of pleasure, veiling the sharp edges of sensation as the September haze veiled the scene at their feet. But Lily, though her attitude was as calm as his, was throbbing inwardly with a rush of thoughts. There were in her at the moment two beings, one drawing deep breaths of freedom and exhilaration, the other gasping for air in a little black prison-house of fears. But gradually the captive's gasps grew fainter, or the other paid less heed to them: the horizon expanded, the air grew stronger, and the free spirit quivered for flight.

She could not herself have explained the sense of buoyancy which seemed to lift and swing her above the sun-suffused world at her feet. Was it love, she wondered, or a mere fortuitous combination of happy thoughts and sensations? How much of it was owing to the spell of the perfect afternoon, the scent of the fading woods, the thought of the dulness she had fled from? Lily had no definite experience by which to test the quality of her feelings. She had several times been in love with fortunes or careers, but only once with a man. That was years ago, when she first came out, and had been smitten with a romantic passion for a young gentleman named Herbert Melson, who had blue eyes and a little wave in his hair. Mr. Melson, who was possessed of no other negotiable securities, had hastened to employ these in capturing the eldest Miss Van Osburgh: since then he had grown stout and wheezy, and was given to telling anecdotes about his children. If Lily recalled this early emotion it was not to compare it with that which now possessed her; the only point of comparison was the sense of lightness, of emancipation, which she remembered feeling, in the whirl of a waltz or the seclusion of a conservatory, during the brief course of her youthful romance. She had not known again till today that lightness, that glow of freedom; but now it was something more than a blind groping of the blood. The peculiar charm of her feeling for Selden was that she understood it; she could put her finger on every link of the chain that was drawing them together. Though his popularity was of the quiet kind, felt rather than actively expressed among his friends, she had never mistaken his inconspicuousness for obscurity. His reputed cultivation was generally regarded as a slight obstacle to easy intercourse, but Lily, who prided herself on her broad-minded recognition of literature, and always carried an Omar Khayam in her travelling-bag, was attracted by this attribute, which she felt would have had its distinction in an older society. It was, moreover, one of his gifts to look his part; to have a height which lifted his head above the crowd, and the keenly-modelled dark features which, in a land of amorphous types, gave him the air of belonging to a more specialized race, of carrying the impress of a concentrated past. Expansive persons found him a little dry, and very young girls thought him sarcastic; but this air of friendly aloofness, as far removed as possible from any assertion of personal advantage, was the quality which piqued Lily's interest. Everything about him accorded with the fastidious element in her taste, even to the light irony with which he surveyed what seemed to her most sacred. She admired him most of all, perhaps, for being able to convey as distinct a sense of superiority as the richest man she had ever met.

It was the unconscious prolongation of this thought which led her to say presently, with a laugh: "I have broken two engagements for you today. How many have you broken for me?"

"None," said Selden calmly. "My only engagement at Bellomont was with you."

She glanced down at him, faintly smiling.

"Did you really come to Bellomont to see me?"

"Of course I did."

Her look deepened meditatively. "Why?" she murmured, with an accent which took all tinge of coquetry from the question.

"Because you're such a wonderful spectacle: I always like to see what you are doing."

"How do you know what I should be doing if you were not here?"

Selden smiled. "I don't flatter myself that my coming has deflected your course of action by a hair's breadth."

"That's absurd—since, if you were not here, I could obviously not be taking a walk with you."

"No; but your taking a walk with me is only another way of making use of your material. You are an artist and I happen to be the bit of colour you are using today. It's a part of your cleverness to be able to produce premeditated effects extemporaneously."

Lily smiled also: his words were too acute not to strike her sense of humour. It was true that she meant to use the accident of his presence as part of a very definite effect; or that, at least, was the secret pretext she had found for breaking her promise to walk with Mr. Gryce. She had sometimes been accused of being too eager—even Judy Trenor had warned her to go slowly. Well, she would not be too eager in this case; she would give her suitor a longer taste of suspense. Where duty and inclination jumped together, it was not in Lily's nature to hold them asunder. She had excused herself from the walk on the plea of a headache: the horrid headache which, in the morning, had prevented her venturing to church. Her appearance at luncheon justified the excuse. She looked languid, full of a suffering sweetness; she carried a scent-bottle in her hand. Mr. Gryce was new to such manifestations; he wondered rather nervously if she were delicate, having far-reaching fears about the future of his progeny. But sympathy won the day, and he besought her not to expose herself: he always connected the outer air with ideas of exposure.

Lily had received his sympathy with languid gratitude, urging him, since she should be such poor company, to join the rest of the party who, after luncheon, were starting in automobiles on a visit to the Van Osburghs at Peekskill. Mr. Gryce was touched by her disinterestedness, and, to escape from the threatened vacuity of the afternoon, had taken her advice and departed mournfully, in a dust-hood and goggles: as the motor-car plunged down the avenue she smiled at his resemblance to a baffled beetle. Selden had watched her manoeuvres with lazy amusement. She had made no reply to his suggestion that they should spend the afternoon together, but as her plan unfolded itself he felt fairly confident of being included in it. The house was empty when at length he heard her step on the stair and strolled out of the billiard-room to join her.

She had on a hat and walking-dress, and the dogs were bounding at her feet.

"I thought, after all, the air might do me good," she explained; and he agreed that so simple a remedy was worth trying.

The excursionists would be gone at least four hours; Lily and Selden had the whole afternoon before them, and the sense of leisure and safety gave the last touch of lightness to her spirit. With so much time to talk, and no definite object to be led up to, she could taste the rare joys of mental vagrancy.

She felt so free from ulterior motives that she took up his charge with a touch of resentment.

"I don't know," she said, "why you are always accusing me of premeditation."

"I thought you confessed to it: you told me the other day that you had to follow a certain line—and if one does a thing at all it is a merit to do it thoroughly."

"If you mean that a girl who has no one to think for her is obliged to think for herself, I am quite willing to accept the imputation. But you must find me a dismal kind of person if you suppose that I never yield to an impulse."

"Ah, but I don't suppose that: haven't I told you that your genius lies in converting impulses into intentions?"

"My genius?" she echoed with a sudden note of weariness. "Is there any final test of genius but success? And I certainly haven't succeeded."

Selden pushed his hat back and took a side-glance at her. "Success—what is success? I shall be interested to have your definition."

"Success?" She hesitated. "Why, to get as much as one can out of life, I suppose. It's a relative quality, after all. Isn't that your idea of it?"

"My idea of it? God forbid!" He sat up with sudden energy, resting his elbows on his knees and staring out upon the mellow fields. "My idea of success," he said, "is personal freedom."

"Freedom? Freedom from worries?"

"From everything—from money, from poverty, from ease and anxiety, from all the material accidents. To keep a kind of republic of the spirit—that's what I call success."

She leaned forward with a responsive flash. "I know—I know—it's strange; but that's just what I've been feeling today."

He met her eyes with the latent sweetness of his. "Is the feeling so rare with you?" he said.

She blushed a little under his gaze. "You think me horribly sordid, don't you? But perhaps it's rather that I never had any choice. There was no one, I mean, to tell me about the republic of the spirit."

"There never is—it's a country one has to find the way to one's self."

"But I should never have found my way there if you hadn't told me."

"Ah, there are sign-posts—but one has to know how to read them."

"Well, I have known, I have known!" she cried with a glow of eagerness. "Whenever I see you, I find myself spelling out a letter of the sign—and yesterday—last evening at dinner—I suddenly saw a little way into your republic."

Selden was still looking at her, but with a changed eye. Hitherto he had found, in her presence and her talk, the aesthetic amusement which a reflective man is apt to seek in desultory intercourse with pretty women. His attitude had been one of admiring spectatorship, and he would have been almost sorry to detect in her any emotional weakness which should interfere with the fulfilment of her aims. But now the hint of this weakness had become the most interesting thing about her. He had come on her that morning in a moment of disarray; her face had been pale and altered, and the diminution of her beauty had lent her a poignant charm. *That is how she looks when she is alone*! had been his first thought; and the second was to note in her the change which his coming produced. It was the danger-point of their intercourse that he could not doubt the spontaneity of her liking. From whatever angle he viewed their dawning intimacy, he could not see it as part of her scheme of life; and to be the unforeseen element in a career so accurately planned was stimulating even to a man who had renounced sentimental experiments.

"Well," he said, "did it make you want to see more? Are you going to become one of us?"

He had drawn out his cigarettes as he spoke, and she reached her hand toward the case.

"Oh, do give me one—I haven't smoked for days!"

"Why such unnatural abstinence? Everybody smokes at Bellomont."

"Yes—but it is not considered becoming in a *jeune fille a marier*; and at the present moment I am a *jeune fille a marier*."

"Ah, then I'm afraid we can't let you into the republic."

"Why not? Is it a celibate order?"

"Not in the least, though I'm bound to say there are not many married people in it. But you will marry some one very rich, and it's as hard for rich people to get into as the kingdom of heaven."

"That's unjust, I think, because, as I understand it, one of the conditions of citizenship is not to think too much about money, and the only way not to think about money is to have a great deal of it."

"You might as well say that the only way not to think about air is to have enough to breathe. That is true enough in a sense; but your lungs are thinking about the air, if you are not. And so it is with your rich people—they may not be thinking of money, but they're breathing it all the while; take them into another element and see how they squirm and gasp!"

Lily sat gazing absently through the blue rings of her cigarette-smoke.

"It seems to me," she said at length, "that you spend a good deal of your time in the element you disapprove of."

Selden received this thrust without discomposure. "Yes; but I have tried to remain amphibious: it's all right as long as one's lungs can work in another air. The real alchemy consists in being able to turn gold back again into something else; and that's the secret that most of your friends have lost."

Lily mused. "Don't you think," she rejoined after a moment, "that the people who find fault with society are too apt to regard it as an end and not a means, just as the people who despise money speak as if its only use were to be kept in bags and gloated over? Isn't it fairer to look at them both as opportunities, which may be used either stupidly or intelligently, according to the capacity of the user?"

"That is certainly the sane view; but the queer thing about society is that the people who regard it as an end are those who are in it, and not the critics on the fence. It's just the other way with most shows—the audience may be under the illusion, but the actors know that real life is on the other side of the footlights. The people who take society as an escape from work are putting it to its proper use; but when it becomes the thing worked for it distorts all the relations of life." Selden raised himself on his elbow. "Good heavens!" he went on, "I don't underrate the decorative side of life. It seems to me the sense of splendour has justified itself by what it has produced. The worst of it is that so much human nature is used up in the process. If we're all the raw stuff of the cosmic effects, one would rather be the fire that tempers a sword than the fish that dyes a purple cloak. And a society like ours wastes such good material in producing its little patch of purple! Look at a boy like Ned Silverton—he's really too good to be used to refurbish anybody's social shabbiness. There's a lad just setting out to discover the universe:

isn't it a pity he should end by finding it in Mrs. Fisher's drawing-room?"

"Ned is a dear boy, and I hope he will keep his illusions long enough to write some nice poetry about them; but do you think it is only in society that he is likely to lose them?"

Selden answered her with a shrug. "Why do we call all our generous ideas illusions, and the mean ones truths? Isn't it a sufficient condemnation of society to find one's self accepting such phraseology? I very nearly acquired the jargon at Silverton's age, and I know how names can alter the colour of beliefs."

She had never heard him speak with such energy of affirmation. His habitual touch was that of the eclectic, who lightly turns over and compares; and she was moved by this sudden glimpse into the laboratory where his faiths were formed.

"Ah, you are as bad as the other sectarians," she exclaimed; "why do you call your republic a republic? It is a closed corporation, and you create arbitrary objections in order to keep people out."

"It is not *my* republic; if it were, I should have a *coup d'etat* and seat you on the throne."

"Whereas, in reality, you think I can never even get my foot across the threshold? Oh, I understand what you mean. You despise my ambitions—you think them unworthy of me!"

Selden smiled, but not ironically. "Well, isn't that a tribute? I think them quite worthy of most of the people who live by them."

She had turned to gaze on him gravely. "But isn't it possible that, if I had the opportunities of these people, I might make a better use of them? Money stands for all kinds of things—its purchasing quality isn't limited to diamonds and motor-cars."

"Not in the least: you might expiate your enjoyment of them by founding a hospital."

"But if you think they are what I should really enjoy, you must think my ambitions are good enough for me."

Selden met this appeal with a laugh. "Ah, my dear Miss Bart, I am not divine Providence, to guarantee your enjoying the things you are trying to get!"

"Then the best you can say for me is, that after struggling to get them I probably shan't like them?" She drew a deep breath. "What a miserable future you foresee for me!"

"Well—have you never foreseen it for yourself?" The slow colour rose to her cheek, not a blush of excitement but drawn from the deep wells of feeling; it was as if the effort of her spirit had produced it.

"Often and often," she said. "But it looks so much darker when you show it to me!"

He made no answer to this exclamation, and for a while they sat silent, while something throbbed between them in the wide quiet of the air.

But suddenly she turned on him with a kind of vehemence. "Why do you do this to me?" she cried. "Why do you make the things I have chosen seem hateful to me, if you have nothing to give me instead?"

The words roused Selden from the musing fit into which he had fallen. He himself did not know why he had led their talk along such lines; it was the last use he would have imagined himself making of an afternoon's solitude with Miss Bart. But it was one of those moments when neither seemed to speak deliberately, when an indwelling voice in each called to the other across unsounded depths of feeling.

"No, I have nothing to give you instead," he said, sitting up and turning so that he faced her. "If I had, it should be yours, you know."

She received this abrupt declaration in a way even stranger than the manner of its making: she dropped her face on her hands and he saw that for a moment she wept.

It was for a moment only, however; for when he leaned nearer and drew down her hands with a gesture less passionate than grave, she turned on him a face softened but not disfigured by emotion, and he said to himself, somewhat cruelly, that even her weeping was an art.

The reflection steadied his voice as he asked, between pity and irony: "Isn't it natural that I should try to belittle all the things I can't offer you?"

Her face brightened at this, but she drew her hand away, not with a gesture of coquetry, but as though renouncing something to which she had no claim.

"But you belittle ME, don't you," she returned gently, "in being so sure they are the only things I care for?"

Selden felt an inner start; but it was only the last quiver of his egoism. Almost at once he answered quite simply: "But you do care for them, don't you? And no wishing of mine can alter that."

He had so completely ceased to consider how far this might carry him, that he had a distinct sense of disappointment when she turned on him a face sparkling with derision.

"Ah," she cried, "for all your fine phrases you're really as great a coward as I am, for you wouldn't have made one of them if you hadn't been so sure of my answer."

The shock of this retort had the effect of crystallizing Selden's wavering intentions.

"I am not so sure of your answer," he said quietly. "And I do you the justice to believe that you are not either."

It was her turn to look at him with surprise; and after a moment—"Do you want to marry me?" she asked.

He broke into a laugh. "No, I don't want to—but perhaps I should if you did!"

"That's what I told you—you're so sure of me that you can amuse yourself with experiments." She drew back the hand he had regained, and sat looking down on him sadly.

"I am not making experiments," he returned. "Or if I am, it is not on you but on myself. I don't know what effect they are going to have on me—but if marrying you is one of them, I will take the risk."

She smiled faintly. "It would be a great risk, certainly—I have never concealed from you how great."

"Ah, it's you who are the coward!" he exclaimed.

She had risen, and he stood facing her with his eyes on hers. The soft isolation of the falling day enveloped them: they seemed lifted into a finer air. All the exquisite influences of the hour trembled in their veins, and drew them to each other as the loosened leaves were drawn to the earth.

"It's you who are the coward," he repeated, catching her hands in his.

She leaned on him for a moment, as if with a drop of tired wings: he felt as though her heart were beating rather with the stress of a long flight than the thrill of new distances. Then, drawing back with a little smile of warning—"I shall look hideous in dowdy clothes; but I can trim my own hats," she declared.

They stood silent for a while after this, smiling at each other like adventurous children who have climbed to a forbidden height from which they discover a new world. The actual world at their feet was veiling itself in dimness, and across the valley a clear moon rose in the denser blue.

Suddenly they heard a remote sound, like the hum of a giant insect, and following the high-road, which wound whiter through the surrounding twilight, a black object rushed across their vision.

Lily started from her attitude of absorption; her smile faded and she began to move toward the lane.

"I had no idea it was so late! We shall not be back till after dark," she said, almost impatiently.

Selden was looking at her with surprise: it took him a moment to regain his usual view of her; then he said, with an uncontrollable note of dryness: "That was not one of our party; the motor was going the other way."

"I know—I know—" She paused, and he saw her redden through the twilight. "But I told them I was not well—that I should not go out. Let us go down!" she murmured.

Selden continued to look at her; then he drew his cigarette-case from his pocket and slowly lit a cigarette. It seemed to him necessary, at that moment, to proclaim, by some habitual gesture of this sort, his recovered hold on the actual: he had an almost puerile wish to let his companion see that, their flight over, he had landed on his feet.

She waited while the spark flickered under his curved palm; then he held out the cigarettes to her.

She took one with an unsteady hand, and putting it to her lips, leaned forward to draw her light from his. In the indistinctness the little red gleam lit up the lower part of her face, and he saw her mouth tremble into a smile.

"Were you serious?" she asked, with an odd thrill of gaiety which she might have caught up, in haste, from a heap of stock inflections, without having time to select the just note. Selden's voice was under better control. "Why not?" he returned. "You see I took no risks in being so." And as she continued to stand before him, a little pale under the retort, he added quickly: "Let us go down."

# Chapter 7

It spoke much for the depth of Mrs. Trenor's friendship that her voice, in admonishing Miss Bart, took the same note of personal despair as if she had been lamenting the collapse of a house-party.

"All I can say is, Lily, that I can't make you out!" She leaned back, sighing, in the morning abandon of lace and muslin, turning an indifferent shoulder to the heaped-up importunities of her desk, while she considered, with the eye of a physician who has given up the case, the erect exterior of the patient confronting her.

"If you hadn't told me you were going in for him seriously—but I'm sure you made that plain enough from the beginning! Why else did you ask me to let you off bridge, and to keep away Carry and Kate Corby? I don't suppose you did it because he amused you; we could none of us imagine your putting up with him for a moment unless you meant to marry him. And I'm sure everybody played fair! They all wanted to help it along. Even Bertha kept her hands off—I will say that—till Lawrence came down and you dragged him away from her. After that she had a right to retaliate—why on earth did you interfere with her? You've known Lawrence Selden for years—why did you behave as if you had just discovered him? If you had a grudge against Bertha it was a stupid time to show it—you could have paid her back just as well after you were married! I told you Bertha was dangerous. She was in an odious mood when she came here, but Lawrence's turning up put her in a good humour, and if you'd only let her think he came for *her* it would have never occurred to her to play you this trick. Oh, Lily, you'll never do anything if you're not serious!"

Miss Bart accepted this exhortation in a spirit of the purest impartiality. Why should she have been angry? It was the voice of her own conscience which spoke to her through Mrs. Trenor's reproachful accents. But even to her own conscience she must trump up a semblance of defence. "I only took a day off—I thought he meant to stay on all this week, and I knew Mr. Selden was leaving this morning."

Mrs. Trenor brushed aside the plea with a gesture which laid bare its weakness.

"He did mean to stay—that's the worst of it. It shows that he's run away from you; that Bertha's done her work and poisoned him thoroughly."

Lily gave a slight laugh. "Oh, if he's running I'll overtake him!"

Her friend threw out an arresting hand. "Whatever you do, Lily, do nothing!"

Miss Bart received the warning with a smile. "I don't mean, literally, to take the next train. There are ways—" But she did not go on to specify them.

Mrs. Trenor sharply corrected the tense. "There *were* ways—plenty of them! I didn't suppose you needed to have them pointed out. But don't deceive yourself—he's thoroughly frightened. He has run straight home to his mother, and she'll protect him!"

"Oh, to the death," Lily agreed, dimpling at the vision.

"How you can *laugh*—" her friend rebuked her; and she dropped back to a soberer perception of things with the question: "What was it Bertha really told him?"

"Don't ask me—horrors! She seemed to have raked up everything. Oh, you know what I mean—of course there isn't anything, *really*; but I suppose she brought in Prince Varigliano—and Lord Hubert—and there was some story of your having borrowed money of old Ned Van Alstyne: did you ever?"

"He is my father's cousin," Miss Bart interposed.

"Well, of course she left *that* out. It seems Ned told Carry Fisher; and she told Bertha, naturally. They're all alike, you know: they hold their tongues for years, and you think you're safe, but when their opportunity comes they remember everything."

Lily had grown pale: her voice had a harsh note in it. "It was some money I lost at bridge at the Van Osburghs'. I repaid it, of course."

"Ah, well, they wouldn't remember that; besides, it was the idea of the gambling debt that frightened Percy. Oh, Bertha knew her man—she knew just what to tell him!"

In this strain Mrs. Trenor continued for nearly an hour to admonish her friend. Miss Bart listened with admirable equanimity. Her naturally good temper had been disciplined by years of enforced compliance, since she had almost always had to attain her ends by the circuitous path of other people's; and, being naturally inclined to face unpleasant facts as soon as they presented themselves, she was not sorry to hear an impartial statement of what her folly was likely to cost, the more so as her own thoughts were still insisting on the other side of the case. Presented in the light of Mrs. Trenor's vigorous comments, the reckoning was certainly a formidable one, and Lily, as she listened, found herself gradually reverting to her friend's view of the situation. Mrs. Trenor's words were moreover emphasized for her hearer by anxieties which she herself could scarcely guess. Affluence, unless stimulated by a keen imagination, forms but the vaguest notion of the practical strain of poverty. Judy knew it must be "horrid" for poor Lily to have to stop to consider whether she could afford real lace on her petticoats, and not to have a motor-car and a steam-yacht at her orders; but the daily friction of unpaid bills, the daily nibble of small temptations to expenditure, were trials as far out of her experience as the domestic problems of the char-woman. Mrs. Trenor's unconsciousness of the real stress of the situation had the effect of making it more galling to Lily. While her friend reproached her for missing the opportunity to eclipse her rivals, she was once more battling in imagination with the mounting tide of indebtedness from which she had so nearly escaped. What wind of folly had driven her out again on those dark seas?

If anything was needed to put the last touch to her self-abasement it was the sense of the way her old life was opening its ruts again to receive her. Yesterday her fancy had fluttered free pinions above a choice of occupations; now she had to drop to the level of the familiar routine, in which moments of seeming brilliancy and freedom alternated with long hours of subjection.

She laid a deprecating hand on her friend's. "Dear Judy! I'm sorry to have been such a bore, and you are very good to me. But you must have some letters for me to answer—let me at least be useful."

She settled herself at the desk, and Mrs. Trenor accepted her resumption of the morning's task with a sigh which implied that, after all, she had proved herself unfit for higher uses.

The luncheon table showed a depleted circle. All the men but Jack Stepney and Dorset had returned to town (it seemed to Lily a last touch of irony that Selden and Percy Gryce should have gone in the same train), and Lady Cressida and the attendant Wetheralls had been despatched by motor to lunch at a distant country-house. At such moments of diminished interest it was usual for Mrs. Dorset to keep her room till the afternoon; but on this occasion she drifted in when luncheon was half over, hollowed-eyed and drooping, but with an edge of malice under her indifference.

She raised her eyebrows as she looked about the table. "How few of us are left! I do so enjoy the quiet—don't you, Lily? I wish the men would always stop away—it's really much nicer without them. Oh, you don't count, George: one doesn't have to talk to one's husband. But I thought Mr. Gryce was to stay for the rest of the week?" she added enquiringly. "Didn't he intend to, Judy? He's such a nice boy—I wonder what drove him away? He is rather shy, and I'm afraid we may have shocked him: he has been brought up in such an old-fashioned way. Do you know, Lily, he told me he had never seen a girl play cards for money till he saw you doing it the other night? And he lives on the interest of his income, and always has a lot left over to invest!"

Mrs. Fisher leaned forward eagerly. "I do believe it is some one's duty to educate that young man. It is shocking that he has never been made to realize his duties as a citizen. Every wealthy man should be compelled to study the laws of his country."

Mrs. Dorset glanced at her quietly. "I think he *has* studied the divorce laws. He told me he had promised the Bishop to sign some kind of a petition against divorce."

Mrs. Fisher reddened under her powder, and Stepney said with a laughing glance at Miss Bart: "I suppose he is thinking of marriage, and wants to tinker up the old ship before he goes aboard."

His betrothed looked shocked at the metaphor, and George Dorset exclaimed with a sardonic growl: "Poor devil! It isn't the ship that will do for him, it's the crew."

"Or the stowaways," said Miss Corby brightly. "If I contemplated a voyage with him I should try to start with a friend in the hold."

Miss Van Osburgh's vague feeling of pique was struggling for appropriate expression. "I'm sure I don't see why you laugh at him; I think he's very nice," she exclaimed; "and, at any rate, a girl who married him would always have enough to be comfortable."

She looked puzzled at the redoubled laughter which hailed her words, but it might have consoled her to know how deeply they had sunk into the breast of one of her hearers.

Comfortable! At that moment the word was more eloquent to Lily Bart than any other in the language. She could not even pause to smile over the heiress's view of a colossal fortune as a mere shelter against want: her mind was filled with the vision of what that shelter might have been to her. Mrs. Dorset's pin-pricks did not smart, for her own irony cut deeper: no one could hurt her as much as she was hurting herself, for no one else—not even Judy Trenor—knew the full magnitude of her folly.

She was roused from these unprofitable considerations by a whispered request from her hostess, who drew her apart as they left the luncheon-table.

"Lily, dear, if you've nothing special to do, may I tell Carry Fisher that you intend to drive to the station and fetch Gus? He will be back at four, and I know she has it in her mind to meet him. Of course I'm very glad to have him amused, but I happen to know that she has bled him rather severely since she's been here, and she is so keen about going to fetch him that I fancy she must have got a lot more bills this morning. It seems to me," Mrs. Trenor feelingly concluded, "that most of her alimony is paid by other women's husbands!"

Miss Bart, on her way to the station, had leisure to muse over her friend's words, and their peculiar application to herself. Why should she have to suffer for having once, for a few hours, borrowed money of an elderly cousin, when a woman like Carry Fisher could make a living unrebuked from the good-nature of her men friends and the tolerance of their wives? It all turned on the tiresome distinction between what a married woman might, and a girl might not, do. Of course it was shocking for a married woman to borrow money—and Lily was expertly aware of the implication involved—but still, it was the mere *Malum prohibitum* which the world decries but condones, and which, though it may be punished by private vengeance, does not provoke the collective disapprobation of society. To Miss Bart, in short, no such opportunities were possible. She could of course borrow from her women friends—a hundred here or there, at the utmost—but they were more ready to give a gown or a trinket, and looked a little askance when she hinted her preference for a cheque. Women are not generous lenders, and those among whom her lot was cast were either in the same case as herself, or else too far removed from it to understand its necessities. The result of her meditations was the decision to join her aunt at Richfield. She could not remain at Bellomont without playing bridge, and being involved in other expenses; and to continue her usual series of autumn visits would merely prolong the same difficulties. She had reached a point where abrupt retrenchment was necessary, and the only cheap life was a dull life. She would start the next morning for Richfield.

At the station she thought Gus Trenor seemed surprised, and not wholly unrelieved, to see her. She yielded up the reins of the light runabout in which she had driven over, and as he climbed heavily to her side, crushing her into a scant third of the seat, he said: "Halloo! It isn't often you honour me. You must have been uncommonly hard up for something to do."

The afternoon was warm, and propinquity made her more than usually conscious that he was red and massive, and that beads of moisture had caused the dust of the train to adhere unpleasantly to the broad expanse of cheek and neck which he turned to her; but she was aware also, from the look in his small dull eyes, that the contact with her freshness and slenderness was as agreeable to him as the sight of a cooling beverage.

The perception of this fact helped her to answer gaily: "It's not often I have the chance. There are too many ladies to dispute the privilege with me."

"The privilege of driving me home? Well, I'm glad you won the race, anyhow. But I know what really happened—my wife sent you. Now didn't she?"

He had the dull man's unexpected flashes of astuteness, and Lily could not help joining in the laugh with which he had pounced on the truth.

"You see, Judy thinks I'm the safest person for you to be with; and she's quite right," she rejoined.

"Oh, is she, though? If she is, it's because you wouldn't waste your time on an old hulk like me. We married men have to put up with what we can get: all the prizes are for the clever chaps who've kept a free foot. Let me light a cigar, will you? I've had a beastly day of it."

He drew up in the shade of the village street, and passed the reins to her while he held a match to his cigar. The little flame under his hand cast a deeper crimson on his puffing face, and Lily averted her eyes with a momentary feeling of repugnance. And yet some women thought him handsome!

As she handed back the reins, she said sympathetically: "Did you have such a lot of tiresome things to do?"

"I should say so—rather!" Trenor, who was seldom listened to, either by his wife or her friends, settled down into the rare enjoyment of a confidential talk. "You don't know how a fellow has to hustle to keep this kind of thing going." He waved his whip in the direction of the Bellomont acres, which lay outspread before them in opulent undulations. "Judy has no idea of what she spends—not that there isn't plenty to keep the thing going," he interrupted himself, "but a man has got to keep his eyes open and pick up all the tips he can. My father and mother used to live like fighting-cocks on their income, and put by a good bit of it too—luckily for me—but at the pace we go now, I don't know where I should be if it weren't for taking a flyer now and then. The women all think—I mean Judy thinks—I've nothing to do but to go down town once a month and cut off coupons, but the truth is it takes a devilish lot of hard work to keep the machinery running. Not that I ought to complain to-day, though," he went on after a moment, "for I did a very neat stroke of business, thanks to Stepney's friend Rosedale: by the way, Miss Lily, I wish you'd try to persuade Judy to be decently civil to that chap. He's going to be rich enough to buy us all out one of these days, and if she'd only ask him to dine now and then I could get almost anything out of him. The man is mad to know the people who don't want to know him, and when a fellow's in that state there is nothing he won't do for the first woman who takes him up."

Lily hesitated a moment. The first part of her companion's discourse had started an interesting train of thought, which was rudely interrupted by the mention of Mr. Rosedale's name. She uttered a faint protest.

"But you know Jack did try to take him about, and he was impossible."

"Oh, hang it—because he's fat and shiny, and has a sloppy manner! Well, all I can say is that the people who are clever enough to be civil to him now will make a mighty good thing of it. A few years from now he'll be in it whether we want him or not, and then he won't be giving away a half-a-million tip for a dinner."

Lily's mind had reverted from the intrusive personality of Mr. Rosedale to the train of thought set in motion by Trenor's first words.

This vast mysterious Wall Street world of "tips" and "deals"—might she not find in it the means of escape from her dreary predicament? She had often heard of women making money in this way through their friends: she had no more notion than most of her sex of the exact nature of the transaction, and its vagueness seemed to diminish its indelicacy. She could not, indeed, imagine herself, in any extremity, stooping to extract a "tip" from Mr. Rosedale; but at her side was a man in possession of that precious commodity, and who, as the husband of her dearest friend, stood to her in a relation of almost fraternal intimacy.

In her inmost heart Lily knew it was not by appealing to the fraternal instinct that she was likely to move Gus Trenor; but this way of explaining the situation helped to drape its crudity, and she was always scrupulous about keeping up appearances to herself. Her personal fastidiousness had a moral equivalent, and when she made a tour of inspection in her own mind there were certain closed doors she did not open.

As they reached the gates of Bellomont she turned to Trenor with a smile. "The afternoon is so perfect—don't you want to drive me a little farther? I've been rather out of spirits all day, and it's so restful to be away from people, with some one who won't mind if I'm a little dull."

She looked so plaintively lovely as she proffered the request, so trustfully sure of his sympathy and understanding, that Trenor felt himself wishing that his wife could see how other women treated him—not battered wire-pullers like Mrs. Fisher, but a girl that most men would have given their boots to get such a look from.

"Out of spirits? Why on earth should you ever be out of spirits? Is your last box of Doucet dresses a failure, or did Judy rook you out of everything at bridge last night?"

Lily shook her head with a sigh. "I have had to give up Doucet; and bridge too—I can't afford it. In fact I can't afford any of the things my friends do, and I am afraid Judy often thinks me a bore because I don't play cards any longer, and because I am not as smartly dressed as the other women. But you will think me a bore too if I talk to you about my worries, and I only mention them because I want you to do me a favour—the very greatest of favours."

Her eyes sought his once more, and she smiled inwardly at the tinge of apprehension that she read in them.

"Why, of course—if it's anything I can manage—" He broke off, and she guessed that his enjoyment was disturbed by the remembrance of Mrs. Fisher's methods.

"The greatest of favours," she rejoined gently. "The fact is, Judy is angry with me, and I want you to make my peace."

"Angry with you? Oh, come, nonsense—" his relief broke through in a laugh. "Why, you know she's devoted to you."

"She is the best friend I have, and that is why I mind having to vex her. But I daresay you know what she has wanted me to do. She has set her heart—poor dear—on my marrying—marrying a great deal of money."

She paused with a slight falter of embarrassment, and Trenor, turning abruptly, fixed on her a look of growing intelligence.

"A great deal of money? Oh, by Jove—you don't mean Gryce? What—you do? Oh, no, of course I won't mention it—you can trust me to keep my mouth shut—but Gryce—good Lord, *Gryce*! Did Judy really think you could bring yourself to marry that portentous little ass? But you couldn't, eh? And so you gave him the sack, and that's the reason why he lit out by the first train this morning?" He leaned back, spreading himself farther across the seat, as if dilated by the joyful sense of his own discernment. "How on earth could Judy think you would do such a thing? I could have told her you'd never put up with such a little milksop!"

Lily sighed more deeply. "I sometimes think," she murmured, "that men understand a woman's motives better than other women do."

"Some men—I'm certain of it! I could have *told* Judy," he repeated, exulting in the implied superiority over his wife.

"I thought you would understand; that's why I wanted to speak to you," Miss Bart rejoined. "I can't make that kind of marriage; it's impossible. But neither can I go on living as all the women in my set do. I am almost entirely dependent on my aunt, and though she is very kind to me she makes me no regular allowance, and lately I've lost money at cards, and I don't dare tell her about it. I have paid my card debts, of course, but there is hardly anything left for my other expenses, and if I go on with my present life I shall be in horrible difficulties. I have a tiny income of my own, but I'm afraid it's badly invested, for it seems to bring in less every year, and I am so ignorant of money matters that I don't know if my aunt's agent, who looks after it, is a good adviser." She paused a moment, and added in a lighter tone: "I didn't mean to bore you with all this, but I want your help in making Judy understand that I can't, at present, go on living as one must live among you all. I am going away tomorrow to join my aunt at Richfield, and I shall stay there for the rest of the autumn, and dismiss my maid and learn how to mend my own clothes."

At this picture of loveliness in distress, the pathos of which was heightened by the light touch with which it was drawn, a murmur of indignant sympathy broke from Trenor. Twenty-four hours earlier, if his wife had consulted him on the subject of Miss Bart's future, he would have said that a girl with extravagant tastes and no money had better marry the first rich man she could get; but with the subject of discussion at his side, turning to him for sympathy, making him feel that he understood her better than her dearest friends, and confirming the assurance by the appeal of her exquisite nearness, he was ready to swear that such a marriage was a desecration, and that, as a man of honour, he was bound to do all he could to protect her from the results of her disinterestedness. This impulse was reinforced by the reflection that if she had married Gryce she would have been surrounded by flattery and approval, whereas, having refused to sacrifice herself to expediency, she was left to bear the whole cost of her resistance. Hang it, if he could find a way out of such difficulties for a professional sponge like Carry Fisher, who was simply a mental habit corresponding to the physical titillations of the cigarette or the cock-tail, he could surely do as much for a girl who appealed to his highest sympathies, and who brought her troubles to him with the trustfulness of a child.

Trenor and Miss Bart prolonged their drive till long after sunset; and before it was over he had tried, with some show of success, to prove to her that, if she would only trust him, he could make a handsome sum of money for her without endangering the small amount she possessed. She was too genuinely ignorant of the manipulations of the stock-market to understand his technical explanations, or even perhaps to perceive that certain points in them were slurred; the haziness enveloping the transaction served as a veil for her embarrassment, and through the general blur her hopes dilated like lamps in a fog. She understood only that her modest investments were to be mysteriously multiplied without risk to herself; and the assurance that this miracle would take place within a short time, that there would be no tedious interval for suspense and reaction, relieved her of her lingering scruples.

Again she felt the lightening of her load, and with it the release of repressed activities. Her immediate worries conjured, it was easy to resolve that she would never again find herself in such straits, and as the need of economy and self-denial receded from her foreground she felt herself ready to meet any other demand which life might make. Even the immediate one of letting Trenor, as they drove homeward, lean a little nearer and rest his hand reassuringly on hers, cost her only a momentary shiver of reluctance. It was part of the game to make him feel that her appeal had been an uncalculated impulse, provoked by the liking he inspired; and the renewed sense of power in handling men, while it consoled her wounded vanity, helped also to obscure the thought of the claim at which his manner hinted. He was a coarse dull man who, under all his show of authority, was a mere supernumerary in the costly show for which his money paid: surely, to a clever girl, it would be easy to hold him by his vanity, and so keep the obligation on his side.

# Chapter 8

The first thousand dollar cheque which Lily received with a blotted scrawl from Gus Trenor strengthened her self-confidence in the exact degree to which it effaced her debts.

The transaction had justified itself by its results: she saw now how absurd it would have been to let any primitive scruple deprive her of this easy means of appeasing her creditors. Lily felt really virtuous as she dispensed the sum in sops to her tradesmen, and the fact that a fresh order accompanied each payment did not lessen her sense of disinterestedness. How many women, in her place, would have given the orders without making the payment!

She had found it reassuringly easy to keep Trenor in a good humour. To listen to his stories, to receive his confidences and laugh at his jokes, seemed for the moment all that was required of her, and the complacency with which her hostess regarded these attentions freed them of the least hint of ambiguity. Mrs. Trenor evidently assumed that Lily's growing intimacy with her husband was simply an indirect way of returning her own kindness.

"I'm so glad you and Gus have become such good friends," she said approvingly. "It's too delightful of you to be so nice to him, and put up with all his tiresome stories. I know what they are, because I had to listen to them when we were engaged—I'm sure he is telling the same ones still. And now I shan't always have to be asking Carry Fisher here to keep him in a good-humour. She's a perfect vulture, you know; and she hasn't the least moral sense. She is always getting Gus to speculate for her, and I'm sure she never pays when she loses."

Miss Bart could shudder at this state of things without the embarrassment of a personal application. Her own position was surely quite different. There could be no question of her not paying when she lost, since Trenor had assured her that she was certain not to lose. In sending her the cheque he had explained that he had made five thousand for her out of Rosedale's "tip," and had put four thousand back in the same venture, as there was the promise of another "big rise"; she understood therefore that he was now speculating with her own money, and that she consequently owed him no more than the gratitude which such a trifling service demanded. She vaguely supposed that, to raise the first sum, he had borrowed on her securities; but this was a point over which her curiosity did not linger. It was concentrated, for the moment, on the probable date of the next "big rise."

The news of this event was received by her some weeks later, on the occasion of Jack Stepney's marriage to Miss Van Osburgh. As a cousin of the bridegroom, Miss Bart had been asked to act as bridesmaid; but she had declined on the plea that, since she was much taller than the other attendant virgins, her presence might mar the symmetry of the group. The truth was, she had attended too many brides to the altar: when next seen there she meant to be the chief figure in the ceremony. She knew the pleasantries made at the expense of young girls who have been too long before the public, and she was resolved to avoid such assumptions of youthfulness as might lead people to think her older than she really was.

The Van Osburgh marriage was celebrated in the village church near the paternal estate on the Hudson. It was the "simple country wedding" to which guests are convoyed in special trains, and from which the hordes of the uninvited have to be fended off by the intervention of the police. While these sylvan rites were taking place, in a church packed with fashion and festooned with orchids, the representatives of the press were threading their way, note-book in hand, through the labyrinth of wedding presents, and the agent of a cinematograph syndicate was setting up his apparatus at the church door. It was the kind of scene in which Lily had often pictured herself as taking the principal part, and on this occasion the fact that she was once more merely a casual spectator, instead of the mystically veiled figure occupying the centre of attention, strengthened her resolve to assume the latter part before the year was over. The fact that her immediate anxieties were relieved did not blind her to a possibility of their recurrence; it merely gave her enough buoyancy to rise once more above her doubts and feel a renewed faith in her beauty, her power, and her general fitness to attract a brilliant destiny. It could not be that one conscious of such aptitudes for mastery and enjoyment was doomed to a perpetuity of failure; and her mistakes looked easily reparable in the light of her restored self-confidence.

A special appositeness was given to these reflections by the discovery, in a neighbouring pew, of the serious profile and neatly-trimmed beard of Mr. Percy Gryce. There was something almost bridal in his own aspect: his large white gardenia had a symbolic air that struck Lily as a good omen. After all, seen in an assemblage of his kind he was not ridiculous-looking: a friendly critic might have called his heaviness weighty, and he was at his best in the attitude of vacant passivity which brings out the oddities of the restless. She fancied he was the kind of man whose sentimental associations would be stirred by the conventional imagery of a wedding, and she pictured herself, in the seclusion of the Van Osburgh conservatories, playing skillfully upon sensibilities thus prepared for her touch. In fact, when she looked at the other women about her, and recalled the image she had brought away from her own glass, it did not seem as though any special skill would be needed to repair her blunder and bring him once more to her feet.

The sight of Selden's dark head, in a pew almost facing her, disturbed for a moment the balance of her complacency. The rise of her blood as their eyes met was succeeded by a contrary motion, a wave of resistance and withdrawal. She did not wish to see him again, not because she feared his influence, but because his presence always had the effect of cheapening her aspirations, of throwing her whole world out of focus. Besides, he was a living reminder of the worst mistake in her career, and the fact that he had been its cause did not soften her feelings toward him. She could still imagine an ideal state of existence in which, all else being superadded, intercourse with Selden might be the last touch of luxury; but in the world as it was, such a privilege was likely to cost more than it was worth.

"Lily, dear, I never saw you look so lovely! You look as if something delightful had just happened to you!"

The young lady who thus formulated her admiration of her brilliant friend did not, in her own person, suggest such happy possibilities. Miss Gertrude Farish, in fact, typified the mediocre and the ineffectual. If there were compensating qualities in her wide frank glance and the freshness of her smile, these were qualities which only the sympathetic observer would perceive before noticing that her eyes were of a workaday grey and her lips without haunting curves. Lily's own view of her wavered between pity for her limitations and impatience at her cheerful acceptance of them. To Miss Bart, as to her mother, acquiescence in dinginess was evidence of stupidity; and there were moments when, in the consciousness of her own power to look and to be so exactly what the occasion required, she almost felt that other girls were plain and inferior from choice. Certainly no one need have confessed such acquiescence in her lot as was revealed in the "useful" colour of Gerty Farish's gown and the subdued lines of her hat: it is almost as stupid to let your clothes betray that you know you are ugly as to have them proclaim that you think you are beautiful.

Of course, being fatally poor and dingy, it was wise of Gerty to have taken up philanthropy and symphony concerts; but there was something irritating in her assumption that existence yielded no higher pleasures, and that one might get as much interest and excitement out of life in a cramped flat as in the splendours of the Van Osburgh establishment. Today, however, her chirping enthusiasms did not irritate Lily. They seemed only to throw her own exceptionalness into becoming relief, and give a soaring vastness to her scheme of life.

"Do let us go and take a peep at the presents before everyone else leaves the dining-room!" suggested Miss Farish, linking her arm in her friend's. It was characteristic of her to take a sentimental and unenvious interest in all the details of a wedding: she was the kind of person who always kept her handkerchief out during the service, and departed clutching a box of wedding-cake.

"Isn't everything beautifully done?" she pursued, as they entered the distant drawing-room assigned to the display of Miss Van Osburgh's bridal spoils. "I always say no one does things better than cousin Grace! Did you ever taste anything more delicious than that MOUSSE of lobster with champagne sauce? I made up my mind weeks ago that I wouldn't miss this wedding, and just fancy how delightfully it all came about. When Lawrence Selden heard I was coming, he insisted on fetching me himself and driving me to the station, and when we go back this evening I am to dine with him at Sherry's. I really feel as excited as if I were getting married myself!"

Lily smiled: she knew that Selden had always been kind to his dull cousin, and she had sometimes wondered why he wasted so much time in such an unremunerative manner; but now the thought gave her a vague pleasure.

"Do you see him often?" she asked.

"Yes; he is very good about dropping in on Sundays. And now and then we do a play together; but lately I haven't seen much of him. He doesn't look well, and he seems nervous and unsettled. The dear fellow! I do wish he would marry some nice girl. I told him so today, but he said he didn't care for the really nice ones, and the other kind didn't care for him—but that was just his joke, of course. He could never marry a girl who *wasn't* nice. Oh, my dear, did you ever see such pearls?"

They had paused before the table on which the bride's jewels were displayed, and Lily's heart gave an envious throb as she caught the refraction of light from their surfaces—the milky gleam of perfectly matched pearls, the flash of rubies relieved against contrasting velvet, the intense blue rays of sapphires kindled into light by surrounding diamonds: all these precious tints enhanced and deepened by the varied art of their setting. The glow of the stones warmed Lily's veins like wine. More completely than any other expression of wealth they symbolized the life she longed to lead, the life of fastidious aloofness and refinement in which every detail should have the finish of a jewel, and the whole form a harmonious setting to her own jewel-like rareness.

"Oh, Lily, do look at this diamond pendant—it's as big as a dinner-plate! Who can have given it?" Miss Farish bent short-sightedly over the accompanying card. "*Mr. Simon Rosedale.* What, that horrid man? Oh, yes—I remember he's a friend of Jack's, and I suppose cousin Grace had to ask him here today; but she must rather hate having to let Gwen accept such a present from him."

Lily smiled. She doubted Mrs. Van Osburgh's reluctance, but was aware of Miss Farish's habit of ascribing her own delicacies of feeling to the persons least likely to be encumbered by them.

"Well, if Gwen doesn't care to be seen wearing it she can always exchange it for something else," she remarked.

"Ah, here is something so much prettier," Miss Farish continued. "Do look at this exquisite white sapphire. I'm sure the person who chose it must have taken particular pains. What is the name? Percy Gryce? Ah, then I'm not surprised!" She smiled significantly as she replaced the card. "Of course you've heard that he's perfectly devoted to Evie Van Osburgh? Cousin Grace is so pleased about it—it's quite a romance! He met her first at the George Dorsets', only about six weeks ago, and it's just the nicest possible marriage for dear Evie. Oh, I don't mean the money—of course she has plenty of her own—but she's such a quiet stay-at-home kind of girl, and it seems he has just the same tastes; so they are exactly suited to each other."

Lily stood staring vacantly at the white sapphire on its velvet bed. Evie Van Osburgh and Percy Gryce? The names rang derisively through her brain. *Evie Van Osburgh?* The youngest, dumpiest, dullest of the four dull and dumpy daughters whom Mrs. Van Osburgh, with unsurpassed astuteness, had "placed" one by one in enviable niches of existence! Ah, lucky girls who grow up in the shelter of a mother's love—a mother who knows how to contrive opportunities without conceding favours, how to take advantage of propinquity without allowing appetite to be dulled by habit! The cleverest girl may miscalculate where her own interests are concerned, may yield too much at one moment and withdraw too far at the next: it takes a mother's unerring vigilance and foresight to land her daughters safely in the arms of wealth and suitability.

Lily's passing light-heartedness sank beneath a renewed sense of failure. Life was too stupid, too blundering! Why should Percy Gryce's millions be joined to another great fortune, why should this clumsy girl be put in possession of powers she would never know how to use?

She was roused from these speculations by a familiar touch on her arm, and turning saw Gus Trenor beside her. She felt a thrill of vexation: what right had he to touch her? Luckily Gerty Farish had wandered off to the next table, and they were alone.

Trenor, looking stouter than ever in his tight frock-coat, and unbecomingly flushed by the bridal libations, gazed at her with undisguised approval.

"By Jove, Lily, you do look a stunner!" He had slipped insensibly into the use of her Christian name, and she had never found the right moment to correct him. Besides, in her set all the men and women called each other by their Christian names; it was only on Trenor's lips that the familiar address had an unpleasant significance.

"Well," he continued, still jovially impervious to her annoyance, "have you made up your mind which of these little trinkets you mean to duplicate at Tiffany's tomorrow? I've got a cheque for you in my pocket that will go a long way in that line!"

Lily gave him a startled look: his voice was louder than usual, and the room was beginning to fill with people. But as her glance assured her that they were still beyond ear-shot a sense of pleasure replaced her apprehension.

"Another dividend?" she asked, smiling and drawing near him in the desire not to be overheard.

"Well, not exactly: I sold out on the rise and I've pulled off four thou' for you. Not so bad for a beginner, eh? I suppose you'll begin to think you're a pretty knowing speculator. And perhaps you won't think poor old Gus such an awful ass as some people do."

"I think you the kindest of friends; but I can't thank you properly now."

She let her eyes shine into his with a look that made up for the hand-clasp he would have claimed if they had been alone—and how glad she was that they were not! The news filled her with the glow produced by a sudden cessation of physical pain. The world was not so stupid and blundering after all: now and then a stroke of luck came to the unluckiest. At the thought her spirits began to rise: it was characteristic of her that one trifling piece of good fortune should give wings to all her hopes. Instantly came the reflection that Percy Gryce was not irretrievably lost; and she smiled to think of the excitement of recapturing him from Evie Van Osburgh. What chance could such a simpleton have against her if she chose to exert herself? She glanced about, hoping to catch a glimpse of Gryce; but her eyes lit instead on the glossy countenance of Mr. Rosedale, who was slipping through the crowd with an air half obsequious, half obtrusive, as though, the moment his presence was recognized, it would swell to the dimensions of the room.

Not wishing to be the means of effecting this enlargement, Lily quickly transferred her glance to Trenor, to whom the expression of her gratitude seemed not to have brought the complete gratification she had meant it to give.

"Hang thanking me—I don't want to be thanked, but I *should* like the chance to say two words to you now and then," he grumbled. "I thought you were going to spend the whole autumn with us, and I've hardly laid eyes on you for the last month. Why can't you come back to Bellomont this evening? We're all alone, and Judy is as cross as two sticks. Do come and cheer a fellow up. If you say yes I'll run you over in the motor, and you can telephone your maid to bring your traps from town by the next train."

Lily shook her head with a charming semblance of regret. "I wish I could—but it's quite impossible. My aunt has come back to town, and I must be with her for the next few days."

"Well, I've seen a good deal less of you since we've got to be such pals than I used to when you were Judy's friend," he continued with unconscious penetration.

"When I was Judy's friend? Am I not her friend still? Really, you say the most absurd things! If I were always at Bellomont you would tire of me much sooner than Judy—but come and see me at my aunt's the next afternoon you are in town; then we can have a nice quiet talk, and you can tell me how I had better invest my fortune."

It was true that, during the last three or four weeks, she had absented herself from Bellomont on the pretext of having other visits to pay; but she now began to feel that the reckoning she had thus contrived to evade had rolled up interest in the interval.

The prospect of the nice quiet talk did not appear as all-sufficing to Trenor as she had hoped, and his brows continued to lower as he said: "Oh, I don't know that I can promise you a fresh tip every day. But there's one thing you might do for me; and that is, just to be a little civil to Rosedale. Judy has promised to ask him to dine when we get to town, but I can't induce her to have him at Bellomont, and if you would let me bring him up now it would make a lot of difference. I don't believe two women have spoken to him this afternoon, and I can tell you he's a chap it pays to be decent to."

Miss Bart made an impatient movement, but suppressed the words which seemed about to accompany it. After all, this was an unexpectedly easy way of acquitting her debt; and had she not reasons of her own for wishing to be civil to Mr. Rosedale?

"Oh, bring him by all means," she said smiling; "perhaps I can get a tip out of him on my own account."

Trenor paused abruptly, and his eyes fixed themselves on hers with a look which made her change colour.

"I say, you know—you'll please remember he's a blooming bounder," he said; and with a slight laugh she turned toward the open window near which they had been standing.

The throng in the room had increased, and she felt a desire for space and fresh air. Both of these she found on the terrace, where only a few men were lingering over cigarettes and liqueur, while scattered couples strolled across the lawn to the autumn-tinted borders of the flower-garden.

As she emerged, a man moved toward her from the knot of smokers, and she found herself face to face with Selden. The stir of the pulses which his nearness always caused was increased by a slight sense of constraint. They had not met since their Sunday afternoon walk at Bellomont, and that episode was still so vivid to her that she could hardly believe him to be less conscious of it. But his greeting expressed no more than the satisfaction which every pretty woman expects to see reflected in masculine eyes; and the discovery, if distasteful to her vanity, was reassuring to her nerves. Between the relief of her escape from Trenor, and the vague apprehension of her meeting with Rosedale, it was pleasant to rest a moment on the sense of complete understanding which Lawrence Selden's manner always conveyed.

"This is luck," he said smiling. "I was wondering if I should be able to have a word with you before the special snatches us away. I came with Gerty Farish, and promised not to let her miss the train, but I am sure she is still extracting sentimental solace from the wedding presents. She appears to regard their number and value as evidence of the disinterested affection of the contracting parties."

There was not the least trace of embarrassment in his voice, and as he spoke, leaning slightly against the jamb of the window, and letting his eyes rest on her in the frank enjoyment of her grace, she felt with a faint chill of regret that he had gone back without an effort to the footing on which they had stood before their last talk together. Her vanity was stung by the sight of his unscathed smile. She longed to be to him something more than a piece of sentient prettiness, a passing diversion to his eye and brain; and the longing betrayed itself in her reply.

"Ah," she said, "I envy Gerty that power she has of dressing up with romance all our ugly and prosaic arrangements! I have never recovered my self-respect since you showed me how poor and unimportant my ambitions were."

The words were hardly spoken when she realized their infelicity. It seemed to be her fate to appear at her worst to Selden.

"I thought, on the contrary," he returned lightly, "that I had been the means of proving they were more important to you than anything else."

It was as if the eager current of her being had been checked by a sudden obstacle which drove it back upon itself. She looked at him helplessly, like a hurt or frightened child: this real self of hers, which he had the faculty of drawing out of the depths, was so little accustomed to go alone!

The appeal of her helplessness touched in him, as it always did, a latent chord of inclination. It would have meant nothing to him to discover that his nearness made her more brilliant, but this glimpse of a twilight mood to which he alone had the clue seemed once more to set him in a world apart with her.

"At least you can't think worse things of me than you say!" she exclaimed with a trembling laugh; but before he could answer, the flow of comprehension between them was abruptly stayed by the reappearance of Gus Trenor, who advanced with Mr. Rosedale in his wake.

"Hang it, Lily, I thought you'd given me the slip: Rosedale and I have been hunting all over for you!"

His voice had a note of conjugal familiarity: Miss Bart fancied she detected in Rosedale's eye a twinkling perception of the fact, and the idea turned her dislike of him to repugnance.

She returned his profound bow with a slight nod, made more disdainful by the sense of Selden's surprise that she should number Rosedale among her acquaintances. Trenor had turned away, and his companion continued to stand before Miss Bart, alert and expectant, his lips parted in a smile at whatever she might be about to say, and his very back conscious of the privilege of being seen with her.

It was the moment for tact; for the quick bridging over of gaps; but Selden still leaned against the window, a detached observer of the scene, and under the spell of his observation Lily felt herself powerless to exert her usual arts. The dread of Selden's suspecting that there was any need for her to propitiate such a man as Rosedale checked the trivial phrases of politeness. Rosedale still stood before her in an expectant attitude, and she continued to face him in silence, her glance just level with his polished baldness. The look put the finishing touch to what her silence implied.

He reddened slowly, shifting from one foot to the other, fingered the plump black pearl in his tie, and gave a nervous twist to his moustache; then, running his eye over her, he drew back, and said, with a side-glance at Selden: "Upon my soul, I never saw a more ripping get-up. Is that the last creation of the dress-maker you go to see at the Benedick? If so, I wonder all the other women don't go to her too!"

The words were projected sharply against Lily's silence, and she saw in a flash that her own act had given them their emphasis. In ordinary talk they might have passed unheeded; but following on her prolonged pause they acquired a special meaning. She felt, without looking, that Selden had immediately seized it, and would inevitably connect the allusion with her visit to himself. The consciousness increased her irritation against Rosedale, but also her feeling that now, if ever, was the moment to propitiate him, hateful as it was to do so in Selden's presence.

"How do you know the other women don't go to my dress-maker?" she returned. "You see I'm not afraid to give her address to my friends!"

Her glance and accent so plainly included Rosedale in this privileged circle that his small eyes puckered with gratification, and a knowing smile drew up his moustache.

"By Jove, you needn't be!" he declared. "You could give 'em the whole outfit and win at a canter!"

"Ah, that's nice of you; and it would be nicer still if you would carry me off to a quiet corner, and get me a glass of lemonade or some innocent drink before we all have to rush for the train."

She turned away as she spoke, letting him strut at her side through the gathering groups on the terrace, while every nerve in her throbbed with the consciousness of what Selden must have thought of the scene.

But under her angry sense of the perverseness of things, and the light surface of her talk with Rosedale, a third idea persisted: she did not mean to leave without an attempt to discover the truth about Percy Gryce. Chance, or perhaps his own resolve, had kept them apart since his hasty withdrawal from Bellomont; but Miss Bart was an expert in making the most of the unexpected, and the distasteful incidents of the last few minutes—the revelation to Selden of precisely that part of her life which she most wished him to ignore—increased her longing for shelter, for escape from such humiliating contingencies. Any definite situation would be more tolerable than this buffeting of chances, which kept her in an attitude of uneasy alertness toward every possibility of life.

Indoors there was a general sense of dispersal in the air, as of an audience gathering itself up for departure after the principal actors had left the stage; but among the remaining groups, Lily could discover neither Gryce nor the youngest Miss Van Osburgh. That both should be missing struck her with foreboding; and she charmed Mr. Rosedale by proposing that they should make their way to the conservatories at the farther end of the house. There were just enough people left in the long suite of rooms to make their progress conspicuous, and Lily was aware of being followed by looks of amusement and interrogation, which glanced off as harmlessly from her indifference as from her companion's self-satisfaction. She cared very little at that moment about being seen with Rosedale: all her thoughts were centred on the object of her search. The latter, however, was not discoverable in the conservatories, and Lily, oppressed by a sudden conviction of failure, was casting about for a way to rid herself of her now superfluous companion, when they came upon Mrs. Van Osburgh, flushed and exhausted, but beaming with the consciousness of duty performed.

She glanced at them a moment with the benign but vacant eye of the tired hostess, to whom her guests have become mere whirling spots in a kaleidoscope of fatigue; then her attention became suddenly fixed, and she seized on Miss Bart with a confidential gesture. "My dear Lily, I haven't had time for a word with you, and now I suppose you are just off. Have you seen Evie? She's been looking everywhere for you: she wanted to tell you her little secret; but I daresay you have guessed it already. The engagement is not to be announced till next week—but you are such a friend of Mr. Gryce's that they both wished you to be the first to know of their happiness."

# Chapter 9

In Mrs. Peniston's youth, fashion had returned to town in October; therefore on the tenth day of the month the blinds of her Fifth Avenue residence were drawn up, and the eyes of the Dying Gladiator in bronze who occupied the drawing-room window resumed their survey of that deserted thoroughfare.

The first two weeks after her return represented to Mrs. Peniston the domestic equivalent of a religious retreat. She "went through" the linen and blankets in the precise spirit of the penitent exploring the inner folds of conscience; she sought for moths as the stricken soul seeks for lurking infirmities. The topmost shelf of every closet was made to yield up its secret, cellar and coal-bin were probed to their darkest depths and, as a final stage in the lustral rites, the entire house was swathed in penitential white and deluged with expiatory soapsuds.

It was on this phase of the proceedings that Miss Bart entered on the afternoon of her return from the Van Osburgh wedding. The journey back to town had not been calculated to soothe her nerves. Though Evie Van Osburgh's engagement was still officially a secret, it was one of which the innumerable intimate friends of the family were already possessed; and the trainful of returning guests buzzed with allusions and anticipations. Lily was acutely aware of her own part in this drama of innuendo: she knew the exact quality of the amusement the situation evoked. The crude forms in which her friends took their pleasure included a loud enjoyment of such complications: the zest of surprising destiny in the act of playing a practical joke. Lily knew well enough how to bear herself in difficult situations. She had, to a shade, the exact manner between victory and defeat: every insinuation was shed without an effort by the bright indifference of her manner. But she was beginning to feel the strain of the attitude; the reaction was more rapid, and she lapsed to a deeper self-disgust.

As was always the case with her, this moral repulsion found a physical outlet in a quickened distaste for her surroundings. She revolted from the complacent ugliness of Mrs. Peniston's black walnut, from the slippery gloss of the vestibule tiles, and the mingled odour of sapolio and furniture-polish that met her at the door.

The stairs were still carpetless, and on the way up to her room she was arrested on the landing by an encroaching tide of soapsuds. Gathering up her skirts, she drew aside with an impatient gesture; and as she did so she had the odd sensation of having already found herself in the same situation but in different surroundings. It seemed to her that she was again descending the staircase from Selden's rooms; and looking down to remonstrate with the dispenser of the soapy flood, she found herself met by a lifted stare which had once before confronted her under similar circumstances. It was the char-woman of the Benedick who, resting on crimson elbows, examined her with the same unflinching curiosity, the same apparent reluctance to let her pass. On this occasion, however, Miss Bart was on her own ground.

"Don't you see that I wish to go by? Please move your pail," she said sharply.

The woman at first seemed not to hear; then, without a word of excuse, she pushed back her pail and dragged a wet floor-cloth across the landing, keeping her eyes fixed on Lily while the latter swept by. It was insufferable that Mrs. Peniston should have such creatures about the house; and Lily entered her room resolved that the woman should be dismissed that evening.

Mrs. Peniston, however, was at the moment inaccessible to remonstrance: since early morning she had been shut up with her maid, going over her furs, a process which formed the culminating episode in the drama of household renovation. In the evening also Lily found herself alone, for her aunt, who rarely dined out, had responded to the summons of a Van Alstyne cousin who was passing through town. The house, in its state of unnatural immaculateness and order, was as dreary as a tomb, and as Lily, turning from her brief repast between shrouded sideboards, wandered into the newly-uncovered glare of the drawing-room she felt as though she were buried alive in the stifling limits of Mrs. Peniston's existence.

She usually contrived to avoid being at home during the season of domestic renewal. On the present occasion, however, a variety of reasons had combined to bring her to town; and foremost among them was the fact that she had fewer invitations than usual for the autumn. She had so long been accustomed to pass from one country-house to another, till the close of the holidays brought her friends to town, that the unfilled gaps of time confronting her produced a sharp sense of waning popularity. It was as she had said to Selden—people were tired of her. They would welcome her in a new character, but as Miss Bart they knew her by heart. She knew herself by heart too, and was sick of the old story. There were moments when she longed blindly for anything different, anything strange, remote and untried; but the utmost reach of her imagination did not go beyond picturing her usual life in a new setting. She could not figure herself as anywhere but in a drawing-room, diffusing elegance as a flower sheds perfume.

Meanwhile, as October advanced she had to face the alternative of returning to the Trenors or joining her aunt in town. Even the desolating dulness of New York in October, and the soapy discomforts of Mrs. Peniston's interior, seemed preferable to what might await her at Bellomont; and with an air of heroic devotion she announced her intention of remaining with her aunt till the holidays.

Sacrifices of this nature are sometimes received with feelings as mixed as those which actuate them; and Mrs. Peniston remarked to her confidential maid that, if any of the family were to be with her at such a crisis (though for forty years she had been thought competent to see to the hanging of her own curtains), she would certainly have preferred Miss Grace to Miss Lily. Grace Stepney was an obscure cousin, of adaptable manners and vicarious interests, who "ran in" to sit with Mrs. Peniston when Lily dined out too continuously; who played bezique, picked up dropped stitches, read out the deaths from the Times, and sincerely admired the purple satin drawing-room curtains, the Dying Gladiator in the window, and the seven-by-five painting of Niagara which represented the one artistic excess of Mr. Peniston's temperate career.

Mrs. Peniston, under ordinary circumstances, was as much bored by her excellent cousin as the recipient of such services usually is by the person who performs them. She greatly preferred the brilliant and unreliable Lily, who did not know one end of a crochet-needle from the other, and had frequently wounded her susceptibilities by suggesting that the drawing-room should be "done over." But when it came to hunting for missing napkins, or helping to decide whether the backstairs needed re-carpeting, Grace's judgment was certainly sounder than Lily's: not to mention the fact that the latter resented the smell of beeswax and brown soap, and behaved as though she thought a house ought to keep clean of itself, without extrancous assistance.

Seated under the cheerless blaze of the drawing-room chandelier—Mrs. Peniston never lit the lamps unless there was "company"—Lily seemed to watch her own figure retreating down vistas of neutral-tinted dulness to a middle age like Grace Stepney's. When she ceased to amuse Judy Trenor and her friends she would have to fall back on amusing Mrs. Peniston; whichever way she looked she saw only a future of servitude to the whims of others, never the possibility of asserting her own eager individuality.

A ring at the door-bell, sounding emphatically through the empty house, roused her suddenly to the extent of her boredom. It was as though all the weariness of the past months had culminated in the vacuity of that interminable evening. If only the ring meant a summons from the outer world—a token that she was still remembered and wanted!

After some delay a parlour-maid presented herself with the announcement that there was a person outside who was asking to see Miss Bart; and on Lily's pressing for a more specific description, she added:

"It's Mrs. Haffen, Miss; she won't say what she wants."

Lily, to whom the name conveyed nothing, opened the door upon a woman in a battered bonnet, who stood firmly planted under the hall-light. The glare of the unshaded gas shone familiarly on her pock-marked face and the reddish baldness visible through thin strands of straw-coloured hair. Lily looked at the char-woman in surprise.

"Do you wish to see me?" she asked.

"I should like to say a word to you, Miss." The tone was neither aggressive nor conciliatory: it revealed nothing of the speaker's errand. Nevertheless, some precautionary instinct warned Lily to withdraw beyond ear-shot of the hovering parlour-maid.

She signed to Mrs. Haffen to follow her into the drawing-room, and closed the door when they had entered.

"What is it that you wish?" she enquired.

The char-woman, after the manner of her kind, stood with her arms folded in her shawl. Unwinding the latter, she produced a small parcel wrapped in dirty newspaper.

"I have something here that you might like to see, Miss Bart." She spoke the name with an unpleasant emphasis, as though her knowing it made a part of her reason for being there. To Lily the intonation sounded like a threat.

"You have found something belonging to me?" she asked, extending her hand.

Mrs. Haffen drew back. "Well, if it comes to that, I guess it's mine as much as anybody's," she returned.

Lily looked at her perplexedly. She was sure, now, that her visitor's manner conveyed a threat; but, expert as she was in certain directions, there was nothing in her experience to prepare her for the exact significance of the present scene. She felt, however, that it must be ended as promptly as possible.

"I don't understand; if this parcel is not mine, why have you asked for me?"

The woman was unabashed by the question. She was evidently prepared to answer it, but like all her class she had to go a long way back to make a beginning, and it was only after a pause that she replied: "My husband was janitor to the Benedick till the first of the month; since then he can't get nothing to do."

Lily remained silent and she continued: "It wasn't no fault of our own, neither: the agent had another man he wanted the place for, and we was put out, bag and baggage, just to suit his fancy. I had a long sickness last winter, and an operation that ate up all we'd put by; and it's hard for me and the children, Haffen being so long out of a job."

After all, then, she had come only to ask Miss Bart to find a place for her husband; or, more probably, to seek the young lady's intervention with Mrs. Peniston. Lily had such an air of always getting what she wanted that she was used to being appealed to as an intermediary, and, relieved of her vague apprehension, shc took refuge in the conventional formula.

"I am sorry you have been in trouble," she said.

"Oh, that we have, Miss, and it's on'y just beginning. If on'y we'd 'a got another situation—but the agent, he's dead against us. It ain't no fault of ours, neither, but—"

At this point Lily's impatience overcame her. "If you have anything to say to me—" she interposed.

The woman's resentment of the rebuff seemed to spur her lagging ideas.

"Yes, Miss; I'm coming to that," she said. She paused again, with her eyes on Lily, and then continued, in a tone of diffuse narrative: "When we was at the Benedick I had charge of some of the gentlemen's rooms; leastways, I swep' 'em out on Saturdays. Some of the gentlemen got the greatest sight of letters: I never saw the like of it. Their waste-paper baskets 'd be fairly brimming, and papers falling over on the floor. Maybe havin' so many is how they get so careless. Some of 'em is worse than others. Mr. Selden, Mr. Lawrence Selden, he was always one of the carefullest: burnt his letters in winter, and tore 'em in little bits in summer. But sometimes he'd have so many he'd just bunch 'em together, the way the others did, and tear the lot through once—like this."

While she spoke she had loosened the string from the parcel in her hand, and now she drew forth a letter which she laid on the table between Miss Bart and herself. As she had said, the letter was torn in two; but with a rapid gesture she laid the torn edges together and smoothed out the page.

A wave of indignation swept over Lily. She felt herself in the presence of something vile, as yet but dimly conjectured—the kind of vileness of which people whispered, but which she had never thought of as touching her own life. She drew back with a motion of disgust, but her withdrawal was checked by a sudden discovery: under the glare of Mrs. Peniston's chandelier she had recognized the hand-writing of the letter. It was a large disjointed hand, with a flourish of masculinity which but slightly disguised its rambling weakness, and the words, scrawled in heavy ink on pale-tinted notepaper, smote on Lily's ear as though she had heard them spoken.

At first she did not grasp the full import of the situation. She understood only that before her lay a letter written by Bertha Dorset, and addressed, presumably, to Lawrence Selden. There was no date, but the blackness of the ink proved the writing to be comparatively recent. The packet in Mrs. Haffen's hand doubtless contained more letters of the same kind—a dozen, Lily conjectured from its thickness. The letter before her was short, but its few words, which had leapt into her brain before she was conscious of reading them, told a long history—a history over which, for the last four years, the friends of the writer had smiled and shrugged, viewing it merely as one among the countless "good situations" of the mundane comedy. Now the other side presented itself to Lily, the volcanic nether side of the surface over which conjecture and innuendo glide so lightly till the first fissure turns their whisper to a shriek. Lily knew that there is nothing society resents so much as having given its protection to those who have not known how to profit by it: it is for having betrayed its connivance that the body social punishes the offender who is found out. And in this case there was no doubt of the issue. The code of Lily's world decreed that a woman's husband should be the only judge of her conduct: she was technically above suspicion while she had the shelter of his approval, or even of his indifference. But with a man of George Dorset's temper there could be no thought of condonation—the possessor of his wife's letters could overthrow with a touch the whole structure of her existence. And into what hands Bertha Dorset's secret had been delivered! For a moment the irony of the coincidence tinged Lily's disgust with a confused sense of triumph. But the disgust prevailed—all her instinctive resistances, of taste, of training, of blind inherited scruples, rose against the other feeling. Her strongest sense was one of personal contamination.

She moved away, as though to put as much distance as possible between herself and her visitor. "I know nothing of these letters," she said; "I have no idea why you have brought them here."

Mrs. Haffen faced her steadily. "I'll tell you why, Miss. I brought 'em to you to sell, because I ain't got no other way of raising money, and if we don't pay our rent by tomorrow night we'll be put out. I never done anythin' of the kind before, and if you'd speak to Mr. Selden or to Mr. Rosedale about getting Haffen taken on again at the Benedick—I seen you talking to Mr. Rosedale on the steps that day you come out of Mr. Selden's rooms—"

The blood rushed to Lily's forehead. She understood now—Mrs. Haffen supposed her to be the writer of the letters. In the first leap of her anger she was about to ring and order the woman out; but an obscure impulse restrained her. The mention of Selden's name had started a new train of thought. Bertha Dorset's letters were nothing to her—they might go where the current of chance carried them! But Selden was inextricably involved in their fate. Men do not, at worst, suffer much from such exposure; and in this instance the flash of divination which had carried the meaning of the letters to Lily's brain had revealed also that they were appeals—repeated and therefore probably unanswered—for the renewal of a tie which time had evidently relaxed. Nevertheless, the fact that the correspondence had been allowed to fall into strange hands would convict Selden of negligence in a matter where the world holds it least pardonable; and there were graver risks to consider where a man of Dorset's ticklish balance was concerned.

If she weighed all these things it was unconsciously: she was aware only of feeling that Selden would wish the letters rescued, and that therefore she must obtain possession of them. Beyond that her mind did not travel. She had, indeed, a quick vision of returning the packet to Bertha Dorset, and of the opportunities the restitution offered; but this thought lit up abysses from which she shrank back ashamed.

Meanwhile Mrs. Haffen, prompt to perceive her hesitation, had already opened the packet and ranged its contents on the table. All the letters had been pieced together with strips of thin paper. Some were in small fragments, the others merely torn in half. Though there were not many, thus spread out they nearly covered the table. Lily's glance fell on a word here and there—then she said in a low voice: "What do you wish me to pay you?"

Mrs. Haffen's face reddened with satisfaction. It was clear that the young lady was badly frightened, and Mrs. Haffen was the woman to make the most of such fears. Anticipating an easier victory than she had foreseen, she named an exorbitant sum.

But Miss Bart showed herself a less ready prey than might have been expected from her imprudent opening. She refused to pay the price named, and after a moment's hesitation, met it by a counter-offer of half the amount.

Mrs. Haffen immediately stiffened. Her hand travelled toward the outspread letters, and folding them slowly, she made as though to restore them to their wrapping.

"I guess they're worth more to you than to me, Miss, but the poor has got to live as well as the rich," she observed sententiously.

Lily was throbbing with fear, but the insinuation fortified her resistance.

"You are mistaken," she said indifferently. "I have offered all I am willing to give for the letters; but there may be other ways of getting them."

Mrs. Haffen raised a suspicious glance: she was too experienced not to know that the traffic she was engaged in had perils as great as its rewards, and she had a vision of the elaborate machinery of revenge which a word of this commanding young lady's might set in motion.

She applied the corner of her shawl to her eyes, and murmured through it that no good came of bearing too hard on the poor, but that for her part she had never been mixed up in such a business before, and that on her honour as a Christian all she and Haffen had thought of was that the letters mustn't go any farther.

Lily stood motionless, keeping between herself and the char-woman the greatest distance compatible with the need of speaking in low tones. The idea of bargaining for the letters was intolerable to her, but she knew that, if she appeared to weaken, Mrs. Haffen would at once increase her original demand.

She could never afterward recall how long the duel lasted, or what was the decisive stroke which finally, after a lapse of time recorded in minutes by the clock, in hours by the precipitate beat of her pulses, put her in possession of the letters; she knew only that the door had finally closed, and that she stood alone with the packet in her hand.

She had no idea of reading the letters; even to unfold Mrs. Haffen's dirty newspaper would have seemed degrading. But what did she intend to do with its contents? The recipient of the letters had meant to destroy them, and it was her duty to carry out his intention. She had no right to keep them—to do so was to lessen whatever merit lay in having secured their possession. But how destroy them so effectually that there should be no second risk of their falling in such hands? Mrs. Peniston's icy drawing-room grate shone with a forbidding lustre: the fire, like the lamps, was never lit except when there was company.

Miss Bart was turning to carry the letters upstairs when she heard the opening of the outer door, and her aunt entered the drawing-room. Mrs. Peniston was a small plump woman, with a colourless skin lined with trivial wrinkles. Her grey hair was arranged with precision, and her clothes looked excessively new and yet slightly old-fashioned. They were always black and tightly fitting, with an expensive glitter: she was the kind of woman who wore jet at breakfast. Lily had never seen her when she was not cuirassed in shining black, with small tight boots, and an air of being packed and ready to start; yet she never started.

She looked about the drawing-room with an expression of minute scrutiny. "I saw a streak of light under one of the blinds as I drove up: it's extraordinary that I can never teach that woman to draw them down evenly."

Having corrected the irregularity, she seated herself on one of the glossy purple arm-chairs; Mrs. Peniston always sat on a chair, never in it.

Then she turned her glance to Miss Bart. "My dear, you look tired; I suppose it's the excitement of the wedding. Cornelia Van Alstyne was full of it: Molly was there, and Gerty Farish ran in for a minute to tell us about it. I think it was odd, their serving melons before the *consomme*: a wedding breakfast should always begin with *consomme*. Molly didn't care for the bridesmaids' dresses. She had it straight from Julia Melson that they cost three hundred dollars apiece at Celeste's, but she says they didn't look it. I'm glad you decided not to be a bridesmaid; that shade of salmon-pink wouldn't have suited you." Mrs. Peniston delighted in discussing the minutest details of festivities in which she had not taken part. Nothing would have induced her to undergo the exertion and fatigue of attending the Van Osburgh wedding, but so great was her interest in the event that, having heard two versions of it, she now prepared to extract a third from her niece. Lily, however, had been deplorably careless in noting the particulars of the entertainment. She had failed to observe the colour of Mrs. Van Osburgh's gown, and could not even say whether the old Van Osburgh

Sevres had been used at the bride's table: Mrs. Peniston, in short, found that she was of more service as a listener than as a narrator.

"Really, Lily, I don't see why you took the trouble to go to the wedding, if you don't remember what happened or whom you saw there. When I was a girl I used to keep the *menu* of every dinner I went to, and write the names of the people on the back; and I never threw away my cotillion favours till after your uncle's death, when it seemed unsuitable to have so many coloured things about the house. I had a whole closet-full, I remember; and I can tell to this day what balls I got them at. Molly Van Alstyne reminds me of what I was at that age; it's wonderful how she notices. She was able to tell her mother exactly how the wedding-dress was cut, and we knew at once, from the fold in the back, that it must have come from Paquin."

Mrs. Peniston rose abruptly, and, advancing to the ormolu clock surmounted by a helmeted Minerva, which throned on the chimney-piece between two malachite vases, passed her lace handkerchief between the helmet and its visor.

"I knew it—the parlour-maid never dusts there!" she exclaimed, triumphantly displaying a minute spot on the handkerchief; then, reseating herself, she went on: "Molly thought Mrs. Dorset the best-dressed woman at the wedding. I've no doubt her dress *did* cost more than any one else's, but I can't quite like the idea—a combination of sable and *point de milan*. It seems she goes to a new man in Paris, who won't take an order till his client has spent a day with him at his villa at Neuilly. He says he must study his subject's home life—a most peculiar arrangement, I should say! But Mrs. Dorset told Molly about it herself: she said the villa was full of the most exquisite things and she was really sorry to leave. Molly said she never saw her looking better; she was in tremendous spirits, and said she had made a match between Evie Van Osburgh and Percy Gryce. She really seems to have a very good influence on young men. I hear she is interesting herself now in that silly Silverton boy, who has had his head turned by Carry Fisher, and has been gambling so dreadfully. Well, as I was saying, Evie is really engaged: Mrs. Dorset had her to stay with Percy Gryce, and managed it all, and Grace Van Osburgh is in the seventh heaven—she had almost despaired of marrying Evie."

Mrs. Peniston again paused, but this time her scrutiny addressed itself, not to the furniture, but to her niece.

"Cornelia Van Alstyne was so surprised: she had heard that you were to marry young Gryce. She saw the Wetheralls just after they had stopped with you at Bellomont, and Alice Wetherall was quite sure there was an engagement. She said that when Mr. Gryce left unexpectedly one morning, they all thought he had rushed to town for the ring."

Lily rose and moved toward the door.

"I believe I *am* tired: I think I will go to bed," she said; and Mrs. Peniston, suddenly distracted by the discovery that the easel sustaining the late Mr. Peniston's crayon-portrait was not exactly in line with the sofa in front of it, presented an absent-minded brow to her kiss.

In her own room Lily turned up the gas-jet and glanced toward the grate. It was as brilliantly polished as the one below, but here at least she could burn a few papers with less risk of incurring her aunt's disapproval. She made no immediate motion to do so, however, but dropping into a chair looked wearily about her. Her room was large and comfortably-furnished—it was the envy and admiration of poor Grace Stepney, who boarded; but, contrasted with the light tints and luxurious appointments of the guest-rooms where so many weeks of Lily's existence were spent, it seemed as dreary as a prison. The monumental wardrobe and bedstead of black walnut had migrated from Mr. Peniston's bedroom, and the magenta "flock" wall-paper, of a pattern dear to the early 'sixties, was hung with large steel engravings of an anecdotic character. Lily had tried to mitigate this charmless background by a few frivolous touches, in the shape of a lace-decked toilet table and a little painted desk surmounted by photographs; but the futility of the attempt struck her as she looked about the room. What a contrast to the subtle elegance of the setting she had pictured for herself—an apartment which should surpass the complicated luxury of her friends' surroundings by the whole extent of that artistic sensibility which made her feel herself their superior; in which every tint and line should combine to enhance her beauty and give distinction to her leisure! Once more the haunting sense of physical ugliness was intensified by her mental depression, so that each piece of the offending furniture seemed to thrust forth its most aggressive angle.

Her aunt's words had told her nothing new; but they had revived the vision of Bertha Dorset, smiling, flattered, victorious, holding her up to ridicule by insinuations intelligible to every member of their little group. The thought of the ridicule struck deeper than any other sensation: Lily knew every turn of the allusive jargon which could flay its victims without the shedding of blood. Her cheek burned at the recollection, and she rose and caught up the letters. She no longer meant to destroy them: that intention had been effaced by the quick corrosion of Mrs. Peniston's words.

Instead, she approached her desk, and lighting a taper, tied and sealed the packet; then she opened the wardrobe, drew out a despatch-box, and deposited the letters within it. As she did so, it struck her with a flash of irony that she was indebted to Gus Trenor for the means of buying them.

# Chapter 10

The autumn dragged on monotonously. Miss Bart had received one or two notes from Judy Trenor, reproaching her for not returning to Bellomont; but she replied evasively, alleging the obligation to remain with her aunt. In truth, however, she was fast wearying of her solitary existence with Mrs. Peniston, and only the excitement of spending her newly-acquired money lightened the dulness of the days.

All her life Lily had seen money go out as quickly as it came in, and whatever theories she cultivated as to the prudence of setting aside a part of her gains, she had unhappily no saving vision of the risks of the opposite course. It was a keen satisfaction to feel that, for a few months at least, she would be independent of her friends' bounty, that she could show herself abroad without wondering whether some penetrating eye would detect in her dress the traces of Judy Trenor's refurbished splendour. The fact that the money freed her temporarily from all minor obligations obscured her sense of the greater one it represented, and having never before known what it was to command so large a sum, she lingered delectably over the amusement of spending it.

It was on one of these occasions that, leaving a shop where she had spent an hour of deliberation over a dressing-case of the most complicated elegance, she ran across Miss Farish, who had entered the same establishment with the modest object of having her watch repaired. Lily was feeling unusually virtuous. She had decided to defer the purchase of the dressing-case till she should receive the bill for her new opera-cloak, and the resolve made her feel much richer than when she had entered the shop. In this mood of self-approval she had a sympathetic eye for others, and she was struck by her friend's air of dejection.

Miss Farish, it appeared, had just left the committee-meeting of a struggling charity in which she was interested. The object of the association was to provide comfortable lodgings, with a reading-room and other modest distractions, where young women of the class employed in down town offices might find a home when out of work, or in need of rest, and the first year's financial report showed so deplorably small a balance that Miss Farish, who was convinced of the urgency of the work, felt proportionately discouraged by the small amount of interest it aroused. The other-regarding sentiments had not been cultivated in Lily, and she was often bored by the relation of her friend's philanthropic efforts, but today her quick dramatizing fancy seized on the contrast between her own situation and that represented by some of Gerty's "cases." These were young girls, like herself; some perhaps pretty, some not without a trace of her finer sensibilities. She pictured herself leading such a life as theirs—a life in which achievement seemed as squalid as failure—and the vision made her shudder sympathetically. The price of the dressing-case was still in her pocket; and drawing out her little gold purse she slipped a liberal fraction of the amount into Miss Farish's hand.

The satisfaction derived from this act was all that the most ardent moralist could have desired. Lily felt a new interest in herself as a person of charitable instincts: she had never before thought of doing good with the wealth she had so often dreamed of possessing, but now her horizon was enlarged by the vision of a prodigal philanthropy. Moreover, by some obscure process of logic, she felt that her momentary burst of generosity had justified all previous extravagances, and excused any in which she might subsequently indulge. Miss Farish's surprise and gratitude confirmed this feeling, and Lily parted from her with a sense of self-esteem which she naturally mistook for the fruits of altruism.

About this time she was farther cheered by an invitation to spend the Thanksgiving week at a camp in the Adirondacks. The invitation was one which, a year earlier, would have provoked a less ready response, for the party, though organized by Mrs. Fisher, was ostensibly given by a lady of obscure origin and indomitable social ambitions, whose acquaintance Lily had hitherto avoided. Now, however, she was disposed to coincide with Mrs. Fisher's view, that it didn't matter who gave the party, as long as things were well done; and doing things well (under competent direction) was Mrs. Wellington Bry's strong point. The lady (whose consort was known as "Welly" Bry on the Stock Exchange and in sporting circles) had already sacrificed one husband, and sundry minor considerations, to her determination to get on; and, having obtained a hold on Carry Fisher, she was astute enough to perceive the wisdom of committing herself entirely to that lady's guidance. Everything, accordingly, was well done, for there was no limit to Mrs. Fisher's prodigality when she was not spending her own money, and as she remarked to her pupil, a good cook was the best introduction to society. If the company was not as select as the CUISINE, the Welly Brys at least had the satisfaction of figuring for the first time in the society columns in company with one or two noticeable names; and foremost among these was of course Miss Bart's. The young lady was treated by her hosts with corresponding deference; and she was in the mood when such attentions are acceptable, whatever their source. Mrs. Bry's admiration was a mirror in which Lily's self-complacency recovered its lost outline. No insect hangs its nest on threads as frail as those which will sustain the weight of human vanity; and the sense of being of importance among the insignificant was enough to restore to Miss Bart the gratifying consciousness of power. If these people paid court to her it proved that she was still conspicuous in the world to which they aspired; and she was not above a certain enjoyment in dazzling them by her fineness, in developing their puzzled perception of her superiorities.

Perhaps, however, her enjoyment proceeded more than she was aware from the physical stimulus of the excursion, the challenge of crisp cold and hard exercise, the responsive thrill of her body to the influences of the winter woods. She returned to town in a glow of rejuvenation, conscious of a clearer colour in her cheeks, a fresh elasticity in her muscles. The future seemed full of a vague promise, and all her apprehensions were swept out of sight on the buoyant current of her mood.

A few days after her return to town she had the unpleasant surprise of a visit from Mr. Rosedale. He came late, at the confidential hour when the tea-table still lingers by the fire in friendly expectancy; and his manner showed a readiness to adapt itself to the intimacy of the occasion.

Lily, who had a vague sense of his being somehow connected with her lucky speculations, tried to give him the welcome he expected; but there was something in the quality of his geniality which chilled her own, and she was conscious of marking each step in their acquaintance by a fresh blunder.

Mr. Rosedale—making himself promptly at home in an adjoining easy-chair, and sipping his tea critically, with the comment: "You ought to go to my man for something really good"—appeared totally unconscious of the repugnance which kept her in frozen erectness behind the urn. It was perhaps her very manner of holding herself aloof that appealed to his collector's passion for the rare and unattainable. He gave, at any rate, no sign of resenting it and seemed prepared to supply in his own manner all the ease that was lacking in hers.

His object in calling was to ask her to go to the opera in his box on the opening night, and seeing her hesitate he said persuasively: "Mrs. Fisher is coming, and I've secured a tremendous admirer of yours, who'll never forgive me if you don't accept."

As Lily's silence left him with this allusion on his hands, he added with a confidential smile: "Gus Trenor has promised to come to town on purpose. I fancy he'd go a good deal farther for the pleasure of seeing you."

Miss Bart felt an inward motion of annoyance: it was distasteful enough to hear her name coupled with Trenor's, and on Rosedale's lips the allusion was peculiarly unpleasant.

"The Trenors are my best friends—I think we should all go a long way to see each other," she said, absorbing herself in the preparation of fresh tea.

Her visitor's smile grew increasingly intimate. "Well, I wasn't thinking of Mrs. Trenor at the moment—they say Gus doesn't always, you know." Then, dimly conscious that he had not struck the right note, he added, with a well-meant effort at diversion: "How's your luck been going in Wall Street, by the way? I hear Gus pulled off a nice little pile for you last month."

Lily put down the tea-caddy with an abrupt gesture. She felt that her hands were trembling, and clasped them on her knee to steady them; but her lip trembled too, and for a moment she was afraid the tremor might communicate itself to her voice. When she spoke, however, it was in a tone of perfect lightness.

"Ah, yes—I had a little bit of money to invest, and Mr. Trenor, who helps me about such matters, advised my putting it in stocks instead of a mortgage, as my aunt's agent wanted me to do; and as it happened, I made a lucky 'turn'—is that what you call it? For you make a great many yourself, I believe."

She was smiling back at him now, relaxing the tension of her attitude, and admitting him, by imperceptible gradations of glance and manner, a step farther toward intimacy. The protective instinct always nerved her to successful dissimulation, and it was not the first time she had used her beauty to divert attention from an inconvenient topic.

When Mr. Rosedale took leave, he carried with him, not only her acceptance of his invitation, but a general sense of having comported himself in a way calculated to advance his cause. He had always believed he had a light touch and a knowing way with women, and the prompt manner in which Miss Bart (as he would have phrased it) had "come into line," confirmed his confidence in his powers of handling this skittish sex. Her way of glossing over the transaction with Trenor he regarded at once as a tribute to his own acuteness, and a confirmation of his suspicions. The girl was evidently nervous, and Mr.

Rosedale, if he saw no other means of advancing his acquaintance with her, was not above taking advantage of her nervousness.

He left Lily to a passion of disgust and fear. It seemed incredible that Gus Trenor should have spoken of her to Rosedale. With all his faults, Trenor had the safeguard of his traditions, and was the less likely to overstep them because they were so purely instinctive. But Lily recalled with a pang that there were convivial moments when, as Judy had confided to her, Gus "talked foolishly": in one of these, no doubt, the fatal word had slipped from him. As for Rosedale, she did not, after the first shock, greatly care what conclusions he had drawn. Though usually adroit enough where her own interests were concerned, she made the mistake, not uncommon to persons in whom the social habits are instinctive, of supposing that the inability to acquire them quickly implies a general dulness. Because a blue-bottle bangs irrationally against a window-pane, the drawing-room naturalist may forget that under less artificial conditions it is capable of measuring distances and drawing conclusions with all the accuracy needful to its welfare; and the fact that Mr. Rosedale's drawing-room manner lacked perspective made Lily class him with Trenor and the other dull men she knew, and assume that a little flattery, and the occasional acceptance of his hospitality, would suffice to render him innocuous. However, there could be no doubt of the expediency of showing herself in his box on the opening night of the opera; and after all, since Judy Trenor had promised to take him up that winter, it was as well to reap the advantage of being first in the field.

For a day or two after Rosedale's visit, Lily's thoughts were dogged by the consciousness of Trenor's shadowy claim, and she wished she had a clearer notion of the exact nature of the transaction which seemed to have put her in his power; but her mind shrank from any unusual application, and she was always helplessly puzzled by figures. Moreover she had not seen Trenor since the day of the Van Osburgh wedding, and in his continued absence the trace of Rosedale's words was soon effaced by other impressions.

When the opening night of the opera came, her apprehensions had so completely vanished that the sight of Trenor's ruddy countenance in the back of Mr. Rosedale's box filled her with a sense of pleasant reassurance. Lily had not quite reconciled herself to the necessity of appearing as Rosedale's guest on so conspicuous an occasion, and it was a relief to find herself supported by any one of her own set—for Mrs. Fisher's social habits were too promiscuous for her presence to justify Miss Bart's.

To Lily, always inspirited by the prospect of showing her beauty in public, and conscious tonight of all the added enhancements of dress, the insistency of Trenor's gaze merged itself in the general stream of admiring looks of which she felt herself the centre. Ah, it was good to be young, to be radiant, to glow with the sense of slenderness, strength and elasticity, of well-poised lines and happy tints, to feel one's self lifted to a height apart by that incommunicable grace which is the bodily counterpart of genius!

All means seemed justifiable to attain such an end, or rather, by a happy shifting of lights with which practice had familiarized Miss Bart, the cause shrank to a pin-point in the general brightness of the effect. But brilliant young ladies, a little blinded by their own effulgence, are apt to forget that the modest satellite drowned in their light is still performing its own revolutions and generating heat at its own rate. If Lily's poetic enjoyment of the moment was undisturbed by the base thought that her gown and opera cloak had been indirectly paid for by Gus Trenor, the latter had not sufficient poetry in his composition to lose sight of these prosaic facts. He knew only that he had never seen Lily look smarter in her life, that there wasn't a woman in the house who showed off good clothes as she did, and that hitherto he, to whom she owed the opportunity of making this display, had reaped no return beyond that of gazing at her in company with several hundred other pairs of eyes.

It came to Lily therefore as a disagreeable surprise when, in the back of the box, where they found themselves alone between two acts,

Trenor said, without preamble, and in a tone of sulky authority: "Look here, Lily, how is a fellow ever to see anything of you? I'm in town three or four days in the week, and you know a line to the club will always find me, but you don't seem to remember my existence nowadays unless you want to get a tip out of me."

The fact that the remark was in distinctly bad taste did not make it any easier to answer, for Lily was vividly aware that it was not the moment for that drawing up of her slim figure and surprised lifting of the brows by which she usually quelled incipient signs of familiarity.

"I'm very much flattered by your wanting to see me," she returned, essaying lightness instead, "but, unless you have mislaid my address, it would have been easy to find me any afternoon at my aunt's—in fact, I rather expected you to look me up there."

If she hoped to mollify him by this last concession the attempt was a failure, for he only replied, with the familiar lowering of the brows that made him look his dullest when he was angry: "Hang going to your aunt's, and wasting the afternoon listening to a lot of other chaps talking to you! You know I'm not the kind to sit in a crowd and jaw—I'd always rather clear out when that sort of circus is going on. But why can't we go off somewhere on a little lark together—a nice quiet little expedition like that drive at Bellomont, the day you met me at the station?"

He leaned unpleasantly close in order to convey this suggestion, and she fancied she caught a significant aroma which explained the dark flush on his face and the glistening dampness of his forehead.

The idea that any rash answer might provoke an unpleasant outburst tempered her disgust with caution, and she answered with a laugh: "I don't see how one can very well take country drives in town, but I am not always surrounded by an admiring throng, and if you will let me know what afternoon you are coming I will arrange things so that we can have a nice quiet talk."

"Hang talking! That's what you always say," returned Trenor, whose expletives lacked variety. "You put me off with that at the Van

Osburgh wedding—but the plain English of it is that, now you've got what you wanted out of me, you'd rather have any other fellow about."

His voice had risen sharply with the last words, and Lily flushed with annoyance, but she kept command of the situation and laid a persuasive hand on his arm.

"Don't be foolish, Gus; I can't let you talk to me in that ridiculous way. If you really want to see me, why shouldn't we take a walk in the Park some afternoon? I agree with you that it's amusing to be rustic in town, and if you like I'll meet you there, and we'll go and feed the squirrels, and you shall take me out on the lake in the steam-gondola."

She smiled as she spoke, letting her eyes rest on his in a way that took the edge from her banter and made him suddenly malleable to her will.

"All right, then: that's a go. Will you come tomorrow? Tomorrow at three o'clock, at the end of the Mall. I'll be there sharp, remember; you won't go back on me, Lily?"

But to Miss Bart's relief the repetition of her promise was cut short by the opening of the box door to admit George Dorset.

Trenor sulkily yielded his place, and Lily turned a brilliant smile on the newcomer. She had not talked with Dorset since their visit at Bellomont, but something in his look and manner told her that he recalled the friendly footing on which they had last met. He was not a man to whom the expression of admiration came easily: his long sallow face and distrustful eyes seemed always barricaded against the expansive emotions. But, where her own influence was concerned, Lily's intuitions sent out thread-like feelers, and as she made room for him on the narrow sofa she was sure he found a dumb pleasure in being near her. Few women took the trouble to make themselves agreeable to Dorset, and Lily had been kind to him at Bellomont, and was now smiling on him with a divine renewal of kindness.

"Well, here we are, in for another six months of caterwauling," he began complainingly. "Not a shade of difference between this year and last, except that the women have got new clothes and the singers haven't got new voices. My wife's musical, you know—puts me through a course of this every winter. It isn't so bad on Italian nights—then she comes late, and there's time to digest. But when they give Wagner we have to rush dinner, and I pay up for it. And the draughts are damnable—asphyxia in front and pleurisy in the back. There's Trenor leaving the box without drawing the curtain! With a hide like that draughts don't make any difference. Did you ever watch Trenor eat? If you did, you'd wonder why he's alive; I suppose he's leather inside too.—But I came to say that my wife wants you to come down to our place next Sunday. Do for heaven's sake say yes. She's got a lot of bores coming—intellectual ones, I mean; that's her new line, you know, and I'm not sure it ain't worse than the music. Some of 'em have long hair, and they start an argument with the soup, and don't notice when things are handed to them. The consequence is the dinner gets cold, and I have dyspepsia. That silly ass Silverton brings them to the house—he writes poetry, you know, and Bertha and he are getting tremendously thick. She could write better than any of 'em if she chose, and I don't blame her for wanting clever fellows about; all I say is: 'Don't let me see 'em eat!'"

The gist of this strange communication gave Lily a distinct thrill of pleasure. Under ordinary circumstances, there would have been nothing surprising in an invitation from Bertha Dorset; but since the Bellomont episode an unavowed hostility had kept the two women apart. Now, with a start of inner wonder, Lily felt that her thirst for retaliation had died Out. *If You Would Forgive Your Enemy*, says the Malay proverb, *First Inflict a Hurt on Him*; and Lily was experiencing the truth of the apothegm. If she had destroyed Mrs. Dorset's letters, she might have continued to hate her; but the fact that they remained in her possession had fed her resentment to satiety.

She uttered a smiling acceptance, hailing in the renewal of the tie an escape from Trenor's importunities.

# Chapter 11

Meanwhile the holidays had gone by and the season was beginning. Fifth Avenue had become a nightly torrent of carriages surging upward to the fashionable quarters about the Park, where illuminated windows and outspread awnings betokened the usual routine of hospitality. Other tributary currents crossed the mainstream, bearing their freight to the theatres, restaurants or opera; and Mrs. Peniston, from the secluded watch-tower of her upper window, could tell to a nicety just when the chronic volume of sound was increased by the sudden influx setting toward a Van Osburgh ball, or when the multiplication of wheels meant merely that the opera was over, or that there was a big supper at Sherry's.

Mrs. Peniston followed the rise and culmination of the season as keenly as the most active sharer in its gaieties; and, as a looker-on, she enjoyed opportunities of comparison and generalization such as those who take part must proverbially forego. No one could have kept a more accurate record of social fluctuations, or have put a more unerring finger on the distinguishing features of each season: its dulness, its extravagance, its lack of balls or excess of divorces. She had a special memory for the vicissitudes of the "new people" who rose to the surface with each recurring tide, and were either submerged beneath its rush or landed triumphantly beyond the reach of envious breakers; and she was apt to display a remarkable retrospective insight into their ultimate fate, so that, when they had fulfilled their destiny, she was almost always able to say to Grace Stepney—the recipient of her prophecies—that she had known exactly what would happen.

This particular season Mrs. Peniston would have characterized as that in which everybody "felt poor" except the Welly Brys and Mr. Simon Rosedale. It had been a bad autumn in Wall Street, where prices fell in accordance with that peculiar law which proves railway stocks and bales of cotton to be more sensitive to the allotment of executive power than many estimable citizens trained to all the advantages of self-government. Even fortunes supposed to be independent of the market either betrayed a secret dependence on it, or suffered from a sympathetic affection: fashion sulked in its country houses, or came to town incognito, general entertainments were discountenanced, and informality and short dinners became the fashion.

But society, amused for a while at playing Cinderella, soon wearied of the hearthside role, and welcomed the Fairy Godmother in the shape of any magician powerful enough to turn the shrunken pumpkin back again into the golden coach. The mere fact of growing richer at a time when most people's investments are shrinking, is calculated to attract envious attention; and according to Wall Street rumours, Welly Bry and Rosedale had found the secret of performing this miracle.

Rosedale, in particular, was said to have doubled his fortune, and there was talk of his buying the newly-finished house of one of the victims of the crash, who, in the space of twelve short months, had made the same number of millions, built a house in Fifth Avenue, filled a picture-gallery with old masters, entertained all New York in it, and been smuggled out of the country between a trained nurse and a doctor, while his creditors mounted guard over the old masters, and his guests explained to each other that they had dined with him only because they wanted to see the pictures. Mr. Rosedale meant to have a less meteoric career. He knew he should have to go slowly, and the instincts of his race fitted him to suffer rebuffs and put up with delays. But he was prompt to perceive that the general dulness of the season afforded him an unusual opportunity to shine, and he set about with patient industry to form a background for his growing glory. Mrs. Fisher was of immense service to him at this period. She had set off so many newcomers on the social stage that she was like one of those pieces of stock scenery which tell the experienced spectator exactly what is going to take place. But Mr. Rosedale wanted, in the long run, a more individual environment. He was sensitive to shades of difference which Miss Bart would never have credited him with perceiving, because he had no corresponding variations of manner; and it was becoming more and more clear to him that Miss Bart herself possessed precisely the complementary qualities needed to round off his social personality.

Such details did not fall within the range of Mrs. Peniston's vision. Like many minds of panoramic sweep, hers was apt to overlook the *minutiae* of the foreground, and she was much more likely to know where Carry Fisher had found the Welly Brys' *chef* for them, than what was happening to her own niece. She was not, however, without purveyors of information ready to supplement her deficiencies. Grace Stepney's mind was like a kind of moral fly-paper, to which the buzzing items of gossip were drawn by a fatal attraction, and where they hung fast in the toils of an inexorable memory. Lily would have been surprised to know how many trivial facts concerning herself were lodged in Miss Stepney's head. She was quite aware that she was of interest to dingy people, but she assumed that there is only one form of dinginess, and that admiration for brilliancy is the natural expression of its inferior state. She knew that Gerty Farish admired her blindly, and therefore supposed that she inspired the same sentiments in Grace Stepney, whom she classified as a Gerty Farish without the saving traits of youth and enthusiasm.

In reality, the two differed from each other as much as they differed from the object of their mutual contemplation. Miss Farish's heart was a fountain of tender illusions, Miss Stepney's a precise register of facts as manifested in their relation to herself. She had sensibilities which, to Lily, would have seemed comic in a person with a freckled nose and red eyelids, who lived in a boarding-house and admired Mrs. Peniston's drawing-room; but poor Grace's limitations gave them a more concentrated inner life, as poor soil starves certain plants into intenser efflorescence. She had in truth no abstract propensity to malice: she did not dislike Lily because the latter was brilliant and predominant, but because she thought that Lily disliked her. It is less mortifying to believe one's self unpopular than insignificant, and vanity prefers to assume that indifference is a latent form of unfriendliness. Even such scant civilities as Lily accorded to Mr. Rosedale would have made Miss Stepney her friend for life; but how could she foresee that such a friend was worth cultivating? How, moreover, can a young woman who has never been ignored measure the pang which this injury inflicts? And, lastly, how could Lily, accustomed to choose between a pressure of engagements, guess that she had mortally offended Miss Stepney by causing her to be excluded from one of Mrs. Peniston's infrequent dinner-parties?

Mrs. Peniston disliked giving dinners, but she had a high sense of family obligation, and on the Jack Stepneys' return from their honeymoon she felt it incumbent upon her to light the drawing-room lamps and extract her best silver from the Safe Deposit vaults. Mrs. Peniston's rare entertainments were preceded by days of heart-rending vacillation as to every detail of the feast, from the seating of the guests to the pattern of the table-cloth, and in the course of one of these preliminary discussions she had imprudently suggested to her cousin Grace that, as the dinner was a family affair, she might be included in it. For a week the prospect had lighted up Miss Stepney's colourless existence; then she had been given to understand that it would be more convenient to have her another day. Miss Stepney knew exactly what had happened. Lily, to whom family reunions were occasions of unalloyed dulness, had persuaded her aunt that a dinner of "smart" people would be much more to the taste of the young couple, and Mrs. Peniston, who leaned helplessly on her niece in social matters, had been prevailed upon to pronounce Grace's exile. After all, Grace could come any other day; why should she mind being put off?

It was precisely because Miss Stepney could come any other day—and because she knew her relations were in the secret of her unoccupied evenings—that this incident loomed gigantically on her horizon. She was aware that she had Lily to thank for it; and dull resentment was turned to active animosity.

Mrs. Peniston, on whom she had looked in a day or two after the dinner, laid down her crochet-work and turned abruptly from her oblique survey of Fifth Avenue.

"Gus Trenor?—Lily and Gus Trenor?" she said, growing so suddenly pale that her visitor was almost alarmed.

"Oh, cousin Julia . . . of course I don't mean . . ."

"I don't know what you *do* mean," said Mrs. Peniston, with a frightened quiver in her small fretful voice. "Such things were never heard of in my day. And my own niece! I'm not sure I understand you. Do people say he's in love with her?"

Mrs. Peniston's horror was genuine. Though she boasted an unequalled familiarity with the secret chronicles of society, she had the innocence of the school-girl who regards wickedness as a part of "history," and to whom it never occurs that the scandals she reads of in lesson-hours may be repeating themselves in the next street. Mrs. Peniston had kept her imagination shrouded, like the drawing-room furniture. She knew, of course, that society was "very much changed," and that many women her mother would have thought "peculiar" were now in a position to be critical about their visiting-lists; she had discussed the perils of divorce with her rector, and had felt thankful at times that Lily was still unmarried; but the idea that any scandal could attach to a young girl's name, above all that it could be lightly coupled with that of a married man, was so new to her that she was as much aghast as if she had been accused of leaving her carpets down all summer, or of violating any of the other cardinal laws of housekeeping.

Miss Stepney, when her first fright had subsided, began to feel the superiority that greater breadth of mind confers. It was really pitiable to be as ignorant of the world as Mrs. Peniston! She smiled at the latter's question. "People always say unpleasant things—and certainly they're a great deal together. A friend of mine met them the other afternoon in the Park-quite late, after the lamps were lit. It's a pity Lily makes herself so conspicuous."

"*Conspicuous!*" gasped Mrs. Peniston. She bent forward, lowering her voice to mitigate the horror. "What sort of things do they say? That he means to get a divorce and marry her?"

Grace Stepney laughed outright. "Dear me, no! He would hardly do that. It—it's a flirtation—nothing more."

"A flirtation? Between my niece and a married man? Do you mean to tell me that, with Lily's looks and advantages, she could find no better use for her time than to waste it on a fat stupid man almost old enough to be her father?" This argument had such a convincing ring that it gave Mrs. Peniston sufficient reassurance to pick up her work, while she waited for Grace Stepney to rally her scattered forces.

But Miss Stepney was on the spot in an instant. "That's the worst of it—people say she isn't wasting her time! Every one knows, as you say, that Lily is too handsome and-and charming—to devote herself to a man like Gus Trenor unless—"

"Unless?" echoed Mrs. Peniston. Her visitor drew breath nervously. It was agreeable to shock Mrs. Peniston, but not to shock her to the verge of anger. Miss Stepney was not sufficiently familiar with the classic drama to have recalled in advance how bearers of bad tidings are proverbially received, but she now had a rapid vision of forfeited dinners and a reduced wardrobe as the possible consequence of her disinterestedness. To the honour of her sex, however, hatred of Lily prevailed over more personal considerations. Mrs. Peniston had chosen the wrong moment to boast of her niece's charms.

"Unless," said Grace, leaning forward to speak with low-toned emphasis, "unless there are material advantages to be gained by making herself agreeable to him."

She felt that the moment was tremendous, and remembered suddenly that Mrs. Peniston's black brocade, with the cut jet fringe, would have been hers at the end of the season.

Mrs. Peniston put down her work again. Another aspect of the same idea had presented itself to her, and she felt that it was beneath her dignity to have her nerves racked by a dependent relative who wore her old clothes.

"If you take pleasure in annoying me by mysterious insinuations," she said coldly, "you might at least have chosen a more suitable time than just as I am recovering from the strain of giving a large dinner."

The mention of the dinner dispelled Miss Stepney's last scruples. "I don't know why I should be accused of taking pleasure in telling you about Lily. I was sure I shouldn't get any thanks for it," she returned with a flare of temper. "But I have some family feeling left, and as you are the only person who has any authority over Lily, I thought you ought to know what is being said of her."

"Well," said Mrs. Peniston, "what I complain of is that you haven't told me yet what IS being said."

"I didn't suppose I should have to put it so plainly. People say that Gus Trenor pays her bills."

"Pays her bills—her bills?" Mrs. Peniston broke into a laugh. "I can't imagine where you can have picked up such rubbish. Lily has her own income—and I provide for her very handsomely—"

"Oh, we all know that," interposed Miss Stepney drily. "But Lily wears a great many smart gowns—"

"I like her to be well-dressed—it's only suitable!"

"Certainly; but then there are her gambling debts besides."

Miss Stepney, in the beginning, had not meant to bring up this point; but Mrs. Peniston had only her own incredulity to blame. She was like the stiff-necked unbelievers of Scripture, who must be annihilated to be convinced.

"Gambling debts? Lily?" Mrs. Peniston's voice shook with anger and bewilderment. She wondered whether Grace Stepney had gone out of her mind. "What do you mean by her gambling debts?"

"Simply that if one plays bridge for money in Lily's set one is liable to lose a great deal—and I don't suppose Lily always wins."

"Who told you that my niece played cards for money?"

"Mercy, cousin Julia, don't look at me as if I were trying to turn you against Lily! Everybody knows she is crazy about bridge. Mrs. Gryce told me herself that it was her gambling that frightened Percy Gryce—it seems he was really taken with her at first. But, of course, among Lily's friends it's quite the custom for girls to play for money. In fact, people are inclined to excuse her on that account—"

"To excuse her for what?"

"For being hard up—and accepting attentions from men like Gus Trenor—and George Dorset—"

Mrs. Peniston gave another cry. "George Dorset? Is there any one else? I should like to know the worst, if you please."

"Don't put it in that way, cousin Julia. Lately Lily has been a good deal with the Dorsets, and he seems to admire her—but of course that's only natural. And I'm sure there is no truth in the horrid things people say; but she *has* been spending a great deal of money this winter. Evie Van Osburgh was at Celeste's ordering her trousseau the other day—yes, the marriage takes place next month—and she told me that Celeste showed her the most exquisite things she was just sending home to Lily. And people say that Judy Trenor has quarrelled with her on account of Gus; but I'm sure I'm sorry I spoke, though I only meant it as a kindness."

Mrs. Peniston's genuine incredulity enabled her to dismiss Miss Stepney with a disdain which boded ill for that lady's prospect of succeeding to the black brocade; but minds impenetrable to reason have generally some crack through which suspicion filters, and her visitor's insinuations did not glide off as easily as she had expected. Mrs. Peniston disliked scenes, and her determination to avoid them had always led her to hold herself aloof from the details of Lily's life. In her youth, girls had not been supposed to require close supervision. They were generally assumed to be taken up with the legitimate business of courtship and marriage, and interference in such affairs on the part of their natural guardians was considered as unwarrantable as a spectator's suddenly joining in a game. There had of course been "fast" girls even in Mrs. Peniston's early experience; but their fastness, at worst, was understood to be a mere excess of animal spirits, against which there could be no graver charge than that of being "unladylike." The modern fastness appeared synonymous with immorality, and the mere idea of immorality was as offensive to Mrs. Peniston as a smell of cooking in the drawing-room: it was one of the conceptions her mind refused to admit.

She had no immediate intention of repeating to Lily what she had heard, or even of trying to ascertain its truth by means of discreet interrogation. To do so might be to provoke a scene; and a scene, in the shaken state of Mrs. Peniston's nerves, with the effects of her dinner not worn off, and her mind still tremulous with new impressions, was a risk she deemed it her duty to avoid. But there remained in her thoughts a settled deposit of resentment against her niece, all the denser because it was not to be cleared by explanation or discussion. It was horrible of a young girl to let herself be talked about; however unfounded the charges against her, she must be to blame for their having been made. Mrs. Peniston felt as if there had been a contagious illness in the house, and she was doomed to sit shivering among her contaminated furniture.

# Chapter 12

Miss Bart had in fact been treading a devious way, and none of her critics could have been more alive to the fact than herself; but she had a fatalistic sense of being drawn from one wrong turning to another, without ever perceiving the right road till it was too late to take it.

Lily, who considered herself above narrow prejudices, had not imagined that the fact of letting Gus Trenor make a little money for her would ever disturb her self-complacency. And the fact in itself still seemed harmless enough; only it was a fertile source of harmful complications. As she exhausted the amusement of spending the money these complications became more pressing, and Lily, whose mind could be severely logical in tracing the causes of her ill-luck to others, justified herself by the thought that she owed all her troubles to the enmity of Bertha Dorset. This enmity, however, had apparently expired in a renewal of friendliness between the two women. Lily's visit to the Dorsets had resulted, for both, in the discovery that they could be of use to each other; and the civilized instinct finds a subtler pleasure in making use of its antagonist than in confounding him. Mrs. Dorset was, in fact, engaged in a new sentimental experiment, of which Mrs. Fisher's late property, Ned Silverton, was the rosy victim; and at such moments, as Judy Trenor had once remarked, she felt a peculiar need of distracting her husband's attention. Dorset was as difficult to amuse as a savage; but even his self-engrossment was not proof against Lily's arts, or rather these were especially adapted to soothe an uneasy egoism. Her experience with Percy Gryce stood her in good stead in ministering to Dorset's humours, and if the incentive to please was less urgent, the difficulties of her situation were teaching her to make much of minor opportunities.

Intimacy with the Dorsets was not likely to lessen such difficulties on the material side. Mrs. Dorset had none of Judy Trenor's lavish impulses, and Dorset's admiration was not likely to express itself in financial "tips," even had Lily cared to renew her experiences in that line. What she required, for the moment, of the Dorsets' friendship, was simply its social sanction. She knew that people were beginning to talk of her; but this fact did not alarm her as it had alarmed Mrs. Peniston. In her set such gossip was not unusual, and a handsome girl who flirted with a married man was merely assumed to be pressing to the limit of her opportunities. It was Trenor himself who frightened her. Their walk in the Park had not been a success. Trenor had married young, and since his marriage his intercourse with women had not taken the form of the sentimental small-talk which doubles upon itself like the paths in a maze. He was first puzzled and then irritated to find himself always led back to the same starting-point, and Lily felt that she was gradually losing control of the situation. Trenor was in truth in an unmanageable mood. In spite of his understanding with Rosedale he had been somewhat heavily "touched" by the fall in stocks; his household expenses weighed on him, and he seemed to be meeting, on all sides, a sullen opposition to his wishes, instead of the easy good luck he had hitherto encountered.

Mrs. Trenor was still at Bellomont, keeping the town-house open, and descending on it now and then for a taste of the world, but preferring the recurrent excitement of week-end parties to the restrictions of a dull season. Since the holidays she had not urged Lily to return to Bellomont, and the first time they met in town Lily fancied there was a shade of coldness in her manner. Was it merely the expression of her displeasure at Miss Bart's neglect, or had disquieting rumours reached her? The latter contingency seemed improbable, yet Lily was not without a sense of uneasiness. If her roaming sympathies had struck root anywhere, it was in her friendship with Judy Trenor. She believed in the sincerity of her friend's affection, though it sometimes showed itself in self-interested ways, and she shrank with peculiar reluctance from any risk of estranging it. But, aside from this, she was keenly conscious of the way in which such an estrangement would react on herself. The fact that Gus Trenor was Judy's husband was at times Lily's strongest reason for disliking him, and for resenting the obligation under which he had placed her. To set her doubts at rest, Miss Bart, soon after the New Year, "proposed" herself for a week-end at Bellomont. She had learned in advance that the presence of a large party would protect her from too great assiduity on Trenor's part, and his wife's telegraphic "come by all means" seemed to assure her of her usual welcome.

Judy received her amicably. The cares of a large party always prevailed over personal feelings, and Lily saw no change in her hostess's manner. Nevertheless, she was soon aware that the experiment of coming to Bellomont was destined not to be successful. The party was made up of what Mrs. Trenor called "poky people"—her generic name for persons who did not play bridge—and, it being her habit to group all such obstructionists in one class, she usually invited them together, regardless of their other characteristics. The result was apt to be an irreducible combination of persons having no other quality in common than their abstinence from bridge, and the antagonisms developed in a group lacking the one taste which might have amalgamated them, were in this case aggravated by bad weather, and by the ill-concealed boredom of their host and hostess. In such emergencies, Judy would usually have turned to Lily to fuse the discordant elements; and Miss Bart, assuming that such a service was expected of her, threw herself into it with her accustomed zeal. But at the outset she perceived a subtle resistance to her efforts. If Mrs. Trenor's manner toward her was unchanged, there was certainly a faint coldness in that of the other ladies. An occasional caustic allusion to "your friends the Wellington Brys," or to "the little Jew who has bought the Greiner house—some one told us you knew him, Miss Bart,"—showed Lily that she was in disfavour with that portion of society which, while contributing least to its amusement, has assumed the right to decide what forms that amusement shall take. The indication was a slight one, and a year ago Lily would have smiled at it, trusting to the charm of her personality to dispel any prejudice against her. But now she had grown more sensitive to criticism and less confident in her power of disarming it. She knew, moreover, that if the ladies at Bellomont permitted themselves to criticize her friends openly, it was a proof that they were not afraid of subjecting her to the same treatment behind her back. The nervous dread lest anything in Trenor's manner should seem to justify their disapproval made her seek every pretext for avoiding him, and she left Bellomont conscious of having failed in every purpose which had taken her there.

In town she returned to preoccupations which, for the moment, had the happy effect of banishing troublesome thoughts. The Welly Brys, after much debate, and anxious counsel with their newly acquired friends, had decided on the bold move of giving a general entertainment. To attack society collectively, when one's means of approach are limited to a few acquaintances, is like advancing into a strange country with an insufficient number of scouts; but such rash tactics have sometimes led to brilliant victories, and the Brys had determined to put their fate to the touch. Mrs. Fisher, to whom they had entrusted the conduct of the affair, had decided that *tableaux vivants* and expensive music were the two baits most likely to attract the desired prey, and after prolonged negotiations, and the kind of wire-pulling in which she was known to excel, she had induced a dozen fashionable women to exhibit themselves in a series of pictures which, by a farther miracle of persuasion, the distinguished portrait painter, Paul Morpeth, had been prevailed upon to organize.

Lily was in her element on such occasions. Under Morpeth's guidance her vivid plastic sense, hitherto nurtured on no higher food than dress-making and upholstery, found eager expression in the disposal of draperies, the study of attitudes, the shifting of lights and shadows. Her dramatic instinct was roused by the choice of subjects, and the gorgeous reproductions of historic dress stirred an imagination which only visual impressions could reach. But keenest of all was the exhilaration of displaying her own beauty under a new aspect: of showing that her loveliness was no mere fixed quality, but an element shaping all emotions to fresh forms of grace.

Mrs. Fisher's measures had been well-taken, and society, surprised in a dull moment, succumbed to the temptation of Mrs. Bry's hospitality. The protesting minority were forgotten in the throng which abjured and came; and the audience was almost as brilliant as the show.

Lawrence Selden was among those who had yielded to the proffered inducements. If he did not often act on the accepted social axiom that a man may go where he pleases, it was because he had long since learned that his pleasures were mainly to be found in a small group of the like-minded. But he enjoyed spectacular effects, and was not insensible to the part money plays in their production: all he asked was that the very rich should live up to their calling as stage-managers, and not spend their money in a dull way. This the Brys could certainly not be charged with doing. Their recently built house, whatever it might lack as a frame for domesticity, was almost as well-designed for the display of a festal assemblage as one of those airy pleasure-halls which the Italian architects improvised to set off the hospitality of princes. The air of improvisation was in fact strikingly present: so recent, so rapidly-evoked was the whole *mise-en-scene* that one had to touch the marble columns to learn they were not of cardboard, to seat one's self in one of the damask-and-gold arm-chairs to be sure it was not painted against the wall.

Selden, who had put one of these seats to the test, found himself, from an angle of the ball-room, surveying the scene with frank enjoyment. The company, in obedience to the decorative instinct which calls for fine clothes in fine surroundings, had dressed rather with an eye to Mrs. Bry's background than to herself. The seated throng, filling the immense room without undue crowding, presented a surface of rich tissues and jewelled shoulders in harmony with the festooned and gilded walls, and the flushed splendours of the Venetian ceiling. At the farther end of the room a stage had been constructed behind a proscenium arch curtained with folds of old damask; but in the pause before the parting of the folds there was little thought of what they might reveal, for every woman who had accepted Mrs. Bry's invitation was engaged in trying to find out how many of her friends had done the same.

Gerty Farish, seated next to Selden, was lost in that indiscriminate and uncritical enjoyment so irritating to Miss Bart's finer perceptions. It may be that Selden's nearness had something to do with the quality of his cousin's pleasure; but Miss Farish was so little accustomed to refer her enjoyment of such scenes to her own share in them, that she was merely conscious of a deeper sense of contentment.

"Wasn't it dear of Lily to get me an invitation? Of course it would never have occurred to Carry Fisher to put me on the list, and I should have been so sorry to miss seeing it all—and especially Lily herself. Some one told me the ceiling was by Veronese—you would know, of course, Lawrence. I suppose it's very beautiful, but his women are so dreadfully fat. Goddesses? Well, I can only say that if they'd been mortals and had to wear corsets, it would have been better for them. I think our women are much handsomer. And this room is wonderfully becoming—every one looks so well! Did you ever see such jewels? Do look at Mrs. George Dorset's pearls—I suppose the smallest of them would pay the rent of our Girls' Club for a year. Not that I ought to complain about the club; every one has been so wonderfully kind. Did I tell you that Lily had given us three hundred dollars? Wasn't it splendid of her? And then she collected a lot of money from her friends—Mrs. Bry gave us five hundred, and Mr. Rosedale a thousand. I wish Lily were not so nice to Mr. Rosedale, but she says it's no use being rude to him, because he doesn't see the difference. She really can't bear to hurt people's feelings—it makes me so angry when I hear her called cold and conceited! The girls at the club don't call her that. Do you know she has been there with me twice?—yes, Lily! And you should have seen their eyes! One of them said it was as good as a day in the country just to look at her. And she sat there, and laughed and talked with them—not a bit as if she were being *charitable*, you know, but as if she liked it as much as they did. They've been asking ever since when she's coming back; and she's promised me—oh!"

Miss Farish's confidences were cut short by the parting of the curtain on the first *tableau*—a group of nymphs dancing across flower-strewn sward in the rhythmic postures of Botticelli's Spring. *Tableaux vivants* depend for their effect not only on the happy disposal of lights and the delusive-interposition of layers of gauze, but on a corresponding adjustment of the mental vision. To unfurnished minds they remain, in spite of every enhancement of art, only a superior kind of wax-works; but to the responsive fancy they may give magic glimpses of the boundary world between fact and imagination. Selden's mind was of this order: he could yield to vision-making influences as completely as a child to the spell of a fairy-tale. Mrs. Bry's *tableaux* wanted none of the qualities which go to the producing of such illusions, and under Morpeth's organizing hand the pictures succceded each other with the rhythmic march of some splendid frieze, in which the fugitive curves of living flesh and the wandering light of young eyes have been subdued to plastic harmony without losing the charm of life.

The scenes were taken from old pictures, and the participators had been cleverly fitted with characters suited to their types. No one, for instance, could have made a more typical Goya than Carry Fisher, with her short dark-skinned face, the exaggerated glow of her eyes, the provocation of her frankly-painted smile. A brilliant Miss Smedden from Brooklyn showed to perfection the sumptuous curves of Titian's Daughter, lifting her gold salver laden with grapes above the harmonizing gold of rippled hair and rich brocade, and a young Mrs. Van Alstyne, who showed the frailer Dutch type, with high blue-veined forehead and pale eyes and lashes, made a characteristic Vandyck, in black satin, against a curtained archway. Then there were Kauffmann nymphs garlanding the altar of Love; a Veronese supper, all sheeny textures, pearl-woven heads and marble architecture; and a Watteau group of lute-playing comedians, lounging by a fountain in a sunlit glade.

Each evanescent picture touched the vision-building faculty in Selden, leading him so far down the vistas of fancy that even Gerty Farish's running commentary—"Oh, how lovely Lulu Melson looks!" or: "That must be Kate Corby, to the right there, in purple"—did not break the spell of the illusion. Indeed, so skilfully had the personality of the actors been subdued to the scenes they figured in that even the least imaginative of the audience must have felt a thrill of contrast when the curtain suddenly parted on a picture which was simply and undisguisedly the portrait of Miss Bart.

Here there could be no mistaking the predominance of personality—the unanimous "Oh!" of the spectators was a tribute, not to the brush-work of Reynolds's "Mrs. Lloyd" but to the flesh and blood loveliness of Lily Bart. She had shown her artistic intelligence in selecting a type so like her own that she could embody the person represented without ceasing to be herself. It was as though she had stepped, not out of, but into, Reynolds's canvas, banishing the phantom of his dead beauty by the beams of her living grace. The impulse to show herself in a splendid setting—she had thought for a moment of representing Tiepolo's Cleopatra—had yielded to the truer instinct of trusting to her unassisted beauty, and she had purposely chosen a picture without distracting accessories of dress or surroundings. Her pale draperies, and the background of foliage against which she stood, served only to relieve the long dryad-like curves that swept upward from her poised foot to her lifted arm. The noble buoyancy of her attitude, its suggestion of soaring grace, revealed the touch of poetry in her beauty that Selden always felt in her presence, yet lost the sense of when he was not with her. Its expression was now so vivid that for the first time he seemed to see before him the real Lily Bart, divested of the trivialities of her little world, and catching for a moment a note of that eternal harmony of which her beauty was a part.

"Deuced bold thing to show herself in that get-up; but, gad, there isn't a break in the lines anywhere, and I suppose she wanted us to know it!"

These words, uttered by that experienced connoisseur, Mr. Ned Van Alstyne, whose scented white moustache had brushed Selden's shoulder whenever the parting of the curtains presented any exceptional opportunity for the study of the female outline, affected their hearer in an unexpected way. It was not the first time that Selden had heard Lily's beauty lightly remarked on, and hitherto the tone of the comments had imperceptibly coloured his view of her. But now it woke only a motion of indignant contempt. This was the world she lived in, these were the standards by which she was fated to be measured! Does one go to Caliban for a judgment on Miranda?

In the long moment before the curtain fell, he had time to feel the whole tragedy of her life. It was as though her beauty, thus detached from all that cheapened and vulgarized it, had held out suppliant hands to him from the world in which he and she had once met for a moment, and where he felt an overmastering longing to be with her again.

He was roused by the pressure of ecstatic fingers. "Wasn't she too beautiful, Lawrence? Don't you like her best in that simple dress? It makes her look like the real Lily—the Lily I know."

He met Gerty Farish's brimming gaze. "The Lily we know," he corrected; and his cousin, beaming at the implied understanding, exclaimed joyfully: "I'll tell her that! She always says you dislike her."

The performance over, Selden's first impulse was to seek Miss Bart. During the interlude of music which succeeded the *tableaux*, the actors had seated themselves here and there in the audience, diversifying its conventional appearance by the varied picturesqueness of their dress. Lily, however, was not among them, and her absence served to protract the effect she had produced on Selden: it would have broken the spell to see her too soon in the surroundings from which accident had so happily detached her. They had not met since the day of the Van Osburgh wedding, and on his side the avoidance had been intentional. Tonight, however, he knew that, sooner or later, he should find himself at her side; and though he let the dispersing crowd drift him whither it would, without making an immediate effort to reach her, his procrastination was not due to any lingering resistance, but to the desire to luxuriate a moment in the sense of complete surrender.

Lily had not an instant's doubt as to the meaning of the murmur greeting her appearance. No other tableau had been received with that precise note of approval: it had obviously been called forth by herself, and not by the picture she impersonated. She had feared at the last moment that she was risking too much in dispensing with the advantages of a more sumptuous setting, and the completeness of her triumph gave her an intoxicating sense of recovered power. Not caring to diminish the impression she had produced, she held herself aloof from the audience till the movement of dispersal before supper, and thus had a second opportunity of showing herself to advantage, as the throng poured slowly into the empty drawing-room where she was standing.

She was soon the centre of a group which increased and renewed itself as the circulation became general, and the individual comments on her success were a delightful prolongation of the collective applause. At such moments she lost something of her natural fastidiousness, and cared less for the quality of the admiration received than for its quantity. Differences of personality were merged in a warm atmosphere of praise, in which her beauty expanded like a flower in sunlight; and if Selden had approached a moment or two sooner he would have seen her turning on Ned Van Alstyne and George Dorset the look he had dreamed of capturing for himself.

Fortune willed, however, that the hurried approach of Mrs. Fisher, as whose aide-de-camp Van Alstyne was acting, should break up the group before Selden reached the threshold of the room. One or two of the men wandered off in search of their partners for supper, and the others, noticing Selden's approach, gave way to him in accordance with the tacit freemasonry of the ball-room. Lily was therefore standing alone when he reached her; and finding the expected look in her eye, he had the satisfaction of supposing he had kindled it. The look did indeed deepen as it rested on him, for even in that moment of self-intoxication Lily felt the quicker beat of life that his nearness always produced. She read, too, in his answering gaze the delicious confirmation of her triumph, and for the moment it seemed to her that it was for him only she cared to be beautiful.

Selden had given her his arm without speaking. She took it in silence, and they moved away, not toward the supper-room, but against the tide which was setting thither. The faces about her flowed by like the streaming images of sleep: she hardly noticed where Selden was leading her, till they passed through a glass doorway at the end of the long suite of rooms and stood suddenly in the fragrant hush of a garden. Gravel grated beneath their feet, and about them was the transparent dimness of a midsummer night. Hanging lights made emerald caverns in the depths of foliage, and whitened the spray of a fountain falling among lilies. The magic place was deserted: there was no sound but the splash of the water on the lily-pads, and a distant drift of music that might have been blown across a sleeping lake.

Selden and Lily stood still, accepting the unreality of the scene as a part of their own dream-like sensations. It would not have surprised them to feel a summer breeze on their faces, or to see the lights among the boughs reduplicated in the arch of a starry sky. The strange solitude about them was no stranger than the sweetness of being alone in it together. At length Lily withdrew her hand, and moved away a step, so that her white-robed slimness was outlined against the dusk of the branches. Selden followed her, and still without speaking they seated themselves on a bench beside the fountain.

Suddenly she raised her eyes with the beseeching earnestness of a child. "You never speak to me—you think hard things of me," she murmured.

"I think of you at any rate, God knows!" he said.

"Then why do we never see each other? Why can't we be friends? You promised once to help me," she continued in the same tone, as though the words were drawn from her unwillingly.

"The only way I can help you is by loving you," Selden said in a low voice.

She made no reply, but her face turned to him with the soft motion of a flower. His own met it slowly, and their lips touched. She drew back and rose from her seat. Selden rose too, and they stood facing each other. Suddenly she caught his hand and pressed it a moment against her cheek.

"Ah, love me, love me—but don't tell me so!" she sighed with her eyes in his; and before he could speak she had turned and slipped through the arch of boughs, disappearing in the brightness of the room beyond.

Selden stood where she had left him. He knew too well the transiency of exquisite moments to attempt to follow her; but presently he reentered the house and made his way through the deserted rooms to the door. A few sumptuously-cloaked ladies were already gathered in the marble vestibule, and in the coat-room he found Van Alstyne and Gus Trenor.

The former, at Selden's approach, paused in the careful selection of a cigar from one of the silver boxes invitingly set out near the door.

"Hallo, Selden, going too? You're an Epicurean like myself, I see: you don't want to see all those goddesses gobbling terrapin. Gad, what a show of good-looking women; but not one of 'em could touch that little cousin of mine. Talk of jewels—what's a woman want with jewels when she's got herself to show? The trouble is that all these fal-bals they wear cover up their figures when they've got 'em. I never knew till tonight what an outline Lily has."

"It's not her fault if everybody don't know it now," growled Trenor, flushed with the struggle of getting into his fur-lined coat. "Damned bad taste, I call it—no, no cigar for me. You can't tell what you're smoking in one of these new houses—likely as not the *chef* buys the cigars. Stay for supper? Not if I know it! When people crowd their rooms so that you can't get near any one you want to speak to, I'd as soon sup in the elevated at the rush hour. My wife was dead right to stay away: she says life's too short to spend it in breaking in new people."

# Chapter 13

Lily woke from happy dreams to find two notes at her bedside.

One was from Mrs. Trenor, who announced that she was coming to town that afternoon for a flying visit, and hoped Miss Bart would be able to dine with her. The other was from Selden. He wrote briefly that an important case called him to Albany, whence he would be unable to return till the evening, and asked Lily to let him know at what hour on the following day she would see him.

Lily, leaning back among her pillows, gazed musingly at his letter. The scene in the Brys' conservatory had been like a part of her dreams; she had not expected to wake to such evidence of its reality. Her first movement was one of annoyance: this unforeseen act of Selden's added another complication to life. It was so unlike him to yield to such an irrational impulse! Did he really mean to ask her to marry him? She had once shown him the impossibility of such a hope, and his subsequent behaviour seemed to prove that he had accepted the situation with a reasonableness somewhat mortifying to her vanity. It was all the more agreeable to find that this reasonableness was maintained only at the cost of not seeing her; but, though nothing in life was as sweet as the sense of her power over him, she saw the danger of allowing the episode of the previous night to have a sequel. Since she could not marry him, it would be kinder to him, as well as easier for herself, to write a line amicably evading his request to see her: he was not the man to mistake such a hint, and when next they met it would be on their usual friendly footing.

Lily sprang out of bed, and went straight to her desk. She wanted to write at once, while she could trust to the strength of her resolve. She was still languid from her brief sleep and the exhilaration of the evening, and the sight of Selden's writing brought back the culminating moment of her triumph: the moment when she had read in his eyes that no philosophy was proof against her power. It would be pleasant to have that sensation again . . . no one else could give it to her in its fulness; and she could not bear to mar her mood of luxurious retrospection by an act of definite refusal. She took up her pen and wrote hastily: "*Tomorrow at Four*;" murmuring to herself, as she slipped the sheet into its envelope: "I can easily put him off when tomorrow comes."

Judy Trenor's summons was very welcome to Lily. It was the first time she had received a direct communication from Bellomont since the close of her last visit there, and she was still visited by the dread of having incurred Judy's displeasure. But this characteristic command seemed to reestablish their former relations; and Lily smiled at the thought that her friend had probably summoned her in order to hear about the Brys' entertainment. Mrs. Trenor had absented herself from the feast, perhaps for the reason so frankly enunciated by her husband, perhaps because, as Mrs. Fisher somewhat differently put it, she "couldn't bear new people when she hadn't discovered them herself." At any rate, though she remained haughtily at Bellomont, Lily suspected in her a devouring eagerness to hear of what she had missed, and to learn exactly in what measure Mrs. Wellington Bry had surpassed all previous competitors for social recognition. Lily was quite ready to gratify this curiosity, but it happened that she was dining out. She determined, however, to see Mrs. Trenor for a few moments, and ringing for her maid she despatched a telegram to say that she would be with her friend that evening at ten.

She was dining with Mrs. Fisher, who had gathered at an informal feast a few of the performers of the previous evening. There was to be plantation music in the studio after dinner—for Mrs. Fisher, despairing of the republic, had taken up modelling, and annexed to her small crowded house a spacious apartment, which, whatever its uses in her hours of plastic inspiration, served at other times for the exercise of an indefatigable hospitality. Lily was reluctant to leave, for the dinner was amusing, and she would have liked to lounge over a cigarette and hear a few songs; but she could not break her engagement with Judy, and shortly after ten she asked her hostess to ring for a hansom, and drove up Fifth Avenue to the Trenors'.

She waited long enough on the doorstep to wonder that Judy's presence in town was not signalized by a greater promptness in admitting her; and her surprise was increased when, instead of the expected footman, pushing his shoulders into a tardy coat, a shabby care-taking person in calico let her into the shrouded hall. Trenor, however, appeared at once on the threshold of the drawing-room, welcoming her with unusual volubility while he relieved her of her cloak and drew her into the room.

"Come along to the den; it's the only comfortable place in the house. Doesn't this room look as if it was waiting for the body to be brought down? Can't see why Judy keeps the house wrapped up in this awful slippery white stuff—it's enough to give a fellow pneumonia to walk through these rooms on a cold day. You look a little pinched yourself, by the way: it's rather a sharp night out. I noticed it walking up from the club. Come along, and I'll give you a nip of brandy, and you can toast yourself over the fire and try some of my new Egyptians—that little Turkish chap at the Embassy put me on to a brand that I want you to try, and if you like 'em I'll get out a lot for you: they don't have 'em here yet, but I'll cable."

He led her through the house to the large room at the back, where Mrs. Trenor usually sat, and where, even in her absence, there was an air of occupancy. Here, as usual, were flowers, newspapers, a littered writing-table, and a general aspect of lamp-lit familiarity, so that it was a surprise not to see Judy's energetic figure start up from the arm-chair near the fire.

It was apparently Trenor himself who had been occupying the seat in question, for it was overhung by a cloud of cigar smoke, and near it stood one of those intricate folding tables which British ingenuity has devised to facilitate the circulation of tobacco and spirits. The sight of such appliances in a drawing-room was not unusual in Lily's set, where smoking and drinking were unrestricted by considerations of time and place, and her first movement was to help herself to one of the cigarettes recommended by Trenor, while she checked his loquacity by asking, with a surprised glance: "Where's Judy?"

Trenor, a little heated by his unusual flow of words, and perhaps by prolonged propinquity with the decanters, was bending over the latter to decipher their silver labels.

"Here, now, Lily, just a drop of cognac in a little fizzy water—you do look pinched, you know: I swear the end of your nose is red. I'll take another glass to keep you company—Judy?—Why, you see, Judy's got a devil of a head ache—quite knocked out with it, poor thing—she asked me to explain—make it all right, you know—Do come up to the fire, though; you look dead-beat, really. Now do let me make you comfortable, there's a good girl."

He had taken her hand, half-banteringly, and was drawing her toward a low seat by the hearth; but she stopped and freed herself quietly.

"Do you mean to say that Judy's not well enough to see me? Doesn't she want me to go upstairs?"

Trenor drained the glass he had filled for himself, and paused to set it down before he answered.

"Why, no—the fact is, she's not up to seeing anybody. It came on suddenly, you know, and she asked me to tell you how awfully sorry she was—if she'd known where you were dining she'd have sent you word."

"She did know where I was dining; I mentioned it in my telegram. But it doesn't matter, of course. I suppose if she's so poorly she won't go back to Bellomont in the morning, and I can come and see her then."

"Yes: exactly—that's capital. I'll tell her you'll pop in tomorrow morning. And now do sit down a minute, there's a dear, and let's have a nice quiet jaw together. You won't take a drop, just for sociability? Tell me what you think of that cigarette. Why, don't you like it? What are you chucking it away for?"

"I am chucking it away because I must go, if you'll have the goodness to call a cab for me," Lily returned with a smile.

She did not like Trenor's unusual excitability, with its too evident explanation, and the thought of being alone with him, with her friend out of reach upstairs, at the other end of the great empty house, did not conduce to a desire to prolong their *tete-a-tete*.

But Trenor, with a promptness which did not escape her, had moved between herself and the door.

"Why must you go, I should like to know? If Judy'd been here you'd have sat gossiping till all hours—and you can't even give me five minutes! It's always the same story. Last night I couldn't get near you—I went to that damned vulgar party just to see you, and there was everybody talking about you, and asking me if I'd ever seen anything so stunning, and when I tried to come up and say a word, you never took any notice, but just went on laughing and joking with a lot of asses who only wanted to be able to swagger about afterward, and look knowing when you were mentioned."

He paused, flushed by his diatribe, and fixing on her a look in which resentment was the ingredient she least disliked. But she had regained her presence of mind, and stood composedly in the middle of the room, while her slight smile seemed to put an ever increasing distance between herself and Trenor.

Across it she said: "Don't be absurd, Gus. It's past eleven, and I must really ask you to ring for a cab."

He remained immovable, with the lowering forehead she had grown to detest.

"And supposing I won't ring for one—what'll you do then?"

"I shall go upstairs to Judy if you force me to disturb her."

Trenor drew a step nearer and laid his hand on her arm. "Look here, Lily: won't you give me five minutes of your own accord?"

"Not tonight, Gus: you—"

"Very good, then: I'll take 'em. And as many more as I want." He had squared himself on the threshold, his hands thrust deep in his pockets. He nodded toward the chair on the hearth.

"Go and sit down there, please: I've got a word to say to you."

Lily's quick temper was getting the better of her fears. She drew herself up and moved toward the door.

"If you have anything to say to me, you must say it another time. I shall go up to Judy unless you call a cab for me at once."

He burst into a laugh. "Go upstairs and welcome, my dear; but you won't find Judy. She ain't there."

Lily cast a startled look upon him. "Do you mean that Judy is not in the house—not in town?" she exclaimed.

"That's just what I do mean," returned Trenor, his bluster sinking to sullenness under her look.

"Nonsense—I don't believe you. I am going upstairs," she said impatiently.

He drew unexpectedly aside, letting her reach the threshold unimpeded.

"Go up and welcome; but my wife is at Bellomont."

But Lily had a flash of reassurance. "If she hadn't come she would have sent me word—"

"She did; she telephoned me this afternoon to let you know."

"I received no message."

"I didn't send any."

The two measured each other for a moment, but Lily still saw her opponent through a blur of scorn that made all other considerations indistinct.

"I can't imagine your object in playing such a stupid trick on me; but if you have fully gratified your peculiar sense of humour I must again ask you to send for a cab."

It was the wrong note, and she knew it as she spoke. To be stung by irony it is not necessary to understand it, and the angry streaks on Trenor's face might have been raised by an actual lash.

"Look here, Lily, don't take that high and mighty tone with me." He had again moved toward the door, and in her instinctive shrinking from him she let him regain command of the threshold. "I *did* play a trick on you; I own up to it; but if you think I'm ashamed you're mistaken. Lord knows I've been patient enough—I've hung round and looked like an ass. And all the while you were letting a lot of other fellows make up to you . . . letting 'em make fun of me, I daresay . . . I'm not sharp, and can't dress my friends up to look funny, as you do . . . but I can tell when it's being done to me . . . I can tell fast enough when I'm made a fool of . . ."

"Ah, I shouldn't have thought that!" flashed from Lily; but her laugh dropped to silence under his look.

"No; you wouldn't have thought it; but you'll know better now. That's what you're here for tonight. I've been waiting for a quiet time to talk things over, and now I've got it I mean to make you hear me out."

His first rush of inarticulate resentment had been followed by a steadiness and concentration of tone more disconcerting to Lily than the excitement preceding it. For a moment her presence of mind forsook her. She had more than once been in situations where a quick sword-play of wit had been needful to cover her retreat; but her frightened heart-throbs told her that here such skill would not avail.

To gain time she repeated: "I don't understand what you want."

Trenor had pushed a chair between herself and the door. He threw himself in it, and leaned back, looking up at her.

"I'll tell you what I want: I want to know just where you and I stand. Hang it, the man who pays for the dinner is generally allowed to have a seat at table."

She flamed with anger and abasement, and the sickening need of having to conciliate where she longed to humble.

"I don't know what you mean—but you must see, Gus, that I can't stay here talking to you at this hour—"

"Gad, you go to men's houses fast enough in broad day light—strikes me you're not always so deuced careful of appearances."

The brutality of the thrust gave her the sense of dizziness that follows on a physical blow. Rosedale had spoken then—this was the way men talked of her—She felt suddenly weak and defenceless: there was a throb of self-pity in her throat. But all the while another self was sharpening her to vigilance, whispering the terrified warning that every word and gesture must be measured.

"If you have brought me here to say insulting things—" she began.

Trenor laughed. "Don't talk stage-rot. I don't want to insult you. But a man's got his feelings—and you've played with mine too long. I didn't begin this business—kept out of the way, and left the track clear for the other chaps, till you rummaged me out and set to work to make an ass of me—and an easy job you had of it, too. That's the trouble—it was too easy for you—you got reckless—thought you could turn me inside out, and chuck me in the gutter like an empty purse. But, by gad, that ain't playing fair: that's dodging the rules of the game. Of course I know now what you wanted—it wasn't my beautiful eyes you were after—but I tell you what, Miss Lily, you've got to pay up for making me think so—"

He rose, squaring his shoulders aggressively, and stepped toward her with a reddening brow; but she held her footing, though every nerve tore at her to retreat as he advanced.

"Pay up?" she faltered. "Do you mean that I owe you money?"

He laughed again. "Oh, I'm not asking for payment in kind. But there's such a thing as fair play—and interest on one's money—and hang me if I've had as much as a look from you—"

"Your money? What have I to do with your money? You advised me how to invest mine . . . you must have seen I knew nothing of business . . . you told me it was all right—"

"It *was* all right—it is, Lily: you're welcome to all of it, and ten times more. I'm only asking for a word of thanks from you." He was closer still, with a hand that grew formidable; and the frightened self in her was dragging the other down.

"I *have* thanked you; I've shown I was grateful. What more have you done than any friend might do, or any one accept from a friend?"

Trenor caught her up with a sneer. "I don't doubt you've accepted as much before—and chucked the other chaps as you'd like to chuck me. I don't care how you settled your score with them—if you fooled 'em I'm that much to the good. Don't stare at me like that—I know I'm not talking the way a man is supposed to talk to a girl—but, hang it, if you don't like it you can stop me quick enough—you know I'm mad about you—damn the money, there's plenty more of it—if *that* bothers you . . . I was a brute, Lily—Lily!—just look at me—"

Over and over her the sea of humiliation broke—wave crashing on wave so close that the moral shame was one with the physical dread. It seemed to her that self-esteem would have made her invulnerable—that it was her own dishonour which put a fearful solitude about her.

His touch was a shock to her drowning consciousness. She drew back from him with a desperate assumption of scorn.

"I've told you I don't understand—but if I owe you money you shall be paid—"

Trenor's face darkened to rage: her recoil of abhorrence had called out the primitive man.

"Ah—you'll borrow from Selden or Rosedale—and take your chances of fooling them as you've fooled me! Unless—unless you've settled your other scores already—and I'm the only one left out in the cold!"

She stood silent, frozen to her place. The words—the words were worse than the touch! Her heart was beating all over her body—in her throat, her limbs, her helpless useless hands. Her eyes travelled despairingly about the room—they lit on the bell, and she remembered that help was in call. Yes, but scandal with it—a hideous mustering of tongues. No, she must fight her way out alone. It was enough that the servants knew her to be in the house with Trenor—there must be nothing to excite conjecture in her way of leaving it.

She raised her head, and achieved a last clear look at him.

"I am here alone with you," she said. "What more have you to say?"

To her surprise, Trenor answered the look with a speechless stare. With his last gust of words the flame had died out, leaving him chill and humbled. It was as though a cold air had dispersed the fumes of his libations, and the situation loomed before him black and naked as the ruins of a fire. Old habits, old restraints, the hand of inherited order, plucked back the bewildered mind which passion had jolted from its ruts. Trenor's eye had the haggard look of the sleep-walker waked on a deathly ledge.

"Go home! Go away from here"—he stammered, and turning his back on her walked toward the hearth.

The sharp release from her fears restored Lily to immediate lucidity. The collapse of Trenor's will left her in control, and she heard herself, in a voice that was her own yet outside herself, bidding him ring for the servant, bidding him give the order for a hansom, directing him to put her in it when it came. Whence the strength came to her she knew not; but an insistent voice warned her that she must leave the house openly, and nerved her, in the hall before the hovering care taker, to exchange light words with Trenor, and charge him with the usual messages for Judy, while all the while she shook with inward loathing. On the doorstep, with the street before her, she felt a mad throb of liberation, intoxicating as the prisoner's first draught of free air; but the clearness of brain continued, and she noted the mute aspect of Fifth Avenue, guessed at the lateness of the hour, and even observed a man's figure—was there something half-familiar in its outline?—which, as she entered the hansom, turned from the opposite corner and vanished in the obscurity of the side street.

But with the turn of the wheels reaction came, and shuddering darkness closed on her. "I can't think—I can't think," she moaned, and leaned her head against the rattling side of the cab. She seemed a stranger to herself, or rather there were two selves in her, the one she had always known, and a new abhorrent being to which it found itself chained. She had once picked up, in a house where she was staying, a translation of the *eumenides*, and her imagination had been seized by the high terror of the scene where Orestes, in the cave of the oracle, finds his implacable huntresses asleep, and snatches an hour's repose. Yes, the Furies might sometimes sleep, but they were there, always there in the dark corners, and now they were awake and the iron clang of their wings was in her brain . . . She opened her eyes and saw the streets passing—the familiar alien streets. All she looked on was the same and yet changed. There was a great gulf fixed between today and yesterday. Everything in the past seemed simple, natural, full of daylight—and she was alone in a place of darkness and pollution.—Alone! It was the loneliness that frightened her. Her eyes fell on an illuminated clock at a street corner, and she saw that the hands marked the half hour after eleven. Only half-past eleven—there were hours and hours left of the night! And she must spend them alone, shuddering sleepless on her bed. Her soft nature recoiled from this ordeal, which had none of the stimulus of conflict to goad her through it. Oh, the slow cold drip of the minutes on her head! She had a vision of herself lying on the black walnut bed—and the darkness would frighten her, and if she left the light burning the dreary details of the room would brand themselves forever on her brain. She had always hated her room at Mrs. Peniston's—its ugliness, its impersonality, the fact that nothing in it was really hers. To a torn heart uncomforted by human nearness a room may open almost human arms, and the being to whom no four walls mean more than any others, is, at such hours, expatriate everywhere.

Lily had no heart to lean on. Her relation with her aunt was as superficial as that of chance lodgers who pass on the stairs. But even had the two been in closer contact, it was impossible to think of Mrs. Peniston's mind as offering shelter or comprehension to such misery as Lily's. As the pain that can be told is but half a pain, so the pity that questions has little healing in its touch. What Lily craved was the darkness made by enfolding arms, the silence which is not solitude, but compassion holding its breath.

She started up and looked forth on the passing streets. Gerty!—they were nearing Gerty's corner. If only she could reach there before this labouring anguish burst from her breast to her lips—if only she could feel the hold of Gerty's arms while she shook in the ague-fit of fear that was coming upon her! She pushed up the door in the roof and called the address to the driver. It was not so late—Gerty might still be waking. And even if she were not, the sound of the bell would penetrate every recess of her tiny apartment, and rouse her to answer her friend's call.

# Chapter 14

Gerty Farish, the morning after the Wellington Brys' entertainment, woke from dreams as happy as Lily's. If they were less vivid in hue, more subdued to the half-tints of her personality and her experience, they were for that very reason better suited to her mental vision. Such flashes of joy as Lily moved in would have blinded Miss Farish, who was accustomed, in the way of happiness, to such scant light as shone through the cracks of other people's lives.

Now she was the centre of a little illumination of her own: a mild but unmistakable beam, compounded of Lawrence Selden's growing kindness to herself and the discovery that he extended his liking to Lily Bart. If these two factors seem incompatible to the student of feminine psychology, it must be remembered that Gerty had always been a parasite in the moral order, living on the crumbs of other tables, and content to look through the window at the banquet spread for her friends. Now that she was enjoying a little private feast of her own, it would have seemed incredibly selfish not to lay a plate for a friend; and there was no one with whom she would rather have shared her enjoyment than Miss Bart.

As to the nature of Selden's growing kindness, Gerty would no more have dared to define it than she would have tried to learn a butterfly's colours by knocking the dust from its wings. To seize on the wonder would be to brush off its bloom, and perhaps see it fade and stiffen in her hand: better the sense of beauty palpitating out of reach, while she held her breath and watched where it would alight. Yet Selden's manner at the Brys' had brought the flutter of wings so close that they seemed to be beating in her own heart. She had never seen him so alert, so responsive, so attentive to what she had to say. His habitual manner had an absent-minded kindliness which she accepted, and was grateful for, as the liveliest sentiment her presence was likely to inspire; but she was quick to feel in him a change implying that for once she could give pleasure as well as receive it.

And it was so delightful that this higher degree of sympathy should be reached through their interest in Lily Bart!

Gerty's affection for her friend—a sentiment that had learned to keep itself alive on the scantiest diet—had grown to active adoration since Lily's restless curiosity had drawn her into the circle of Miss Farish's work. Lily's taste of beneficence had wakened in her a momentary appetite for well-doing. Her visit to the Girls' Club had first brought her in contact with the dramatic contrasts of life. She had always accepted with philosophic calm the fact that such existences as hers were pedestalled on foundations of obscure humanity. The dreary limbo of dinginess lay all around and beneath that little illuminated circle in which life reached its finest efflorescence, as the mud and sleet of a winter night enclose a hot-house filled with tropical flowers. All this was in the natural order of things, and the orchid basking in its artificially created atmosphere could round the delicate curves of its petals undisturbed by the ice on the panes.

But it is one thing to live comfortably with the abstract conception of poverty, another to be brought in contact with its human embodiments. Lily had never conceived of these victims of fate otherwise than in the mass. That the mass was composed of individual lives, innumerable separate centres of sensation, with her own eager reachings for pleasure, her own fierce revulsions from pain—that some of these bundles of feeling were clothed in shapes not so unlike her own, with eyes meant to look on gladness, and young lips shaped for love—this discovery gave Lily one of those sudden shocks of pity that sometimes decentralize a life. Lily's nature was incapable of such renewal: she could feel other demands only through her own, and no pain was long vivid which did not press on an answering nerve. But for the moment she was drawn out of herself by the interest of her direct relation with a world so unlike her own. She had supplemented her first gift by personal assistance to one or two of Miss Farish's most appealing subjects, and the admiration and interest her presence excited among the tired workers at the club ministered in a new form to her insatiable desire to please.

Gerty Farish was not a close enough reader of character to disentangle the mixed threads of which Lily's philanthropy was woven. She supposed her beautiful friend to be actuated by the same motive as herself—that sharpening of the moral vision which makes all human suffering so near and insistent that the other aspects of life fade into remoteness. Gerty lived by such simple formulas that she did not hesitate to class her friend's state with the emotional "change of heart" to which her dealings with the poor had accustomed her; and she rejoiced in the thought that she had been the humble instrument of this renewal. Now she had an answer to all criticisms of Lily's conduct: as she had said, she knew "the real Lily," and the discovery that Selden shared her knowledge raised her placid acceptance of life to a dazzled sense of its possibilities—a sense farther enlarged, in the course of the afternoon, by the receipt of a telegram from Selden asking if he might dine with her that evening.

While Gerty was lost in the happy bustle which this announcement produced in her small household, Selden was at one with her in thinking with intensity of Lily Bart. The case which had called him to Albany was not complicated enough to absorb all his attention, and he had the professional faculty of keeping a part of his mind free when its services were not needed. This part—which at the moment seemed dangerously like the whole—was filled to the brim with the sensations of the previous evening. Selden understood the symptoms: he recognized the fact that he was paying up, as there had always been a chance of his having to pay up, for the voluntary exclusions of his past. He had meant to keep free from permanent ties, not from any poverty of feeling, but because, in a different way, he was, as much as Lily, the victim of his environment. There had been a germ of truth in his declaration to Gerty Farish that he had never wanted to marry a "nice" girl: the adjective connoting, in his cousin's vocabulary, certain utilitarian qualities which are apt to preclude the luxury of charm. Now it had been Selden's fate to have a charming mother: her graceful portrait, all smiles and Cashmere, still emitted a faded scent of the undefinable quality. His father was the kind of man who delights in a charming woman: who quotes her, stimulates her, and keeps her perennially charming. Neither one of the couple cared for money, but their disdain of it took the form of always spending a little more than was prudent. If their house was shabby, it was exquisitely kept; if there were good books on the shelves there were also good dishes on the table. Selden senior had an eye for a picture, his wife an understanding of old lace; and both were so conscious of restraint and discrimination in buying that they never quite knew how it was that the bills mounted up.

Though many of Selden's friends would have called his parents poor, he had grown up in an atmosphere where restricted means were felt only as a check on aimless profusion: where the few possessions were so good that their rarity gave them a merited relief, and abstinence was combined with elegance in a way exemplified by Mrs. Selden's knack of wearing her old velvet as if it were new. A man has the advantage of being delivered early from the home point of view, and before Selden left college he had learned that there are as many different ways of going without money as of spending it. Unfortunately, he found no way as agreeable as that practised at home; and his views of womankind in especial were tinged by the remembrance of the one woman who had given him his sense of "values." It was from her that he inherited his detachment from the sumptuary side of life: the stoic's carelessness of material things, combined with the Epicurean's pleasure in them. Life shorn of either feeling appeared to him a diminished thing; and nowhere was the blending of the two ingredients so essential as in the character of a pretty woman.

It had always seemed to Selden that experience offered a great deal besides the sentimental adventure, yet he could vividly conceive of a love which should broaden and deepen till it became the central fact of life. What he could not accept, in his own case, was the makeshift alternative of a relation that should be less than this: that should leave some portions of his nature unsatisfied, while it put an undue strain on others. He would not, in other words, yield to the growth of an affection which might appeal to pity yet leave the understanding untouched: sympathy should no more delude him than a trick of the eyes, the grace of helplessness than a curve of the cheek.

But now—that little *but* passed like a sponge over all his vows. His reasoned-out resistances seemed for the moment so much less important than the question as to when Lily would receive his note! He yielded himself to the charm of trivial preoccupations, wondering at what hour her reply would be sent, with what words it would begin. As to its import he had no doubt—he was as sure of her surrender as of his own. And so he had leisure to muse on all its exquisite details, as a hard worker, on a holiday morning, might lie still and watch the beam of light travel gradually across his room. But if the new light dazzled, it did not blind him. He could still discern the outline of facts, though his own relation to them had changed. He was no less conscious than before of what was said of Lily Bart, but he could separate the woman he knew from the vulgar estimate of her. His mind turned to Gerty Farish's words, and the wisdom of the world seemed a groping thing beside the insight of innocence. *Blessed Are the Pure in Heart, for They Shall See God*—even the hidden god in their neighbour's breast! Selden was in the state of impassioned self-absorption that the first surrender to love produces. His craving was for the companionship of one whose point of view should justify his own, who should confirm, by deliberate observation, the truth to which his intuitions had leaped. He could not wait for the midday recess, but seized a moment's leisure in court to scribble his telegram to Gerty Farish.

Reaching town, he was driven direct to his club, where he hoped a note from Miss Bart might await him. But his box contained only a line of rapturous assent from Gerty, and he was turning away disappointed when he was hailed by a voice from the smoking room.

"Hallo, Lawrence! Dining here? Take a bite with me—I've ordered a canvas-back."

He discovered Trenor, in his day clothes, sitting, with a tall glass at his elbow, behind the folds of a sporting journal.

Selden thanked him, but pleaded an engagement.

"Hang it, I believe every man in town has an engagement tonight. I shall have the club to myself. You know how I'm living this winter, rattling round in that empty house. My wife meant to come to town today, but she's put it off again, and how is a fellow to dine alone in a room with the looking-glasses covered, and nothing but a bottle of Harvey sauce on the side-board? I say, Lawrence, chuck your engagement and take pity on me—it gives me the blue devils to dine alone, and there's nobody but that canting ass Wetherall in the club."

"Sorry, Gus—I can't do it."

As Selden turned away, he noticed the dark flush on Trenor's face, the unpleasant moisture of his intensely white forehead, the way his jewelled rings were wedged in the creases of his fat red fingers. Certainly the beast was predominating—the beast at the bottom of the glass. And he had heard this man's name coupled with Lily's! Bah—the thought sickened him; all the way back to his rooms he was haunted by the sight of Trenor's fat creased hands—

On his table lay the note: Lily had sent it to his rooms. He knew what was in it before he broke the seal—a grey seal with *beyond*! beneath a flying ship. Ah, he would take her beyond—beyond the ugliness, the pettiness, the attrition and corrosion of the soul—

Gerty's little sitting-room sparkled with welcome when Selden entered it. Its modest "effects," compact of enamel paint and ingenuity, spoke to him in the language just then sweetest to his ear. It is surprising how little narrow walls and a low ceiling matter, when the roof of the soul has suddenly been raised. Gerty sparkled too; or at least shone with a tempered radiance. He had never before noticed that she had "points"—really, some good fellow might do worse . . . Over the little dinner (and here, again, the effects were wonderful) he told her she ought to marry—he was in a mood to pair off the whole world. She had made the caramel custard with her own hands? It was sinful to keep such gifts to herself. He reflected with a throb of pride that Lily could trim her own hats—she had told him so the day of their walk at Bellomont.

He did not speak of Lily till after dinner. During the little repast he kept the talk on his hostess, who, fluttered at being the centre of observation, shone as rosy as the candle-shades she had manufactured for the occasion. Selden evinced an extraordinary interest in her household arrangements: complimented her on the ingenuity with which she had utilized every inch of her small quarters, asked how her servant managed about afternoons out, learned that one may improvise delicious dinners in a chafing-dish, and uttered thoughtful generalizations on the burden of a large establishment.

When they were in the sitting-room again, where they fitted as snugly as bits in a puzzle, and she had brewed the coffee, and poured it into her grandmother's egg-shell cups, his eye, as he leaned back, basking in the warm fragrance, lighted on a recent photograph of Miss Bart, and the desired transition was effected without an effort. The photograph was well enough—but to catch her as she had looked last night! Gerty agreed with him—never had she been so radiant. But could photography capture that light? There had been a new look in her face—something different; yes, Selden agreed there had been something different. The coffee was so exquisite that he asked for a second cup: such a contrast to the watery stuff at the club! Ah, your poor bachelor with his impersonal club fare, alternating with the equally impersonal *cuisine* of the dinner-party! A man who lived in lodgings missed the best part of life—he pictured the flavourless solitude of Trenor's repast, and felt a moment's compassion for the man . . . But to return to Lily—and again and again he returned, questioning, conjecturing, leading Gerty on, draining her inmost thoughts of their stored tenderness for her friend.

At first she poured herself out unstintingly, happy in this perfect communion of their sympathies. His understanding of Lily helped to confirm her own belief in her friend. They dwelt together on the fact that Lily had had no chance. Gerty instanced her generous impulses—her restlessness and discontent. The fact that her life had never satisfied her proved that she was made for better things. She might have married more than once—the conventional rich marriage which she had been taught to consider the sole end of existence—but when the opportunity came she had always shrunk from it. Percy Gryce, for instance, had been in love with her—every one at Bellomont had supposed them to be engaged, and her dismissal of him was thought inexplicable. This view of the Gryce incident chimed too well with Selden's mood not to be instantly adopted by him, with a flash of retrospective contempt for what had once seemed the obvious solution. If rejection there had been—and he wondered now that he had ever doubted it!—then he held the key to the secret, and the hillsides of Bellomont were lit up, not with sunset, but with dawn. It was he who had wavered and disowned the face of opportunity—and the joy now warming his breast might have been a familiar inmate if he had captured it in its first flight.

It was at this point, perhaps, that a joy just trying its wings in Gerty's heart dropped to earth and lay still. She sat facing Selden, repeating mechanically: "No, she has never been understood—" and all the while she herself seemed to be sitting in the centre of a great glare of comprehension. The little confidential room, where a moment ago their thoughts had touched elbows like their chairs, grew to unfriendly vastness, separating her from Selden by all the length of her new vision of the future—and that future stretched out interminably, with her lonely figure toiling down it, a mere speck on the solitude.

"She is herself with a few people only; and you are one of them," she heard Selden saying. And again: "Be good to her, Gerty, won't you?" and: "She has it in her to become whatever she is believed to be—you'll help her by believing the best of her?"

The words beat on Gerty's brain like the sound of a language which has seemed familiar at a distance, but on approaching is found to be unintelligible. He had come to talk to her of Lily—that was all! There had been a third at the feast she had spread for him, and that third had taken her own place. She tried to follow what he was saying, to cling to her own part in the talk—but it was all as meaningless as the boom of waves in a drowning head, and she felt, as the drowning may feel, that to sink would be nothing beside the pain of struggling to keep up.

Selden rose, and she drew a deep breath, feeling that soon she could yield to the blessed waves.

"Mrs. Fisher's? You say she was dining there? There's music afterward; I believe I had a card from her." He glanced at the foolish pink-faced clock that was drumming out this hideous hour. "A quarter past ten? I might look in there now; the Fisher evenings are amusing. I haven't kept you up too late, Gerty? You look tired—I've rambled on and bored you." And in the unwonted overflow of his feelings, he left a cousinly kiss upon her cheek.

At Mrs. Fisher's, through the cigar-smoke of the studio, a dozen voices greeted Selden. A song was pending as he entered, and he dropped into a seat near his hostess, his eyes roaming in search of Miss Bart. But she was not there, and the discovery gave him a pang out of all proportion to its seriousness; since the note in his breast-pocket assured him that at four the next day they would meet. To his impatience it seemed immeasurably long to wait, and half-ashamed of the impulse, he leaned to Mrs. Fisher to ask, as the music ceased, if Miss Bart had not dined with her.

"Lily? She's just gone. She had to run off, I forget where. Wasn't she wonderful last night?"

"Who's that? Lily?" asked Jack Stepney, from the depths of a neighbouring arm-chair. "Really, you know, I'm no prude, but when it comes to a girl standing there as if she was up at auction—I thought seriously of speaking to cousin Julia."

"You didn't know Jack had become our social censor?" Mrs. Fisher said to Selden with a laugh; and Stepney spluttered, amid the general derision: "But she's a cousin, hang it, and when a man's married—*town talk* was full of her this morning."

"Yes: lively reading that was," said Mr. Ned Van Alstyne, stroking his moustache to hide the smile behind it. "Buy the dirty sheet? No, of course not; some fellow showed it to me—but I'd heard the stories before. When a girl's as good-looking as that she'd better marry; then no questions are asked. In our imperfectly organized society there is no provision as yet for the young woman who claims the privileges of marriage without assuming its obligations."

"Well, I understand Lily is about to assume them in the shape of Mr. Rosedale," Mrs. Fisher said with a laugh.

"Rosedale—good heavens!" exclaimed Van Alstyne, dropping his eye-glass. "Stepney, that's your fault for foisting the brute on us."

"Oh, confound it, you know, we don't *marry* Rosedale in our family," Stepney languidly protested; but his wife, who sat in oppressive bridal finery at the other side of the room, quelled him with the judicial reflection: "In Lily's circumstances it's a mistake to have too high a standard."

"I hear even Rosedale has been scared by the talk lately," Mrs. Fisher rejoined; "but the sight of her last night sent him off his head. What do you think he said to me after her *tableau*? 'My God, Mrs. Fisher, if I could get Paul Morpeth to paint her like that, the picture'd appreciate a hundred per cent in ten years.'"

"By Jove,—but isn't she about somewhere?" exclaimed Van Alstyne, restoring his glass with an uneasy glance.

"No; she ran off while you were all mixing the punch down stairs. Where was she going, by the way? What's on tonight? I hadn't heard of anything."

"Oh, not a party, I think," said an inexperienced young Farish who had arrived late. "I put her in her cab as I was coming in, and she gave the driver the Trenors' address."

"The Trenors'?" exclaimed Mrs. Jack Stepney. "Why, the house is closed—Judy telephoned me from Bellomont this evening."

"Did she? That's queer. I'm sure I'm not mistaken. Well, come now, Trenor's there, anyhow—I—oh, well—the fact is, I've no head for numbers," he broke off, admonished by the nudge of an adjoining foot, and the smile that circled the room.

In its unpleasant light Selden had risen and was shaking hands with his hostess. The air of the place stifled him, and he wondered why he had stayed in it so long.

On the doorstep he stood still, remembering a phrase of Lily's: "It seems to me you spend a good deal of time in the element you disapprove of."

Well—what had brought him there but the quest of her? It was her element, not his. But he would lift her out of it, take her beyond! That *beyond*! on her letter was like a cry for rescue. He knew that Perseus's task is not done when he has loosed Andromeda's chains, for her limbs are numb with bondage, and she cannot rise and walk, but clings to him with dragging arms as he beats back to land with his burden. Well, he had strength for both—it was her weakness which had put the strength in him. It was not, alas, a clean rush of waves they had to win through, but a clogging morass of old associations and habits, and for the moment its vapours were in his throat. But he would see clearer, breathe freer in her presence: she was at once the dead weight at his breast and the spar which should float them to safety. He smiled at the whirl of metaphor with which he was trying to build up a defence against the influences of the last hour. It was pitiable that he, who knew the mixed motives on which social judgments depend, should still feel himself so swayed by them. How could he lift Lily to a freer vision of life, if his own view of her was to be coloured by any mind in which he saw her reflected?

The moral oppression had produced a physical craving for air, and he strode on, opening his lungs to the reverberating coldness of the night.

At the corner of Fifth Avenue Van Alstyne hailed him with an offer of company.

"Walking? A good thing to blow the smoke out of one's head. Now that women have taken to tobacco we live in a bath of nicotine. It would be a curious thing to study the effect of cigarettes on the relation of the sexes. Smoke is almost as great a solvent as divorce: both tend to obscure the moral issue."

Nothing could have been less consonant with Selden's mood than Van Alstyne's after-dinner aphorisms, but as long as the latter confined himself to generalities his listener's nerves were in control. Happily Van Alstyne prided himself on his summing up of social aspects, and with Selden for audience was eager to show the sureness of his touch. Mrs. Fisher lived in an East side street near the Park, and as the two men walked down Fifth Avenue the new architectural developments of that versatile thoroughfare invited Van Alstyne's comment.

"That Greiner house, now—a typical rung in the social ladder! The man who built it came from a *milieu* where all the dishes are put on the table at once. His facade is a complete architectural meal; if he had omitted a style his friends might have thought the money had given out. Not a bad purchase for Rosedale, though: attracts attention, and awes the Western sight-seer. By and bye he'll get out of that phase, and want something that the crowd will pass and the few pause before. Especially if he marries my clever cousin—"

Selden dashed in with the query: "And the Wellington Brys'? Rather clever of its kind, don't you think?"

They were just beneath the wide white facade, with its rich restraint of line, which suggested the clever corseting of a redundant figure.

"That's the next stage: the desire to imply that one has been to Europe, and has a standard. I'm sure Mrs. Bry thinks her house a copy of the *trianon*; in America every marble house with gilt furniture is thought to be a copy of the *trianon*. What a clever chap that architect is, though—how he takes his client's measure! He has put the whole of Mrs. Bry in his use of the composite order. Now for the Trenors, you remember, he chose the Corinthian: exuberant, but based on the best precedent. The Trenor house is one of his best things—doesn't look like a banqueting-hall turned inside out. I hear Mrs. Trenor wants to build out a new ball-room, and that divergence from Gus on that point keeps her at Bellomont. The dimensions of the Brys' ball-room must rankle: you may be sure she knows 'em as well as if she'd been there last night with a yard-measure. Who said she was in town, by the way? That Farish boy? She isn't, I know; Mrs. Stepney was right; the house is dark, you see: I suppose Gus lives in the back."

He had halted opposite the Trenors' corner, and Selden perforce stayed his steps also. The house loomed obscure and uninhabited; only an oblong gleam above the door spoke of provisional occupancy.

"They've bought the house at the back: it gives them a hundred and fifty feet in the side street. There's where the ball-room's to be, with a gallery connecting it: billiard-room and so on above. I suggested changing the entrance, and carrying the drawing-room across the whole Fifth Avenue front; you see the front door corresponds with the windows—"

The walking-stick which Van Alstyne swung in demonstration dropped to a startled "Hallo!" as the door opened and two figures were seen silhouetted against the hall-light. At the same moment a hansom halted at the curb-stone, and one of the figures floated down to it in a haze of evening draperies; while the other, black and bulky, remained persistently projected against the light.

For an immeasurable second the two spectators of the incident were silent; then the house-door closed, the hansom rolled off, and the whole scene slipped by as if with the turn of a stereopticon.

Van Alstyne dropped his eye-glass with a low whistle.

"A—hem—nothing of this, eh, Selden? As one of the family, I know I may count on you—appearances are deceptive—and Fifth Avenue is so imperfectly lighted—"

"Goodnight," said Selden, turning sharply down the side street without seeing the other's extended hand.

Alone with her cousin's kiss, Gerty stared upon her thoughts. He had kissed her before—but not with another woman on his lips. If he had spared her that she could have drowned quietly, welcoming the dark flood as it submerged her. But now the flood was shot through with glory, and it was harder to drown at sunrise than in darkness. Gerty hid her face from the light, but it pierced to the crannies of her soul. She had been so contented, life had seemed so simple and sufficient—why had he come to trouble her with new hopes? And Lily—Lily, her best friend! Woman-like, she accused the woman. Perhaps, had it not been for Lily, her fond imagining might have become truth. Selden had always liked her—had understood and sympathized with the modest independence of her life. He, who had the reputation of weighing all things in the nice balance of fastidious perceptions, had been uncritical and simple in his view of her: his cleverness had never overawed her because she had felt at home in his heart. And now she was thrust out, and the door barred against her by Lily's hand! Lily, for whose admission there she herself had pleaded! The situation was lighted up by a dreary flash of irony. She knew Selden—she saw how the force of her faith in Lily must have helped to dispel his hesitations. She remembered, too, how Lily had talked of him—she saw herself bringing the two together, making them known to each other. On Selden's part, no doubt, the wound inflicted was inconscient; he had never guessed her foolish secret; but Lily—Lily must have known! When, in such matters, are a woman's perceptions at fault? And if she knew, then she had deliberately despoiled her friend, and in mere wantonness of power, since, even to Gerty's suddenly flaming jealousy, it seemed incredible that Lily should wish to be Selden's wife. Lily might be incapable of marrying for money, but she was equally incapable of living without it, and Selden's eager investigations into the small economies of house-keeping made him appear to Gerty as tragically duped as herself.

She remained long in her sitting-room, where the embers were crumbling to cold grey, and the lamp paled under its gay shade. Just beneath it stood the photograph of Lily Bart, looking out imperially on the cheap gimcracks, the cramped furniture of the little room. Could Selden picture her in such an interior? Gerty felt the poverty, the insignificance of her surroundings: she beheld her life as it must appear to Lily. And the cruelty of Lily's judgments smote upon her memory. She saw that she had dressed her idol with attributes of her own making. When had Lily ever really felt, or pitied, or understood? All she wanted was the taste of new experiences: she seemed like some cruel creature experimenting in a laboratory.

The pink-faced clock drummed out another hour, and Gerty rose with a start. She had an appointment early the next morning with a district visitor on the East side. She put out her lamp, covered the fire, and went into her bedroom to undress. In the little glass above her dressing-table she saw her face reflected against the shadows of the room, and tears blotted the reflection. What right had she to dream the dreams of loveliness? A dull face invited a dull fate. She cried quietly as she undressed, laying aside her clothes with her habitual precision, setting everything in order for the next day, when the old life must be taken up as though there had been no break in its routine. Her servant did not come till eight o'clock, and she prepared her own tea-tray and placed it beside the bed. Then she locked the door of the flat, extinguished her light and lay down. But on her bed sleep would not come, and she lay face to face with the fact that she hated Lily Bart. It closed with her in the darkness like some formless evil to be blindly grappled with. Reason, judgment, renunciation, all the sane daylight forces, were beaten back in the sharp struggle for self-preservation. She wanted happiness—wanted it as fiercely and unscrupulously as Lily did, but without Lily's power of obtaining it. And in her conscious impotence she lay shivering, and hated her friend—

A ring at the door-bell caught her to her feet. She struck a light and stood startled, listening. For a moment her heart beat incoherently, then she felt the sobering touch of fact, and remembered that such calls were not unknown in her charitable work. She flung on her dressing-gown to answer the summons, and unlocking her door, confronted the shining vision of Lily Bart.

Gerty's first movement was one of revulsion. She shrank back as though Lily's presence flashed too sudden a light upon her misery. Then she heard her name in a cry, had a glimpse of her friend's face, and felt herself caught and clung to.

"Lily—what is it?" she exclaimed.

Miss Bart released her, and stood breathing brokenly, like one who has gained shelter after a long flight.

"I was so cold—I couldn't go home. Have you a fire?"

Gerty's compassionate instincts, responding to the swift call of habit, swept aside all her reluctances. Lily was simply some one who needed help—for what reason, there was no time to pause and conjecture: disciplined sympathy checked the wonder on Gerty's lips, and made her draw her friend silently into the sitting-room and seat her by the darkened hearth.

"There is kindling wood here: the fire will burn in a minute."

She knelt down, and the flame leapt under her rapid hands. It flashed strangely through the tears which still blurred her eyes, and smote on the white ruin of Lily's face. The girls looked at each other in silence; then Lily repeated: "I couldn't go home."

"No—no—you came here, dear! You're cold and tired—sit quiet, and I'll make you some tea."

Gerty had unconsciously adopted the soothing note of her trade: all personal feeling was merged in the sense of ministry, and experience had taught her that the bleeding must be stayed before the wound is probed.

Lily sat quiet, leaning to the fire: the clatter of cups behind her soothed her as familiar noises hush a child whom silence has kept wakeful. But when Gerty stood at her side with the tea she pushed it away, and turned an estranged eye on the familiar room.

"I came here because I couldn't bear to be alone," she said.

Gerty set down the cup and knelt beside her.

"Lily! Something has happened—can't you tell me?"

"I couldn't bear to lie awake in my room till morning. I hate my room at Aunt Julia's—so I came here—"

She stirred suddenly, broke from her apathy, and clung to Gerty in a fresh burst of fear.

"Oh, Gerty, the furies . . . you know the noise of their wings—alone, at night, in the dark? But you don't know—there is nothing to make the dark dreadful to you—"

The words, flashing back on Gerty's last hours, struck from her a faint derisive murmur; but Lily, in the blaze of her own misery, was blinded to everything outside it.

"You'll let me stay? I shan't mind when daylight comes—Is it late? Is the night nearly over? It must be awful to be sleepless—everything stands by the bed and stares—"

Miss Farish caught her straying hands. "Lily, look at me! Something has happened—an accident? You have been frightened—what has frightened you? Tell me if you can—a word or two—so that I can help you."

Lily shook her head.

"I am not frightened: that's not the word. Can you imagine looking into your glass some morning and seeing a disfigurement—some hideous change that has come to you while you slept? Well, I seem to myself like that—I can't bear to see myself in my own thoughts—I hate ugliness, you know—I've always turned from it—but I can't explain to you—you wouldn't understand."

She lifted her head and her eyes fell on the clock.

"How long the night is! And I know I shan't sleep tomorrow. Some one told me my father used to lie sleepless and think of horrors. And he was not wicked, only unfortunate—and I see now how he must have suffered, lying alone with his thoughts! But I am bad—a bad girl—all my thoughts are bad—I have always had bad people about me. Is that any excuse? I thought I could manage my own life—I was proud—proud! but now I'm on their level—"

Sobs shook her, and she bowed to them like a tree in a dry storm.

Gerty knelt beside her, waiting, with the patience born of experience, till this gust of misery should loosen fresh speech. She had first imagined some physical shock, some peril of the crowded streets, since Lily was presumably on her way home from Carry Fisher's; but she now saw that other nerve-centres were smitten, and her mind trembled back from conjecture.

Lily's sobs ceased, and she lifted her head.

"There are bad girls in your slums. Tell me—do they ever pick themselves up? Ever forget, and feel as they did before?"

"Lily! you mustn't speak so—you're dreaming."

"Don't they always go from bad to worse? There's no turning back—your old self rejects you, and shuts you out."

She rose, stretching her arms as if in utter physical weariness. "Go to bed, dear! You work hard and get up early. I'll watch here by the fire, and you'll leave the light, and your door open. All I want is to feel that you are near me." She laid both hands on Gerty's shoulders, with a smile that was like sunrise on a sea strewn with wreckage.

"I can't leave you, Lily. Come and lie on my bed. Your hands are frozen—you must undress and be made warm." Gerty paused with sudden compunction. "But Mrs. Peniston—it's past midnight! What will she think?"

"She goes to bed. I have a latch-key. It doesn't matter—I can't go back there."

"There's no need to: you shall stay here. But you must tell me where you have been. Listen, Lily—it will help you to speak!" She regained Miss Bart's hands, and pressed them against her. "Try to tell me—it will clear your poor head. Listen—you were dining at Carry Fisher's." Gerty paused and added with a flash of heroism: "Lawrence Selden went from here to find you."

At the word, Lily's face melted from locked anguish to the open misery of a child. Her lips trembled and her gaze widened with tears.

"He went to find me? And I missed him! Oh, Gerty, he tried to help me. He told me—he warned me long ago—he foresaw that I should grow hateful to myself!"

The name, as Gerty saw with a clutch at the heart, had loosened the springs of self-pity in her friend's dry breast, and tear by tear Lily poured out the measure of her anguish. She had dropped sideways in Gerty's big arm-chair, her head buried where lately Selden's had leaned, in a beauty of abandonment that drove home to Gerty's aching senses the inevitableness of her own defeat. Ah, it needed no deliberate purpose on Lily's part to rob her of her dream! To look on that prone loveliness was to see in it a natural force, to recognize that love and power belong to such as Lily, as renunciation and service are the lot of those they despoil. But if Selden's infatuation seemed a fatal necessity, the effect that his name produced shook Gerty's steadfastness with a last pang. Men pass through such superhuman loves and outlive them: they are the probation subduing the heart to human joys. How gladly Gerty would have welcomed the ministry of healing: how willingly have soothed the sufferer back to tolerance of life! But Lily's self-betrayal took this last hope from her. The mortal maid on the shore is helpless against the siren who loves her prey: such victims are floated back dead from their adventure.

Lily sprang up and caught her with strong hands. "Gerty, you know him—you understand him—tell me; if I went to him, if I told him everything—if I said: 'I am bad through and through—I want admiration, I want excitement, I want money—' yes, *money*! That's my shame, Gerty—and it's known, it's said of me—it's what men think of me—If I said it all to him—told him the whole story—said plainly: 'I've sunk lower than the lowest, for I've taken what they take, and not paid as they pay'—oh, Gerty, you know him, you can speak for him: if I told him everything would he loathe me? Or would he pity me, and understand me, and save me from loathing myself?"

Gerty stood cold and passive. She knew the hour of her probation had come, and her poor heart beat wildly against its destiny. As a dark river sweeps by under a lightning flash, she saw her chance of happiness surge past under a flash of temptation. What prevented her from saying: "He is like other men?" She was not so sure of him, after all! But to do so would have been like blaspheming her love. She could not put him before herself in any light but the noblest: she must trust him to the height of her own passion.

"Yes: I know him; he will help you," she said; and in a moment Lily's passion was weeping itself out against her breast.

There was but one bed in the little flat, and the two girls lay down on it side by side when Gerty had unlaced Lily's dress and persuaded her to put her lips to the warm tea. The light extinguished, they lay still in the darkness, Gerty shrinking to the outer edge of the narrow couch to avoid contact with her bed-fellow. Knowing that Lily disliked to be caressed, she had long ago learned to check her demonstrative impulses toward her friend. But tonight every fibre in her body shrank from Lily's nearness: it was torture to listen to her breathing, and feel the sheet stir with it. As Lily turned, and settled to completer rest, a strand of her hair swept Gerty's cheek with its fragrance. Everything about her was warm and soft and scented: even the stains of her grief became her as rain-drops do the beaten rose. But as Gerty lay with arms drawn down her side, in the motionless narrowness of an effigy, she felt a stir of sobs from the breathing warmth beside her, and Lily flung out her hand, groped for her friend's, and held it fast.

"Hold me, Gerty, hold me, or I shall think of things," she moaned; and Gerty silently slipped an arm under her, pillowing her head in its hollow as a mother makes a nest for a tossing child. In the warm hollow Lily lay still and her breathing grew low and regular. Her hand still clung to Gerty's as if to ward off evil dreams, but the hold of her fingers relaxed, her head sank deeper into its shelter, and Gerty felt that she slept.

# Chapter 15

When lily woke she had the bed to herself, and the winter light was in the room.

She sat up, bewildered by the strangeness of her surroundings; then memory returned, and she looked about her with a shiver. In the cold slant of light reflected from the back wall of a neighbouring building, she saw her evening dress and opera cloak lying in a tawdry heap on a chair. Finery laid off is as unappetizing as the remains of a feast, and it occurred to Lily that, at home, her maid's vigilance had always spared her the sight of such incongruities. Her body ached with fatigue, and with the constriction of her attitude in Gerty's bed. All through her troubled sleep she had been conscious of having no space to toss in, and the long effort to remain motionless made her feel as if she had spent her night in a train.

This sense of physical discomfort was the first to assert itself; then she perceived, beneath it, a corresponding mental prostration, a languor of horror more insufferable than the first rush of her disgust. The thought of having to wake every morning with this weight on her breast roused her tired mind to fresh effort. She must find some way out of the slough into which she had stumbled: it was not so much compunction as the dread of her morning thoughts that pressed on her the need of action. But she was unutterably tired; it was weariness to think connectedly. She lay back, looking about the poor slit of a room with a renewal of physical distaste. The outer air, penned between high buildings, brought no freshness through the window; steam-heat was beginning to sing in a coil of dingy pipes, and a smell of cooking penetrated the crack of the door.

The door opened, and Gerty, dressed and hatted, entered with a cup of tea. Her face looked sallow and swollen in the dreary light, and her dull hair shaded imperceptibly into the tones of her skin.

She glanced shyly at Lily, asking in an embarrassed tone how she felt; Lily answered with the same constraint, and raised herself up to drink the tea.

"I must have been over-tired last night; I think I had a nervous attack in the carriage," she said, as the drink brought clearness to her sluggish thoughts.

"You were not well; I am so glad you came here," Gerty returned.

"But how am I to get home? And Aunt Julia—?"

"She knows; I telephoned early, and your maid has brought your things. But won't you eat something? I scrambled the eggs myself."

Lily could not eat; but the tea strengthened her to rise and dress under her maid's searching gaze. It was a relief to her that Gerty was obliged to hasten away: the two kissed silently, but without a trace of the previous night's emotion.

Lily found Mrs. Peniston in a state of agitation. She had sent for Grace Stepney and was taking digitalis. Lily breasted the storm of enquiries as best she could, explaining that she had had an attack of faintness on her way back from Carry Fisher's; that, fearing she would not have strength to reach home, she had gone to Miss Farish's instead; but that a quiet night had restored her, and that she had no need of a doctor.

This was a relief to Mrs. Peniston, who could give herself up to her own symptoms, and Lily was advised to go and lie down, her aunt's panacea for all physical and moral disorders. In the solitude of her own room she was brought back to a sharp contemplation of facts. Her daylight view of them necessarily differed from the cloudy vision of the night. The winged furies were now prowling gossips who dropped in on each other for tea. But her fears seemed the uglier, thus shorn of their vagueness; and besides, she had to act, not rave. For the first time she forced herself to reckon up the exact amount of her debt to Trenor; and the result of this hateful computation was the discovery that she had, in all, received nine thousand dollars from him. The flimsy pretext on which it had been given and received shrivelled up in the blaze of her shame: she knew that not a penny of it was her own, and that to restore her self-respect she must at once repay the whole amount. The inability thus to solace her outraged feelings gave her a paralyzing sense of insignificance. She was realizing for the first time that a woman's dignity may cost more to keep up than her carriage; and that the maintenance of a moral attribute should be dependent on dollars and cents, made the world appear a more sordid place than she had conceived it.

After luncheon, when Grace Stepney's prying eyes had been removed, Lily asked for a word with her aunt. The two ladies went upstairs to the sitting-room, where Mrs. Peniston seated herself in her black satin arm-chair tufted with yellow buttons, beside a bead-work table bearing a bronze box with a miniature of Beatrice Cenci in the lid. Lily felt for these objects the same distaste which the prisoner may entertain for the fittings of the court-room. It was here that her aunt received her rare confidences, and the pink-eyed smirk of the turbaned Beatrice was associated in her mind with the gradual fading of the smile from Mrs. Peniston's lips. That lady's dread of a scene gave her an inexorableness which the greatest strength of character could not have produced, since it was independent of all considerations of right or wrong; and knowing this, Lily seldom ventured to assail it. She had never felt less like making the attempt than on the present occasion; but she had sought in vain for any other means of escape from an intolerable situation.

Mrs. Peniston examined her critically. "You're a bad colour, Lily: this incessant rushing about is beginning to tell on you," she said.

Miss Bart saw an opening. "I don't think it's that, Aunt Julia; I've had worries," she replied.

"Ah," said Mrs. Peniston, shutting her lips with the snap of a purse closing against a beggar.

"I'm sorry to bother you with them," Lily continued, "but I really believe my faintness last night was brought on partly by anxious thoughts—"

"I should have said Carry Fisher's cook was enough to account for it. She has a woman who was with Maria Melson in 1891—the spring of the year we went to Aix—and I remember dining there two days before we sailed, and feeling *sure* the coppers hadn't been scoured."

"I don't think I ate much; I can't eat or sleep." Lily paused, and then said abruptly: "The fact is, Aunt Julia, I owe some money."

Mrs. Peniston's face clouded perceptibly, but did not express the astonishment her niece had expected. She was silent, and Lily was forced to continue: "I have been foolish—"

"No doubt you have: extremely foolish," Mrs. Peniston interposed. "I fail to see how any one with your income, and no expenses—not to mention the handsome presents I've always given you—"

"Oh, you've been most generous, Aunt Julia; I shall never forget your kindness. But perhaps you don't quite realize the expense a girl is put to nowadays—"

"I don't realize that *you* are put to any expense except for your clothes and your railway fares. I expect you to be handsomely dressed; but I paid Celeste's bill for you last October."

Lily hesitated: her aunt's implacable memory had never been more inconvenient. "You were as kind as possible; but I have had to get a few things since—"

"What kind of things? Clothes? How much have you spent? Let me see the bill—I daresay the woman is swindling you."

"Oh, no, I think not: clothes have grown so frightfully expensive; and one needs so many different kinds, with country visits, and golf and skating, and Aiken and Tuxedo—"

"Let me see the bill," Mrs. Peniston repeated.

Lily hesitated again. In the first place, Mme. Celeste had not yet sent in her account, and secondly, the amount it represented was only a fraction of the sum that Lily needed.

"She hasn't sent in the bill for my winter things, but I *know* it's large; and there are one or two other things; I've been careless and imprudent—I'm frightened to think of what I owe—"

She raised the troubled loveliness of her face to Mrs. Peniston, vainly hoping that a sight so moving to the other sex might not be without effect upon her own. But the effect produced was that of making Mrs. Peniston shrink back apprehensively.

"Really, Lily, you are old enough to manage your own affairs, and after frightening me to death by your performance of last night you might at least choose a better time to worry me with such matters." Mrs. Peniston glanced at the clock, and swallowed a tablet of digitalis. "If you owe Celeste another thousand, she may send me her account," she added, as though to end the discussion at any cost.

"I am very sorry, Aunt Julia; I hate to trouble you at such a time; but I have really no choice—I ought to have spoken sooner—I owe a great deal more than a thousand dollars."

"A great deal more? Do you owe two? She must have robbed you!"

"I told you it was not only Celeste. I—there are other bills—more pressing—that must be settled."

"What on earth have you been buying? Jewelry? You must have gone off your head," said Mrs. Peniston with asperity. "But if you have run into debt, you must suffer the consequences, and put aside your monthly income till your bills are paid. If you stay quietly here until next spring, instead of racing about all over the country, you will have no expenses at all, and surely in four or five months you can settle the rest of your bills if I pay the dress-maker now."

Lily was again silent. She knew she could not hope to extract even a thousand dollars from Mrs. Peniston on the mere plea of paying Celeste's bill: Mrs. Peniston would expect to go over the dress-maker's account, and would make out the cheque to her and not to Lily. And yet the money must be obtained before the day was over!

"The debts I speak of are—different—not like tradesmen's bills," she began confusedly; but Mrs. Peniston's look made her almost afraid to continue. Could it be that her aunt suspected anything? The idea precipitated Lily's avowal.

"The fact is, I've played cards a good deal—bridge; the women all do it; girls too—it's expected. Sometimes I've won—won a good deal—but lately I've been unlucky—and of course such debts can't be paid off gradually—"

She paused: Mrs. Peniston's face seemed to be petrifying as she listened.

"Cards—you've played cards for money? It's true, then: when I was told so I wouldn't believe it. I won't ask if the other horrors I was told were true too; I've heard enough for the state of my nerves. When I think of the example you've had in this house! But I suppose it's your foreign bringing-up—no one knew where your mother picked up her friends. And her Sundays were a scandal—that I know."

Mrs. Peniston wheeled round suddenly. "You play cards on Sunday?"

Lily flushed with the recollection of certain rainy Sundays at Bellomont and with the Dorsets.

"You're hard on me, Aunt Julia: I have never really cared for cards, but a girl hates to be thought priggish and superior, and one drifts into doing what the others do. I've had a dreadful lesson, and if you'll help me out this time I promise you—"

Mrs. Peniston raised her hand warningly. "You needn't make any promises: it's unnecessary. When I offered you a home I didn't undertake to pay your gambling debts."

"Aunt Julia! You don't mean that you won't help me?"

"I shall certainly not do anything to give the impression that I countenance your behaviour. If you really owe your dress-maker, I will settle with her—beyond that I recognize no obligation to assume your debts."

Lily had risen, and stood pale and quivering before her aunt. Pride stormed in her, but humiliation forced the cry from her lips: "Aunt Julia, I shall be disgraced—I—" But she could go no farther. If her aunt turned such a stony ear to the fiction of the gambling debts, in what spirit would she receive the terrible avowal of the truth?

"I consider that you *are* disgraced, Lily: disgraced by your conduct far more than by its results. You say your friends have persuaded you to play cards with them; well, they may as well learn a lesson too. They can probably afford to lose a little money—and at any rate, I am not going to waste any of mine in paying them. And now I must ask you to leave me—this scene has been extremely painful, and I have my own health to consider. Draw down the blinds, please; and tell Jennings I will see no one this afternoon but Grace Stepney."

Lily went up to her own room and bolted the door. She was trembling with fear and anger—the rush of the furies' wings was in her ears. She walked up and down the room with blind irregular steps. The last door of escape was closed—she felt herself shut in with her dishonour.

Suddenly her wild pacing brought her before the clock on the chimney-piece. Its hands stood at half-past three, and she remembered that Selden was to come to her at four. She had meant to put him off with a word—but now her heart leaped at the thought of seeing him. Was there not a promise of rescue in his love? As she had lain at Gerty's side the night before, she had thought of his coming, and of the sweetness of weeping out her pain upon his breast. Of course she had meant to clear herself of its consequences before she met him—she had never really doubted that Mrs. Peniston would come to her aid. And she had felt, even in the full storm of her misery, that Selden's love could not be her ultimate refuge; only it would be so sweet to take a moment's shelter there, while she gathered fresh strength to go on.

But now his love was her only hope, and as she sat alone with her wretchedness the thought of confiding in him became as seductive as the river's flow to the suicide. The first plunge would be terrible—but afterward, what blessedness might come! She remembered Gerty's words: "I know him—he will help you"; and her mind clung to them as a sick person might cling to a healing relic. Oh, if he really understood—if he would help her to gather up her broken life, and put it together in some new semblance in which no trace of the past should remain! He had always made her feel that she was worthy of better things, and she had never been in greater need of such solace. Once and again she shrank at the thought of imperilling his love by her confession: for love was what she needed—it would take the glow of passion to weld together the shattered fragments of her self-esteem. But she recurred to Gerty's words and held fast to them. She was sure that Gerty knew Selden's feeling for her, and it had never dawned upon her blindness that Gerty's own judgment of him was coloured by emotions far more ardent than her own.

Four o'clock found her in the drawing-room: she was sure that Selden would be punctual. But the hour came and passed—it moved on feverishly, measured by her impatient heart-beats. She had time to take a fresh survey of her wretchedness, and to fluctuate anew between the impulse to confide in Selden and the dread of destroying his illusions. But as the minutes passed the need of throwing herself on his comprehension became more urgent: she could not bear the weight of her misery alone. There would be a perilous moment, perhaps: but could she not trust to her beauty to bridge it over, to land her safe in the shelter of his devotion?

But the hour sped on and Selden did not come. Doubtless he had been detained, or had misread her hurriedly scrawled note, taking the four for a five. The ringing of the door-bell a few minutes after five confirmed this supposition, and made Lily hastily resolve to write more legibly in future. The sound of steps in the hall, and of the butler's voice preceding them, poured fresh energy into her veins. She felt herself once more the alert and competent moulder of emergencies, and the remembrance of her power over Selden flushed her with sudden confidence. But when the drawing-room door opened it was Rosedale who came in.

The reaction caused her a sharp pang, but after a passing movement of irritation at the clumsiness of fate, and at her own carelessness in not denying the door to all but Selden, she controlled herself and greeted Rosedale amicably. It was annoying that Selden, when he came, should find that particular visitor in possession, but Lily was mistress of the art of ridding herself of superfluous company, and to her present mood Rosedale seemed distinctly negligible.

His own view of the situation forced itself upon her after a few moments' conversation. She had caught at the Brys' entertainment as an easy impersonal subject, likely to tide them over the interval till Selden appeared, but Mr. Rosedale, tenaciously planted beside the tea-table, his hands in his pockets, his legs a little too freely extended, at once gave the topic a personal turn.

"Pretty well done—well, yes, I suppose it was: Welly Bry's got his back up and don't mean to let go till he's got the hang of the thing. Of course, there were things here and there—things Mrs. Fisher couldn't be expected to see to—the champagne wasn't cold, and the coats got mixed in the coat-room. I would have spent more money on the music. But that's my character: if I want a thing I'm willing to pay: I don't go up to the counter, and then wonder if the article's worth the price. I wouldn't be satisfied to entertain like the Welly Brys; I'd want something that would look more easy and natural, more as if I took it in my stride. And it takes just two things to do that, Miss Bart: money, and the right woman to spend it."

He paused, and examined her attentively while she affected to rearrange the tea-cups.

"I've got the money," he continued, clearing his throat, "and what I want is the woman—and I mean to have her too."

He leaned forward a little, resting his hands on the head of his walking-stick. He had seen men of Ned Van Alstyne's type bring their hats and sticks into a drawing-room, and he thought it added a touch of elegant familiarity to their appearance.

Lily was silent, smiling faintly, with her eyes absently resting on his face. She was in reality reflecting that a declaration would take some time to make, and that Selden must surely appear before the moment of refusal had been reached. Her brooding look, as of a mind withdrawn yet not averted, seemed to Mr. Rosedale full of a subtle encouragement. He would not have liked any evidence of eagerness.

"I mean to have her too," he repeated, with a laugh intended to strengthen his self-assurance. "I generally *have* got what I wanted in life, Miss Bart. I wanted money, and I've got more than I know how to invest; and now the money doesn't seem to be of any account unless I can spend it on the right woman. That's what I want to do with it: I want my wife to make all the other women feel small. I'd never grudge a dollar that was spent on that. But it isn't every woman can do it, no matter how much you spend on her. There was a girl in some history book who wanted gold shields, or something, and the fellows threw 'em at her, and she was crushed under 'em: they killed her. Well, that's true enough: some women looked buried under their jewelry. What I want is a woman who'll hold her head higher the more diamonds I put on it. And when I looked at you the other night at the Brys', in that plain white dress, looking as if you had a crown on, I said to myself: 'By gad, if she had one she'd wear it as if it grew on her.'"

Still Lily did not speak, and he continued, warming with his theme: "Tell you what it is, though, that kind of woman costs more than all the rest of 'em put together. If a woman's going to ignore her pearls, they want to be better than anybody else's—and so it is with everything else. You know what I mean—you know it's only the showy things that are cheap. Well, I should want my wife to be able to take the earth for granted if she wanted to. I know there's one thing vulgar about money, and that's the thinking about it; and my wife would never have to demean herself in that way." He paused, and then added, with an unfortunate lapse to an earlier manner: "I guess you know the lady I've got in view, Miss Bart."

Lily raised her head, brightening a little under the challenge. Even through the dark tumult of her thoughts, the clink of Mr. Rosedale's millions had a faintly seductive note. Oh, for enough of them to cancel her one miserable debt! But the man behind them grew increasingly repugnant in the light of Selden's expected coming. The contrast was too grotesque: she could scarcely suppress the smile it provoked. She decided that directness would be best.

"If you mean me, Mr. Rosedale, I am very grateful—very much flattered; but I don't know what I have ever done to make you think—"

"Oh, if you mean you're not dead in love with me, I've got sense enough left to see that. And I ain't talking to you as if you were—I presume I know the kind of talk that's expected under those circumstances. I'm confoundedly gone on you—that's about the size of it—and I'm just giving you a plain business statement of the consequences. You're not very fond of me—*yet*—but you're fond of luxury, and style, and amusement, and of not having to worry about cash. You like to have a good time, and not have to settle for it; and what I propose to do is to provide for the good time and do the settling."

He paused, and she returned with a chilling smile: "You are mistaken in one point, Mr. Rosedale: whatever I enjoy I am prepared to settle for."

She spoke with the intention of making him see that, if his words implied a tentative allusion to her private affairs, she was prepared to meet and repudiate it. But if he recognized her meaning it failed to abash him, and he went on in the same tone: "I didn't mean to give offence; excuse me if I've spoken too plainly. But why ain't you straight with me—why do you put up that kind of bluff? You know there've been times when you were bothered—damned bothered—and as a girl gets older, and things keep moving along, why, before she knows it, the things she wants are liable to move past her and not come back. I don't say it's anywhere near that with you yet; but you've had a taste of bothers that a girl like yourself ought never to have known about, and what I'm offering you is the chance to turn your back on them once for all."

The colour burned in Lily's face as he ended; there was no mistaking the point he meant to make, and to permit it to pass unheeded was a fatal confession of weakness, while to resent it too openly was to risk offending him at a perilous moment. Indignation quivered on her lip; but it was quelled by the secret voice which warned her that she must not quarrel with him. He knew too much about her, and even at the moment when it was essential that he should show himself at his best, he did not scruple to let her see how much he knew. How then would he use his power when her expression of contempt had dispelled his one motive for restraint? Her whole future might hinge on her way of answering him: she had to stop and consider that, in the stress of her other anxieties, as a breathless fugitive may have to pause at the cross-roads and try to decide coolly which turn to take.

"You are quite right, Mr. Rosedale. I *have* had bothers; and I am grateful to you for wanting to relieve me of them. It is not always easy to be quite independent and self-respecting when one is poor and lives among rich people; I have been careless about money, and have worried about my bills. But I should be selfish and ungrateful if I made that a reason for accepting all you offer, with no better return to make than the desire to be free from my anxieties. You must give me time—time to think of your kindness—and of what I could give you in return for it—"

She held out her hand with a charming gesture in which dismissal was shorn of its rigour. Its hint of future leniency made Rosedale rise in obedience to it, a little flushed with his unhoped-for success, and disciplined by the tradition of his blood to accept what was conceded, without undue haste to press for more. Something in his prompt acquiescence frightened her; she felt behind it the stored force of a patience that might subdue the strongest will. But at least they had parted amicably, and he was out of the house without meeting Selden—Selden, whose continued absence now smote her with a new alarm. Rosedale had remained over an hour, and she understood that it was now too late to hope for Selden. He would write explaining his absence, of course; there would be a note from him by the late post. But her confession would have to be postponed; and the chill of the delay settled heavily on her fagged spirit.

It lay heavier when the postman's last ring brought no note for her, and she had to go upstairs to a lonely night—a night as grim and sleepless as her tortured fancy had pictured it to Gerty. She had never learned to live with her own thoughts, and to be confronted with them through such hours of lucid misery made the confused wretchedness of her previous vigil seem easily bearable.

Daylight disbanded the phantom crew, and made it clear to her that she would hear from Selden before noon; but the day passed without his writing or coming. Lily remained at home, lunching and dining alone with her aunt, who complained of flutterings of the heart, and talked icily on general topics. Mrs. Peniston went to bed early, and when she had gone Lily sat down and wrote a note to Selden. She was about to ring for a messenger to despatch it when her eye fell on a paragraph in the evening paper which lay at her elbow: "Mr. Lawrence Selden was among the passengers sailing this afternoon for Havana and the West Indies on the Windward Liner Antilles."

She laid down the paper and sat motionless, staring at her note. She understood now that he was never coming—that he had gone away because he was afraid that he might come. She rose, and walking across the floor stood gazing at herself for a long time in the brightly-lit mirror above the mantel-piece. The lines in her face came out terribly—she looked old; and when a girl looks old to herself, how does she look to other people? She moved away, and began to wander aimlessly about the room, fitting her steps with mechanical precision between the monstrous roses of Mrs. Peniston's Axminster. Suddenly she noticed that the pen with which she had written to Selden still rested against the uncovered inkstand. She seated herself again, and taking out an envelope, addressed it rapidly to Rosedale. Then she laid out a sheet of paper, and sat over it with suspended pen. It had been easy enough to write the date, and "Dear Mr. Rosedale"—but after that her inspiration flagged. She meant to tell him to come to her, but the words refused to shape themselves. At length she began: "I have been thinking—" then she laid the pen down, and sat with her elbows on the table and her face hidden in her hands.

Suddenly she started up at the sound of the door-bell. It was not late—barely ten o'clock—and there might still be a note from Selden, or a message—or he might be there himself, on the other side of the door! The announcement of his sailing might have been a mistake—it might be another Lawrence Selden who had gone to Havana—all these possibilities had time to flash through her mind, and build up the conviction that she was after all to see or hear from him, before the drawing-room door opened to admit a servant carrying a telegram.

Lily tore it open with shaking hands, and read Bertha Dorset's name below the message: "Sailing unexpectedly tomorrow. Will you join us on a cruise in Mediterranean?"

# Book 2
## Chapter 1

It came vividly to Selden on the Casino steps that Monte Carlo had, more than any other place he knew, the gift of accommodating itself to each man's humour. His own, at the moment, lent it a festive readiness of welcome that might well, in a disenchanted eye, have turned to paint and facility. So frank an appeal for participation—so outspoken a recognition of the holiday vein in human nature—struck refreshingly on a mind jaded by prolonged hard work in surroundings made for the discipline of the senses. As he surveyed the white square set in an exotic coquetry of architecture, the studied tropicality of the gardens, the groups loitering in the foreground against mauve mountains which suggested a sublime stage-setting forgotten in a hurried shifting of scenes—as he took in the whole outspread effect of light and leisure, he felt a movement of revulsion from the last few months of his life.

The New York winter had presented an interminable perspective of snow-burdened days, reaching toward a spring of raw sunshine and furious air, when the ugliness of things rasped the eye as the gritty wind ground into the skin. Selden, immersed in his work, had told himself that external conditions did not matter to a man in his state, and that cold and ugliness were a good tonic for relaxed sensibilities. When an urgent case summoned him abroad to confer with a client in Paris, he broke reluctantly with the routine of the office; and it was only now that, having despatched his business, and slipped away for a week in the south, he began to feel the renewed zest of spectatorship that is the solace of those who take an objective interest in life.

The multiplicity of its appeals—the perpetual surprise of its contrasts and resemblances! All these tricks and turns of the show were upon him with a spring as he descended the Casino steps and paused on the pavement at its doors. He had not been abroad for seven years—and what changes the renewed contact produced! If the central depths were untouched, hardly a pin-point of surface remained the same. And this was the very place to bring out the completeness of the renewal. The sublimities, the perpetuities, might have left him as he was: but this tent pitched for a day's revelry spread a roof of oblivion between himself and his fixed sky.

It was mid-April, and one felt that the revelry had reached its climax and that the desultory groups in the square and gardens would soon dissolve and re-form in other scenes. Meanwhile the last moments of the performance seemed to gain an added brightness from the hovering threat of the curtain. The quality of the air, the exuberance of the flowers, the blue intensity of sea and sky, produced the effect of a closing *tableau*, when all the lights are turned on at once. This impression was presently heightened by the way in which a consciously conspicuous group of people advanced to the middle front, and stood before Selden with the air of the chief performers gathered together by the exigencies of the final effect. Their appearance confirmed the impression that the show had been staged regardless of expense, and emphasized its resemblance to one of those "costume-plays" in which the protagonists walk through the passions without displacing a drapery. The ladies stood in unrelated attitudes calculated to isolate their effects, and the men hung about them as irrelevantly as stage heroes whose tailors are named in the programme. It was Selden himself who unwittingly fused the group by arresting the attention of one of its members.

"Why, Mr. Selden!" Mrs. Fisher exclaimed in surprise; and with a gesture toward Mrs. Jack Stepney and Mrs. Wellington Bry, she added plaintively: "We're starving to death because we can't decide where to lunch."

Welcomed into their group, and made the confidant of their difficulty, Selden learned with amusement that there were several places where one might miss something by not lunching, or forfeit something by lunching; so that eating actually became a minor consideration on the very spot consecrated to its rites.

"Of course one gets the best things at the *terrasse*—but that looks as if one hadn't any other reason for being there: the Americans who don't know any one always rush for the best food. And the Duchess of Beltshire has taken up Becassin's lately," Mrs. Bry earnestly summed up.

Mrs. Bry, to Mrs. Fisher's despair, had not progressed beyond the point of weighing her social alternatives in public. She could not acquire the air of doing things because she wanted to, and making her choice the final seal of their fitness.

Mr. Bry, a short pale man, with a business face and leisure clothes, met the dilemma hilariously.

"I guess the Duchess goes where it's cheapest, unless she can get her meal paid for. If you offered to blow her off at the *terrasse* she'd turn up fast enough."

But Mrs. Jack Stepney interposed. "The Grand Dukes go to that little place at the Condamine. Lord Hubert says it's the only restaurant in Europe where they can cook peas."

Lord Hubert Dacey, a slender shabby-looking man, with a charming worn smile, and the air of having spent his best years in piloting the wealthy to the right restaurant, assented with gentle emphasis: "It's quite that."

"*Peas?*" said Mr. Bry contemptuously. "Can they cook terrapin? It just shows," he continued, "what these European markets are, when a fellow can make a reputation cooking peas!"

Jack Stepney intervened with authority. "I don't know that I quite agree with Dacey: there's a little hole in Paris, off the Quai Voltaire—but in any case, I can't advise the Condamine *gargote*; at least not with ladies."

Stepney, since his marriage, had thickened and grown prudish, as the Van Osburgh husbands were apt to do; but his wife, to his surprise and discomfiture, had developed an earth-shaking fastness of gait which left him trailing breathlessly in her wake.

"That's where we'll go then!" she declared, with a heavy toss of her plumage. "I'm so tired of the *terrasse*: it's as dull as one of mother's dinners. And Lord Hubert has promised to tell us who all the awful people are at the other place—hasn't he, Carry? Now, Jack, don't look so solemn!"

"Well," said Mrs. Bry, "all I want to know is who their dress-makers are."

"No doubt Dacey can tell you that too," remarked Stepney, with an ironic intention which the other received with the light murmur, "I can at least *find out*, my dear fellow"; and Mrs. Bry having declared that she couldn't walk another step, the party hailed two or three of the light phaetons which hover attentively on the confines of the gardens, and rattled off in procession toward the Condamine.

Their destination was one of the little restaurants overhanging the boulevard which dips steeply down from Monte Carlo to the low intermediate quarter along the quay. From the window in which they presently found themselves installed, they overlooked the intense blue curve of the harbour, set between the verdure of twin promontories: to the right, the cliff of Monaco, topped by the mediaeval silhouette of its church and castle, to the left the terraces and pinnacles of the gambling-house. Between the two, the waters of the bay were furrowed by a light coming and going of pleasure-craft, through which, just at the culminating moment of luncheon, the majestic advance of a great steam-yacht drew the company's attention from the peas.

"By Jove, I believe that's the Dorsets back!" Stepney exclaimed; and Lord Hubert, dropping his single eye-glass, corroborated: "It's the Sabrina—yes."

"So soon? They were to spend a month in Sicily," Mrs. Fisher observed.

"I guess they feel as if they had: there's only one up-to-date hotel in the whole place," said Mr. Bry disparagingly.

"It was Ned Silverton's idea—but poor Dorset and Lily Bart must have been horribly bored." Mrs. Fisher added in an undertone to Selden: "I do hope there hasn't been a row."

"It's most awfully jolly having Miss Bart back," said Lord Hubert, in his mild deliberate voice; and Mrs. Bry added ingenuously: "I daresay the Duchess will dine with us, now that Lily's here."

"The Duchess admires her immensely: I'm sure she'd be charmed to have it arranged," Lord Hubert agreed, with the professional promptness of the man accustomed to draw his profit from facilitating social contacts: Selden was struck by the businesslike change in his manner.

"Lily has been a tremendous success here," Mrs. Fisher continued, still addressing herself confidentially to Selden. "She looks ten years younger—I never saw her so handsome. Lady Skiddaw took her everywhere in Cannes, and the Crown Princess of Macedonia had her to stop for a week at Cimiez. People say that was one reason why Bertha whisked the yacht off to Sicily: the Crown Princess didn't take much notice of her, and she couldn't bear to look on at Lily's triumph."

Selden made no reply. He was vaguely aware that Miss Bart was cruising in the Mediterranean with the Dorsets, but it had not occurred to him that there was any chance of running across her on the Riviera, where the season was virtually at an end. As he leaned back, silently contemplating his filigree cup of Turkish coffee, he was trying to put some order in his thoughts, to tell himself how the news of her nearness was really affecting him. He had a personal detachment enabling him, even in moments of emotional high-pressure, to get a fairly clear view of his feelings, and he was sincerely surprised by the disturbance which the sight of the Sabrina had produced in him. He had reason to think that his three months of engrossing professional work, following on the sharp shock of his disillusionment, had cleared his mind of its sentimental vapours. The feeling he had nourished and given prominence to was one of thankfulness for his escape: he was like a traveller so grateful for rescue from a dangerous accident that at first he is hardly conscious of his bruises. Now he suddenly felt the latent ache, and realized that after all he had not come off unhurt.

An hour later, at Mrs. Fisher's side in the Casino gardens, he was trying to find fresh reasons for forgetting the injury received in the contemplation of the peril avoided. The party had dispersed with the loitering indecision characteristic of social movements at Monte Carlo, where the whole place, and the long gilded hours of the day, seem to offer an infinity of ways of being idle. Lord Hubert Dacey had finally gone off in quest of the Duchess of Beltshire, charged by Mrs. Bry with the delicate negotiation of securing that lady's presence at dinner, the Stepneys had left for Nice in their motor-car, and Mr. Bry had departed to take his place in the pigeon shooting match which was at the moment engaging his highest faculties.

Mrs. Bry, who had a tendency to grow red and stertorous after luncheon, had been judiciously prevailed upon by Carry Fisher to withdraw to her hotel for an hour's repose; and Selden and his companion were thus left to a stroll propitious to confidences. The stroll soon resolved itself into a tranquil session on a bench overhung with laurel and Banksian roses, from which they caught a dazzle of blue sea between marble balusters, and the fiery shafts of cactus-blossoms shooting meteor-like from the rock. The soft shade of their niche, and the adjacent glitter of the air, were conducive to an easy lounging mood, and to the smoking of many cigarettes; and Selden, yielding to these influences, suffered Mrs. Fisher to unfold to him the history of her recent experiences. She had come abroad with the Welly Brys at the moment when fashion flees the inclemency of the New York spring. The Brys, intoxicated by their first success, already thirsted for new kingdoms, and Mrs. Fisher, viewing the Riviera as an easy introduction to London society, had guided their course thither. She had affiliations of her own in every capital, and a facility for picking them up again after long absences; and the carefully disseminated rumour of the Brys' wealth had at once gathered about them a group of cosmopolitan pleasure-seekers.

"But things are not going as well as I expected," Mrs. Fisher frankly admitted. "It's all very well to say that every body with money can get into society; but it would be truer to say that *nearly* everybody can. And the London market is so glutted with new Americans that, to succeed there now, they must be either very clever or awfully queer. The Brys are neither. *He* would get on well enough if she'd let him alone; they like his slang and his brag and his blunders. But Louisa spoils it all by trying to repress him and put herself forward. If she'd be natural herself—fat and vulgar and bouncing—it would be all right; but as soon as she meets anybody smart she tries to be slender and queenly. She tried it with the Duchess of Beltshire and Lady Skiddaw, and they fled. I've done my best to make her see her mistake—I've said to her again and again: 'Just let yourself go, Louisa'; but she keeps up the humbug even with me—I believe she keeps on being queenly in her own room, with the door shut.

"The worst of it is," Mrs. Fisher went on, "that she thinks it's all *my* fault. When the Dorsets turned up here six weeks ago, and everybody began to make a fuss about Lily Bart, I could see Louisa thought that if she'd had Lily in tow instead of me she would have been hob-nobbing with all the royalties by this time. She doesn't realize that it's Lily's beauty that does it: Lord Hubert tells me Lily is thought even handsomer than when he knew her at Aix ten years ago. It seems she was tremendously admired there. An Italian Prince, rich and the real thing, wanted to marry her; but just at the critical moment a good-looking step-son turned up, and Lily was silly enough to flirt with him while her marriage-settlements with the step-father were being drawn up. Some people said the young man did it on purpose. You can fancy the scandal: there was an awful row between the men, and people began to look at Lily so queerly that Mrs. Peniston had to pack up and finish her cure elsewhere. Not that *she* ever understood: to this day she thinks that Aix didn't suit her, and mentions her having been sent there as proof of the incompetence of French doctors. That's Lily all over, you know: she works like a slave preparing the ground and sowing her seed; but the day she ought to be reaping the harvest she over-sleeps herself or goes off on a picnic."

Mrs. Fisher paused and looked reflectively at the deep shimmer of sea between the cactus-flowers. "Sometimes," she added, "I think it's just flightiness—and sometimes I think it's because, at heart, she despises the things she's trying for. And it's the difficulty of deciding that makes her such an interesting study." She glanced tentatively at Selden's motionless profile, and resumed with a slight sigh: "Well, all I can say is, I wish she'd give *me* some of her discarded opportunities. I wish we could change places now, for instance. She could make a very good thing out of the Brys if she managed them properly, and I should know just how to look after George Dorset while Bertha is reading Verlaine with Neddy Silverton."

She met Selden's sound of protest with a sharp derisive glance. "Well, what's the use of mincing matters? We all know that's what Bertha brought her abroad for. When Bertha wants to have a good time she has to provide occupation for George. At first I thought Lily was going to play her cards well *this* time, but there are rumours that Bertha is jealous of her success here and at Cannes, and I shouldn't be surprised if there were a break any day. Lily's only safeguard is that Bertha needs her badly—oh, very badly. The Silverton affair is in the acute stage: it's necessary that George's attention should be pretty continuously distracted. And I'm bound to say Lily *does* distract it: I believe he'd marry her tomorrow if he found out there was anything wrong with Bertha. But you know him—he's as blind as he's jealous; and of course Lily's present business is to keep him blind. A clever woman might know just the right moment to tear off the bandage: but Lily isn't clever in that way, and when George does open his eyes she'll probably contrive not to be in his line of vision."

Selden tossed away his cigarette. "By Jove—it's time for my train," he exclaimed, with a glance at his watch; adding, in reply to Mrs. Fisher's surprised comment—"Why, I thought of course you were at

Monte!"—a murmured word to the effect that he was making Nice his head-quarters.

"The worst of it is, she snubs the Brys now," he heard irrelevantly flung after him.

Ten minutes later, in the high-perched bedroom of an hotel overlooking the Casino, he was tossing his effects into a couple of gaping portmanteaux, while the porter waited outside to transport them to the cab at the door. It took but a brief plunge down the steep white road to the station to land him safely in the afternoon express for Nice; and not till he was installed in the corner of an empty carriage, did he exclaim to himself, with a reaction of self-contempt: "What the deuce am I running away from?"

The pertinence of the question checked Selden's fugitive impulse before the train had started. It was ridiculous to be flying like an emotional coward from an infatuation his reason had conquered. He had instructed his bankers to forward some important business letters to Nice, and at Nice he would quietly await them. He was already annoyed with himself for having left Monte Carlo, where he had intended to pass the week which remained to him before sailing; but it would now be difficult to return on his steps without an appearance of inconsistency from which his pride recoiled. In his inmost heart he was not sorry to put himself beyond the probability of meeting Miss Bart. Completely as he had detached himself from her, he could not yet regard her merely as a social instance; and viewed in a more personal ways she was not likely to be a reassuring object of study. Chance encounters, or even the repeated mention of her name, would send his thoughts back into grooves from which he had resolutely detached them; whereas, if she could be entirely excluded from his life, the pressure of new and varied impressions, with which no thought of her was connected, would soon complete the work of separation. Mrs. Fisher's conversation had, indeed, operated to that end; but the treatment was too painful to be voluntarily chosen while milder remedies were untried; and Selden thought he could trust himself to return gradually to a reasonable view of Miss Bart, if only he did not see her.

Having reached the station early, he had arrived at this point in his reflections before the increasing throng on the platform warned him that he could not hope to preserve his privacy; the next moment there was a hand on the door, and he turned to confront the very face he was fleeing.

Miss Bart, glowing with the haste of a precipitate descent upon the train, headed a group composed of the Dorsets, young Silverton and Lord Hubert Dacey, who had barely time to spring into the carriage, and envelop Selden in ejaculations of surprise and welcome, before the whistle of departure sounded. The party, it appeared, were hastening to Nice in response to a sudden summons to dine with the Duchess of Beltshire and to see the water-fete in the bay; a plan evidently improvised—in spite of Lord Hubert's protesting "Oh, I say, you know,"—for the express purpose of defeating Mrs. Bry's endeavour to capture the Duchess.

During the laughing relation of this manoeuvre, Selden had time for a rapid impression of Miss Bart, who had seated herself opposite to him in the golden afternoon light. Scarcely three months had elapsed since he had parted from her on the threshold of the Brys' conservatory; but a subtle change had passed over the quality of her beauty. Then it had had a transparency through which the fluctuations of the spirit were sometimes tragically visible; now its impenetrable surface suggested a process of crystallization which had fused her whole being into one hard brilliant substance. The change had struck Mrs. Fisher as a rejuvenation: to Selden it seemed like that moment of pause and arrest when the warm fluidity of youth is chilled into its final shape.

He felt it in the way she smiled on him, and in the readiness and competence with which, flung unexpectedly into his presence, she took up the thread of their intercourse as though that thread had not been snapped with a violence from which he still reeled. Such facility sickened him—but he told himself that it was with the pang which precedes recovery. Now he would really get well—would eject the last drop of poison from his blood. Already he felt himself calmer in her presence than he had learned to be in the thought of her. Her assumptions and elisions, her short-cuts and long *detours*, the skill with which she contrived to meet him at a point from which no inconvenient glimpses of the past were visible, suggested what opportunities she had had for practising such arts since their last meeting. He felt that she had at last arrived at an understanding with herself: had made a pact with her rebellious impulses, and achieved a uniform system of self-government, under which all vagrant tendencies were either held captive or forced into the service of the state.

And he saw other things too in her manner: saw how it had adjusted itself to the hidden intricacies of a situation in which, even after Mrs. Fisher's elucidating flashes, he still felt himself agrope. Surely Mrs. Fisher could no longer charge Miss Bart with neglecting her opportunities! To Selden's exasperated observation she was only too completely alive to them. She was "perfect" to every one: subservient to Bertha's anxious predominance, good-naturedly watchful of Dorset's moods, brightly companionable to Silverton and Dacey, the latter of whom met her on an evident footing of old admiration, while young Silverton, portentously self-absorbed, seemed conscious of her only as of something vaguely obstructive. And suddenly, as Selden noted the fine shades of manner by which she harmonized herself with her surroundings, it flashed on him that, to need such adroit handling, the situation must indeed be desperate. She was on the edge of something—that was the impression left with him. He seemed to see her poised on the brink of a chasm, with one graceful foot advanced to assert her unconsciousness that the ground was failing her.

On the Promenade des Anglais, where Ned Silverton hung on him for the half hour before dinner, he received a deeper impression of the general insecurity. Silverton was in a mood of Titanic pessimism. How any one could come to such a damned hole as the Riviera—any one with a grain of imagination—with the whole Mediterranean to choose from: but then, if one's estimate of a place depended on the way they broiled a spring chicken! Gad! what a study might be made of the tyranny of the stomach—the way a sluggish liver or insufficient gastric juices might affect the whole course of the universe, overshadow everything in reach—chronic dyspepsia ought to be among the "statutory causes"; a woman's life might be ruined by a man's inability to digest fresh bread. Grotesque? Yes—and tragic—like most absurdities. There's nothing grimmer than the tragedy that wears a comic mask.... Where was he? Oh—the reason they chucked Sicily and rushed back? Well—partly, no doubt, Miss Bart's desire to get back to bridge and smartness. Dead as a stone to art and poetry—the light never *was* on sea or land for her! And of course she persuaded Dorset that the Italian food was bad for him. Oh, she could make him believe anything—*anything*! Mrs. Dorset was aware of it—oh, perfectly: nothing *she* didn't see! But she could hold her tongue—she'd had to, often enough. Miss Bart was an intimate friend—she wouldn't hear a word against her. Only it hurts a woman's pride—there are some things one doesn't get used to . . . All this in confidence, of course? Ah—and there were the ladies signalling from the balcony of the hotel.... He plunged across the Promenade, leaving Selden to a meditative cigar.

The conclusions it led him to were fortified, later in the evening, by some of those faint corroborative hints that generate a light of their own in the dusk of a doubting mind. Selden, stumbling on a chance acquaintance, had dined with him, and adjourned, still in his company, to the brightly lit Promenade, where a line of crowded stands commanded the glittering darkness of the waters. The night was soft and persuasive. Overhead hung a summer sky furrowed with the rush of rockets; and from the east a late moon, pushing up beyond the lofty bend of the coast, sent across the bay a shaft of brightness which paled to ashes in the red glitter of the illuminated boats. Down the lantern-hung Promenade, snatches of band-music floated above the hum of the crowd and the soft tossing of boughs in dusky gardens; and between these gardens and the backs of the stands there flowed a stream of people in whom the vociferous carnival mood seemed tempered by the growing languor of the season.

Selden and his companion, unable to get seats on one of the stands facing the bay, had wandered for a while with the throng, and then found a point of vantage on a high garden-parapet above the Promenade. Thence they caught but a triangular glimpse of the water, and of the flashing play of boats across its surface; but the crowd in the street was under their immediate view, and seemed to Selden, on the whole, of more interest than the show itself. After a while, however, he wearied of his perch and, dropping alone to the pavement, pushed his way to the first corner and turned into the moonlit silence of a side street. Long garden-walls overhung by trees made a dark boundary to the pavement; an empty cab trailed along the deserted thoroughfare, and presently Selden saw two persons emerge from the opposite shadows, signal to the cab, and drive off in it toward the centre of the town. The moonlight touched them as they paused to enter the carriage, and he recognized Mrs. Dorset and young Silverton.

Beneath the nearest lamp-post he glanced at his watch and saw that the time was close on eleven. He took another cross street, and without breasting the throng on the Promenade, made his way to the fashionable club which overlooks that thoroughfare. Here, amid the blaze of crowded baccarat tables, he caught sight of Lord Hubert Dacey, seated with his habitual worn smile behind a rapidly dwindling heap of gold. The heap being in due course wiped out, Lord Hubert rose with a shrug, and joining Selden, adjourned with him to the deserted terrace of the club. It was now past midnight, and the throng on the stands was dispersing, while the long trails of red-lit boats scattered and faded beneath a sky repossessed by the tranquil splendour of the moon.

Lord Hubert looked at his watch. "By Jove, I promised to join the Duchess for supper at the *London House*; but it's past twelve, and I suppose they've all scattered. The fact is, I lost them in the crowd soon after dinner, and took refuge here, for my sins. They had seats on one of the stands, but of course they couldn't stop quiet: the Duchess never can. She and Miss Bart went off in quest of what they call adventures—gad, it ain't their fault if they don't have some queer ones!" He added tentatively, after pausing to grope for a cigarette: "Miss Bart's an old friend of yours, I believe? So she told me.—Ah, thanks—I don't seem to have one left." He lit Selden's proffered cigarette, and continued, in his high-pitched drawling tone: "None of my business, of course, but I didn't introduce her to the Duchess. Charming woman, the Duchess, you understand; and a very good friend of mine; but *rather* a liberal education."

Selden received this in silence, and after a few puffs Lord Hubert broke out again: "Sort of thing one can't communicate to the young lady—though young ladies nowadays are so competent to judge for themselves; but in this case—I'm an old friend too, you know . . . and there seemed no one else to speak to. The whole situation's a little mixed, as I see it—but there used to be an aunt somewhere, a diffuse and innocent person, who was great at bridging over chasms she didn't see . . . Ah, in New York, is she? Pity New York's such a long way off!"

## Chapter 2

Miss Bart, emerging late the next morning from her cabin, found herself alone on the deck of the Sabrina. The cushioned chairs, disposed expectantly under the wide awning, showed no signs of recent occupancy, and she presently learned from a steward that Mrs. Dorset had not yet appeared, and that the gentlemen—separately—had gone ashore as soon as they had breakfasted. Supplied with these facts, Lily leaned awhile over the side, giving herself up to a leisurely enjoyment of the spectacle before her. Unclouded sunlight enveloped sea and shore in a bath of purest radiancy. The purpling waters drew a sharp white line of foam at the base of the shore; against its irregular eminences, hotels and villas flashed from the greyish verdure of olive and eucalyptus; and the background of bare and finely-pencilled mountains quivered in a pale intensity of light.

How beautiful it was—and how she loved beauty! She had always felt that her sensibility in this direction made up for certain obtusenesses of feeling of which she was less proud; and during the last three months she had indulged it passionately. The Dorsets' invitation to go abroad with them had come as an almost miraculous release from crushing difficulties; and her faculty for renewing herself in new scenes, and casting off problems of conduct as easily as the surroundings in which they had arisen, made the mere change from one place to another seem, not merely a postponement, but a solution of her troubles. Moral complications existed for her only in the environment that had produced them; she did not mean to slight or ignore them, but they lost their reality when they changed their background. She could not have remained in New York without repaying the money she owed to Trenor; to acquit herself of that odious debt she might even have faced a marriage with Rosedale; but the accident of placing the

Atlantic between herself and her obligations made them dwindle out of sight as if they had been milestones and she had travelled past them.

Her two months on the Sabrina had been especially calculated to aid this illusion of distance. She had been plunged into new scenes, and had found in them a renewal of old hopes and ambitions. The cruise itself charmed her as a romantic adventure. She was vaguely touched by the names and scenes amid which she moved, and had listened to Ned Silverton reading Theocritus by moonlight, as the yacht rounded the Sicilian promontories, with a thrill of the nerves that confirmed her belief in her intellectual superiority. But the weeks at Cannes and Nice had really given her more pleasure. The gratification of being welcomed in high company, and of making her own ascendency felt there, so that she found herself figuring once more as the "beautiful Miss Bart" in the interesting journal devoted to recording the least movements of her cosmopolitan companions—all these experiences tended to throw into the extreme background of memory the prosaic and sordid difficulties from which she had escaped.

If she was faintly aware of fresh difficulties ahead, she was sure of her ability to meet them: it was characteristic of her to feel that the only problems she could not solve were those with which she was familiar. Meanwhile she could honestly be proud of the skill with which she had adapted herself to somewhat delicate conditions. She had reason to think that she had made herself equally necessary to her host and hostess; and if only she had seen any perfectly irreproachable means of drawing a financial profit from the situation, there would have been no cloud on her horizon. The truth was that her funds, as usual, were inconveniently low; and to neither Dorset nor his wife could this vulgar embarrassment be safely hinted. Still, the need was not a pressing one; she could worry along, as she had so often done before, with the hope of some happy change of fortune to sustain her; and meanwhile life was gay and beautiful and easy, and she was conscious of figuring not unworthily in such a setting.

She was engaged to breakfast that morning with the Duchess of Beltshire, and at twelve o'clock she asked to be set ashore in the gig. Before this she had sent her maid to enquire if she might see Mrs. Dorset; but the reply came back that the latter was tired, and trying to sleep. Lily thought she understood the reason of the rebuff. Her hostess had not been included in the Duchess's invitation, though she herself had made the most loyal efforts in that direction. But her grace was impervious to hints, and invited or omitted as she chose. It was not Lily's fault if Mrs. Dorset's complicated attitudes did not fall in with the Duchess's easy gait. The Duchess, who seldom explained herself, had not formulated her objection beyond saying: "She's rather a bore, you know. The only one of your friends I like is that little Mr. Bry—HE'S funny—" but Lily knew enough not to press the point, and was not altogether sorry to be thus distinguished at her friend's expense. Bertha certainly *had* grown tiresome since she had taken to poetry and Ned Silverton.

On the whole, it was a relief to break away now and then from the Sabrina; and the Duchess's little breakfast, organized by Lord Hubert with all his usual virtuosity, was the pleasanter to Lily for not including her travelling-companions. Dorset, of late, had grown more than usually morose and incalculable, and Ned Silverton went about with an air that seemed to challenge the universe. The freedom and lightness of the ducal intercourse made an agreeable change from these complications, and Lily was tempted, after luncheon, to adjourn in the wake of her companions to the hectic atmosphere of the Casino. She did not mean to play; her diminished pocket-money offered small scope for the adventure; but it amused her to sit on a divan, under the doubtful protection of the Duchess's back, while the latter hung above her stakes at a neighbouring table.

The rooms were packed with the gazing throng which, in the afternoon hours, trickles heavily between the tables, like the Sunday crowd in a lion-house. In the stagnant flow of the mass, identities were hardly distinguishable; but Lily presently saw Mrs. Bry cleaving her determined way through the doors, and, in the broad wake she left, the light figure of Mrs. Fisher bobbing after her like a row-boat at the stern of a tug. Mrs. Bry pressed on, evidently animated by the resolve to reach a certain point in the rooms; but Mrs. Fisher, as she passed Lily, broke from her towing-line, and let herself float to the girl's side.

"Lose her?" she echoed the latter's query, with an indifferent glance at Mrs. Bry's retreating back. "I daresay—it doesn't matter: I *have* lost her already." And, as Lily exclaimed, she added: "We had an awful row this morning. You know, of course, that the Duchess chucked her at dinner last night, and she thinks it was my fault—my want of management. The worst of it is, the message—just a mere word by telephone—came so late that the dinner *had* to be paid for; and Becassin *had* run it up—it had been so drummed into him that the Duchess was coming!" Mrs. Fisher indulged in a faint laugh at the remembrance. "Paying for what she doesn't get rankles so dreadfully with Louisa: I can't make her see that it's one of the preliminary steps to getting what you haven't paid for—and as I was the nearest thing to smash, she smashed me to atoms, poor dear!"

Lily murmured her commiseration. Impulses of sympathy came naturally to her, and it was instinctive to proffer her help to Mrs. Fisher.

"If there's anything I can do—if it's only a question of meeting the Duchess! I heard her say she thought Mr. Bry amusing—"

But Mrs. Fisher interposed with a decisive gesture. "My dear, I have my pride: the pride of my trade. I couldn't manage the Duchess, and I can't palm off your arts on Louisa Bry as mine. I've taken the final step: I go to Paris tonight with the Sam Gormers. *They're* still in the elementary stage; an Italian Prince is a great deal more than a Prince to them, and they're always on the brink of taking a courier for one. To save them from that is my present mission." She laughed again at the picture. "But before I go I want to make my last will and testament—I want to leave you the Brys."

"Me?" Miss Bart joined in her amusement. "It's charming of you to remember me, dear; but really—"

"You're already so well provided for?" Mrs. Fisher flashed a sharp glance at her. "*Are* you, though, Lily—to the point of rejecting my offer?"

Miss Bart coloured slowly. "What I really meant was, that the Brys wouldn't in the least care to be so disposed of."

Mrs. Fisher continued to probe her embarrassment with an unflinching eye. "What you really meant was that you've snubbed the Brys horribly; and you know that they know—"

"Carry!"

"Oh, on certain sides Louisa bristles with perceptions. If you'd even managed to have them asked once on the Sabrina—especially when royalties were coming! But it's not too late," she ended earnestly, "it's not too late for either of you."

Lily smiled. "Stay over, and I'll get the Duchess to dine with them."

"I shan't stay over—the Gormers have paid for my *salon-lit*," said Mrs. Fisher with simplicity. "But get the Duchess to dine with them all the same."

Lily's smile again flowed into a slight laugh: her friend's importunity was beginning to strike her as irrelevant. "I'm sorry I have been negligent about the Brys—" she began.

"Oh, as to the Brys—it's you I'm thinking of," said Mrs. Fisher abruptly. She paused, and then, bending forward, with a lowered voice: "You know we all went on to Nice last night when the Duchess chucked us. It was Louisa's idea—I told her what I thought of it."

Miss Bart assented. "Yes—I caught sight of you on the way back, at the station."

"Well, the man who was in the carriage with you and George Dorset—that horrid little Dabham who does 'Society Notes from the Riviera'—had been dining with us at Nice. And he's telling everybody that you and Dorset came back alone after midnight."

"Alone—? When he was with us?" Lily laughed, but her laugh faded into gravity under the prolonged implication of Mrs. Fisher's look. "We *did* come back alone—if that's so very dreadful! But whose fault was it? The Duchess was spending the night at Cimiez with the Crown Princess; Bertha got bored with the show, and went off early, promising to meet us at the station. We turned up on time, but she didn't—she didn't turn up at all!"

Miss Bart made this announcement in the tone of one who presents, with careless assurance, a complete vindication; but Mrs. Fisher received it in a manner almost inconsequent. She seemed to have lost sight of her friend's part in the incident: her inward vision had taken another slant.

"Bertha never turned up at all? Then how on earth did she get back?"

"Oh, by the next train, I suppose; there were two extra ones for the *fete*. At any rate, I know she's safe on the yacht, though I haven't yet seen her; but you see it was not my fault," Lily summed up.

"Not your fault that Bertha didn't turn up? My poor child, if only you don't have to pay for it!" Mrs. Fisher rose—she had seen Mrs. Bry surging back in her direction. "There's Louisa, and I must be off—oh, we're on the best of terms externally; we're lunching together; but at heart it's *me* she's lunching on," she explained; and with a last hand-clasp and a last look, she added: "Remember, I leave her to you; she's hovering now, ready to take you in."

Lily carried the impression of Mrs. Fisher's leave-taking away with her from the Casino doors. She had accomplished, before leaving, the first step toward her reinstatement in Mrs. Bry's good graces. An affable advance—a vague murmur that they must see more of each other—an allusive glance to a near future that was felt to include the Duchess as well as the Sabrina—how easily it was all done, if one possessed the knack of doing it! She wondered at herself, as she had so often wondered, that, possessing the knack, she did not more consistently exercise it. But sometimes she was forgetful—and sometimes, could it be that she was proud? Today, at any rate, she had been vaguely conscious of a reason for sinking her pride, had in fact even sunk it to the point of suggesting to Lord Hubert Dacey, whom she ran across on the Casino steps, that he might really get the Duchess to dine with the Brys, if *she* undertook to have them asked on the Sabrina. Lord Hubert had promised his help, with the readiness on which she could always count: it was his only way of ever reminding her that he had once been ready to do so much more for her. Her path, in short, seemed to smooth itself before her as she advanced; yet the faint stir of uneasiness persisted. Had it been produced, she wondered, by her chance meeting with Selden? She thought not—time and change seemed so completely to have relegated him to his proper distance. The sudden and exquisite reaction from her anxieties had had the effect of throwing the recent past so far back that even Selden, as part of it, retained a certain air of unreality. And he had made it so clear that they were not to meet again; that he had merely dropped down to Nice for a day or two, and had almost his foot on the next steamer. No—that part of the past had merely surged up for a moment on the fleeing surface of events; and now that it was submerged again, the uncertainty, the apprehension persisted.

They grew to sudden acuteness as she caught sight of George Dorset descending the steps of the Hotel de Paris and making for her across the square. She had meant to drive down to the quay and regain the yacht; but she now had the immediate impression that something more was to happen first.

"Which way are you going? Shall we walk a bit?" he began, putting the second question before the first was answered, and not waiting for a reply to either before he directed her silently toward the comparative seclusion of the lower gardens.

She detected in him at once all the signs of extreme nervous tension. The skin was puffed out under his sunken eyes, and its sallowness had paled to a leaden white against which his irregular eyebrows and long reddish moustache were relieved with a saturnine effect. His appearance, in short, presented an odd mixture of the bedraggled and the ferocious.

He walked beside her in silence, with quick precipitate steps, till they reached the embowered slopes to the east of the Casino; then, pulling up abruptly, he said: "Have you seen Bertha?"

"No—when I left the yacht she was not yet up."

He received this with a laugh like the whirring sound in a disabled clock. "Not yet up? Had she gone to bed? Do you know at what time she came on board? This morning at seven!" he exclaimed.

"At seven?" Lily started. "What happened—an accident to the train?"

He laughed again. "They missed the train—all the trains—they had to drive back."

"Well—?" She hesitated, feeling at once how little even this necessity accounted for the fatal lapse of hours.

"Well, they couldn't get a carriage at once—at that time of night, you know—" the explanatory note made it almost seem as though he were putting the case for his wife—"and when they finally did, it was only a one-horse cab, and the horse was lame!"

"How tiresome! I see," she affirmed, with the more earnestness because she was so nervously conscious that she did not; and after a pause she added: "I'm so sorry—but ought we to have waited?"

"Waited for the one-horse cab? It would scarcely have carried the four of us, do you think?"

She took this in what seemed the only possible way, with a laugh intended to sink the question itself in his humorous treatment of it. "Well, it would have been difficult; we should have had to walk by turns. But it would have been jolly to see the sunrise."

"Yes: the sunrise *was* jolly," he agreed.

"Was it? You saw it, then?"

"I saw it, yes; from the deck. I waited up for them."

"Naturally—I suppose you were worried. Why didn't you call on me to share your vigil?"

He stood still, dragging at his moustache with a lean weak hand. "I don't think you would have cared for its *denouement*," he said with sudden grimness.

Again she was disconcerted by the abrupt change in his tone, and as in one flash she saw the peril of the moment, and the need of keeping her sense of it out of her eyes.

"*Denouement*—isn't that too big a word for such a small incident? The worst of it, after all, is the fatigue which Bertha has probably slept off by this time."

She clung to the note bravely, though its futility was now plain to her in the glare of his miserable eyes.

"Don't—don't—!" he broke out, with the hurt cry of a child; and while she tried to merge her sympathy, and her resolve to ignore any cause for it, in one ambiguous murmur of deprecation, he dropped down on the bench near which they had paused, and poured out the wretchedness of his soul.

It was a dreadful hour—an hour from which she emerged shrinking and seared, as though her lids had been scorched by its actual glare. It was not that she had never had premonitory glimpses of such an outbreak; but rather because, here and there throughout the three months, the surface of life had shown such ominous cracks and vapours that her fears had always been on the alert for an upheaval. There had been moments when the situation had presented itself under a homelier yet more vivid image—that of a shaky vehicle, dashed by unbroken steeds over a bumping road, while she cowered within, aware that the harness wanted mending, and wondering what would give way first. Well—everything had given way now; and the wonder was that the crazy outfit had held together so long. Her sense of being involved in the crash, instead of merely witnessing it from the road, was intensified by the way in which Dorset, through his furies of denunciation and wild reactions of self-contempt, made her feel the need he had of her, the place she had taken in his life. But for her, what ear would have been open to his cries? And what hand but hers could drag him up again to a footing of sanity and self-respect? All through the stress of the struggle with him, she had been conscious of something faintly maternal in her efforts to guide and uplift him. But for the present, if he clung to her, it was not in order to be dragged up, but to feel some one floundering in the depths with him: he wanted her to suffer with him, not to help him to suffer less.

Happily for both, there was little physical strength to sustain his frenzy. It left him, collapsed and breathing heavily, to an apathy so deep and prolonged that Lily almost feared the passers-by would think it the result of a seizure, and stop to offer their aid. But Monte Carlo is, of all places, the one where the human bond is least close, and odd sights are the least arresting. If a glance or two lingered on the couple, no intrusive sympathy disturbed them; and it was Lily herself who broke the silence by rising from her seat. With the clearing of her vision the sweep of peril had extended, and she saw that the post of danger was no longer at Dorset's side.

"If you won't go back, I must—don't make me leave you!" she urged.

But he remained mutely resistant, and she added: "What are you going to do? You really can't sit here all night."

"I can go to an hotel. I can telegraph my lawyers." He sat up, roused by a new thought. "By Jove, Selden's at Nice—I'll send for Selden!"

Lily, at this, reseated herself with a cry of alarm. "No, no, *no*!" she protested.

He swung round on her distrustfully. "Why not Selden? He's a lawyer isn't he? One will do as well as another in a case like this."

"As badly as another, you mean. I thought you relied on *me* to help you."

"You do—by being so sweet and patient with me. If it hadn't been for you I'd have ended the thing long ago. But now it's got to end." He rose suddenly, straightening himself with an effort. "You can't want to see me ridiculous."

She looked at him kindly. "That's just it." Then, after a moment's pondering, almost to her own surprise she broke out with a flash of inspiration: "Well, go over and see Mr. Selden. You'll have time to do it before dinner."

"Oh, *dinner*—" he mocked her; but she left him with the smiling rejoinder: "Dinner on board, remember; we'll put it off till nine if you like."

It was past four already; and when a cab had dropped her at the quay, and she stood waiting for the gig to put off for her, she began to wonder what had been happening on the yacht. Of Silverton's whereabouts there had been no mention. Had he returned to the Sabrina? Or could Bertha—the dread alternative sprang on her suddenly—could Bertha, left to herself, have gone ashore to rejoin him? Lily's heart stood still at the thought. All her concern had hitherto been for young Silverton, not only because, in such affairs, the woman's instinct is to side with the man, but because his case made a peculiar appeal to her sympathies. He was so desperately in earnest, poor youth, and his earnestness was of so different a quality from Bertha's, though hers too was desperate enough. The difference was that Bertha was in earnest only about herself, while he was in earnest about her. But now, at the actual crisis, this difference seemed to throw the weight of destitution on Bertha's side, since at least he had her to suffer for, and she had only herself. At any rate, viewed less ideally, all the disadvantages of such a situation were for the woman; and it was to Bertha that Lily's sympathies now went out. She was not fond of Bertha Dorset, but neither was she without a sense of obligation, the heavier for having so little personal liking to sustain it. Bertha had been kind to her, they had lived together, during the last months, on terms of easy friendship, and the sense of friction of which Lily had recently become aware seemed to make it the more urgent that she should work undividedly in her friend's interest.

It was in Bertha's interest, certainly, that she had despatched Dorset to consult with Lawrence Selden. Once the grotesqueness of the situation accepted, she had seen at a glance that it was the safest in which Dorset could find himself. Who but Selden could thus miraculously combine the skill to save Bertha with the obligation of doing so? The consciousness that much skill would be required made Lily rest thankfully in the greatness of the obligation. Since he would *have* to pull Bertha through she could trust him to find a way; and she put the fulness of her trust in the telegram she managed to send him on her way to the quay.

Thus far, then, Lily felt that she had done well; and the conviction strengthened her for the task that remained. She and Bertha had never been on confidential terms, but at such a crisis the barriers of reserve must surely fall: Dorset's wild allusions to the scene of the morning made Lily feel that they were down already, and that any attempt to rebuild them would be beyond Bertha's strength. She pictured the poor creature shivering behind her fallen defences and awaiting with suspense the moment when she could take refuge in the first shelter that offered. If only that shelter had not already offered itself elsewhere! As the gig traversed the short distance between the quay and the yacht, Lily grew more than ever alarmed at the possible consequences of her long absence. What if the wretched Bertha, finding in all the long hours no soul to turn to—but by this time Lily's eager foot was on the side-ladder, and her first step on the Sabrina showed the worst of her apprehensions to be unfounded; for there, in the luxurious shade of the after-deck, the wretched Bertha, in full command of her usual attenuated elegance, sat dispensing tea to the Duchess of Beltshire and Lord Hubert.

The sight filled Lily with such surprise that she felt that Bertha, at least, must read its meaning in her look, and she was proportionately disconcerted by the blankness of the look returned. But in an instant she saw that Mrs. Dorset had, of necessity, to look blank before the others, and that, to mitigate the effect of her own surprise, she must at once produce some simple reason for it. The long habit of rapid transitions made it easy for her to exclaim to the Duchess: "Why, I thought you'd gone back to the Princess!" and this sufficed for the lady she addressed, if it was hardly enough for Lord Hubert.

At least it opened the way to a lively explanation of how the Duchess was, in fact, going back the next moment, but had first rushed out to the yacht for a word with Mrs. Dorset on the subject of tomorrow's dinner—the dinner with the Brys, to which Lord Hubert had finally insisted on dragging them.

"To save my neck, you know!" he explained, with a glance that appealed to Lily for some recognition of his promptness; and the Duchess added, with her noble candour: "Mr. Bry has promised him a tip, and he says if we go he'll pass it onto us."

This led to some final pleasantries, in which, as it seemed to Lily, Mrs. Dorset bore her part with astounding bravery, and at the close of which Lord Hubert, from half way down the side-ladder, called back, with an air of numbering heads: "And of course we may count on Dorset too?"

"Oh, count on him," his wife assented gaily. She was keeping up well to the last—but as she turned back from waving her adieux over the side, Lily said to herself that the mask must drop and the soul of fear look out.

Mrs. Dorset turned back slowly; perhaps she wanted time to steady her muscles; at any rate, they were still under perfect control when, dropping once more into her seat behind the tea-table, she remarked to Miss Bart with a faint touch of irony: "I suppose I ought to say good morning."

If it was a cue, Lily was ready to take it, though with only the vaguest sense of what was expected of her in return. There was something unnerving in the contemplation of Mrs. Dorset's composure, and she had to force the light tone in which she answered: "I tried to see you this morning, but you were not yet up."

"No—I got to bed late. After we missed you at the station I thought we ought to wait for you till the last train." She spoke very gently, but with just the least tinge of reproach.

"You missed us? You waited for us at the station?" Now indeed Lily was too far adrift in bewilderment to measure the other's words or keep watch on her own. "But I thought you didn't get to the station till after the last train had left!"

Mrs. Dorset, examining her between lowered lids, met this with the immediate query: "Who told you that?"

"George—I saw him just now in the gardens."

"Ah, is that George's version? Poor George—he was in no state to remember what I told him. He had one of his worst attacks this morning, and I packed him off to see the doctor. Do you know if he found him?"

Lily, still lost in conjecture, made no reply, and Mrs. Dorset settled herself indolently in her seat. "He'll wait to see him; he was horribly frightened about himself. It's very bad for him to be worried, and whenever anything upsetting happens, it always brings on an attack."

This time Lily felt sure that a cue was being pressed on her; but it was put forth with such startling suddenness, and with so incredible an air of ignoring what it led up to, that she could only falter out doubtfully: "Anything upsetting?"

"Yes—such as having you so conspicuously on his hands in the small hours. You know, my dear, you're rather a big responsibility in such a scandalous place after midnight."

At that—at the complete unexpectedness and the inconceivable audacity of it—Lily could not restrain the tribute of an astonished laugh.

"Well, really—considering it was you who burdened him with the responsibility!"

Mrs. Dorset took this with an exquisite mildness. "By not having the superhuman cleverness to discover you in that frightful rush for the train? Or the imagination to believe that you'd take it without us—you and he all alone—instead of waiting quietly in the station till we *did* manage to meet you?"

Lily's colour rose: it was growing clear to her that Bertha was pursuing an object, following a line she had marked out for herself. Only, with such a doom impending, why waste time in these childish efforts to avert it? The puerility of the attempt disarmed Lily's indignation: did it not prove how horribly the poor creature was frightened?

"No; by our simply all keeping together at Nice," she returned.

"Keeping together? When it was you who seized the first opportunity to rush off with the Duchess and her friends? My dear Lily, you are not a child to be led by the hand!"

"No—nor to be lectured, Bertha, really; if that's what you are doing to me now."

Mrs. Dorset smiled on her reproachfully. "Lecture you—I? Heaven forbid! I was merely trying to give you a friendly hint. But it's usually the other way round, isn't it? I'm expected to take hints, not to give them: I've positively lived on them all these last months."

"Hints—from me to you?" Lily repeated.

"Oh, negative ones merely—what not to be and to do and to see. And I think I've taken them to admiration. Only, my dear, if you'll let me say so, I didn't understand that one of my negative duties was *not* to warn you when you carried your imprudence too far."

A chill of fear passed over Miss Bart: a sense of remembered treachery that was like the gleam of a knife in the dusk. But compassion, in a moment, got the better of her instinctive recoil. What was this outpouring of senseless bitterness but the tracked creature's attempt to cloud the medium through which it was fleeing? It was on Lily's lips to exclaim: "You poor soul, don't double and turn—come straight back to me, and we'll find a way out!" But the words died under the impenetrable insolence of Bertha's smile. Lily sat silent, taking the brunt of it quietly, letting it spend itself on her to the last drop of its accumulated falseness; then, without a word, she rose and went down to her cabin.

# Chapter 3

Miss Bart's telegram caught Lawrence Selden at the door of his hotel; and having read it, he turned back to wait for Dorset. The message necessarily left large gaps for conjecture; but all that he had recently heard and seen made these but too easy to fill in. On the whole he was surprised; for though he had perceived that the situation contained all the elements of an explosion, he had often enough, in the range of his personal experience, seen just such combinations subside into harmlessness. Still, Dorset's spasmodic temper, and his wife's reckless disregard of appearances, gave the situation a peculiar insecurity; and it was less from the sense of any special relation to the case than from a purely professional zeal, that Selden resolved to guide the pair to safety. Whether, in the present instance, safety for either lay in repairing so damaged a tie, it was no business of his to consider: he had only, on general principles, to think of averting a scandal, and his desire to avert it was increased by his fear of its involving Miss Bart. There was nothing specific in this apprehension; he merely wished to spare her the embarrassment of being ever so remotely connected with the public washing of the Dorset linen.

How exhaustive and unpleasant such a process would be, he saw even more vividly after his two hours' talk with poor Dorset. If anything came out at all, it would be such a vast unpacking of accumulated moral rags as left him, after his visitor had gone, with the feeling that he must fling open the windows and have his room swept out. But nothing should come out; and happily for his side of the case, the dirty rags, however pieced together, could not, without considerable difficulty, be turned into a homogeneous grievance. The torn edges did not always fit—there were missing bits, there were disparities of size and colour, all of which it was naturally Selden's business to make the most of in putting them under his client's eye. But to a man in Dorset's mood the completest demonstration could not carry conviction, and Selden saw that for the moment all he could do was to soothe and temporize, to offer sympathy and to counsel prudence. He let Dorset depart charged to the brim with the sense that, till their next meeting, he must maintain a strictly noncommittal attitude; that, in short, his share in the game consisted for the present in looking on. Selden knew, however, that he could not long keep such violences in equilibrium; and he promised to meet Dorset, the next morning, at an hotel in Monte Carlo. Meanwhile he counted not a little on the reaction of weakness and self-distrust that, in such natures, follows on every unwonted expenditure of moral force; and his telegraphic reply to Miss Bart consisted simply in the injunction: "Assume that everything is as usual."

On this assumption, in fact, the early part of the following day was lived through. Dorset, as if in obedience to Lily's imperative bidding, had actually returned in time for a late dinner on the yacht. The repast had been the most difficult moment of the day. Dorset was sunk in one of the abysmal silences which so commonly followed on what his wife called his "attacks" that it was easy, before the servants, to refer it to this cause; but Bertha herself seemed, perversely enough, little disposed to make use of this obvious means of protection. She simply left the brunt of the situation on her husband's hands, as if too absorbed in a grievance of her own to suspect that she might be the object of one herself. To Lily this attitude was the most ominous, because the most perplexing, element in the situation. As she tried to fan the weak flicker of talk, to build up, again and again, the crumbling structure of "appearances," her own attention was perpetually distracted by the question: "What on earth can she be driving at?" There was something positively exasperating in Bertha's attitude of isolated defiance. If only she would have given her friend a hint they might still have worked together successfully; but how could Lily be of use, while she was thus obstinately shut out from participation? To be of use was what she honestly wanted; and not for her own sake but for the Dorsets'. She had not thought of her own situation at all: she was simply engrossed in trying to put a little order in theirs. But the close of the short dreary evening left her with a sense of effort hopelessly wasted. She had not tried to see Dorset alone: she had positively shrunk from a renewal of his confidences. It was Bertha whose confidence she sought, and who should as eagerly have invited her own; and Bertha, as if in the infatuation of self-destruction, was actually pushing away her rescuing hand.

Lily, going to bed early, had left the couple to themselves; and it seemed part of the general mystery in which she moved that more than an hour should elapse before she heard Bertha walk down the silent passage and regain her room. The morrow, rising on an apparent continuance of the same conditions, revealed nothing of what had occurred between the confronted pair. One fact alone outwardly proclaimed the change they were all conspiring to ignore; and that was the non-appearance of Ned Silverton. No one referred to it, and this tacit avoidance of the subject kept it in the immediate foreground of consciousness. But there was another change, perceptible only to Lily; and that was that Dorset now avoided her almost as pointedly as his wife. Perhaps he was repenting his rash outpourings of the previous day; perhaps only trying, in his clumsy way, to conform to Selden's counsel to behave "as usual." Such instructions no more make for easiness of attitude than the photographer's behest to "look natural"; and in a creature as unconscious as poor Dorset of the appearance he habitually presented, the struggle to maintain a pose was sure to result in queer contortions.

It resulted, at any rate, in throwing Lily strangely on her own resources. She had learned, on leaving her room, that Mrs. Dorset was still invisible, and that Dorset had left the yacht early; and feeling too restless to remain alone, she too had herself ferried ashore. Straying toward the Casino, she attached herself to a group of acquaintances from Nice, with whom she lunched, and in whose company she was returning to the rooms when she encountered Selden crossing the square. She could not, at the moment, separate herself definitely from her party, who had hospitably assumed that she would remain with them till they took their departure; but she found time for a momentary pause of enquiry, to which he promptly returned: "I've seen him again—he's just left me."

She waited before him anxiously. "Well? what has happened? What *will* happen?"

"Nothing as yet—and nothing in the future, I think."

"It's over, then? It's settled? You're sure?"

He smiled. "Give me time. I'm not sure—but I'm a good deal surer." And with that she had to content herself, and hasten on to the expectant group on the steps.

Selden had in fact given her the utmost measure of his sureness, had even stretched it a shade to meet the anxiety in her eyes. And now, as he turned away, strolling down the hill toward the station, that anxiety remained with him as the visible justification of his own. It was not, indeed, anything specific that he feared: there had been a literal truth in his declaration that he did not think anything would happen. What troubled him was that, though Dorset's attitude had perceptibly changed, the change was not clearly to be accounted for. It had certainly not been produced by Selden's arguments, or by the action of his own soberer reason. Five minutes' talk sufficed to show that some alien influence had been at work, and that it had not so much subdued his resentment as weakened his will, so that he moved under it in a state of apathy, like a dangerous lunatic who has been drugged. Temporarily, no doubt, however exerted, it worked for the general safety: the question was how long it would last, and by what kind of reaction it was likely to be followed. On these points Selden could gain no light; for he saw that one effect of the transformation had been to shut him off from free communion with Dorset. The latter, indeed, was still moved by the irresistible desire to discuss his wrong; but, though he revolved about it with the same forlorn tenacity, Selden was aware that something always restrained him from full expression. His state was one to produce first weariness and then impatience in his hearer; and when their talk was over, Selden began to feel that he had done his utmost, and might justifiably wash his hands of the sequel.

It was in this mind that he had been making his way back to the station when Miss Bart crossed his path; but though, after his brief word with her, he kept mechanically on his course, he was conscious of a gradual change in his purpose. The change had been produced by the look in her eyes; and in his eagerness to define the nature of that look, he dropped into a seat in the gardens, and sat brooding upon the question. It was natural enough, in all conscience, that she should appear anxious: a young woman placed, in the close intimacy of a yachting-cruise, between a couple on the verge of disaster, could hardly, aside from her concern for her friends, be insensible to the awkwardness of her own position. The worst of it was that, in interpreting Miss Bart's state of mind, so many alternative readings were possible; and one of these, in Selden's troubled mind, took the ugly form suggested by Mrs. Fisher. If the girl was afraid, was she afraid for herself or for her friends? And to what degree was her dread of a catastrophe intensified by the sense of being fatally involved in it? The burden of offence lying manifestly with Mrs. Dorset, this conjecture seemed on the face of it gratuitously unkind; but Selden knew that in the most one-sided matrimonial quarrel there are generally counter-charges to be brought, and that they are brought with the greater audacity where the original grievance is so emphatic. Mrs. Fisher had not hesitated to suggest the likelihood of Dorset's marrying Miss Bart if "anything happened"; and though Mrs. Fisher's conclusions were notoriously rash, she was shrewd enough in reading the signs from which they were drawn. Dorset had apparently shown marked interest in the girl, and this interest might be used to cruel advantage in his wife's struggle for rehabilitation. Selden knew that Bertha would fight to the last round of powder: the rashness of her conduct was illogically combined with a cold determination to escape its consequences. She could be as unscrupulous in fighting for herself as she was reckless in courting danger, and whatever came to her hand at such moments was likely to be used as a defensive missile. He did not, as yet, see clearly just what course she was likely to take, but his perplexity increased his apprehension, and with it the sense that, before leaving, he must speak again with Miss Bart. Whatever her share in the situation—and he had always honestly tried to resist judging her by her surroundings—however free she might be from any personal connection with it, she would be better out of the way of a possible crash; and since she had appealed to him for help, it was clearly his business to tell her so.

This decision at last brought him to his feet, and carried him back to the gambling rooms, within whose doors he had seen her disappearing; but a prolonged exploration of the crowd failed to put him on her traces. He saw instead, to his surprise, Ned Silverton loitering somewhat ostentatiously about the tables; and the discovery that this actor in the drama was not only hovering in the wings, but actually inviting the exposure of the footlights, though it might have seemed to imply that all peril was over, served rather to deepen Selden's sense of foreboding. Charged with this impression he returned to the square, hoping to see Miss Bart move across it, as every one in Monte Carlo seemed inevitably to do at least a dozen times a day; but here again he waited vainly for a glimpse of her, and the conclusion was slowly forced on him that she had gone back to the Sabrina. It would be difficult to follow her there, and still more difficult, should he do so, to contrive the opportunity for a private word; and he had almost decided on the unsatisfactory alternative of writing, when the ceaseless diorama of the square suddenly unrolled before him the figures of Lord Hubert and Mrs. Bry.

Hailing them at once with his question, he learned from Lord Hubert that Miss Bart had just returned to the Sabrina in Dorset's company; an announcement so evidently disconcerting to him that Mrs. Bry, after a glance from her companion, which seemed to act like the pressure on a spring, brought forth the prompt proposal that he should come and meet his friends at dinner that evening—"At Becassin's—a little dinner to the Duchess," she flashed out before Lord Hubert had time to remove the pressure.

Selden's sense of the privilege of being included in such company brought him early in the evening to the door of the restaurant, where he paused to scan the ranks of diners approaching down the brightly lit terrace. There, while the Brys hovered within over the last agitating alternatives of the *menu*, he kept watch for the guests from the Sabrina, who at length rose on the horizon in company with the Duchess, Lord and Lady Skiddaw and the Stepneys. From this group it was easy for him to detach Miss Bart on the pretext of a moment's glance into one of the brilliant shops along the terrace, and to say to her, while they lingered together in the white dazzle of a jeweller's window: "I stopped over to see you—to beg of you to leave the yacht."

The eyes she turned on him showed a quick gleam of her former fear. "To leave—? What do you mean? What has happened?"

"Nothing. But if anything should, why be in the way of it?"

The glare from the jeweller's window, deepening the pallour of her face, gave to its delicate lines the sharpness of a tragic mask. "Nothing will, I am sure; but while there's even a doubt left, how can you think I would leave Bertha?"

The words rang out on a note of contempt—was it possibly of contempt for himself? Well, he was willing to risk its renewal to the extent of insisting, with an undeniable throb of added interest: "You have yourself to think of, you know—" to which, with a strange fall of sadness in her voice, she answered, meeting his eyes: "If you knew how little difference that makes!"

"Oh, well, nothing *will* happen," he said, more for his own reassurance than for hers; and "Nothing, nothing, of course!" she valiantly assented, as they turned to overtake their companions.

In the thronged restaurant, taking their places about Mrs. Bry's illuminated board, their confidence seemed to gain support from the familiarity of their surroundings. Here were Dorset and his wife once more presenting their customary faces to the world, she engrossed in establishing her relation with an intensely new gown, he shrinking with dyspeptic dread from the multiplied solicitations of the MENU. The mere fact that they thus showed themselves together, with the utmost openness the place afforded, seemed to declare beyond a doubt that their differences were composed. How this end had been attained was still matter for wonder, but it was clear that for the moment Miss Bart rested confidently in the result; and Selden tried to achieve the same view by telling himself that her opportunities for observation had been ampler than his own.

Meanwhile, as the dinner advanced through a labyrinth of courses, in which it became clear that Mrs. Bry had occasionally broken away from Lord Hubert's restraining hand, Selden's general watchfulness began to lose itself in a particular study of Miss Bart. It was one of the days when she was so handsome that to be handsome was enough, and all the rest—her grace, her quickness, her social felicities—seemed the overflow of a bounteous nature. But what especially struck him was the way in which she detached herself, by a hundred undefinable shades, from the persons who most abounded in her own style. It was in just such company, the fine flower and complete expression of the state she aspired to, that the differences came out with special poignancy, her grace cheapening the other women's smartness as her finely-discriminated silences made their chatter dull. The strain of the last hours had restored to her face the deeper eloquence which Selden had lately missed in it, and the bravery of her words to him still fluttered in her voice and eyes. Yes, she was matchless—it was the one word for her; and he could give his admiration the freer play because so little personal feeling remained in it. His real detachment from her had taken place, not at the lurid moment of disenchantment, but now, in the sober after-light of discrimination, where he saw her definitely divided from him by the crudeness of a choice which seemed to deny the very differences he felt in her. It was before him again in its completeness—the choice in which she was content to rest: in the stupid costliness of the food and the showy dulness of the talk, in the freedom of speech which never arrived at wit and the freedom of act which never made for romance. The strident setting of the restaurant, in which their table seemed set apart in a special glare of publicity, and the presence at it of little Dabham of the "Riviera Notes," emphasized the ideals of a world where conspicuousness passed for distinction, and the society column had become the roll of fame.

It was as the immortalizer of such occasions that little Dabham, wedged in modest watchfulness between two brilliant neighbours, suddenly became the centre of Selden's scrutiny. How much did he know of what was going on, and how much, for his purpose, was still worth finding out? His little eyes were like tentacles thrown out to catch the floating intimations with which, to Selden, the air at moments seemed thick; then again it cleared to its normal emptiness, and he could see nothing in it for the journalist but leisure to note the elegance of the ladies' gowns. Mrs. Dorset's, in particular, challenged all the wealth of Mr. Dabham's vocabulary: it had surprises and subtleties worthy of what he would have called "the literary style." At first, as Selden had noticed, it had been almost too preoccupying to its wearer; but now she was in full command of it, and was even producing her effects with unwonted freedom. Was she not, indeed, too free, too fluent, for perfect naturalness? And was not Dorset, to whom his glance had passed by a natural transition, too jerkily wavering between the same extremes? Dorset indeed was always jerky; but it seemed to Selden that tonight each vibration swung him farther from his centre.

The dinner, meanwhile, was moving to its triumphant close, to the evident satisfaction of Mrs. Bry, who, throned in apoplectic majesty between Lord Skiddaw and Lord Hubert, seemed in spirit to be calling on Mrs. Fisher to witness her achievement. Short of Mrs. Fisher her audience might have been called complete; for the restaurant was crowded with persons mainly gathered there for the purpose of spectatorship, and accurately posted as to the names and faces of the celebrities they had come to see. Mrs. Bry, conscious that all her feminine guests came under that heading, and that each one looked her part to admiration, shone on Lily with all the pent-up gratitude that Mrs. Fisher had failed to deserve. Selden, catching the glance, wondered what part Miss Bart had played in organizing the entertainment. She did, at least, a great deal to adorn it; and as he watched the bright security with which she bore herself, he smiled to think that he should have fancied her in need of help. Never had she appeared more serenely mistress of the situation than when, at the moment of dispersal, detaching herself a little from the group about the table, she turned with a smile and a graceful slant of the shoulders to receive her cloak from Dorset.

The dinner had been protracted over Mr. Bry's exceptional cigars and a bewildering array of liqueurs, and many of the other tables were empty; but a sufficient number of diners still lingered to give relief to the leave-taking of Mrs. Bry's distinguished guests. This ceremony was drawn out and complicated by the fact that it involved, on the part of the Duchess and Lady Skiddaw, definite farewells, and pledges of speedy reunion in Paris, where they were to pause and replenish their wardrobes on the way to England. The quality of Mrs. Bry's hospitality, and of the tips her husband had presumably imparted, lent to the manner of the English ladies a general effusiveness which shed the rosiest light over their hostess's future. In its glow Mrs. Dorset and the Stepneys were also visibly included, and the whole scene had touches of intimacy worth their weight in gold to the watchful pen of Mr. Dabham.

A glance at her watch caused the Duchess to exclaim to her sister that they had just time to dash for their train, and the flurry of this departure over, the Stepneys, who had their motor at the door, offered to convey the Dorsets and Miss Bart to the quay. The offer was accepted, and Mrs. Dorset moved away with her husband in attendance. Miss Bart had lingered for a last word with Lord Hubert, and Stepney, on whom Mr. Bry was pressing a final, and still more expensive, cigar, called out: "Come on, Lily, if you're going back to the yacht."

Lily turned to obey; but as she did so, Mrs. Dorset, who had paused on her way out, moved a few steps back toward the table.

"Miss Bart is not going back to the yacht," she said in a voice of singular distinctness.

A startled look ran from eye to eye; Mrs. Bry crimsoned to the verge of congestion, Mrs. Stepney slipped nervously behind her husband, and Selden, in the general turmoil of his sensations, was mainly conscious of a longing to grip Dabham by the collar and fling him out into the street.

Dorset, meanwhile, had stepped back to his wife's side. His face was white, and he looked about him with cowed angry eyes. "Bertha!—Miss Bart . . . this is some misunderstanding . . . some mistake . . ."

"Miss Bart remains here," his wife rejoined incisively. "And, I think, George, we had better not detain Mrs. Stepney any longer."

Miss Bart, during this brief exchange of words, remained in admirable erectness, slightly isolated from the embarrassed group about her. She had paled a little under the shock of the insult, but the discomposure of the surrounding faces was not reflected in her own. The faint disdain of her smile seemed to lift her high above her antagonist's reach, and it was not till she had given Mrs. Dorset the full measure of the distance between them that she turned and extended her hand to her hostess.

"I am joining the Duchess tomorrow," she explained, "and it seemed easier for me to remain on shore for the night."

She held firmly to Mrs. Bry's wavering eye while she gave this explanation, but when it was over Selden saw her send a tentative glance from one to another of the women's faces. She read their incredulity in their averted looks, and in the mute wretchedness of the men behind them, and for a miserable half-second he thought she quivered on the brink of failure. Then, turning to him with an easy gesture, and the pale bravery of her recovered smile—"Dear Mr. Selden," she said, "you promised to see me to my cab."

Outside, the sky was gusty and overcast, and as Lily and Selden moved toward the deserted gardens below the restaurant, spurts of warm rain blew fitfully against their faces. The fiction of the cab had been tacitly abandoned; they walked on in silence, her hand on his arm, till the deeper shade of the gardens received them, and pausing beside a bench, he said: "Sit down a moment."

She dropped to the seat without answering, but the electric lamp at the bend of the path shed a gleam on the struggling misery of her face. Selden sat down beside her, waiting for her to speak, fearful lest any word he chose should touch too roughly on her wound, and kept also from free utterance by the wretched doubt which had slowly renewed itself within him. What had brought her to this pass? What weakness had placed her so abominably at her enemy's mercy? And why should Bertha Dorset have turned into an enemy at the very moment when she so obviously needed the support of her sex? Even while his nerves raged at the subjection of husbands to their wives, and at the cruelty of women to their kind, reason obstinately harped on the proverbial relation between smoke and fire. The memory of Mrs. Fisher's hints, and the corroboration of his own impressions, while they deepened his pity also increased his constraint, since, whichever way he sought a free outlet for sympathy, it was blocked by the fear of committing a blunder.

Suddenly it struck him that his silence must seem almost as accusatory as that of the men he had despised for turning from her; but before he could find the fitting word she had cut him short with a question.

"Do you know of a quiet hotel? I can send for my maid in the morning."

"An hotel—*here*—that you can go to alone? It's not possible."

She met this with a pale gleam of her old playfulness. "What *is*, then? It's too wet to sleep in the gardens."

"But there must be some one—"

"Some one to whom I can go? Of course—any number—but at *this* hour? You see my change of plan was rather sudden—"

"Good God—if you'd listened to me!" he cried, venting his helplessness in a burst of anger.

She still held him off with the gentle mockery of her smile. "But haven't I?" she rejoined. "You advised me to leave the yacht, and I'm leaving it."

He saw then, with a pang of self-reproach, that she meant neither to explain nor to defend herself; that by his miserable silence he had forfeited all chance of helping her, and that the decisive hour was past.

She had risen, and stood before him in a kind of clouded majesty, like some deposed princess moving tranquilly to exile.

"Lily!" he exclaimed, with a note of despairing appeal; but—"Oh, not now," she gently admonished him; and then, in all the sweetness of her recovered composure: "Since I must find shelter somewhere, and since you're so kindly here to help me—"

He gathered himself up at the challenge. "You will do as I tell you? There's but one thing, then; you must go straight to your cousins, the Stepneys."

"Oh—" broke from her with a movement of instinctive resistance; but he insisted: "Come—it's late, and you must appear to have gone there directly."

He had drawn her hand into his arm, but she held him back with a last gesture of protest. "I can't—I can't—not that—you don't know Gwen: you mustn't ask me!"

"I *must* ask you—you must obey me," he persisted, though infected at heart by her own fear.

Her voice sank to a whisper: "And if she refuses?"—but, "Oh, trust me—trust me!" he could only insist in return; and yielding to his touch, she let him lead her back in silence to the edge of the square.

In the cab they continued to remain silent through the brief drive which carried them to the illuminated portals of the Stepneys' hotel. Here he left her outside, in the darkness of the raised hood, while his name was sent up to Stepney, and he paced the showy hall, awaiting the latter's descent. Ten minutes later the two men passed out together between the gold-laced custodians of the threshold; but in the vestibule Stepney drew up with a last flare of reluctance.

"It's understood, then?" he stipulated nervously, with his hand on Selden's arm. "She leaves tomorrow by the early train—and my wife's asleep, and can't be disturbed."

# Chapter 4

The blinds of Mrs. Peniston's drawing-room were drawn down against the oppressive June sun, and in the sultry twilight the faces of her assembled relatives took on a fitting shadow of bereavement. They were all there: Van Alstynes, Stepneys and Melsons—even a stray Peniston or two, indicating, by a greater latitude in dress and manner, the fact of remoter relationship and more settled hopes. The Peniston side was, in fact, secure in the knowledge that the bulk of Mr. Peniston-'s property "went back"; while the direct connection hung suspended on the disposal of his widow's private fortune and on the uncertainty of its extent. Jack Stepney, in his new character as the richest nephew, tacitly took the lead, emphasizing his importance by the deeper gloss of his mourning and the subdued authority of his manner; while his wife's bored attitude and frivolous gown proclaimed the heiress's disregard of the insignificant interests at stake. Old Ned Van Alstyne, seated next to her in a coat that made affliction dapper, twirled his white moustache to conceal the eager twitch of his lips; and Grace Stepney, red-nosed and smelling of crape, whispered emotionally to Mrs. Herbert Melson: "I couldn't *bear* to see the Niagara anywhere else!"

A rustle of weeds and quick turning of heads hailed the opening of the door, and Lily Bart appeared, tall and noble in her black dress, with Gerty Farish at her side. The women's faces, as she paused interrogatively on the threshold, were a study in hesitation. One or two made faint motions of recognition, which might have been subdued either by the solemnity of the scene, or by the doubt as to how far the others meant to go; Mrs. Jack Stepney gave a careless nod, and Grace Stepney, with a sepulchral gesture, indicated a seat at her side. But Lily, ignoring the invitation, as well as Jack Stepney's official attempt to direct her, moved across the room with her smooth free gait, and seated herself in a chair which seemed to have been purposely placed apart from the others.

It was the first time that she had faced her family since her return from Europe, two weeks earlier; but if she perceived any uncertainty in their welcome, it served only to add a tinge of irony to the usual composure of her bearing. The shock of dismay with which, on the dock, she had heard from Gerty Farish of Mrs. Peniston's sudden death, had been mitigated, almost at once, by the irrepressible thought that now, at last, she would be able to pay her debts. She had looked forward with considerable uneasiness to her first encounter with her aunt. Mrs. Peniston had vehemently opposed her niece's departure with the Dorsets, and had marked her continued disapproval by not writing during Lily's absence. The certainty that she had heard of the rupture with the Dorsets made the prospect of the meeting more formidable; and how should Lily have repressed a quick sense of relief at the thought that, instead of undergoing the anticipated ordeal, she had only to enter gracefully on a long-assured inheritance? It had been, in the consecrated phrase, "always understood" that Mrs. Peniston was to provide handsomely for her niece; and in the latter's mind the understanding had long since crystallized into fact.

"She gets everything, of course—I don't see what we're here for," Mrs. Jack Stepney remarked with careless loudness to Ned Van Alstyne; and the latter's deprecating murmur—"Julia was always a just woman"—might have been interpreted as signifying either acquiescence or doubt.

"Well, it's only about four hundred thousand," Mrs. Stepney rejoined with a yawn; and Grace Stepney, in the silence produced by the lawyer's preliminary cough, was heard to sob out: "They won't find a towel missing—I went over them with her the very day—"

Lily, oppressed by the close atmosphere, and the stifling odour of fresh mourning, felt her attention straying as Mrs. Peniston's lawyer, solemnly erect behind the Buhl table at the end of the room, began to rattle through the preamble of the will.

"It's like being in church," she reflected, wondering vaguely where Gwen Stepney had got such an awful hat. Then she noticed how stout Jack had grown—he would soon be almost as plethoric as Herbert Melson, who sat a few feet off, breathing puffily as he leaned his black-gloved hands on his stick.

"I wonder why rich people always grow fat—I suppose it's because there's nothing to worry them. If I inherit, I shall have to be careful of my figure," she mused, while the lawyer droned on through a labyrinth of legacies. The servants came first, then a few charitable institutions, then several remoter Melsons and Stepneys, who stirred consciously as their names rang out, and then subsided into a state of impassiveness befitting the solemnity of the occasion. Ned Van Alstyne, Jack Stepney, and a cousin or two followed, each coupled with the mention of a few thousands: Lily wondered that Grace Stepney was not among them. Then she heard her own name—"to my niece Lily Bart ten thousand dollars—" and after that the lawyer again lost himself in a coil of unintelligible periods, from which the concluding phrase flashed out with startling distinctness: "and the residue of my estate to my dear cousin and name-sake, Grace Julia Stepney."

There was a subdued gasp of surprise, a rapid turning of heads, and a surging of sable figures toward the corner in which Miss Stepney wailed out her sense of unworthiness through the crumpled ball of a black-edged handkerchief.

Lily stood apart from the general movement, feeling herself for the first time utterly alone. No one looked at her, no one seemed aware of her presence; she was probing the very depths of insignificance. And under her sense of the collective indifference came the acuter pang of hopes deceived. Disinherited—she had been disinherited—and for Grace Stepney! She met Gerty's lamentable eyes, fixed on her in a despairing effort at consolation, and the look brought her to herself. There was something to be done before she left the house: to be done with all the nobility she knew how to put into such gestures. She advanced to the group about Miss Stepney, and holding out her hand said simply: "Dear Grace, I am so glad."

The other ladies had fallen back at her approach, and a space created itself about her. It widened as she turned to go, and no one advanced to fill it up. She paused a moment, glancing about her, calmly taking the measure of her situation. She heard some one ask a question about the date of the will; she caught a fragment of the lawyer's answer—something about a sudden summons, and an "earlier instrument." Then the tide of dispersal began to drift past her; Mrs. Jack Stepney and Mrs. Herbert Melson stood on the doorstep awaiting their motor; a sympathizing group escorted Grace Stepney to the cab it was felt to be fitting she should take, though she lived but a street or two away; and Miss Bart and Gerty found themselves almost alone in the purple drawing-room, which more than ever, in its stuffy dimness, resembled a well-kept family vault, in which the last corpse had just been decently deposited.

In Gerty Farish's sitting-room, whither a hansom had carried the two friends, Lily dropped into a chair with a faint sound of laughter: it struck her as a humorous coincidence that her aunt's legacy should so nearly represent the amount of her debt to Trenor. The need of discharging that debt had reasserted itself with increased urgency since her return to America, and she spoke her first thought in saying to the anxiously hovering Gerty: "I wonder when the legacies will be paid."

But Miss Farish could not pause over the legacies; she broke into a larger indignation. "Oh, Lily, it's unjust; it's cruel—Grace Stepney must *feel* she has no right to all that money!"

"Any one who knew how to please Aunt Julia has a right to her money," Miss Bart rejoined philosophically.

"But she was devoted to you—she led every one to think—" Gerty checked herself in evident embarrassment, and Miss Bart turned to her with a direct look. "Gerty, be honest: this will was made only six weeks ago. She had heard of my break with the Dorsets?"

"Every one heard, of course, that there had been some disagreement—some misunderstanding—"

"Did she hear that Bertha turned me off the yacht?"

"Lily!"

"That was what happened, you know. She said I was trying to marry George Dorset. She did it to make him think she was jealous. Isn't that what she told Gwen Stepney?"

"I don't know—I don't listen to such horrors."

"I *must* listen to them—I must know where I stand." She paused, and again sounded a faint note of derision. "Did you notice the women? They were afraid to snub me while they thought I was going to get the money—afterward they scuttled off as if I had the plague." Gerty remained silent, and she continued: "I stayed on to see what would happen. They took their cue from Gwen Stepney and Lulu Melson—I saw them watching to see what Gwen would do.—Gerty, I must know just what is being said of me."

"I tell you I don't listen—"

"One hears such things without listening." She rose and laid her resolute hands on Miss Farish's shoulders. "Gerty, are people going to cut me?"

"Your *friends*, Lily—how can you think it?"

"Who are one's friends at such a time? Who, but you, you poor trustful darling? And heaven knows what *you* suspect me of!" She kissed Gerty with a whimsical murmur. "You'd never let it make any difference—but then you're fond of criminals, Gerty! How about the irreclaimable ones, though? For I'm absolutely impenitent, you know."

She drew herself up to the full height of her slender majesty, towering like some dark angel of defiance above the troubled Gerty, who could only falter out: "Lily, Lily—how can you laugh about such things?"

"So as not to weep, perhaps. But no—I'm not of the tearful order. I discovered early that crying makes my nose red, and the knowledge has helped me through several painful episodes." She took a restless turn about the room, and then, reseating herself, lifted the bright mockery of her eyes to Gerty's anxious countenance.

"I shouldn't have minded, you know, if I'd got the money—" and at Miss Farish's protesting "Oh!" she repeated calmly: "Not a straw, my dear; for, in the first place, they wouldn't have quite dared to ignore me; and if they had, it wouldn't have mattered, because I should have been independent of them. But now—!" The irony faded from her eyes, and she bent a clouded face upon her friend.

"How can you talk so, Lily? Of course the money ought to have been yours, but after all that makes no difference. The important thing—" Gerty paused, and then continued firmly: "The important thing is that you should clear yourself—should tell your friends the whole truth."

"The whole truth?" Miss Bart laughed. "What is truth? Where a woman is concerned, it's the story that's easiest to believe. In this case it's a great deal easier to believe Bertha Dorset's story than mine, because she has a big house and an opera box, and it's convenient to be on good terms with her."

Miss Farish still fixed her with an anxious gaze. "But what IS your story, Lily? I don't believe any one knows it yet."

"My story?—I don't believe I know it myself. You see I never thought of preparing a version in advance as Bertha did—and if I had, I don't think I should take the trouble to use it now."

But Gerty continued with her quiet reasonableness: "I don't want a version prepared in advance—but I want you to tell me exactly what happened from the beginning."

"From the beginning?" Miss Bart gently mimicked her. "Dear Gerty, how little imagination you good people have! Why, the beginning was in my cradle, I suppose—in the way I was brought up, and the things I was taught to care for. Or no—I won't blame anybody for my faults: I'll say it was in my blood, that I got it from some wicked pleasure-loving ancestress, who reacted against the homely virtues of New Amsterdam, and wanted to be back at the court of the Charleses!" And as Miss Farish continued to press her with troubled eyes, she went on impatiently: "You asked me just now for the truth—well, the truth about any girl is that once she's talked about she's done for; and the more she explains her case the worse it looks.—My good Gerty, you don't happen to have a cigarette about you?"

In her stuffy room at the hotel to which she had gone on landing, Lily Bart that evening reviewed her situation. It was the last week in June, and none of her friends were in town. The few relatives who had stayed on, or returned, for the reading of Mrs. Peniston's will, had taken flight again that afternoon to Newport or Long Island; and not one of them had made any proffer of hospitality to Lily. For the first time in her life she found herself utterly alone except for Gerty Farish. Even at the actual moment of her break with the Dorsets she had not had so keen a sense of its consequences, for the Duchess of Beltshire, hearing of the catastrophe from Lord Hubert, had instantly offered her protection, and under her sheltering wing Lily had made an almost triumphant progress to London. There she had been sorely tempted to linger on in a society which asked of her only to amuse and charm it, without enquiring too curiously how she had acquired her gift for doing so; but Selden, before they parted, had pressed on her the urgent need of returning at once to her aunt, and Lord Hubert, when he presently reappeared in London, abounded in the same counsel. Lily did not need to be told that the Duchess's championship was not the best road to social rehabilitation, and as she was besides aware that her noble defender might at any moment drop her in favour of a new *protegee*, she reluctantly decided to return to America. But she had not been ten minutes on her native shore before she realized that she had delayed too long to regain it. The Dorsets, the Stepneys, the Brys—all the actors and witnesses in the miserable drama—had preceded her with their version of the case; and, even had she seen the least chance of gaining a hearing for her own, some obscure disdain and reluctance would have restrained her. She knew it was not by explanations and counter-charges that she could ever hope to recover her lost standing;

but even had she felt the least trust in their efficacy, she would still have been held back by the feeling which had kept her from defending herself to Gerty Farish—a feeling that was half pride and half humiliation. For though she knew she had been ruthlessly sacrificed to Bertha Dorset's determination to win back her husband, and though her own relation to Dorset had been that of the merest good-fellowship, yet she had been perfectly aware from the outset that her part in the affair was, as Carry Fisher brutally put it, to distract Dorset's attention from his wife. That was what she was "there for": it was the price she had chosen to pay for three months of luxury and freedom from care. Her habit of resolutely facing the facts, in her rare moments of introspection, did not now allow her to put any false gloss on the situation. She had suffered for the very faithfulness with which she had carried out her part of the tacit compact, but the part was not a handsome one at best, and she saw it now in all the ugliness of failure.

She saw, too, in the same uncompromising light, the train of consequences resulting from that failure; and these became clearer to her with every day of her weary lingering in town. She stayed on partly for the comfort of Gerty Farish's nearness, and partly for lack of knowing where to go. She understood well enough the nature of the task before her. She must set out to regain, little by little, the position she had lost; and the first step in the tedious task was to find out, as soon as possible, on how many of her friends she could count. Her hopes were mainly centred on Mrs. Trenor, who had treasures of easy-going tolerance for those who were amusing or useful to her, and in the noisy rush of whose existence the still small voice of detraction was slow to make itself heard. But Judy, though she must have been apprised of Miss Bart's return, had not even recognized it by the formal note of condolence which her friend's bereavement demanded. Any advance on Lily's side might have been perilous: there was nothing to do but to trust to the happy chance of an accidental meeting, and Lily knew that, even so late in the season, there was always a hope of running across her friends in their frequent passages through town.

To this end she assiduously showed herself at the restaurants they frequented, where, attended by the troubled Gerty, she lunched luxuriously, as she said, on her expectations.

"My dear Gerty, you wouldn't have me let the head-waiter see that I've nothing to live on but Aunt Julia's legacy? Think of Grace Stepney's satisfaction if she came in and found us lunching on cold mutton and tea! What sweet shall we have today, Dear—*Coupe Jacques* or *Peches a La Melba?*"

She dropped the *menu* abruptly, with a quick heightening of colour, and Gerty, following her glance, was aware of the advance, from an inner room, of a party headed by Mrs. Trenor and Carry Fisher. It was impossible for these ladies and their companions—among whom Lily had at once distinguished both Trenor and Rosedale—not to pass, in going out, the table at which the two girls were seated; and Gerty's sense of the fact betrayed itself in the helpless trepidation of her manner. Miss Bart, on the contrary, borne forward on the wave of her buoyant grace, and neither shrinking from her friends nor appearing to lie in wait for them, gave to the encounter the touch of naturalness which she could impart to the most strained situations. Such embarrassment as was shown was on Mrs. Trenor's side, and manifested itself in the mingling of exaggerated warmth with imperceptible reservations. Her loudly affirmed pleasure at seeing Miss Bart took the form of a nebulous generalization, which included neither enquiries as to her future nor the expression of a definite wish to see her again. Lily, well-versed in the language of these omissions, knew that they were equally intelligible to the other members of the party: even Rosedale, flushed as he was with the importance of keeping such company, at once took the temperature of Mrs. Trenor's cordiality, and reflected it in his off-hand greeting of Miss Bart. Trenor, red and uncomfortable, had cut short his salutations on the pretext of a word to say to the head-waiter; and the rest of the group soon melted away in Mrs. Trenor's wake.

It was over in a moment—the waiter, *menu* in hand, still hung on the result of the choice between *Coupe Jacques* and *Peches a La Melba*—but Miss Bart, in the interval, had taken the measure of her fate. Where Judy Trenor led, all the world would follow; and Lily had the doomed sense of the castaway who has signalled in vain to fleeing sails.

In a flash she remembered Mrs. Trenor's complaints of Carry Fisher's rapacity, and saw that they denoted an unexpected acquaintance with her husband's private affairs. In the large tumultuous disorder of the life at Bellomont, where no one seemed to have time to observe any one else, and private aims and personal interests were swept along unheeded in the rush of collective activities, Lily had fancied herself sheltered from inconvenient scrutiny; but if Judy knew when Mrs. Fisher borrowed money of her husband, was she likely to ignore the same transaction on Lily's part? If she was careless of his affections she was plainly jealous of his pocket; and in that fact Lily read the explanation of her rebuff. The immediate result of these conclusions was the passionate resolve to pay back her debt to Trenor. That obligation discharged, she would have but a thousand dollars of Mrs. Peniston's legacy left, and nothing to live on but her own small income, which was considerably less than Gerty Farish's wretched pittance; but this consideration gave way to the imperative claim of her wounded pride. She must be quits with the Trenors first; after that she would take thought for the future.

In her ignorance of legal procrastinations she had supposed that her legacy would be paid over within a few days of the reading of her aunt's will; and after an interval of anxious suspense, she wrote to enquire the cause of the delay. There was another interval before Mrs. Peniston's lawyer, who was also one of the executors, replied to the effect that, some questions having arisen relative to the interpretation of the will, he and his associates might not be in a position to pay the legacies till the close of the twelvemonth legally allotted for their settlement. Bewildered and indignant, Lily resolved to try the effect of a personal appeal; but she returned from her expedition with a sense of the powerlessness of beauty and charm against the unfeeling processes of the law. It seemed intolerable to live on for another year under the weight of her debt; and in her extremity she decided to turn to Miss Stepney, who still lingered in town, immersed in the delectable duty of "going over" her benefactress's effects. It was bitter enough for Lily to ask a favour of Grace Stepney, but the alternative was bitterer still; and one morning she presented herself at Mrs. Peniston's, where Grace, for the facilitation of her pious task, had taken up a provisional abode.

The strangeness of entering as a suppliant the house where she had so long commanded, increased Lily's desire to shorten the ordeal; and when Miss Stepney entered the darkened drawing-room, rustling with the best quality of crape, her visitor went straight to the point: would she be willing to advance the amount of the expected legacy?

Grace, in reply, wept and wondered at the request, bemoaned the inexorableness of the law, and was astonished that Lily had not realized the exact similarity of their positions. Did she think that only the payment of the legacies had been delayed? Why, Miss Stepney herself had not received a penny of her inheritance, and was paying rent—yes, actually!—for the privilege of living in a house that belonged to her. She was sure it was not what poor dear cousin Julia would have wished—she had told the executors so to their faces; but they were inaccessible to reason, and there was nothing to do but to wait. Let Lily take example by her, and be patient—let them both remember how beautifully patient cousin Julia had always been.

Lily made a movement which showed her imperfect assimilation of this example. "But you will have everything, Grace—it would be easy for you to borrow ten times the amount I am asking for."

"Borrow—easy for me to borrow?" Grace Stepney rose up before her in sable wrath. "Do you imagine for a moment that I would raise money on my expectations from cousin Julia, when I know so well her unspeakable horror of every transaction of the sort? Why, Lily, if you must know the truth, it was the idea of your being in debt that brought on her illness—you remember she had a slight attack before you sailed.

Oh, I don't know the particulars, of course—I don't *want* to know them—but there were rumours about your affairs that made her most unhappy—no one could be with her without seeing that. I can't help it if you are offended by my telling you this now—if I can do anything to make you realize the folly of your course, and how deeply *she* disapproved of it, I shall feel it is the truest way of making up to you for her loss."

# Chapter 5

It seemed to Lily, as Mrs. Peniston's door closed on her, that she was taking a final leave of her old life. The future stretched before her dull and bare as the deserted length of Fifth Avenue, and opportunities showed as meagrely as the few cabs trailing in quest of fares that did not come. The completeness of the analogy was, however, disturbed as she reached the sidewalk by the rapid approach of a hansom which pulled up at sight of her.

From beneath its luggage-laden top, she caught the wave of a signalling hand; and the next moment Mrs. Fisher, springing to the street, had folded her in a demonstrative embrace.

"My dear, you don't mean to say you're still in town? When I saw you the other day at Sherry's I didn't have time to ask—" She broke off, and added with a burst of frankness: "The truth is I was *horrid*, Lily, and I've wanted to tell you so ever since."

"Oh—" Miss Bart protested, drawing back from her penitent clasp; but Mrs. Fisher went on with her usual directness: "Look here, Lily, don't let's beat about the bush: half the trouble in life is caused by pretending there isn't any. That's not my way, and I can only say I'm thoroughly ashamed of myself for following the other women's lead. But we'll talk of that by and bye—tell me now where you're staying and what your plans are. I don't suppose you're keeping house in there with Grace Stepney, eh?—and it struck me you might be rather at loose ends."

In Lily's present mood there was no resisting the honest friendliness of this appeal, and she said with a smile: "I am at loose ends for the moment, but Gerty Farish is still in town, and she's good enough to let me be with her whenever she can spare the time."

Mrs. Fisher made a slight grimace. "H'm—that's a temperate joy. Oh, I know—Gerty's a trump, and worth all the rest of us put together;

but *a la longue* you're used to a little higher seasoning, aren't you, dear? And besides, I suppose she'll be off herself before long—the first of August, you say? Well, look here, you can't spend your summer in town; we'll talk of that later too. But meanwhile, what do you say to putting a few things in a trunk and coming down with me to the Sam Gormers' tonight?"

And as Lily stared at the breathless suddenness of the suggestion, she continued with her easy laugh: "You don't know them and they don't know you; but that don't make a rap of difference. They've taken the Van Alstyne place at Roslyn, and I've got *Carte Blanche* to bring my friends down there—the more the merrier. They do things awfully well, and there's to be rather a jolly party there this week—" she broke off, checked by an undefinable change in Miss Bart's expression. "Oh, I don't mean *your* particular set, you know: rather a different crowd, but very good fun. The fact is, the Gormers have struck out on a line of their own: what they want is to have a good time, and to have it in their own way. They gave the other thing a few months' trial, under my distinguished auspices, and they were really doing extremely well—getting on a good deal faster than the Brys, just because they didn't care as much—but suddenly they decided that the whole business bored them, and that what they wanted was a crowd they could really feel at home with. Rather original of them, don't you think so? Mattie Gormer *has* got aspirations still; women always have; but she's awfully easy-going, and Sam won't be bothered, and they both like to be the most important people in sight, so they've started a sort of continuous performance of their own, a kind of social Coney Island, where everybody is welcome who can make noise enough and doesn't put on airs. I think it's awfully good fun myself—some of the artistic set, you know, any pretty actress that's going, and so on. This week, for instance, they have Audrey Anstell, who made such a hit last spring in 'The Winning of Winny'; and Paul Morpeth—he's painting Mattie Gormer—and the Dick Bellingers, and Kate Corby—well, every one you can think of who's jolly and makes a row. Now don't stand there with your nose in the air, my dear—it will be a good deal better than a broiling Sunday in town, and you'll find clever people as well as noisy ones—Morpeth, who admires Mattie enormously, always brings one or two of his set."

Mrs. Fisher drew Lily toward the hansom with friendly authority. "Jump in now, there's a dear, and we'll drive round to your hotel and have your things packed, and then we'll have tea, and the two maids can meet us at the train."

It was a good deal better than a broiling Sunday in town—of that no doubt remained to Lily as, reclining in the shade of a leafy verandah, she looked seaward across a stretch of greensward picturesquely dotted with groups of ladies in lace raiment and men in tennis flannels. The huge Van Alstyne house and its rambling dependencies were packed to their fullest capacity with the Gormers' week-end guests, who now, in the radiance of the Sunday forenoon, were dispersing themselves over the grounds in quest of the various distractions the place afforded: distractions ranging from tennis-courts to shooting-galleries, from bridge and whiskey within doors to motors and steam-launches without. Lily had the odd sense of having been caught up into the crowd as carelessly as a passenger is gathered in by an express train. The blonde and genial Mrs. Gormer might, indeed, have figured the conductor, calmly assigning seats to the rush of travellers, while Carry Fisher represented the porter pushing their bags into place, giving them their numbers for the dining-car, and warning them when their station was at hand. The train, meanwhile, had scarcely slackened speed—life whizzed on with a deafening' rattle and roar, in which one traveller at least found a welcome refuge from the sound of her own thoughts. The Gormer *Milieu* represented a social out-skirt which Lily had always fastidiously avoided; but it struck her, now that she was in it, as only a flamboyant copy of her own world, a caricature approximating the real thing as the "society play" approaches the manners of the drawing-room. The people about her were doing the same things as the

Trenors, the Van Osburghs and the Dorsets: the difference lay in a hundred shades of aspect and manner, from the pattern of the men's waistcoats to the inflexion of the women's voices. Everything was pitched in a higher key, and there was more of each thing: more noise, more colour, more champagne, more familiarity—but also greater good-nature, less rivalry, and a fresher capacity for enjoyment.

Miss Bart's arrival had been welcomed with an uncritical friendliness that first irritated her pride and then brought her to a sharp sense of her own situation—of the place in life which, for the moment, she must accept and make the best of. These people knew her story—of that her first long talk with Carry Fisher had left no doubt: she was publicly branded as the heroine of a "queer" episode—but instead of shrinking from her as her own friends had done, they received her without question into the easy promiscuity of their lives. They swallowed her past as easily as they did Miss Anstell's, and with no apparent sense of any difference in the size of the mouthful: all they asked was that she should—in her own way, for they recognized a diversity of gifts—contribute as much to the general amusement as that graceful actress, whose talents, when off the stage, were of the most varied order. Lily felt at once that any tendency to be "stuck-up," to mark a sense of differences and distinctions, would be fatal to her continuance in the Gormer set. To be taken in on such terms—and into such a world!—was hard enough to the lingering pride in her; but she realized, with a pang of self-contempt, that to be excluded from it would, after all, be harder still. For, almost at once, she had felt the insidious charm of slipping back into a life where every material difficulty was smoothed away. The sudden escape from a stifling hotel in a dusty deserted city to the space and luxury of a great country-house fanned by sea breezes, had produced a state of moral lassitude agreeable enough after the nervous tension and physical discomfort of the past weeks. For the moment she must yield to the refreshment her senses craved—after that she would reconsider her situation, and take counsel with her dignity. Her enjoyment of her surroundings was, indeed, tinged by the unpleasant consideration that she was accepting the hospitality and courting the approval of people she had disdained under other conditions. But she was growing less sensitive on such points: a hard glaze of indifference was fast forming over her delicacies and susceptibilities, and each concession to expediency hardened the surface a little more.

On the Monday, when the party disbanded with uproarious adieux, the return to town threw into stronger relief the charms of the life she was leaving. The other guests were dispersing to take up the same existence in a different setting: some at Newport, some at Bar Harbour, some in the elaborate rusticity of an Adirondack camp. Even Gerty Farish, who welcomed Lily's return with tender solicitude, would soon be preparing to join the aunt with whom she spent her summers on Lake George: only Lily herself remained without plan or purpose, stranded in a backwater of the great current of pleasure. But Carry Fisher, who had insisted on transporting her to her own house, where she herself was to perch for a day or two on the way to the Brys' camp, came to the rescue with a new suggestion.

"Look here, Lily—I'll tell you what it is: I want you to take my place with Mattie Gormer this summer. They're taking a party out to Alaska next month in their private car, and Mattie, who is the laziest woman alive, wants me to go with them, and relieve her of the bother of arranging things; but the Brys want me too—oh, yes, we've made it up: didn't I tell you?—and, to put it frankly, though I like the Gormers best, there's more profit for me in the Brys. The fact is, they want to try Newport this summer, and if I can make it a success for them they—well, they'll make it a success for me." Mrs. Fisher clasped her hands enthusiastically. "Do you know, Lily, the more I think of my idea the better I like it—quite as much for you as for myself. The Gormers have both taken a tremendous fancy to you, and the trip to Alaska is—well—the very thing I should want for you just at present."

Miss Bart lifted her eyes with a keen glance. "To take me out of my friends' way, you mean?" she said quietly; and Mrs. Fisher responded with a deprecating kiss: "To keep you out of their sight till they realize how much they miss you."

Miss Bart went with the Gormers to Alaska; and the expedition, if it did not produce the effect anticipated by her friend, had at least the negative advantage of removing her from the fiery centre of criticism and discussion. Gerty Farish had opposed the plan with all the energy of her somewhat inarticulate nature. She had even offered to give up her visit to Lake George, and remain in town with Miss Bart, if the latter would renounce her journey; but Lily could disguise her real distaste for this plan under a sufficiently valid reason.

"You dear innocent, don't you see," she protested, "that Carry is quite right, and that I must take up my usual life, and go about among people as much as possible? If my old friends choose to believe lies about me I shall have to make new ones, that's all; and you know beggars mustn't be choosers. Not that I don't like Mattie Gormer—I *do* like her: she's kind and honest and unaffected; and don't you suppose I feel grateful to her for making me welcome at a time when, as you've yourself seen, my own family have unanimously washed their hands of me?"

Gerty shook her head, mutely unconvinced. She felt not only that Lily was cheapening herself by making use of an intimacy she would never have cultivated from choice, but that, in drifting back now to her former manner of life, she was forfeiting her last chance of ever escaping from it. Gerty had but an obscure conception of what Lily's actual experience had been: but its consequences had established a lasting hold on her pity since the memorable night when she had offered up her own secret hope to her friend's extremity. To characters like Gerty's such a sacrifice constitutes a moral claim on the part of the person in whose behalf it has been made. Having once helped Lily, she must continue to help her; and helping her, must believe in her, because faith is the main-spring of such natures. But even if Miss Bart, after her renewed taste of the amenities of life, could have returned to the barrenness of a New York August, mitigated only by poor Gerty's presence, her worldly wisdom would have counselled her against such an act of abnegation. She knew that Carry Fisher was right: that an opportune absence might be the first step toward rehabilitation, and that, at any rate, to linger on in town out of season was a fatal admission of defeat. From the Gormers' tumultuous progress across their native continent, she returned with an altered view of her situation. The renewed habit of luxury—the daily waking to an assured absence of care and presence of material ease—gradually blunted her appreciation of these values, and left her more conscious of the void they could not fill. Mattie Gormer's undiscriminating good-nature, and the slap-dash sociability of her friends, who treated Lily precisely as they treated each other—all these characteristic notes of difference began to wear upon her endurance; and the more she saw to criticize in her companions, the less justification she found for making use of them. The longing to get back to her former surroundings hardened to a fixed idea; but with the strengthening of her purpose came the inevitable perception that, to attain it, she must exact fresh concessions from her pride. These, for the moment, took the unpleasant form of continuing to cling to her hosts after their return from Alaska. Little as she was in the key of their *Milieu*, her immense social facility, her long habit of adapting herself to others without suffering her own outline to be blurred, the skilled manipulation of all the polished implements of her craft, had won for her an important place in the Gormer group. If their resonant hilarity could never be hers, she contributed a note of easy elegance more valuable to Mattie Gormer than the louder passages of the band. Sam Gormer and his special cronies stood indeed a little in awe of her; but Mattie's following, headed by Paul Morpeth, made her feel that they prized her for the very qualities they most conspicuously lacked. If Morpeth, whose social indolence was as great as his artistic activity, had abandoned himself to the easy current of the Gormer existence, where the minor exactions of politeness were unknown or ignored, and a man could either break his engagements, or keep them in a painting-jacket and slippers, he still preserved his sense of differences, and his appreciation of graces he had no time to cultivate. During the preparations for the Brys' *tableaux* he had been immensely struck by Lily's plastic possibilities—"not the face: too self-controlled for expression; but the rest of her—gad, what a model she'd make!"—and though his abhorrence of the world in which he had seen her was too great for him to think of seeking her there, he was fully alive to the privilege of having her to look at and listen to while he lounged in Mattie Gormer's dishevelled drawing-room.

Lily had thus formed, in the tumult of her surroundings, a little nucleus of friendly relations which mitigated the crudeness of her course in lingering with the Gormers after their return. Nor was she without pale glimpses of her own world, especially since the breaking-up of the Newport season had set the social current once more toward Long Island. Kate Corby, whose tastes made her as promiscuous as Carry Fisher was rendered by her necessities, occasionally descended on the Gormers, where, after a first stare of surprise, she took Lily's presence almost too much as a matter of course. Mrs. Fisher, too, appearing frequently in the neighbourhood, drove over to impart her experiences and give Lily what she called the latest report from the weather-bureau; and the latter, who had never directly invited her confidence, could yet talk with her more freely than with Gerty Farish, in whose presence it was impossible even to admit the existence of much that Mrs. Fisher conveniently took for granted.

Mrs. Fisher, moreover, had no embarrassing curiosity. She did not wish to probe the inwardness of Lily's situation, but simply to view it from the outside, and draw her conclusions accordingly; and these conclusions, at the end of a confidential talk, she summed up to her friend in the succinct remark: "You must marry as soon as you can."

Lily uttered a faint laugh—for once Mrs. Fisher lacked originality. "Do you mean, like Gerty Farish, to recommend the unfailing panacea of 'a good man's love'?"

"No—I don't think either of my candidates would answer to that description," said Mrs. Fisher after a pause of reflection.

"Either? Are there actually two?"

"Well, perhaps I ought to say one and a half—for the moment."

Miss Bart received this with increasing amusement. "Other things being equal, I think I should prefer a half-husband: who is he?"

"Don't fly out at me till you hear my reasons—George Dorset."

"Oh—" Lily murmured reproachfully; but Mrs. Fisher pressed on unrebuffed. "Well, why not? They had a few weeks' honeymoon when they first got back from Europe, but now things are going badly with them again. Bertha has been behaving more than ever like a madwoman, and George's powers of credulity are very nearly exhausted. They're at their place here, you know, and I spent last Sunday with them. It was a ghastly party—no one else but poor Neddy Silverton, who looks like a galley-slave (they used to talk of my making that poor boy unhappy!)—and after luncheon George carried me off on a long walk, and told me the end would have to come soon."

Miss Bart made an incredulous gesture. "As far as that goes, the end will never come—Bertha will always know how to get him back when she wants him."

Mrs. Fisher continued to observe her tentatively. "Not if he has any one else to turn to! Yes—that's just what it comes to: the poor creature can't stand alone. And I remember him such a good fellow, full of life and enthusiasm." She paused, and went on, dropping her glance from Lily's: "He wouldn't stay with her ten minutes if he *knew*—"

"Knew—?" Miss Bart repeated.

"What *you* must, for instance—with the opportunities you've had! If he had positive proof, I mean—"

Lily interrupted her with a deep blush of displeasure. "Please let us drop the subject, Carry: it's too odious to me." And to divert her companion's attention she added, with an attempt at lightness: "And your second candidate? We must not forget him."

Mrs. Fisher echoed her laugh. "I wonder if you'll cry out just as loud if I say—Sim Rosedale?"

Miss Bart did not cry out: she sat silent, gazing thoughtfully at her friend. The suggestion, in truth, gave expression to a possibility which, in the last weeks, had more than once recurred to her; but after a moment she said carelessly: "Mr. Rosedale wants a wife who can establish him in the bosom of the Van Osburghs and Trenors."

Mrs. Fisher caught her up eagerly. "And so *you* could—with his money! Don't you see how beautifully it would work out for you both?"

"I don't see any way of making him see it," Lily returned, with a laugh intended to dismiss the subject.

But in reality it lingered with her long after Mrs. Fisher had taken leave. She had seen very little of Rosedale since her annexation by the Gormers, for he was still steadily bent on penetrating to the inner Paradise from which she was now excluded; but once or twice, when nothing better offered, he had turned up for a Sunday, and on these occasions he had left her in no doubt as to his view of her situation. That he still admired her was, more than ever, offensively evident; for in the Gormer circle, where he expanded as in his native element, there were no puzzling conventions to check the full expression of his approval. But it was in the quality of his admiration that she read his shrewd estimate of her case. He enjoyed letting the Gormers see that he had known "Miss Lily"—she was "Miss Lily" to him now—before they had had the faintest social existence: enjoyed more especially impressing Paul Morpeth with the distance to which their intimacy dated back. But he let it be felt that that intimacy was a mere ripple on the surface of a rushing social current, the kind of relaxation which a man of large interests and manifold preoccupations permits himself in his hours of ease.

The necessity of accepting this view of their past relation, and of meeting it in the key of pleasantry prevalent among her new friends, was deeply humiliating to Lily. But she dared less than ever to quarrel with Rosedale. She suspected that her rejection rankled among the most unforgettable of his rebuffs, and the fact that he knew something of her wretched transaction with Trenor, and was sure to put the basest construction on it, seemed to place her hopelessly in his power. Yet at

Carry Fisher's suggestion a new hope had stirred in her. Much as she disliked Rosedale, she no longer absolutely despised him. For he was gradually attaining his object in life, and that, to Lily, was always less despicable than to miss it. With the slow unalterable persistency which she had always felt in him, he was making his way through the dense mass of social antagonisms. Already his wealth, and the masterly use he had made of it, were giving him an enviable prominence in the world of affairs, and placing Wall Street under obligations which only Fifth Avenue could repay. In response to these claims, his name began to figure on municipal committees and charitable boards; he appeared at banquets to distinguished strangers, and his candidacy at one of the fashionable clubs was discussed with diminishing opposition. He had figured once or twice at the Trenor dinners, and had learned to speak with just the right note of disdain of the big Van Osburgh crushes; and all he now needed was a wife whose affiliations would shorten the last tedious steps of his ascent. It was with that object that, a year earlier, he had fixed his affections on Miss Bart; but in the interval he had mounted nearer to the goal, while she had lost the power to abbreviate the remaining steps of the way. All this she saw with the clearness of vision that came to her in moments of despondency. It was success that dazzled her—she could distinguish facts plainly enough in the twilight of failure. And the twilight, as she now sought to pierce it, was gradually lighted by a faint spark of reassurance. Under the utilitarian motive of Rosedale's wooing she had felt, clearly enough, the heat of personal inclination. She would not have detested him so heartily had she not known that he dared to admire her. What, then, if the passion persisted, though the other motive had ceased to sustain it? She had never even tried to please him—he had been drawn to her in spite of her manifest disdain. What if she now chose to exert the power which, even in its passive state, he had felt so strongly? What if she made him marry her for love, now that he had no other reason for marrying her?

# Chapter 6

As became persons of their rising consequence, the Gormers were engaged in building a country-house on Long Island; and it was a part of Miss Bart's duty to attend her hostess on frequent visits of inspection to the new estate. There, while Mrs. Gormer plunged into problems of lighting and sanitation, Lily had leisure to wander, in the bright autumn air, along the tree-fringed bay to which the land declined. Little as she was addicted to solitude, there had come to be moments when it seemed a welcome escape from the empty noises of her life. She was weary of being swept passively along a current of pleasure and business in which she had no share; weary of seeing other people pursue amusement and squander money, while she felt herself of no more account among them than an expensive toy in the hands of a spoiled child.

It was in this frame of mind that, striking back from the shore one morning into the windings of an unfamiliar lane, she came suddenly upon the figure of George Dorset. The Dorset place was in the immediate neighbourhood of the Gormers' newly-acquired estate, and in her motor-flights thither with Mrs. Gormer, Lily had caught one or two passing glimpses of the couple; but they moved in so different an orbit that she had not considered the possibility of a direct encounter.

Dorset, swinging along with bent head, in moody abstraction, did not see Miss Bart till he was close upon her; but the sight, instead of bringing him to a halt, as she had half-expected, sent him toward her with an eagerness which found expression in his opening words.

"Miss Bart!—You'll shake hands, won't you? I've been hoping to meet you—I should have written to you if I'd dared." His face, with its tossed red hair and straggling moustache, had a driven uneasy look, as though life had become an unceasing race between himself and the thoughts at his heels.

The look drew a word of compassionate greeting from Lily, and he pressed on, as if encouraged by her tone: "I wanted to apologize—to ask you to forgive me for the miserable part I played—"

She checked him with a quick gesture. "Don't let us speak of it: I was very sorry for you," she said, with a tinge of disdain which, as she instantly perceived, was not lost on him.

He flushed to his haggard eyes, flushed so cruelly that she repented the thrust. "You might well be; you don't know—you must let me explain. I was deceived: abominably deceived—"

"I am still more sorry for you, then," she interposed, without irony; "but you must see that I am not exactly the person with whom the subject can be discussed."

He met this with a look of genuine wonder. "Why not? Isn't it to you, of all people, that I owe an explanation—"

"No explanation is necessary: the situation was perfectly clear to me."

"Ah—" he murmured, his head drooping again, and his irresolute hand switching at the underbrush along the lane. But as Lily made a movement to pass on, he broke out with fresh vehemence: "Miss Bart, for God's sake don't turn from me! We used to be good friends—you were always kind to me—and you don't know how I need a friend now."

The lamentable weakness of the words roused a motion of pity in Lily's breast. She too needed friends—she had tasted the pang of loneliness; and her resentment of Bertha Dorset's cruelty softened her heart to the poor wretch who was after all the chief of Bertha's victims.

"I still wish to be kind; I feel no ill-will toward you," she said. "But you must understand that after what has happened we can't be friends again—we can't see each other."

"Ah, you *are* kind—you're merciful—you always were!" He fixed his miserable gaze on her. "But why can't we be friends—why not, when I've repented in dust and ashes? Isn't it hard that you should condemn me to suffer for the falseness, the treachery of others? I was punished enough at the time—is there to be no respite for me?"

"I should have thought you had found complete respite in the reconciliation which was effected at my expense," Lily began, with renewed impatience; but he broke in imploringly: "Don't put it in that way—when that's been the worst of my punishment. My God! what could I do—wasn't I powerless? You were singled out as a sacrifice: any word I might have said would have been turned against you—"

"I have told you I don't blame you; all I ask you to understand is that, after the use Bertha chose to make of me—after all that her behaviour has since implied—it's impossible that you and I should meet."

He continued to stand before her, in his dogged weakness. "Is it—need it be? Mightn't there be circumstances—?" he checked himself, slashing at the wayside weeds in a wider radius. Then he began again: "Miss Bart, listen—give me a minute. If we're not to meet again, at least let me have a hearing now. You say we can't be friends after—after what has happened. But can't I at least appeal to your pity? Can't I move you if I ask you to think of me as a prisoner—a prisoner you alone can set free?"

Lily's inward start betrayed itself in a quick blush: was it possible that this was really the sense of Carry Fisher's adumbrations?

"I can't see how I can possibly be of any help to you," she murmured, drawing back a little from the mounting excitement of his look.

Her tone seemed to sober him, as it had so often done in his stormiest moments. The stubborn lines of his face relaxed, and he said, with an abrupt drop to docility: "You *would* see, if you'd be as merciful as you used to be: and heaven knows I've never needed it more!"

She paused a moment, moved in spite of herself by this reminder of her influence over him. Her fibres had been softened by suffering, and the sudden glimpse into his mocked and broken life disarmed her contempt for his weakness.

"I am very sorry for you—I would help you willingly; but you must have other friends, other advisers."

"I never had a friend like you," he answered simply. "And besides—can't you see?—you're the only person"—his voice dropped to a whisper—"the only person who knows."

Again she felt her colour change; again her heart rose in precipitate throbs to meet what she felt was coming. He lifted his eyes to her entreatingly. "You do see, don't you? You understand? I'm desperate—I'm at the end of my tether. I want to be free, and you can free me. I know you can. You don't want to keep me bound fast in hell, do you? You can't want to take such a vengeance as that. You were always kind—your eyes are kind now. You say you're sorry for me. Well, it rests with you to show it; and heaven knows there's nothing to keep you back. You understand, of course—there wouldn't be a hint of publicity—not a sound or a syllable to connect you with the thing. It would never come to that, you know: all I need is to be able to say definitely: 'I know this—and this—and this'—and the fight would drop, and the way be cleared, and the whole abominable business swept out of sight in a second."

He spoke pantingly, like a tired runner, with breaks of exhaustion between his words; and through the breaks she caught, as through the shifting rents of a fog, great golden vistas of peace and safety. For there was no mistaking the definite intention behind his vague appeal; she could have filled up the blanks without the help of Mrs. Fisher's insinuations. Here was a man who turned to her in the extremity of his loneliness and his humiliation: if she came to him at such a moment he would be hers with all the force of his deluded faith. And the power to make him so lay in her hand—lay there in a completeness he could not even remotely conjecture. Revenge and rehabilitation might be hers at a stroke—there was something dazzling in the completeness of the opportunity.

She stood silent, gazing away from him down the autumnal stretch of the deserted lane. And suddenly fear possessed her—fear of herself, and of the terrible force of the temptation. All her past weaknesses were like so many eager accomplices drawing her toward the path their feet had already smoothed. She turned quickly, and held out her hand to Dorset.

"Goodbye—I'm sorry; there's nothing in the world that I can do."

"Nothing? Ah, don't say that," he cried; "say what's true: that you abandon me like the others. You, the only creature who could have saved me!"

"Goodbye—goodbye," she repeated hurriedly; and as she moved away she heard him cry out on a last note of entreaty: "At least you'll let me see you once more?"

Lily, on regaining the Gormer grounds, struck rapidly across the lawn toward the unfinished house, where she fancied that her hostess might be speculating, not too resignedly, on the cause of her delay; for, like many unpunctual persons, Mrs. Gormer disliked to be kept waiting.

As Miss Bart reached the avenue, however, she saw a smart phaeton with a high-stepping pair disappear behind the shrubbery in the direction of the gate; and on the doorstep stood Mrs. Gormer, with a glow of retrospective pleasure on her open countenance. At sight of Lily the glow deepened to an embarrassed red, and she said with a slight laugh: "Did you see my visitor? Oh, I thought you came back by the avenue. It was Mrs. George Dorset—she said she'd dropped in to make a neighbourly call."

Lily met the announcement with her usual composure, though her experience of Bertha's idiosyncrasies would not have led her to include the neighbourly instinct among them; and Mrs. Gormer, relieved to see that she gave no sign of surprise, went on with a deprecating laugh: "Of course what really brought her was curiosity—she made me take her all over the house. But no one could have been nicer—no airs, you know, and so good-natured: I can quite see why people think her so fascinating."

This surprising event, coinciding too completely with her meeting with Dorset to be regarded as contingent upon it, had yet immediately struck Lily with a vague sense of foreboding. It was not in Bertha's habits to be neighbourly, much less to make advances to any one outside the immediate circle of her affinities. She had always consistently ignored the world of outer aspirants, or had recognized its individual members only when prompted by motives of self-interest; and the very capriciousness of her condescensions had, as Lily was aware, given them special value in the eyes of the persons she distinguished. Lily saw this now in Mrs. Gormer's unconcealable complacency, and in the happy irrelevance with which, for the next day or two, she quoted Bertha's opinions and speculated on the origin of her gown. All the secret ambitions which Mrs. Gormer's native indolence, and the attitude of her companions, kept in habitual abeyance, were now germinating afresh in the glow of Bertha's advances; and whatever the cause of the latter, Lily saw that, if they were followed up, they were likely to have a disturbing effect upon her own future.

She had arranged to break the length of her stay with her new friends by one or two visits to other acquaintances as recent; and on her return from this somewhat depressing excursion she was immediately conscious that Mrs. Dorset's influence was still in the air. There had been another exchange of visits, a tea at a country-club, an encounter at a hunt ball; there was even a rumour of an approaching dinner, which Mattie Gormer, with an unnatural effort at discretion, tried to smuggle out of the conversation whenever Miss Bart took part in it.

The latter had already planned to return to town after a farewell Sunday with her friends; and, with Gerty Farish's aid, had discovered a small private hotel where she might establish herself for the winter. The hotel being on the edge of a fashionable neighbourhood, the price of the few square feet she was to occupy was considerably in excess of her means; but she found a justification for her dislike of poorer quarters in the argument that, at this particular juncture, it was of the utmost importance to keep up a show of prosperity. In reality, it was impossible for her, while she had the means to pay her way for a week ahead, to lapse into a form of existence like Gerty Farish's. She had never been so near the brink of insolvency; but she could at least manage to meet her weekly hotel bill, and having settled the heaviest of her previous debts out of the money she had received from Trenor, she had a still fair margin of credit to go upon. The situation, however, was not agreeable enough to lull her to complete unconsciousness of its insecurity. Her rooms, with their cramped outlook down a sallow vista of brick walls and fire-escapes, her lonely meals in the dark restaurant with its surcharged ceiling and haunting smell of coffee—all these material discomforts, which were yet to be accounted as so many privileges soon to be withdrawn, kept constantly before her the disadvantages of her state; and her mind reverted the more insistently to Mrs. Fisher's counsels. Beat about the question as she would, she knew the outcome of it was that she must try to marry Rosedale; and in this conviction she was fortified by an unexpected visit from George Dorset.

She found him, on the first Sunday after her return to town, pacing her narrow sitting-room to the imminent peril of the few knick-knacks with which she had tried to disguise its plush exuberances; but the sight of her seemed to quiet him, and he said meekly that he hadn't come to bother her—that he asked only to be allowed to sit for half an hour and talk of anything she liked. In reality, as she knew, he had but one subject: himself and his wretchedness; and it was the need of her sympathy that had drawn him back. But he began with a pretence of questioning her about herself, and as she replied, she saw that, for the first time, a faint realization of her plight penetrated the dense surface of his self-absorption. Was it possible that her old beast of an aunt had actually cut her off? That she was living alone like this because there was no one else for her to go to, and that she really hadn't more than enough to keep alive on till the wretched little legacy was paid? The fibres of sympathy were nearly atrophied in him, but he was suffering so intensely that he had a faint glimpse of what other sufferings might mean—and, as she perceived, an almost simultaneous perception of the way in which her particular misfortunes might serve him.

When at length she dismissed him, on the pretext that she must dress for dinner, he lingered entreatingly on the threshold to blurt out: "It's been such a comfort—do say you'll let me see you again—" But to this direct appeal it was impossible to give an assent; and she said with friendly decisiveness: "I'm sorry—but you know why I can't."

He coloured to the eyes, pushed the door shut, and stood before her embarrassed but insistent. "I know how you might, if you would—if things were different—and it lies with you to make them so. It's just a word to say, and you put me out of my misery!"

Their eyes met, and for a second she trembled again with the nearness of the temptation. "You're mistaken; I know nothing; I saw nothing," she exclaimed, striving, by sheer force of reiteration, to build a barrier between herself and her peril; and as he turned away, groaning out "You sacrifice us both," she continued to repeat, as if it were a charm: "I know nothing—absolutely nothing."

Lily had seen little of Rosedale since her illuminating talk with Mrs. Fisher, but on the two or three occasions when they had met she was conscious of having distinctly advanced in his favour. There could be no doubt that he admired her as much as ever, and she believed it rested with herself to raise his admiration to the point where it should bear down the lingering counsels of expediency. The task was not an easy one; but neither was it easy, in her long sleepless nights, to face the thought of what George Dorset was so clearly ready to offer. Baseness for baseness, she hated the other least: there were even moments when a marriage with Rosedale seemed the only honourable solution of her difficulties. She did not indeed let her imagination range beyond the day of plighting: after that everything faded into a haze of material well-being, in which the personality of her benefactor remained mercifully vague. She had learned, in her long vigils, that there were certain things not good to think of, certain midnight images that must at any cost be exorcised—and one of these was the image of herself as Rosedale's wife.

Carry Fisher, on the strength, as she frankly owned, of the Brys' Newport success, had taken for the autumn months a small house at Tuxedo; and thither Lily was bound on the Sunday after Dorset's visit. Though it was nearly dinner-time when she arrived, her hostess was still out, and the firelit quiet of the small silent house descended on her spirit with a sense of peace and familiarity. It may be doubted if such an emotion had ever before been evoked by Carry Fisher's surroundings; but, contrasted to the world in which Lily had lately lived, there was an air of repose and stability in the very placing of the furniture, and in the quiet competence of the parlour-maid who led her up to her room. Mrs. Fisher's unconventionality was, after all, a merely superficial divergence from an inherited social creed, while the manners of the Gormer circle represented their first attempt to formulate such a creed for themselves.

It was the first time since her return from Europe that Lily had found herself in a congenial atmosphere, and the stirring of familiar associations had almost prepared her, as she descended the stairs before dinner, to enter upon a group of her old acquaintances. But this expectation was instantly checked by the reflection that the friends who remained loyal were precisely those who would be least willing to expose her to such encounters; and it was hardly with surprise that she found, instead, Mr. Rosedale kneeling domestically on the drawing-room hearth before his hostess's little girl.

Rosedale in the paternal role was hardly a figure to soften Lily; yet she could not but notice a quality of homely goodness in his advances to the child. They were not, at any rate, the premeditated and perfunctory endearments of the guest under his hostess's eye, for he and the little girl had the room to themselves; and something in his attitude made him seem a simple and kindly being compared to the small critical creature who endured his homage. Yes, he would be kind—Lily, from the threshold, had time to feel—kind in his gross, unscrupulous, rapacious way, the way of the predatory creature with his mate. She had but a moment in which to consider whether this glimpse of the fireside man mitigated her repugnance, or gave it, rather, a more concrete and intimate form; for at sight of her he was immediately on his feet again, the florid and dominant Rosedale of Mattie Gormer's drawing-room.

It was no surprise to Lily to find that he had been selected as her only fellow-guest. Though she and her hostess had not met since the latter's tentative discussion of her future, Lily knew that the acuteness which enabled Mrs. Fisher to lay a safe and pleasant course through a world of antagonistic forces was not infrequently exercised for the benefit of her friends. It was, in fact, characteristic of Carry that, while she actively gleaned her own stores from the fields of affluence, her real sympathies were on the other side—with the unlucky, the unpopular, the unsuccessful, with all her hungry fellow-toilers in the shorn stubble of success.

Mrs. Fisher's experience guarded her against the mistake of exposing Lily, for the first evening, to the unmitigated impression of Rosedale's personality. Kate Corby and two or three men dropped in to dinner, and Lily, alive to every detail of her friend's method, saw that such opportunities as had been contrived for her were to be deferred till she had, as it were, gained courage to make effectual use of them. She had a sense of acquiescing in this plan with the passiveness of a sufferer resigned to the surgeon's touch; and this feeling of almost lethargic helplessness continued when, after the departure of the guests, Mrs. Fisher followed her upstairs.

"May I come in and smoke a cigarette over your fire? If we talk in my room we shall disturb the child." Mrs. Fisher looked about her with the eye of the solicitous hostess. "I hope you've managed to make yourself comfortable, dear? Isn't it a jolly little house? It's such a blessing to have a few quiet weeks with the baby."

Carry, in her rare moments of prosperity, became so expansively maternal that Miss Bart sometimes wondered whether, if she could ever get time and money enough, she would not end by devoting them both to her daughter.

"It's a well-earned rest: I'll say that for myself," she continued, sinking down with a sigh of content on the pillowed lounge near the fire. "Louisa Bry is a stern task-master: I often used to wish myself back with the Gormers. Talk of love making people jealous and suspicious—it's nothing to social ambition! Louisa used to lie awake at night wondering whether the women who called on us called on *me* because I was with her, or on *her* because she was with me; and she was always laying traps to find out what I thought. Of course I had to disown my oldest friends, rather than let her suspect she owed me the chance of making a single acquaintance—when, all the while, that was what she had me there for, and what she wrote me a handsome cheque for when the season was over!"

Mrs. Fisher was not a woman who talked of herself without cause, and the practice of direct speech, far from precluding in her an occasional resort to circuitous methods, served rather, at crucial moments, the purpose of the juggler's chatter while he shifts the contents of his sleeves. Through the haze of her cigarette smoke she continued to gaze meditatively at Miss Bart, who, having dismissed her maid, sat before the toilet-table shaking out over her shoulders the loosened undulations of her hair.

"Your hair's wonderful, Lily. Thinner—? What does that matter, when it's so light and alive? So many women's worries seem to go straight to their hair—but yours looks as if there had never been an anxious thought under it. I never saw you look better than you did this evening. Mattie Gormer told me that Morpeth wanted to paint you—why don't you let him?"

Miss Bart's immediate answer was to address a critical glance to the reflection of the countenance under discussion. Then she said, with a slight touch of irritation: "I don't care to accept a portrait from Paul Morpeth."

Mrs. Fisher mused. "N—no. And just now, especially—well, he can do you after you're married." She waited a moment, and then went on:

"By the way, I had a visit from Mattie the other day. She turned up here last Sunday—and with Bertha Dorset, of all people in the world!"

She paused again to measure the effect of this announcement on her hearer, but the brush in Miss Bart's lifted hand maintained its unwavering stroke from brow to nape.

"I never was more astonished," Mrs. Fisher pursued. "I don't know two women less predestined to intimacy—from Bertha's standpoint, that is; for of course poor Mattie thinks it natural enough that she should be singled out—I've no doubt the rabbit always thinks it is fascinating the anaconda. Well, you know I've always told you that Mattie secretly longed to bore herself with the really fashionable; and now that the chance has come, I see that she's capable of sacrificing all her old friends to it."

Lily laid aside her brush and turned a penetrating glance upon her friend. "Including *me*?" she suggested.

"Ah, my dear," murmured Mrs. Fisher, rising to push back a log from the hearth.

"That's what Bertha means, isn't it?" Miss Bart went on steadily. "For of course she always means something; and before I left Long Island I saw that she was beginning to lay her toils for Mattie."

Mrs. Fisher sighed evasively. "She has her fast now, at any rate. To think of that loud independence of Mattie's being only a subtler form of snobbishness! Bertha can already make her believe anything she pleases—and I'm afraid she's begun, my poor child, by insinuating horrors about you."

Lily flushed under the shadow of her drooping hair. "The world is too vile," she murmured, averting herself from Mrs. Fisher's anxious scrutiny.

"It's not a pretty place; and the only way to keep a footing in it is to fight it on its own terms—and above all, my dear, not alone!" Mrs. Fisher gathered up her floating implications in a resolute grasp. "You've told me so little that I can only guess what has been happening; but in the rush we all live in there's no time to keep on hating any one without a cause, and if Bertha is still nasty enough to want to injure you with other people it must be because she's still afraid of you. From her standpoint there's only one reason for being afraid of you; and my own idea is that, if you want to punish her, you hold the means in your hand. I believe you can marry George Dorset tomorrow; but if you don't care for that particular form of retaliation, the only thing to save you from Bertha is to marry somebody else."

# Chapter 7

The light projected on the situation by Mrs. Fisher had the cheerless distinctness of a winter dawn. It outlined the facts with a cold precision unmodified by shade or colour, and refracted, as it were, from the blank walls of the surrounding limitations: she had opened windows from which no sky was ever visible. But the idealist subdued to vulgar necessities must employ vulgar minds to draw the inferences to which he cannot stoop; and it was easier for Lily to let Mrs. Fisher formulate her case than to put it plainly to herself. Once confronted with it, however, she went the full length of its consequences; and these had never been more clearly present to her than when, the next afternoon, she set out for a walk with Rosedale.

It was one of those still November days when the air is haunted with the light of summer, and something in the lines of the landscape, and in the golden haze which bathed them, recalled to Miss Bart the September afternoon when she had climbed the slopes of Bellomont with Selden. The importunate memory was kept before her by its ironic contrast to her present situation, since her walk with Selden had represented an irresistible flight from just such a climax as the present excursion was designed to bring about. But other memories importuned her also; the recollection of similar situations, as skillfully led up to, but through some malice of fortune, or her own unsteadiness of purpose, always failing of the intended result. Well, her purpose was steady enough now. She saw that the whole weary work of rehabilitation must begin again, and against far greater odds, if Bertha Dorset should succeed in breaking up her friendship with the Gormers; and her longing for shelter and security was intensified by the passionate desire to triumph over Bertha, as only wealth and predominance could triumph over her. As the wife of Rosedale—the Rosedale she felt it in her power to create—she would at least present an invulnerable front to her enemy.

She had to draw upon this thought, as upon some fiery stimulant, to keep up her part in the scene toward which Rosedale was too frankly tending. As she walked beside him, shrinking in every nerve from the way in which his look and tone made free of her, yet telling herself that this momentary endurance of his mood was the price she must pay for her ultimate power over him, she tried to calculate the exact point at which concession must turn to resistance, and the price *he* would have to pay be made equally clear to him. But his dapper self-confidence seemed impenetrable to such hints, and she had a sense of something hard and self-contained behind the superficial warmth of his manner.

They had been seated for some time in the seclusion of a rocky glen above the lake, when she suddenly cut short the culmination of an impassioned period by turning upon him the grave loveliness of her gaze.

"I *do* believe what you say, Mr. Rosedale," she said quietly; "and I am ready to marry you whenever you wish."

Rosedale, reddening to the roots of his glossy hair, received this announcement with a recoil which carried him to his feet, where he halted before her in an attitude of almost comic discomfiture.

"For I suppose that is what you do wish," she continued, in the same quiet tone. "And, though I was unable to consent when you spoke to me in this way before, I am ready, now that I know you so much better, to trust my happiness to your hands."

She spoke with the noble directness which she could command on such occasions, and which was like a large steady light thrown across the tortuous darkness of the situation. In its inconvenient brightness Rosedale seemed to waver a moment, as though conscious that every avenue of escape was unpleasantly illuminated.

Then he gave a short laugh, and drew out a gold cigarette-case, in which, with plump jewelled fingers, he groped for a gold-tipped cigarette. Selecting one, he paused to contemplate it a moment before saying: "My dear Miss Lily, I'm sorry if there's been any little misapprehension between us-but you made me feel my suit was so hopeless that I had really no intention of renewing it."

Lily's blood tingled with the grossness of the rebuff; but she checked the first leap of her anger, and said in a tone of gentle dignity: "I have no one but myself to blame if I gave you the impression that my decision was final."

Her word-play was always too quick for him, and this reply held him in puzzled silence while she extended her hand and added, with the faintest inflection of sadness in her voice: "Before we bid each other goodbye, I want at least to thank you for having once thought of me as you did."

The touch of her hand, the moving softness of her look, thrilled a vulnerable fibre in Rosedale. It was her exquisite inaccessibleness, the sense of distance she could convey without a hint of disdain, that made it most difficult for him to give her up.

"Why do you talk of saying goodbye? Ain't we going to be good friends all the same?" he urged, without releasing her hand.

She drew it away quietly. "What is your idea of being good friends?" she returned with a slight smile. "Making love to me without asking me to marry you?" Rosedale laughed with a recovered sense of ease.

"Well, that's about the size of it, I suppose. I can't help making love to you—I don't see how any man could; but I don't mean to ask you to marry me as long as I can keep out of it."

She continued to smile. "I like your frankness; but I am afraid our friendship can hardly continue on those terms." She turned away, as though to mark that its final term had in fact been reached, and he followed her for a few steps with a baffled sense of her having after all kept the game in her own hands.

"Miss Lily—" he began impulsively; but she walked on without seeming to hear him.

He overtook her in a few quick strides, and laid an entreating hand on her arm. "Miss Lily—don't hurry away like that. You're beastly hard on a fellow; but if you don't mind speaking the truth I don't see why you shouldn't allow me to do the same."

She had paused a moment with raised brows, drawing away instinctively from his touch, though she made no effort to evade his words.

"I was under the impression," she rejoined, "that you had done so without waiting for my permission."

"Well—why shouldn't you hear my reasons for doing it, then? We're neither of us such new hands that a little plain speaking is going to hurt us. I'm all broken up on you: there's nothing new in that. I'm more in love with you than I was this time last year; but I've got to face the fact that the situation is changed."

She continued to confront him with the same air of ironic composure. "You mean to say that I'm not as desirable a match as you thought me?"

"Yes; that's what I do mean," he answered resolutely. "I won't go into what's happened. I don't believe the stories about you—I don't *want* to believe them. But they're there, and my not believing them ain't going to alter the situation."

She flushed to her temples, but the extremity of her need checked the retort on her lip and she continued to face him composedly. "If they are not true," she said, "doesn't *that* alter the situation?"

He met this with a steady gaze of his small stock-taking eyes, which made her feel herself no more than some superfine human merchandise. "I believe it does in novels; but I'm certain it don't in real life. You know that as well as I do: if we're speaking the truth, let's speak the whole truth. Last year I was wild to marry you, and you wouldn't look at me: this year—well, you appear to be willing. Now, what has changed in the interval? Your situation, that's all. Then you thought you could do better; now—"

"You think you can?" broke from her ironically.

"Why, yes, I do: in one way, that is." He stood before her, his hands in his pockets, his chest sturdily expanded under its vivid waistcoat.

"It's this way, you see: I've had a pretty steady grind of it these last years, working up my social position. Think it's funny I should say that? Why should I mind saying I want to get into society? A man ain't ashamed to say he wants to own a racing stable or a picture gallery. Well, a taste for society's just another kind of hobby. Perhaps I want to get even with some of the people who cold-shouldered me last year—put it that way if it sounds better. Anyhow, I want to have the run of the best houses; and I'm getting it too, little by little. But I know the quickest way to queer yourself with the right people is to be seen with the wrong ones; and that's the reason I want to avoid mistakes."

Miss Bart continued to stand before him in a silence that might have expressed either mockery or a half-reluctant respect for his candour, and after a moment's pause he went on: "There it is, you see. I'm more in love with you than ever, but if I married you now I'd queer myself for good and all, and everything I've worked for all these years would be wasted."

She received this with a look from which all tinge of resentment had faded. After the tissue of social falsehoods in which she had so long moved it was refreshing to step into the open daylight of an avowed expediency.

"I understand you," she said. "A year ago I should have been of use to you, and now I should be an encumbrance; and I like you for telling me so quite honestly." She extended her hand with a smile.

Again the gesture had a disturbing effect upon Mr. Rosedale's self-command. "By George, you're a dead game sport, you are!" he exclaimed; and as she began once more to move away, he broke out suddenly—"Miss Lily—stop. You know I don't believe those stories—I believe they were all got up by a woman who didn't hesitate to sacrifice you to her own convenience—"

Lily drew away with a movement of quick disdain: it was easier to endure his insolence than his commiseration.

"You are very kind; but I don't think we need discuss the matter farther."

But Rosedale's natural imperviousness to hints made it easy for him to brush such resistance aside. "I don't want to discuss anything; I just want to put a plain case before you," he persisted.

She paused in spite of herself, held by the note of a new purpose in his look and tone; and he went on, keeping his eyes firmly upon her: "The wonder to me is that you've waited so long to get square with that woman, when you've had the power in your hands." She continued silent under the rush of astonishment that his words produced, and he moved a step closer to ask with low-toned directness: "Why don't you use those letters of hers you bought last year?"

Lily stood speechless under the shock of the interrogation. In the words preceding it she had conjectured, at most, an allusion to her supposed influence over George Dorset; nor did the astonishing indelicacy of the reference diminish the likelihood of Rosedale's resorting to it. But now she saw how far short of the mark she had fallen; and the surprise of learning that he had discovered the secret of the letters left her, for the moment, unconscious of the special use to which he was in the act of putting his knowledge.

Her temporary loss of self-possession gave him time to press his point; and he went on quickly, as though to secure completer control of the situation: "You see I know where you stand—I know how completely she's in your power. That sounds like stage-talk, don't it?—but there's a lot of truth in some of those old gags; and I don't suppose you bought those letters simply because you're collecting autographs."

She continued to look at him with a deepening bewilderment: her only clear impression resolved itself into a scared sense of his power.

"You're wondering how I found out about 'em?" he went on, answering her look with a note of conscious pride. "Perhaps you've forgotten that I'm the owner of the Benedick-but never mind about that now. Getting on to things is a mighty useful accomplishment in business, and I've simply extended it to my private affairs. For this *is* partly my affair, you see—at least, it depends on you to make it so. Let's look the situation straight in the eye. Mrs. Dorset, for reasons we needn't go into, did you a beastly bad turn last spring. Everybody knows what Mrs. Dorset is, and her best friends wouldn't believe her on oath where their own interests were concerned; but as long as they're out of the row it's much easier to follow her lead than to set themselves against it, and you've simply been sacrificed to their laziness and selfishness. Isn't that a pretty fair statement of the case?—Well, some people say you've got the neatest kind of an answer in your hands: that George Dorset would marry you tomorrow, if you'd tell him all you know, and give him the chance to show the lady the door. I daresay he would; but you don't seem to care for that particular form of getting even, and, taking a purely business view of the question, I think you're right. In a deal like that, nobody comes out with perfectly clean hands, and the only way for you to start fresh is to get Bertha Dorset to back you up, instead of trying to fight her."

He paused long enough to draw breath, but not to give her time for the expression of her gathering resistance; and as he pressed on, expounding and elucidating his idea with the directness of the man who has no doubts of his cause, she found the indignation gradually freezing on her lip, found herself held fast in the grasp of his argument by the mere cold strength of its presentation. There was no time now to wonder how he had heard of her obtaining the letters: all her world was dark outside the monstrous glare of his scheme for using them. And it was not, after the first moment, the horror of the idea that held her spell-bound, subdued to his will; it was rather its subtle affinity to her own inmost cravings. He would marry her tomorrow if she could regain Bertha Dorset's friendship; and to induce the open resumption of that friendship, and the tacit retractation of all that had caused its withdrawal, she had only to put to the lady the latent menace contained in the packet so miraculously delivered into her hands. Lily saw in a flash the advantage of this course over that which poor Dorset had pressed upon her. The other plan depended for its success on the infliction of an open injury, while this reduced the transaction to a private understanding, of which no third person need have the remotest hint. Put by Rosedale in terms of business-like give-and-take, this understanding took on the harmless air of a mutual accommodation, like a transfer of property or a revision of boundary lines. It certainly simplified life to view it as a perpetual adjustment, a play of party politics, in which every concession had its recognized equivalent: Lily's tired mind was fascinated by this escape from fluctuating ethical estimates into a region of concrete weights and measures.

Rosedale, as she listened, seemed to read in her silence not only a gradual acquiescence in his plan, but a dangerously far-reaching perception of the chances it offered; for as she continued to stand before him without speaking, he broke out, with a quick return upon himself: "You see how simple it is, don't you? Well, don't be carried away by the idea that it's *too* simple. It isn't exactly as if you'd started in with a clean bill of health. Now we're talking let's call things by their right names, and clear the whole business up. You know well enough that Bertha Dorset couldn't have touched you if there hadn't been—well—questions asked before—little points of interrogation, eh? Bound to happen to a good-looking girl with stingy relatives, I suppose; anyhow, they *did* happen, and she found the ground prepared for her. Do you see where I'm coming out? You don't want these little questions cropping up again. It's one thing to get Bertha Dorset into line—but what you want is to keep her there. You can frighten her fast enough—but how are you going to keep her frightened? By showing her that you're as powerful as she is. All the letters in the world won't do that for you as you are now; but with a big backing behind you, you'll keep her just where you want her to be. That's *my* share in the business—that's what I'm offering you. You can't put the thing through without me—don't run away with any idea that you can. In six months you'd be back again among your old worries, or worse ones; and here I am, ready to lift you out of 'em tomorrow if you say so. *Do* you say so, Miss Lily?" he added, moving suddenly nearer.

The words, and the movement which accompanied them, combined to startle Lily out of the state of tranced subservience into which she had insensibly slipped. Light comes in devious ways to the groping consciousness, and it came to her now through the disgusted perception that her would-be accomplice assumed, as a matter of course, the likelihood of her distrusting him and perhaps trying to cheat him of his share of the spoils. This glimpse of his inner mind seemed to present the whole transaction in a new aspect, and she saw that the essential baseness of the act lay in its freedom from risk.

She drew back with a quick gesture of rejection, saying, in a voice that was a surprise to her own ears: "You are mistaken—quite mistaken—both in the facts and in what you infer from them."

Rosedale stared a moment, puzzled by her sudden dash in a direction so different from that toward which she had appeared to be letting him guide her.

"Now what on earth does that mean? I thought we understood each other!" he exclaimed; and to her murmur of "Ah, we do *now*," he retorted with a sudden burst of violence: "I suppose it's because the letters are to *him*, then? Well, I'll be damned if I see what thanks you've got from him!"

# Chapter 8

The autumn days declined to winter. Once more the leisure world was in transition between country and town, and Fifth Avenue, still deserted at the week-end, showed from Monday to Friday a broadening stream of carriages between house-fronts gradually restored to consciousness.

The Horse Show, some two weeks earlier, had produced a passing semblance of reanimation, filling the theatres and restaurants with a human display of the same costly and high-stepping kind as circled daily about its ring. In Miss Bart's world the Horse Show, and the public it attracted, had ostensibly come to be classed among the spectacles disdained of the elect; but, as the feudal lord might sally forth to join in the dance on his village green, so society, unofficially and incidentally, still condescended to look in upon the scene. Mrs. Gormer, among the rest, was not above seizing such an occasion for the display of herself and her horses; and Lily was given one or two opportunities of appearing at her friend's side in the most conspicuous box the house afforded. But this lingering semblance of intimacy made her only the more conscious of a change in the relation between Mattie and herself, of a dawning discrimination, a gradually formed social standard, emerging from Mrs. Gormer's chaotic view of life. It was inevitable that Lily herself should constitute the first sacrifice to this new ideal, and she knew that, once the Gormers were established in town, the whole drift of fashionable life would facilitate Mattie's detachment from her. She had, in short, failed to make herself indispensable; or rather, her attempt to do so had been thwarted by an influence stronger than any she could exert. That influence, in its last analysis, was simply the power of money: Bertha Dorset's social credit was based on an impregnable bank-account.

Lily knew that Rosedale had overstated neither the difficulty of her own position nor the completeness of the vindication he offered: once Bertha's match in material resources, her superior gifts would make it easy for her to dominate her adversary. An understanding of what such domination would mean, and of the disadvantages accruing from her rejection of it, was brought home to Lily with increasing clearness during the early weeks of the winter. Hitherto, she had kept up a semblance of movement outside the main flow of the social current; but with the return to town, and the concentrating of scattered activities, the mere fact of not slipping back naturally into her old habits of life marked her as being unmistakably excluded from them. If one were not a part of the season's fixed routine, one swung unsphered in a void of social non-existence. Lily, for all her dissatisfied dreaming, had never really conceived the possibility of revolving about a different centre: it was easy enough to despise the world, but decidedly difficult to find any other habitable region. Her sense of irony never quite deserted her, and she could still note, with self-directed derision, the abnormal value suddenly acquired by the most tiresome and insignificant details of her former life. Its very drudgeries had a charm now that she was involuntarily released from them: card-leaving, note-writing, enforced civilities to the dull and elderly, and the smiling endurance of tedious dinners—how pleasantly such obligations would have filled the emptiness of her days! She did indeed leave cards in plenty; she kept herself, with a smiling and valiant persistence, well in the eye of her world; nor did she suffer any of those gross rebuffs which sometimes produce a wholesome reaction of contempt in their victim. Society did not turn away from her, it simply drifted by, preoccupied and inattentive, letting her feel, to the full measure of her humbled pride, how completely she had been the creature of its favour.

She had rejected Rosedale's suggestion with a promptness of scorn almost surprising to herself: she had not lost her capacity for high flashes of indignation. But she could not breathe long on the heights; there had been nothing in her training to develop any continuity of moral strength: what she craved, and really felt herself entitled to, was a situation in which the noblest attitude should also be the easiest. Hitherto her intermittent impulses of resistance had sufficed to maintain her self-respect. If she slipped she recovered her footing, and it was only afterward that she was aware of having recovered it each time on a slightly lower level. She had rejected Rosedale's offer without conscious effort; her whole being had risen against it; and she did not yet perceive that, by the mere act of listening to him, she had learned to live with ideas which would once have been intolerable to her.

To Gerty Farish, keeping watch over her with a tenderer if less discerning eye than Mrs. Fisher's, the results of the struggle were already distinctly visible. She did not, indeed, know what hostages Lily had already given to expediency; but she saw her passionately and irretrievably pledged to the ruinous policy of "keeping up." Gerty could smile now at her own early dream of her friend's renovation through adversity: she understood clearly enough that Lily was not of those to whom privation teaches the unimportance of what they have lost. But this very fact, to Gerty, made her friend the more piteously in want of aid, the more exposed to the claims of a tenderness she was so little conscious of needing.

Lily, since her return to town, had not often climbed Miss Farish's stairs. There was something irritating to her in the mute interrogation of Gerty's sympathy: she felt the real difficulties of her situation to be incommunicable to any one whose theory of values was so different from her own, and the restrictions of Gerty's life, which had once had the charm of contrast, now reminded her too painfully of the limits to which her own existence was shrinking. When at length, one afternoon, she put into execution the belated resolve to visit her friend, this sense of shrunken opportunities possessed her with unusual intensity. The walk up Fifth Avenue, unfolding before her, in the brilliance of the hard winter sunlight, an interminable procession of fastidiously-equipped carriages—giving her, through the little squares of brougham-windows, peeps of familiar profiles bent above visiting-lists, of hurried hands dispensing notes and cards to attendant footmen—this glimpse of the ever-revolving wheels of the great social machine made Lily more than ever conscious of the steepness and narrowness of Gerty's stairs, and of the cramped blind alley of life to which they led. Dull stairs destined to be mounted by dull people: how many thousands of insignificant figures were going up and down such stairs all over the world at that very moment—figures as shabby and uninteresting as that of the middle-aged lady in limp black who descended Gerty's flight as Lily climbed to it!

"That was poor Miss Jane Silverton—she came to talk things over with me: she and her sister want to do something to support themselves," Gerty explained, as Lily followed her into the sitting-room.

"To support themselves? Are they so hard up?" Miss Bart asked with a touch of irritation: she had not come to listen to the woes of other people.

"I'm afraid they have nothing left: Ned's debts have swallowed up everything. They had such hopes, you know, when he broke away from Carry Fisher; they thought Bertha Dorset would be such a good influence, because she doesn't care for cards, and—well, she talked quite beautifully to poor Miss Jane about feeling as if Ned were her younger brother, and wanting to carry him off on the yacht, so that he might have a chance to drop cards and racing, and take up his literary work again."

Miss Farish paused with a sigh which reflected the perplexity of her departing visitor. "But that isn't all; it isn't even the worst. It seems that Ned has quarrelled with the Dorsets; or at least Bertha won't allow him to see her, and he is so unhappy about it that he has taken to gambling again, and going about with all sorts of queer people. And cousin Grace Van Osburgh accuses him of having had a very bad influence on Freddy, who left Harvard last spring, and has been a great deal with Ned ever since. She sent for Miss Jane, and made a dreadful scene; and Jack Stepney and Herbert Melson, who were there too, told Miss Jane that Freddy was threatening to marry some dreadful woman to whom Ned had introduced him, and that they could do nothing with him because now he's of age he has his own money. You can fancy how poor Miss Jane felt—she came to me at once, and seemed to think that if I could get her something to do she could earn enough to pay Ned's debts and send him away—I'm afraid she has no idea how long it would take her to pay for one of his evenings at bridge. And he was horribly in debt when he came back from the cruise—I can't see why he should have spent so much more money under Bertha's influence than Carry's: can you?"

Lily met this query with an impatient gesture. "My dear Gerty, I always understand how people can spend much more money—never how they can spend any less!"

She loosened her furs and settled herself in Gerty's easy-chair, while her friend busied herself with the tea-cups.

"But what can they do—the Miss Silvertons? How do they mean to support themselves?" she asked, conscious that the note of irritation still persisted in her voice. It was the very last topic she had meant to discuss—it really did not interest her in the least—but she was seized by a sudden perverse curiosity to know how the two colourless shrinking victims of young Silverton's sentimental experiments meant to cope with the grim necessity which lurked so close to her own threshold.

"I don't know—I am trying to find something for them. Miss Jane reads aloud very nicely—but it's so hard to find any one who is willing to be read to. And Miss Annie paints a little—"

"Oh, I know—apple-blossoms on blotting-paper; just the kind of thing I shall be doing myself before long!" exclaimed Lily, starting up with a vehemence of movement that threatened destruction to Miss Farish's fragile tea-table.

Lily bent over to steady the cups; then she sank back into her seat. "I'd forgotten there was no room to dash about in—how beautifully one does have to behave in a small flat! Oh, Gerty, I wasn't meant to be good," she sighed out incoherently.

Gerty lifted an apprehensive look to her pale face, in which the eyes shone with a peculiar sleepless lustre.

"You look horribly tired, Lily; take your tea, and let me give you this cushion to lean against."

Miss Bart accepted the cup of tea, but put back the cushion with an impatient hand.

"Don't give me that! I don't want to lean back—I shall go to sleep if I do."

"Well, why not, dear? I'll be as quiet as a mouse," Gerty urged affectionately.

"No—no; don't be quiet; talk to me—keep me awake! I don't sleep at night, and in the afternoon a dreadful drowsiness creeps over me."

"You don't sleep at night? Since when?"

"I don't know—I can't remember." She rose and put the empty cup on the tea-tray. "Another, and stronger, please; if I don't keep awake now I shall see horrors tonight—perfect horrors!"

"But they'll be worse if you drink too much tea."

"No, no—give it to me; and don't preach, please," Lily returned imperiously. Her voice had a dangerous edge, and Gerty noticed that her hand shook as she held it out to receive the second cup.

"But you look so tired: I'm sure you must be ill—"

Miss Bart set down her cup with a start. "Do I look ill? Does my face show it?" She rose and walked quickly toward the little mirror above the writing-table. "What a horrid looking-glass—it's all blotched and discoloured. Any one would look ghastly in it!" She turned back, fixing her plaintive eyes on Gerty. "You stupid dear, why do you say such odious things to me? It's enough to make one ill to be told one looks so! And looking ill means looking ugly." She caught Gerty's wrists, and drew her close to the window. "After all, I'd rather know the truth. Look me straight in the face, Gerty, and tell me: am I perfectly frightful?"

"You're perfectly beautiful now, Lily: your eyes are shining, and your cheeks have grown so pink all of a sudden—"

"Ah, they *were* pale, then—ghastly pale, when I came in? Why don't you tell me frankly that I'm a wreck? My eyes are bright now because I'm so nervous—but in the mornings they look like lead. And I can see the lines coming in my face—the lines of worry and disappointment and failure! Every sleepless night leaves a new one—and how can I sleep, when I have such dreadful things to think about?"

"Dreadful things—what things?" asked Gerty, gently detaching her wrists from her friend's feverish fingers.

"What things? Well, poverty, for one—and I don't know any that's more dreadful." Lily turned away and sank with sudden weariness into the easy-chair near the tea-table. "You asked me just now if I could understand why Ned Silverton spent so much money. Of course I understand—he spends it on living with the rich. You think we live ON the rich, rather than with them: and so we do, in a sense—but it's a privilege we have to pay for! We eat their dinners, and drink their wine, and smoke their cigarettes, and use their carriages and their opera-boxes and their private cars—yes, but there's a tax to pay on every one of those luxuries. The man pays it by big tips to the servants, by playing cards beyond his means, by flowers and presents—and—and—lots of other things that cost; the girl pays it by tips and cards too—oh, yes, I've had to take up bridge again—and by going to the best dress-makers, and having just the right dress for every occasion, and always keeping herself fresh and exquisite and amusing!"

She leaned back for a moment, closing her eyes, and as she sat there, her pale lips slightly parted, and the lids dropped above her fagged brilliant gaze, Gerty had a startled perception of the change in her face—of the way in which an ashen daylight seemed suddenly to extinguish its artificial brightness. She looked up, and the vision vanished.

"It doesn't sound very amusing, does it? And it isn't—I'm sick to death of it! And yet the thought of giving it all up nearly kills me—it's what keeps me awake at night, and makes me so crazy for your strong tea. For I can't go on in this way much longer, you know—I'm nearly at the end of my tether. And then what can I do—how on earth am I to keep myself alive? I see myself reduced to the fate of that poor Silverton woman—slinking about to employment agencies, and trying to sell painted blotting-pads to Women's Exchanges! And there are thousands and thousands of women trying to do the same thing already, and not one of the number who has less idea how to earn a dollar than I have!"

She rose again with a hurried glance at the clock. "It's late, and I must be off—I have an appointment with Carry Fisher. Don't look so worried, you dear thing—don't think too much about the nonsense I've been talking." She was before the mirror again, adjusting her hair with a light hand, drawing down her veil, and giving a dexterous touch to her furs. "Of course, you know, it hasn't come to the employment agencies and the painted blotting-pads yet; but I'm rather hard-up just for the moment, and if I could find something to do—notes to write and visiting-lists to make up, or that kind of thing—it would tide me over till the legacy is paid. And Carry has promised to find somebody who wants a kind of social secretary—you know she makes a specialty of the helpless rich."

Miss Bart had not revealed to Gerty the full extent of her anxiety. She was in fact in urgent and immediate need of money: money to meet the vulgar weekly claims which could neither be deferred nor evaded. To give up her apartment, and shrink to the obscurity of a boarding-house, or the provisional hospitality of a bed in Gerty Farish's sitting-room, was an expedient which could only postpone the problem confronting her; and it seemed wiser as well as more agreeable to remain where she was and find some means of earning her living. The possibility of having to do this was one which she had never before seriously considered, and the discovery that, as a bread-winner, she was likely to prove as helpless and ineffectual as poor Miss Silverton, was a severe shock to her self-confidence.

Having been accustomed to take herself at the popular valuation, as a person of energy and resource, naturally fitted to dominate any situation in which she found herself, she vaguely imagined that such gifts would be of value to seekers after social guidance; but there was unfortunately no specific head under which the art of saying and doing the right thing could be offered in the market, and even Mrs. Fisher's resourcefulness failed before the difficulty of discovering a workable vein in the vague wealth of Lily's graces. Mrs. Fisher was full of indirect expedients for enabling her friends to earn a living, and could conscientiously assert that she had put several opportunities of this kind before Lily; but more legitimate methods of bread-winning were as much out of her line as they were beyond the capacity of the sufferers she was generally called upon to assist. Lily's failure to profit by the chances already afforded her might, moreover, have justified the abandonment of farther effort on her behalf; but Mrs. Fisher's inexhaustible good-nature made her an adept at creating artificial demands in response to an actual supply. In the pursuance of this end she at once started on a voyage of discovery in Miss Bart's behalf; and as the result of her explorations she now summoned the latter with the announcement that she had "found something."

Left to herself, Gerty mused distressfully upon her friend's plight, and her own inability to relieve it. It was clear to her that Lily, for the present, had no wish for the kind of help she could give. Miss Farish could see no hope for her friend but in a life completely reorganized and detached from its old associations; whereas all Lily's energies were centred in the determined effort to hold fast to those associations, to keep herself visibly identified with them, as long as the illusion could be maintained. Pitiable as such an attitude seemed to Gerty, she could not judge it as harshly as Selden, for instance, might have done. She had not forgotten the night of emotion when she and Lily had lain in each other's arms, and she had seemed to feel her very heart's blood passing into her friend. The sacrifice she had made had seemed unavailing enough; no trace remained in Lily of the subduing influences of that hour; but Gerty's tenderness, disciplined by long years of contact with obscure and inarticulate suffering, could wait on its object with a silent forbearance which took no account of time. She could not, however, deny herself the solace of taking anxious counsel with Lawrence Selden, with whom, since his return from Europe, she had renewed her old relation of cousinly confidence.

Selden himself had never been aware of any change in their relation. He found Gerty as he had left her, simple, undemanding and devoted, but with a quickened intelligence of the heart which he recognized without seeking to explain it. To Gerty herself it would once have seemed impossible that she should ever again talk freely with him of Lily Bart; but what had passed in the secrecy of her own breast seemed to resolve itself, when the mist of the struggle cleared, into a breaking down of the bounds of self, a deflecting of the wasted personal emotion into the general current of human understanding.

It was not till some two weeks after her visit from Lily that Gerty had the opportunity of communicating her fears to Selden. The latter, having presented himself on a Sunday afternoon, had lingered on through the dowdy animation of his cousin's tea-hour, conscious of something in her voice and eye which solicited a word apart; and as soon as the last visitor was gone Gerty opened her case by asking how lately he had seen Miss Bart.

Selden's perceptible pause gave her time for a slight stir of surprise.

"I haven't seen her at all—I've perpetually missed seeing her since she came back."

This unexpected admission made Gerty pause too; and she was still hesitating on the brink of her subject when he relieved her by adding: "I've wanted to see her—but she seems to have been absorbed by the Gormer set since her return from Europe."

"That's all the more reason: she's been very unhappy."

"Unhappy at being with the Gormers?"

"Oh, I don't defend her intimacy with the Gormers; but that too is at an end now, I think. You know people have been very unkind since Bertha Dorset quarrelled with her."

"Ah—" Selden exclaimed, rising abruptly to walk to the window, where he remained with his eyes on the darkening street while his cousin continued to explain: "Judy Trenor and her own family have deserted her too—and all because Bertha Dorset has said such horrible things. And she is very poor—you know Mrs. Peniston cut her off with a small legacy, after giving her to understand that she was to have everything."

"Yes—I know," Selden assented curtly, turning back into the room, but only to stir about with restless steps in the circumscribed space between door and window. "Yes—she's been abominably treated; but it's unfortunately the precise thing that a man who wants to show his sympathy can't say to her."

His words caused Gerty a slight chill of disappointment. "There would be other ways of showing your sympathy," she suggested.

Selden, with a slight laugh, sat down beside her on the little sofa which projected from the hearth. "What are you thinking of, you incorrigible missionary?" he asked.

Gerty's colour rose, and her blush was for a moment her only answer. Then she made it more explicit by saying: "I am thinking of the fact that you and she used to be great friends—that she used to care immensely for what you thought of her—and that, if she takes your staying away as a sign of what you think now, I can imagine its adding a great deal to her unhappiness."

"My dear child, don't add to it still more—at least to your conception of it—by attributing to her all sorts of susceptibilities of your own." Selden, for his life, could not keep a note of dryness out of his voice; but he met Gerty's look of perplexity by saying more mildly: "But, though you immensely exaggerate the importance of anything I could do for Miss Bart, you can't exaggerate my readiness to do it—if you ask me to." He laid his hand for a moment on hers, and there passed between them, on the current of the rare contact, one of those exchanges of meaning which fill the hidden reservoirs of affection. Gerty had the feeling that he measured the cost of her request as plainly as she read the significance of his reply; and the sense of all that was suddenly clear between them made her next words easier to find.

"I do ask you, then; I ask you because she once told me that you had been a help to her, and because she needs help now as she has never needed it before. You know how dependent she has always been on ease and luxury—how she has hated what was shabby and ugly and uncomfortable. She can't help it—she was brought up with those ideas, and has never been able to find her way out of them. But now all the things she cared for have been taken from her, and the people who taught her to care for them have abandoned her too; and it seems to me that if some one could reach out a hand and show her the other side—show her how much is left in life and in herself—" Gerty broke off, abashed at the sound of her own eloquence, and impeded by the difficulty of giving precise expression to her vague yearning for her friend's retrieval. "I can't help her myself: she's passed out of my reach," she continued. "I think she's afraid of being a burden to me. When she was last here, two weeks ago, she seemed dreadfully worried about her future: she said Carry Fisher was trying to find something for her to do. A few days later she wrote me that she had taken a position as private secretary, and that I was not to be anxious, for everything was all right, and she would come in and tell me about it when she had time; but she has never come, and I don't like to go to her, because I am afraid of forcing myself on her when I'm not wanted. Once, when we were children, and I had rushed up after a long separation, and thrown my arms about her, she said: 'Please don't kiss me unless I ask you to, Gerty'—and she *did* ask me, a minute later; but since then I've always waited to be asked."

Selden had listened in silence, with the concentrated look which his thin dark face could assume when he wished to guard it against any involuntary change of expression. When his cousin ended, he said with a slight smile: "Since you've learned the wisdom of waiting, I don't see why you urge me to rush in—" but the troubled appeal of her eyes made him add, as he rose to take leave: "Still, I'll do what you wish, and not hold you responsible for my failure."

Selden's avoidance of Miss Bart had not been as unintentional as he had allowed his cousin to think. At first, indeed, while the memory of their last hour at Monte Carlo still held the full heat of his indignation, he had anxiously watched for her return; but she had disappointed him by lingering in England, and when she finally reappeared it happened that business had called him to the West, whence he came back only to learn that she was starting for Alaska with the Gormers. The revelation of this suddenly-established intimacy effectually chilled his desire to see her. If, at a moment when her whole life seemed to be breaking up, she could cheerfully commit its reconstruction to the Gormers, there was no reason why such accidents should ever strike her as irreparable. Every step she took seemed in fact to carry her farther from the region where, once or twice, he and she had met for an illumined moment; and the recognition of this fact, when its first pang had been surmounted, produced in him a sense of negative relief. It was much simpler for him to judge Miss Bart by her habitual conduct than by the rare deviations from it which had thrown her so disturbingly in his way; and every act of hers which made the recurrence of such deviations more unlikely, confirmed the sense of relief with which he returned to the conventional view of her.

But Gerty Farish's words had sufficed to make him see how little this view was really his, and how impossible it was for him to live quietly with the thought of Lily Bart. To hear that she was in need of help—even such vague help as he could offer—was to be at once repossessed by that thought; and by the time he reached the street he had sufficiently convinced himself of the urgency of his cousin's appeal to turn his steps directly toward Lily's hotel.

There his zeal met a check in the unforeseen news that Miss Bart had moved away; but, on his pressing his enquiries, the clerk remembered that she had left an address, for which he presently began to search through his books.

It was certainly strange that she should have taken this step without letting Gerty Farish know of her decision; and Selden waited with a vague sense of uneasiness while the address was sought for. The process lasted long enough for uneasiness to turn to apprehension; but when at length a slip of paper was handed him, and he read on it: "Care of Mrs. Norma Hatch, Emporium Hotel," his apprehension passed into an incredulous stare, and this into the gesture of disgust with which he tore the paper in two, and turned to walk quickly homeward.

# Chapter 9

When Lily woke on the morning after her translation to the Emporium Hotel, her first feeling was one of purely physical satisfaction. The force of contrast gave an added keenness to the luxury of lying once more in a soft-pillowed bed, and looking across a spacious sunlit room at a breakfast-table set invitingly near the fire. Analysis and introspection might come later; but for the moment she was not even troubled by the excesses of the upholstery or the restless convolutions of the furniture. The sense of being once more lapped and folded in ease, as in some dense mild medium impenetrable to discomfort, effectually stilled the faintest note of criticism.

When, the afternoon before, she had presented herself to the lady to whom Carry Fisher had directed her, she had been conscious of entering a new world. Carry's vague presentment of Mrs. Norma Hatch (whose reversion to her Christian name was explained as the result of her latest divorce), left her under the implication of coming "from the West," with the not unusual extenuation of having brought a great deal of money with her. She was, in short, rich, helpless, unplaced: the very subject for Lily's hand. Mrs. Fisher had not specified the line her friend was to take; she owned herself unacquainted with Mrs. Hatch, whom she "knew about" through Melville Stancy, a lawyer in his leisure moments, and the Falstaff of a certain section of festive dub life. Socially, Mr. Stancy might have been said to form a connecting link between the Gormer world and the more dimly-lit region on which Miss Bart now found herself entering. It was, however, only figuratively that the illumination of Mrs. Hatch's world could be described as dim: in actual fact, Lily found her seated in a blaze of electric light, impartially projected from various ornamental excrescences on a vast concavity of pink damask and gilding, from which she rose like Venus from her shell. The analogy was justified by the appearance of the lady, whose large-eyed prettiness had the fixity of something impaled and shown under glass. This did not preclude the immediate discovery that she was some years younger than her visitor, and that under her showiness, her ease, the aggression of her dress and voice, there persisted that ineradicable innocence which, in ladies of her nationality, so curiously coexists with startling extremes of experience.

The environment in which Lily found herself was as strange to her as its inhabitants. She was unacquainted with the world of the fashionable New York hotel—a world over-heated, over-upholstered, and over-fitted with mechanical appliances for the gratification of fantastic requirements, while the comforts of a civilized life were as unattainable as in a desert. Through this atmosphere of torrid splendour moved wan beings as richly upholstered as the furniture, beings without definite pursuits or permanent relations, who drifted on a languid tide of curiosity from restaurant to concert-hall, from palm-garden to music-room, from "art exhibit" to dress-maker's opening. High-stepping horses or elaborately equipped motors waited to carry these ladies into vague metropolitan distances, whence they returned, still more wan from the weight of their sables, to be sucked back into the stifling inertia of the hotel routine. Somewhere behind them, in the background of their lives, there was doubtless a real past, peopled by real human activities: they themselves were probably the product of strong ambitions, persistent energies, diversified contacts with the wholesome roughness of life; yet they had no more real existence than the poet's shades in limbo.

Lily had not been long in this pallid world without discovering that Mrs. Hatch was its most substantial figure. That lady, though still floating in the void, showed faint symptoms of developing an outline; and in this endeavour she was actively seconded by Mr. Melville Stancy. It was Mr. Stancy, a man of large resounding presence, suggestive of convivial occasions and of a chivalry finding expression in "first-night" boxes and thousand dollar bonbonnieres, who had transplanted Mrs. Hatch from the scene of her first development to the higher stage of hotel life in the metropolis. It was he who had selected the horses with which she had taken the blue ribbon at the Show, had introduced her to the photographer whose portraits of her formed the recurring ornament of "Sunday Supplements," and had got together the group which constituted her social world. It was a small group still, with heterogeneous figures suspended in large unpeopled spaces; but Lily did not take long to learn that its regulation was no longer in Mr. Stancy's hands. As often happens, the pupil had outstripped the teacher, and Mrs. Hatch was already aware of heights of elegance as well as depths of luxury beyond the world of the Emporium. This discovery at once produced in her a craving for higher guidance, for the adroit feminine hand which should give the right turn to her correspondence, the right "look" to her hats, the right succession to the items of her MENUS. It was, in short, as the regulator of a germinating social life that Miss Bart's guidance was required; her ostensible duties as secretary being restricted by the fact that Mrs. Hatch, as yet, knew hardly any one to write to.

The daily details of Mrs. Hatch's existence were as strange to Lily as its general tenor. The lady's habits were marked by an Oriental indolence and disorder peculiarly trying to her companion. Mrs. Hatch and her friends seemed to float together outside the bounds of time and space. No definite hours were kept; no fixed obligations existed: night and day flowed into one another in a blur of confused and retarded engagements, so that one had the impression of lunching at the tea-hour, while dinner was often merged in the noisy after-theatre supper which prolonged Mrs. Hatch's vigil till daylight.

Through this jumble of futile activities came and went a strange throng of hangers-on—manicures, beauty-doctors, hair-dressers, teachers of bridge, of French, of "physical development": figures sometimes indistinguishable, by their appearance, or by Mrs. Hatch's relation to them, from the visitors constituting her recognized society. But strangest of all to Lily was the encounter, in this latter group, of several of her acquaintances. She had supposed, and not without relief, that she was passing, for the moment, completely out of her own circle; but she found that Mr. Stancy, one side of whose sprawling existence overlapped the edge of Mrs. Fisher's world, had drawn several of its brightest ornaments into the circle of the Emporium. To find Ned Silverton among the habitual frequenters of Mrs. Hatch's drawing-room was one of Lily's first astonishments; but she soon discovered that he was not Mr. Stancy's most important recruit. It was on little Freddy Van Osburgh, the small slim heir of the Van Osburgh millions, that the attention of Mrs. Hatch's group was centred. Freddy, barely out of college, had risen above the horizon since Lily's eclipse, and she now saw with surprise what an effulgence he shed on the outer twilight of Mrs. Hatch's existence. This, then, was one of the things that young men "went in" for when released from the official social routine; this was the kind of "previous engagement" that so frequently caused them to disappoint the hopes of anxious hostesses. Lily had an odd sense of being behind the social tapestry, on the side where the threads were knotted and the loose ends hung. For a moment she found a certain amusement in the show, and in her own share of it: the situation had an ease and unconventionality distinctly refreshing after her experience of the irony of conventions. But these flashes of amusement were but brief reactions from the long disgust of her days. Compared with the vast gilded void of Mrs. Hatch's existence, the life of Lily's former friends seemed packed with ordered activities. Even the most irresponsible pretty woman of her acquaintance had her inherited obligations, her conventional benevolences, her share in the working of the great civic machine; and all hung together in the solidarity of these traditional functions. The performance of specific duties would have simplified Miss Bart's position; but the vague attendance on Mrs. Hatch was not without its perplexities.

It was not her employer who created these perplexities. Mrs. Hatch showed from the first an almost touching desire for Lily's approval. Far from asserting the superiority of wealth, her beautiful eyes seemed to urge the plea of inexperience: she wanted to do what was "nice," to be taught how to be "lovely." The difficulty was to find any point of contact between her ideals and Lily's.

Mrs. Hatch swam in a haze of indeterminate enthusiasms, of aspirations culled from the stage, the newspapers, the fashion journals, and a gaudy world of sport still more completely beyond her companion's ken. To separate from these confused conceptions those most likely to advance the lady on her way, was Lily's obvious duty; but its performance was hampered by rapidly-growing doubts. Lily was in fact becoming more and more aware of a certain ambiguity in her situation. It was not that she had, in the conventional sense, any doubt of Mrs. Hatch's irreproachableness. The lady's offences were always against taste rather than conduct; her divorce record seemed due to geographical rather than ethical conditions; and her worst laxities were likely to proceed from a wandering and extravagant good-nature. But if Lily did not mind her detaining her manicure for luncheon, or offering the "Beauty-Doctor" a seat in Freddy Van Osburgh's box at the play, she was not equally at ease in regard to some less apparent lapses from convention. Ned Silverton's relation to Stancy seemed, for instance, closer and less clear than any natural affinities would warrant; and both appeared united in the effort to cultivate Freddy Van Osburgh's growing taste for Mrs. Hatch. There was as yet nothing definable in the situation, which might well resolve itself into a huge joke on the part of the other two; but Lily had a vague sense that the subject of their experiment was too young, too rich and too credulous. Her embarrassment was increased by the fact that Freddy seemed to regard her as cooperating with himself in the social development of Mrs. Hatch: a view that suggested, on his part, a permanent interest in the lady's future. There were moments when Lily found an ironic amusement in this aspect of the case. The thought of launching such a missile as Mrs. Hatch at the perfidious bosom of society was not without its charm: Miss Bart had even beguiled her leisure with visions of the fair Norma introduced for the first time to a family banquet at the Van Osburghs'. But the thought of being personally connected with the transaction was less agreeable; and her momentary flashes of amusement were followed by increasing periods of doubt.

The sense of these doubts was uppermost when, late one afternoon, she was surprised by a visit from Lawrence Selden. He found her alone in the wilderness of pink damask, for in Mrs. Hatch's world the tea-hour was not dedicated to social rites, and the lady was in the hands of her masseuse.

Selden's entrance had caused Lily an inward start of embarrassment; but his air of constraint had the effect of restoring her self-possession, and she took at once the tone of surprise and pleasure, wondering frankly that he should have traced her to so unlikely a place, and asking what had inspired him to make the search.

Selden met this with an unusual seriousness: she had never seen him so little master of the situation, so plainly at the mercy of any obstructions she might put in his way. "I wanted to see you," he said; and she could not resist observing in reply that he had kept his wishes under remarkable control. She had in truth felt his long absence as one of the chief bitternesses of the last months: his desertion had wounded sensibilities far below the surface of her pride.

Selden met the challenge with directness. "Why should I have come, unless I thought I could be of use to you? It is my only excuse for imagining you could want me."

This struck her as a clumsy evasion, and the thought gave a flash of keenness to her answer. "Then you have come now because you think you can be of use to me?"

He hesitated again. "Yes: in the modest capacity of a person to talk things over with."

For a clever man it was certainly a stupid beginning; and the idea that his awkwardness was due to the fear of her attaching a personal significance to his visit, chilled her pleasure in seeing him. Even under the most adverse conditions, that pleasure always made itself felt: she might hate him, but she had never been able to wish him out of the room. She was very near hating him now; yet the sound of his voice, the way the light fell on his thin dark hair, the way he sat and moved and wore his clothes—she was conscious that even these trivial things were inwoven with her deepest life. In his presence a sudden stillness came upon her, and the turmoil of her spirit ceased; but an impulse of resistance to this stealing influence now prompted her to say: "It's very good of you to present yourself in that capacity; but what makes you think I have anything particular to talk about?"

Though she kept the even tone of light intercourse, the question was framed in a way to remind him that his good offices were unsought; and for a moment Selden was checked by it. The situation between them was one which could have been cleared up only by a sudden explosion of feeling; and their whole training and habit of mind were against the chances of such an explosion. Selden's calmness seemed rather to harden into resistance, and Miss Bart's into a surface of glittering irony, as they faced each other from the opposite corners of one of Mrs. Hatch's elephantine sofas. The sofa in question, and the apartment peopled by its monstrous mates, served at length to suggest the turn of Selden's reply.

"Gerty told me that you were acting as Mrs. Hatch's secretary; and I knew she was anxious to hear how you were getting on."

Miss Bart received this explanation without perceptible softening. "Why didn't she look me up herself, then?" she asked.

"Because, as you didn't send her your address, she was afraid of being importunate." Selden continued with a smile: "You see no such scruples restrained me; but then I haven't as much to risk if I incur your displeasure."

Lily answered his smile. "You haven't incurred it as yet; but I have an idea that you are going to."

"That rests with you, doesn't it? You see my initiative doesn't go beyond putting myself at your disposal."

"But in what capacity? What am I to do with you?" she asked in the same light tone.

Selden again glanced about Mrs. Hatch's drawing-room; then he said, with a decision which he seemed to have gathered from this final inspection: "You are to let me take you away from here."

Lily flushed at the suddenness of the attack; then she stiffened under it and said coldly: "And may I ask where you mean me to go?"

"Back to Gerty in the first place, if you will; the essential thing is that it should be away from here."

The unusual harshness of his tone might have shown her how much the words cost him; but she was in no state to measure his feelings while her own were in a flame of revolt. To neglect her, perhaps even to avoid her, at a time when she had most need of her friends, and then suddenly and unwarrantably to break into her life with this strange assumption of authority, was to rouse in her every instinct of pride and self-defence.

"I am very much obliged to you," she said, "for taking such an interest in my plans; but I am quite contented where I am, and have no intention of leaving."

Selden had risen, and was standing before her in an attitude of uncontrollable expectancy.

"That simply means that you don't know where you are!" he exclaimed.

Lily rose also, with a quick flash of anger. "If you have come here to say disagreeable things about Mrs. Hatch—"

"It is only with your relation to Mrs. Hatch that I am concerned."

"My relation to Mrs. Hatch is one I have no reason to be ashamed of. She has helped me to earn a living when my old friends were quite resigned to seeing me starve."

"Nonsense! Starvation is not the only alternative. You know you can always find a home with Gerty till you are independent again."

"You show such an intimate acquaintance with my affairs that I suppose you mean—till my aunt's legacy is paid?"

"I do mean that; Gerty told me of it," Selden acknowledged without embarrassment. He was too much in earnest now to feel any false constraint in speaking his mind.

"But Gerty does not happen to know," Miss Bart rejoined, "that I owe every penny of that legacy."

"Good God!" Selden exclaimed, startled out of his composure by the abruptness of the statement.

"Every penny of it, and more too," Lily repeated; "and you now perhaps see why I prefer to remain with Mrs. Hatch rather than take advantage of Gerty's kindness. I have no money left, except my small income, and I must earn something more to keep myself alive."

Selden hesitated a moment; then he rejoined in a quieter tone: "But with your income and Gerty's—since you allow me to go so far into the details of the situation—you and she could surely contrive a life together which would put you beyond the need of having to support yourself. Gerty, I know, is eager to make such an arrangement, and would be quite happy in it—"

"But I should not," Miss Bart interposed. "There are many reasons why it would be neither kind to Gerty nor wise for myself." She paused a moment, and as he seemed to await a farther explanation, added with a quick lift of her head: "You will perhaps excuse me from giving you these reasons."

"I have no claim to know them," Selden answered, ignoring her tone; "no claim to offer any comment or suggestion beyond the one I have already made. And my right to make that is simply the universal right of a man to enlighten a woman when he sees her unconsciously placed in a false position."

Lily smiled. "I suppose," she rejoined, "that by a false position you mean one outside of what we call society; but you must remember that I had been excluded from those sacred precincts long before I met Mrs. Hatch. As far as I can see, there is very little real difference in being inside or out, and I remember your once telling me that it was only those inside who took the difference seriously."

She had not been without intention in making this allusion to their memorable talk at Bellomont, and she waited with an odd tremor of the nerves to see what response it would bring; but the result of the experiment was disappointing. Selden did not allow the allusion to deflect him from his point; he merely said with completer fulness of emphasis: "The question of being inside or out is, as you say, a small one, and it happens to have nothing to do with the case, except in so far as Mrs. Hatch's desire to be inside may put you in the position I call false."

In spite of the moderation of his tone, each word he spoke had the effect of confirming Lily's resistance. The very apprehensions he aroused hardened her against him: she had been on the alert for the note of personal sympathy, for any sign of recovered power over him; and his attitude of sober impartiality, the absence of all response to her appeal, turned her hurt pride to blind resentment of his interference. The conviction that he had been sent by Gerty, and that, whatever straits he conceived her to be in, he would never voluntarily have come to her aid, strengthened her resolve not to admit him a hair's breadth farther into her confidence. However doubtful she might feel her situation to be, she would rather persist in darkness than owe her enlightenment to Selden.

"I don't know," she said, when he had ceased to speak, "why you imagine me to be situated as you describe; but as you have always told me that the sole object of a bringing-up like mine was to teach a girl to get what she wants, why not assume that that is precisely what I am doing?"

The smile with which she summed up her case was like a clear barrier raised against farther confidences: its brightness held him at such a distance that he had a sense of being almost out of hearing as he rejoined: "I am not sure that I have ever called you a successful example of that kind of bringing-up."

Her colour rose a little at the implication, but she steeled herself with a light laugh. "Ah, wait a little longer—give me a little more time before you decide!" And as he wavered before her, still watching for a break in the impenetrable front she presented: "Don't give me up; I may still do credit to my training!" she affirmed.

# Chapter 10

"Look at those spangles, Miss Bart—every one of 'em sewed on crooked."

The tall forewoman, a pinched perpendicular figure, dropped the condemned structure of wire and net on the table at Lily's side, and passed on to the next figure in the line.

There were twenty of them in the work-room, their fagged profiles, under exaggerated hair, bowed in the harsh north light above the utensils of their art; for it was something more than an industry, surely, this creation of ever-varied settings for the face of fortunate womanhood. Their own faces were sallow with the unwholesomeness of hot air and sedentary toil, rather than with any actual signs of want: they were employed in a fashionable millinery establishment, and were fairly well clothed and well paid; but the youngest among them was as dull and colourless as the middle-aged. In the whole work-room there was only one skin beneath which the blood still visibly played; and that now burned with vexation as Miss Bart, under the lash of the forewoman's comment, began to strip the hat-frame of its over-lapping spangles.

To Gerty Farish's hopeful spirit a solution appeared to have been reached when she remembered how beautifully Lily could trim hats. Instances of young lady-milliners establishing themselves under fashionable patronage, and imparting to their "creations" that indefinable touch which the professional hand can never give, had flattered Gerty's visions of the future, and convinced even Lily that her separation from Mrs. Norma Hatch need not reduce her to dependence on her friends.

The parting had occurred a few weeks after Selden's visit, and would have taken place sooner had it not been for the resistance set up in Lily by his ill-starred offer of advice. The sense of being involved in a transaction she would not have cared to examine too closely had soon afterward defined itself in the light of a hint from Mr. Stancy that, if she "saw them through," she would have no reason to be sorry. The implication that such loyalty would meet with a direct reward had hastened her flight, and flung her back, ashamed and penitent, on the broad bosom of Gerty's sympathy. She did not, however, propose to lie there prone, and Gerty's inspiration about the hats at once revived her hopes of profitable activity. Here was, after all, something that her charming listless hands could really do; she had no doubt of their capacity for knotting a ribbon or placing a flower to advantage. And of course only these finishing touches would be expected of her: subordinate fingers, blunt, grey, needle-pricked fingers, would prepare the shapes and stitch the linings, while she presided over the charming little front shop—a shop all white panels, mirrors, and moss-green hangings—where her finished creations, hats, wreaths, aigrettes and the rest, perched on their stands like birds just poising for flight.

But at the very outset of Gerty's campaign this vision of the green-and-white shop had been dispelled. Other young ladies of fashion had been thus "set-up," selling their hats by the mere attraction of a name and the reputed knack of tying a bow; but these privileged beings could command a faith in their powers materially expressed by the readiness to pay their shop-rent and advance a handsome sum for current expenses. Where was Lily to find such support? And even could it have been found, how were the ladies on whose approval she depended to be induced to give her their patronage? Gerty learned that whatever sympathy her friend's case might have excited a few months since had been imperilled, if not lost, by her association with Mrs. Hatch. Once again, Lily had withdrawn from an ambiguous situation in time to save her self-respect, but too late for public vindication. Freddy Van Osburgh was not to marry Mrs. Hatch; he had been rescued at the eleventh hour—some said by the efforts of Gus Trenor and Rosedale—and despatched to Europe with old Ned Van Alstyne; but the risk he had run would always be ascribed to Miss Bart's connivance, and would somehow serve as a summing-up and corroboration of the vague general distrust of her. It was a relief to those who had hung back from her to find themselves thus justified, and they were inclined to insist a little on her connection with the Hatch case in order to show that they had been right.

Gerty's quest, at any rate, brought up against a solid wall of resistance; and even when Carry Fisher, momentarily penitent for her share in the Hatch affair, joined her efforts to Miss Farish's, they met with no better success. Gerty had tried to veil her failure in tender ambiguities; but Carry, always the soul of candour, put the case squarely to her friend.

"I went straight to Judy Trenor; she has fewer prejudices than the others, and besides she's always hated Bertha Dorset. But what *have* you done to her, Lily? At the very first word about giving you a start she flamed out about some money you'd got from Gus; I never knew her so hot before. You know she'll let him do anything but spend money on his friends: the only reason she's decent to me now is that she knows I'm not hard up.—He speculated for you, you say? Well, what's the harm? He had no business to lose. He *didn't* lose? Then what on earth—but I never *could* understand you, Lily!"

The end of it was that, after anxious enquiry and much deliberation, Mrs. Fisher and Gerty, for once oddly united in their effort to help their friend, decided on placing her in the work-room of Mme. Regina's renowned millinery establishment. Even this arrangement was not effected without considerable negotiation, for Mme. Regina had a strong prejudice against untrained assistance, and was induced to yield only by the fact that she owed the patronage of Mrs. Bry and Mrs. Gormer to Carry Fisher's influence. She had been willing from the first to employ Lily in the show-room: as a displayer of hats, a fashionable beauty might be a valuable asset. But to this suggestion Miss Bart opposed a negative which Gerty emphatically supported, while Mrs. Fisher, inwardly unconvinced, but resigned to this latest proof of Lily's unreason, agreed that perhaps in the end it would be more useful that she should learn the trade. To Regina's work-room Lily was therefore committed by her friends, and there Mrs. Fisher left her with a sigh of relief, while Gerty's watchfulness continued to hover over her at a distance.

Lily had taken up her work early in January: it was now two months later, and she was still being rebuked for her inability to sew spangles on a hat-frame. As she returned to her work she heard a titter pass down the tables. She knew she was an object of criticism and amusement to the other work-women. They were, of course, aware of her history—the exact situation of every girl in the room was known and freely discussed by all the others—but the knowledge did not produce in them any awkward sense of class distinction: it merely explained why her untutored fingers were still blundering over the rudiments of the trade. Lily had no desire that they should recognize any social difference in her; but she had hoped to be received as their equal, and perhaps before long to show herself their superior by a special deftness of touch, and it was humiliating to find that, after two months of drudgery, she still betrayed her lack of early training. Remote was the day when she might aspire to exercise the talents she felt confident of possessing; only experienced workers were entrusted with the delicate art of shaping and trimming the hat, and the forewoman still held her inexorably to the routine of preparatory work.

She began to rip the spangles from the frame, listening absently to the buzz of talk which rose and fell with the coming and going of Miss Haines's active figure. The air was closer than usual, because Miss Haines, who had a cold, had not allowed a window to be opened even during the noon recess; and Lily's head was so heavy with the weight of a sleepless night that the chatter of her companions had the incoherence of a dream.

"I *told* her he'd never look at her again; and he didn't. I wouldn't have, either—I think she acted real mean to him. He took her to the Arion Ball, and had a hack for her both ways.... She's taken ten bottles, and her headaches don't seem no better—but she's written a testimonial to say the first bottle cured her, and she got five dollars and her picture in the paper.... Mrs. Trenor's hat? The one with the green Paradise? Here, Miss Haines—it'll be ready right off.... That was one of the Trenor girls here yesterday with Mrs. George Dorset. How'd I know? Why, Madam sent for me to alter the flower in that Virot hat—the blue tulle: she's tall and slight, with her hair fuzzed out—a good deal like Mamie Leach, on'y thinner...."

On and on it flowed, a current of meaningless sound, on which, startlingly enough, a familiar name now and then floated to the surface. It was the strangest part of Lily's strange experience, the hearing of these names, the seeing the fragmentary and distorted image of the world she had lived in reflected in the mirror of the working-girls' minds. She had never before suspected the mixture of insatiable curiosity and contemptuous freedom with which she and her kind were discussed in this underworld of toilers who lived on their vanity and self-indulgence. Every girl in Mme. Regina's work-room knew to whom the headgear in her hands was destined, and had her opinion of its future wearer, and a definite knowledge of the latter's place in the social system. That Lily was a star fallen from that sky did not, after the first stir of curiosity had subsided, materially add to their interest in her. She had fallen, she had "gone under," and true to the ideal of their race, they were awed only by success—by the gross tangible image of material achievement. The consciousness of her different point of view merely kept them at a little distance from her, as though she were a foreigner with whom it was an effort to talk.

"Miss Bart, if you can't sew those spangles on more regular I guess you'd better give the hat to Miss Kilroy."

Lily looked down ruefully at her handiwork. The forewoman was right: the sewing on of the spangles was inexcusably bad. What made her so much more clumsy than usual? Was it a growing distaste for her task, or actual physical disability? She felt tired and confused: it was an effort to put her thoughts together. She rose and handed the hat to Miss Kilroy, who took it with a suppressed smile.

"I'm sorry; I'm afraid I am not well," she said to the forewoman.

Miss Haines offered no comment. From the first she had augured ill of Mme. Regina's consenting to include a fashionable apprentice among her workers. In that temple of art no raw beginners were wanted, and Miss Haines would have been more than human had she not taken a certain pleasure in seeing her forebodings confirmed.

"You'd better go back to binding edges," she said drily. Lily slipped out last among the band of liberated work-women. She did not care to be mingled in their noisy dispersal: once in the street, she always felt an irresistible return to her old standpoint, an instinctive shrinking from all that was unpolished and promiscuous. In the days—how distant they now seemed!—when she had visited the Girls' Club with Gerty Farish, she had felt an enlightened interest in the working-classes; but that was because she looked down on them from above, from the happy altitude of her grace and her beneficence. Now that she was on a level with them, the point of view was less interesting.

She felt a touch on her arm, and met the penitent eye of Miss Kilroy. "Miss Bart, I guess you can sew those spangles on as well as I can when you're feeling right. Miss Haines didn't act fair to you."

Lily's colour rose at the unexpected advance: it was a long time since real kindness had looked at her from any eyes but Gerty's.

"Oh, thank you: I'm not particularly well, but Miss Haines was right. I *am* clumsy."

"Well, it's mean work for anybody with a headache." Miss Kilroy paused irresolutely. "You ought to go right home and lay down. Ever try orangeine?"

"Thank you." Lily held out her hand. "It's very kind of you—I mean to go home."

She looked gratefully at Miss Kilroy, but neither knew what more to say. Lily was aware that the other was on the point of offering to go home with her, but she wanted to be alone and silent—even kindness, the sort of kindness that Miss Kilroy could give, would have jarred on her just then.

"Thank you," she repeated as she turned away.

She struck westward through the dreary March twilight, toward the street where her boarding-house stood. She had resolutely refused Gerty's offer of hospitality. Something of her mother's fierce shrinking from observation and sympathy was beginning to develop in her, and the promiscuity of small quarters and close intimacy seemed, on the whole, less endurable than the solitude of a hall bedroom in a house where she could come and go unremarked among other workers. For a while she had been sustained by this desire for privacy and independence; but now, perhaps from increasing physical weariness, the lassitude brought about by hours of unwonted confinement, she was beginning to feel acutely the ugliness and discomfort of her surroundings. The day's task done, she dreaded to return to her narrow room, with its blotched wallpaper and shabby paint; and she hated every step of the walk thither, through the degradation of a New York street in the last stages of decline from fashion to commerce.

But what she dreaded most of all was having to pass the chemist's at the corner of Sixth Avenue. She had meant to take another street: she had usually done so of late. But today her steps were irresistibly drawn toward the flaring plate-glass corner; she tried to take the lower crossing, but a laden dray crowded her back, and she struck across the street obliquely, reaching the sidewalk just opposite the chemist's door.

Over the counter she caught the eye of the clerk who had waited on her before, and slipped the prescription into his hand. There could be no question about the prescription: it was a copy of one of Mrs. Hatch's, obligingly furnished by that lady's chemist. Lily was confident that the clerk would fill it without hesitation; yet the nervous dread of a refusal, or even of an expression of doubt, communicated itself to her restless hands as she affected to examine the bottles of perfume stacked on the glass case before her.

The clerk had read the prescription without comment; but in the act of handing out the bottle he paused.

"You don't want to increase the dose, you know," he remarked. Lily's heart contracted.

What did he mean by looking at her in that way?

"Of course not," she murmured, holding out her hand.

"That's all right: it's a queer-acting drug. A drop or two more, and off you go—the doctors don't know why."

The dread lest he should question her, or keep the bottle back, choked the murmur of acquiescence in her throat; and when at length she emerged safely from the shop she was almost dizzy with the intensity of her relief. The mere touch of the packet thrilled her tired nerves with the delicious promise of a night of sleep, and in the reaction from her momentary fear she felt as if the first fumes of drowsiness were already stealing over her.

In her confusion she stumbled against a man who was hurrying down the last steps of the elevated station. He drew back, and she heard her name uttered with surprise. It was Rosedale, fur-coated, glossy and prosperous—but why did she seem to see him so far off, and as if through a mist of splintered crystals? Before she could account for the phenomenon she found herself shaking hands with him. They had parted with scorn on her side and anger upon his; but all trace of these emotions seemed to vanish as their hands met, and she was only aware of a confused wish that she might continue to hold fast to him.

"Why, what's the matter, Miss Lily? You're not well!" he exclaimed; and she forced her lips into a pallid smile of reassurance.

"I'm a little tired—it's nothing. Stay with me a moment, please," she faltered. That she should be asking this service of Rosedale!

He glanced at the dirty and unpropitious corner on which they stood, with the shriek of the "elevated" and the tumult of trams and waggons contending hideously in their ears.

"We can't stay here; but let me take you somewhere for a cup of tea. The *Longworth* is only a few yards off, and there'll be no one there at this hour."

A cup of tea in quiet, somewhere out of the noise and ugliness, seemed for the moment the one solace she could bear. A few steps brought them to the ladies' door of the hotel he had named, and a moment later he was seated opposite to her, and the waiter had placed the tea-tray between them.

"Not a drop of brandy or whiskey first? You look regularly done up, Miss Lily. Well, take your tea strong, then; and, waiter, get a cushion for the lady's back."

Lily smiled faintly at the injunction to take her tea strong. It was the temptation she was always struggling to resist. Her craving for the keen stimulant was forever conflicting with that other craving for sleep—the midnight craving which only the little phial in her hand could still. But today, at any rate, the tea could hardly be too strong: she counted on it to pour warmth and resolution into her empty veins.

As she leaned back before him, her lids drooping in utter lassitude, though the first warm draught already tinged her face with returning life, Rosedale was seized afresh by the poignant surprise of her beauty. The dark pencilling of fatigue under her eyes, the morbid blue-veined pallour of the temples, brought out the brightness of her hair and lips, as though all her ebbing vitality were centred there. Against the dull chocolate-coloured background of the restaurant, the purity of her head stood out as it had never done in the most brightly-lit ball-room. He looked at her with a startled uncomfortable feeling, as though her beauty were a forgotten enemy that had lain in ambush and now sprang out on him unawares.

To clear the air he tried to take an easy tone with her. "Why, Miss Lily, I haven't seen you for an age. I didn't know what had become of you."

As he spoke, he was checked by an embarrassing sense of the complications to which this might lead. Though he had not seen her he had heard of her; he knew of her connection with Mrs. Hatch, and of the talk resulting from it. Mrs. Hatch's *milieu* was one which he had once assiduously frequented, and now as devoutly shunned.

Lily, to whom the tea had restored her usual clearness of mind, saw what was in his thoughts and said with a slight smile: "You would not be likely to know about me. I have joined the working classes."

He stared in genuine wonder. "You don't mean—? Why, what on earth are you doing?"

"Learning to be a milliner—at least *trying* to learn," she hastily qualified the statement.

Rosedale suppressed a low whistle of surprise. "Come off—you ain't serious, are you?"

"Perfectly serious. I'm obliged to work for my living."

"But I understood—I thought you were with Norma Hatch."

"You heard I had gone to her as her secretary?"

"Something of the kind, I believe." He leaned forward to refill her cup.

Lily guessed the possibilities of embarrassment which the topic held for him, and raising her eyes to his, she said suddenly: "I left her two months ago."

Rosedale continued to fumble awkwardly with the tea-pot, and she felt sure that he had heard what had been said of her. But what was there that Rosedale did not hear?

"Wasn't it a soft berth?" he enquired, with an attempt at lightness.

"Too soft—one might have sunk in too deep." Lily rested one arm on the edge of the table, and sat looking at him more intently than she had ever looked before. An uncontrollable impulse was urging her to put her case to this man, from whose curiosity she had always so fiercely defended herself.

"You know Mrs. Hatch, I think? Well, perhaps you can understand that she might make things too easy for one."

Rosedale looked faintly puzzled, and she remembered that allusiveness was lost on him.

"It was no place for you, anyhow," he agreed, so suffused and immersed in the light of her full gaze that he found himself being drawn into strange depths of intimacy. He who had had to subsist on mere fugitive glances, looks winged in flight and swiftly lost under covert, now found her eyes settling on him with a brooding intensity that fairly dazzled him.

"I left," Lily continued, "lest people should say I was helping Mrs. Hatch to marry Freddy Van Osburgh—who is not in the least too good for her—and as they still continue to say it, I see that I might as well have stayed where I was."

"Oh, Freddy—" Rosedale brushed aside the topic with an air of its unimportance which gave a sense of the immense perspective he had acquired. "Freddy don't count—but I knew *you* weren't mixed up in that. It ain't your style."

Lily coloured slightly: she could not conceal from herself that the words gave her pleasure. She would have liked to sit there, drinking more tea, and continuing to talk of herself to Rosedale. But the old habit of observing the conventions reminded her that it was time to bring their colloquy to an end, and she made a faint motion to push back her chair.

Rosedale stopped her with a protesting gesture. "Wait a minute—don't go yet; sit quiet and rest a little longer. You look thoroughly played out. And you haven't told me—" He broke off, conscious of going farther than he had meant. She saw the struggle and understood it; understood also the nature of the spell to which he yielded as, with his eyes on her face, he began again abruptly: "What on earth did you mean by saying just now that you were learning to be a milliner?"

"Just what I said. I am an apprentice at Regina's."

"Good Lord—*you*? But what for? I knew your aunt had turned you down: Mrs. Fisher told me about it. But I understood you got a legacy from her—"

"I got ten thousand dollars; but the legacy is not to be paid till next summer."

"Well, but—look here: you could *borrow* on it any time you wanted."

She shook her head gravely. "No; for I owe it already."

"Owe it? The whole ten thousand?"

"Every penny." She paused, and then continued abruptly, with her eyes on his face: "I think Gus Trenor spoke to you once about having made some money for me in stocks."

She waited, and Rosedale, congested with embarrassment, muttered that he remembered something of the kind.

"He made about nine thousand dollars," Lily pursued, in the same tone of eager communicativeness. "At the time, I understood that he was speculating with my own money: it was incredibly stupid of me, but I knew nothing of business. Afterward I found out that he had *not* used my money—that what he said he had made for me he had really given me. It was meant in kindness, of course; but it was not the sort of obligation one could remain under. Unfortunately I had spent the money before I discovered my mistake; and so my legacy will have to go to pay it back. That is the reason why I am trying to learn a trade."

She made the statement clearly, deliberately, with pauses between the sentences, so that each should have time to sink deeply into her hearer's mind. She had a passionate desire that some one should know the truth about this transaction, and also that the rumour of her intention to repay the money should reach Judy Trenor's ears. And it had suddenly occurred to her that Rosedale, who had surprised Trenor's confidence, was the fitting person to receive and transmit her version of the facts. She had even felt a momentary exhilaration at the thought of thus relieving herself of her detested secret; but the sensation gradually faded in the telling, and as she ended her pallour was suffused with a deep blush of misery.

Rosedale continued to stare at her in wonder; but the wonder took the turn she had least expected.

"But see here—if that's the case, it cleans you out altogether?"

He put it to her as if she had not grasped the consequences of her act; as if her incorrigible ignorance of business were about to precipitate her into a fresh act of folly.

"Altogether—yes," she calmly agreed.

He sat silent, his thick hands clasped on the table, his little puzzled eyes exploring the recesses of the deserted restaurant.

"See here—that's fine," he exclaimed abruptly.

Lily rose from her seat with a deprecating laugh. "Oh, no—it's merely a bore," she asserted, gathering together the ends of her feather scarf.

Rosedale remained seated, too intent on his thoughts to notice her movement. "Miss Lily, if you want any backing—I like pluck—" broke from him disconnectedly.

"Thank you." She held out her hand. "Your tea has given me a tremendous backing. I feel equal to anything now."

Her gesture seemed to show a definite intention of dismissal, but her companion had tossed a bill to the waiter, and was slipping his short arms into his expensive overcoat.

"Wait a minute—you've got to let me walk home with you," he said.

Lily uttered no protest, and when he had paused to make sure of his change they emerged from the hotel and crossed Sixth Avenue again. As she led the way westward past a long line of areas which, through the distortion of their paintless rails, revealed with increasing candour the *disjecta membra* of bygone dinners, Lily felt that Rosedale was taking contemptuous note of the neighbourhood; and before the doorstep at which she finally paused he looked up with an air of incredulous disgust.

"This isn't the place? Some one told me you were living with Miss Farish."

"No: I am boarding here. I have lived too long on my friends."

He continued to scan the blistered brown stone front, the windows draped with discoloured lace, and the Pompeian decoration of the muddy vestibule; then he looked back at her face and said with a visible effort: "You'll let me come and see you some day?"

She smiled, recognizing the heroism of the offer to the point of being frankly touched by it. "Thank you—I shall be very glad," she made answer, in the first sincere words she had ever spoken to him.

That evening in her own room Miss Bart—who had fled early from the heavy fumes of the basement dinner-table—sat musing upon the impulse which had led her to unbosom herself to Rosedale. Beneath it she discovered an increasing sense of loneliness—a dread of returning to the solitude of her room, while she could be anywhere else, or in any company but her own. Circumstances, of late, had combined to cut her off more and more from her few remaining friends. On Carry Fisher's part the withdrawal was perhaps not quite involuntary. Having made her final effort on Lily's behalf, and landed her safely in Mme. Regina's work-room, Mrs. Fisher seemed disposed to rest from her labours; and Lily, understanding the reason, could not condemn her. Carry had in fact come dangerously near to being involved in the episode of Mrs. Norma Hatch, and it had taken some verbal ingenuity to extricate herself. She frankly owned to having brought Lily and Mrs. Hatch together, but then she did not know Mrs. Hatch—she had expressly warned Lily that she did not know Mrs. Hatch—and besides, she was not Lily's keeper, and really the girl was old enough to take care of herself. Carry did not put her own case so brutally, but she allowed it to be thus put for her by her latest bosom friend, Mrs. Jack Stepney: Mrs. Stepney, trembling over the narrowness of her only brother's escape, but eager to vindicate Mrs. Fisher, at whose house she could count on the "jolly parties" which had become a necessity to her since marriage had emancipated her from the Van Osburgh point of view.

Lily understood the situation and could make allowances for it. Carry had been a good friend to her in difficult days, and perhaps only a friendship like Gerty's could be proof against such an increasing strain. Gerty's friendship did indeed hold fast; yet Lily was beginning to avoid her also. For she could not go to Gerty's without risk of meeting Selden; and to meet him now would be pure pain. It was pain enough even to think of him, whether she considered him in the distinctness of her waking thoughts, or felt the obsession of his presence through the blur of her tormented nights. That was one of the reasons why she had turned again to Mrs. Hatch's prescription. In the uneasy snatches of her natural dreams he came to her sometimes in the old guise of fellowship and tenderness; and she would rise from the sweet delusion mocked and emptied of her courage. But in the sleep which the phial procured she sank far below such half-waking visitations, sank into depths of dreamless annihilation from which she woke each morning with an obliterated past.

Gradually, to be sure, the stress of the old thoughts would return; but at least they did not importune her waking hour. The drug gave her a momentary illusion of complete renewal, from which she drew strength to take up her daily work. The strength was more and more needed as the perplexities of her future increased. She knew that to Gerty and Mrs. Fisher she was only passing through a temporary period of probation, since they believed that the apprenticeship she was serving at Mme. Regina's would enable her, when Mrs. Peniston's legacy was paid, to realize the vision of the green-and-white shop with the fuller competence acquired by her preliminary training. But to Lily herself, aware that the legacy could not be put to such a use, the preliminary training seemed a wasted effort. She understood clearly enough that, even if she could ever learn to compete with hands formed from childhood for their special work, the small pay she received would not be a sufficient addition to her income to compensate her for such drudgery. And the realization of this fact brought her recurringly face to face with the temptation to use the legacy in establishing her business. Once installed, and in command of her own work-women, she believed she had sufficient tact and ability to attract a fashionable *clientele*; and if the business succeeded she could gradually lay aside money enough to discharge her debt to Trenor. But the task might take years to accomplish, even if she continued to stint herself to the utmost; and meanwhile her pride would be crushed under the weight of an intolerable obligation.

These were her superficial considerations; but under them lurked the secret dread that the obligation might not always remain intolerable. She knew she could not count on her continuity of purpose, and what really frightened her was the thought that she might gradually accommodate herself to remaining indefinitely in Trenor's debt, as she had accommodated herself to the part allotted her on the Sabrina, and as she had so nearly drifted into acquiescing with Stancy's scheme for the advancement of Mrs. Hatch. Her danger lay, as she knew, in her old incurable dread of discomfort and poverty; in the fear of that mounting tide of dinginess against which her mother had so passionately warned her. And now a new vista of peril opened before her. She understood that Rosedale was ready to lend her money; and the longing to take advantage of his offer began to haunt her insidiously. It was of course impossible to accept a loan from Rosedale; but proximate possibilities hovered temptingly before her. She was quite sure that he would come and see her again, and almost sure that, if he did, she could bring him to the point of offering to marry her on the terms she had previously rejected. Would she still reject them if they were offered? More and more, with every fresh mischance befalling her, did the pursuing furies seem to take the shape of Bertha Dorset; and close at hand, safely locked among her papers, lay the means of ending their pursuit. The temptation, which her scorn of Rosedale had once enabled her to reject, now insistently returned upon her; and how much strength was left her to oppose it?

What little there was must at any rate be husbanded to the utmost; she could not trust herself again to the perils of a sleepless night. Through the long hours of silence the dark spirit of fatigue and loneliness crouched upon her breast, leaving her so drained of bodily strength that her morning thoughts swam in a haze of weakness. The only hope of renewal lay in the little bottle at her bed-side; and how much longer that hope would last she dared not conjecture.

# Chapter 11

Lily, lingering for a moment on the corner, looked out on the afternoon spectacle of Fifth Avenue. It was a day in late April, and the sweetness of spring was in the air. It mitigated the ugliness of the long crowded thoroughfare, blurred the gaunt roof-lines, threw a mauve veil over the discouraging perspective of the side streets, and gave a touch of poetry to the delicate haze of green that marked the entrance to the Park.

As Lily stood there, she recognized several familiar faces in the passing carriages. The season was over, and its ruling forces had disbanded; but a few still lingered, delaying their departure for Europe, or passing through town on their return from the South. Among them was Mrs. Van Osburgh, swaying majestically in her C-spring barouche, with Mrs. Percy Gryce at her side, and the new heir to the Gryce millions enthroned before them on his nurse's knees. They were succeeded by Mrs. Hatch's electric victoria, in which that lady reclined in the lonely splendour of a spring toilet obviously designed for company; and a moment or two later came Judy Trenor, accompanied by Lady Skiddaw, who had come over for her annual tarpon fishing and a dip into "the street."

This fleeting glimpse of her past served to emphasize the sense of aimlessness with which Lily at length turned toward home. She had nothing to do for the rest of the day, nor for the days to come; for the season was over in millinery as well as in society, and a week earlier Mme. Regina had notified her that her services were no longer required. Mme. Regina always reduced her staff on the first of May, and Miss Bart's attendance had of late been so irregular—she had so often been unwell, and had done so little work when she came—that it was only as a favour that her dismissal had hitherto been deferred.

Lily did not question the justice of the decision. She was conscious of having been forgetful, awkward and slow to learn. It was bitter to acknowledge her inferiority even to herself, but the fact had been brought home to her that as a bread-winner she could never compete with professional ability. Since she had been brought up to be ornamental, she could hardly blame herself for failing to serve any practical purpose; but the discovery put an end to her consoling sense of universal efficiency.

As she turned homeward her thoughts shrank in anticipation from the fact that there would be nothing to get up for the next morning. The luxury of lying late in bed was a pleasure belonging to the life of ease; it had no part in the utilitarian existence of the boarding-house. She liked to leave her room early, and to return to it as late as possible; and she was walking slowly now in order to postpone the detested approach to her doorstep.

But the doorstep, as she drew near it, acquired a sudden interest from the fact that it was occupied—and indeed filled—by the conspicuous figure of Mr. Rosedale, whose presence seemed to take on an added amplitude from the meanness of his surroundings.

The sight stirred Lily with an irresistible sense of triumph. Rosedale, a day or two after their chance meeting, had called to enquire if she had recovered from her indisposition; but since then she had not seen or heard from him, and his absence seemed to betoken a struggle to keep away, to let her pass once more out of his life. If this were the case, his return showed that the struggle had been unsuccessful, for Lily knew he was not the man to waste his time in an ineffectual sentimental dalliance. He was too busy, too practical, and above all too much preoccupied with his own advancement, to indulge in such unprofitable asides.

In the peacock-blue parlour, with its bunches of dried pampas grass, and discoloured steel engravings of sentimental episodes, he looked about him with unconcealed disgust, laying his hat distrustfully on the dusty console adorned with a Rogers statuette.

Lily sat down on one of the plush and rosewood sofas, and he deposited himself in a rocking-chair draped with a starched antimacassar which scraped unpleasantly against the pink fold of skin above his collar.

"My goodness—you can't go on living here!" he exclaimed.

Lily smiled at his tone. "I am not sure that I can; but I have gone over my expenses very carefully, and I rather think I shall be able to manage it."

"Be able to manage it? That's not what I mean—it's no place for you!"

"It's what I mean; for I have been out of work for the last week."

"Out of work—out of work! What a way for you to talk! The idea of your having to work—it's preposterous." He brought out his sentences in short violent jerks, as though they were forced up from a deep inner crater of indignation. "It's a farce—a crazy farce," he repeated, his eyes fixed on the long vista of the room reflected in the blotched glass between the windows.

Lily continued to meet his expostulations with a smile. "I don't know why I should regard myself as an exception—" she began.

"Because you ARE; that's why; and your being in a place like this is a damnable outrage. I can't talk of it calmly."

She had in truth never seen him so shaken out of his usual glibness; and there was something almost moving to her in his inarticulate struggle with his emotions.

He rose with a start which left the rocking-chair quivering on its beam ends, and placed himself squarely before her.

"Look here, Miss Lily, I'm going to Europe next week: going over to Paris and London for a couple of months—and I can't leave you like this. I can't do it. I know it's none of my business—you've let me understand that often enough; but things are worse with you now than they have been before, and you must see that you've got to accept help from somebody. You spoke to me the other day about some debt to

Trenor. I know what you mean—and I respect you for feeling as you do about it."

A blush of surprise rose to Lily's pale face, but before she could interrupt him he had continued eagerly: "Well, I'll lend you the money to pay Trenor; and I won't—I—see here, don't take me up till I've finished. What I mean is, it'll be a plain business arrangement, such as one man would make with another. Now, what have you got to say against that?"

Lily's blush deepened to a glow in which humiliation and gratitude were mingled; and both sentiments revealed themselves in the unexpected gentleness of her reply.

"Only this: that it is exactly what Gus Trenor proposed; and that I can never again be sure of understanding the plainest business arrangement." Then, realizing that this answer contained a germ of injustice, she added, even more kindly: "Not that I don't appreciate your kindness—that I'm not grateful for it. But a business arrangement between us would in any case be impossible, because I shall have no security to give when my debt to Gus Trenor has been paid."

Rosedale received this statement in silence: he seemed to feel the note of finality in her voice, yet to be unable to accept it as closing the question between them.

In the silence Lily had a clear perception of what was passing through his mind. Whatever perplexity he felt as to the inexorableness of her course—however little he penetrated its motive—she saw that it unmistakably tended to strengthen her hold over him. It was as though the sense in her of unexplained scruples and resistances had the same attraction as the delicacy of feature, the fastidiousness of manner, which gave her an external rarity, an air of being impossible to match. As he advanced in social experience this uniqueness had acquired a greater value for him, as though he were a collector who had learned to distinguish minor differences of design and quality in some long-coveted object.

Lily, perceiving all this, understood that he would marry her at once, on the sole condition of a reconciliation with Mrs. Dorset; and the temptation was the less easy to put aside because, little by little, circumstances were breaking down her dislike for Rosedale. The dislike, indeed, still subsisted; but it was penetrated here and there by the perception of mitigating qualities in him: of a certain gross kindliness, a rather helpless fidelity of sentiment, which seemed to be struggling through the hard surface of his material ambitions.

Reading his dismissal in her eyes, he held out his hand with a gesture which conveyed something of this inarticulate conflict.

"If you'd only let me, I'd set you up over them all—I'd put you where you could wipe your feet on 'em!" he declared; and it touched her oddly to see that his new passion had not altered his old standard of values.

Lily took no sleeping-drops that night. She lay awake viewing her situation in the crude light which Rosedale's visit had shed on it. In fending off the offer he was so plainly ready to renew, had she not sacrificed to one of those abstract notions of honour that might be called the conventionalities of the moral life? What debt did she owe to a social order which had condemned and banished her without trial? She had never been heard in her own defence; she was innocent of the charge on which she had been found guilty; and the irregularity of her conviction might seem to justify the use of methods as irregular in recovering her lost rights. Bertha Dorset, to save herself, had not scrupled to ruin her by an open falsehood; why should she hesitate to make private use of the facts that chance had put in her way? After all, half the opprobrium of such an act lies in the name attached to it. Call it blackmail and it becomes unthinkable; but explain that it injures no one, and that the rights regained by it were unjustly forfeited, and he must be a formalist indeed who can find no plea in its defence.

The arguments pleading for it with Lily were the old unanswerable ones of the personal situation: the sense of injury, the sense of failure, the passionate craving for a fair chance against the selfish despotism of society. She had learned by experience that she had neither the aptitude nor the moral constancy to remake her life on new lines; to become a worker among workers, and let the world of luxury and pleasure sweep by her unregarded. She could not hold herself much to blame for this ineffectiveness, and she was perhaps less to blame than she believed. Inherited tendencies had combined with early training to make her the highly specialized product she was: an organism as helpless out of its narrow range as the sea-anemone torn from the rock. She had been fashioned to adorn and delight; to what other end does nature round the rose-leaf and paint the humming-bird's breast? And was it her fault that the purely decorative mission is less easily and harmoniously fulfilled among social beings than in the world of nature? That it is apt to be hampered by material necessities or complicated by moral scruples?

These last were the two antagonistic forces which fought out their battle in her breast during the long watches of the night; and when she rose the next morning she hardly knew where the victory lay. She was exhausted by the reaction of a night without sleep, coming after many nights of rest artificially obtained; and in the distorting light of fatigue the future stretched out before her grey, interminable and desolate.

She lay late in bed, refusing the coffee and fried eggs which the friendly Irish servant thrust through her door, and hating the intimate domestic noises of the house and the cries and rumblings of the street. Her week of idleness had brought home to her with exaggerated force these small aggravations of the boarding-house world, and she yearned for that other luxurious world, whose machinery is so carefully concealed that one scene flows into another without perceptible agency.

At length she rose and dressed. Since she had left Mme. Regina's she had spent her days in the streets, partly to escape from the uncongenial promiscuities of the boarding-house, and partly in the hope that physical fatigue would help her to sleep. But once out of the house, she could not decide where to go; for she had avoided Gerty since her dismissal from the milliner's, and she was not sure of a welcome anywhere else.

The morning was in harsh contrast to the previous day. A cold grey sky threatened rain, and a high wind drove the dust in wild spirals up and down the streets. Lily walked up Fifth Avenue toward the Park, hoping to find a sheltered nook where she might sit; but the wind chilled her, and after an hour's wandering under the tossing boughs she yielded to her increasing weariness, and took refuge in a little restaurant in Fifty-ninth Street. She was not hungry, and had meant to go without luncheon; but she was too tired to return home, and the long perspective of white tables showed alluringly through the windows.

The room was full of women and girls, all too much engaged in the rapid absorption of tea and pie to remark her entrance. A hum of shrill voices reverberated against the low ceiling, leaving Lily shut out in a little circle of silence. She felt a sudden pang of profound loneliness. She had lost the sense of time, and it seemed to her as though she had not spoken to any one for days. Her eyes sought the faces about her, craving a responsive glance, some sign of an intuition of her trouble. But the sallow preoccupied women, with their bags and note-books and rolls of music, were all engrossed in their own affairs, and even those who sat by themselves were busy running over proof-sheets or devouring magazines between their hurried gulps of tea. Lily alone was stranded in a great waste of disoccupation.

She drank several cups of the tea which was served with her portion of stewed oysters, and her brain felt clearer and livelier when she emerged once more into the street. She realized now that, as she sat in the restaurant, she had unconsciously arrived at a final decision. The discovery gave her an immediate illusion of activity: it was exhilarating to think that she had actually a reason for hurrying home. To prolong her enjoyment of the sensation she decided to walk; but the distance was so great that she found herself glancing nervously at the clocks on the way. One of the surprises of her unoccupied state was the discovery that time, when it is left to itself and no definite demands are made on it, cannot be trusted to move at any recognized pace. Usually it loiters; but just when one has come to count upon its slowness, it may suddenly break into a wild irrational gallop.

She found, however, on reaching home, that the hour was still early enough for her to sit down and rest a few minutes before putting her plan into execution. The delay did not perceptibly weaken her resolve. She was frightened and yet stimulated by the reserved force of resolution which she felt within herself: she saw it was going to be easier, a great deal easier, than she had imagined.

At five o'clock she rose, unlocked her trunk, and took out a sealed packet which she slipped into the bosom of her dress. Even the contact with the packet did not shake her nerves as she had half-expected it would. She seemed encased in a strong armour of indifference, as though the vigorous exertion of her will had finally benumbed her finer sensibilities.

She dressed herself once more for the street, locked her door and went out. When she emerged on the pavement, the day was still high, but a threat of rain darkened the sky and cold gusts shook the signs projecting from the basement shops along the street. She reached Fifth Avenue and began to walk slowly northward. She was sufficiently familiar with Mrs. Dorset's habits to know that she could always be found at home after five. She might not, indeed, be accessible to visitors, especially to a visitor so unwelcome, and against whom it was quite possible that she had guarded herself by special orders; but Lily had written a note which she meant to send up with her name, and which she thought would secure her admission.

She had allowed herself time to walk to Mrs. Dorset's, thinking that the quick movement through the cold evening air would help to steady her nerves; but she really felt no need of being tranquillized. Her survey of the situation remained calm and unwavering.

As she reached Fiftieth Street the clouds broke abruptly, and a rush of cold rain slanted into her face. She had no umbrella and the moisture quickly penetrated her thin spring dress. She was still half a mile from her destination, and she decided to walk across to Madison Avenue and take the electric car. As she turned into the side street, a vague memory stirred in her. The row of budding trees, the new brick and limestone house-fronts, the Georgian flat-house with flowerboxes on its balconies, were merged together into the setting of a familiar scene. It was down this street that she had walked with Selden, that September day two years ago; a few yards ahead was the doorway they had entered together. The recollection loosened a throng of benumbed sensations—longings, regrets, imaginings, the throbbing brood of the only spring her heart had ever known. It was strange to find herself passing his house on such an errand. She seemed suddenly to see her action as he would see it—and the fact of his own connection with it, the fact that, to attain her end, she must trade on his name, and profit by a secret of his past, chilled her blood with shame. What a long way she had travelled since the day of their first talk together! Even then her feet had been set in the path she was now following—even then she had resisted the hand he had held out.

All her resentment of his fancied coldness was swept away in this overwhelming rush of recollection. Twice he had been ready to help her—to help her by loving her, as he had said—and if, the third time, he had seemed to fail her, whom but herself could she accuse? . . . Well, that part of her life was over; she did not know why her thoughts still clung to it. But the sudden longing to see him remained; it grew to hunger as she paused on the pavement opposite his door. The street was dark and empty, swept by the rain. She had a vision of his quiet room, of the bookshelves, and the fire on the hearth. She looked up and saw a light in his window; then she crossed the street and entered the house.

# Chapter 12

The library looked as she had pictured it. The green-shaded lamps made tranquil circles of light in the gathering dusk, a little fire flickered on the hearth, and Selden's easy-chair, which stood near it, had been pushed aside when he rose to admit her.

He had checked his first movement of surprise, and stood silent, waiting for her to speak, while she paused a moment on the threshold, assailed by a rush of memories.

The scene was unchanged. She recognized the row of shelves from which he had taken down his La Bruyere, and the worn arm of the chair he had leaned against while she examined the precious volume. But then the wide September light had filled the room, making it seem a part of the outer world: now the shaded lamps and the warm hearth, detaching it from the gathering darkness of the street, gave it a sweeter touch of intimacy.

Becoming gradually aware of the surprise under Selden's silence, Lily turned to him and said simply: "I came to tell you that I was sorry for the way we parted—for what I said to you that day at Mrs. Hatch's."

The words rose to her lips spontaneously. Even on her way up the stairs, she had not thought of preparing a pretext for her visit, but she now felt an intense longing to dispel the cloud of misunderstanding that hung between them.

Selden returned her look with a smile. "I was sorry too that we should have parted in that way; but I am not sure I didn't bring it on myself. Luckily I had foreseen the risk I was taking—"

"So that you really didn't care—?" broke from her with a flash of her old irony.

"So that I was prepared for the consequences," he corrected good-humouredly. "But we'll talk of all this later. Do come and sit by the fire. I can recommend that arm-chair, if you'll let me put a cushion behind you."

While he spoke she had moved slowly to the middle of the room, and paused near his writing-table, where the lamp, striking upward, cast exaggerated shadows on the pallour of her delicately-hollowed face.

"You look tired—do sit down," he repeated gently.

She did not seem to hear the request. "I wanted you to know that I left Mrs. Hatch immediately after I saw you," she said, as though continuing her confession.

"Yes—yes; I know," he assented, with a rising tinge of embarrassment.

"And that I did so because you told me to. Before you came I had already begun to see that it would be impossible to remain with her—for the reasons you gave me; but I wouldn't admit it—I wouldn't let you see that I understood what you meant."

"Ah, I might have trusted you to find your own way out—don't overwhelm me with the sense of my officiousness!"

His light tone, in which, had her nerves been steadier, she would have recognized the mere effort to bridge over an awkward moment, jarred on her passionate desire to be understood. In her strange state of extra-lucidity, which gave her the sense of being already at the heart of the situation, it seemed incredible that any one should think it necessary to linger in the conventional outskirts of word-play and evasion.

"It was not that—I was not ungrateful," she insisted. But the power of expression failed her suddenly; she felt a tremor in her throat, and two tears gathered and fell slowly from her eyes.

Selden moved forward and took her hand. "You are very tired. Why won't you sit down and let me make you comfortable?"

He drew her to the arm-chair near the fire, and placed a cushion behind her shoulders.

"And now you must let me make you some tea: you know I always have that amount of hospitality at my command."

She shook her head, and two more tears ran over. But she did not weep easily, and the long habit of self-control reasserted itself, though she was still too tremulous to speak.

"You know I can coax the water to boil in five minutes," Selden continued, speaking as though she were a troubled child.

His words recalled the vision of that other afternoon when they had sat together over his tea-table and talked jestingly of her future. There were moments when that day seemed more remote than any other event in her life; and yet she could always relive it in its minutest detail.

She made a gesture of refusal. "No: I drink too much tea. I would rather sit quiet—I must go in a moment," she added confusedly.

Selden continued to stand near her, leaning against the mantelpiece. The tinge of constraint was beginning to be more distinctly perceptible under the friendly ease of his manner. Her self-absorption had not allowed her to perceive it at first; but now that her consciousness was once more putting forth its eager feelers, she saw that her presence was becoming an embarrassment to him. Such a situation can be saved only by an immediate outrush of feeling; and on Selden's side the determining impulse was still lacking.

The discovery did not disturb Lily as it might once have done. She had passed beyond the phase of well-bred reciprocity, in which every demonstration must be scrupulously proportioned to the emotion it elicits, and generosity of feeling is the only ostentation condemned. But the sense of loneliness returned with redoubled force as she saw herself forever shut out from Selden's inmost self. She had come to him with no definite purpose; the mere longing to see him had directed her; but the secret hope she had carried with her suddenly revealed itself in its death-pang.

"I must go," she repeated, making a motion to rise from her chair. "But I may not see you again for a long time, and I wanted to tell you that I have never forgotten the things you said to me at Bellomont, and that sometimes—sometimes when I seemed farthest from remembering them—they have helped me, and kept me from mistakes; kept me from really becoming what many people have thought me."

Strive as she would to put some order in her thoughts, the words would not come more clearly; yet she felt that she could not leave him without trying to make him understand that she had saved herself whole from the seeming ruin of her life.

A change had come over Selden's face as she spoke. Its guarded look had yielded to an expression still untinged by personal emotion, but full of a gentle understanding.

"I am glad to have you tell me that; but nothing I have said has really made the difference. The difference is in yourself—it will always be there. And since it IS there, it can't really matter to you what people think: you are so sure that your friends will always understand you."

"Ah, don't say that—don't say that what you have told me has made no difference. It seems to shut me out—to leave me all alone with the other people." She had risen and stood before him, once more completely mastered by the inner urgency of the moment. The consciousness of his half-divined reluctance had vanished. Whether he wished it or not, he must see her wholly for once before they parted.

Her voice had gathered strength, and she looked him gravely in the eyes as she continued. "Once—twice—you gave me the chance to escape from my life, and I refused it: refused it because I was a coward. Afterward I saw my mistake—I saw I could never be happy with what had contented me before. But it was too late: you had judged me—I understood. It was too late for happiness—but not too late to be helped by the thought of what I had missed. That is all I have lived on—don't take it from me now! Even in my worst moments it has been like a little light in the darkness. Some women are strong enough to be good by themselves, but I needed the help of your belief in me. Perhaps I might have resisted a great temptation, but the little ones would have pulled me down. And then I remembered—I remembered your saying that such a life could never satisfy me; and I was ashamed to admit to myself that it could. That is what you did for me—that is what I wanted to thank you for. I wanted to tell you that I have always remembered; and that I have tried—tried hard . . ."

She broke off suddenly. Her tears had risen again, and in drawing out her handkerchief her fingers touched the packet in the folds of her dress. A wave of colour suffused her, and the words died on her lips. Then she lifted her eyes to his and went on in an altered voice.

"I have tried hard—but life is difficult, and I am a very useless person. I can hardly be said to have an independent existence. I was just a screw or a cog in the great machine I called life, and when I dropped out of it I found I was of no use anywhere else. What can one do when one finds that one only fits into one hole? One must get back to it or be thrown out into the rubbish heap—and you don't know what it's like in the rubbish heap!"

Her lips wavered into a smile—she had been distracted by the whimsical remembrance of the confidences she had made to him, two years earlier, in that very room. Then she had been planning to marry Percy Gryce—what was it she was planning now?

The blood had risen strongly under Selden's dark skin, but his emotion showed itself only in an added seriousness of manner.

"You have something to tell me—do you mean to marry?" he said abruptly.

Lily's eyes did not falter, but a look of wonder, of puzzled self-interrogation, formed itself slowly in their depths. In the light of his question, she had paused to ask herself if her decision had really been taken when she entered the room.

"You always told me I should have to come to it sooner or later!" she said with a faint smile.

"And you have come to it now?"

"I shall have to come to it—presently. But there is something else I must come to first." She paused again, trying to transmit to her voice the steadiness of her recovered smile. "There is some one I must say goodbye to. Oh, not *you*—we are sure to see each other again—but the Lily Bart you knew. I have kept her with me all this time, but now we are going to part, and I have brought her back to you—I am going to leave her here. When I go out presently she will not go with me. I shall like to think that she has stayed with you—and she'll be no trouble, she'll take up no room."

She went toward him, and put out her hand, still smiling. "Will you let her stay with you?" she asked.

He caught her hand, and she felt in his the vibration of feeling that had not yet risen to his lips. "Lily—can't I help you?" he exclaimed.

She looked at him gently. "Do you remember what you said to me once? That you could help me only by loving me? Well—you did love me for a moment; and it helped me. It has always helped me. But the moment is gone—it was I who let it go. And one must go on living. Goodbye."

She laid her other hand on his, and they looked at each other with a kind of solemnity, as though they stood in the presence of death. Something in truth lay dead between them—the love she had killed in him and could no longer call to life. But something lived between them also, and leaped up in her like an imperishable flame: it was the love his love had kindled, the passion of her soul for his.

In its light everything else dwindled and fell away from her. She understood now that she could not go forth and leave her old self with him: that self must indeed live on in his presence, but it must still continue to be hers.

Selden had retained her hand, and continued to scrutinize her with a strange sense of foreboding. The external aspect of the situation had vanished for him as completely as for her: he felt it only as one of those rare moments which lift the veil from their faces as they pass.

"Lily," he said in a low voice, "you mustn't speak in this way. I can't let you go without knowing what you mean to do. Things may change—but they don't pass. You can never go out of my life."

She met his eyes with an illumined look. "No," she said. "I see that now. Let us always be friends. Then I shall feel safe, whatever happens."

"Whatever happens? What do you mean? What is going to happen?"

She turned away quietly and walked toward the hearth.

"Nothing at present—except that I am very cold, and that before I go you must make up the fire for me."

She knelt on the hearth-rug, stretching her hands to the embers. Puzzled by the sudden change in her tone, he mechanically gathered a handful of wood from the basket and tossed it on the fire. As he did so, he noticed how thin her hands looked against the rising light of the flames. He saw too, under the loose lines of her dress, how the curves of her figure had shrunk to angularity; he remembered long afterward how the red play of the flame sharpened the depression of her nostrils, and intensified the blackness of the shadows which struck up from her cheekbones to her eyes. She knelt there for a few moments in silence; a silence which he dared not break. When she rose he fancied that he saw her draw something from her dress and drop it into the fire; but he hardly noticed the gesture at the time. His faculties seemed tranced, and he was still groping for the word to break the spell. She went up to him and laid her hands on his shoulders. "Goodbye," she said, and as he bent over her she touched his forehead with her lips.

# Chapter 13

The street-lamps were lit, but the rain had ceased, and there was a momentary revival of light in the upper sky. Lily walked on unconscious of her surroundings. She was still treading the buoyant ether which emanates from the high moments of life. But gradually it shrank away from her and she felt the dull pavement beneath her feet. The sense of weariness returned with accumulated force, and for a moment she felt that she could walk no farther. She had reached the corner of Forty-first Street and Fifth Avenue, and she remembered that in Bryant Park there were seats where she might rest.

That melancholy pleasure-ground was almost deserted when she entered it, and she sank down on an empty bench in the glare of an electric street-lamp. The warmth of the fire had passed out of her veins, and she told herself that she must not sit long in the penetrating dampness which struck up from the wet asphalt. But her will-power seemed to have spent itself in a last great effort, and she was lost in the blank reaction which follows on an unwonted expenditure of energy. And besides, what was there to go home to? Nothing but the silence of her cheerless room—that silence of the night which may be more racking to tired nerves than the most discordant noises: that, and the bottle of chloral by her bed. The thought of the chloral was the only spot of light in the dark prospect: she could feel its lulling influence stealing over her already. But she was troubled by the thought that it was losing its power—she dared not go back to it too soon. Of late the sleep it had brought her had been more broken and less profound; there had been nights when she was perpetually floating up through it to consciousness. What if the effect of the drug should gradually fail, as all narcotics were said to fail? She remembered the chemist's warning against increasing the dose; and she had heard before of the capricious and incalculable action of the drug. Her dread of returning to a sleepless night was so great that she lingered on, hoping that excessive weariness would reinforce the waning power of the chloral.

Night had now closed in, and the roar of traffic in Forty-second Street was dying out. As complete darkness fell on the square the lingering occupants of the benches rose and dispersed; but now and then a stray figure, hurrying homeward, struck across the path where Lily sat, looming black for a moment in the white circle of electric light. One or two of these passers-by slackened their pace to glance curiously at her lonely figure; but she was hardly conscious of their scrutiny.

Suddenly, however, she became aware that one of the passing shadows remained stationary between her line of vision and the gleaming asphalt; and raising her eyes she saw a young woman bending over her.

"Excuse me—are you sick?—Why, it's Miss Bart!" a half-familiar voice exclaimed.

Lily looked up. The speaker was a poorly-dressed young woman with a bundle under her arm. Her face had the air of unwholesome refinement which ill-health and over-work may produce, but its common prettiness was redeemed by the strong and generous curve of the lips.

"You don't remember me," she continued, brightening with the pleasure of recognition, "but I'd know you anywhere, I've thought of you such a lot. I guess my folks all know your name by heart. I was one of the girls at Miss Farish's club—you helped me to go to the country that time I had lung-trouble. My name's Nettie Struther. It was Nettie Crane then—but I daresay you don't remember that either."

Yes: Lily was beginning to remember. The episode of Nettie Crane's timely rescue from disease had been one of the most satisfying incidents of her connection with Gerty's charitable work. She had furnished the girl with the means to go to a sanatorium in the mountains: it struck her now with a peculiar irony that the money she had used had been Gus Trenor's.

She tried to reply, to assure the speaker that she had not forgotten; but her voice failed in the effort, and she felt herself sinking under a great wave of physical weakness. Nettie Struther, with a startled exclamation, sat down and slipped a shabbily-clad arm behind her back.

"Why, Miss Bart, you *are* sick. Just lean on me a little till you feel better."

A faint glow of returning strength seemed to pass into Lily from the pressure of the supporting arm.

"I'm only tired—it is nothing," she found voice to say in a moment; and then, as she met the timid appeal of her companion's eyes, she added involuntarily: "I have been unhappy—in great trouble."

"*You* in trouble? I've always thought of you as being so high up, where everything was just grand. Sometimes, when I felt real mean, and got to wondering why things were so queerly fixed in the world, I used to remember that you were having a lovely time, anyhow, and that seemed to show there was a kind of justice somewhere. But you mustn't sit here too long—it's fearfully damp. Don't you feel strong enough to walk on a little ways now?" she broke off.

"Yes—yes; I must go home," Lily murmured, rising.

Her eyes rested wonderingly on the thin shabby figure at her side. She had known Nettie Crane as one of the discouraged victims of over-work and anaemic parentage: one of the superfluous fragments of life destined to be swept prematurely into that social refuse-heap of which Lily had so lately expressed her dread. But Nettie Struther's frail envelope was now alive with hope and energy: whatever fate the future reserved for her, she would not be cast into the refuse-heap without a struggle.

"I am very glad to have seen you," Lily continued, summoning a smile to her unsteady lips. "It'll be my turn to think of you as happy—and the world will seem a less unjust place to me too."

"Oh, but I can't leave you like this—you're not fit to go home alone. And I can't go with you either!" Nettie Struther wailed with a start of recollection. "You see, it's my husband's night-shift—he's a motor-man—and the friend I leave the baby with has to step upstairs to get *her* husband's supper at seven. I didn't tell you I had a baby, did I? She'll be four months old day after tomorrow, and to look at her you wouldn't think I'd ever had a sick day. I'd give anything to show you the baby, Miss Bart, and we live right down the street here—it's only three blocks off." She lifted her eyes tentatively to Lily's face, and then added with a burst of courage: "Why won't you get right into the cars and come home with me while I get baby's supper? It's real warm in our kitchen, and you can rest there, and I'll take *you* home as soon as ever she drops off to sleep."

It WAS warm in the kitchen, which, when Nettie Struther's match had made a flame leap from the gas-jet above the table, revealed itself to Lily as extraordinarily small and almost miraculously clean. A fire shone through the polished flanks of the iron stove, and near it stood a crib in which a baby was sitting upright, with incipient anxiety struggling for expression on a countenance still placid with sleep.

Having passionately celebrated her reunion with her offspring, and excused herself in cryptic language for the lateness of her return, Nettie restored the baby to the crib and shyly invited Miss Bart to the rocking-chair near the stove.

"We've got a parlour too," she explained with pardonable pride; "but I guess it's warmer in here, and I don't want to leave you alone while I'm getting baby's supper."

On receiving Lily's assurance that she much preferred the friendly proximity of the kitchen fire, Mrs. Struther proceeded to prepare a bottle of infantile food, which she tenderly applied to the baby's impatient lips; and while the ensuing degustation went on, she seated herself with a beaming countenance beside her visitor.

"You're sure you won't let me warm up a drop of coffee for you, Miss Bart? There's some of baby's fresh milk left over—well, maybe you'd rather just sit quiet and rest a little while. It's too lovely having you here. I've thought of it so often that I can't believe it's really come true. I've said to George again and again: 'I just wish Miss Bart could see me

*Now*—' and I used to watch for your name in the papers, and we'd talk over what you were doing, and read the descriptions of the dresses you wore. I haven't seen your name for a long time, though, and I began to be afraid you were sick, and it worried me so that George said I'd get sick myself, fretting about it." Her lips broke into a reminiscent smile. "Well, I can't afford to be sick again, that's a fact: the last spell nearly finished me. When you sent me off that time I never thought I'd come back alive, and I didn't much care if I did. You see I didn't know about George and the baby then."

She paused to readjust the bottle to the child's bubbling mouth.

"You precious—don't you be in too much of a hurry! Was it mad with mommer for getting its supper so late? Marry Anto'nette—that's what we call her: after the French queen in that play at the Garden—I told George the actress reminded me of you, and that made me fancy the name . . . I never thought I'd get married, you know, and I'd never have had the heart to go on working just for myself."

She broke off again, and meeting the encouragement in Lily's eyes, went on, with a flush rising under her anaemic skin: "You see I wasn't only just *sick* that time you sent me off—I was dreadfully unhappy too. I'd known a gentleman where I was employed—I don't know as you remember I did type-writing in a big importing firm—and—well—I thought we were to be married: he'd gone steady with me six months and given me his mother's wedding ring. But I presume he was too stylish for me—he travelled for the firm, and had seen a great deal of society. Work girls aren't looked after the way you are, and they don't always know how to look after themselves. I didn't . . . and it pretty near killed me when he went away and left off writing . . .

"It was then I came down sick—I thought it was the end of everything. I guess it would have been if you hadn't sent me off. But when I found I was getting well I began to take heart in spite of myself. And then, when I got back home, George came round and asked me to marry him. At first I thought I couldn't, because we'd been brought up together, and I knew he knew about me. But after a while I began to see that that made it easier. I never could have told another man, and I'd never have married without telling; but if George cared for me enough to have me as I was, I didn't see why I shouldn't begin over again—and I did."

The strength of the victory shone forth from her as she lifted her irradiated face from the child on her knees. "But, mercy, I didn't mean to go on like this about myself, with you sitting there looking so fagged out. Only it's so lovely having you here, and letting you see just how you've helped me." The baby had sunk back blissfully replete, and Mrs. Struther softly rose to lay the bottle aside. Then she paused before Miss Bart.

"I only wish I could help *you*—but I suppose there's nothing on earth I could do," she murmured wistfully.

Lily, instead of answering, rose with a smile and held out her arms; and the mother, understanding the gesture, laid her child in them.

The baby, feeling herself detached from her habitual anchorage, made an instinctive motion of resistance; but the soothing influences of digestion prevailed, and Lily felt the soft weight sink trustfully against her breast. The child's confidence in its safety thrilled her with a sense of warmth and returning life, and she bent over, wondering at the rosy blur of the little face, the empty clearness of the eyes, the vague tendrilly motions of the folding and unfolding fingers. At first the burden in her arms seemed as light as a pink cloud or a heap of down, but as she continued to hold it the weight increased, sinking deeper, and penetrating her with a strange sense of weakness, as though the child entered into her and became a part of herself.

She looked up, and saw Nettie's eyes resting on her with tenderness and exultation.

"Wouldn't it be too lovely for anything if she could grow up to be just like you? Of course I know she never *could*—but mothers are always dreaming the craziest things for their children."

Lily clasped the child close for a moment and laid her back in her mother's arms.

"Oh, she must not do that—I should be afraid to come and see her too often!" she said with a smile; and then, resisting Mrs. Struther's anxious offer of companionship, and reiterating the promise that of course she would come back soon, and make George's acquaintance, and see the baby in her bath, she passed out of the kitchen and went alone down the tenement stairs.

As she reached the street she realized that she felt stronger and happier: the little episode had done her good. It was the first time she had ever come across the results of her spasmodic benevolence, and the surprised sense of human fellowship took the mortal chill from her heart.

It was not till she entered her own door that she felt the reaction of a deeper loneliness. It was long after seven o'clock, and the light and odours proceeding from the basement made it manifest that the boarding-house dinner had begun. She hastened up to her room, lit the gas, and began to dress. She did not mean to pamper herself any longer, to go without food because her surroundings made it unpalatable. Since it was her fate to live in a boarding-house, she must learn to fall in with the conditions of the life. Nevertheless she was glad that, when she descended to the heat and glare of the dining-room, the repast was nearly over.

In her own room again, she was seized with a sudden fever of activity. For weeks past she had been too listless and indifferent to set her possessions in order, but now she began to examine systematically the contents of her drawers and cupboard. She had a few handsome dresses left—survivals of her last phase of splendour, on the Sabrina and in London—but when she had been obliged to part with her maid she had given the woman a generous share of her cast-off apparel. The remaining dresses, though they had lost their freshness, still kept the long unerring lines, the sweep and amplitude of the great artist's stroke, and as she spread them out on the bed the scenes in which they had been worn rose vividly before her. An association lurked in every fold: each fall of lace and gleam of embroidery was like a letter in the record of her past. She was startled to find how the atmosphere of her old life enveloped her. But, after all, it was the life she had been made for: every dawning tendency in her had been carefully directed toward it, all her interests and activities had been taught to centre around it. She was like some rare flower grown for exhibition, a flower from which every bud had been nipped except the crowning blossom of her beauty.

Last of all, she drew forth from the bottom of her trunk a heap of white drapery which fell shapelessly across her arm. It was the Reynolds dress she had worn in the Bry *tableaux*. It had been impossible for her to give it away, but she had never seen it since that night, and the long flexible folds, as she shook them out, gave forth an odour of violets which came to her like a breath from the flower-edged fountain where she had stood with Lawrence Selden and disowned her fate. She put back the dresses one by one, laying away with each some gleam of light, some note of laughter, some stray waft from the rosy shores of pleasure. She was still in a state of highly-wrought impressionability, and every hint of the past sent a lingering tremor along her nerves.

She had just closed her trunk on the white folds of the Reynolds dress when she heard a tap at her door, and the red fist of the Irish maid-servant thrust in a belated letter. Carrying it to the light, Lily read with surprise the address stamped on the upper corner of the envelope. It was a business communication from the office of her aunt's executors, and she wondered what unexpected development had caused them to break silence before the appointed time. She opened the envelope and a cheque fluttered to the floor. As she stooped to pick it up the blood rushed to her face. The cheque represented the full amount of Mrs. Peniston's legacy, and the letter accompanying it explained that the executors, having adjusted the business of the estate with less delay than they had expected, had decided to anticipate the date fixed for the payment of the bequests.

Lily sat down beside the desk at the foot of her bed, and spreading out the cheque, read over and over the *ten thousand dollars* written across it in a steely business hand. Ten months earlier the amount it stood for had represented the depths of penury; but her standard of values had changed in the interval, and now visions of wealth lurked in every flourish of the pen. As she continued to gaze at it, she felt the glitter of the visions mounting to her brain, and after a while she lifted the lid of the desk and slipped the magic formula out of sight. It was easier to think without those five figures dancing before her eyes; and she had a great deal of thinking to do before she slept.

She opened her cheque-book, and plunged into such anxious calculations as had prolonged her vigil at Bellomont on the night when she had decided to marry Percy Gryce. Poverty simplifies book-keeping, and her financial situation was easier to ascertain than it had been then; but she had not yet learned the control of money, and during her transient phase of luxury at the Emporium she had slipped back into habits of extravagance which still impaired her slender balance. A careful examination of her cheque-book, and of the unpaid bills in her desk, showed that, when the latter had been settled, she would have barely enough to live on for the next three or four months; and even after that, if she were to continue her present way of living, without earning any additional money, all incidental expenses must be reduced to the vanishing point. She hid her eyes with a shudder, beholding herself at the entrance of that ever-narrowing perspective down which she had seen Miss Silverton's dowdy figure take its despondent way.

It was no longer, however, from the vision of material poverty that she turned with the greatest shrinking. She had a sense of deeper empoverishment—of an inner destitution compared to which outward conditions dwindled into insignificance. It was indeed miserable to be poor—to look forward to a shabby, anxious middle-age, leading by dreary degrees of economy and self-denial to gradual absorption in the dingy communal existence of the boarding-house. But there was something more miserable still—it was the clutch of solitude at her heart, the sense of being swept like a stray uprooted growth down the heedless current of the years. That was the feeling which possessed her now—the feeling of being something rootless and ephemeral, mere spin-drift of the whirling surface of existence, without anything to which the poor little tentacles of self could cling before the awful flood submerged them. And as she looked back she saw that there had never been a time when she had had any real relation to life. Her parents too had been rootless, blown hither and thither on every wind of fashion, without any personal existence to shelter them from its shifting gusts. She herself had grown up without any one spot of earth being dearer to her than another: there was no centre of early pieties, of grave endearing traditions, to which her heart could revert and from which it could draw strength for itself and tenderness for others. In whatever form a slowly-accumulated past lives in the blood—whether in the concrete image of the old house stored with visual memories, or in the conception of the house not built with hands, but made up of inherited passions and loyalties—it has the same power of broadening and deepening the individual existence, of attaching it by mysterious links of kinship to all the mighty sum of human striving.

Such a vision of the solidarity of life had never before come to Lily. She had had a premonition of it in the blind motions of her mating-instinct; but they had been checked by the disintegrating influences of the life about her. All the men and women she knew were like atoms whirling away from each other in some wild centrifugal dance: her first glimpse of the continuity of life had come to her that evening in Nettie Struther's kitchen.

The poor little working-girl who had found strength to gather up the fragments of her life, and build herself a shelter with them, seemed to Lily to have reached the central truth of existence. It was a meagre enough life, on the grim edge of poverty, with scant margin for possibilities of sickness or mischance, but it had the frail audacious permanence of a bird's nest built on the edge of a cliff—a mere wisp of leaves and straw, yet so put together that the lives entrusted to it may hang safely over the abyss.

Yes—but it had taken two to build the nest; the man's faith as well as the woman's courage. Lily remembered Nettie's words: *I knew he knew about me.* Her husband's faith in her had made her renewal possible—it is so easy for a woman to become what the man she loves believes her to be! Well—Selden had twice been ready to stake his faith on Lily Bart; but the third trial had been too severe for his endurance. The very quality of his love had made it the more impossible to recall to life. If it had been a simple instinct of the blood, the power of her beauty might have revived it. But the fact that it struck deeper, that it was inextricably wound up with inherited habits of thought and feeling, made it as impossible to restore to growth as a deep-rooted plant torn from its bed. Selden had given her of his best; but he was as incapable as herself of an uncritical return to former states of feeling.

There remained to her, as she had told him, the uplifting memory of his faith in her; but she had not reached the age when a woman can live on her memories. As she held Nettie Struther's child in her arms the frozen currents of youth had loosed themselves and run warm in her veins: the old life-hunger possessed her, and all her being clamoured for its share of personal happiness. Yes—it was happiness she still wanted, and the glimpse she had caught of it made everything else of no account. One by one she had detached herself from the baser possibilities, and she saw that nothing now remained to her but the emptiness of renunciation.

It was growing late, and an immense weariness once more possessed her. It was not the stealing sense of sleep, but a vivid wakeful fatigue, a wan lucidity of mind against which all the possibilities of the future were shadowed forth gigantically. She was appalled by the intense cleanness of the vision; she seemed to have broken through the merciful veil which intervenes between intention and action, and to see exactly what she would do in all the long days to come. There was the cheque in her desk, for instance—she meant to use it in paying her debt to Trenor; but she foresaw that when the morning came she would put off doing so, would slip into gradual tolerance of the debt. The thought terrified her—she dreaded to fall from the height of her last moment with Lawrence Selden. But how could she trust herself to keep her footing? She knew the strength of the opposing impulses-she could feel the countless hands of habit dragging her back into some fresh compromise with fate. She felt an intense longing to prolong, to perpetuate, the momentary exaltation of her spirit. If only life could end now—end on this tragic yet sweet vision of lost possibilities, which gave her a sense of kinship with all the loving and foregoing in the world!

She reached out suddenly and, drawing the cheque from her writing-desk, enclosed it in an envelope which she addressed to her bank. She then wrote out a cheque for Trenor, and placing it, without an accompanying word, in an envelope inscribed with his name, laid the two letters side by side on her desk. After that she continued to sit at the table, sorting her papers and writing, till the intense silence of the house reminded her of the lateness of the hour. In the street the noise of wheels had ceased, and the rumble of the "elevated" came only at long intervals through the deep unnatural hush. In the mysterious nocturnal separation from all outward signs of life, she felt herself more strangely confronted with her fate. The sensation made her brain reel, and she tried to shut out consciousness by pressing her hands against her eyes. But the terrible silence and emptiness seemed to symbolize her future—she felt as though the house, the street, the world were all empty, and she alone left sentient in a lifeless universe.

But this was the verge of delirium . . . she had never hung so near the dizzy brink of the unreal. Sleep was what she wanted—she remembered that she had not closed her eyes for two nights. The little bottle was at her bed-side, waiting to lay its spell upon her. She rose and undressed hastily, hungering now for the touch of her pillow. She felt so profoundly tired that she thought she must fall asleep at once; but as soon as she had lain down every nerve started once more into separate wakefulness. It was as though a great blaze of electric light had been turned on in her head, and her poor little anguished self shrank and cowered in it, without knowing where to take refuge.

She had not imagined that such a multiplication of wakefulness was possible: her whole past was reenacting itself at a hundred different points of consciousness. Where was the drug that could still this legion of insurgent nerves? The sense of exhaustion would have been sweet compared to this shrill beat of activities; but weariness had dropped from her as though some cruel stimulant had been forced into her veins.

She could bear it—yes, she could bear it; but what strength would be left her the next day? Perspective had disappeared—the next day pressed close upon her, and on its heels came the days that were to follow—they swarmed about her like a shrieking mob. She must shut them out for a few hours; she must take a brief bath of oblivion. She put out her hand, and measured the soothing drops into a glass; but as she did so, she knew they would be powerless against the supernatural lucidity of her brain. She had long since raised the dose to its highest limit, but tonight she felt she must increase it. She knew she took a slight risk in doing so—she remembered the chemist's warning. If sleep came at all, it might be a sleep without waking. But after all that was but one chance in a hundred: the action of the drug was incalculable, and the addition of a few drops to the regular dose would probably do no more than procure for her the rest she so desperately needed....

She did not, in truth, consider the question very closely—the physical craving for sleep was her only sustained sensation. Her mind shrank from the glare of thought as instinctively as eyes contract in a blaze of light—darkness, darkness was what she must have at any cost. She raised herself in bed and swallowed the contents of the glass; then she blew out her candle and lay down.

She lay very still, waiting with a sensuous pleasure for the first effects of the soporific. She knew in advance what form they would take—the gradual cessation of the inner throb, the soft approach of passiveness, as though an invisible hand made magic passes over her in the darkness. The very slowness and hesitancy of the effect increased its fascination: it was delicious to lean over and look down into the dim abysses of unconsciousness. Tonight the drug seemed to work more slowly than usual: each passionate pulse had to be stilled in turn, and it was long before she felt them dropping into abeyance, like sentinels falling asleep at their posts. But gradually the sense of complete subjugation came over her, and she wondered languidly what had made her feel so uneasy and excited. She saw now that there was nothing to be excited about—she had returned to her normal view of life. Tomorrow would not be so difficult after all: she felt sure that she would have the strength to meet it. She did not quite remember what it was that she had been afraid to meet, but the uncertainty no longer troubled her. She had been unhappy, and now she was happy—she had felt herself alone, and now the sense of loneliness had vanished.

She stirred once, and turned on her side, and as she did so, she suddenly understood why she did not feel herself alone. It was odd—but Nettie Struther's child was lying on her arm: she felt the pressure of its little head against her shoulder. She did not know how it had come there, but she felt no great surprise at the fact, only a gentle penetrating thrill of warmth and pleasure. She settled herself into an easier position, hollowing her arm to pillow the round downy head, and holding her breath lest a sound should disturb the sleeping child.

As she lay there she said to herself that there was something she must tell Selden, some word she had found that should make life clear between them. She tried to repeat the word, which lingered vague and luminous on the far edge of thought—she was afraid of not remembering it when she woke; and if she could only remember it and say it to him, she felt that everything would be well.

Slowly the thought of the word faded, and sleep began to enfold her. She struggled faintly against it, feeling that she ought to keep awake on account of the baby; but even this feeling was gradually lost in an indistinct sense of drowsy peace, through which, of a sudden, a dark flash of loneliness and terror tore its way.

She started up again, cold and trembling with the shock: for a moment she seemed to have lost her hold of the child. But no—she was mistaken—the tender pressure of its body was still close to hers: the recovered warmth flowed through her once more, she yielded to it, sank into it, and slept.

# Chapter 14

The next morning rose mild and bright, with a promise of summer in the air. The sunlight slanted joyously down Lily's street, mellowed the blistered house-front, gilded the paintless railings of the door-step, and struck prismatic glories from the panes of her darkened window.

When such a day coincides with the inner mood there is intoxication in its breath; and Selden, hastening along the street through the squalor of its morning confidences, felt himself thrilling with a youthful sense of adventure. He had cut loose from the familiar shores of habit, and launched himself on uncharted seas of emotion; all the old tests and measures were left behind, and his course was to be shaped by new stars.

That course, for the moment, led merely to Miss Bart's boarding-house; but its shabby door-step had suddenly become the threshold of the untried. As he approached he looked up at the triple row of windows, wondering boyishly which one of them was hers. It was nine o'clock, and the house, being tenanted by workers, already showed an awakened front to the street. He remembered afterward having noticed that only one blind was down. He noticed too that there was a pot of pansies on one of the window sills, and at once concluded that the window must be hers: it was inevitable that he should connect her with the one touch of beauty in the dingy scene.

Nine o'clock was an early hour for a visit, but Selden had passed beyond all such conventional observances. He only knew that he must see Lily Bart at once—he had found the word he meant to say to her, and it could not wait another moment to be said. It was strange that it had not come to his lips sooner—that he had let her pass from him the evening before without being able to speak it. But what did that matter, now that a new day had come? It was not a word for twilight, but for the morning.

Selden ran eagerly up the steps and pulled the bell; and even in his state of self-absorption it came as a sharp surprise to him that the door should open so promptly. It was still more of a surprise to see, as he entered, that it had been opened by Gerty Farish—and that behind her, in an agitated blur, several other figures ominously loomed.

"Lawrence!" Gerty cried in a strange voice, "how could you get here so quickly?"—and the trembling hand she laid on him seemed instantly to close about his heart.

He noticed the other faces, vague with fear and conjecture—he saw the landlady's imposing bulk sway professionally toward him; but he shrank back, putting up his hand, while his eyes mechanically mounted the steep black walnut stairs, up which he was immediately aware that his cousin was about to lead him.

A voice in the background said that the doctor might be back at any minute—and that nothing, upstairs, was to be disturbed. Some one else exclaimed: "It was the greatest mercy—" then Selden felt that Gerty had taken him gently by the hand, and that they were to be suffered to go up alone.

In silence they mounted the three flights, and walked along the passage to a closed door. Gerty opened the door, and Selden went in after her. Though the blind was down, the irresistible sunlight poured a tempered golden flood into the room, and in its light Selden saw a narrow bed along the wall, and on the bed, with motionless hands and calm unrecognizing face, the semblance of Lily Bart.

That it was her real self, every pulse in him ardently denied. Her real self had lain warm on his heart but a few hours earlier—what had he to do with this estranged and tranquil face which, for the first time, neither paled nor brightened at his coming?

Gerty, strangely tranquil too, with the conscious self-control of one who has ministered to much pain, stood by the bed, speaking gently, as if transmitting a final message.

"The doctor found a bottle of chloral—she had been sleeping badly for a long time, and she must have taken an overdose by mistake....

There is no doubt of that—no doubt—there will be no question—he has been very kind. I told him that you and I would like to be left alone with her—to go over her things before any one else comes. I know it is what she would have wished."

Selden was hardly conscious of what she said. He stood looking down on the sleeping face which seemed to lie like a delicate impalpable mask over the living lineaments he had known. He felt that the real Lily was still there, close to him, yet invisible and inaccessible; and the tenuity of the barrier between them mocked him with a sense of helplessness. There had never been more than a little impalpable barrier between them—and yet he had suffered it to keep them apart! And now, though it seemed slighter and frailer than ever, it had suddenly hardened to adamant, and he might beat his life out against it in vain.

He had dropped on his knees beside the bed, but a touch from Gerty aroused him. He stood up, and as their eyes met he was struck by the extraordinary light in his cousin's face.

"You understand what the doctor has gone for? He has promised that there shall be no trouble—but of course the formalities must be gone through. And I asked him to give us time to look through her things first—"

He nodded, and she glanced about the small bare room. "It won't take long," she concluded.

"No—it won't take long," he agreed.

She held his hand in hers a moment longer, and then, with a last look at the bed, moved silently toward the door. On the threshold she paused to add: "You will find me downstairs if you want me."

Selden roused himself to detain her. "But why are you going? She would have wished—"

Gerty shook her head with a smile. "No: this is what she would have wished—" and as she spoke a light broke through Selden's stony misery, and he saw deep into the hidden things of love.

The door closed on Gerty, and he stood alone with the motionless sleeper on the bed. His impulse was to return to her side, to fall on his knees, and rest his throbbing head against the peaceful cheek on the pillow. They had never been at peace together, they two; and now he felt himself drawn downward into the strange mysterious depths of her tranquillity.

But he remembered Gerty's warning words—he knew that, though time had ceased in this room, its feet were hastening relentlessly toward the door. Gerty had given him this supreme half-hour, and he must use it as she willed.

He turned and looked about him, sternly compelling himself to regain his consciousness of outward things. There was very little furniture in the room. The shabby chest of drawers was spread with a lace cover, and set out with a few gold-topped boxes and bottles, a rose-coloured pin-cushion, a glass tray strewn with tortoise-shell hair-pins—he shrank from the poignant intimacy of these trifles, and from the blank surface of the toilet-mirror above them.

These were the only traces of luxury, of that clinging to the minute observance of personal seemliness, which showed what her other renunciations must have cost. There was no other token of her personality about the room, unless it showed itself in the scrupulous neatness of the scant articles of furniture: a washing-stand, two chairs, a small writing-desk, and the little table near the bed. On this table stood the empty bottle and glass, and from these also he averted his eyes.

The desk was closed, but on its slanting lid lay two letters which he took up. One bore the address of a bank, and as it was stamped and sealed, Selden, after a moment's hesitation, laid it aside. On the other letter he read Gus Trenor's name; and the flap of the envelope was still ungummed.

Temptation leapt on him like the stab of a knife. He staggered under it, steadying himself against the desk. Why had she been writing to Trenor—writing, presumably, just after their parting of the previous evening? The thought unhallowed the memory of that last hour, made a mock of the word he had come to speak, and defiled even the reconciling silence upon which it fell. He felt himself flung back on all the ugly uncertainties from which he thought he had cast loose forever. After all, what did he know of her life? Only as much as she had chosen to show him, and measured by the world's estimate, how little that was! By what right—the letter in his hand seemed to ask—by what right was it he who now passed into her confidence through the gate which death had left unbarred? His heart cried out that it was by right of their last hour together, the hour when she herself had placed the key in his hand. Yes—but what if the letter to Trenor had been written afterward?

He put it from him with sudden loathing, and setting his lips, addressed himself resolutely to what remained of his task. After all, that task would be easier to perform, now that his personal stake in it was annulled.

He raised the lid of the desk, and saw within it a cheque-book and a few packets of bills and letters, arranged with the orderly precision which characterized all her personal habits. He looked through the letters first, because it was the most difficult part of the work. They proved to be few and unimportant, but among them he found, with a strange commotion of the heart, the note he had written her the day after the Brys' entertainment.

"When may I come to you?"—his words overwhelmed him with a realization of the cowardice which had driven him from her at the very moment of attainment. Yes—he had always feared his fate, and he was too honest to disown his cowardice now; for had not all his old doubts started to life again at the mere sight of Trenor's name?

He laid the note in his card-case, folding it away carefully, as something made precious by the fact that she had held it so; then, growing once more aware of the lapse of time, he continued his examination of the papers.

To his surprise, he found that all the bills were receipted; there was not an unpaid account among them. He opened the cheque-book, and saw that, the very night before, a cheque of ten thousand dollars from Mrs. Peniston's executors had been entered in it. The legacy, then, had been paid sooner than Gerty had led him to expect. But, turning another page or two, he discovered with astonishment that, in spite of this recent accession of funds, the balance had already declined to a few dollars. A rapid glance at the stubs of the last cheques, all of which bore the date of the previous day, showed that between four or five hundred dollars of the legacy had been spent in the settlement of bills, while the remaining thousands were comprehended in one cheque, made out, at the same time, to Charles Augustus Trenor.

Selden laid the book aside, and sank into the chair beside the desk. He leaned his elbows on it, and hid his face in his hands. The bitter waters of life surged high about him, their sterile taste was on his lips. Did the cheque to Trenor explain the mystery or deepen it? At first his mind refused to act—he felt only the taint of such a transaction between a man like Trenor and a girl like Lily Bart. Then, gradually, his troubled vision cleared, old hints and rumours came back to him, and out of the very insinuations he had feared to probe, he constructed an explanation of the mystery. It was true, then, that she had taken money from Trenor; but true also, as the contents of the little desk declared, that the obligation had been intolerable to her, and that at the first opportunity she had freed herself from it, though the act left her face to face with bare unmitigated poverty.

That was all he knew—all he could hope to unravel of the story. The mute lips on the pillow refused him more than this—unless indeed they had told him the rest in the kiss they had left upon his forehead. Yes, he could now read into that farewell all that his heart craved to find there; he could even draw from it courage not to accuse himself for having failed to reach the height of his opportunity.

He saw that all the conditions of life had conspired to keep them apart; since his very detachment from the external influences which swayed her had increased his spiritual fastidiousness, and made it more difficult for him to live and love uncritically. But at least he HAD loved her—had been willing to stake his future on his faith in her—and if the moment had been fated to pass from them before they could seize it, he saw now that, for both, it had been saved whole out of the ruin of their lives.

It was this moment of love, this fleeting victory over themselves, which had kept them from atrophy and extinction; which, in her, had reached out to him in every struggle against the influence of her surroundings, and in him, had kept alive the faith that now drew him penitent and reconciled to her side.

He knelt by the bed and bent over her, draining their last moment to its lees; and in the silence there passed between them the word which made all clear.

THE END

# The Age of Innocence

# Book I

## I.

On a January evening of the early seventies, Christine Nilsson was singing in Faust at the Academy of Music in New York.

Though there was already talk of the erection, in remote metropolitan distances "above the Forties," of a new Opera House which should compete in costliness and splendour with those of the great European capitals, the world of fashion was still content to reassemble every winter in the shabby red and gold boxes of the sociable old Academy. Conservatives cherished it for being small and inconvenient, and thus keeping out the "new people" whom New York was beginning to dread and yet be drawn to; and the sentimental clung to it for its historic associations, and the musical for its excellent acoustics, always so problematic a quality in halls built for the hearing of music.

It was Madame Nilsson's first appearance that winter, and what the daily press had already learned to describe as "an exceptionally brilliant audience" had gathered to hear her, transported through the slippery, snowy streets in private broughams, in the spacious family landau, or in the humbler but more convenient "Brown coupe." To come to the Opera in a Brown coupe was almost as honourable a way of arriving as in one's own carriage; and departure by the same means had the immense advantage of enabling one (with a playful allusion to democratic principles) to scramble into the first Brown conveyance in the line, instead of waiting till the cold-and-gin congested nose of one's own coachman gleamed under the portico of the Academy. It was one of the great livery-stableman's most masterly intuitions to have discovered that Americans want to get away from amusement even more quickly than they want to get to it.

When Newland Archer opened the door at the back of the club box the curtain had just gone up on the garden scene. There was no reason why the young man should not have come earlier, for he had dined at seven, alone with his mother and sister, and had lingered afterward over a cigar in the Gothic library with glazed black-walnut bookcases and finial-topped chairs which was the only room in the house where Mrs. Archer allowed smoking.

But, in the first place, New York was a metropolis, and perfectly aware that in metropolises it was "not the thing" to arrive early at the opera; and what was or was not "the thing" played a part as important in Newland Archer's New York as the inscrutable totem terrors that had ruled the destinies of his forefathers thousands of years ago.

The second reason for his delay was a personal one. He had dawdled over his cigar because he was at heart a dilettante, and thinking over a pleasure to come often gave him a subtler satisfaction than its realisation. This was especially the case when the pleasure was a delicate one, as his pleasures mostly were; and on this occasion the moment he looked forward to was so rare and exquisite in quality that—well, if he had timed his arrival in accord with the prima donna's stage-manager he could not have entered the Academy at a more significant moment than just as she was singing: "He loves me—he loves me not—*he loves me!*—" and sprinkling the falling daisy petals with notes as clear as dew.

She sang, of course, "M'ama!" and not "he loves me," since an unalterable and unquestioned law of the musical world required that the German text of French operas sung by Swedish artists should be translated into Italian for the clearer understanding of English-speaking audiences. This seemed as natural to Newland Archer as all the other conventions on which his life was moulded: such as the duty of using two silver-backed brushes with his monogram in blue enamel to part his hair, and of never appearing in society without a flower (preferably a gardenia) in his buttonhole.

"M'ama ... non m'ama ..." the prima donna sang, and "M'ama!", with a final burst of love triumphant, as she pressed the dishevelled daisy to her lips and lifted her large eyes to the sophisticated countenance of the little brown Faust-Capoul, who was vainly trying, in a tight purple velvet doublet and plumed cap, to look as pure and true as his artless victim.

Newland Archer, leaning against the wall at the back of the club box, turned his eyes from the stage and scanned the opposite side of the house. Directly facing him was the box of old Mrs. Manson Mingott, whose monstrous obesity had long since made it impossible for her to attend the Opera, but who was always represented on fashionable nights by some of the younger members of the family. On this occasion, the front of the box was filled by her daughter-in-law, Mrs. Lovell Mingott, and her daughter, Mrs. Welland; and slightly withdrawn behind these brocaded matrons sat a young girl in white with eyes ecstatically fixed on the stagelovers. As Madame Nilsson's "M'ama!" thrilled out above the silent house (the boxes always stopped talking during the Daisy Song) a warm pink mounted to the girl's cheek, mantled her brow to the roots of her fair braids, and suffused the young slope of her breast to the line where it met a modest tulle tucker fastened with a single gardenia. She dropped her eyes to the immense bouquet of lilies-of-the-valley on her knee, and Newland Archer saw her white-gloved finger-tips touch the flowers softly. He drew a breath of satisfied vanity and his eyes returned to the stage.

No expense had been spared on the setting, which was acknowledged to be very beautiful even by people who shared his acquaintance with the Opera houses of Paris and Vienna. The foreground, to the footlights, was covered with emerald green cloth. In the middle distance symmetrical mounds of woolly green moss bounded by croquet hoops formed the base of shrubs shaped like orange-trees but studded with large pink and red roses. Gigantic pansies, considerably larger than the roses, and closely resembling the floral pen-wipers made by female parishioners for fashionable clergymen, sprang from the moss beneath the rose-trees; and here and there a daisy grafted on a rose-branch flowered with a luxuriance prophetic of Mr. Luther Burbank's far-off prodigies.

In the centre of this enchanted garden Madame Nilsson, in white cashmere slashed with pale blue satin, a reticule dangling from a blue girdle, and large yellow braids carefully disposed on each side of her muslin chemisette, listened with downcast eyes to M. Capoul's impassioned wooing, and affected a guileless incomprehension of his designs whenever, by word or glance, he persuasively indicated the ground floor window of the neat brick villa projecting obliquely from the right wing.

"The darling!" thought Newland Archer, his glance flitting back to the young girl with the lilies-of-the-valley. "She doesn't even guess what it's all about." And he contemplated her absorbed young face with a thrill of possessorship in which pride in his own masculine initiation was mingled with a tender reverence for her abysmal purity. "We'll read Faust together ... by the Italian lakes ..." he thought, somewhat hazily confusing the scene of his projected honey-moon with the masterpieces of literature which it would be his manly privilege to reveal to his bride. It was only that afternoon that May Welland had let him guess that she "cared" (New York's consecrated phrase of maiden avowal), and already his imagination, leaping ahead of the engagement ring, the betrothal kiss and the march from Lohengrin, pictured her at his side in some scene of old European witchery.

He did not in the least wish the future Mrs. Newland Archer to be a simpleton. He meant her (thanks to his enlightening companionship) to develop a social tact and readiness of wit enabling her to hold her own with the most popular married women of the "younger set," in which it was the recognised custom to attract masculine homage while playfully discouraging it. If he had probed to the bottom of his vanity (as he sometimes nearly did) he would have found there the wish that his wife should be as worldly-wise and as eager to please as the married lady whose charms had held his fancy through two mildly agitated years; without, of course, any hint of the frailty which had so nearly marred that unhappy being's life, and had disarranged his own plans for a whole winter.

How this miracle of fire and ice was to be created, and to sustain itself in a harsh world, he had never taken the time to think out; but he was content to hold his view without analysing it, since he knew it was that of all the carefully-brushed, white-waistcoated, button-hole-flowered gentlemen who succeeded each other in the club box, exchanged friendly greetings with him, and turned their opera-glasses critically on the circle of ladies who were the product of the system. In matters intellectual and artistic Newland Archer felt himself distinctly the superior of these chosen specimens of old New York gentility; he had probably read more, thought more, and even seen a good deal more of the world, than any other man of the number. Singly they betrayed their inferiority; but grouped together they represented "New York," and the habit of masculine solidarity made him accept their doctrine on all the issues called moral. He instinctively felt that in this respect it would be troublesome—and also rather bad form—to strike out for himself.

"Well—upon my soul!" exclaimed Lawrence Lefferts, turning his opera-glass abruptly away from the stage. Lawrence Lefferts was, on the whole, the foremost authority on "form" in New York. He had probably devoted more time than any one else to the study of this intricate and fascinating question; but study alone could not account for his complete and easy competence. One had only to look at him, from the slant of his bald forehead and the curve of his beautiful fair moustache to the long patent-leather feet at the other end of his lean and elegant person, to feel that the knowledge of "form" must be congenital in any one who knew how to wear such good clothes so carelessly and carry such height with so much lounging grace. As a young admirer had once said of him: "If anybody can tell a fellow just when to wear a black tie with evening clothes and when not to, it's Larry Lefferts." And on the question of pumps versus patent-leather "Oxfords" his authority had never been disputed.

"My God!" he said; and silently handed his glass to old Sillerton Jackson.

Newland Archer, following Lefferts's glance, saw with surprise that his exclamation had been occasioned by the entry of a new figure into old Mrs. Mingott's box. It was that of a slim young woman, a little less tall than May Welland, with brown hair growing in close curls about her temples and held in place by a narrow band of diamonds. The suggestion of this headdress, which gave her what was then called a "Josephine look," was carried out in the cut of the dark blue velvet gown rather theatrically caught up under her bosom by a girdle with a large old-fashioned clasp. The wearer of this unusual dress, who seemed quite unconscious of the attention it was attracting, stood a moment in the centre of the box, discussing with Mrs. Welland the propriety of taking the latter's place in the front right-hand corner; then she yielded with a slight smile, and seated herself in line with Mrs. Welland's sister-in-law, Mrs. Lovell Mingott, who was installed in the opposite corner.

Mr. Sillerton Jackson had returned the opera-glass to Lawrence Lefferts. The whole of the club turned instinctively, waiting to hear what the old man had to say; for old Mr. Jackson was as great an authority on "family" as Lawrence Lefferts was on "form." He knew all the ramifications of New York's cousinships; and could not only elucidate such complicated questions as that of the connection between the Mingotts (through the Thorleys) with the Dallases of South Carolina, and that of the relationship of the elder branch of Philadelphia Thorleys to the Albany Chiverses (on no account to be confused with the Manson Chiverses of University Place), but could also enumerate the leading characteristics of each family: as, for instance, the fabulous stinginess of the younger lines of Leffertses (the Long Island ones); or the fatal tendency of the Rushworths to make foolish matches; or the insanity recurring in every second generation of the Albany Chiverses, with whom their New York cousins had always refused to intermarry—with the disastrous exception of poor Medora Manson, who, as everybody knew ... but then her mother was a Rushworth.

In addition to this forest of family trees, Mr. Sillerton Jackson carried between his narrow hollow temples, and under his soft thatch of silver hair, a register of most of the scandals and mysteries that had smouldered under the unruffled surface of New York society within the last fifty years. So far indeed did his information extend, and so acutely retentive was his memory, that he was supposed to be the only man who could have told you who Julius Beaufort, the banker, really was, and what had become of handsome Bob Spicer, old Mrs. Manson Mingott's father, who had disappeared so mysteriously (with a large sum of trust money) less than a year after his marriage, on the very day that a beautiful Spanish dancer who had been delighting thronged audiences in the old Opera-house on the Battery had taken ship for Cuba. But these mysteries, and many others, were closely locked in Mr. Jackson's breast; for not only did his keen sense of honour forbid his repeating anything privately imparted, but he was fully aware that his reputation for discretion increased his opportunities of finding out what he wanted to know.

The club box, therefore, waited in visible suspense while Mr. Sillerton Jackson handed back Lawrence Lefferts's opera-glass. For a moment he silently scrutinised the attentive group out of his filmy blue eyes overhung by old veined lids; then he gave his moustache a thoughtful twist, and said simply: "I didn't think the Mingotts would have tried it on."

## II.

Newland Archer, during this brief episode, had been thrown into a strange state of embarrassment.

It was annoying that the box which was thus attracting the undivided attention of masculine New York should be that in which his betrothed was seated between her mother and aunt; and for a moment he could not identify the lady in the Empire dress, nor imagine why her presence created such excitement among the initiated. Then light dawned on him, and with it came a momentary rush of indignation. No, indeed; no one would have thought the Mingotts would have tried it on!

But they had; they undoubtedly had; for the low-toned comments behind him left no doubt in Archer's mind that the young woman was May Welland's cousin, the cousin always referred to in the family as "poor Ellen Olenska." Archer knew that she had suddenly arrived from Europe a day or two previously; he had even heard from Miss Welland (not disapprovingly) that she had been to see poor Ellen, who was staying with old Mrs. Mingott. Archer entirely approved of family solidarity, and one of the qualities he most admired in the Mingotts was their resolute championship of the few black sheep that their blameless stock had produced. There was nothing mean or ungenerous in the young man's heart, and he was glad that his future wife should not be restrained by false prudery from being kind (in private) to her unhappy cousin; but to receive Countess Olenska in the family circle was a different thing from producing her in public, at the Opera of all places, and in the very box with the young girl whose engagement to him, Newland Archer, was to be announced within a few weeks. No, he felt as old Sillerton Jackson felt; he did not think the Mingotts would have tried it on!

He knew, of course, that whatever man dared (within Fifth Avenue's limits) that old Mrs. Manson Mingott, the Matriarch of the line, would dare. He had always admired the high and mighty old lady, who, in spite of having been only Catherine Spicer of Staten Island, with a father mysteriously discredited, and neither money nor position enough to make people forget it, had allied herself with the head of the wealthy Mingott line, married two of her daughters to "foreigners" (an Italian marquis and an English banker), and put the crowning touch to her audacities by building a large house of pale cream-coloured stone (when brown sandstone seemed as much the only wear as a frock-coat in the afternoon) in an inaccessible wilderness near the Central Park.

Old Mrs. Mingott's foreign daughters had become a legend. They never came back to see their mother, and the latter being, like many persons of active mind and dominating will, sedentary and corpulent in her habit, had philosophically remained at home. But the cream-coloured house (supposed to be modelled on the private hotels of the Parisian aristocracy) was there as a visible proof of her moral courage; and she throned in it, among pre-Revolutionary furniture and souvenirs of the Tuileries of Louis Napoleon (where she had shone in her middle age), as placidly as if there were nothing peculiar in living above Thirty-fourth Street, or in having French windows that opened like doors instead of sashes that pushed up.

Every one (including Mr. Sillerton Jackson) was agreed that old Catherine had never had beauty—a gift which, in the eyes of New York, justified every success, and excused a certain number of failings. Unkind people said that, like her Imperial namesake, she had won her way to success by strength of will and hardness of heart, and a kind of haughty effrontery that was somehow justified by the extreme decency and dignity of her private life. Mr. Manson Mingott had died when she was only twenty-eight, and had "tied up" the money with an additional caution born of the general distrust of the Spicers; but his bold young widow went her way fearlessly, mingled freely in foreign society, married her daughters in heaven knew what corrupt and fashionable circles, hobnobbed with Dukes and Ambassadors, associated familiarly with Papists, entertained Opera singers, and was the intimate friend of Mme. Taglioni; and all the while (as Sillerton Jackson was the first to proclaim) there had never been a breath on her reputation; the only respect, he always added, in which she differed from the earlier Catherine.

Mrs. Manson Mingott had long since succeeded in untying her husband's fortune, and had lived in affluence for half a century; but memories of her early straits had made her excessively thrifty, and though, when she bought a dress or a piece of furniture, she took care that it should be of the best, she could not bring herself to spend much on the transient pleasures of the table. Therefore, for totally different reasons, her food was as poor as Mrs. Archer's, and her wines did nothing to redeem it. Her relatives considered that the penury of her table discredited the Mingott name, which had always been associated with good living; but people continued to come to her in spite of the "made dishes" and flat champagne, and in reply to the remonstrances of her son Lovell (who tried to retrieve the family credit by having the best chef in New York) she used to say laughingly: "What's the use of two good cooks in one family, now that I've married the girls and can't eat sauces?"

Newland Archer, as he mused on these things, had once more turned his eyes toward the Mingott box. He saw that Mrs. Welland and her sister-in-law were facing their semicircle of critics with the Mingottian APLOMB which old Catherine had inculcated in all her tribe, and that only May Welland betrayed, by a heightened colour (perhaps due to the knowledge that he was watching her) a sense of the gravity of the situation. As for the cause of the commotion, she sat gracefully in her corner of the box, her eyes fixed on the stage, and revealing, as she leaned forward, a little more shoulder and bosom than New York was accustomed to seeing, at least in ladies who had reasons for wishing to pass unnoticed.

Few things seemed to Newland Archer more awful than an offence against "Taste," that far-off divinity of whom "Form" was the mere visible representative and vicegerent. Madame Olenska's pale and serious face appealed to his fancy as suited to the occasion and to her unhappy situation; but the way her dress (which had no tucker) sloped away from her thin shoulders shocked and troubled him. He hated to think of May Welland's being exposed to the influence of a young woman so careless of the dictates of Taste.

"After all," he heard one of the younger men begin behind him (everybody talked through the Mephistopheles-and-Martha scenes), "after all, just *what* happened?"

"Well—she left him; nobody attempts to deny that."

"He's an awful brute, isn't he?" continued the young enquirer, a candid Thorley, who was evidently preparing to enter the lists as the lady's champion.

"The very worst; I knew him at Nice," said Lawrence Lefferts with authority. "A half-paralysed white sneering fellow—rather handsome head, but eyes with a lot of lashes. Well, I'll tell you the sort: when he wasn't with women he was collecting china. Paying any price for both, I understand."

There was a general laugh, and the young champion said: "Well, then——?"

"Well, then; she bolted with his secretary."

"Oh, I see." The champion's face fell.

"It didn't last long, though: I heard of her a few months later living alone in Venice. I believe Lovell Mingott went out to get her. He said she was desperately unhappy. That's all right—but this parading her at the Opera's another thing."

"Perhaps," young Thorley hazarded, "she's too unhappy to be left at home."

This was greeted with an irreverent laugh, and the youth blushed deeply, and tried to look as if he had meant to insinuate what knowing people called a "double entendre."

"Well—it's queer to have brought Miss Welland, anyhow," some one said in a low tone, with a side-glance at Archer.

"Oh, that's part of the campaign: Granny's orders, no doubt," Lefferts laughed. "When the old lady does a thing she does it thoroughly."

The act was ending, and there was a general stir in the box. Suddenly Newland Archer felt himself impelled to decisive action. The desire to be the first man to enter Mrs. Mingott's box, to proclaim to the waiting world his engagement to May Welland, and to see her through whatever difficulties her cousin's anomalous situation might involve her in; this impulse had abruptly overruled all scruples and hesitations, and sent him hurrying through the red corridors to the farther side of the house.

As he entered the box his eyes met Miss Welland's, and he saw that she had instantly understood his motive, though the family dignity which both considered so high a virtue would not permit her to tell him so. The persons of their world lived in an atmosphere of faint implications and pale delicacies, and the fact that he and she understood each other without a word seemed to the young man to bring them nearer than any explanation would have done. Her eyes said: "You see why Mamma brought me," and his answered: "I would not for the world have had you stay away."

"You know my niece Countess Olenska?" Mrs. Welland enquired as she shook hands with her future son-in-law. Archer bowed without extending his hand, as was the custom on being introduced to a lady; and Ellen Olenska bent her head slightly, keeping her own pale-gloved hands clasped on her huge fan of eagle feathers. Having greeted Mrs. Lovell Mingott, a large blonde lady in creaking satin, he sat down beside his betrothed, and said in a low tone: "I hope you've told Madame Olenska that we're engaged? I want everybody to know—I want you to let me announce it this evening at the ball."

Miss Welland's face grew rosy as the dawn, and she looked at him with radiant eyes. "If you can persuade Mamma," she said; "but why should we change what is already settled?" He made no answer but that which his eyes returned, and she added, still more confidently smiling: "Tell my cousin yourself: I give you leave. She says she used to play with you when you were children."

She made way for him by pushing back her chair, and promptly, and a little ostentatiously, with the desire that the whole house should see what he was doing, Archer seated himself at the Countess Olenska's side.

"We *did* use to play together, didn't we?" she asked, turning her grave eyes to his. "You were a horrid boy, and kissed me once behind a door; but it was your cousin Vandie Newland, who never looked at me, that I was in love with." Her glance swept the horse-shoe curve of boxes. "Ah, how this brings it all back to me—I see everybody here in knickerbockers and pantalettes," she said, with her trailing slightly foreign accent, her eyes returning to his face.

Agreeable as their expression was, the young man was shocked that they should reflect so unseemly a picture of the august tribunal before which, at that very moment, her case was being tried. Nothing could be in worse taste than misplaced flippancy; and he answered somewhat stiffly: "Yes, you have been away a very long time."

"Oh, centuries and centuries; so long," she said, "that I'm sure I'm dead and buried, and this dear old place is heaven;" which, for reasons he could not define, struck Newland Archer as an even more disrespectful way of describing New York society.

## III.

It invariably happened in the same way.

Mrs. Julius Beaufort, on the night of her annual ball, never failed to appear at the Opera; indeed, she always gave her ball on an Opera night in order to emphasise her complete superiority to household cares, and her possession of a staff of servants competent to organise every detail of the entertainment in her absence.

The Beauforts' house was one of the few in New York that possessed a ball-room (it antedated even Mrs. Manson Mingott's and the Headly Chiverses'); and at a time when it was beginning to be thought "provincial" to put a "crash" over the drawing-room floor and move the furniture upstairs, the possession of a ball-room that was used for no other purpose, and left for three-hundred-and-sixty-four days of the year to shuttered darkness, with its gilt chairs stacked in a corner and its chandelier in a bag; this undoubted superiority was felt to compensate for whatever was regrettable in the Beaufort past.

Mrs. Archer, who was fond of coining her social philosophy into axioms, had once said: "We all have our pet common people —" and though the phrase was a daring one, its truth was secretly admitted in many an exclusive bosom. But the Beauforts were not exactly common; some people said they were even worse. Mrs. Beaufort belonged indeed to one of America's most honoured families; she had been the lovely Regina Dallas (of the South

Carolina branch), a penniless beauty introduced to New York society by her cousin, the imprudent Medora Manson, who was always doing the wrong thing from the right motive. When one was related to the Mansons and the Rushworths one had a "droit de cite" (as Mr. Sillerton Jackson, who had frequented the Tuileries, called it) in New York society; but did one not forfeit it in marrying Julius Beaufort?

The question was: who was Beaufort? He passed for an Englishman, was agreeable, handsome, ill-tempered, hospitable and witty. He had come to America with letters of recommendation from old Mrs. Manson Mingott's English son-in-law, the banker, and had speedily made himself an important position in the world of affairs; but his habits were dissipated, his tongue was bitter, his antecedents were mysterious; and when Medora Manson announced her cousin's engagement to him it was felt to be one more act of folly in poor Medora's long record of imprudences.

But folly is as often justified of her children as wisdom, and two years after young Mrs. Beaufort's marriage it was admitted that she had the most distinguished house in New York. No one knew exactly how the miracle was accomplished. She was indolent, passive, the caustic even called her dull; but dressed like an idol, hung with pearls, growing younger and blonder and more beautiful each year, she throned in Mr. Beaufort's heavy brown-stone palace, and drew all the world there without lifting her jewelled little finger. The knowing people said it was Beaufort himself who trained the servants, taught the chef new dishes, told the gardeners what hot-house flowers to grow for the dinner-table and the drawing-rooms, selected the guests, brewed the after-dinner punch and dictated the little notes his wife wrote to her friends. If he did, these domestic activities were privately performed, and he presented to the world the appearance of a careless and hospitable millionaire strolling into his own drawing-room with the detachment of an invited guest, and saying: "My wife's gloxinias are a marvel, aren't they? I believe she gets them out from Kew."

Mr. Beaufort's secret, people were agreed, was the way he carried things off. It was all very well to whisper that he had been "helped" to leave England by the international banking-house in which he had been employed; he carried off that rumour as easily as the rest—though New York's business conscience was no less sensitive than its moral standard—he carried everything before him, and all New York into his drawing-rooms, and for over twenty years now people had said they were "going to the Beauforts'" with the same tone of security as if they had said they were going to Mrs. Manson Mingott's, and with the added satisfaction of knowing they would get hot canvas-back ducks and vintage wines, instead of tepid Veuve Clicquot without a year and warmed-up croquettes from Philadelphia.

Mrs. Beaufort, then, had as usual appeared in her box just before the Jewel Song; and when, again as usual, she rose at the end of the third act, drew her opera cloak about her lovely shoulders, and disappeared, New York knew that meant that half an hour later the ball would begin.

The Beaufort house was one that New Yorkers were proud to show to foreigners, especially on the night of the annual ball. The Beauforts had been among the first people in New York to own their own red velvet carpet and have it rolled down the steps by their own footmen, under their own awning, instead of hiring it with the supper and the ball-room chairs. They had also inaugurated the custom of letting the ladies take their cloaks off in the hall, instead of shuffling up to the hostess's bedroom and recurling their hair with the aid of the gas-burner; Beaufort was understood to have said that he supposed all his wife's friends had maids who saw to it that they were properly coiffees when they left home.

Then the house had been boldly planned with a ball-room, so that, instead of squeezing through a narrow passage to get to it (as at the Chiverses') one marched solemnly down a vista of enfiladed drawing-rooms (the sea-green, the crimson and the bouton d'or), seeing from afar the many-candled lustres reflected in the polished parquetry, and beyond that the depths of a conservatory where camellias and tree-ferns arched their costly foliage over seats of black and gold bamboo.

Newland Archer, as became a young man of his position, strolled in somewhat late. He had left his overcoat with the silk-stockinged footmen (the stockings were one of Beaufort's few fatuities), had dawdled a while in the library hung with Spanish leather and furnished with Buhl and malachite, where a few men were chatting and putting on their dancing-gloves, and had finally joined the line of guests whom Mrs. Beaufort was receiving on the threshold of the crimson drawing-room.

Archer was distinctly nervous. He had not gone back to his club after the Opera (as the young bloods usually did), but, the night being fine, had walked for some distance up Fifth Avenue before turning back in the direction of the

Beauforts' house. He was definitely afraid that the Mingotts might be going too far; that, in fact, they might have Granny Mingott's orders to bring the Countess Olenska to the ball.

From the tone of the club box he had perceived how grave a mistake that would be; and, though he was more than ever determined to "see the thing through," he felt less chivalrously eager to champion his betrothed's cousin than before their brief talk at the Opera.

Wandering on to the bouton d'or drawing-room (where Beaufort had had the audacity to hang "Love Victorious," the much-discussed nude of Bouguereau) Archer found Mrs. Welland and her daughter standing near the ball-room door. Couples were already gliding over the floor beyond: the light of the wax candles fell on revolving tulle skirts, on girlish heads wreathed with modest blossoms, on the dashing aigrettes and ornaments of the young married women's coiffures, and on the glitter of highly glazed shirt-fronts and fresh glace gloves.

Miss Welland, evidently about to join the dancers, hung on the threshold, her lilies-of-the-valley in her hand (she carried no other bouquet), her face a little pale, her eyes burning with a candid excitement. A group of young men and girls were gathered about her, and there was much hand-clasping, laughing and pleasantry on which Mrs. Welland, standing slightly apart, shed the beam of a qualified approval. It was evident that Miss Welland was in the act of announcing her engagement, while her mother affected the air of parental reluctance considered suitable to the occasion.

Archer paused a moment. It was at his express wish that the announcement had been made, and yet it was not thus that he would have wished to have his happiness known. To proclaim it in the heat and noise of a crowded ball-room was to rob it of the fine bloom of privacy which should belong to things nearest the heart. His joy was so deep that this blurring of the surface left its essence untouched; but he would have liked to keep the surface pure too. It was something of a satisfaction to find that May Welland shared this feeling. Her eyes fled to his beseechingly, and their look said: "Remember, we're doing this because it's right."

No appeal could have found a more immediate response in Archer's breast; but he wished that the necessity of their action had been represented by some ideal reason, and not simply by poor Ellen Olenska. The group about Miss Welland made way for him with significant smiles, and after taking his share of the felicitations he drew his betrothed into the middle of the ball-room floor and put his arm about her waist.

"Now we shan't have to talk," he said, smiling into her candid eyes, as they floated away on the soft waves of the Blue Danube.

She made no answer. Her lips trembled into a smile, but the eyes remained distant and serious, as if bent on some ineffable vision. "Dear," Archer whispered, pressing her to him: it was borne in on him that the first hours of being engaged, even if spent in a ball-room, had in them something grave and sacramental. What a new life it was going to be, with this whiteness, radiance, goodness at one's side!

The dance over, the two, as became an affianced couple, wandered into the conservatory; and sitting behind a tall screen of tree-ferns and camellias Newland pressed her gloved hand to his lips.

"You see I did as you asked me to," she said.

"Yes: I couldn't wait," he answered smiling. After a moment he added: "Only I wish it hadn't had to be at a ball."

"Yes, I know." She met his glance comprehendingly. "But after all—even here we're alone together, aren't we?"

"Oh, dearest—always!" Archer cried.

Evidently she was always going to understand; she was always going to say the right thing. The discovery made the cup of his bliss overflow, and he went on gaily: "The worst of it is that I want to kiss you and I can't." As he spoke he took a swift glance about the conservatory, assured himself of their momentary privacy, and catching her to him laid a fugitive pressure on her lips. To counteract the audacity of this proceeding he led her to a bamboo sofa in a less secluded part of the conservatory, and sitting down beside her broke a lily-of-the-valley from her bouquet. She sat silent, and the world lay like a sunlit valley at their feet.

"Did you tell my cousin Ellen?" she asked presently, as if she spoke through a dream.

He roused himself, and remembered that he had not done so. Some invincible repugnance to speak of such things to the strange foreign woman had checked the words on his lips.

"No—I hadn't the chance after all," he said, fibbing hastily.

"Ah." She looked disappointed, but gently resolved on gaining her point. "You must, then, for I didn't either; and I shouldn't like her to think —"

"Of course not. But aren't you, after all, the person to do it?"

She pondered on this. "If I'd done it at the right time, yes: but now that there's been a delay I think you must explain that I'd asked you to tell her at the Opera, before our speaking about it to everybody here. Otherwise she might think I had forgotten her. You see, she's one of the family, and she's been away so long that she's rather—sensitive."

Archer looked at her glowingly. "Dear and great angel! Of course I'll tell her." He glanced a trifle apprehensively toward the crowded ball-room. "But I haven't seen her yet. Has she come?"

"No; at the last minute she decided not to."

"At the last minute?" he echoed, betraying his surprise that she should ever have considered the alternative possible.

"Yes. She's awfully fond of dancing," the young girl answered simply. "But suddenly she made up her mind that her dress wasn't smart enough for a ball, though we thought it so lovely; and so my aunt had to take her home."

"Oh, well —" said Archer with happy indifference. Nothing about his betrothed pleased him more than her resolute determination to carry to its utmost limit that ritual of ignoring the "unpleasant" in which they had both been brought up.

"She knows as well as I do," he reflected, "the real reason of her cousin's staying away; but I shall never let her see by the least sign that I am conscious of there being a shadow of a shade on poor Ellen Olenska's reputation."

## IV.

In the course of the next day the first of the usual betrothal visits were exchanged. The New York ritual was precise and inflexible in such matters; and in conformity with it Newland Archer first went with his mother and sister to call on Mrs. Welland, after which he and Mrs. Welland and May drove out to old Mrs. Manson Mingott's to receive that venerable ancestress's blessing.

A visit to Mrs. Manson Mingott was always an amusing episode to the young man. The house in itself was already an historic document, though not, of course, as venerable as certain other old family houses in University Place and lower Fifth Avenue. Those were of the purest 1830, with a grim harmony of cabbage-rose-garlanded carpets, rosewood consoles, round-arched fire-places with black marble mantels, and immense glazed book-cases of mahogany; whereas old Mrs. Mingott, who had built her house later, had bodily cast out the massive furniture of her prime, and mingled with the Mingott heirlooms the frivolous upholstery of the Second Empire. It was her habit to sit in a window of her sitting-room on the ground floor, as if watching calmly for life and fashion to flow northward to her solitary doors. She seemed in no hurry to have them come, for her patience was equalled by her confidence. She was sure that presently the hoardings, the quarries, the one-story saloons, the wooden green-houses in ragged gardens, and the rocks from which goats surveyed the scene, would vanish before the advance of residences as stately as her own—perhaps (for she was an impartial woman) even statelier; and that the cobble-stones over which the old clattering omnibuses bumped would be replaced by smooth asphalt, such as people reported having seen in Paris. Meanwhile, as every one she cared to see came to *her* (and she could fill her rooms as easily as the Beauforts, and without adding a single item to the menu of her suppers), she did not suffer from her geographic isolation.

The immense accretion of flesh which had descended on her in middle life like a flood of lava on a doomed city had changed her from a plump active little woman with a neatly-turned foot and ankle into something as vast and august as a natural phenomenon. She had accepted this submergence as philosophically as all her other trials, and now, in extreme old age, was rewarded by presenting to her mirror an almost unwrinkled expanse of firm pink and white flesh, in the centre of which the traces of a small face survived as if awaiting excavation. A flight of smooth double chins led down to the dizzy depths of a still-snowy bosom veiled in snowy muslins that were held in place by a miniature portrait of the late Mr. Mingott; and around and below, wave after wave of black silk surged away over the edges of a capacious armchair, with two tiny white hands poised like gulls on the surface of the billows.

The burden of Mrs. Manson Mingott's flesh had long since made it impossible for her to go up and down stairs, and with characteristic independence she had made her reception rooms upstairs and established herself (in flagrant violation of all the New York proprieties) on the ground floor of her house; so that, as you sat in her sitting-room window with her, you caught (through a door that was always open, and a looped-back yellow damask portiere) the unexpected vista of a bedroom with a huge low bed upholstered like a sofa, and a toilet-table with frivolous lace flounces and a gilt-framed mirror.

Her visitors were startled and fascinated by the foreignness of this arrangement, which recalled scenes in French fiction, and architectural incentives to immorality such as the simple American had never dreamed of. That was how women with lovers lived in the wicked old societies, in apartments with all the rooms on one floor, and all the indecent propinquities that their novels described. It amused Newland Archer (who had secretly situated the love-scenes of "Monsieur de Camors" in Mrs. Mingott's bedroom) to picture her blameless life led in the stage-setting of adultery; but he said to himself, with considerable admiration, that if a lover had been what she wanted, the intrepid woman would have had him too.

To the general relief the Countess Olenska was not present in her grandmother's drawing-room during the visit of the betrothed couple. Mrs. Mingott said she had gone out; which, on a day of such glaring sunlight, and at the "shopping hour," seemed in itself an indelicate thing for a compromised woman to do. But at any rate it spared them the embarrassment of her presence, and the faint shadow that her unhappy past might seem to shed on their radiant future. The visit went off successfully, as was to have been expected. Old Mrs. Mingott was delighted with the engagement, which, being long foreseen by watchful relatives, had been carefully passed upon in family council; and the engagement ring, a large thick sapphire set in invisible claws, met with her unqualified admiration.

"It's the new setting: of course it shows the stone beautifully, but it looks a little bare to old-fashioned eyes," Mrs. Welland had explained, with a conciliatory side-glance at her future son-in-law.

"Old-fashioned eyes? I hope you don't mean mine, my dear? I like all the novelties," said the ancestress, lifting the stone to her small bright orbs, which no glasses had ever disfigured. "Very handsome," she added, returning the jewel; "very liberal. In my time a cameo set in pearls was thought sufficient. But it's the hand that sets off the ring, isn't it, my dear Mr. Archer?" and she waved one of her tiny hands, with small pointed nails and rolls of aged fat encircling the wrist like ivory bracelets. "Mine was modelled in Rome by the great Ferrigiani. You should have May's done: no doubt he'll have it done, my child. Her hand is large—it's these modern sports that spread the joints—but the skin is white.—And when's the wedding to be?" she broke off, fixing her eyes on Archer's face.

"Oh —" Mrs. Welland murmured, while the young man, smiling at his betrothed, replied: "As soon as ever it can, if only you'll back me up, Mrs. Mingott."

"We must give them time to get to know each other a little better, mamma," Mrs. Welland interposed, with the proper affectation of reluctance; to which the ancestress rejoined: "Know each other? Fiddlesticks! Everybody in New York has always known everybody. Let the young man have his way, my dear; don't wait till the bubble's off the wine. Marry them before Lent; I may catch pneumonia any winter now, and I want to give the wedding-breakfast."

These successive statements were received with the proper expressions of amusement, incredulity and gratitude; and the visit was breaking up in a vein of mild pleasantry when the door opened to admit the Countess Olenska, who entered in bonnet and mantle followed by the unexpected figure of Julius Beaufort.

There was a cousinly murmur of pleasure between the ladies, and Mrs. Mingott held out Ferrigiani's model to the banker. "Ha! Beaufort, this is a rare favour!" (She had an odd foreign way of addressing men by their surnames.)

"Thanks. I wish it might happen oftener," said the visitor in his easy arrogant way. "I'm generally so tied down; but I met the Countess Ellen in Madison Square, and she was good enough to let me walk home with her."

"Ah—I hope the house will be gayer, now that Ellen's here!" cried Mrs. Mingott with a glorious effrontery. "Sit down—sit down, Beaufort: push up the yellow armchair; now I've got you I want a good gossip. I hear your ball was magnificent; and I understand you invited Mrs. Lemuel Struthers? Well—I've a curiosity to see the woman myself."

She had forgotten her relatives, who were drifting out into the hall under Ellen Olenska's guidance. Old Mrs. Mingott had always professed a great admiration for Julius Beaufort, and there was a kind of kinship in their cool domineering way and their short-cuts through the conventions. Now she was eagerly curious to know what had decided the Beauforts to invite (for the first time) Mrs. Lemuel Struthers, the widow of Struthers's Shoe-polish, who had returned the previous year from a long initiatory sojourn in Europe to lay siege to the tight little citadel of New York. "Of course if you and Regina invite her the thing is settled. Well, we need new blood and new money—and I hear she's still very good-looking," the carnivorous old lady declared.

In the hall, while Mrs. Welland and May drew on their furs, Archer saw that the Countess Olenska was looking at him with a faintly questioning smile.

"Of course you know already—about May and me," he said, answering her look with a shy laugh. "She scolded me for not giving you the news last night at the Opera: I had her orders to tell you that we were engaged—but I couldn't, in that crowd."

The smile passed from Countess Olenska's eyes to her lips: she looked younger, more like the bold brown Ellen Mingott of his boyhood. "Of course I know; yes. And I'm so glad. But one doesn't tell such things first in a crowd." The ladies were on the threshold and she held out her hand.

"Good-bye; come and see me some day," she said, still looking at Archer.

In the carriage, on the way down Fifth Avenue, they talked pointedly of Mrs. Mingott, of her age, her spirit, and all her wonderful attributes. No one alluded to Ellen Olenska; but Archer knew that Mrs. Welland was thinking: "It's a mistake for Ellen to be seen, the very day after her arrival, parading up Fifth Avenue at the crowded hour with Julius Beaufort —" and the young man himself mentally added: "And she ought to know that a man who's just engaged doesn't spend his time calling on married women. But I daresay in the set she's lived in they do—they never do anything else." And, in spite of the cosmopolitan views on which he prided himself, he thanked heaven that he was a New Yorker, and about to ally himself with one of his own kind.

## V.

The next evening old Mr. Sillerton Jackson came to dine with the Archers.

Mrs. Archer was a shy woman and shrank from society; but she liked to be well-informed as to its doings. Her old friend Mr. Sillerton Jackson applied to the investigation of his friends' affairs the patience of a collector and the science of a naturalist; and his sister, Miss Sophy Jackson, who lived with him, and was entertained by all the people who could not secure her much-sought-after brother, brought home bits of minor gossip that filled out usefully the gaps in his picture.

Therefore, whenever anything happened that Mrs. Archer wanted to know about, she asked Mr. Jackson to dine; and as she honoured few people with her invitations, and as she and her daughter Janey were an excellent audience, Mr. Jackson usually came himself instead of sending his sister. If he could have dictated all the conditions, he would have chosen the evenings when Newland was out; not because the young man was uncongenial to him (the two got on capitally at their club) but because the old anecdotist sometimes felt, on Newland's part, a tendency to weigh his evidence that the ladies of the family never showed.

Mr. Jackson, if perfection had been attainable on earth, would also have asked that Mrs. Archer's food should be a little better. But then New York, as far back as the mind of man could travel, had been divided into the two great fundamental groups of the Mingotts and Mansons and all their clan, who cared about eating and clothes and money, and the Archer-Newland-van-der-Luyden tribe, who were devoted to travel, horticulture and the best fiction, and looked down on the grosser forms of pleasure.

You couldn't have everything, after all. If you dined with the Lovell Mingotts you got canvas-back and terrapin and vintage wines; at Adeline Archer's you could talk about Alpine scenery and "The Marble Faun"; and luckily the Archer Madeira had gone round the Cape. Therefore when a friendly summons came from Mrs. Archer, Mr. Jackson, who was a true eclectic, would usually say to his sister: "I've been a little gouty since my last dinner at the Lovell Mingotts'—it will do me good to diet at Adeline's."

Mrs. Archer, who had long been a widow, lived with her son and daughter in West Twenty-eighth Street. An upper floor was dedicated to Newland, and the two women squeezed themselves into narrower quarters below. In an unclouded harmony of tastes and interests they cultivated ferns in Wardian cases, made macrame lace and wool embroidery on linen, collected American revolutionary glazed ware, subscribed to "Good Words," and read Ouida's novels for the sake of the Italian atmosphere. (They preferred those about peasant life, because of the descriptions of scenery and the pleasanter sentiments, though in general they liked novels about people in society, whose motives and habits were more comprehensible, spoke severely of

Dickens, who "had never drawn a gentleman," and considered Thackeray less at home in the great world than Bulwer—who, however, was beginning to be thought old-fashioned.) Mrs. and Miss Archer were both great lovers of scenery. It was what they principally sought and admired on their occasional travels abroad; considering architecture and painting as subjects for men, and chiefly for learned persons who read Ruskin. Mrs. Archer had been born a Newland, and mother and daughter, who were as like as sisters, were both, as people said, "true Newlands"; tall, pale, and slightly round-shouldered, with long noses, sweet smiles and a kind of drooping distinction like that in certain faded Reynolds portraits. Their physical resemblance would have been complete if an elderly embonpoint had not stretched Mrs. Archer's black brocade, while Miss Archer's brown and purple poplins hung, as the years went on, more and more slackly on her virgin frame.

Mentally, the likeness between them, as Newland was aware, was less complete than their identical mannerisms often made it appear. The long habit of living together in mutually dependent intimacy had given them the same vocabulary, and the same habit of beginning their phrases "Mother thinks" or "Janey thinks," according as one or the other wished to advance an opinion of her own; but in reality, while Mrs. Archer's serene unimaginativeness rested easily in the accepted and familiar, Janey was subject to starts and aberrations of fancy welling up from springs of suppressed romance.

Mother and daughter adored each other and revered their son and brother; and Archer loved them with a tenderness made compunctious and uncritical by the sense of their exaggerated admiration, and by his secret satisfaction in it. After all, he thought it a good thing for a man to have his authority respected in his own house, even if his sense of humour sometimes made him question the force of his mandate.

On this occasion the young man was very sure that Mr. Jackson would rather have had him dine out; but he had his own reasons for not doing so.

Of course old Jackson wanted to talk about Ellen Olenska, and of course Mrs. Archer and Janey wanted to hear what he had to tell. All three would be slightly embarrassed by Newland's presence, now that his prospective relation to the Mingott clan had been made known; and the young man waited with an amused curiosity to see how they would turn the difficulty.

They began, obliquely, by talking about Mrs. Lemuel Struthers.

"It's a pity the Beauforts asked her," Mrs. Archer said gently. "But then Regina always does what he tells her; and *Beaufort* —"

"Certain nuances escape Beaufort," said Mr. Jackson, cautiously inspecting the broiled shad, and wondering for the thousandth time why Mrs. Archer's cook always burnt the roe to a cinder. (Newland, who had long shared his wonder, could always detect it in the older man's expression of melancholy disapproval.)

"Oh, necessarily; Beaufort is a vulgar man," said Mrs. Archer. "My grandfather Newland always used to say to my mother: 'Whatever you do, don't let that fellow Beaufort be introduced to the girls.' But at least he's had the advantage of associating with gentlemen; in England too, they say. It's all very mysterious —" She glanced at Janey and paused. She and Janey knew every fold of the Beaufort mystery, but in public Mrs. Archer continued to assume that the subject was not one for the unmarried.

"But this Mrs. Struthers," Mrs. Archer continued; "what did you say *she* was, Sillerton?"

"Out of a mine: or rather out of the saloon at the head of the pit. Then with Living Wax-Works, touring New England. After the police broke *that* up, they say she lived —" Mr. Jackson in his turn glanced at Janey, whose eyes began to bulge from under her prominent lids. There were still hiatuses for her in Mrs. Struthers's past.

"Then," Mr. Jackson continued (and Archer saw he was wondering why no one had told the butler never to slice cucumbers with a steel knife), "then Lemuel Struthers came along. They say his advertiser used the girl's head for the shoe-polish posters; her hair's intensely black, you know—the Egyptian style. Anyhow, he—eventually—married her." There were volumes of innuendo in the way the "eventually" was spaced, and each syllable given its due stress.

"Oh, well—at the pass we've come to nowadays, it doesn't matter," said Mrs. Archer indifferently. The ladies were not really interested in Mrs. Struthers just then; the subject of Ellen Olenska was too fresh and too absorbing to them. Indeed, Mrs. Struthers's name had been introduced by Mrs. Archer only that she might presently be able to say: "And Newland's new cousin—Countess Olenska? Was *she* at the ball too?"

There was a faint touch of sarcasm in the reference to her son, and Archer knew it and had expected it. Even Mrs. Archer, who was seldom unduly pleased with human events, had been altogether glad of her son's engagement. ("Especially after that silly business with Mrs. Rushworth," as she had remarked to Janey, alluding to what had once seemed to Newland a tragedy of which his soul would always bear the scar.)

There was no better match in New York than May Welland, look at the question from whatever point you chose. Of course such a marriage was only what Newland was entitled to; but young men are so foolish and incalculable—and some women so ensnaring and unscrupulous—that it was nothing short of a miracle to see one's only son safe past the Siren Isle and in the haven of a blameless domesticity.

All this Mrs. Archer felt, and her son knew she felt; but he knew also that she had been perturbed by the premature announcement of his engagement, or rather by its cause; and it was for that reason—because on the whole he was a tender and indulgent master—that he had stayed at home that evening. "It's not that I don't approve of the Mingotts' esprit de corps; but why Newland's engagement should be mixed up with that Olenska woman's comings and goings I don't see," Mrs. Archer grumbled to Janey, the only witness of her slight lapses from perfect sweetness.

She had behaved beautifully—and in beautiful behaviour she was unsurpassed—during the call on Mrs. Welland; but Newland knew (and his betrothed doubtless guessed) that all through the visit she and Janey were nervously on the watch for Madame Olenska's possible intrusion; and when they left the house together she had permitted herself to say to her son: "I'm thankful that Augusta Welland received us alone."

These indications of inward disturbance moved Archer the more that he too felt that the Mingotts had gone a little too far. But, as it was against all the rules of their code that the mother and son should ever allude to what was uppermost in their thoughts, he simply replied: "Oh, well, there's always a phase of family parties to be gone through when one gets engaged, and the sooner it's over the better." At which his mother merely pursed her lips under the lace veil that hung down from her grey velvet bonnet trimmed with frosted grapes.

Her revenge, he felt—her lawful revenge—would be to "draw" Mr. Jackson that evening on the Countess Olenska; and, having publicly done his duty as a future member of the Mingott clan, the young man had no objection to hearing the lady discussed in private—except that the subject was already beginning to bore him.

Mr. Jackson had helped himself to a slice of the tepid filet which the mournful butler had handed him with a look as sceptical as his own, and had rejected the mushroom sauce after a scarcely perceptible sniff. He looked baffled and hungry, and Archer reflected that he would probably finish his meal on Ellen Olenska.

Mr. Jackson leaned back in his chair, and glanced up at the candlelit Archers, Newlands and van der Luydens hanging in dark frames on the dark walls.

"Ah, how your grandfather Archer loved a good dinner, my dear Newland!" he said, his eyes on the portrait of a plump full-chested young man in a stock and a blue coat, with a view of a white-columned country-house behind him. "Well—well—well ... I wonder what he would have said to all these foreign marriages!"

Mrs. Archer ignored the allusion to the ancestral cuisine and Mr. Jackson continued with deliberation: "No, she was *not* at the ball."

"Ah —" Mrs. Archer murmured, in a tone that implied: "She had that decency."

"Perhaps the Beauforts don't know her," Janey suggested, with her artless malice.

Mr. Jackson gave a faint sip, as if he had been tasting invisible Madeira. "Mrs. Beaufort may not—but Beaufort certainly does, for she was seen walking up Fifth Avenue this afternoon with him by the whole of New York."

"Mercy —" moaned Mrs. Archer, evidently perceiving the uselessness of trying to ascribe the actions of foreigners to a sense of delicacy.

"I wonder if she wears a round hat or a bonnet in the afternoon," Janey speculated. "At the Opera I know she had on dark blue velvet, perfectly plain and flat—like a night-gown."

"Janey!" said her mother; and Miss Archer blushed and tried to look audacious.

"It was, at any rate, in better taste not to go to the ball," Mrs. Archer continued.

A spirit of perversity moved her son to rejoin: "I don't think it was a question of taste with her. May said she meant to go, and then decided that the dress in question wasn't smart enough."

Mrs. Archer smiled at this confirmation of her inference. "Poor Ellen," she simply remarked; adding compassionately: "We must always bear in mind what an eccentric bringing-up Medora Manson gave her. What can you expect of a girl who was allowed to wear black satin at her coming-out ball?"

"Ah—don't I remember her in it!" said Mr. Jackson; adding: "Poor girl!" in the tone of one who, while enjoying the memory, had fully understood at the time what the sight portended.

"It's odd," Janey remarked, "that she should have kept such an ugly name as Ellen. I should have changed it to Elaine." She glanced about the table to see the effect of this.

Her brother laughed. "Why Elaine?"

"I don't know; it sounds more—more Polish," said Janey, blushing.

"It sounds more conspicuous; and that can hardly be what she wishes," said Mrs. Archer distantly.

"Why not?" broke in her son, growing suddenly argumentative. "Why shouldn't she be conspicuous if she chooses? Why should she slink about as if it were she who had disgraced herself? She's 'poor Ellen' certainly, because she had the bad luck to make a wretched marriage; but I don't see that that's a reason for hiding her head as if she were the culprit."

"That, I suppose," said Mr. Jackson, speculatively, "is the line the Mingotts mean to take."

The young man reddened. "I didn't have to wait for their cue, if that's what you mean, sir. Madame Olenska has had an unhappy life: that doesn't make her an outcast."

"There are rumours," began Mr. Jackson, glancing at Janey.

"Oh, I know: the secretary," the young man took him up. "Nonsense, mother; Janey's grown-up. They say, don't they," he went on, "that the secretary helped her to get away from her brute of a husband, who kept her practically a prisoner? Well, what if he did? I hope there isn't a man among us who wouldn't have done the same in such a case."

Mr. Jackson glanced over his shoulder to say to the sad butler: "Perhaps ... that sauce ... just a little, after all —"; then, having helped himself, he remarked: "I'm told she's looking for a house. She means to live here."

"I hear she means to get a divorce," said Janey boldly.

"I hope she will!" Archer exclaimed.

The word had fallen like a bombshell in the pure and tranquil atmosphere of the Archer dining-room. Mrs. Archer raised her delicate eye-brows in the particular curve that signified: "The butler —" and the young man, himself mindful of the bad taste of discussing such intimate matters in public, hastily branched off into an account of his visit to old Mrs. Mingott.

After dinner, according to immemorial custom, Mrs. Archer and Janey trailed their long silk draperies up to the drawing-room, where, while the gentlemen smoked below stairs, they sat beside a Carcel lamp with an engraved globe, facing each other across a rosewood work-table with a green silk bag under it, and stitched at the two ends of a tapestry band of field-flowers destined to adorn an "occasional" chair in the drawing-room of young Mrs. Newland Archer.

While this rite was in progress in the drawing-room, Archer settled Mr. Jackson in an armchair near the fire in the Gothic library and handed him a cigar. Mr. Jackson sank into the armchair with satisfaction, lit his cigar with perfect confidence (it was Newland who bought them), and stretching his thin old ankles to the coals, said: "You say the secretary merely helped her to get away, my dear fellow? Well, he was still helping her a year later, then; for somebody met 'em living at Lausanne together."

Newland reddened. "Living together? Well, why not? Who had the right to make her life over if she hadn't? I'm sick of the hypocrisy that would bury alive a woman of her age if her husband prefers to live with harlots."

He stopped and turned away angrily to light his cigar. "Women ought to be free—as free as we are," he declared, making a discovery of which he was too irritated to measure the terrific consequences.

Mr. Sillerton Jackson stretched his ankles nearer the coals and emitted a sardonic whistle.

"Well," he said after a pause, "apparently Count Olenski takes your view; for I never heard of his having lifted a finger to get his wife back."

## VI.

That evening, after Mr. Jackson had taken himself away, and the ladies had retired to their chintz-curtained bedroom, Newland Archer mounted thoughtfully to his own study. A vigilant hand had, as usual, kept the fire alive and the lamp trimmed; and the room, with its rows and rows of books, its bronze and steel statuettes of "The Fencers" on the mantelpiece and its many photographs of famous pictures, looked singularly home-like and welcoming.

As he dropped into his armchair near the fire his eyes rested on a large photograph of May Welland, which the young girl had given him in the first days of their romance, and which had now displaced all the other portraits on the table. With a new sense of awe he looked at the frank forehead, serious eyes and gay innocent mouth of the young creature whose soul's custodian he was to be. That terrifying product of the social system he belonged to and believed in, the young girl who knew nothing and expected everything, looked back at him like a stranger through May Welland's familiar features; and once more it was borne in on him that marriage was not the safe anchorage he had been taught to think, but a voyage on uncharted seas.

The case of the Countess Olenska had stirred up old settled convictions and set them drifting dangerously through his mind. His own exclamation: "Women should be free—as free as we are," struck to the root of a problem that it was agreed in his world to regard as non-existent. "Nice" women, however wronged, would never claim the kind of freedom he meant, and generous-minded men like himself were therefore—in the heat of argument—the more chivalrously ready to concede it to them. Such verbal generosities were in fact only a humbugging disguise of the inexorable conventions that tied things together and bound people down to the old pattern. But here he was pledged to defend, on the part of his betrothed's cousin, conduct that, on his own wife's part, would justify him in calling down on her all the thunders of Church and State. Of course the dilemma was purely hypothetical; since he wasn't a blackguard Polish nobleman, it was absurd to speculate what his wife's rights would be if he *were*. But Newland Archer was too imaginative not to feel that, in his case and May's, the tie might gall for reasons far less gross and palpable. What could he and she really know of each other, since it was his duty, as a "decent" fellow, to conceal his past from her, and hers, as a marriageable girl, to have no past to conceal? What if, for some one of the subtler reasons that would tell with both of them, they should tire of each other, misunderstand or irritate each other? He reviewed his friends' marriages—the supposedly happy ones—and saw none that answered, even remotely, to the passionate and tender comradeship which he pictured as his permanent relation with May Welland. He perceived that such a picture presupposed, on her part, the experience, the versatility, the freedom of judgment, which she had been carefully trained not to possess; and with a shiver of foreboding he saw his marriage becoming what most of the other marriages about him were: a dull association of material and social interests held together by ignorance on the one side and hypocrisy on the other. Lawrence Lefferts occurred to him as the husband who had most completely realised this enviable ideal. As became the high-priest of form, he had formed a wife so completely to his own convenience that, in the most conspicuous moments of his frequent love-affairs with other men's wives, she went about in smiling unconsciousness, saying that "Lawrence was so frightfully strict"; and had been known to blush indignantly, and avert her gaze, when some one alluded in her presence to the fact that Julius Beaufort (as became a "foreigner" of doubtful origin) had what was known in New York as "another establishment."

Archer tried to console himself with the thought that he was not quite such an ass as Larry Lefferts, nor May such a simpleton as poor Gertrude; but the difference was after all one of intelligence and not of standards. In reality they all lived in a kind of hieroglyphic world, where the real thing was never said or done or even thought, but only represented by a set of arbitrary signs; as when Mrs. Welland, who knew exactly why Archer had pressed her to announce her daughter's engagement at the Beaufort ball (and had indeed expected him to do no less), yet felt obliged to simulate reluctance, and the air of having had her hand forced, quite as, in the books on Primitive Man that people of advanced culture were beginning to read, the savage bride is dragged with shrieks from her parents' tent.

The result, of course, was that the young girl who was the centre of this elaborate system of mystification remained the more inscrutable for her very frankness and assurance. She was frank, poor darling, because she had nothing to conceal, assured because she knew of nothing to be on her guard against; and with no better preparation than this, she was to be plunged overnight into what people evasively called "the facts of life."

The young man was sincerely but placidly in love. He delighted in the radiant good looks of his betrothed, in her health, her horsemanship, her grace and quickness at games, and the shy interest in books and ideas that she was beginning to develop under his guidance. (She had advanced far enough to join him in ridiculing the Idyls of the King, but not to feel the beauty of

Ulysses and the Lotus Eaters.) She was straightforward, loyal and brave; she had a sense of humour (chiefly proved by her laughing at *his* jokes); and he suspected, in the depths of her innocently-gazing soul, a glow of feeling that it would be a joy to waken. But when he had gone the brief round of her he returned discouraged by the thought that all this frankness and innocence were only an artificial product. Untrained human nature was not frank and innocent; it was full of the twists and defences of an instinctive guile. And he felt himself oppressed by this creation of factitious purity, so cunningly manufactured by a conspiracy of mothers and aunts and grandmothers and long-dead ancestresses, because it was supposed to be what he wanted, what he had a right to, in order that he might exercise his lordly pleasure in smashing it like an image made of snow.

There was a certain triteness in these reflections: they were those habitual to young men on the approach of their wedding day. But they were generally accompanied by a sense of compunction and self-abasement of which Newland Archer felt no trace. He could not deplore (as Thackeray's heroes so often exasperated him by doing) that he had not a blank page to offer his bride in exchange for the unblemished one she was to give to him. He could not get away from the fact that if he had been brought up as she had they would have been no more fit to find their way about than the Babes in the Wood; nor could he, for all his anxious cogitations, see any honest reason (any, that is, unconnected with his own momentary pleasure, and the passion of masculine vanity) why his bride should not have been allowed the same freedom of experience as himself.

Such questions, at such an hour, were bound to drift through his mind; but he was conscious that their uncomfortable persistence and precision were due to the inopportune arrival of the Countess Olenska. Here he was, at the very moment of his betrothal—a moment for pure thoughts and cloudless hopes—pitchforked into a coil of scandal which raised all the special problems he would have preferred to let lie. "Hang Ellen Olenska!" he grumbled, as he covered his fire and began to undress. He could not really see why her fate should have the least bearing on his; yet he dimly felt that he had only just begun to measure the risks of the championship which his engagement had forced upon him.

A few days later the bolt fell.

The Lovell Mingotts had sent out cards for what was known as "a formal dinner" (that is, three extra footmen, two dishes for each course, and a Roman punch in the middle), and had headed their invitations with the words "To meet the Countess Olenska," in accordance with the hospitable American fashion, which treats strangers as if they were royalties, or at least as their ambassadors.

The guests had been selected with a boldness and discrimination in which the initiated recognised the firm hand of Catherine the Great. Associated with such immemorial standbys as the Selfridge Merrys, who were asked everywhere because they always had been, the Beauforts, on whom there was a claim of relationship, and Mr. Sillerton Jackson and his sister Sophy (who went wherever her brother told her to), were some of the most fashionable and yet most irreproachable of the dominant "young married" set; the Lawrence Leffertses, Mrs. Lefferts Rushworth (the lovely widow), the Harry Thorleys, the Reggie Chiverses and young Morris Dagonet and his wife (who was a van der Luyden). The company indeed was perfectly assorted, since all the members belonged to the little inner group of people who, during the long New York season, disported themselves together daily and nightly with apparently undiminished zest.

Forty-eight hours later the unbelievable had happened; every one had refused the Mingotts' invitation except the Beauforts and old Mr. Jackson and his sister. The intended slight was emphasised by the fact that even the Reggie Chiverses, who were of the Mingott clan, were among those inflicting it; and by the uniform wording of the notes, in all of which the writers "regretted that they were unable to accept," without the mitigating plea of a "previous engagement" that ordinary courtesy prescribed.

New York society was, in those days, far too small, and too scant in its resources, for every one in it (including livery-stable-keepers, butlers and cooks) not to know exactly on which evenings people were free; and it was thus possible for the recipients of Mrs. Lovell Mingott's invitations to make cruelly clear their determination not to meet the Countess Olenska.

The blow was unexpected; but the Mingotts, as their way was, met it gallantly. Mrs. Lovell Mingott confided the case to Mrs. Welland, who confided it to Newland Archer; who, aflame at the outrage, appealed passionately and authoritatively to his mother; who, after a painful period of inward resistance and outward temporising, succumbed to his instances (as she always did), and immediately embracing his cause with an energy redoubled by her previous hesitations, put on her grey velvet bonnet and said: "I'll go and see Louisa van der Luyden."

The New York of Newland Archer's day was a small and slippery pyramid, in which, as yet, hardly a fissure had been made or a foothold gained. At its base was a firm foundation of what Mrs. Archer called "plain people"; an honourable but obscure majority of respectable families who (as in the case of the Spicers or the Leffertses or the Jacksons) had been raised above their level by marriage with one of the ruling clans. People, Mrs. Archer always said, were not as particular as they used to be; and with old Catherine Spicer ruling one end of Fifth Avenue, and Julius Beaufort the other, you couldn't expect the old traditions to last much longer.

Firmly narrowing upward from this wealthy but inconspicuous substratum was the compact and dominant group which the Mingotts, Newlands, Chiverses and Mansons so actively represented. Most people imagined them to be the very apex of the pyramid; but they themselves (at least those of Mrs. Archer's generation) were aware that, in the eyes of the professional genealogist, only a still smaller number of families could lay claim to that eminence.

"Don't tell me," Mrs. Archer would say to her children, "all this modern newspaper rubbish about a New York aristocracy. If there is one, neither the Mingotts nor the Mansons belong to it; no, nor the Newlands or the Chiverses either. Our grandfathers and great-grandfathers were just respectable English or Dutch merchants, who came to the colonies to make their fortune, and stayed here because they did so well. One of your great-grandfathers signed the Declaration, and another was a general on Washington's staff, and received General Burgoyne's sword after the battle of Saratoga. These are things to be proud of, but they have nothing to do with rank or class. New York has always been a commercial community, and there are not more than three families in it who can claim an aristocratic origin in the real sense of the word."

Mrs. Archer and her son and daughter, like every one else in New York, knew who these privileged beings were: the Dagonets of Washington Square, who came of an old English county family allied with the Pitts and Foxes; the Lannings, who had intermarried with the descendants of Count de Grasse, and the van der Luydens, direct descendants of the first Dutch governor of

Manhattan, and related by pre-revolutionary marriages to several members of the French and British aristocracy.

The Lannings survived only in the person of two very old but lively Miss Lannings, who lived cheerfully and reminiscently among family portraits and Chippendale; the Dagonets were a considerable clan, allied to the best names in Baltimore and Philadelphia; but the van der Luydens, who stood above all of them, had faded into a kind of super-terrestrial twilight, from which only two figures impressively emerged; those of Mr. and Mrs. Henry van der Luyden.

Mrs. Henry van der Luyden had been Louisa Dagonet, and her mother had been the granddaughter of Colonel du Lac, of an old Channel Island family, who had fought under Cornwallis and had settled in Maryland, after the war, with his bride, Lady Angelica Trevenna, fifth daughter of the Earl of St. Austrey. The tie between the Dagonets, the du Lacs of Maryland, and their aristocratic Cornish kinsfolk, the Trevennas, had always remained close and cordial. Mr. and Mrs. van der Luyden had more than once paid long visits to the present head of the house of Trevenna, the Duke of St. Austrey, at his country-seat in Cornwall and at St. Austrey in Gloucestershire; and his Grace had frequently announced his intention of some day returning their visit (without the Duchess, who feared the Atlantic).

Mr. and Mrs. van der Luyden divided their time between Trevenna, their place in Maryland, and Skuytercliff, the great estate on the Hudson which had been one of the colonial grants of the Dutch government to the famous first Governor, and of which Mr. van der Luyden was still "Patroon." Their large solemn house in Madison Avenue was seldom opened, and when they came to town they received in it only their most intimate friends.

"I wish you would go with me, Newland," his mother said, suddenly pausing at the door of the Brown coupe. "Louisa is fond of you; and of course it's on account of dear May that I'm taking this step—and also because, if we don't all stand together, there'll be no such thing as Society left."

## VII.

Mrs. Henry van der Luyden listened in silence to her cousin Mrs. Archer's narrative.

It was all very well to tell yourself in advance that Mrs. van der Luyden was always silent, and that, though non-committal by nature and training, she was very kind to the people she really liked. Even personal experience of these facts was not always a protection from the chill that descended on one in the high-ceilinged white-walled Madison Avenue drawing-room, with the pale brocaded armchairs so obviously uncovered for the occasion, and the gauze still veiling the ormolu mantel ornaments and the beautiful old carved frame of Gainsborough's "Lady Angelica du Lac."

Mrs. van der Luyden's portrait by Huntington (in black velvet and Venetian point) faced that of her lovely ancestress. It was generally considered "as fine as a Cabanel," and, though twenty years had elapsed since its execution, was still "a perfect likeness." Indeed the Mrs. van der Luyden who sat beneath it listening to Mrs. Archer might have been the twin-sister of the fair and still youngish woman drooping against a gilt armchair before a green rep curtain. Mrs. van der Luyden still wore black velvet and Venetian point when she went into society—or rather (since she never dined out) when she threw open her own doors to receive it. Her fair hair, which had faded without turning grey, was still parted in flat overlapping points on her forehead, and the straight nose that divided her pale blue eyes was only a little more pinched about the nostrils than when the portrait had been painted. She always, indeed, struck Newland Archer as having been rather gruesomely preserved in the airless atmosphere of a perfectly irreproachable existence, as bodies caught in glaciers keep for years a rosy life-in-death.

Like all his family, he esteemed and admired Mrs. van der Luyden; but he found her gentle bending sweetness less approachable than the grimness of some of his mother's old aunts, fierce spinsters who said "No" on principle before they knew what they were going to be asked.

Mrs. van der Luyden's attitude said neither yes nor no, but always appeared to incline to clemency till her thin lips, wavering into the shadow of a smile, made the almost invariable reply: "I shall first have to talk this over with my husband."

She and Mr. van der Luyden were so exactly alike that Archer often wondered how, after forty years of the closest conjugality, two such merged identities ever separated themselves enough for anything as controversial as a talking-over. But as neither had ever reached a decision without prefacing it by this mysterious conclave, Mrs. Archer and her son, having set forth their case, waited resignedly for the familiar phrase.

Mrs. van der Luyden, however, who had seldom surprised any one, now surprised them by reaching her long hand toward the bell-rope.

"I think," she said, "I should like Henry to hear what you have told me."

A footman appeared, to whom she gravely added: "If Mr. van der Luyden has finished reading the newspaper, please ask him to be kind enough to come."

She said "reading the newspaper" in the tone in which a Minister's wife might have said: "Presiding at a Cabinet meeting"—not from any arrogance of mind, but because the habit of a life-time, and the attitude of her friends and relations, had led her to consider Mr. van der Luyden's least gesture as having an almost sacerdotal importance.

Her promptness of action showed that she considered the case as pressing as Mrs. Archer; but, lest she should be thought to have committed herself in advance, she added, with the sweetest look: "Henry always enjoys seeing you, dear Adeline; and he will wish to congratulate Newland."

The double doors had solemnly reopened and between them appeared Mr. Henry van der Luyden, tall, spare and frock-coated, with faded fair hair, a straight nose like his wife's and the same look of frozen gentleness in eyes that were merely pale grey instead of pale blue.

Mr. van der Luyden greeted Mrs. Archer with cousinly affability, proffered to Newland low-voiced congratulations couched in the same language as his wife's, and seated himself in one of the brocade armchairs with the simplicity of a reigning sovereign.

"I had just finished reading the Times," he said, laying his long finger-tips together. "In town my mornings are so much occupied that I find it more convenient to read the newspapers after luncheon."

"Ah, there's a great deal to be said for that plan—indeed I think my uncle Egmont used to say he found it less agitating not to read the morning papers till after dinner," said Mrs. Archer responsively.

"Yes: my good father abhorred hurry. But now we live in a constant rush," said Mr. van der Luyden in measured tones, looking with pleasant deliberation about the large shrouded room which to Archer was so complete an image of its owners.

"But I hope you *had* finished your reading, Henry?" his wife interposed.

"Quite—quite," he reassured her.

"Then I should like Adeline to tell you —"

"Oh, it's really Newland's story," said his mother smiling; and proceeded to rehearse once more the monstrous tale of the affront inflicted on Mrs. Lovell Mingott.

"Of course," she ended, "Augusta Welland and Mary Mingott both felt that, especially in view of Newland's engagement, you and Henry *ought to know.*"

"Ah —" said Mr. van der Luyden, drawing a deep breath.

There was a silence during which the tick of the monumental ormolu clock on the white marble mantelpiece grew as loud as the boom of a minute-gun. Archer contemplated with awe the two slender faded figures, seated side by side in a kind of viceregal rigidity, mouthpieces of some remote ancestral authority which fate compelled them to wield, when they would so much rather have lived in simplicity and seclusion, digging invisible weeds out of the perfect lawns of Skuytercliff, and playing Patience together in the evenings.

Mr. van der Luyden was the first to speak.

"You really think this is due to some—some intentional interference of Lawrence Lefferts's?" he enquired, turning to Archer.

"I'm certain of it, sir. Larry has been going it rather harder than usual lately—if cousin Louisa won't mind my mentioning it—having rather a stiff affair with the postmaster's wife in their village, or some one of that sort; and whenever poor Gertrude Lefferts begins to suspect anything, and he's afraid of trouble, he gets up a fuss of this kind, to show how awfully moral he is, and talks at the top of his voice about the impertinence of inviting his wife to meet people he doesn't wish her to know. He's simply using Madame Olenska as a lightning-rod; I've seen him try the same thing often before."

"The *Leffertses!*—" said Mrs. van der Luyden.

"The *leffertses!*—" echoed Mrs. Archer. "What would uncle Egmont have said of Lawrence Lefferts's pronouncing on anybody's social position? It shows what Society has come to."

"We'll hope it has not quite come to that," said Mr. van der Luyden firmly.

"Ah, if only you and Louisa went out more!" sighed Mrs. Archer.

But instantly she became aware of her mistake. The van der Luydens were morbidly sensitive to any criticism of their secluded existence. They were the arbiters of fashion, the Court of last Appeal, and they knew it, and bowed to their fate. But being shy and retiring persons, with no natural inclination for their part, they lived as much as possible in the sylvan solitude of Skuytercliff, and when they came to town, declined all invitations on the plea of Mrs. van der Luyden's health.

Newland Archer came to his mother's rescue. "Everybody in New York knows what you and cousin Louisa represent. That's why Mrs. Mingott felt she ought not to allow this slight on Countess Olenska to pass without consulting you."

Mrs. van der Luyden glanced at her husband, who glanced back at her.

"It is the principle that I dislike," said Mr. van der Luyden. "As long as a member of a well-known family is backed up by that family it should be considered—final."

"It seems so to me," said his wife, as if she were producing a new thought.

"I had no idea," Mr. van der Luyden continued, "that things had come to such a pass." He paused, and looked at his wife again. "It occurs to me, my dear, that the Countess Olenska is already a sort of relation—through Medora Manson's first husband. At any rate, she will be when Newland marries." He turned toward the young man. "Have you read this morning's Times, Newland?"

"Why, yes, sir," said Archer, who usually tossed off half a dozen papers with his morning coffee.

Husband and wife looked at each other again. Their pale eyes clung together in prolonged and serious consultation; then a faint smile fluttered over Mrs. van der Luyden's face. She had evidently guessed and approved.

Mr. van der Luyden turned to Mrs. Archer. "If Louisa's health allowed her to dine out—I wish you would say to Mrs. Lovell Mingott—she and I would have been happy to—er—fill the places of the Lawrence Leffertses at her dinner." He paused to let the irony of this sink in. "As you know, this is impossible." Mrs. Archer sounded a sympathetic assent. "But Newland tells me he has read this morning's Times; therefore he has probably seen that Louisa's relative, the Duke of St. Austrey, arrives next week on the Russia. He is coming to enter his new sloop, the Guinevere, in next summer's International Cup Race; and also to have a little canvasback shooting at Trevenna." Mr. van der Luyden paused again, and continued with increasing benevolence: "Before taking him down to Maryland we are inviting a few friends to meet him here—only a little dinner—with a reception afterward. I am sure Louisa will be as glad as I am if Countess Olenska will let us include her among our guests." He got up, bent his long body with a stiff friendliness toward his cousin, and added: "I think I have Louisa's authority for saying that she will herself leave the invitation to dine when she drives out presently: with our cards—of course with our cards."

Mrs. Archer, who knew this to be a hint that the seventeen-hand chestnuts which were never kept waiting were at the door, rose with a hurried murmur of thanks. Mrs. van der Luyden beamed on her with the smile of Esther interceding with Ahasuerus; but her husband raised a protesting hand.

"There is nothing to thank me for, dear Adeline; nothing whatever. This kind of thing must not happen in New York; it shall not, as long as I can help it," he pronounced with sovereign gentleness as he steered his cousins to the door.

Two hours later, every one knew that the great C-spring barouche in which Mrs. van der Luyden took the air at all seasons had been seen at old Mrs. Mingott's door, where a large square envelope was handed in; and that evening at the Opera Mr. Sillerton Jackson was able to state that the envelope contained a card inviting the Countess Olenska to the dinner which the van der Luydens were giving the following week for their cousin, the Duke of St. Austrey.

Some of the younger men in the club box exchanged a smile at this announcement, and glanced sideways at Lawrence Lefferts, who sat carelessly in the front of the box, pulling his long fair moustache, and who remarked with authority, as the soprano paused: "No one but Patti ought to attempt the Sonnambula."

## VIII.

It was generally agreed in New York that the Countess Olenska had "lost her looks."

She had appeared there first, in Newland Archer's boyhood, as a brilliantly pretty little girl of nine or ten, of whom people said that she "ought to be painted." Her parents had been continental wanderers, and after a roaming babyhood she had lost them both, and been taken in charge by her aunt, Medora Manson, also a wanderer, who was herself returning to New York to "settle down."

Poor Medora, repeatedly widowed, was always coming home to settle down (each time in a less expensive house), and bringing with her a new husband or an adopted child; but after a few months she invariably parted from her husband or quarrelled with her ward, and, having got rid of her house at a loss, set out again on her wanderings. As her mother had been a Rushworth, and her last unhappy marriage had linked her to one of the crazy Chiverses, New York looked indulgently on her eccentricities; but when she returned with her little orphaned niece, whose parents had been popular in spite of their regrettable taste for travel, people thought it a pity that the pretty child should be in such hands.

Every one was disposed to be kind to little Ellen Mingott, though her dusky red cheeks and tight curls gave her an air of gaiety that seemed unsuitable in a child who should still have been in black for her parents. It was one of the misguided Medora's many peculiarities to flout the unalterable rules that regulated American mourning, and when she stepped from the steamer her family were scandalised to see that the crape veil she wore for her own brother was seven inches shorter than those of her sisters-in-law, while little Ellen was in crimson merino and amber beads, like a gipsy foundling.

But New York had so long resigned itself to Medora that only a few old ladies shook their heads over Ellen's gaudy clothes, while her other relations fell under the charm of her high colour and high spirits. She was a fearless and familiar little thing, who asked disconcerting questions, made precocious comments, and possessed outlandish arts, such as dancing a Spanish shawl dance and singing Neapolitan love-songs to a guitar. Under the direction of her aunt (whose real name was Mrs. Thorley Chivers, but who, having received a Papal title, had resumed her first husband's patronymic, and called herself the Marchioness Manson, because in Italy she could turn it into Manzoni) the little girl received an expensive but incoherent education, which included "drawing from the model," a thing never dreamed of before, and playing the piano in quintets with professional musicians.

Of course no good could come of this; and when, a few years later, poor Chivers finally died in a madhouse, his widow (draped in strange weeds) again pulled up stakes and departed with Ellen, who had grown into a tall bony girl with conspicuous eyes. For some time no more was heard of them; then news came of Ellen's marriage to an immensely rich Polish nobleman of legendary fame, whom she had met at a ball at the Tuileries, and who was said to have princely establishments in Paris, Nice and Florence, a yacht at Cowes, and many square miles of shooting in Transylvania. She disappeared in a kind of sulphurous apotheosis, and when a few years later Medora again came back to New York, subdued, impoverished, mourning a third husband, and in quest of a still smaller house, people wondered that her rich niece had not been able to do something for her. Then came the news that Ellen's own marriage had ended in disaster, and that she was herself returning home to seek rest and oblivion among her kinsfolk.

These things passed through Newland Archer's mind a week later as he watched the Countess Olenska enter the van der Luyden drawing-room on the evening of the momentous dinner. The occasion was a solemn one, and he wondered a little nervously how she would carry it off. She came rather late, one hand still ungloved, and fastening a bracelet about her wrist; yet she entered without any appearance of haste or embarrassment the drawing-room in which New York's most chosen company was somewhat awfully assembled.

In the middle of the room she paused, looking about her with a grave mouth and smiling eyes; and in that instant Newland Archer rejected the general verdict on her looks. It was true that her early radiance was gone. The red cheeks had paled; she was thin, worn, a little older-looking than her age, which must have been nearly thirty. But there was about her the mysterious authority of beauty, a sureness in the carriage of the head, the movement of the eyes, which, without being in the least theatrical, struck his as highly trained and full of a conscious power. At the same time she was simpler in manner than most of the ladies present, and many people (as he heard afterward from Janey) were disappointed that her appearance was not more "stylish"—for stylishness was what New York most valued. It was, perhaps, Archer reflected, because her early vivacity had disappeared; because she was so quiet—quiet in her movements, her voice, and the tones of her low-pitched voice. New York had expected something a good deal more reasonant in a young woman with such a history.

The dinner was a somewhat formidable business. Dining with the van der Luydens was at best no light matter, and dining there with a Duke who was their cousin was almost a religious solemnity. It pleased Archer to think that only an old New Yorker could perceive the shade of difference (to New York) between being merely a Duke and being the van der Luydens' Duke. New York took stray noblemen calmly, and even (except in the Struthers set) with a certain distrustful hauteur; but when they presented such credentials as these they were received with an old-fashioned cordiality that they would have been greatly mistaken in ascribing solely to their standing in Debrett. It was for just such distinctions that the young man cherished his old New York even while he smiled at it.

The van der Luydens had done their best to emphasise the importance of the occasion. The du Lac Sevres and the Trevenna George II plate were out; so was the van der Luyden "Lowestoft" (East India Company) and the Dagonet Crown Derby. Mrs. van der Luyden looked more than ever like a Cabanel, and Mrs. Archer, in her grandmother's seed-pearls and emeralds, reminded her son of an Isabey miniature. All the ladies had on their handsomest jewels, but it was characteristic of the house and the occasion that these were mostly in rather heavy old-fashioned settings; and old Miss Lanning, who had been persuaded to come, actually wore her mother's cameos and a Spanish blonde shawl.

The Countess Olenska was the only young woman at the dinner; yet, as Archer scanned the smooth plump elderly faces between their diamond necklaces and towering ostrich feathers, they struck him as curiously immature compared with hers. It frightened him to think what must have gone to the making of her eyes.

The Duke of St. Austrey, who sat at his hostess's right, was naturally the chief figure of the evening. But if the Countess Olenska was less conspicuous than had been hoped, the Duke was almost invisible. Being a well-bred man he had not (like another recent ducal visitor) come to the dinner in a shooting-jacket; but his evening clothes were so shabby and baggy, and he wore them with such an air of their being homespun, that (with his stooping way of sitting, and the vast beard spreading over his shirt-front) he hardly gave the appearance of being in dinner attire. He was short, round-shouldered, sunburnt, with a thick nose, small eyes and a sociable smile; but he seldom spoke, and when he did it was in such low tones that, despite the frequent silences of expectation about the table, his remarks were lost to all but his neighbours.

When the men joined the ladies after dinner the Duke went straight up to the Countess Olenska, and they sat down in a corner and plunged into animated talk. Neither seemed aware that the Duke should first have paid his respects to Mrs. Lovell Mingott and Mrs. Headly Chivers, and the Countess have conversed with that amiable hypochondriac, Mr. Urban Dagonet of Washington Square, who, in order to have the pleasure of meeting her, had broken through his fixed rule of not dining out between January and April. The two chatted together for nearly twenty minutes; then the Countess rose and, walking alone across the wide drawing-room, sat down at Newland Archer's side.

It was not the custom in New York drawing-rooms for a lady to get up and walk away from one gentleman in order to seek the company of another. Etiquette required that she should wait, immovable as an idol, while the men who wished to converse with her succeeded each other at her side. But the Countess was apparently unaware of having broken any rule; she sat at perfect ease in a corner of the sofa beside Archer, and looked at him with the kindest eyes.

"I want you to talk to me about May," she said.

Instead of answering her he asked: "You knew the Duke before?"

"Oh, yes—we used to see him every winter at Nice. He's very fond of gambling—he used to come to the house a great deal." She said it in the simplest manner, as if she had said: "He's fond of wild-flowers"; and after a moment she added candidly: "I think he's the dullest man I ever met."

This pleased her companion so much that he forgot the slight shock her previous remark had caused him. It was undeniably exciting to meet a lady who found the van der Luydens' Duke dull, and dared to utter the opinion. He longed to question her, to hear more about the life of which her careless words had given him so illuminating a glimpse; but he feared to touch on distressing memories, and before he could think of anything to say she had strayed back to her original subject.

"May is a darling; I've seen no young girl in New York so handsome and so intelligent. Are you very much in love with her?"

Newland Archer reddened and laughed. "As much as a man can be."

She continued to consider him thoughtfully, as if not to miss any shade of meaning in what he said, "Do you think, then, there is a limit?"

"To being in love? If there is, I haven't found it!"

She glowed with sympathy. "Ah—it's really and truly a romance?"

"The most romantic of romances!"

"How delightful! And you found it all out for yourselves—it was not in the least arranged for you?"

Archer looked at her incredulously. "Have you forgotten," he asked with a smile, "that in our country we don't allow our marriages to be arranged for us?"

A dusky blush rose to her cheek, and he instantly regretted his words.

"Yes," she answered, "I'd forgotten. You must forgive me if I sometimes make these mistakes. I don't always remember that everything here is good that was—that was bad where I've come from." She looked down at her Viennese fan of eagle feathers, and he saw that her lips trembled.

"I'm so sorry," he said impulsively; "but you ARE among friends here, you know."

"Yes—I know. Wherever I go I have that feeling. That's why I came home. I want to forget everything else, to become a complete American again, like the Mingotts and Wellands, and you and your delightful mother, and all the other good people here tonight. Ah, here's May arriving, and you will want to hurry away to her," she added, but without moving; and her eyes turned back from the door to rest on the young man's face.

The drawing-rooms were beginning to fill up with after-dinner guests, and following Madame Olenska's glance Archer saw May Welland entering with her mother. In her dress of white and silver, with a wreath of silver blossoms in her hair, the tall girl looked like a Diana just alight from the chase.

"Oh," said Archer, "I have so many rivals; you see she's already surrounded. There's the Duke being introduced."

"Then stay with me a little longer," Madame Olenska said in a low tone, just touching his knee with her plumed fan. It was the lightest touch, but it thrilled him like a caress.

"Yes, let me stay," he answered in the same tone, hardly knowing what he said; but just then Mr. van der Luyden came up, followed by old Mr. Urban Dagonet. The Countess greeted them with her grave smile, and Archer, feeling his host's admonitory glance on him, rose and surrendered his seat.

Madame Olenska held out her hand as if to bid him goodbye.

"Tomorrow, then, after five—I shall expect you," she said; and then turned back to make room for Mr. Dagonet.

"Tomorrow —" Archer heard himself repeating, though there had been no engagement, and during their talk she had given him no hint that she wished to see him again.

As he moved away he saw Lawrence Lefferts, tall and resplendent, leading his wife up to be introduced; and heard Gertrude Lefferts say, as she beamed on the Countess with her large unperceiving smile: "But I think we used to go to dancing-school together when we were children—." Behind her, waiting their turn to name themselves to the Countess, Archer noticed a number of the recalcitrant couples who had declined to meet her at Mrs. Lovell Mingott's. As Mrs. Archer remarked: when the van der Luydens chose, they knew how to give a lesson. The wonder was that they chose so seldom.

The young man felt a touch on his arm and saw Mrs. van der Luyden looking down on him from the pure eminence of black velvet and the family diamonds. "It was good of you, dear Newland, to devote yourself so unselfishly to Madame Olenska. I told your cousin Henry he must really come to the rescue."

He was aware of smiling at her vaguely, and she added, as if condescending to his natural shyness: "I've never seen May looking lovelier. The Duke thinks her the handsomest girl in the room."

## IX.

The Countess Olenska had said "after five"; and at half after the hour Newland Archer rang the bell of the peeling stucco house with a giant wisteria throttling its feeble cast-iron balcony, which she had hired, far down West Twenty-third Street, from the vagabond Medora.

It was certainly a strange quarter to have settled in. Small dress-makers, bird-stuffers and "people who wrote" were her nearest neighbours; and further down the dishevelled street Archer recognised a dilapidated wooden house, at the end of a paved path, in which a writer and journalist called Winsett, whom he used to come across now and then, had mentioned that he lived. Winsett did not invite people to his house; but he had once pointed it out to Archer in the course of a nocturnal stroll, and the latter had asked himself, with a little shiver, if the humanities were so meanly housed in other capitals.

Madame Olenska's own dwelling was redeemed from the same appearance only by a little more paint about the window-frames; and as Archer mustered its modest front he said to himself that the Polish Count must have robbed her of her fortune as well as of her illusions.

The young man had spent an unsatisfactory day. He had lunched with the Wellands, hoping afterward to carry off May for a walk in the Park. He wanted to have her to himself, to tell her how enchanting she had looked the night before, and how proud he was of her, and to press her to hasten their marriage. But Mrs. Welland had firmly reminded him that the round of family visits was not half over, and, when he hinted at advancing the date of the wedding, had raised reproachful eye-brows and sighed out: "Twelve dozen of everything—hand-embroidered —"

Packed in the family landau they rolled from one tribal doorstep to another, and Archer, when the afternoon's round was over, parted from his betrothed with the feeling that he had been shown off like a wild animal cunningly trapped. He supposed that his readings in anthropology caused him to take such a coarse view of what was after all a simple and natural demonstration of family feeling; but when he remembered that the Wellands did not expect the wedding to take place till the following autumn, and pictured what his life would be till then, a dampness fell upon his spirit.

"Tomorrow," Mrs. Welland called after him, "we'll do the Chiverses and the Dallases"; and he perceived that she was going through their two families alphabetically, and that they were only in the first quarter of the alphabet.

He had meant to tell May of the Countess Olenska's request—her command, rather—that he should call on her that afternoon; but in the brief moments when they were alone he had had more pressing things to say. Besides, it struck him as a little absurd to allude to the matter. He knew that May most particularly wanted him to be kind to her cousin; was it not that wish which had hastened the announcement of their engagement? It gave him an odd sensation to reflect that, but for the Countess's arrival, he might have been, if not still a free man, at least a man less irrevocably pledged. But May had willed it so, and he felt himself somehow relieved of further responsibility—and therefore at liberty, if he chose, to call on her cousin without telling her.

As he stood on Madame Olenska's threshold curiosity was his uppermost feeling. He was puzzled by the tone in which she had summoned him; he concluded that she was less simple than she seemed.

The door was opened by a swarthy foreign-looking maid, with a prominent bosom under a gay neckerchief, whom he vaguely fancied to be Sicilian. She welcomed him with all her white teeth, and answering his enquiries by a head-shake of incomprehension led him through the narrow hall into a low firelit drawing-room. The room was empty, and she left him, for an appreciable time, to wonder whether she had gone to find her mistress, or whether she had not understood what he was there for, and thought it might be to wind the clock—of which he perceived that the only visible specimen had stopped. He knew that the southern races communicated with each other in the language of pantomime, and was mortified to find her shrugs and smiles so unintelligible. At length she returned with a lamp; and Archer, having meanwhile put together a phrase out of Dante and Petrarch, evoked the answer: "La signora e fuori; ma verra subito"; which he took to mean: "She's out—but you'll soon see."

What he saw, meanwhile, with the help of the lamp, was the faded shadowy charm of a room unlike any room he had known. He knew that the Countess Olenska had brought some of her possessions with her—bits of wreckage, she called them—and these, he supposed, were represented by some small slender tables of dark wood, a delicate little Greek bronze on the chimney-piece, and a stretch of red damask nailed on the discoloured wallpaper behind a couple of Italian-looking pictures in old frames.

Newland Archer prided himself on his knowledge of Italian art. His boyhood had been saturated with Ruskin, and he had read all the latest books: John Addington Symonds, Vernon Lee's "Euphorion," the essays of P. G. Hamerton, and a wonderful new volume called "The Renaissance" by Walter Pater. He talked easily of Botticelli, and spoke of Fra Angelico with a faint condescension. But these pictures bewildered him, for they were like nothing that he was accustomed to look at (and therefore able to see) when he travelled in Italy; and perhaps, also, his powers of observation were impaired by the oddness of finding himself in this strange empty house, where apparently no one expected him. He was sorry that he had not told May Welland of Countess Olenska's request, and a little disturbed by the thought that his betrothed might come in to see her cousin. What would she think if she found him sitting there with the air of intimacy implied by waiting alone in the dusk at a lady's fireside?

But since he had come he meant to wait; and he sank into a chair and stretched his feet to the logs.

It was odd to have summoned him in that way, and then forgotten him; but Archer felt more curious than mortified. The atmosphere of the room was so different from any he had ever breathed that self-consciousness vanished in the sense of adventure. He had been before in drawing-rooms hung with red damask, with pictures "of the Italian school"; what struck him was the way in which Medora Manson's shabby hired house, with its blighted background of pampas grass and Rogers statuettes, had, by a turn of the hand, and the skilful use of a few properties, been transformed into something intimate, "foreign," subtly suggestive of old romantic scenes and sentiments. He tried to analyse the trick, to find a clue to it in the way the chairs and tables were grouped, in the fact that only two Jacqueminot roses (of which nobody ever bought less than a dozen) had been placed in the slender vase at his elbow, and in the vague pervading perfume that was not what one put on handkerchiefs, but rather like the scent of some far-off bazaar, a smell made up of Turkish coffee and ambergris and dried roses.

His mind wandered away to the question of what May's drawing-room would look like. He knew that Mr. Welland, who was behaving "very handsomely," already had his eye on a newly built house in East Thirty-ninth Street. The neighbourhood was thought remote, and the house was built in a ghastly greenish-yellow stone that the younger architects were beginning to employ as a protest against the brownstone of which the uniform hue coated New York like a cold chocolate sauce; but the plumbing was perfect. Archer would have liked to travel, to put off the housing question; but, though the Wellands approved of an extended European honeymoon (perhaps even a winter in Egypt), they were firm as to the need of a house for the returning couple. The young man felt that his fate was sealed: for the rest of his life he would go up every evening between the cast-iron railings of that greenish-yellow doorstep, and pass through a Pompeian vestibule into a hall with a wainscoting of varnished yellow wood. But beyond that his imagination could not travel. He knew the drawing-room above had a bay window, but he could not fancy how May would deal with it. She submitted cheerfully to the purple satin and yellow tuftings of the Welland drawing-room, to its sham Buhl tables and gilt vitrines full of modern Saxe. He saw no reason to suppose that she would want anything different in her own house; and his only comfort was to reflect that she would probably let him arrange his library as he pleased—which would be, of course, with "sincere" Eastlake furniture, and the plain new bookcases without glass doors.

The round-bosomed maid came in, drew the curtains, pushed back a log, and said consolingly: "Verra—verra." When she had gone Archer stood up and began to wander about. Should he wait any longer? His position was becoming rather foolish. Perhaps he had misunderstood Madame Olenska—perhaps she had not invited him after all.

Down the cobblestones of the quiet street came the ring of a stepper's hoofs; they stopped before the house, and he caught the opening of a carriage door. Parting the curtains he looked out into the early dusk. A street-lamp faced him, and in its light he saw Julius Beaufort's compact English brougham, drawn by a big roan, and the banker descending from it, and helping out Madame Olenska.

Beaufort stood, hat in hand, saying something which his companion seemed to negative; then they shook hands, and he jumped into his carriage while she mounted the steps.

When she entered the room she showed no surprise at seeing Archer there; surprise seemed the emotion that she was least addicted to.

"How do you like my funny house?" she asked. "To me it's like heaven."

As she spoke she untied her little velvet bonnet and tossing it away with her long cloak stood looking at him with meditative eyes.

"You've arranged it delightfully," he rejoined, alive to the flatness of the words, but imprisoned in the conventional by his consuming desire to be simple and striking.

"Oh, it's a poor little place. My relations despise it. But at any rate it's less gloomy than the van der Luydens'."

The words gave him an electric shock, for few were the rebellious spirits who would have dared to call the stately home of the van der Luydens gloomy. Those privileged to enter it shivered there, and spoke of it as "handsome." But suddenly he was glad that she had given voice to the general shiver.

"It's delicious—what you've done here," he repeated.

"I like the little house," she admitted; "but I suppose what I like is the blessedness of its being here, in my own country and my own town; and then, of being alone in it." She spoke so low that he hardly heard the last phrase; but in his awkwardness he took it up.

"You like so much to be alone?"

"Yes; as long as my friends keep me from feeling lonely." She sat down near the fire, said: "Nastasia will bring the tea presently," and signed to him to return to his armchair, adding: "I see you've already chosen your corner."

Leaning back, she folded her arms behind her head, and looked at the fire under drooping lids.

"This is the hour I like best—don't you?"

A proper sense of his dignity caused him to answer: "I was afraid you'd forgotten the hour. Beaufort must have been very engrossing."

She looked amused. "Why—have you waited long? Mr. Beaufort took me to see a number of houses—since it seems I'm not to be allowed to stay in this one." She appeared to dismiss both Beaufort and himself from her mind, and went on: "I've never been in a city where there seems to be such a feeling against living in des quartiers excentriques. What does it matter where one lives? I'm told this street is respectable."

"It's not fashionable."

"Fashionable! Do you all think so much of that? Why not make one's own fashions? But I suppose I've lived too independently; at any rate, I want to do what you all do—I want to feel cared for and safe."

He was touched, as he had been the evening before when she spoke of her need of guidance.

"That's what your friends want you to feel. New York's an awfully safe place," he added with a flash of sarcasm.

"Yes, isn't it? One feels that," she cried, missing the mockery. "Being here is like—like—being taken on a holiday when one has been a good little girl and done all one's lessons."

The analogy was well meant, but did not altogether please him. He did not mind being flippant about New York, but disliked to hear any one else take the same tone. He wondered if she did not begin to see what a powerful engine it was, and how nearly it had crushed her. The Lovell Mingotts' dinner, patched up in extremis out of all sorts of social odds and ends, ought to have taught her the narrowness of her escape; but either she had been all along unaware of having skirted disaster, or else she had lost sight of it in the triumph of the van der Luyden evening. Archer inclined to the former theory; he fancied that her New York was still completely undifferentiated, and the conjecture nettled him.

"Last night," he said, "New York laid itself out for you. The van der Luydens do nothing by halves."

"No: how kind they are! It was such a nice party. Every one seems to have such an esteem for them."

The terms were hardly adequate; she might have spoken in that way of a tea-party at the dear old Miss Lannings'.

"The van der Luydens," said Archer, feeling himself pompous as he spoke, "are the most powerful influence in New York society. Unfortunately—owing to her health—they receive very seldom."

She unclasped her hands from behind her head, and looked at him meditatively.

"Isn't that perhaps the reason?"

"The reason—?"

"For their great influence; that they make themselves so rare."

He coloured a little, stared at her—and suddenly felt the penetration of the remark. At a stroke she had pricked the van der Luydens and they collapsed. He laughed, and sacrificed them.

Nastasia brought the tea, with handleless Japanese cups and little covered dishes, placing the tray on a low table.

"But you'll explain these things to me—you'll tell me all I ought to know," Madame Olenska continued, leaning forward to hand him his cup.

"It's you who are telling me; opening my eyes to things I'd looked at so long that I'd ceased to see them."

She detached a small gold cigarette-case from one of her bracelets, held it out to him, and took a cigarette herself. On the chimney were long spills for lighting them.

"Ah, then we can both help each other. But I want help so much more. You must tell me just what to do."

It was on the tip of his tongue to reply: "Don't be seen driving about the streets with Beaufort —" but he was being too deeply drawn into the atmosphere of the room, which was her atmosphere, and to give advice of that sort would have been like telling some one who was bargaining for attar-of-roses in Samarkand that one should always be provided with arctics for a New York winter. New York seemed much farther off than Samarkand, and if they were indeed to help each other she was rendering what might prove the first of their mutual services by making him look at his native city objectively. Viewed thus, as through the wrong end of a telescope, it looked disconcertingly small and distant; but then from Samarkand it would.

A flame darted from the logs and she bent over the fire, stretching her thin hands so close to it that a faint halo shone about the oval nails. The light touched to russet the rings of dark hair escaping from her braids, and made her pale face paler.

"There are plenty of people to tell you what to do," Archer rejoined, obscurely envious of them.

"Oh—all my aunts? And my dear old Granny?" She considered the idea impartially. "They're all a little vexed with me for setting up for myself—poor Granny especially. She wanted to keep me with her; but I had to be free —" He was impressed by this light way of speaking of the formidable Catherine, and moved by the thought of what must have given Madame Olenska this thirst for even the loneliest kind of freedom. But the idea of Beaufort gnawed him.

"I think I understand how you feel," he said. "Still, your family can advise you; explain differences; show you the way."

She lifted her thin black eyebrows. "Is New York such a labyrinth? I thought it so straight up and down—like Fifth Avenue. And with all the cross streets numbered!" She seemed to guess his faint disapproval of this, and added, with the rare smile that enchanted her whole face: "If you knew how I like it for just *that*—the straight-up-and-downness, and the big honest labels on everything!"

He saw his chance. "Everything may be labelled—but everybody is not."

"Perhaps. I may simplify too much—but you'll warn me if I do." She turned from the fire to look at him. "There are only two people here who make me feel as if they understood what I mean and could explain things to me: you and Mr. Beaufort."

Archer winced at the joining of the names, and then, with a quick readjustment, understood, sympathised and pitied. So close to the powers of evil she must have lived that she still breathed more freely in their air. But since she felt that he understood her also, his business would be to make her see Beaufort as he really was, with all he represented—and abhor it.

He answered gently: "I understand. But just at first don't let go of your old friends' hands: I mean the older women, your Granny Mingott, Mrs. Welland, Mrs. van der Luyden. They like and admire you—they want to help you."

She shook her head and sighed. "Oh, I know—I know! But on condition that they don't hear anything unpleasant. Aunt Welland put it in those very words when I tried.... Does no one want to know the truth here, Mr. Archer? The real loneliness is living among all these kind people who only ask one to pretend!" She lifted her hands to her face, and he saw her thin shoulders shaken by a sob.

"Madame Olenska!—Oh, don't, Ellen," he cried, starting up and bending over her. He drew down one of her hands, clasping and chafing it like a child's while he murmured reassuring words; but in a moment she freed herself, and looked up at him with wet lashes.

"Does no one cry here, either? I suppose there's no need to, in heaven," she said, straightening her loosened braids with a laugh, and bending over the tea-kettle. It was burnt into his consciousness that he had called her "Ellen"—called her so twice; and that she had not noticed it. Far down the inverted telescope he saw the faint white figure of May Welland—in New York.

Suddenly Nastasia put her head in to say something in her rich Italian.

Madame Olenska, again with a hand at her hair, uttered an exclamation of assent—a flashing "Gia—gia"—and the Duke of St. Austrey entered, piloting a tremendous blackwigged and red-plumed lady in overflowing furs.

"My dear Countess, I've brought an old friend of mine to see you—Mrs. Struthers. She wasn't asked to the party last night, and she wants to know you."

The Duke beamed on the group, and Madame Olenska advanced with a murmur of welcome toward the queer couple. She seemed to have no idea how oddly matched they were, nor what a liberty the Duke had taken in bringing his companion—and to do him justice, as Archer perceived, the Duke seemed as unaware of it himself.

"Of course I want to know you, my dear," cried Mrs. Struthers in a round rolling voice that matched her bold feathers and her brazen wig. "I want to know everybody who's young and interesting and charming. And the Duke tells me you like music—didn't you, Duke? You're a pianist yourself, I believe? Well, do you want to hear Sarasate play tomorrow evening at my house? You know I've something going on every Sunday evening—it's the day when New York doesn't know what to do with itself, and so I say to it:

'Come and be amused.' And the Duke thought you'd be tempted by Sarasate. You'll find a number of your friends."

Madame Olenska's face grew brilliant with pleasure. "How kind! How good of the Duke to think of me!" She pushed a chair up to the tea-table and Mrs. Struthers sank into it delectably. "Of course I shall be too happy to come."

"That's all right, my dear. And bring your young gentleman with you." Mrs. Struthers extended a hail-fellow hand to Archer. "I can't put a name to you—but I'm sure I've met you—I've met everybody, here, or in Paris or London. Aren't you in diplomacy? All the diplomatists come to me. You like music too? Duke, you must be sure to bring him."

The Duke said "Rather" from the depths of his beard, and Archer withdrew with a stiffly circular bow that made him feel as full of spine as a self-conscious school-boy among careless and unnoticing elders.

He was not sorry for the denouement of his visit: he only wished it had come sooner, and spared him a certain waste of emotion. As he went out into the wintry night, New York again became vast and imminent, and May Welland the loveliest woman in it. He turned into his florist's to send her the daily box of lilies-of-the-valley which, to his confusion, he found he had forgotten that morning.

As he wrote a word on his card and waited for an envelope he glanced about the embowered shop, and his eye lit on a cluster of yellow roses. He had never seen any as sun-golden before, and his first impulse was to send them to May instead of the lilies. But they did not look like her—there was something too rich, too strong, in their fiery beauty. In a sudden revulsion of mood, and almost without knowing what he did, he signed to the florist to lay the roses in another long box, and slipped his card into a second envelope, on which he wrote the name of the Countess Olenska; then, just as he was turning away, he drew the card out again, and left the empty envelope on the box.

"They'll go at once?" he enquired, pointing to the roses.

The florist assured him that they would.

## X.

The next day he persuaded May to escape for a walk in the Park after luncheon. As was the custom in old-fashioned Episcopalian New York, she usually accompanied her parents to church on Sunday afternoons; but Mrs. Welland condoned her truancy, having that very morning won her over to the necessity of a long engagement, with time to prepare a hand-embroidered trousseau containing the proper number of dozens.

The day was delectable. The bare vaulting of trees along the Mall was ceiled with lapis lazuli, and arched above snow that shone like splintered crystals. It was the weather to call out May's radiance, and she burned like a young maple in the frost. Archer was proud of the glances turned on her, and the simple joy of possessorship cleared away his underlying perplexities.

"It's so delicious—waking every morning to smell lilies-of-the-valley in one's room!" she said.

"Yesterday they came late. I hadn't time in the morning —"

"But your remembering each day to send them makes me love them so much more than if you'd given a standing order, and they came every morning on the minute, like one's music-teacher—as I know Gertrude Lefferts's did, for instance, when she and Lawrence were engaged."

"Ah—they would!" laughed Archer, amused at her keenness. He looked sideways at her fruit-like cheek and felt rich and secure enough to add: "When I sent your lilies yesterday afternoon I saw some rather gorgeous yellow roses and packed them off to Madame Olenska. Was that right?"

"How dear of you! Anything of that kind delights her. It's odd she didn't mention it: she lunched with us today, and spoke of Mr. Beaufort's having sent her wonderful orchids, and cousin Henry van der Luyden a whole hamper of carnations from Skuytercliff. She seems so surprised to receive flowers. Don't people send them in Europe? She thinks it such a pretty custom."

"Oh, well, no wonder mine were overshadowed by Beaufort's," said Archer irritably. Then he remembered that he had not put a card with the roses, and was vexed at having spoken of them. He wanted to say: "I called on your cousin yesterday," but hesitated. If Madame Olenska had not spoken of his visit it might seem awkward that he should. Yet not to do so gave the affair an air of mystery that he disliked. To shake off the question he began to talk of their own plans, their future, and Mrs. Welland's insistence on a long engagement.

"If you call it long! Isabel Chivers and Reggie were engaged for two years: Grace and Thorley for nearly a year and a half. Why aren't we very well off as we are?"

It was the traditional maidenly interrogation, and he felt ashamed of himself for finding it singularly childish. No doubt she simply echoed what was said for her; but she was nearing her twenty-second birthday, and he wondered at what age "nice" women began to speak for themselves.

"Never, if we won't let them, I suppose," he mused, and recalled his mad outburst to Mr. Sillerton Jackson: "Women ought to be as free as we are —"

It would presently be his task to take the bandage from this young woman's eyes, and bid her look forth on the world. But how many generations of the women who had gone to her making had descended bandaged to the family vault? He shivered a little, remembering some of the new ideas in his scientific books, and the much-cited instance of the Kentucky cave-fish, which had ceased to develop eyes because they had no use for them. What if, when he had bidden May Welland to open hers, they could only look out blankly at blankness?

"We might be much better off. We might be altogether together—we might travel."

Her face lit up. "That would be lovely," she owned: she would love to travel. But her mother would not understand their wanting to do things so differently.

"As if the mere 'differently' didn't account for it!" the wooer insisted.

"Newland! You're so original!" she exulted.

His heart sank, for he saw that he was saying all the things that young men in the same situation were expected to say, and that she was making the answers that instinct and tradition taught her to make—even to the point of calling him original.

"Original! We're all as like each other as those dolls cut out of the same folded paper. We're like patterns stencilled on a wall. Can't you and I strike out for ourselves, May?"

He had stopped and faced her in the excitement of their discussion, and her eyes rested on him with a bright unclouded admiration.

"Mercy—shall we elope?" she laughed.

"If you would —"

"You *do* love me, Newland! I'm so happy."

"But then—why not be happier?"

"We can't behave like people in novels, though, can we?"

"Why not—why not—why not?"

She looked a little bored by his insistence. She knew very well that they couldn't, but it was troublesome to have to produce a reason. "I'm not clever enough to argue with you. But that kind of thing is rather—vulgar, isn't it?" she suggested, relieved to have hit on a word that would assuredly extinguish the whole subject.

"Are you so much afraid, then, of being vulgar?"

She was evidently staggered by this. "Of course I should hate it—so would you," she rejoined, a trifle irritably.

He stood silent, beating his stick nervously against his boot-top; and feeling that she had indeed found the right way of closing the discussion, she went on light-heartedly: "Oh, did I tell you that I showed Ellen my ring? She thinks it the most beautiful setting she ever saw. There's nothing like it in the rue de la Paix, she said. I do love you, Newland, for being so artistic!"

The next afternoon, as Archer, before dinner, sat smoking sullenly in his study, Janey wandered in on him. He had failed to stop at his club on the way up from the office where he exercised the profession of the law in the leisurely manner common to well-to-do New Yorkers of his class. He was out of spirits and slightly out of temper, and a haunting horror of doing the same thing every day at the same hour besieged his brain.

"Sameness—sameness!" he muttered, the word running through his head like a persecuting tune as he saw the familiar tall-hatted figures lounging behind the plate-glass; and because he usually dropped in at the club at that hour he had gone home instead. He knew not only what they were likely to be talking about, but the part each one would take in the discussion. The Duke of course would be their principal theme; though the appearance in Fifth Avenue of a golden-haired lady in a small canary-coloured brougham with a pair of black cobs (for which Beaufort was generally thought responsible) would also doubtless be thoroughly gone into. Such "women" (as they were called) were few in New York, those driving their own carriages still fewer, and the appearance of Miss Fanny Ring in Fifth Avenue at the fashionable hour had profoundly agitated society. Only the day before, her carriage had passed Mrs. Lovell Mingott's, and the latter had instantly rung the little bell at her elbow and ordered the coachman to drive her home.

"What if it had happened to Mrs. van der Luyden?" people asked each other with a shudder. Archer could hear Lawrence Lefferts, at that very hour, holding forth on the disintegration of society.

He raised his head irritably when his sister Janey entered, and then quickly bent over his book (Swinburne's "Chastelard"—just out) as if he had not seen her. She glanced at the writing-table heaped with books, opened a volume of the "Contes Drolatiques," made a wry face over the archaic French, and sighed: "What learned things you read!"

"Well—?" he asked, as she hovered Cassandra-like before him.

"Mother's very angry."

"Angry? With whom? About what?"

"Miss Sophy Jackson has just been here. She brought word that her brother would come in after dinner: she couldn't say very much, because he forbade her to: he wishes to give all the details himself. He's with cousin Louisa van der Luyden now."

"For heaven's sake, my dear girl, try a fresh start. It would take an omniscient Deity to know what you're talking about."

"It's not a time to be profane, Newland.... Mother feels badly enough about your not going to church ..."

With a groan he plunged back into his book.

"*Newland*! Do listen. Your friend Madame Olenska was at Mrs. Lemuel Struthers's party last night: she went there with the Duke and Mr. Beaufort."

At the last clause of this announcement a senseless anger swelled the young man's breast. To smother it he laughed. "Well, what of it? I knew she meant to."

Janey paled and her eyes began to project. "You knew she meant to—and you didn't try to stop her? To warn her?"

"Stop her? Warn her?" He laughed again. "I'm not engaged to be married to the Countess Olenska!" The words had a fantastic sound in his own ears.

"You're marrying into her family."

"Oh, family—family!" he jeered.

"Newland—don't you care about Family?"

"Not a brass farthing."

"Nor about what cousin Louisa van der Luyden will think?"

"Not the half of one—if she thinks such old maid's rubbish."

"Mother is not an old maid," said his virgin sister with pinched lips.

He felt like shouting back: "Yes, she is, and so are the van der Luydens, and so we all are, when it comes to being so much as brushed by the wing-tip of Reality." But he saw her long gentle face puckering into tears, and felt ashamed of the useless pain he was inflicting.

"Hang Countess Olenska! Don't be a goose, Janey—I'm not her keeper."

"No; but you DID ask the Wellands to announce your engagement sooner so that we might all back her up; and if it hadn't been for that cousin Louisa would never have invited her to the dinner for the Duke."

"Well—what harm was there in inviting her? She was the best-looking woman in the room; she made the dinner a little less funereal than the usual van der Luyden banquet."

"You know cousin Henry asked her to please you: he persuaded cousin Louisa. And now they're so upset that they're going back to Skuytercliff tomorrow. I think, Newland, you'd better come down. You don't seem to understand how mother feels."

In the drawing-room Newland found his mother. She raised a troubled brow from her needlework to ask: "Has Janey told you?"

"Yes." He tried to keep his tone as measured as her own. "But I can't take it very seriously."

"Not the fact of having offended cousin Louisa and cousin Henry?"

"The fact that they can be offended by such a trifle as Countess Olenska's going to the house of a woman they consider common."

"Consider—!"

"Well, who is; but who has good music, and amuses people on Sunday evenings, when the whole of New York is dying of inanition."

"Good music? All I know is, there was a woman who got up on a table and sang the things they sing at the places you go to in Paris. There was smoking and champagne."

"Well—that kind of thing happens in other places, and the world still goes on."

"I don't suppose, dear, you're really defending the French Sunday?"

"I've heard you often enough, mother, grumble at the English Sunday when we've been in London."

"New York is neither Paris nor London."

"Oh, no, it's not!" her son groaned.

"You mean, I suppose, that society here is not as brilliant? You're right, I daresay; but we belong here, and people should respect our ways when they come among us. Ellen Olenska especially: she came back to get away from the kind of life people lead in brilliant societies."

Newland made no answer, and after a moment his mother ventured: "I was going to put on my bonnet and ask you to take me to see cousin Louisa for a moment before dinner." He frowned, and she continued: "I thought you might explain to her what you've just said: that society abroad is different ... that people are not as particular, and that Madame Olenska may not have realised how we feel about such things. It would be, you know, dear," she added with an innocent adroitness, "in Madame Olenska's interest if you did."

"Dearest mother, I really don't see how we're concerned in the matter. The Duke took Madame Olenska to Mrs. Struthers's—in fact he brought Mrs. Struthers to call on her. I was there when they came. If the van der Luydens want to quarrel with anybody, the real culprit is under their own roof."

"Quarrel? Newland, did you ever know of cousin Henry's quarrelling? Besides, the Duke's his guest; and a stranger too. Strangers don't discriminate: how should they? Countess Olenska is a New Yorker, and should have respected the feelings of New York."

"Well, then, if they must have a victim, you have my leave to throw Madame Olenska to them," cried her son, exasperated. "I don't see myself—or you either—offering ourselves up to expiate her crimes."

"Oh, of course you see only the Mingott side," his mother answered, in the sensitive tone that was her nearest approach to anger.

The sad butler drew back the drawing-room portieres and announced: "Mr. Henry van der Luyden."

Mrs. Archer dropped her needle and pushed her chair back with an agitated hand.

"Another lamp," she cried to the retreating servant, while Janey bent over to straighten her mother's cap.

Mr. van der Luyden's figure loomed on the threshold, and Newland Archer went forward to greet his cousin.

"We were just talking about you, sir," he said.

Mr. van der Luyden seemed overwhelmed by the announcement. He drew off his glove to shake hands with the ladies, and smoothed his tall hat shyly, while Janey pushed an arm-chair forward, and Archer continued: "And the Countess Olenska."

Mrs. Archer paled.

"Ah—a charming woman. I have just been to see her," said Mr. van der Luyden, complacency restored to his brow. He sank into the chair, laid his hat and gloves on the floor beside him in the old-fashioned way, and went on: "She has a real gift for arranging flowers. I had sent her a few carnations from Skuytercliff, and I was astonished. Instead of massing them in big bunches as our head-gardener does, she had scattered them about loosely, here and there ... I can't say how. The Duke had told me: he said: 'Go and see how cleverly she's arranged her drawing-room.' And she has. I should really like to take Louisa to see her, if the neighbourhood were not so—unpleasant."

A dead silence greeted this unusual flow of words from Mr. van der Luyden. Mrs. Archer drew her embroidery out of the basket into which she had nervously tumbled it, and Newland, leaning against the chimney-place and twisting a humming-bird-feather screen in his hand, saw Janey's gaping countenance lit up by the coming of the second lamp.

"The fact is," Mr. van der Luyden continued, stroking his long grey leg with a bloodless hand weighed down by the Patroon's great signet-ring, "the fact is, I dropped in to thank her for the very pretty note she wrote me about my flowers; and also—but this is between ourselves, of course—to give her a friendly warning about allowing the Duke to carry her off to parties with him. I don't know if you've heard —"

Mrs. Archer produced an indulgent smile. "Has the Duke been carrying her off to parties?"

"You know what these English grandees are. They're all alike. Louisa and I are very fond of our cousin—but it's hopeless to expect people who are accustomed to the European courts to trouble themselves about our little republican distinctions. The Duke goes where he's amused." Mr. van der Luyden paused, but no one spoke. "Yes—it seems he took her with him last night to Mrs. Lemuel Struthers's. Sillerton Jackson has just been to us with the foolish story, and Louisa was rather troubled. So I thought the shortest way was to go straight to Countess Olenska and explain—by the merest hint, you know—how we feel in New York about certain things. I felt I might, without indelicacy, because the evening she dined with us she rather suggested ... rather let me see that she would be grateful for guidance. And she *was*."

Mr. van der Luyden looked about the room with what would have been self-satisfaction on features less purged of the vulgar passions. On his face it became a mild benevolence which Mrs. Archer's countenance dutifully reflected.

"How kind you both are, dear Henry—always! Newland will particularly appreciate what you have done because of dear May and his new relations."

She shot an admonitory glance at her son, who said: "Immensely, sir. But I was sure you'd like Madame Olenska."

Mr. van der Luyden looked at him with extreme gentleness. "I never ask to my house, my dear Newland," he said, "any one whom I do not like. And so I have just told Sillerton Jackson." With a glance at the clock he rose and added: "But Louisa will be waiting. We are dining early, to take the Duke to the Opera."

After the portieres had solemnly closed behind their visitor a silence fell upon the Archer family.

"Gracious—how romantic!" at last broke explosively from Janey. No one knew exactly what inspired her elliptic comments, and her relations had long since given up trying to interpret them.

Mrs. Archer shook her head with a sigh. "Provided it all turns out for the best," she said, in the tone of one who knows how surely it will not. "Newland, you must stay and see Sillerton Jackson when he comes this evening: I really shan't know what to say to him."

"Poor mother! But he won't come —" her son laughed, stooping to kiss away her frown.

## XI.

Some two weeks later, Newland Archer, sitting in abstracted idleness in his private compartment of the office of Letterblair, Lamson and Low, attorneys at law, was summoned by the head of the firm.

Old Mr. Letterblair, the accredited legal adviser of three generations of New York gentility, throned behind his mahogany desk in evident perplexity. As he stroked his closeclipped white whiskers and ran his hand through the rumpled grey locks above his jutting brows, his disrespectful junior partner thought how much he looked like the Family Physician annoyed with a patient whose symptoms refuse to be classified.

"My dear sir —" he always addressed Archer as "sir"—"I have sent for you to go into a little matter; a matter which, for the moment, I prefer not to mention either to Mr. Skipworth or Mr. Redwood." The gentlemen he spoke of were the other senior partners of the firm; for, as was always the case with legal associations of old standing in New York, all the partners named on the office letter-head were long since dead; and Mr. Letterblair, for example, was, professionally speaking, his own grandson.

He leaned back in his chair with a furrowed brow. "For family reasons —" he continued.

Archer looked up.

"The Mingott family," said Mr. Letterblair with an explanatory smile and bow. "Mrs. Manson Mingott sent for me yesterday. Her grand-daughter the Countess Olenska wishes to sue her husband for divorce. Certain papers have been placed in my hands." He paused and drummed on his desk. "In view of your prospective alliance with the family I should like to consult you—to consider the case with you—before taking any farther steps."

Archer felt the blood in his temples. He had seen the Countess Olenska only once since his visit to her, and then at the Opera, in the Mingott box. During this interval she had become a less vivid and importunate image, receding from his foreground as May Welland resumed her rightful place in it. He had not heard her divorce spoken of since Janey's first random allusion to it, and had dismissed the tale as unfounded gossip. Theoretically, the idea of divorce was almost as distasteful to him as to his mother; and he was annoyed that Mr. Letterblair (no doubt prompted by old Catherine Mingott) should be so evidently planning to draw him into the affair. After all, there were plenty of Mingott men for such jobs, and as yet he was not even a Mingott by marriage.

He waited for the senior partner to continue. Mr. Letterblair unlocked a drawer and drew out a packet. "If you will run your eye over these papers —"

Archer frowned. "I beg your pardon, sir; but just because of the prospective relationship, I should prefer your consulting Mr. Skipworth or Mr. Redwood."

Mr. Letterblair looked surprised and slightly offended. It was unusual for a junior to reject such an opening.

He bowed. "I respect your scruple, sir; but in this case I believe true delicacy requires you to do as I ask. Indeed, the suggestion is not mine but Mrs. Manson Mingott's and her son's. I have seen Lovell Mingott; and also Mr. Welland. They all named you."

Archer felt his temper rising. He had been somewhat languidly drifting with events for the last fortnight, and letting May's fair looks and radiant nature obliterate the rather importunate pressure of the Mingott claims. But this behest of old Mrs. Mingott's roused him to a sense of what the clan thought they had the right to exact from a prospective son-in-law; and he chafed at the role.

"Her uncles ought to deal with this," he said.

"They have. The matter has been gone into by the family. They are opposed to the Countess's idea; but she is firm, and insists on a legal opinion."

The young man was silent: he had not opened the packet in his hand.

"Does she want to marry again?"

"I believe it is suggested; but she denies it."

"Then —"

"Will you oblige me, Mr. Archer, by first looking through these papers? Afterward, when we have talked the case over, I will give you my opinion."

Archer withdrew reluctantly with the unwelcome documents. Since their last meeting he had half-unconsciously collaborated with events in ridding himself of the burden of Madame Olenska. His hour alone with her by the firelight had drawn them into a momentary intimacy on which the Duke of St. Austrey's intrusion with Mrs. Lemuel Struthers, and the Countess's joyous greeting of them, had rather providentially broken. Two days later Archer had assisted at the comedy of her reinstatement in the van der Luydens' favour, and had said to himself, with a touch of tartness, that a lady who knew how to thank all-powerful elderly gentlemen to such good purpose for a bunch of flowers did not need either the private consolations or the public championship of a young man of his small compass. To look at the matter in this light simplified his own case and surprisingly furbished up all the dim domestic virtues. He could not picture May Welland, in whatever conceivable emergency, hawking about her private difficulties and lavishing her confidences on strange men; and she had never seemed to him finer or fairer than in the week that followed. He had even yielded to her wish for a long engagement, since she had found the one disarming answer to his plea for haste.

"You know, when it comes to the point, your parents have always let you have your way ever since you were a little girl," he argued; and she had answered, with her clearest look: "Yes; and that's what makes it so hard to refuse the very last thing they'll ever ask of me as a little girl."

That was the old New York note; that was the kind of answer he would like always to be sure of his wife's making. If one had habitually breathed the New York air there were times when anything less crystalline seemed stifling.

The papers he had retired to read did not tell him much in fact; but they plunged him into an atmosphere in which he choked and spluttered. They consisted mainly of an exchange of letters between Count Olenski's solicitors and a French legal firm to whom the Countess had applied for the settlement of her financial situation. There was also a short letter from the Count to his wife: after reading it, Newland Archer rose, jammed the papers back into their envelope, and reentered Mr. Letterblair's office.

"Here are the letters, sir. If you wish, I'll see Madame Olenska," he said in a constrained voice.

"Thank you—thank you, Mr. Archer. Come and dine with me tonight if you're free, and we'll go into the matter afterward: in case you wish to call on our client tomorrow."

Newland Archer walked straight home again that afternoon. It was a winter evening of transparent clearness, with an innocent young moon above the house-tops; and he wanted to fill his soul's lungs with the pure radiance, and not exchange a word with any one till he and Mr. Letterblair were closeted together after dinner. It was impossible to decide otherwise than he had done: he must see Madame Olenska himself rather than let her secrets be bared to other eyes. A great wave of compassion had swept away his indifference and impatience: she stood before him as an exposed and pitiful figure, to be saved at all costs from farther wounding herself in her mad plunges against fate.

He remembered what she had told him of Mrs. Welland's request to be spared whatever was "unpleasant" in her history, and winced at the thought that it was perhaps this attitude of mind which kept the New York air so pure. "Are we only Pharisees after all?" he wondered, puzzled by the effort to reconcile his instinctive disgust at human vileness with his equally instinctive pity for human frailty.

For the first time he perceived how elementary his own principles had always been. He passed for a young man who had not been afraid of risks, and he knew that his secret love-affair with poor silly Mrs. Thorley Rushworth had not been too secret to invest him with a becoming air of adventure. But Mrs. Rushworth was "that kind of woman"; foolish, vain, clandestine by nature, and far more attracted by the secrecy and peril of the affair than by such charms and qualities as he possessed. When the fact dawned on him it nearly broke his heart, but now it seemed the redeeming feature of the case. The affair, in short, had been of the kind that most of the young men of his age had been through, and emerged from with calm consciences and an undisturbed belief in the abysmal distinction between the women one loved and respected and those one enjoyed—and pitied. In this view they were sedulously abetted by their mothers, aunts and other elderly female relatives, who all shared Mrs. Archer's belief that when "such things happened" it was undoubtedly foolish of the man, but somehow always criminal of the woman. All the elderly ladies whom Archer knew regarded any woman who loved imprudently as necessarily unscrupulous and designing, and mere simple-minded man as powerless in her clutches. The only thing to do was to persuade him, as early as possible, to marry a nice girl, and then trust to her to look after him.

In the complicated old European communities, Archer began to guess, love-problems might be less simple and less easily classified. Rich and idle and ornamental societies must produce many more such situations; and there might even be one in which a woman naturally sensitive and aloof would yet, from the force of circumstances, from sheer defencelessness and loneliness, be drawn into a tie inexcusable by conventional standards.

On reaching home he wrote a line to the Countess Olenska, asking at what hour of the next day she could receive him, and despatched it by a messenger-boy, who returned presently with a word to the effect that she was going to Skuytercliff the next morning to stay over Sunday with the van der Luydens, but that he would find her alone that evening after dinner. The note was written on a rather untidy half-sheet, without date or address, but her hand was firm and free. He was amused at the idea of her week-ending in the stately solitude of Skuytercliff, but immediately afterward felt that there, of all places, she would most feel the chill of minds rigorously averted from the "unpleasant."

He was at Mr. Letterblair's punctually at seven, glad of the pretext for excusing himself soon after dinner. He had formed his own opinion from the papers entrusted to him, and did not especially want to go into the matter with his senior partner. Mr. Letterblair was a widower, and they dined alone, copiously and slowly, in a dark shabby room hung with yellowing prints of "The Death of Chatham" and "The Coronation of Napoleon." On the sideboard, between fluted Sheraton knife-cases, stood a decanter of Haut Brion, and another of the old Lanning port (the gift of a client), which the wastrel Tom Lanning had sold off a year or two before his mysterious and discreditable death in San Francisco—an incident less publicly humiliating to the family than the sale of the cellar.

After a velvety oyster soup came shad and cucumbers, then a young broiled turkey with corn fritters, followed by a canvas-back with currant jelly and a celery mayonnaise. Mr. Letterblair, who lunched on a sandwich and tea, dined deliberately and deeply, and insisted on his guest's doing the same. Finally, when the closing rites had been accomplished, the cloth was removed, cigars were lit, and Mr. Letterblair, leaning back in his chair and pushing the port westward, said, spreading his back agreeably to the coal fire behind him: "The whole family are against a divorce. And I think rightly."

Archer instantly felt himself on the other side of the argument. "But why, sir? If there ever was a case —"

"Well—what's the use? *She's* here—he's there; the Atlantic's between them. She'll never get back a dollar more of her money than what he's voluntarily returned to her: their damned heathen marriage settlements take precious good care of that. As things go over there, Olenski's acted generously: he might have turned her out without a penny."

The young man knew this and was silent.

"I understand, though," Mr. Letterblair continued, "that she attaches no importance to the money. Therefore, as the family say, why not let well enough alone?"

Archer had gone to the house an hour earlier in full agreement with Mr. Letterblair's view; but put into words by this selfish, well-fed and supremely indifferent old man it suddenly became the Pharisaic voice of a society wholly absorbed in barricading itself against the unpleasant.

"I think that's for her to decide."

"H'm—have you considered the consequences if she decides for divorce?"

"You mean the threat in her husband's letter? What weight would that carry? It's no more than the vague charge of an angry blackguard."

"Yes; but it might make some unpleasant talk if he really defends the suit."

"Unpleasant—!" said Archer explosively.

Mr. Letterblair looked at him from under enquiring eyebrows, and the young man, aware of the uselessness of trying to explain what was in his mind, bowed acquiescently while his senior continued: "Divorce is always unpleasant."

"You agree with me?" Mr. Letterblair resumed, after a waiting silence.

"Naturally," said Archer.

"Well, then, I may count on you; the Mingotts may count on you; to use your influence against the idea?"

Archer hesitated. "I can't pledge myself till I've seen the Countess Olenska," he said at length.

"Mr. Archer, I don't understand you. Do you want to marry into a family with a scandalous divorce-suit hanging over it?"

"I don't think that has anything to do with the case."

Mr. Letterblair put down his glass of port and fixed on his young partner a cautious and apprehensive gaze.

Archer understood that he ran the risk of having his mandate withdrawn, and for some obscure reason he disliked the prospect. Now that the job had been thrust on him he did not propose to relinquish it; and, to guard against the possibility, he saw that he must reassure the unimaginative old man who was the legal conscience of the Mingotts.

"You may be sure, sir, that I shan't commit myself till I've reported to you; what I meant was that I'd rather not give an opinion till I've heard what Madame Olenska has to say."

Mr. Letterblair nodded approvingly at an excess of caution worthy of the best New York tradition, and the young man, glancing at his watch, pleaded an engagement and took leave.

## XII.

Old-fashioned New York dined at seven, and the habit of after-dinner calls, though derided in Archer's set, still generally prevailed. As the young man strolled up Fifth Avenue from Waverley Place, the long thoroughfare was deserted but for a group of carriages standing before the Reggie Chiverses' (where there was a dinner for the Duke), and the occasional figure of an elderly gentleman in heavy overcoat and muffler ascending a brownstone doorstep and disappearing into a gas-lit hall. Thus, as Archer crossed Washington Square, he remarked that old Mr. du Lac was calling on his cousins the Dagonets, and turning down the corner of West Tenth Street he saw Mr. Skipworth, of his own firm, obviously bound on a visit to the Miss Lannings. A little farther up Fifth Avenue, Beaufort appeared on his doorstep, darkly projected against a blaze of light, descended to his private brougham, and rolled away to a mysterious and probably unmentionable destination. It was not an Opera night, and no one was giving a party, so that Beaufort's outing was undoubtedly of a clandestine nature. Archer connected it in his mind with a little house beyond Lexington Avenue in which beribboned window curtains and flower-boxes had recently appeared, and before whose newly painted door the canary-coloured brougham of Miss Fanny Ring was frequently seen to wait.

Beyond the small and slippery pyramid which composed Mrs. Archer's world lay the almost unmapped quarter inhabited by artists, musicians and "people who wrote." These scattered fragments of humanity had never shown any desire to be amalgamated with the social structure. In spite of odd ways they were said to be, for the most part, quite respectable; but they preferred to keep to themselves. Medora Manson, in her prosperous days, had inaugurated a "literary salon"; but it had soon died out owing to the reluctance of the literary to frequent it.

Others had made the same attempt, and there was a household of Blenkers—an intense and voluble mother, and three blowsy daughters who imitated her—where one met Edwin Booth and Patti and William Winter, and the new Shakespearian actor George Rignold, and some of the magazine editors and musical and literary critics.

Mrs. Archer and her group felt a certain timidity concerning these persons. They were odd, they were uncertain, they had things one didn't know about in the background of their lives and minds. Literature and art were deeply respected in the Archer set, and Mrs. Archer was always at pains to tell her children how much more agreeable and cultivated society had been when it included such figures as Washington Irving, Fitz-Greene Halleck and the poet of "The Culprit Fay." The most celebrated authors of that generation had been "gentlemen"; perhaps the unknown persons who succeeded them had gentlemanly sentiments, but their origin, their appearance, their hair, their intimacy with the stage and the Opera, made any old New York criterion inapplicable to them.

"When I was a girl," Mrs. Archer used to say, "we knew everybody between the Battery and Canal Street; and only the people one knew had carriages. It was perfectly easy to place any one then; now one can't tell, and I prefer not to try."

Only old Catherine Mingott, with her absence of moral prejudices and almost parvenu indifference to the subtler distinctions, might have bridged the abyss; but she had never opened a book or looked at a picture, and cared for music only because it reminded her of gala nights at the Italiens, in the days of her triumph at the Tuileries. Possibly Beaufort, who was her match in daring, would have succeeded in bringing about a fusion; but his grand house and silk-stockinged footmen were an obstacle to informal sociability. Moreover, he was as illiterate as old Mrs. Mingott, and considered "fellows who wrote" as the mere paid purveyors of rich men's pleasures; and no one rich enough to influence his opinion had ever questioned it.

Newland Archer had been aware of these things ever since he could remember, and had accepted them as part of the structure of his universe. He knew that there were societies where painters and poets and novelists and men of science, and even great actors, were as sought after as Dukes; he had often pictured to himself what it would have been to live in the intimacy of drawing-rooms dominated by the talk of Merimee (whose "Lettres a une Inconnue" was one of his inseparables), of Thackeray, Browning or William Morris. But such things were inconceivable in New York, and unsettling to think of. Archer knew most of the "fellows who wrote," the musicians and the painters: he met them at the Century, or at the little musical and theatrical clubs that were beginning to come into existence. He enjoyed them there, and was bored with them at the Blenkers', where they were mingled with fervid and dowdy women who passed them about like captured curiosities; and even after his most exciting talks with Ned Winsett he always came away with the feeling that if his world was small, so was theirs, and that the only way to enlarge either was to reach a stage of manners where they would naturally merge.

He was reminded of this by trying to picture the society in which the Countess Olenska had lived and suffered, and also—perhaps—tasted mysterious joys. He remembered with what amusement she had told him that her grandmother Mingott and the Wellands objected to her living in a "Bohemian" quarter given over to "people who wrote." It was not the peril but the poverty that her family disliked; but that shade escaped her, and she supposed they considered literature compromising.

She herself had no fears of it, and the books scattered about her drawing-room (a part of the house in which books were usually supposed to be "out of place"), though chiefly works of fiction, had whetted Archer's interest with such new names as those of Paul Bourget, Huysmans, and the Goncourt brothers. Ruminating on these things as he approached her door, he was once more conscious of the curious way in which she reversed his values, and of the need of thinking himself into conditions incredibly different from any that he knew if he were to be of use in her present difficulty.

Nastasia opened the door, smiling mysteriously. On the bench in the hall lay a sable-lined overcoat, a folded opera hat of dull silk with a gold J. B. on the lining, and a white silk muffler: there was no mistaking the fact that these costly articles were the property of Julius Beaufort.

Archer was angry: so angry that he came near scribbling a word on his card and going away; then he remembered that in writing to Madame Olenska he had been kept by excess of discretion from saying that he wished to see her privately. He had therefore no one but himself to blame if she had opened her doors to other visitors; and he entered the drawing-room with the dogged determination to make Beaufort feel himself in the way, and to outstay him.

The banker stood leaning against the mantelshelf, which was draped with an old embroidery held in place by brass candelabra containing church candies of yellowish wax. He had thrust his chest out, supporting his shoulders against the mantel and resting his weight on one large patent-leather foot. As Archer entered he was smiling and looking down on his hostess, who sat on a sofa placed at right angles to the chimney. A table banked with flowers formed a screen behind it, and against the orchids and azaleas which the young man recognised as tributes from the Beaufort hot-houses, Madame Olenska sat half-reclined, her head propped on a hand and her wide sleeve leaving the arm bare to the elbow.

It was usual for ladies who received in the evenings to wear what were called "simple dinner dresses": a close-fitting armour of whale-boned silk, slightly open in the neck, with lace ruffles filling in the crack, and tight sleeves with a flounce uncovering just enough wrist to show an Etruscan gold bracelet or a velvet band. But Madame Olenska, heedless of tradition, was attired in a long robe of red velvet bordered about the chin and down the front with glossy black fur. Archer remembered, on his last visit to Paris, seeing a portrait by the new painter, Carolus Duran, whose pictures were the sensation of the Salon, in which the lady wore one of these bold sheath-like robes with her chin nestling in fur. There was something perverse and provocative in the notion of fur worn in the evening in a heated drawing-room, and in the combination of a muffled throat and bare arms; but the effect was undeniably pleasing.

"Lord love us—three whole days at Skuytercliff!" Beaufort was saying in his loud sneering voice as Archer entered. "You'd better take all your furs, and a hot-water-bottle."

"Why? Is the house so cold?" she asked, holding out her left hand to Archer in a way mysteriously suggesting that she expected him to kiss it.

"No; but the missus is," said Beaufort, nodding carelessly to the young man.

"But I thought her so kind. She came herself to invite me. Granny says I must certainly go."

"Granny would, of course. And I say it's a shame you're going to miss the little oyster supper I'd planned for you at Delmonico's next Sunday, with Campanini and Scalchi and a lot of jolly people."

She looked doubtfully from the banker to Archer.

"Ah—that does tempt me! Except the other evening at Mrs. Struthers's I've not met a single artist since I've been here."

"What kind of artists? I know one or two painters, very good fellows, that I could bring to see you if you'd allow me," said Archer boldly.

"Painters? Are there painters in New York?" asked Beaufort, in a tone implying that there could be none since he did not buy their pictures; and Madame Olenska said to Archer, with her grave smile: "That would be charming. But I was really thinking of dramatic artists, singers, actors, musicians. My husband's house was always full of them."

She said the words "my husband" as if no sinister associations were connected with them, and in a tone that seemed almost to sigh over the lost delights of her married life. Archer looked at her perplexedly, wondering if it were lightness or dissimulation that enabled her to touch so easily on the past at the very moment when she was risking her reputation in order to break with it.

"I do think," she went on, addressing both men, "that the imprevu adds to one's enjoyment. It's perhaps a mistake to see the same people every day."

"It's confoundedly dull, anyhow; New York is dying of dullness," Beaufort grumbled. "And when I try to liven it up for you, you go back on me. Come—think better of it! Sunday is your last chance, for Campanini leaves next week for Baltimore and Philadelphia; and I've a private room, and a Steinway, and they'll sing all night for me."

"How delicious! May I think it over, and write to you tomorrow morning?"

She spoke amiably, yet with the least hint of dismissal in her voice. Beaufort evidently felt it, and being unused to dismissals, stood staring at her with an obstinate line between his eyes.

"Why not now?"

"It's too serious a question to decide at this late hour."

"Do you call it late?"

She returned his glance coolly. "Yes; because I have still to talk business with Mr. Archer for a little while."

"Ah," Beaufort snapped. There was no appeal from her tone, and with a slight shrug he recovered his composure, took her hand, which he kissed with a practised air, and calling out from the threshold: "I say, Newland, if you can persuade the Countess to stop in town of course you're included in the supper," left the room with his heavy important step.

For a moment Archer fancied that Mr. Letterblair must have told her of his coming; but the irrelevance of her next remark made him change his mind.

"You know painters, then? You live in their milieu?" she asked, her eyes full of interest.

"Oh, not exactly. I don't know that the arts have a milieu here, any of them; they're more like a very thinly settled outskirt."

"But you care for such things?"

"Immensely. When I'm in Paris or London I never miss an exhibition. I try to keep up."

She looked down at the tip of the little satin boot that peeped from her long draperies.

"I used to care immensely too: my life was full of such things. But now I want to try not to."

"You want to try not to?"

"Yes: I want to cast off all my old life, to become just like everybody else here."

Archer reddened. "You'll never be like everybody else," he said.

She raised her straight eyebrows a little. "Ah, don't say that. If you knew how I hate to be different!"

Her face had grown as sombre as a tragic mask. She leaned forward, clasping her knee in her thin hands, and looking away from him into remote dark distances.

"I want to get away from it all," she insisted.

He waited a moment and cleared his throat. "I know. Mr. Letterblair has told me."

"Ah?"

"That's the reason I've come. He asked me to—you see I'm in the firm."

She looked slightly surprised, and then her eyes brightened. "You mean you can manage it for me? I can talk to you instead of Mr. Letterblair? Oh, that will be so much easier!"

Her tone touched him, and his confidence grew with his self-satisfaction. He perceived that she had spoken of business to Beaufort simply to get rid of him; and to have routed Beaufort was something of a triumph.

"I am here to talk about it," he repeated.

She sat silent, her head still propped by the arm that rested on the back of the sofa. Her face looked pale and extinguished, as if dimmed by the rich red of her dress. She struck Archer, of a sudden, as a pathetic and even pitiful figure.

"Now we're coming to hard facts," he thought, conscious in himself of the same instinctive recoil that he had so often criticised in his mother and her contemporaries. How little practice he had had in dealing with unusual situations! Their very vocabulary was unfamiliar to him, and seemed to belong to fiction and the stage. In face of what was coming he felt as awkward and embarrassed as a boy.

After a pause Madame Olenska broke out with unexpected vehemence: "I want to be free; I want to wipe out all the past."

"I understand that."

Her face warmed. "Then you'll help me?"

"First —" he hesitated—"perhaps I ought to know a little more."

She seemed surprised. "You know about my husband—my life with him?"

He made a sign of assent.

"Well—then—what more is there? In this country are such things tolerated? I'm a Protestant—our church does not forbid divorce in such cases."

"Certainly not."

They were both silent again, and Archer felt the spectre of Count Olenski's letter grimacing hideously between them. The letter filled only half a page, and was just what he had described it to be in speaking of it to Mr. Letterblair: the vague charge of an angry blackguard. But how much truth was behind it? Only Count Olenski's wife could tell.

"I've looked through the papers you gave to Mr. Letterblair," he said at length.

"Well—can there be anything more abominable?"

"No."

She changed her position slightly, screening her eyes with her lifted hand.

"Of course you know," Archer continued, "that if your husband chooses to fight the case—as he threatens to —"

"Yes—?"

"He can say things—things that might be unpl—might be disagreeable to you: say them publicly, so that they would get about, and harm you even if —"

"If—?"

"I mean: no matter how unfounded they were."

She paused for a long interval; so long that, not wishing to keep his eyes on her shaded face, he had time to imprint on his mind the exact shape of her other hand, the one on her knee, and every detail of the three rings on her fourth and fifth fingers; among which, he noticed, a wedding ring did not appear.

"What harm could such accusations, even if he made them publicly, do me here?"

It was on his lips to exclaim: "My poor child—far more harm than anywhere else!" Instead, he answered, in a voice that sounded in his ears like Mr. Letterblair's: "New York society is a very small world compared with the one you've lived in. And it's ruled, in spite of appearances, by a few people with—well, rather old-fashioned ideas."

She said nothing, and he continued: "Our ideas about marriage and divorce are particularly old-fashioned. Our legislation favours divorce—our social customs don't."

"Never?"

"Well—not if the woman, however injured, however irreproachable, has appearances in the least degree against her, has exposed herself by any unconventional action to—to offensive insinuations —"

She drooped her head a little lower, and he waited again, intensely hoping for a flash of indignation, or at least a brief cry of denial. None came.

A little travelling clock ticked purringly at her elbow, and a log broke in two and sent up a shower of sparks. The whole hushed and brooding room seemed to be waiting silently with Archer.

"Yes," she murmured at length, "that's what my family tell me."

He winced a little. "It's not unnatural —"

"*Our* family," she corrected herself; and Archer coloured. "For you'll be my cousin soon," she continued gently.

"I hope so."

"And you take their view?"

He stood up at this, wandered across the room, stared with void eyes at one of the pictures against the old red damask, and came back irresolutely to her side. How could he say: "Yes, if what your husband hints is true, or if you've no way of disproving it?"

"Sincerely —" she interjected, as he was about to speak.

He looked down into the fire. "Sincerely, then—what should you gain that would compensate for the possibility—the certainty—of a lot of beastly talk?"

"But my freedom—is that nothing?"

It flashed across him at that instant that the charge in the letter was true, and that she hoped to marry the partner of her guilt. How was he to tell her that, if she really cherished such a plan, the laws of the State were inexorably opposed to it? The mere suspicion that the thought was in her mind made him feel harshly and impatiently toward her. "But aren't you as free as air as it is?" he returned. "Who can touch you? Mr. Letterblair tells me the financial question has been settled —"

"Oh, yes," she said indifferently.

"Well, then: is it worth while to risk what may be infinitely disagreeable and painful? Think of the newspapers—their vileness! It's all stupid and narrow and unjust—but one can't make over society."

"No," she acquiesced; and her tone was so faint and desolate that he felt a sudden remorse for his own hard thoughts.

"The individual, in such cases, is nearly always sacrificed to what is supposed to be the collective interest: people cling to any convention that keeps the family together—protects the children, if there are any," he rambled on, pouring out all the stock phrases that rose to his lips in his intense desire to cover over the ugly reality which her silence seemed to have laid bare. Since she would not or could not say the one word that would have cleared the air, his wish was not to let her feel that he was trying to probe into her secret. Better keep on the surface, in the prudent old New York way, than risk uncovering a wound he could not heal.

"It's my business, you know," he went on, "to help you to see these things as the people who are fondest of you see them. The Mingotts, the Wellands, the van der Luydens, all your friends and relations: if I didn't show you honestly how they judge such questions, it wouldn't be fair of me, would it?" He spoke insistently, almost pleading with her in his eagerness to cover up that yawning silence.

She said slowly: "No; it wouldn't be fair."

The fire had crumbled down to greyness, and one of the lamps made a gurgling appeal for attention. Madame Olenska rose, wound it up and returned to the fire, but without resuming her seat.

Her remaining on her feet seemed to signify that there was nothing more for either of them to say, and Archer stood up also.

"Very well; I will do what you wish," she said abruptly. The blood rushed to his forehead; and, taken aback by the suddenness of her surrender, he caught her two hands awkwardly in his.

"I—I do want to help you," he said.

"You do help me. Good night, my cousin."

He bent and laid his lips on her hands, which were cold and lifeless. She drew them away, and he turned to the door, found his coat and hat under the faint gas-light of the hall, and plunged out into the winter night bursting with the belated eloquence of the inarticulate.

## XIII.

It was a crowded night at Wallack's theatre.

The play was "The Shaughraun," with Dion Boucicault in the title role and Harry Montague and Ada Dyas as the lovers. The popularity of the admirable English company was at its height, and the Shaughraun always packed the house. In the galleries the enthusiasm was unreserved; in the stalls and boxes, people smiled a little at the hackneyed sentiments and clap-trap situations, and enjoyed the play as much as the galleries did.

There was one episode, in particular, that held the house from floor to ceiling. It was that in which Harry Montague, after a sad, almost monosyllabic scene of parting with Miss Dyas, bade her good-bye, and turned to go. The actress, who was standing near the mantelpiece and looking down into the fire, wore a gray cashmere dress without fashionable loopings or trimmings, moulded to her tall figure and flowing in long lines about her feet. Around her neck was a narrow black velvet ribbon with the ends falling down her back.

When her wooer turned from her she rested her arms against the mantel-shelf and bowed her face in her hands. On the threshold he paused to look at her; then he stole back, lifted one of the ends of velvet ribbon, kissed it, and left the room without her hearing him or changing her attitude. And on this silent parting the curtain fell.

It was always for the sake of that particular scene that Newland Archer went to see "The Shaughraun." He thought the adieux of Montague and Ada Dyas as fine as anything he had ever seen Croisette and Bressant do in Paris, or Madge Robertson and Kendal in London; in its reticence, its dumb sorrow, it moved him more than the most famous histrionic outpourings.

On the evening in question the little scene acquired an added poignancy by reminding him—he could not have said why—of his leave-taking from Madame Olenska after their confidential talk a week or ten days earlier.

It would have been as difficult to discover any resemblance between the two situations as between the appearance of the persons concerned. Newland Archer could not pretend to anything approaching the young English actor's romantic good looks, and Miss Dyas was a tall red-haired woman of monumental build whose pale and pleasantly ugly face was utterly unlike Ellen Olenska's vivid countenance. Nor were Archer and Madame Olenska two lovers parting in heart-broken silence; they were client and lawyer separating after a talk which had given the lawyer the worst possible impression of the client's case. Wherein, then, lay the resemblance that made the young man's heart beat with a kind of retrospective excitement? It seemed to be in Madame Olenska's mysterious faculty of suggesting tragic and moving possibilities outside the daily run of experience. She had hardly ever said a word to him to produce this impression, but it was a part of her, either a projection of her mysterious and outlandish background or of something inherently dramatic, passionate and unusual in herself. Archer had always been inclined to think that chance and circumstance played a small part in shaping people's lots compared with their innate tendency to have things happen to them. This tendency he had felt from the first in Madame Olenska. The quiet, almost passive young woman struck him as exactly the kind of person to whom things were bound to happen, no matter how much she shrank from them and went out of her way to avoid them. The exciting fact was her having lived in an atmosphere so thick with drama that her own tendency to provoke it had apparently passed unperceived. It was precisely the odd absence of surprise in her that gave him the sense of her having been plucked out of a very maelstrom: the things she took for granted gave the measure of those she had rebelled against.

Archer had left her with the conviction that Count Olenski's accusation was not unfounded. The mysterious person who figured in his wife's past as "the secretary" had probably not been unrewarded for his share in her escape. The conditions from which she had fled were intolerable, past speaking of, past believing: she was young, she was frightened, she was desperate—what more natural than that she should be grateful to her rescuer? The pity was that her gratitude put her, in the law's eyes and the world's, on a par with her abominable husband. Archer had made her understand this, as he was bound to do; he had also made her understand that simplehearted kindly New York, on whose larger charity she had apparently counted, was precisely the place where she could least hope for indulgence.

To have to make this fact plain to her—and to witness her resigned acceptance of it—had been intolerably painful to him. He felt himself drawn to her by obscure feelings of jealousy and pity, as if her dumbly-confessed error had put her at his mercy, humbling yet endearing her. He was glad it was to him she had revealed her secret, rather than to the cold scrutiny of Mr. Letterblair, or the embarrassed gaze of her family. He immediately took it upon himself to assure them both that she had given up her idea of seeking a divorce, basing her decision on the fact that she had understood the uselessness of the proceeding; and with infinite relief they had all turned their eyes from the "unpleasantness" she had spared them.

"I was sure Newland would manage it," Mrs. Welland had said proudly of her future son-in-law; and old Mrs. Mingott, who had summoned him for a confidential interview, had congratulated him on his cleverness, and added impatiently: "Silly goose! I told her myself what nonsense it was. Wanting to pass herself off as Ellen Mingott and an old maid, when she has the luck to be a married woman and a Countess!"

These incidents had made the memory of his last talk with Madame Olenska so vivid to the young man that as the curtain fell on the parting of the two actors his eyes filled with tears, and he stood up to leave the theatre.

In doing so, he turned to the side of the house behind him, and saw the lady of whom he was thinking seated in a box with the Beauforts, Lawrence Lefferts and one or two other men. He had not spoken with her alone since their evening together, and had tried to avoid being with her in company; but now their eyes met, and as Mrs. Beaufort recognised him at the same time, and made her languid little gesture of invitation, it was impossible not to go into the box.

Beaufort and Lefferts made way for him, and after a few words with Mrs. Beaufort, who always preferred to look beautiful and not have to talk, Archer seated himself behind Madame Olenska. There was no one else in the box but Mr. Sillerton Jackson, who was telling Mrs. Beaufort in a confidential undertone about Mrs. Lemuel Struthers's last Sunday reception (where some people reported that there had been dancing). Under cover of this circumstantial narrative, to which Mrs. Beaufort listened with her perfect smile, and her head at just the right angle to be seen in profile from the stalls, Madame Olenska turned and spoke in a low voice.

"Do you think," she asked, glancing toward the stage, "he will send her a bunch of yellow roses tomorrow morning?"

Archer reddened, and his heart gave a leap of surprise. He had called only twice on Madame Olenska, and each time he had sent her a box of yellow roses, and each time without a card. She had never before made any allusion to the flowers, and he supposed she had never thought of him as the sender.

Now her sudden recognition of the gift, and her associating it with the tender leave-taking on the stage, filled him with an agitated pleasure.

"I was thinking of that too—I was going to leave the theatre in order to take the picture away with me," he said.

To his surprise her colour rose, reluctantly and duskily. She looked down at the mother-of-pearl opera-glass in her smoothly gloved hands, and said, after a pause: "What do you do while May is away?"

"I stick to my work," he answered, faintly annoyed by the question.

In obedience to a long-established habit, the Wellands had left the previous week for St. Augustine, where, out of regard for the supposed susceptibility of Mr. Welland's bronchial tubes, they always spent the latter part of the winter. Mr. Welland was a mild and silent man, with no opinions but with many habits. With these habits none might interfere; and one of them demanded that his wife and daughter should always go with him on his annual journey to the south. To preserve an unbroken domesticity was essential to his peace of mind; he would not have known where his hair-brushes were, or how to provide stamps for his letters, if Mrs. Welland had not been there to tell him.

As all the members of the family adored each other, and as Mr. Welland was the central object of their idolatry, it never occurred to his wife and May to let him go to St. Augustine alone; and his sons, who were both in the law, and could not leave New York during the winter, always joined him for Easter and travelled back with him.

It was impossible for Archer to discuss the necessity of May's accompanying her father. The reputation of the Mingotts' family physician was largely based on the attack of pneumonia which Mr. Welland had never had; and his insistence on St. Augustine was therefore inflexible. Originally, it had been intended that May's engagement should not be announced till her return from Florida, and the fact that it had been made known sooner could not be expected to alter Mr. Welland's plans. Archer would have liked to join the travellers and have a few weeks of sunshine and boating with his betrothed; but he too was bound by custom and conventions. Little arduous as his professional duties were, he would have been convicted of frivolity by the whole Mingott clan if he had suggested asking for a holiday in mid-winter; and he accepted May's departure with the resignation which he perceived would have to be one of the principal constituents of married life.

He was conscious that Madame Olenska was looking at him under lowered lids. "I have done what you wished—what you advised," she said abruptly.

"Ah—I'm glad," he returned, embarrassed by her broaching the subject at such a moment.

"I understand—that you were right," she went on a little breathlessly; "but sometimes life is difficult ... perplexing..."

"I know."

"And I wanted to tell you that I *do* feel you were right; and that I'm grateful to you," she ended, lifting her opera-glass quickly to her eyes as the door of the box opened and Beaufort's resonant voice broke in on them.

Archer stood up, and left the box and the theatre.

Only the day before he had received a letter from May Welland in which, with characteristic candour, she had asked him to "be kind to Ellen" in their absence. "She likes you and admires you so much—and you know, though she doesn't show it, she's still very lonely and unhappy. I don't think Granny understands her, or uncle Lovell Mingott either; they really think she's much worldlier and fonder of society than she is. And I can quite see that New York must seem dull to her, though the family won't admit it. I think she's been used to lots of things we haven't got; wonderful music, and picture shows, and celebrities—artists and authors and all the clever people you admire. Granny can't understand her wanting anything but lots of dinners and clothes—but I can see that you're almost the only person in New York who can talk to her about what she really cares for."

His wise May—how he had loved her for that letter! But he had not meant to act on it; he was too busy, to begin with, and he did not care, as an engaged man, to play too conspicuously the part of Madame Olenska's champion. He had an idea that she knew how to take care of herself a good deal better than the ingenuous May imagined. She had Beaufort at her feet, Mr. van der Luyden hovering above her like a protecting deity, and any number of candidates (Lawrence Lefferts among them) waiting their opportunity in the middle distance. Yet he never saw her, or exchanged a word with her, without feeling that, after all, May's ingenuousness almost amounted to a gift of divination. Ellen Olenska was lonely and she was unhappy.

## XIV.

As he came out into the lobby Archer ran across his friend Ned Winsett, the only one among what Janey called his "clever people" with whom he cared to probe into things a little deeper than the average level of club and chop-house banter.

He had caught sight, across the house, of Winsett's shabby round-shouldered back, and had once noticed his eyes turned toward the Beaufort box. The two men shook hands, and Winsett proposed a bock at a little German restaurant around the corner. Archer, who was not in the mood for the kind of talk they were likely to get there, declined on the plea that he had work to do at home; and Winsett said: "Oh, well so have I for that matter, and I'll be the Industrious Apprentice too."

They strolled along together, and presently Winsett said: "Look here, what I'm really after is the name of the dark lady in that swell box of yours—with the Beauforts, wasn't she? The one your friend Lefferts seems so smitten by."

Archer, he could not have said why, was slightly annoyed. What the devil did Ned Winsett want with Ellen Olenska's name? And above all, why did he couple it with Lefferts's? It was unlike Winsett to manifest such curiosity; but after all, Archer remembered, he was a journalist.

"It's not for an interview, I hope?" he laughed.

"Well—not for the press; just for myself," Winsett rejoined. "The fact is she's a neighbour of mine—queer quarter for such a beauty to settle in—and she's been awfully kind to my little boy, who fell down her area chasing his kitten, and gave himself a nasty cut. She rushed in bareheaded, carrying him in her arms, with his knee all beautifully bandaged, and was so sympathetic and beautiful that my wife was too dazzled to ask her name."

A pleasant glow dilated Archer's heart. There was nothing extraordinary in the tale: any woman would have done as much for a neighbour's child. But it was just like Ellen, he felt, to have rushed in bareheaded, carrying the boy in her arms, and to have dazzled poor Mrs. Winsett into forgetting to ask who she was.

"That is the Countess Olenska—a granddaughter of old Mrs. Mingott's."

"Whew—a Countess!" whistled Ned Winsett. "Well, I didn't know Countesses were so neighbourly. Mingotts ain't."

"They would be, if you'd let them."

"Ah, well —" It was their old interminable argument as to the obstinate unwillingness of the "clever people" to frequent the fashionable, and both men knew that there was no use in prolonging it.

"I wonder," Winsett broke off, "how a Countess happens to live in our slum?"

"Because she doesn't care a hang about where she lives—or about any of our little social sign-posts," said Archer, with a secret pride in his own picture of her.

"H'm—been in bigger places, I suppose," the other commented. "Well, here's my corner."

He slouched off across Broadway, and Archer stood looking after him and musing on his last words.

Ned Winsett had those flashes of penetration; they were the most interesting thing about him, and always made Archer wonder why they had allowed him to accept failure so stolidly at an age when most men are still struggling.

Archer had known that Winsett had a wife and child, but he had never seen them. The two men always met at the Century, or at some haunt of journalists and theatrical people, such as the restaurant where Winsett had proposed to go for a bock. He had given Archer to understand that his wife was an invalid; which might be true of the poor lady, or might merely mean that she was lacking in social gifts or in evening clothes, or in both. Winsett himself had a savage abhorrence of social observances: Archer, who dressed in the evening because he thought it cleaner and more comfortable to do so, and who had never stopped to consider that cleanliness and comfort are two of the costliest items in a modest budget, regarded Winsett's attitude as part of the boring "Bohemian" pose that always made fashionable people, who changed their clothes without talking about it, and were not forever harping on the number of servants one kept, seem so much simpler and less self-conscious than the others. Nevertheless, he was always stimulated by Winsett, and whenever he caught sight of the journalist's lean bearded face and melancholy eyes he would rout him out of his corner and carry him off for a long talk.

Winsett was not a journalist by choice. He was a pure man of letters, untimely born in a world that had no need of letters; but after publishing one volume of brief and exquisite literary appreciations, of which one hundred and twenty copies were sold, thirty given away, and the balance eventually destroyed by the publishers (as per contract) to make room for more marketable material, he had abandoned his real calling, and taken a sub-editorial job on a women's weekly, where fashion-plates and paper patterns alternated with New England love-stories and advertisements of temperance drinks.

On the subject of "Hearth-fires" (as the paper was called) he was inexhaustibly entertaining; but beneath his fun lurked the sterile bitterness of the still young man who has tried and given up. His conversation always made Archer take the measure of his own life, and feel how little it contained; but Winsett's, after all, contained still less, and though their common fund of intellectual interests and curiosities made their talks exhilarating, their exchange of views usually remained within the limits of a pensive dilettantism.

"The fact is, life isn't much a fit for either of us," Winsett had once said. "I'm down and out; nothing to be done about it. I've got only one ware to produce, and there's no market for it here, and won't be in my time. But you're free and you're well-off. Why don't you get into touch? There's only one way to do it: to go into politics."

Archer threw his head back and laughed. There one saw at a flash the unbridgeable difference between men like Winsett and the others—Archer's kind. Every one in polite circles knew that, in America, "a gentleman couldn't go into politics." But, since he could hardly put it in that way to Winsett, he answered evasively: "Look at the career of the honest man in American politics! They don't want us."

"Who's 'they'? Why don't you all get together and be 'they' yourselves?"

Archer's laugh lingered on his lips in a slightly condescending smile. It was useless to prolong the discussion: everybody knew the melancholy fate of the few gentlemen who had risked their clean linen in municipal or state politics in New York. The day was past when that sort of thing was possible: the country was in possession of the bosses and the emigrant, and decent people had to fall back on sport or culture.

"Culture! Yes—if we had it! But there are just a few little local patches, dying out here and there for lack of—well, hoeing and cross-fertilising: the last remnants of the old European tradition that your forebears brought with them. But you're in a pitiful little minority: you've got no centre, no competition, no audience. You're like the pictures on the walls of a deserted house: 'The Portrait of a Gentleman.' You'll never amount to anything, any of you, till you roll up your sleeves and get right down into the muck. That, or emigrate ... God! If I could emigrate ..."

Archer mentally shrugged his shoulders and turned the conversation back to books, where Winsett, if uncertain, was always interesting. Emigrate! As if a gentleman could abandon his own country! One could no more do that than one could roll up one's sleeves and go down into the muck. A gentleman simply stayed at home and abstained. But you couldn't make a man like Winsett see that; and that was why the New York of literary clubs and exotic restaurants, though a first shake made it seem more of a kaleidoscope, turned out, in the end, to be a smaller box, with a more monotonous pattern, than the assembled atoms of Fifth Avenue.

The next morning Archer scoured the town in vain for more yellow roses. In consequence of this search he arrived late at the office, perceived that his doing so made no difference whatever to any one, and was filled with sudden exasperation at the elaborate futility of his life. Why should he not be, at that moment, on the sands of St. Augustine with May Welland? No one was deceived by his pretense of professional activity. In old-fashioned legal firms like that of which Mr. Letterblair was the head, and which were mainly engaged in the management of large estates and "conservative" investments, there were always two or three young men, fairly well-off, and without professional ambition, who, for a certain number of hours of each day, sat at their desks accomplishing trivial tasks, or simply reading the newspapers. Though it was supposed to be proper for them to have an occupation, the crude fact of money-making was still regarded as derogatory, and the law, being a profession, was accounted a more gentlemanly pursuit than business. But none of these young men had much hope of really advancing in his profession, or any earnest desire to do so; and over many of them the green mould of the perfunctory was already perceptibly spreading.

It made Archer shiver to think that it might be spreading over him too. He had, to be sure, other tastes and interests; he spent his vacations in European travel, cultivated the "clever people" May spoke of, and generally tried to "keep up," as he had somewhat wistfully put it to Madame Olenska. But once he was married, what would become of this narrow margin of life in which his real experiences were lived? He had seen enough of other young men who had dreamed his dream, though perhaps less ardently, and who had gradually sunk into the placid and luxurious routine of their elders.

From the office he sent a note by messenger to Madame Olenska, asking if he might call that afternoon, and begging her to let him find a reply at his club; but at the club he found nothing, nor did he receive any letter the following day. This unexpected silence mortified him beyond reason, and though the next morning he saw a glorious cluster of yellow roses behind a florist's window-pane, he left it there. It was only on the third morning that he received a line by post from the Countess Olenska. To his surprise it was dated from Skuytercliff, whither the van der Luydens had promptly retreated after putting the Duke on board his steamer.

"I ran away," the writer began abruptly (without the usual preliminaries), "the day after I saw you at the play, and these kind friends have taken me in. I wanted to be quiet, and think things over. You were right in telling me how kind they were; I feel myself so safe here. I wish that you were with us." She ended with a conventional "Yours sincerely," and without any allusion to the date of her return.

The tone of the note surprised the young man. What was Madame Olenska running away from, and why did she feel the need to be safe? His first thought was of some dark menace from abroad; then he reflected that he did not know her epistolary style, and that it might run to picturesque exaggeration. Women always exaggerated; and moreover she was not wholly at her ease in English, which she often spoke as if she were translating from the French. "Je me suis evadee —" put in that way, the opening sentence immediately suggested that she might merely have wanted to escape from a boring round of engagements; which was very likely true, for he judged her to be capricious, and easily wearied of the pleasure of the moment.

It amused him to think of the van der Luydens' having carried her off to Skuytercliff on a second visit, and this time for an indefinite period. The doors of Skuytercliff were rarely and grudgingly opened to visitors, and a chilly week-end was the most ever offered to the few thus privileged. But Archer had seen, on his last visit to Paris, the delicious play of Labiche, "Le Voyage de M. Perrichon," and he remembered M. Perrichon's dogged and undiscouraged attachment to the young man whom he had pulled out of the glacier. The van der Luydens had rescued Madame Olenska from a doom almost as icy; and though there were many other reasons for being attracted to her, Archer knew that beneath them all lay the gentle and obstinate determination to go on rescuing her.

He felt a distinct disappointment on learning that she was away; and almost immediately remembered that, only the day before, he had refused an invitation to spend the following Sunday with the Reggie Chiverses at their house on the Hudson, a few miles below Skuytercliff.

He had had his fill long ago of the noisy friendly parties at Highbank, with coasting, ice-boating, sleighing, long tramps in the snow, and a general flavour of mild flirting and milder practical jokes. He had just received a box of new books from his London book-seller, and had preferred the prospect of a quiet Sunday at home with his spoils. But he now went into the club writing-room, wrote a hurried telegram, and told the servant to send it immediately. He knew that Mrs. Reggie didn't object to her visitors' suddenly changing their minds, and that there was always a room to spare in her elastic house.

## XV.

Newland Archer arrived at the Chiverses' on Friday evening, and on Saturday went conscientiously through all the rites appertaining to a week-end at Highbank.

In the morning he had a spin in the ice-boat with his hostess and a few of the hardier guests; in the afternoon he "went over the farm" with Reggie, and listened, in the elaborately appointed stables, to long and impressive disquisitions on the horse; after tea he talked in a corner of the firelit hall with a young lady who had professed herself broken-hearted when his engagement was announced, but was now eager to tell him of her own matrimonial hopes; and finally, about midnight, he assisted in putting a gold-fish in one visitor's bed, dressed up a burglar in the bath-room of a nervous aunt, and saw in the small hours by joining in a pillow-fight that ranged from the nurseries to the basement. But on Sunday after luncheon he borrowed a cutter, and drove over to Skuytercliff.

People had always been told that the house at Skuytercliff was an Italian villa. Those who had never been to Italy believed it; so did some who had. The house had been built by Mr. van der Luyden in his youth, on his return from the "grand tour," and in anticipation of his approaching marriage with Miss Louisa Dagonet. It was a large square wooden structure, with tongued and grooved walls painted pale green and white, a Corinthian portico, and fluted pilasters between the windows. From the high ground on which it stood a series of terraces bordered by balustrades and urns descended in the steel-engraving style to a small irregular lake with an asphalt edge overhung by rare weeping conifers. To the right and left, the famous weedless lawns studded with "specimen" trees (each of a different variety) rolled away to long ranges of grass crested with elaborate cast-iron ornaments; and below, in a hollow, lay the four-roomed stone house which the first Patroon had built on the land granted him in 1612.

Against the uniform sheet of snow and the greyish winter sky the Italian villa loomed up rather grimly; even in summer it kept its distance, and the boldest coleus bed had never ventured nearer than thirty feet from its awful front. Now, as Archer rang the bell, the long tinkle seemed to echo through a mausoleum; and the surprise of the butler who at length responded to the call was as great as though he had been summoned from his final sleep.

Happily Archer was of the family, and therefore, irregular though his arrival was, entitled to be informed that the Countess Olenska was out, having driven to afternoon service with Mrs. van der Luyden exactly three quarters of an hour earlier.

"Mr. van der Luyden," the butler continued, "is in, sir; but my impression is that he is either finishing his nap or else reading yesterday's Evening Post. I heard him say, sir, on his return from church this morning, that he intended to look through the Evening Post after luncheon; if you like, sir, I might go to the library door and listen —"

But Archer, thanking him, said that he would go and meet the ladies; and the butler, obviously relieved, closed the door on him majestically.

A groom took the cutter to the stables, and Archer struck through the park to the high-road. The village of Skuytercliff was only a mile and a half away, but he knew that Mrs. van der Luyden never walked, and that he must keep to the road to meet the carriage. Presently, however, coming down a foot-path that crossed the highway, he caught sight of a slight figure in a red cloak, with a big dog running ahead. He hurried forward, and Madame Olenska stopped short with a smile of welcome.

"Ah, you've come!" she said, and drew her hand from her muff.

The red cloak made her look gay and vivid, like the Ellen Mingott of old days; and he laughed as he took her hand, and answered: "I came to see what you were running away from."

Her face clouded over, but she answered: "Ah, well—you will see, presently."

The answer puzzled him. "Why—do you mean that you've been overtaken?"

She shrugged her shoulders, with a little movement like Nastasia's, and rejoined in a lighter tone: "Shall we walk on? I'm so cold after the sermon. And what does it matter, now you're here to protect me?"

The blood rose to his temples and he caught a fold of her cloak. "Ellen—what is it? You must tell me."

"Oh, presently—let's run a race first: my feet are freezing to the ground," she cried; and gathering up the cloak she fled away across the snow, the dog leaping about her with challenging barks. For a moment Archer stood watching, his gaze delighted by the flash of the red meteor against the snow; then he started after her, and they met, panting and laughing, at a wicket that led into the park.

She looked up at him and smiled. "I knew you'd come!"

"That shows you wanted me to," he returned, with a disproportionate joy in their nonsense. The white glitter of the trees filled the air with its own mysterious brightness, and as they walked on over the snow the ground seemed to sing under their feet.

"Where did you come from?" Madame Olenska asked.

He told her, and added: "It was because I got your note."

After a pause she said, with a just perceptible chill in her voice: "May asked you to take care of me."

"I didn't need any asking."

"You mean—I'm so evidently helpless and defenceless? What a poor thing you must all think me! But women here seem not—seem never to feel the need: any more than the blessed in heaven."

He lowered his voice to ask: "What sort of a need?"

"Ah, don't ask me! I don't speak your language," she retorted petulantly.

The answer smote him like a blow, and he stood still in the path, looking down at her.

"What did I come for, if I don't speak yours?"

"Oh, my friend—!" She laid her hand lightly on his arm, and he pleaded earnestly: "Ellen—why won't you tell me what's happened?"

She shrugged again. "Does anything ever happen in heaven?"

He was silent, and they walked on a few yards without exchanging a word. Finally she said: "I will tell you—but where, where, where? One can't be alone for a minute in that great seminary of a house, with all the doors wide open, and always a servant bringing tea, or a log for the fire, or the newspaper! Is there nowhere in an American house where one may be by one's self? You're so shy, and yet you're so public. I always feel as if I were in the convent again—or on the stage, before a dreadfully polite audience that never applauds."

"Ah, you don't like us!" Archer exclaimed.

They were walking past the house of the old Patroon, with its squat walls and small square windows compactly grouped about a central chimney. The shutters stood wide, and through one of the newly-washed windows Archer caught the light of a fire.

"Why—the house is open!" he said.

She stood still. "No; only for today, at least. I wanted to see it, and Mr. van der Luyden had the fire lit and the windows opened, so that we might stop there on the way back from church this morning." She ran up the steps and tried the door. "It's still unlocked—what luck! Come in and we can have a quiet talk. Mrs. van der Luyden has driven over to see her old aunts at Rhinebeck and we shan't be missed at the house for another hour."

He followed her into the narrow passage. His spirits, which had dropped at her last words, rose with an irrational leap. The homely little house stood there, its panels and brasses shining in the firelight, as if magically created to receive them. A big bed of embers still gleamed in the kitchen chimney, under an iron pot hung from an ancient crane. Rush-bottomed arm-chairs faced each other across the tiled hearth, and rows of Delft plates stood on shelves against the walls. Archer stooped over and threw a log upon the embers.

Madame Olenska, dropping her cloak, sat down in one of the chairs. Archer leaned against the chimney and looked at her.

"You're laughing now; but when you wrote me you were unhappy," he said.

"Yes." She paused. "But I can't feel unhappy when you're here."

"I sha'n't be here long," he rejoined, his lips stiffening with the effort to say just so much and no more.

"No; I know. But I'm improvident: I live in the moment when I'm happy."

The words stole through him like a temptation, and to close his senses to it he moved away from the hearth and stood gazing out at the black tree-boles against the snow. But it was as if she too had shifted her place, and he still saw her, between himself and the trees, drooping over the fire with her indolent smile. Archer's heart was beating insubordinately. What if it were from him that she had been running away, and if she had waited to tell him so till they were here alone together in this secret room?

"Ellen, if I'm really a help to you—if you really wanted me to come—tell me what's wrong, tell me what it is you're running away from," he insisted.

He spoke without shifting his position, without even turning to look at her: if the thing was to happen, it was to happen in this way, with the whole width of the room between them, and his eyes still fixed on the outer snow.

For a long moment she was silent; and in that moment Archer imagined her, almost heard her, stealing up behind him to throw her light arms about his neck. While he waited, soul and body throbbing with the miracle to come, his eyes mechanically received the image of a heavily-coated man with his fur collar turned up who was advancing along the path to the house. The man was Julius Beaufort.

"Ah—!" Archer cried, bursting into a laugh.

Madame Olenska had sprung up and moved to his side, slipping her hand into his; but after a glance through the window her face paled and she shrank back.

"So that was it?" Archer said derisively.

"I didn't know he was here," Madame Olenska murmured. Her hand still clung to Archer's; but he drew away from her, and walking out into the passage threw open the door of the house.

"Hallo, Beaufort—this way! Madame Olenska was expecting you," he said.

During his journey back to New York the next morning, Archer relived with a fatiguing vividness his last moments at Skuytercliff.

Beaufort, though clearly annoyed at finding him with Madame Olenska, had, as usual, carried off the situation high-handedly. His way of ignoring people whose presence inconvenienced him actually gave them, if they were sensitive to it, a feeling of invisibility, of nonexistence. Archer, as the three strolled back through the park, was aware of this odd sense of disembodiment; and humbling as it was to his vanity it gave him the ghostly advantage of observing unobserved.

Beaufort had entered the little house with his usual easy assurance; but he could not smile away the vertical line between his eyes. It was fairly clear that Madame Olenska had not known that he was coming, though her words to Archer had hinted at the possibility; at any rate, she had evidently not told him where she was going when she left New York, and her unexplained departure had exasperated him. The ostensible reason of his appearance was the discovery, the very night before, of a "perfect little house," not in the market, which was really just the thing for her, but would be snapped up instantly if she didn't take it; and he was loud in mock-reproaches for the dance she had led him in running away just as he had found it.

"If only this new dodge for talking along a wire had been a little bit nearer perfection I might have told you all this from town, and been toasting my toes before the club fire at this minute, instead of tramping after you through the snow," he grumbled, disguising a real irritation under the pretence of it; and at this opening Madame Olenska twisted the talk away to the fantastic possibility that they might one day actually converse with each other from street to street, or even—incredible dream!—from one town to another. This struck from all three allusions to Edgar Poe and Jules Verne, and such platitudes as naturally rise to the lips of the most intelligent when they are talking against time, and dealing with a new invention in which it would seem ingenuous to believe too soon; and the question of the telephone carried them safely back to the big house.

Mrs. van der Luyden had not yet returned; and Archer took his leave and walked off to fetch the cutter, while Beaufort followed the Countess Olenska indoors. It was probable that, little as the van der Luydens encouraged unannounced visits, he could count on being asked to dine, and sent back to the station to catch the nine o'clock train; but more than that he would certainly not get, for it would be inconceivable to his hosts that a gentleman travelling without luggage should wish to spend the night, and distasteful to them to propose it to a person with whom they were on terms of such limited cordiality as Beaufort.

Beaufort knew all this, and must have foreseen it; and his taking the long journey for so small a reward gave the measure of his impatience. He was undeniably in pursuit of the Countess Olenska; and Beaufort had only one object in view in his pursuit of pretty women. His dull and childless home had long since palled on him; and in addition to more permanent consolations he was always in quest of amorous adventures in his own set. This was the man from whom Madame Olenska was avowedly flying: the question was whether she had fled because his importunities displeased her, or because she did not wholly trust herself to resist them; unless, indeed, all her talk of flight had been a blind, and her departure no more than a manoeuvre.

Archer did not really believe this. Little as he had actually seen of Madame Olenska, he was beginning to think that he could read her face, and if not her face, her voice; and both had betrayed annoyance, and even dismay, at Beaufort's sudden appearance. But, after all, if this were the case, was it not worse than if she had left New York for the express purpose of meeting him? If she had done that, she ceased to be an object of interest, she threw in her lot with the vulgarest of dissemblers: a woman engaged in a love affair with Beaufort "classed" herself irretrievably.

No, it was worse a thousand times if, judging Beaufort, and probably despising him, she was yet drawn to him by all that gave him an advantage over the other men about her: his habit of two continents and two societies, his familiar association with artists and actors and people generally in the world's eye, and his careless contempt for local prejudices. Beaufort was vulgar, he was uneducated, he was purse-proud; but the circumstances of his life, and a certain native shrewdness, made him better worth talking to than many men, morally and socially his betters, whose horizon was bounded by the Battery and the Central Park. How should any one coming from a wider world not feel the difference and be attracted by it?

Madame Olenska, in a burst of irritation, had said to Archer that he and she did not talk the same language; and the young man knew that in some respects this was true. But Beaufort understood every turn of her dialect, and spoke it fluently: his view of life, his tone, his attitude, were merely a coarser reflection of those revealed in Count Olenski's letter. This might seem to be to his disadvantage with Count Olenski's wife; but Archer was too intelligent to think that a young woman like Ellen Olenska would necessarily recoil from everything that reminded her of her past. She might believe herself wholly in revolt against it; but what had charmed her in it would still charm her, even though it were against her will.

Thus, with a painful impartiality, did the young man make out the case for Beaufort, and for Beaufort's victim. A longing to enlighten her was strong in him; and there were moments when he imagined that all she asked was to be enlightened.

That evening he unpacked his books from London. The box was full of things he had been waiting for impatiently; a new volume of Herbert Spencer, another collection of the prolific Alphonse Daudet's brilliant tales, and a novel called "Middlemarch," as to which there had lately been interesting things said in the reviews. He had declined three dinner invitations in favour of this feast; but though he turned the pages with the sensuous joy of the book-lover, he did not know what he was reading, and one book after another dropped from his hand. Suddenly, among them, he lit on a small volume of verse which he had ordered because the name had attracted him: "The House of Life." He took it up, and found himself plunged in an atmosphere unlike any he had ever breathed in books; so warm, so rich, and yet so ineffably tender, that it gave a new and haunting beauty to the most elementary of human passions. All through the night he pursued through those enchanted pages the vision of a woman who had the face of Ellen Olenska; but when he woke the next morning, and looked out at the brownstone houses across the street, and thought of his desk in Mr. Letterblair's office, and the family pew in Grace Church, his hour in the park of Skuytercliff became as far outside the pale of probability as the visions of the night.

"Mercy, how pale you look, Newland!" Janey commented over the coffee-cups at breakfast; and his mother added: "Newland, dear, I've noticed lately that you've been coughing; I do hope you're not letting yourself be overworked?" For it was the conviction of both ladies that, under the iron despotism of his senior partners, the young man's life was spent in the most exhausting professional labours—and he had never thought it necessary to undeceive them.

The next two or three days dragged by heavily. The taste of the usual was like cinders in his mouth, and there were moments when he felt as if he were being buried alive under his future. He heard nothing of the Countess Olenska, or of the perfect little house, and though he met Beaufort at the club they merely nodded at each other across the whist-tables. It was not till the fourth evening that he found a note awaiting him on his return home. "Come late tomorrow: I must explain to you. Ellen." These were the only words it contained.

The young man, who was dining out, thrust the note into his pocket, smiling a little at the Frenchness of the "to you." After dinner he went to a play; and it was not until his return home, after midnight, that he drew Madame Olenska's missive out again and re-read it slowly a number of times. There were several ways of answering it, and he gave considerable thought to each one during the watches of an agitated night. That on which, when morning came, he finally decided was to pitch some clothes into a portmanteau and jump on board a boat that was leaving that very afternoon for St. Augustine.

## XVI.

When Archer walked down the sandy main street of St. Augustine to the house which had been pointed out to him as Mr. Welland's, and saw May Welland standing under a magnolia with the sun in her hair, he wondered why he had waited so long to come.

Here was the truth, here was reality, here was the life that belonged to him; and he, who fancied himself so scornful of arbitrary restraints, had been afraid to break away from his desk because of what people might think of his stealing a holiday!

Her first exclamation was: "Newland—has anything happened?" and it occurred to him that it would have been more "feminine" if she had instantly read in his eyes why he had come. But when he answered: "Yes—I found I had to see you," her happy blushes took the chill from her surprise, and he saw how easily he would be forgiven, and how soon even Mr. Letterblair's mild disapproval would be smiled away by a tolerant family.

Early as it was, the main street was no place for any but formal greetings, and Archer longed to be alone with May, and to pour out all his tenderness and his impatience. It still lacked an hour to the late Welland breakfast-time, and instead of asking him to come in she proposed that they should walk out to an old orange-garden beyond the town. She had just been for a row on the river, and the sun that netted the little waves with gold seemed to have caught her in its meshes. Across the warm brown of her cheek her blown hair glittered like silver wire; and her eyes too looked lighter, almost pale in their youthful limpidity. As she walked beside Archer with her long swinging gait her face wore the vacant serenity of a young marble athlete.

To Archer's strained nerves the vision was as soothing as the sight of the blue sky and the lazy river. They sat down on a bench under the orange-trees and he put his arm about her and kissed her. It was like drinking at a cold spring with the sun on it; but his pressure may have been more vehement than he had intended, for the blood rose to her face and she drew back as if he had startled her.

"What is it?" he asked, smiling; and she looked at him with surprise, and answered: "Nothing."

A slight embarrassment fell on them, and her hand slipped out of his. It was the only time that he had kissed her on the lips except for their fugitive embrace in the Beaufort conservatory, and he saw that she was disturbed, and shaken out of her cool boyish composure.

"Tell me what you do all day," he said, crossing his arms under his tilted-back head, and pushing his hat forward to screen the sun-dazzle. To let her talk about familiar and simple things was the easiest way of carrying on his own independent train of thought; and he sat listening to her simple chronicle of swimming, sailing and riding, varied by an occasional dance at the primitive inn when a man-of-war came in. A few pleasant people from Philadelphia and Baltimore were picknicking at the inn, and the Selfridge Merrys had come down for three weeks because Kate Merry had had bronchitis. They were planning to lay out a lawn tennis court on the sands; but no one but Kate and May had racquets, and most of the people had not even heard of the game.

All this kept her very busy, and she had not had time to do more than look at the little vellum book that Archer had sent her the week before (the "Sonnets from the Portuguese"); but she was learning by heart "How they brought the Good News from Ghent to Aix," because it was one of the first things he had ever read to her; and it amused her to be able to tell him that Kate Merry had never even heard of a poet called Robert Browning.

Presently she started up, exclaiming that they would be late for breakfast; and they hurried back to the tumble-down house with its pointless porch and unpruned hedge of plumbago and pink geraniums where the Wellands were installed for the winter. Mr. Welland's sensitive domesticity shrank from the discomforts of the slovenly southern hotel, and at immense expense, and in face of almost insuperable difficulties, Mrs. Welland was obliged, year after year, to improvise an establishment partly made up of discontented New York servants and partly drawn from the local African supply.

"The doctors want my husband to feel that he is in his own home; otherwise he would be so wretched that the climate would not do him any good," she explained, winter after winter, to the sympathising Philadelphians and Baltimoreans; and Mr. Welland, beaming across a breakfast table miraculously supplied with the most varied delicacies, was presently saying to Archer: "You see, my dear fellow, we camp—we literally camp. I tell my wife and May that I want to teach them how to rough it."

Mr. and Mrs. Welland had been as much surprised as their daughter by the young man's sudden arrival; but it had occurred to him to explain that he had felt himself on the verge of a nasty cold, and this seemed to Mr. Welland an all-sufficient reason for abandoning any duty.

"You can't be too careful, especially toward spring," he said, heaping his plate with straw-coloured griddle-cakes and drowning them in golden syrup. "If I'd only been as prudent at your age May would have been dancing at the Assemblies now, instead of spending her winters in a wilderness with an old invalid."

"Oh, but I love it here, Papa; you know I do. If only Newland could stay I should like it a thousand times better than New York."

"Newland must stay till he has quite thrown off his cold," said Mrs. Welland indulgently; and the young man laughed, and said he supposed there was such a thing as one's profession.

He managed, however, after an exchange of telegrams with the firm, to make his cold last a week; and it shed an ironic light on the situation to know that Mr. Letterblair's indulgence was partly due to the satisfactory way in which his brilliant young junior partner had settled the troublesome matter of the Olenski divorce. Mr. Letterblair had let Mrs. Welland know that Mr. Archer had "rendered an invaluable service" to the whole family, and that old Mrs. Manson Mingott had been particularly pleased; and one day when May had gone for a drive with her father in the only vehicle the place produced

Mrs. Welland took occasion to touch on a topic which she always avoided in her daughter's presence.

"I'm afraid Ellen's ideas are not at all like ours. She was barely eighteen when Medora Manson took her back to Europe—you remember the excitement when she appeared in black at her coming-out ball? Another of Medora's fads—really this time it was almost prophetic! That must have been at least twelve years ago; and since then Ellen has never been to America. No wonder she is completely Europeanised."

"But European society is not given to divorce: Countess Olenska thought she would be conforming to American ideas in asking for her freedom." It was the first time that the young man had pronounced her name since he had left Skuytercliff, and he felt the colour rise to his cheek.

Mrs. Welland smiled compassionately. "That is just like the extraordinary things that foreigners invent about us. They think we dine at two o'clock and countenance divorce! That is why it seems to me so foolish to entertain them when they come to New York. They accept our hospitality, and then they go home and repeat the same stupid stories."

Archer made no comment on this, and Mrs. Welland continued: "But we do most thoroughly appreciate your persuading Ellen to give up the idea. Her grandmother and her uncle Lovell could do nothing with her; both of them have written that her changing her mind was entirely due to your influence—in fact she said so to her grandmother. She has an unbounded admiration for you. Poor Ellen—she was always a wayward child. I wonder what her fate will be?"

"What we've all contrived to make it," he felt like answering. "If you'd all of you rather she should be Beaufort's mistress than some decent fellow's wife you've certainly gone the right way about it."

He wondered what Mrs. Welland would have said if he had uttered the words instead of merely thinking them. He could picture the sudden decomposure of her firm placid features, to which a lifelong mastery over trifles had given an air of factitious authority. Traces still lingered on them of a fresh beauty like her daughter's; and he asked himself if May's face was doomed to thicken into the same middle-aged image of invincible innocence.

Ah, no, he did not want May to have that kind of innocence, the innocence that seals the mind against imagination and the heart against experience!

"I verily believe," Mrs. Welland continued, "that if the horrible business had come out in the newspapers it would have been my husband's death-blow. I don't know any of the details; I only ask not to, as I told poor Ellen when she tried to talk to me about it. Having an invalid to care for, I have to keep my mind bright and happy. But Mr. Welland was terribly upset; he had a slight temperature every morning while we were waiting to hear what had been decided. It was the horror of his girl's learning that such things were possible—but of course, dear Newland, you felt that too. We all knew that you were thinking of May."

"I'm always thinking of May," the young man rejoined, rising to cut short the conversation.

He had meant to seize the opportunity of his private talk with Mrs. Welland to urge her to advance the date of his marriage. But he could think of no arguments that would move her, and with a sense of relief he saw Mr. Welland and May driving up to the door.

His only hope was to plead again with May, and on the day before his departure he walked with her to the ruinous garden of the Spanish Mission. The background lent itself to allusions to European scenes; and May, who was looking her loveliest under a wide-brimmed hat that cast a shadow of mystery over her too-clear eyes, kindled into eagerness as he spoke of Granada and the Alhambra.

"We might be seeing it all this spring—even the Easter ceremonies at Seville," he urged, exaggerating his demands in the hope of a larger concession.

"Easter in Seville? And it will be Lent next week!" she laughed.

"Why shouldn't we be married in Lent?" he rejoined; but she looked so shocked that he saw his mistake.

"Of course I didn't mean that, dearest; but soon after Easter—so that we could sail at the end of April. I know I could arrange it at the office."

She smiled dreamily upon the possibility; but he perceived that to dream of it sufficed her. It was like hearing him read aloud out of his poetry books the beautiful things that could not possibly happen in real life.

"Oh, do go on, Newland; I do love your descriptions."

"But why should they be only descriptions? Why shouldn't we make them real?"

"We shall, dearest, of course; next year." Her voice lingered over it.

"Don't you want them to be real sooner? Can't I persuade you to break away now?"

She bowed her head, vanishing from him under her conniving hat-brim.

"Why should we dream away another year? Look at me, dear! Don't you understand how I want you for my wife?"

For a moment she remained motionless; then she raised on him eyes of such despairing dearness that he half-released her waist from his hold. But suddenly her look changed and deepened inscrutably. "I'm not sure if I *do* understand," she said. "Is it—is it because you're not certain of continuing to care for me?"

Archer sprang up from his seat. "My God—perhaps—I don't know," he broke out angrily.

May Welland rose also; as they faced each other she seemed to grow in womanly stature and dignity. Both were silent for a moment, as if dismayed by the unforeseen trend of their words: then she said in a low voice: "If that is it—is there some one else?"

"Some one else—between you and me?" He echoed her words slowly, as though they were only half-intelligible and he wanted time to repeat the question to himself. She seemed to catch the uncertainty of his voice, for she went on in a deepening tone: "Let us talk frankly, Newland. Sometimes I've felt a difference in you; especially since our engagement has been announced."

"Dear—what madness!" he recovered himself to exclaim.

She met his protest with a faint smile. "If it is, it won't hurt us to talk about it." She paused, and added, lifting her head with one of her noble movements: "Or even if it's true: why shouldn't we speak of it? You might so easily have made a mistake."

He lowered his head, staring at the black leaf-pattern on the sunny path at their feet. "Mistakes are always easy to make; but if I had made one of the kind you suggest, is it likely that I should be imploring you to hasten our marriage?"

She looked downward too, disturbing the pattern with the point of her sunshade while she struggled for expression. "Yes," she said at length. "You might want—once for all—to settle the question: it's one way."

Her quiet lucidity startled him, but did not mislead him into thinking her insensible. Under her hat-brim he saw the pallor of her profile, and a slight tremor of the nostril above her resolutely steadied lips.

"Well—?" he questioned, sitting down on the bench, and looking up at her with a frown that he tried to make playful.

She dropped back into her seat and went on: "You mustn't think that a girl knows as little as her parents imagine. One hears and one notices—one has one's feelings and ideas. And of course, long before you told me that you cared for me, I'd known that there was some one else you were interested in; every one was talking about it two years ago at Newport. And once I saw you sitting together on the verandah at a dance—and when she came back into the house her face was sad, and I felt sorry for her; I remembered it afterward, when we were engaged."

Her voice had sunk almost to a whisper, and she sat clasping and unclasping her hands about the handle of her sunshade. The young man laid his upon them with a gentle pressure; his heart dilated with an inexpressible relief.

"My dear child—was *that* it? If you only knew the truth!"

She raised her head quickly. "Then there is a truth I don't know?"

He kept his hand over hers. "I meant, the truth about the old story you speak of."

"But that's what I want to know, Newland—what I ought to know. I couldn't have my happiness made out of a wrong—an unfairness—to somebody else. And I want to believe that it would be the same with you. What sort of a life could we build on such foundations?"

Her face had taken on a look of such tragic courage that he felt like bowing himself down at her feet. "I've wanted to say this for a long time," she went on. "I've wanted to tell you that, when two people really love each other, I understand that there may be situations which make it right that they should—should go against public opinion. And if you feel yourself in any way pledged ... pledged to the person we've spoken of ... and if there is any way ... any way in which you can fulfill your pledge ... even by her getting a divorce ... Newland, don't give her up because of me!"

His surprise at discovering that her fears had fastened upon an episode so remote and so completely of the past as his love-affair with Mrs. Thorley Rushworth gave way to wonder at the generosity of her view. There was something superhuman in an attitude so recklessly unorthodox, and if other problems had not pressed on him he would have been lost in wonder at the prodigy of the Wellands' daughter urging him to marry his former mistress. But he was still dizzy with the glimpse of the precipice they had skirted, and full of a new awe at the mystery of young-girlhood.

For a moment he could not speak; then he said: "There is no pledge—no obligation whatever—of the kind you think. Such cases don't always—present themselves quite as simply as ... But that's no matter ... I love your generosity, because I feel as you do about those things ... I feel that each case must be judged individually, on its own merits ... irrespective of stupid conventionalities ... I mean, each woman's right to her liberty —" He pulled himself up, startled by the turn his thoughts had taken, and went on, looking at her with a smile: "Since you understand so many things, dearest, can't you go a little farther, and understand the uselessness of our submitting to another form of the same foolish conventionalities? If there's no one and nothing between us, isn't that an argument for marrying quickly, rather than for more delay?"

She flushed with joy and lifted her face to his; as he bent to it he saw that her eyes were full of happy tears. But in another moment she seemed to have descended from her womanly eminence to helpless and timorous girlhood; and he understood that her courage and initiative were all for others, and that she had none for herself. It was evident that the effort of speaking had been much greater than her studied composure betrayed, and that at his first word of reassurance she had dropped back into the usual, as a too-adventurous child takes refuge in its mother's arms.

Archer had no heart to go on pleading with her; he was too much disappointed at the vanishing of the new being who had cast that one deep look at him from her transparent eyes. May seemed to be aware of his disappointment, but without knowing how to alleviate it; and they stood up and walked silently home.

## XVII.

"Your cousin the Countess called on mother while you were away," Janey Archer announced to her brother on the evening of his return.

The young man, who was dining alone with his mother and sister, glanced up in surprise and saw Mrs. Archer's gaze demurely bent on her plate. Mrs.

Archer did not regard her seclusion from the world as a reason for being forgotten by it; and Newland guessed that she was slightly annoyed that he should be surprised by Madame Olenska's visit.

"She had on a black velvet polonaise with jet buttons, and a tiny green monkey muff; I never saw her so stylishly dressed," Janey continued. "She came alone, early on Sunday afternoon; luckily the fire was lit in the drawing-room. She had one of those new card-cases. She said she wanted to know us because you'd been so good to her."

Newland laughed. "Madame Olenska always takes that tone about her friends. She's very happy at being among her own people again."

"Yes, so she told us," said Mrs. Archer. "I must say she seems thankful to be here."

"I hope you liked her, mother."

Mrs. Archer drew her lips together. "She certainly lays herself out to please, even when she is calling on an old lady."

"Mother doesn't think her simple," Janey interjected, her eyes screwed upon her brother's face.

"It's just my old-fashioned feeling; dear May is my ideal," said Mrs. Archer.

"Ah," said her son, "they're not alike."

Archer had left St. Augustine charged with many messages for old Mrs. Mingott; and a day or two after his return to town he called on her.

The old lady received him with unusual warmth; she was grateful to him for persuading the Countess Olenska to give up the idea of a divorce; and when he told her that he had deserted the office without leave, and rushed down to St. Augustine simply because he wanted to see May, she gave an adipose chuckle and patted his knee with her puff-ball hand.

"Ah, ah—so you kicked over the traces, did you? And I suppose Augusta and Welland pulled long faces, and behaved as if the end of the world had come? But little May—she knew better, I'll be bound?"

"I hoped she did; but after all she wouldn't agree to what I'd gone down to ask for."

"Wouldn't she indeed? And what was that?"

"I wanted to get her to promise that we should be married in April. What's the use of our wasting another year?"

Mrs. Manson Mingott screwed up her little mouth into a grimace of mimic prudery and twinkled at him through malicious lids. "'Ask Mamma,' I suppose—the usual story. Ah, these Mingotts—all alike! Born in a rut, and you can't root 'em out of it. When I built this house you'd have thought I was moving to California! Nobody ever *had* built above Fortieth Street—no, says I, nor above the Battery either, before Christopher Columbus discovered America. No, no; not one of them wants to be different; they're as scared of it as the small-pox. Ah, my dear Mr. Archer, I thank my stars I'm nothing but a vulgar Spicer; but there's not one of my own children that takes after me but my little Ellen." She broke off, still twinkling at him, and asked, with the casual irrelevance of old age: "Now, why in the world didn't you marry my little Ellen?"

Archer laughed. "For one thing, she wasn't there to be married."

"No—to be sure; more's the pity. And now it's too late; her life is finished." She spoke with the cold-blooded complacency of the aged throwing earth into the grave of young hopes. The young man's heart grew chill, and he said hurriedly: "Can't I persuade you to use your influence with the Wellands, Mrs. Mingott? I wasn't made for long engagements."

Old Catherine beamed on him approvingly. "No; I can see that. You've got a quick eye. When you were a little boy I've no doubt you liked to be helped first." She threw back her head with a laugh that made her chins ripple like little waves. "Ah, here's my Ellen now!" she exclaimed, as the portieres parted behind her.

Madame Olenska came forward with a smile. Her face looked vivid and happy, and she held out her hand gaily to Archer while she stooped to her grandmother's kiss.

"I was just saying to him, my dear: 'Now, why didn't you marry my little Ellen?'"

Madame Olenska looked at Archer, still smiling. "And what did he answer?"

"Oh, my darling, I leave you to find that out! He's been down to Florida to see his sweetheart."

"Yes, I know." She still looked at him. "I went to see your mother, to ask where you'd gone. I sent a note that you never answered, and I was afraid you were ill."

He muttered something about leaving unexpectedly, in a great hurry, and having intended to write to her from St. Augustine.

"And of course once you were there you never thought of me again!" She continued to beam on him with a gaiety that might have been a studied assumption of indifference.

"If she still needs me, she's determined not to let me see it," he thought, stung by her manner. He wanted to thank her for having been to see his mother, but under the ancestress's malicious eye he felt himself tongue-tied and constrained.

"Look at him—in such hot haste to get married that he took French leave and rushed down to implore the silly girl on his knees! That's something like a lover—that's the way handsome Bob Spicer carried off my poor mother; and then got tired of her before I was weaned—though they only had to wait eight months for me! But there—you're not a Spicer, young man; luckily for you and for May. It's only my poor Ellen that has kept any of their wicked blood; the rest of them are all model Mingotts," cried the old lady scornfully.

Archer was aware that Madame Olenska, who had seated herself at her grandmother's side, was still thoughtfully scrutinising him. The gaiety had faded from her eyes, and she said with great gentleness: "Surely, Granny, we can persuade them between us to do as he wishes."

Archer rose to go, and as his hand met Madame Olenska's he felt that she was waiting for him to make some allusion to her unanswered letter.

"When can I see you?" he asked, as she walked with him to the door of the room.

"Whenever you like; but it must be soon if you want to see the little house again. I am moving next week."

A pang shot through him at the memory of his lamplit hours in the low-studded drawing-room. Few as they had been, they were thick with memories.

"Tomorrow evening?"

She nodded. "Tomorrow; yes; but early. I'm going out."

The next day was a Sunday, and if she were "going out" on a Sunday evening it could, of course, be only to Mrs. Lemuel Struthers's. He felt a slight movement of annoyance, not so much at her going there (for he rather liked her going where she pleased in spite of the van der Luydens), but because it was the kind of house at which she was sure to meet Beaufort, where she must have known beforehand that she would meet him—and where she was probably going for that purpose.

"Very well; tomorrow evening," he repeated, inwardly resolved that he would not go early, and that by reaching her door late he would either prevent her from going to Mrs. Struthers's, or else arrive after she had started—which, all things considered, would no doubt be the simplest solution.

It was only half-past eight, after all, when he rang the bell under the wisteria; not as late as he had intended by half an hour—but a singular restlessness had driven him to her door. He reflected, however, that Mrs. Struthers's Sunday evenings were not like a ball, and that her guests, as if to minimise their delinquency, usually went early.

The one thing he had not counted on, in entering Madame Olenska's hall, was to find hats and overcoats there. Why had she bidden him to come early if she was having people to dine? On a closer inspection of the garments besides which Nastasia was laying his own, his resentment gave way to curiosity. The overcoats were in fact the very strangest he had ever seen under a polite roof; and it took but a glance to assure himself that neither of them belonged to Julius Beaufort. One was a shaggy yellow ulster of "reach-me-down" cut, the other a very old and rusty cloak with a cape—something like what the French called a "Macfarlane." This garment, which appeared to be made for a person of prodigious size, had evidently seen long and hard wear, and its greenish-black folds gave out a moist sawdusty smell suggestive of prolonged sessions against bar-room walls. On it lay a ragged grey scarf and an odd felt hat of semiclerical shape.

Archer raised his eyebrows enquiringly at Nastasia, who raised hers in return with a fatalistic "Gia!" as she threw open the drawing-room door.

The young man saw at once that his hostess was not in the room; then, with surprise, he discovered another lady standing by the fire. This lady, who was long, lean and loosely put together, was clad in raiment intricately looped and fringed, with plaids and stripes and bands of plain colour disposed in a design to which the clue seemed missing. Her hair, which had tried to turn white and only succeeded in fading, was surmounted by a Spanish comb and black lace scarf, and silk mittens, visibly darned, covered her rheumatic hands.

Beside her, in a cloud of cigar-smoke, stood the owners of the two overcoats, both in morning clothes that they had evidently not taken off since morning. In one of the two, Archer, to his surprise, recognised Ned Winsett;

the other and older, who was unknown to him, and whose gigantic frame declared him to be the wearer of the "Macfarlane," had a feebly leonine head with crumpled grey hair, and moved his arms with large pawing gestures, as though he were distributing lay blessings to a kneeling multitude.

These three persons stood together on the hearth-rug, their eyes fixed on an extraordinarily large bouquet of crimson roses, with a knot of purple pansies at their base, that lay on the sofa where Madame Olenska usually sat.

"What they must have cost at this season—though of course it's the sentiment one cares about!" the lady was saying in a sighing staccato as Archer came in.

The three turned with surprise at his appearance, and the lady, advancing, held out her hand.

"Dear Mr. Archer—almost my cousin Newland!" she said. "I am the Marchioness Manson."

Archer bowed, and she continued: "My Ellen has taken me in for a few days. I came from Cuba, where I have been spending the winter with Spanish friends—such delightful distinguished people: the highest nobility of old Castile—how I wish you could know them! But I was called away by our dear great friend here, Dr. Carver. You don't know Dr. Agathon Carver, founder of the Valley of Love Community?"

Dr. Carver inclined his leonine head, and the Marchioness continued: "Ah, New York—New York—how little the life of the spirit has reached it! But I see you do know Mr. Winsett."

"Oh, yes—I reached him some time ago; but not by that route," Winsett said with his dry smile.

The Marchioness shook her head reprovingly. "How do you know, Mr. Winsett? The spirit bloweth where it listeth."

"List—oh, list!" interjected Dr. Carver in a stentorian murmur.

"But do sit down, Mr. Archer. We four have been having a delightful little dinner together, and my child has gone up to dress. She expects you; she will be down in a moment. We were just admiring these marvellous flowers, which will surprise her when she reappears."

Winsett remained on his feet. "I'm afraid I must be off. Please tell Madame Olenska that we shall all feel lost when she abandons our street. This house has been an oasis."

"Ah, but she won't abandon *you*. Poetry and art are the breath of life to her. It *is* poetry you write, Mr. Winsett?"

"Well, no; but I sometimes read it," said Winsett, including the group in a general nod and slipping out of the room.

"A caustic spirit—un peu sauvage. But so witty; Dr. Carver, you DO think him witty?"

"I never think of wit," said Dr. Carver severely.

"Ah—ah—you never think of wit! How merciless he is to us weak mortals, Mr. Archer! But he lives only in the life of the spirit; and tonight he is mentally preparing the lecture he is to deliver presently at Mrs. Blenker's. Dr. Carver, would there be time, before you start for the Blenkers' to explain to Mr. Archer your illuminating discovery of the Direct Contact? But no; I see it is nearly nine o'clock, and we have no right to detain you while so many are waiting for your message."

Dr. Carver looked slightly disappointed at this conclusion, but, having compared his ponderous gold time-piece with Madame Olenska's little travelling-clock, he reluctantly gathered up his mighty limbs for departure.

"I shall see you later, dear friend?" he suggested to the Marchioness, who replied with a smile: "As soon as Ellen's carriage comes I will join you; I do hope the lecture won't have begun."

Dr. Carver looked thoughtfully at Archer. "Perhaps, if this young gentleman is interested in my experiences, Mrs. Blenker might allow you to bring him with you?"

"Oh, dear friend, if it were possible—I am sure she would be too happy. But I fear my Ellen counts on Mr. Archer herself."

"That," said Dr. Carver, "is unfortunate—but here is my card." He handed it to Archer, who read on it, in Gothic characters:

Agathon Carver
The Valley of Love
Kittasquattamy, N. Y.

Dr. Carver bowed himself out, and Mrs. Manson, with a sigh that might have been either of regret or relief, again waved Archer to a seat.

"Ellen will be down in a moment; and before she comes, I am so glad of this quiet moment with you."

Archer murmured his pleasure at their meeting, and the Marchioness continued, in her low sighing accents: "I know everything, dear Mr. Archer—my child has told me all you have done for her. Your wise advice: your courageous firmness—thank heaven it was not too late!"

The young man listened with considerable embarrassment. Was there any one, he wondered, to whom Madame Olenska had not proclaimed his intervention in her private affairs?

"Madame Olenska exaggerates; I simply gave her a legal opinion, as she asked me to."

"Ah, but in doing it—in doing it you were the unconscious instrument of—of—what word have we moderns for Providence, Mr. Archer?" cried the lady, tilting her head on one side and drooping her lids mysteriously. "Little did you know that at that very moment I was being appealed to: being approached, in fact—from the other side of the Atlantic!"

She glanced over her shoulder, as though fearful of being overheard, and then, drawing her chair nearer, and raising a tiny ivory fan to her lips, breathed behind it: "By the Count himself—my poor, mad, foolish Olenski; who asks only to take her back on her own terms."

"Good God!" Archer exclaimed, springing up.

"You are horrified? Yes, of course; I understand. I don't defend poor Stanislas, though he has always called me his best friend. He does not defend himself—he casts himself at her feet: in my person." She tapped her emaciated bosom. "I have his letter here."

"A letter?—Has Madame Olenska seen it?" Archer stammered, his brain whirling with the shock of the announcement.

The Marchioness Manson shook her head softly. "Time—time; I must have time. I know my Ellen—haughty, intractable; shall I say, just a shade unforgiving?"

"But, good heavens, to forgive is one thing; to go back into that hell —"

"Ah, yes," the Marchioness acquiesced. "So she describes it—my sensitive child! But on the material side, Mr. Archer, if one may stoop to consider such things; do you know what she is giving up? Those roses there on the sofa—acres like them, under glass and in the open, in his matchless terraced gardens at Nice! Jewels—historic pearls: the Sobieski emeralds—sables,—but she cares nothing for all these! Art and beauty, those she does care for, she lives for, as I always have; and those also surrounded her. Pictures, priceless furniture, music, brilliant conversation—ah, that, my dear young man, if you'll excuse me, is what you've no conception of here! And she had it all; and the homage of the greatest. She tells me she is not thought handsome in New York—good heavens! Her portrait has been painted nine times; the greatest artists in Europe have begged for the privilege. Are these things nothing? And the remorse of an adoring husband?"

As the Marchioness Manson rose to her climax her face assumed an expression of ecstatic retrospection which would have moved Archer's mirth had he not been numb with amazement.

He would have laughed if any one had foretold to him that his first sight of poor Medora Manson would have been in the guise of a messenger of Satan; but he was in no mood for laughing now, and she seemed to him to come straight out of the hell from which Ellen Olenska had just escaped.

"She knows nothing yet—of all this?" he asked abruptly.

Mrs. Manson laid a purple finger on her lips. "Nothing directly—but does she suspect? Who can tell? The truth is, Mr. Archer, I have been waiting to see you. From the moment I heard of the firm stand you had taken, and of your influence over her, I hoped it might be possible to count on your support—to convince you ..."

"That she ought to go back? I would rather see her dead!" cried the young man violently.

"Ah," the Marchioness murmured, without visible resentment. For a while she sat in her arm-chair, opening and shutting the absurd ivory fan between her mittened fingers; but suddenly she lifted her head and listened.

"Here she comes," she said in a rapid whisper; and then, pointing to the bouquet on the sofa: "Am I to understand that you prefer *that*, Mr. Archer? After all, marriage is marriage ... and my niece is still a wife..."

## XVIII.

"What are you two plotting together, aunt Medora?" Madame Olenska cried as she came into the room.

She was dressed as if for a ball. Everything about her shimmered and glimmered softly, as if her dress had been woven out of candle-beams; and she carried her head high, like a pretty woman challenging a roomful of rivals.

"We were saying, my dear, that here was something beautiful to surprise you with," Mrs. Manson rejoined, rising to her feet and pointing archly to the flowers.

Madame Olenska stopped short and looked at the bouquet. Her colour did not change, but a sort of white radiance of anger ran over her like summer lightning. "Ah," she exclaimed, in a shrill voice that the young man had never heard, "who is ridiculous enough to send me a bouquet? Why a bouquet? And why tonight of all nights? I am not going to a ball; I am not a girl engaged to be married. But some people are always ridiculous."

She turned back to the door, opened it, and called out: "Nastasia!"

The ubiquitous handmaiden promptly appeared, and Archer heard Madame Olenska say, in an Italian that she seemed to pronounce with intentional deliberateness in order that he might follow it: "Here—throw this into the dustbin!" and then, as Nastasia stared protestingly: "But no—it's not the fault of the poor flowers. Tell the boy to carry them to the house three doors away, the house of Mr. Winsett, the dark gentleman who dined here. His wife is ill—they may give her pleasure ... The boy is out, you say? Then, my dear one, run yourself; here, put my cloak over you and fly. I want the thing out of the house immediately! And, as you live, don't say they come from me!"

She flung her velvet opera cloak over the maid's shoulders and turned back into the drawing-room, shutting the door sharply. Her bosom was rising high under its lace, and for a moment Archer thought she was about to cry; but she burst into a laugh instead, and looking from the Marchioness to Archer, asked abruptly: "And you two—have you made friends!"

"It's for Mr. Archer to say, darling; he has waited patiently while you were dressing."

"Yes—I gave you time enough: my hair wouldn't go," Madame Olenska said, raising her hand to the heaped-up curls of her chignon. "But that reminds me: I see Dr. Carver is gone, and you'll be late at the Blenkers'. Mr. Archer, will you put my aunt in the carriage?"

She followed the Marchioness into the hall, saw her fitted into a miscellaneous heap of overshoes, shawls and tippets, and called from the doorstep: "Mind, the carriage is to be back for me at ten!" Then she returned to the drawing-room, where Archer, on re-entering it, found her standing by the mantelpiece, examining herself in the mirror. It was not usual, in New

York society, for a lady to address her parlour-maid as "my dear one," and send her out on an errand wrapped in her own opera-cloak; and Archer, through all his deeper feelings, tasted the pleasurable excitement of being in a world where action followed on emotion with such Olympian speed.

Madame Olenska did not move when he came up behind her, and for a second their eyes met in the mirror; then she turned, threw herself into her sofa-corner, and sighed out: "There's time for a cigarette."

He handed her the box and lit a spill for her; and as the flame flashed up into her face she glanced at him with laughing eyes and said: "What do you think of me in a temper?"

Archer paused a moment; then he answered with sudden resolution: "It makes me understand what your aunt has been saying about you."

"I knew she'd been talking about me. Well?"

"She said you were used to all kinds of things—splendours and amusements and excitements—that we could never hope to give you here."

Madame Olenska smiled faintly into the circle of smoke about her lips.

"Medora is incorrigibly romantic. It has made up to her for so many things!"

Archer hesitated again, and again took his risk. "Is your aunt's romanticism always consistent with accuracy?"

"You mean: does she speak the truth?" Her niece considered. "Well, I'll tell you: in almost everything she says, there's something true and something untrue. But why do you ask? What has she been telling you?"

He looked away into the fire, and then back at her shining presence. His heart tightened with the thought that this was their last evening by that fireside, and that in a moment the carriage would come to carry her away.

"She says—she pretends that Count Olenski has asked her to persuade you to go back to him."

Madame Olenska made no answer. She sat motionless, holding her cigarette in her half-lifted hand. The expression of her face had not changed; and Archer remembered that he had before noticed her apparent incapacity for surprise.

"You knew, then?" he broke out.

She was silent for so long that the ash dropped from her cigarette. She brushed it to the floor. "She has hinted about a letter: poor darling! Medora's hints —"

"Is it at your husband's request that she has arrived here suddenly?"

Madame Olenska seemed to consider this question also. "There again: one can't tell. She told me she had had a 'spiritual summons,' whatever that is, from Dr. Carver. I'm afraid she's going to marry Dr. Carver ... poor Medora, there's always some one she wants to marry. But perhaps the people in Cuba just got tired of her! I think she was with them as a sort of paid companion. Really, I don't know why she came."

"But you do believe she has a letter from your husband?"

Again Madame Olenska brooded silently; then she said: "After all, it was to be expected."

The young man rose and went to lean against the fireplace. A sudden restlessness possessed him, and he was tongue-tied by the sense that their minutes were numbered, and that at any moment he might hear the wheels of the returning carriage.

"You know that your aunt believes you will go back?"

Madame Olenska raised her head quickly. A deep blush rose to her face and spread over her neck and shoulders. She blushed seldom and painfully, as if it hurt her like a burn.

"Many cruel things have been believed of me," she said.

"Oh, Ellen—forgive me; I'm a fool and a brute!"

She smiled a little. "You are horribly nervous; you have your own troubles. I know you think the Wellands are unreasonable about your marriage, and of course I agree with you. In Europe people don't understand our long American engagements; I suppose they are not as calm as we are." She pronounced the "we" with a faint emphasis that gave it an ironic sound.

Archer felt the irony but did not dare to take it up. After all, she had perhaps purposely deflected the conversation from her own affairs, and after the pain his last words had evidently caused her he felt that all he could do was to follow her lead. But the sense of the waning hour made him desperate: he could not bear the thought that a barrier of words should drop between them again.

"Yes," he said abruptly; "I went south to ask May to marry me after Easter. There's no reason why we shouldn't be married then."

"And May adores you—and yet you couldn't convince her? I thought her too intelligent to be the slave of such absurd superstitions."

"She IS too intelligent—she's not their slave."

Madame Olenska looked at him. "Well, then—I don't understand."

Archer reddened, and hurried on with a rush. "We had a frank talk—almost the first. She thinks my impatience a bad sign."

"Merciful heavens—a bad sign?"

"She thinks it means that I can't trust myself to go on caring for her. She thinks, in short, I want to marry her at once to get away from some one that I—care for more."

Madame Olenska examined this curiously. "But if she thinks that—why isn't she in a hurry too?"

"Because she's not like that: she's so much nobler. She insists all the more on the long engagement, to give me time —"

"Time to give her up for the other woman?"

"If I want to."

Madame Olenska leaned toward the fire and gazed into it with fixed eyes. Down the quiet street Archer heard the approaching trot of her horses.

"That *is* noble," she said, with a slight break in her voice.

"Yes. But it's ridiculous."

"Ridiculous? Because you don't care for any one else?"

"Because I don't mean to marry any one else."

"Ah." There was another long interval. At length she looked up at him and asked: "This other woman—does she love you?"

"Oh, there's no other woman; I mean, the person that May was thinking of is—was never —"

"Then, why, after all, are you in such haste?"

"There's your carriage," said Archer.

She half-rose and looked about her with absent eyes. Her fan and gloves lay on the sofa beside her and she picked them up mechanically.

"Yes; I suppose I must be going."

"You're going to Mrs. Struthers's?"

"Yes." She smiled and added: "I must go where I am invited, or I should be too lonely. Why not come with me?"

Archer felt that at any cost he must keep her beside him, must make her give him the rest of her evening. Ignoring her question, he continued to lean against the chimney-piece, his eyes fixed on the hand in which she held her gloves and fan, as if watching to see if he had the power to make her drop them.

"May guessed the truth," he said. "There is another woman—but not the one she thinks."

Ellen Olenska made no answer, and did not move. After a moment he sat down beside her, and, taking her hand, softly unclasped it, so that the gloves and fan fell on the sofa between them.

She started up, and freeing herself from him moved away to the other side of the hearth. "Ah, don't make love to me! Too many people have done that," she said, frowning.

Archer, changing colour, stood up also: it was the bitterest rebuke she could have given him. "I have never made love to you," he said, "and I never shall. But you are the woman I would have married if it had been possible for either of us."

"Possible for either of us?" She looked at him with unfeigned astonishment. "And you say that—when it's you who've made it impossible?"

He stared at her, groping in a blackness through which a single arrow of light tore its blinding way.

"*I've* made it impossible—?"

"You, you, *you*!" she cried, her lip trembling like a child's on the verge of tears. "Isn't it you who made me give up divorcing—give it up because you showed me how selfish and wicked it was, how one must sacrifice one's self to preserve the dignity of marriage ... and to spare one's family the publicity, the scandal? And because my family was going to be your family—for May's sake and for yours—I did what you told me, what you proved to me that I ought to do. Ah," she broke out with a sudden laugh, "I've made no secret of having done it for you!"

She sank down on the sofa again, crouching among the festive ripples of her dress like a stricken masquerader; and the young man stood by the fireplace and continued to gaze at her without moving.

"Good God," he groaned. "When I thought —"

"You thought?"

"Ah, don't ask me what I thought!"

Still looking at her, he saw the same burning flush creep up her neck to her face. She sat upright, facing him with a rigid dignity.

"I do ask you."

"Well, then: there were things in that letter you asked me to read —"

"My husband's letter?"

"Yes."

"I had nothing to fear from that letter: absolutely nothing! All I feared was to bring notoriety, scandal, on the family—on you and May."

"Good God," he groaned again, bowing his face in his hands.

The silence that followed lay on them with the weight of things final and irrevocable. It seemed to Archer to be crushing him down like his own grave-stone; in all the wide future he saw nothing that would ever lift that load from his heart. He did not move from his place, or raise his head from his hands; his hidden eyeballs went on staring into utter darkness.

"At least I loved you —" he brought out.

On the other side of the hearth, from the sofa-corner where he supposed that she still crouched, he heard a faint stifled crying like a child's. He started up and came to her side.

"Ellen! What madness! Why are you crying? Nothing's done that can't be undone. I'm still free, and you're going to be." He had her in his arms, her face like a wet flower at his lips, and all their vain terrors shrivelling up like ghosts at sunrise. The one thing that astonished him now was that he should have stood for five minutes arguing with her across the width of the room, when just touching her made everything so simple.

She gave him back all his kiss, but after a moment he felt her stiffening in his arms, and she put him aside and stood up.

"Ah, my poor Newland—I suppose this had to be. But it doesn't in the least alter things," she said, looking down at him in her turn from the hearth.

"It alters the whole of life for me."

"No, no—it mustn't, it can't. You're engaged to May Welland; and I'm married."

He stood up too, flushed and resolute. "Nonsense! It's too late for that sort of thing. We've no right to lie to other people or to ourselves. We won't talk of your marriage; but do you see me marrying May after this?"

She stood silent, resting her thin elbows on the mantelpiece, her profile reflected in the glass behind her. One of the locks of her chignon had become loosened and hung on her neck; she looked haggard and almost old.

"I don't see you," she said at length, "putting that question to May. Do you?"

He gave a reckless shrug. "It's too late to do anything else."

"You say that because it's the easiest thing to say at this moment—not because it's true. In reality it's too late to do anything but what we'd both decided on."

"Ah, I don't understand you!"

She forced a pitiful smile that pinched her face instead of smoothing it. "You don't understand because you haven't yet guessed how you've changed things for me: oh, from the first—long before I knew all you'd done."

"All I'd done?"

"Yes. I was perfectly unconscious at first that people here were shy of me—that they thought I was a dreadful sort of person. It seems they had even refused to meet me at dinner. I found that out afterward; and how you'd made your mother go with you to the van der Luydens'; and how you'd insisted on announcing your engagement at the Beaufort ball, so that I might have two families to stand by me instead of one —"

At that he broke into a laugh.

"Just imagine," she said, "how stupid and unobservant I was! I knew nothing of all this till Granny blurted it out one day. New York simply meant peace and freedom to me: it was coming home. And I was so happy at being among my own people that every one I met seemed kind and good, and glad to see me. But from the very beginning," she continued, "I felt there was no one as kind as you; no one who gave me reasons that I understood for doing what at first seemed so hard and—unnecessary. The very good people didn't convince me; I felt they'd never been tempted. But you knew; you understood; you had felt the world outside tugging at one with all its golden hands—and yet you hated the things it asks of one; you hated happiness bought by disloyalty and cruelty and indifference. That was what I'd never known before—and it's better than anything I've known."

She spoke in a low even voice, without tears or visible agitation; and each word, as it dropped from her, fell into his breast like burning lead. He sat bowed over, his head between his hands, staring at the hearthrug, and at the tip of the satin shoe that showed under her dress. Suddenly he knelt down and kissed the shoe.

She bent over him, laying her hands on his shoulders, and looking at him with eyes so deep that he remained motionless under her gaze.

"Ah, don't let us undo what you've done!" she cried. "I can't go back now to that other way of thinking. I can't love you unless I give you up."

His arms were yearning up to her; but she drew away, and they remained facing each other, divided by the distance that her words had created. Then, abruptly, his anger overflowed.

"And Beaufort? Is he to replace me?"

As the words sprang out he was prepared for an answering flare of anger; and he would have welcomed it as fuel for his own. But Madame Olenska only grew a shade paler, and stood with her arms hanging down before her, and her head slightly bent, as her way was when she pondered a question.

"He's waiting for you now at Mrs. Struthers's; why don't you go to him?" Archer sneered.

She turned to ring the bell. "I shall not go out this evening; tell the carriage to go and fetch the Signora Marchesa," she said when the maid came.

After the door had closed again Archer continued to look at her with bitter eyes. "Why this sacrifice? Since you tell me that you're lonely I've no right to keep you from your friends."

She smiled a little under her wet lashes. "I shan't be lonely now. I *was* lonely; I *was* afraid. But the emptiness and the darkness are gone; when I turn back into myself now I'm like a child going at night into a room where there's always a light."

Her tone and her look still enveloped her in a soft inaccessibility, and Archer groaned out again: "I don't understand you!"

"Yet you understand May!"

He reddened under the retort, but kept his eyes on her. "May is ready to give me up."

"What! Three days after you've entreated her on your knees to hasten your marriage?"

"She's refused; that gives me the right —"

"Ah, you've taught me what an ugly word that is," she said.

He turned away with a sense of utter weariness. He felt as though he had been struggling for hours up the face of a steep precipice, and now, just as he had fought his way to the top, his hold had given way and he was pitching down headlong into darkness.

If he could have got her in his arms again he might have swept away her arguments; but she still held him at a distance by something inscrutably aloof in her look and attitude, and by his own awed sense of her sincerity. At length he began to plead again.

"If we do this now it will be worse afterward—worse for every one —"

"No—no—no!" she almost screamed, as if he frightened her.

At that moment the bell sent a long tinkle through the house. They had heard no carriage stopping at the door, and they stood motionless, looking at each other with startled eyes.

Outside, Nastasia's step crossed the hall, the outer door opened, and a moment later she came in carrying a telegram which she handed to the Countess Olenska.

"The lady was very happy at the flowers," Nastasia said, smoothing her apron. "She thought it was her signor marito who had sent them, and she cried a little and said it was a folly."

Her mistress smiled and took the yellow envelope. She tore it open and carried it to the lamp; then, when the door had closed again, she handed the telegram to Archer.

It was dated from St. Augustine, and addressed to the Countess Olenska. In it he read: "Granny's telegram successful. Papa and Mamma agree marriage after Easter. Am telegraphing Newland. Am too happy for words and love you dearly. Your grateful May."

Half an hour later, when Archer unlocked his own front-door, he found a similar envelope on the hall-table on top of his pile of notes and letters. The message inside the envelope was also from May Welland, and ran as follows: "Parents consent wedding Tuesday after Easter at twelve Grace Church eight bridesmaids please see Rector so happy love May."

Archer crumpled up the yellow sheet as if the gesture could annihilate the news it contained. Then he pulled out a small pocket-diary and turned over the pages with trembling fingers; but he did not find what he wanted, and cramming the telegram into his pocket he mounted the stairs.

A light was shining through the door of the little hall-room which served Janey as a dressing-room and boudoir, and her brother rapped impatiently on the panel. The door opened, and his sister stood before him in her immemorial purple flannel dressing-gown, with her hair "on pins." Her face looked pale and apprehensive.

"Newland! I hope there's no bad news in that telegram? I waited on purpose, in case —" (No item of his correspondence was safe from Janey.)

He took no notice of her question. "Look here—what day is Easter this year?"

She looked shocked at such unchristian ignorance. "Easter? Newland! Why, of course, the first week in April. Why?"

"The first week?" He turned again to the pages of his diary, calculating rapidly under his breath. "The first week, did you say?" He threw back his head with a long laugh.

"For mercy's sake what's the matter?"

"Nothing's the matter, except that I'm going to be married in a month."

Janey fell upon his neck and pressed him to her purple flannel breast. "Oh Newland, how wonderful! I'm so glad! But, dearest, why do you keep on laughing? Do hush, or you'll wake Mamma."

# Book II

## XIX.

The day was fresh, with a lively spring wind full of dust. All the old ladies in both families had got out their faded sables and yellowing ermines, and the smell of camphor from the front pews almost smothered the faint spring scent of the lilies banking the altar.

Newland Archer, at a signal from the sexton, had come out of the vestry and placed himself with his best man on the chancel step of Grace Church.

The signal meant that the brougham bearing the bride and her father was in sight; but there was sure to be a considerable interval of adjustment and consultation in the lobby, where the bridesmaids were already hovering like a cluster of Easter blossoms. During this unavoidable lapse of time the bridegroom, in proof of his eagerness, was expected to expose himself alone to the gaze of the assembled company; and Archer had gone through this formality as resignedly as through all the others which made of a nineteenth century New York wedding a rite that seemed to belong to the dawn of history. Everything was equally easy—or equally painful, as one chose to put it—in the path he was committed to tread, and he had obeyed the flurried injunctions of his best man as piously as other bridegrooms had obeyed his own, in the days when he had guided them through the same labyrinth.

So far he was reasonably sure of having fulfilled all his obligations. The bridesmaids' eight bouquets of white lilac and lilies-of-the-valley had been sent in due time, as well as the gold and sapphire sleeve-links of the eight ushers and the best man's cat's-eye scarf-pin; Archer had sat up half the night trying to vary the wording of his thanks for the last batch of presents from men friends and ex-lady-loves; the fees for the Bishop and the Rector were safely in the pocket of his best man; his own luggage was already at Mrs. Manson Mingott's, where the wedding-breakfast was to take place, and so were the travelling clothes into which he was to change; and a private compartment had been engaged in the train that was to carry the young couple to their unknown destination—concealment of the spot in which the bridal night was to be spent being one of the most sacred taboos of the prehistoric ritual.

"Got the ring all right?" whispered young van der Luyden Newland, who was inexperienced in the duties of a best man, and awed by the weight of his responsibility.

Archer made the gesture which he had seen so many bridegrooms make: with his ungloved right hand he felt in the pocket of his dark grey waistcoat, and assured himself that the little gold circlet (engraved inside: Newland to May, April —-, 187-) was in its place; then, resuming his former attitude, his tall hat and pearl-grey gloves with black stitchings grasped in his left hand, he stood looking at the door of the church.

Overhead, Handel's March swelled pompously through the imitation stone vaulting, carrying on its waves the faded drift of the many weddings at which, with cheerful indifference, he had stood on the same chancel step watching other brides float up the nave toward other bridegrooms.

"How like a first night at the Opera!" he thought, recognising all the same faces in the same boxes (no, pews), and wondering if, when the Last Trump sounded, Mrs. Selfridge Merry would be there with the same towering ostrich feathers in her bonnet, and Mrs. Beaufort with the same diamond earrings and the same smile—and whether suitable proscenium seats were already prepared for them in another world.

After that there was still time to review, one by one, the familiar countenances in the first rows; the women's sharp with curiosity and excitement, the men's sulky with the obligation of having to put on their frock-coats before luncheon, and fight for food at the wedding-breakfast.

"Too bad the breakfast is at old Catherine's," the bridegroom could fancy Reggie Chivers saying. "But I'm told that Lovell Mingott insisted on its being cooked by his own chef, so it ought to be good if one can only get at it." And he could imagine Sillerton Jackson adding with authority: "My dear fellow, haven't you heard? It's to be served at small tables, in the new English fashion."

Archer's eyes lingered a moment on the left-hand pew, where his mother, who had entered the church on Mr. Henry van der Luyden's arm, sat weeping softly under her Chantilly veil, her hands in her grandmother's ermine muff.

"Poor Janey!" he thought, looking at his sister, "even by screwing her head around she can see only the people in the few front pews; and they're mostly dowdy Newlands and Dagonets."

On the hither side of the white ribbon dividing off the seats reserved for the families he saw Beaufort, tall and redfaced, scrutinising the women with his arrogant stare. Beside him sat his wife, all silvery chinchilla and violets; and on the far side of the ribbon, Lawrence Lefferts's sleekly brushed head seemed to mount guard over the invisible deity of "Good Form" who presided at the ceremony.

Archer wondered how many flaws Lefferts's keen eyes would discover in the ritual of his divinity; then he suddenly recalled that he too had once thought such questions important. The things that had filled his days seemed now like a nursery parody of life, or like the wrangles of mediaeval schoolmen over metaphysical terms that nobody had ever understood. A stormy discussion as to whether the wedding presents should be "shown" had darkened the last hours before the wedding; and it seemed inconceivable to Archer that grown-up people should work themselves into a state of agitation over such trifles, and that the matter should have been decided (in the negative) by Mrs. Welland's saying, with indignant tears: "I should as soon turn the reporters loose in my house." Yet there was a time when Archer had had definite and rather aggressive opinions on all such problems, and when everything concerning the manners and customs of his little tribe had seemed to him fraught with world-wide significance.

"And all the while, I suppose," he thought, "real people were living somewhere, and real things happening to them ..."

"*There they come!*" breathed the best man excitedly; but the bridegroom knew better.

The cautious opening of the door of the church meant only that Mr. Brown the livery-stable keeper (gowned in black in his intermittent character of sexton) was taking a preliminary survey of the scene before marshalling his forces. The door was softly shut again; then after another interval it swung majestically open, and a murmur ran through the church: "The family!"

Mrs. Welland came first, on the arm of her eldest son. Her large pink face was appropriately solemn, and her plum-coloured satin with pale blue side-panels, and blue ostrich plumes in a small satin bonnet, met with general approval; but before she had settled herself with a stately rustle in the pew opposite Mrs. Archer's the spectators were craning their necks to see who was coming after her. Wild rumours had been abroad the day before to the effect that Mrs. Manson Mingott, in spite of her physical disabilities, had resolved on being present at the ceremony; and the idea was so much in keeping with her sporting character that bets ran high at the clubs as to her being able to walk up the nave and squeeze into a seat. It was known that she had insisted on sending her own carpenter to look into the possibility of taking down the end panel of the front pew, and to measure the space between the seat and the front; but the result had been discouraging, and for one anxious day her family had watched her dallying with the plan of being wheeled up the nave in her enormous Bath chair and sitting enthroned in it at the foot of the chancel.

The idea of this monstrous exposure of her person was so painful to her relations that they could have covered with gold the ingenious person who suddenly discovered that the chair was too wide to pass between the iron uprights of the awning which extended from the church door to the curbstone. The idea of doing away with this awning, and revealing the bride to the mob of dressmakers and newspaper reporters who stood outside fighting to get near the joints of the canvas, exceeded even old Catherine's courage, though for a moment she had weighed the possibility. "Why, they might take a photograph of my child *and put it in the papers*!" Mrs. Welland exclaimed when her mother's last plan was hinted to her; and from this unthinkable indecency the clan recoiled with a collective shudder. The ancestress had had to give in; but her concession was bought only by the promise that the wedding-breakfast should take place under her roof, though (as the Washington Square connection said) with the Wellands' house in easy reach it was hard to have to make a special price with Brown to drive one to the other end of nowhere.

Though all these transactions had been widely reported by the Jacksons a sporting minority still clung to the belief that old Catherine would appear in church, and there was a distinct lowering of the temperature when she was found to have been replaced by her daughter-in-law. Mrs. Lovell Mingott had the high colour and glassy stare induced in ladies of her age and habit by the effort of getting into a new dress; but once the disappointment occasioned by her mother-in-law's non-appearance had subsided, it was agreed that her black Chantilly over lilac satin, with a bonnet of Parma violets, formed the happiest contrast to Mrs. Welland's blue and plum-colour. Far different was the impression produced by the gaunt and mincing lady who followed on Mr. Mingott's arm, in a wild dishevelment of stripes and fringes and floating scarves; and as this last apparition glided into view Archer's heart contracted and stopped beating.

He had taken it for granted that the Marchioness Manson was still in Washington, where she had gone some four weeks previously with her niece, Madame Olenska. It was generally understood that their abrupt departure was due to Madame Olenska's desire to remove her aunt from the baleful eloquence of Dr. Agathon Carver, who had nearly succeeded in enlisting her as a recruit for the Valley of Love; and in the circumstances no one had expected either of the ladies to return for the wedding. For a moment Archer stood with his eyes fixed on Medora's fantastic figure, straining to see who came behind her; but the little procession was at an end, for all the lesser members of the family had taken their seats, and the eight tall ushers, gathering themselves together like birds or insects preparing for some migratory manoeuvre, were already slipping through the side doors into the lobby.

"Newland—I say: *she's here!*" the best man whispered.

Archer roused himself with a start.

A long time had apparently passed since his heart had stopped beating, for the white and rosy procession was in fact half way up the nave, the Bishop, the Rector and two white-winged assistants were hovering about the flower-banked altar, and the first chords of the Spohr symphony were strewing their flower-like notes before the bride.

Archer opened his eyes (but could they really have been shut, as he imagined?), and felt his heart beginning to resume its usual task. The music, the scent of the lilies on the altar, the vision of the cloud of tulle and orange-blossoms floating nearer and nearer, the sight of Mrs. Archer's face suddenly convulsed with happy sobs, the low benedictory murmur of the Rector's voice, the ordered evolutions of the eight pink bridesmaids and the eight black ushers: all these sights, sounds and sensations, so familiar in themselves, so unutterably strange and meaningless in his new relation to them, were confusedly mingled in his brain.

"My God," he thought, "*have* I got the ring?"—and once more he went through the bridegroom's convulsive gesture.

Then, in a moment, May was beside him, such radiance streaming from her that it sent a faint warmth through his numbness, and he straightened himself and smiled into her eyes.

"Dearly beloved, we are gathered together here," the Rector began ...

The ring was on her hand, the Bishop's benediction had been given, the bridesmaids were a-poise to resume their place in the procession, and the organ was showing preliminary symptoms of breaking out into the Mendelssohn March, without which no newly-wedded couple had ever emerged upon New York.

"Your arm—I *Say, give her your arm!*" young Newland nervously hissed; and once more Archer became aware of having been adrift far off in the unknown. What was it that had sent him there, he wondered? Perhaps the glimpse, among the anonymous spectators in the transept, of a dark coil of hair under a hat which, a moment later, revealed itself as belonging to an unknown lady with a long nose, so laughably unlike the person whose image she had evoked that he asked himself if he were becoming subject to hallucinations.

And now he and his wife were pacing slowly down the nave, carried forward on the light Mendelssohn ripples, the spring day beckoning to them through widely opened doors, and Mrs. Welland's chestnuts, with big white favours on their frontlets, curvetting and showing off at the far end of the canvas tunnel.

The footman, who had a still bigger white favour on his lapel, wrapped May's white cloak about her, and Archer jumped into the brougham at her side. She turned to him with a triumphant smile and their hands clasped under her veil.

"Darling!" Archer said—and suddenly the same black abyss yawned before him and he felt himself sinking into it, deeper and deeper, while his voice rambled on smoothly and cheerfully: "Yes, of course I thought I'd lost the ring; no wedding would be complete if the poor devil of a bridegroom didn't go through that. But you *did* keep me waiting, you know! I had time to think of every horror that might possibly happen."

She surprised him by turning, in full Fifth Avenue, and flinging her arms about his neck. "But none ever *can* happen now, can it, Newland, as long as we two are together?"

Every detail of the day had been so carefully thought out that the young couple, after the wedding-breakfast, had ample time to put on their travelling-clothes, descend the wide Mingott stairs between laughing bridesmaids and weeping parents, and get into the brougham under the traditional shower of rice and satin slippers; and there was still half an hour left in which to drive to the station, buy the last weeklies at the bookstall with the air of seasoned travellers, and settle themselves in the reserved compartment in which May's maid had already placed her dove-coloured travelling cloak and glaringly new dressing-bag from London.

The old du Lac aunts at Rhinebeck had put their house at the disposal of the bridal couple, with a readiness inspired by the prospect of spending a week in New York with Mrs. Archer; and Archer, glad to escape the usual "bridal suite" in a Philadelphia or Baltimore hotel, had accepted with an equal alacrity.

May was enchanted at the idea of going to the country, and childishly amused at the vain efforts of the eight bridesmaids to discover where their mysterious retreat was situated. It was thought "very English" to have a country-house lent to one, and the fact gave a last touch of distinction to what was generally conceded to be the most brilliant wedding of the year; but where the house was no one was permitted to know, except the parents of bride and groom, who, when taxed with the knowledge, pursed their lips and said mysteriously: "Ah, they didn't tell us —" which was manifestly true, since there was no need to.

Once they were settled in their compartment, and the train, shaking off the endless wooden suburbs, had pushed out into the pale landscape of spring, talk became easier than Archer had expected. May was still, in look and tone, the simple girl of yesterday, eager to compare notes with him as to the incidents of the wedding, and discussing them as impartially as a bridesmaid talking it all over with an usher. At first Archer had fancied that this detachment was the disguise of an inward tremor; but her clear eyes revealed only the most tranquil unawareness. She was alone for the first time with her husband; but her husband was only the charming comrade of yesterday. There was no one whom she liked as much, no one whom she trusted as completely, and the culminating "lark" of the whole delightful adventure of engagement and marriage was to be off with him alone on a journey, like a grownup person, like a "married woman," in fact.

It was wonderful that—as he had learned in the Mission garden at St. Augustine—such depths of feeling could coexist with such absence of imagination. But he remembered how, even then, she had surprised him by dropping back to inexpressive girlishness as soon as her conscience had been eased of its burden; and he saw that she would probably go through life dealing to the best of her ability with each experience as it came, but never anticipating any by so much as a stolen glance.

Perhaps that faculty of unawareness was what gave her eyes their transparency, and her face the look of representing a type rather than a person; as if she might have been chosen to pose for a Civic Virtue or a Greek goddess. The blood that ran so close to her fair skin might have been a preserving fluid rather than a ravaging element; yet her look of indestructible youthfulness made her seem neither hard nor dull, but only primitive and pure. In the thick of this meditation Archer suddenly felt himself looking at her with the startled gaze of a stranger, and plunged into a reminiscence of the wedding-breakfast and of Granny Mingott's immense and triumphant pervasion of it.

May settled down to frank enjoyment of the subject. "I was surprised, though—weren't you?—that aunt Medora came after all. Ellen wrote that they were neither of them well enough to take the journey; I do wish it had been she who had recovered! Did you see the exquisite old lace she sent me?"

He had known that the moment must come sooner or later, but he had somewhat imagined that by force of willing he might hold it at bay.

"Yes—I—no: yes, it was beautiful," he said, looking at her blindly, and wondering if, whenever he heard those two syllables, all his carefully built-up world would tumble about him like a house of cards.

"Aren't you tired? It will be good to have some tea when we arrive—I'm sure the aunts have got everything beautifully ready," he rattled on, taking her hand in his; and her mind rushed away instantly to the magnificent tea and coffee service of Baltimore silver which the Beauforts had sent, and which "went" so perfectly with uncle Lovell Mingott's trays and side-dishes.

In the spring twilight the train stopped at the Rhinebeck station, and they walked along the platform to the waiting carriage.

"Ah, how awfully kind of the van der Luydens—they've sent their man over from Skuytercliff to meet us," Archer exclaimed, as a sedate person out of livery approached them and relieved the maid of her bags.

"I'm extremely sorry, sir," said this emissary, "that a little accident has occurred at the Miss du Lacs': a leak in the water-tank. It happened yesterday, and Mr. van der Luyden, who heard of it this morning, sent a housemaid up by the early train to get the Patroon's house ready. It will be quite comfortable, I think you'll find, sir; and the Miss du Lacs have sent their cook over, so that it will be exactly the same as if you'd been at Rhinebeck."

Archer stared at the speaker so blankly that he repeated in still more apologetic accents: "It'll be exactly the same, sir, I do assure you —" and May's eager voice broke out, covering the embarrassed silence: "The same as Rhinebeck? The Patroon's house? But it will be a hundred thousand times better—won't it, Newland? It's too dear and kind of Mr. van der Luyden to have thought of it."

And as they drove off, with the maid beside the coachman, and their shining bridal bags on the seat before them, she went on excitedly: "Only fancy, I've never been inside it—have you? The van der Luydens show it to so few people. But they opened it for Ellen, it seems, and she told me what a darling little place it was: she says it's the only house she's seen in America that she could imagine being perfectly happy in."

"Well—that's what we're going to be, isn't it?" cried her husband gaily; and she answered with her boyish smile: "Ah, it's just our luck beginning—the wonderful luck we're always going to have together!"

## XX.

"Of course we must dine with Mrs. Carfry, dearest," Archer said; and his wife looked at him with an anxious frown across the monumental Britannia ware of their lodging house breakfast-table.

In all the rainy desert of autumnal London there were only two people whom the Newland Archers knew; and these two they had sedulously avoided, in conformity with the old New York tradition that it was not "dignified" to force one's self on the notice of one's acquaintances in foreign countries.

Mrs. Archer and Janey, in the course of their visits to Europe, had so unflinchingly lived up to this principle, and met the friendly advances of their fellow-travellers with an air of such impenetrable reserve, that they had almost achieved the record of never having exchanged a word with a "foreigner" other than those employed in hotels and railway-stations. Their own compatriots—save those previously known or properly accredited—they treated with an even more pronounced disdain; so that, unless they ran across a Chivers, a Dagonet or a Mingott, their months abroad were spent in an unbroken tete-a-tete. But the utmost precautions are sometimes unavailing;

and one night at Botzen one of the two English ladies in the room across the passage (whose names, dress and social situation were already intimately known to Janey) had knocked on the door and asked if Mrs. Archer had a bottle of liniment. The other lady—the intruder's sister, Mrs. Carfry—had been seized with a sudden attack of bronchitis; and Mrs. Archer, who never travelled without a complete family pharmacy, was fortunately able to produce the required remedy.

Mrs. Carfry was very ill, and as she and her sister Miss Harle were travelling alone they were profoundly grateful to the Archer ladies, who supplied them with ingenious comforts and whose efficient maid helped to nurse the invalid back to health.

When the Archers left Botzen they had no idea of ever seeing Mrs. Carfry and Miss Harle again. Nothing, to Mrs. Archer's mind, would have been more "undignified" than to force one's self on the notice of a "foreigner" to whom one had happened to render an accidental service. But Mrs. Carfry and her sister, to whom this point of view was unknown, and who would have found it utterly incomprehensible, felt themselves linked by an eternal gratitude to the "delightful Americans" who had been so kind at Botzen. With touching fidelity they seized every chance of meeting Mrs. Archer and Janey in the course of their continental travels, and displayed a supernatural acuteness in finding out when they were to pass through London on their way to or from the States. The intimacy became indissoluble, and Mrs. Archer and Janey, whenever they alighted at Brown's Hotel, found themselves awaited by two affectionate friends who, like themselves, cultivated ferns in Wardian cases, made macrame lace, read the memoirs of the Baroness Bunsen and had views about the occupants of the leading London pulpits. As Mrs. Archer said, it made "another thing of London" to know Mrs. Carfry and Miss Harle; and by the time that Newland became engaged the tie between the families was so firmly established that it was thought "only right" to send a wedding invitation to the two English ladies, who sent, in return, a pretty bouquet of pressed Alpine flowers under glass. And on the dock, when Newland and his wife sailed for England, Mrs. Archer's last word had been: "You must take May to see Mrs. Carfry."

Newland and his wife had had no idea of obeying this injunction; but Mrs. Carfry, with her usual acuteness, had run them down and sent them an invitation to dine; and it was over this invitation that May Archer was wrinkling her brows across the tea and muffins.

"It's all very well for you, Newland; you *know* them. But I shall feel so shy among a lot of people I've never met. And what shall I wear?"

Newland leaned back in his chair and smiled at her. She looked handsomer and more Diana-like than ever. The moist English air seemed to have deepened the bloom of her cheeks and softened the slight hardness of her virginal features; or else it was simply the inner glow of happiness, shining through like a light under ice.

"Wear, dearest? I thought a trunkful of things had come from Paris last week."

"Yes, of course. I meant to say that I shan't know *which* to wear." She pouted a little. "I've never dined out in London; and I don't want to be ridiculous."

He tried to enter into her perplexity. "But don't Englishwomen dress just like everybody else in the evening?"

"Newland! How can you ask such funny questions? When they go to the theatre in old ball-dresses and bare heads."

"Well, perhaps they wear new ball-dresses at home; but at any rate Mrs. Carfry and Miss Harle won't. They'll wear caps like my mother's—and shawls; very soft shawls."

"Yes; but how will the other women be dressed?"

"Not as well as you, dear," he rejoined, wondering what had suddenly developed in her Janey's morbid interest in clothes.

She pushed back her chair with a sigh. "That's dear of you, Newland; but it doesn't help me much."

He had an inspiration. "Why not wear your wedding-dress? That can't be wrong, can it?"

"Oh, dearest! If I only had it here! But it's gone to Paris to be made over for next winter, and Worth hasn't sent it back."

"Oh, well —" said Archer, getting up. "Look here—the fog's lifting. If we made a dash for the National Gallery we might manage to catch a glimpse of the pictures."

The Newland Archers were on their way home, after a three months' wedding-tour which May, in writing to her girl friends, vaguely summarised as "blissful."

They had not gone to the Italian Lakes: on reflection, Archer had not been able to picture his wife in that particular setting. Her own inclination (after a month with the Paris dressmakers) was for mountaineering in July and swimming in August. This plan they punctually fulfilled, spending July at Interlaken and Grindelwald, and August at a little place called Etretat, on the Normandy coast, which some one had recommended as quaint and quiet. Once or twice, in the mountains, Archer had pointed southward and said: "There's Italy"; and May, her feet in a gentian-bed, had smiled cheerfully, and replied: "It would be lovely to go there next winter, if only you didn't have to be in New York."

But in reality travelling interested her even less than he had expected. She regarded it (once her clothes were ordered) as merely an enlarged opportunity for walking, riding, swimming, and trying her hand at the fascinating new game of lawn tennis; and when they finally got back to London (where they were to spend a fortnight while he ordered *his* clothes) she no longer concealed the eagerness with which she looked forward to sailing.

In London nothing interested her but the theatres and the shops; and she found the theatres less exciting than the Paris cafes chantants where, under the blossoming horse-chestnuts of the Champs Elysees, she had had the novel experience of looking down from the restaurant terrace on an audience of "cocottes," and having her husband interpret to her as much of the songs as he thought suitable for bridal ears.

Archer had reverted to all his old inherited ideas about marriage. It was less trouble to conform with the tradition and treat May exactly as all his friends treated their wives than to try to put into practice the theories with which his untrammelled bachelorhood had dallied. There was no use in trying to emancipate a wife who had not the dimmest notion that she was not free; and he had long since discovered that May's only use of the liberty she supposed herself to possess would be to lay it on the altar of her wifely adoration. Her innate dignity would always keep her from making the gift abjectly; and a day might even come (as it once had) when she would find strength to take it altogether back if she thought she were doing it for his own good. But with a conception of marriage so uncomplicated and incurious as hers such a crisis could be brought about only by something visibly outrageous in his own conduct; and the fineness of her feeling for him made that unthinkable. Whatever happened, he knew, she would always be loyal, gallant and unresentful; and that pledged him to the practice of the same virtues.

All this tended to draw him back into his old habits of mind. If her simplicity had been the simplicity of pettiness he would have chafed and rebelled; but since the lines of her character, though so few, were on the same fine mould as her face, she became the tutelary divinity of all his old traditions and reverences.

Such qualities were scarcely of the kind to enliven foreign travel, though they made her so easy and pleasant a companion; but he saw at once how they would fall into place in their proper setting. He had no fear of being oppressed by them, for his artistic and intellectual life would go on, as it always had, outside the domestic circle; and within it there would be nothing small and stifling—coming back to his wife would never be like entering a stuffy room after a tramp in the open. And when they had children the vacant corners in both their lives would be filled.

All these things went through his mind during their long slow drive from Mayfair to South Kensington, where Mrs. Carfry and her sister lived. Archer too would have preferred to escape their friends' hospitality: in conformity with the family tradition he had always travelled as a sight-seer and looker-on, affecting a haughty unconsciousness of the presence of his fellow-beings. Once only, just after Harvard, he had spent a few gay weeks at Florence with a band of queer Europeanised Americans, dancing all night with titled ladies in palaces, and gambling half the day with the rakes and dandies of the fashionable club; but it had all seemed to him, though the greatest fun in the world, as unreal as a carnival. These queer cosmopolitan women, deep in complicated love-affairs which they appeared to feel the need of retailing to every one they met, and the magnificent young officers and elderly dyed wits who were the subjects or the recipients of their confidences, were too different from the people Archer had grown up among, too much like expensive and rather malodorous hot-house exotics, to detain his imagination long. To introduce his wife into such a society was out of the question; and in the course of his travels no other had shown any marked eagerness for his company.

Not long after their arrival in London he had run across the Duke of St. Austrey, and the Duke, instantly and cordially recognising him, had said: "Look me up, won't you?"—but no proper-spirited American would have considered that a suggestion to be acted on, and the meeting was without a sequel. They had even managed to avoid May's English aunt, the banker's wife, who was still in Yorkshire; in fact, they had purposely postponed going to London till the autumn in order that their arrival during the season might not appear pushing and snobbish to these unknown relatives.

"Probably there'll be nobody at Mrs. Carfry's—London's a desert at this season, and you've made yourself much too beautiful," Archer said to May, who sat at his side in the hansom so spotlessly splendid in her sky-blue cloak edged with swansdown that it seemed wicked to expose her to the London grime.

"I don't want them to think that we dress like savages," she replied, with a scorn that Pocahontas might have resented; and he was struck again by the religious reverence of even the most unworldly American women for the social advantages of dress.

"It's their armour," he thought, "their defence against the unknown, and their defiance of it." And he understood for the first time the earnestness with which May, who was incapable of tying a ribbon in her hair to charm him, had gone through the solemn rite of selecting and ordering her extensive wardrobe.

He had been right in expecting the party at Mrs. Carfry's to be a small one. Besides their hostess and her sister, they found, in the long chilly drawing-room, only another shawled lady, a genial Vicar who was her husband, a silent lad whom Mrs. Carfry named as her nephew, and a small dark gentleman with lively eyes whom she introduced as his tutor, pronouncing a French name as she did so.

Into this dimly-lit and dim-featured group May Archer floated like a swan with the sunset on her: she seemed larger, fairer, more voluminously rustling than her husband had ever seen her; and he perceived that the rosiness and rustlingness were the tokens of an extreme and infantile shyness.

"What on earth will they expect me to talk about?" her helpless eyes implored him, at the very moment that her dazzling apparition was calling forth the same anxiety in their own bosoms. But beauty, even when distrustful of itself, awakens confidence in the manly heart; and the Vicar and the French-named tutor were soon manifesting to May their desire to put her at her ease.

In spite of their best efforts, however, the dinner was a languishing affair. Archer noticed that his wife's way of showing herself at her ease with foreigners was to become more uncompromisingly local in her references, so that, though her loveliness was an encouragement to admiration, her conversation was a chill to repartee. The Vicar soon abandoned the struggle; but the tutor, who spoke the most fluent and accomplished English, gallantly continued to pour it out to her until the ladies, to the manifest relief of all concerned, went up to the drawing-room.

The Vicar, after a glass of port, was obliged to hurry away to a meeting, and the shy nephew, who appeared to be an invalid, was packed off to bed. But Archer and the tutor continued to sit over their wine, and suddenly Archer found himself talking as he had not done since his last symposium with Ned Winsett. The Carfry nephew, it turned out, had been threatened with consumption, and had had to leave Harrow for Switzerland, where he had spent two years in the milder air of Lake Leman. Being a bookish youth, he had been entrusted to M. Riviere, who had brought him back to England, and was to remain with him till he went up to Oxford the following spring; and M. Riviere added with simplicity that he should then have to look out for another job.

It seemed impossible, Archer thought, that he should be long without one, so varied were his interests and so many his gifts. He was a man of about thirty, with a thin ugly face (May would certainly have called him common-looking) to which the play of his ideas gave an intense expressiveness; but there was nothing frivolous or cheap in his animation.

His father, who had died young, had filled a small diplomatic post, and it had been intended that the son should follow the same career; but an insatiable taste for letters had thrown the young man into journalism, then into authorship (apparently unsuccessful), and at length—after other experiments and vicissitudes which he spared his listener—into tutoring English youths in Switzerland. Before that, however, he had lived much in Paris, frequented the Goncourt grenier, been advised by Maupassant not to attempt to write (even that seemed to Archer a dazzling honour!), and had often talked with Merimee in his mother's house. He had obviously always been desperately poor and anxious (having a mother and an unmarried sister to provide for), and it was apparent that his literary ambitions had failed. His situation, in fact, seemed, materially speaking, no more brilliant than Ned

Winsett's; but he had lived in a world in which, as he said, no one who loved ideas need hunger mentally. As it was precisely of that love that poor Winsett was starving to death, Archer looked with a sort of vicarious envy at this eager impecunious young man who had fared so richly in his poverty.

"You see, Monsieur, it's worth everything, isn't it, to keep one's intellectual liberty, not to enslave one's powers of appreciation, one's critical independence? It was because of that that I abandoned journalism, and took to so much duller work: tutoring and private secretaryship. There is a good deal of drudgery, of course; but one preserves one's moral freedom, what we call in French one's quant a soi. And when one hears good talk one can join in it without compromising any opinions but one's own; or one can listen, and answer it inwardly. Ah, good conversation—there's nothing like it, is there? The air of ideas is the only air worth breathing. And so I have never regretted giving up either diplomacy or journalism—two different forms of the same self-abdication." He fixed his vivid eyes on Archer as he lit another cigarette. "Voyez-vous, Monsieur, to be able to look life in the face: that's worth living in a garret for, isn't it? But, after all, one must earn enough to pay for the garret; and I confess that to grow old as a private tutor—or a 'private' anything—is almost as chilling to the imagination as a second secretaryship at Bucharest. Sometimes I feel I must make a plunge: an immense plunge. Do you suppose, for instance, there would be any opening for me in America—in New York?"

Archer looked at him with startled eyes. New York, for a young man who had frequented the Goncourts and Flaubert, and who thought the life of ideas the only one worth living! He continued to stare at M. Riviere perplexedly, wondering how to tell him that his very superiorities and advantages would be the surest hindrance to success.

"New York—New York—but must it be especially New York?" he stammered, utterly unable to imagine what lucrative opening his native city could offer to a young man to whom good conversation appeared to be the only necessity.

A sudden flush rose under M. Riviere's sallow skin. "I—I thought it your metropolis: is not the intellectual life more active there?" he rejoined; then, as if fearing to give his hearer the impression of having asked a favour, he went on hastily: "One throws out random suggestions—more to one's self than to others. In reality, I see no immediate prospect —" and rising from his seat he added, without a trace of constraint: "But Mrs. Carfry will think that I ought to be taking you upstairs."

During the homeward drive Archer pondered deeply on this episode. His hour with M. Riviere had put new air into his lungs, and his first impulse had been to invite him to dine the next day; but he was beginning to understand why married men did not always immediately yield to their first impulses.

"That young tutor is an interesting fellow: we had some awfully good talk after dinner about books and things," he threw out tentatively in the hansom.

May roused herself from one of the dreamy silences into which he had read so many meanings before six months of marriage had given him the key to them.

"The little Frenchman? Wasn't he dreadfully common?" she questioned coldly; and he guessed that she nursed a secret disappointment at having been invited out in London to meet a clergyman and a French tutor. The disappointment was not occasioned by the sentiment ordinarily defined as snobbishness, but by old New York's sense of what was due to it when it risked its dignity in foreign lands. If May's parents had entertained the Carfrys in Fifth Avenue they would have offered them something more substantial than a parson and a schoolmaster.

But Archer was on edge, and took her up.

"Common—common *where?*" he queried; and she returned with unusual readiness: "Why, I should say anywhere but in his school-room. Those people are always awkward in society. But then," she added disarmingly, "I suppose I shouldn't have known if he was clever."

Archer disliked her use of the word "clever" almost as much as her use of the word "common"; but he was beginning to fear his tendency to dwell on the things he disliked in her. After all, her point of view had always been the same. It was that of all the people he had grown up among, and he had always regarded it as necessary but negligible. Until a few months ago he had never known a "nice" woman who looked at life differently; and if a man married it must necessarily be among the nice.

"Ah—then I won't ask him to dine!" he concluded with a laugh; and May echoed, bewildered: "Goodness—ask the Carfrys' tutor?"

"Well, not on the same day with the Carfrys, if you prefer I shouldn't. But I did rather want another talk with him. He's looking for a job in New York."

Her surprise increased with her indifference: he almost fancied that she suspected him of being tainted with "foreignness."

"A job in New York? What sort of a job? People don't have French tutors: what does he want to do?"

"Chiefly to enjoy good conversation, I understand," her husband retorted perversely; and she broke into an appreciative laugh. "Oh, Newland, how funny! Isn't that *French?*"

On the whole, he was glad to have the matter settled for him by her refusing to take seriously his wish to invite M. Riviere. Another after-dinner talk would have made it difficult to avoid the question of New York; and the more Archer considered it the less he was able to fit M. Riviere into any conceivable picture of New York as he knew it.

He perceived with a flash of chilling insight that in future many problems would be thus negatively solved for him; but as he paid the hansom and followed his wife's long train into the house he took refuge in the comforting platitude that the first six months were always the most difficult in marriage. "After that I suppose we shall have pretty nearly finished rubbing off each other's angles," he reflected; but the worst of it was that May's pressure was already bearing on the very angles whose sharpness he most wanted to keep.

## XXI.

The small bright lawn stretched away smoothly to the big bright sea.

The turf was hemmed with an edge of scarlet geranium and coleus, and cast-iron vases painted in chocolate colour, standing at intervals along the winding path that led to the sea, looped their garlands of petunia and ivy geranium above the neatly raked gravel.

Half way between the edge of the cliff and the square wooden house (which was also chocolate-coloured, but with the tin roof of the verandah striped in yellow and brown to represent an awning) two large targets had been placed against a background of shrubbery. On the other side of the lawn, facing the targets, was pitched a real tent, with benches and garden-seats about it. A number of ladies in summer dresses and gentlemen in grey frock-coats and tall hats stood on the lawn or sat upon the benches; and every now and then a slender girl in starched muslin would step from the tent, bow in hand, and speed her shaft at one of the targets, while the spectators interrupted their talk to watch the result.

Newland Archer, standing on the verandah of the house, looked curiously down upon this scene. On each side of the shiny painted steps was a large blue china flower-pot on a bright yellow china stand. A spiky green plant filled each pot, and below the verandah ran a wide border of blue hydrangeas edged with more red geraniums. Behind him, the French windows of the drawing-rooms through which he had passed gave glimpses, between swaying lace curtains, of glassy parquet floors islanded with chintz poufs, dwarf armchairs, and velvet tables covered with trifles in silver.

The Newport Archery Club always held its August meeting at the Beauforts'. The sport, which had hitherto known no rival but croquet, was beginning to be discarded in favour of lawn-tennis; but the latter game was still considered too rough and inelegant for social occasions, and as an opportunity to show off pretty dresses and graceful attitudes the bow and arrow held their own.

Archer looked down with wonder at the familiar spectacle. It surprised him that life should be going on in the old way when his own reactions to it had so completely changed. It was Newport that had first brought home to him the extent of the change. In New York, during the previous winter, after he and May had settled down in the new greenish-yellow house with the bow-window and the Pompeian vestibule, he had dropped back with relief into the old routine of the office, and the renewal of this daily activity had served as a link with his former self. Then there had been the pleasurable excitement of choosing a showy grey stepper for May's brougham (the Wellands had given the carriage), and the abiding occupation and interest of arranging his new library, which, in spite of family doubts and disapprovals, had been carried out as he had dreamed, with a dark embossed paper, Eastlake book-cases and "sincere" arm-chairs and tables. At the Century he had found Winsett again, and at the Knickerbocker the fashionable young men of his own set; and what with the hours dedicated to the law and those given to dining out or entertaining friends at home, with an occasional evening at the Opera or the play, the life he was living had still seemed a fairly real and inevitable sort of business.

But Newport represented the escape from duty into an atmosphere of unmitigated holiday-making. Archer had tried to persuade May to spend the summer on a remote island off the coast of Maine (called, appropriately enough, Mount Desert), where a few hardy Bostonians and Philadelphians were camping in "native" cottages, and whence came reports of enchanting scenery and a wild, almost trapper-like existence amid woods and waters.

But the Wellands always went to Newport, where they owned one of the square boxes on the cliffs, and their son-in-law could adduce no good reason why he and May should not join them there. As Mrs. Welland rather tartly pointed out, it was hardly worth while for May to have worn herself out trying on summer clothes in Paris if she was not to be allowed to wear them; and this argument was of a kind to which Archer had as yet found no answer.

May herself could not understand his obscure reluctance to fall in with so reasonable and pleasant a way of spending the summer. She reminded him that he had always liked Newport in his bachelor days, and as this was indisputable he could only profess that he was sure he was going to like it better than ever now that they were to be there together. But as he stood on the Beaufort verandah and looked out on the brightly peopled lawn it came home to him with a shiver that he was not going to like it at all.

It was not May's fault, poor dear. If, now and then, during their travels, they had fallen slightly out of step, harmony had been restored by their return to the conditions she was used to. He had always foreseen that she would not disappoint him; and he had been right. He had married (as most young men did) because he had met a perfectly charming girl at the moment when a series of rather aimless sentimental adventures were ending in premature disgust; and she had represented peace, stability, comradeship, and the steadying sense of an unescapable duty.

He could not say that he had been mistaken in his choice, for she had fulfilled all that he had expected. It was undoubtedly gratifying to be the husband of one of the handsomest and most popular young married women in New York, especially when she was also one of the sweetest-tempered and most reasonable of wives; and Archer had never been insensible to such advantages. As for the momentary madness which had fallen upon him on the eve of his marriage, he had trained himself to regard it as the last of his discarded experiments. The idea that he could ever, in his senses, have dreamed of marrying the Countess Olenska had become almost unthinkable, and she remained in his memory simply as the most plaintive and poignant of a line of ghosts.

But all these abstractions and eliminations made of his mind a rather empty and echoing place, and he supposed that was one of the reasons why the busy animated people on the Beaufort lawn shocked him as if they had been children playing in a grave-yard.

He heard a murmur of skirts beside him, and the Marchioness Manson fluttered out of the drawing-room window. As usual, she was extraordinarily festooned and bedizened, with a limp Leghorn hat anchored to her head by many windings of faded gauze, and a little black velvet parasol on a carved ivory handle absurdly balanced over her much larger hatbrim.

"My dear Newland, I had no idea that you and May had arrived! You yourself came only yesterday, you say? Ah, business—business—professional duties ... I understand. Many husbands, I know, find it impossible to join their wives here except for the week-end." She cocked her head on one side and languished at him through screwed-up eyes. "But marriage is one long sacrifice, as I used often to remind my Ellen —"

Archer's heart stopped with the queer jerk which it had given once before, and which seemed suddenly to slam a door between himself and the outer world; but this break of continuity must have been of the briefest, for he presently heard Medora answering a question he had apparently found voice to put.

"No, I am not staying here, but with the Blenkers, in their delicious solitude at Portsmouth. Beaufort was kind enough to send his famous trotters for me this morning, so that I might have at least a glimpse of one of Regina's garden-parties; but this evening I go back to rural life. The Blenkers, dear original beings, have hired a primitive old farm-house at Portsmouth where they gather about them representative people ..." She drooped slightly beneath her protecting brim, and added with a faint blush: "This week Dr. Agathon Carver is holding a series of Inner Thought meetings there. A contrast indeed to this gay scene of worldly pleasure—but then I have always lived on contrasts! To me the only death is monotony. I always say to Ellen: Beware of monotony; it's the mother of all the deadly sins. But my poor child is going through a phase of exaltation, of abhorrence of the world. You know, I suppose, that she has declined all invitations to stay at Newport, even with her grandmother Mingott? I could hardly persuade her to come with me to the Blenkers', if you will believe it! The life she leads is morbid, unnatural. Ah, if she had only listened to me when it was still possible ... When the door was still open ... But shall we go down and watch this absorbing match? I hear your May is one of the competitors."

Strolling toward them from the tent Beaufort advanced over the lawn, tall, heavy, too tightly buttoned into a London frock-coat, with one of his own orchids in its buttonhole. Archer, who had not seen him for two or three months, was struck by the change in his appearance. In the hot summer light his floridness seemed heavy and bloated, and but for his erect square-shouldered walk he would have looked like an over-fed and over-dressed old man.

There were all sorts of rumours afloat about Beaufort. In the spring he had gone off on a long cruise to the West Indies in his new steam-yacht, and it was reported that, at various points where he had touched, a lady resembling Miss Fanny Ring had been seen in his company. The steam-yacht, built in the Clyde, and fitted with tiled bath-rooms and other unheard-of luxuries, was said to have cost him half a million; and the pearl necklace which he had presented to his wife on his return was as magnificent as such expiatory offerings are apt to be. Beaufort's fortune was substantial enough to stand the strain; and yet the disquieting rumours persisted, not only in Fifth Avenue but in Wall Street. Some people said he had speculated unfortunately in railways, others that he was being bled by one of the most insatiable members of her profession; and to every report of threatened insolvency Beaufort replied by a fresh extravagance: the building of a new row of orchid-houses, the purchase of a new string of race-horses, or the addition of a new Meissonnier or Cabanel to his picture-gallery.

He advanced toward the Marchioness and Newland with his usual half-sneering smile. "Hullo, Medora! Did the trotters do their business? Forty minutes, eh? ... Well, that's not so bad, considering your nerves had to be spared." He shook hands with Archer, and then, turning back with them, placed himself on Mrs. Manson's other side, and said, in a low voice, a few words which their companion did not catch.

The Marchioness replied by one of her queer foreign jerks, and a "Que voulez-vous?" which deepened Beaufort's frown; but he produced a good semblance of a congratulatory smile as he glanced at Archer to say: "You know May's going to carry off the first prize."

"Ah, then it remains in the family," Medora rippled; and at that moment they reached the tent and Mrs. Beaufort met them in a girlish cloud of mauve muslin and floating veils.

May Welland was just coming out of the tent. In her white dress, with a pale green ribbon about the waist and a wreath of ivy on her hat, she had the same Diana-like aloofness as when she had entered the Beaufort ball-room on the night of her engagement. In the interval not a thought seemed to have passed behind her eyes or a feeling through her heart; and though her husband knew that she had the capacity for both he marvelled afresh at the way in which experience dropped away from her.

She had her bow and arrow in her hand, and placing herself on the chalk-mark traced on the turf she lifted the bow to her shoulder and took aim. The attitude was so full of a classic grace that a murmur of appreciation followed her appearance, and Archer felt the glow of proprietorship that so often cheated him into momentary well-being. Her rivals—Mrs. Reggie Chivers, the Merry girls, and divers rosy Thorleys, Dagonets and Mingotts, stood behind her in a lovely anxious group, brown heads and golden bent above the scores, and pale muslins and flower-wreathed hats mingled in a tender rainbow. All were young and pretty, and bathed in summer bloom; but not one had the nymph-like ease of his wife, when, with tense muscles and happy frown, she bent her soul upon some feat of strength.

"Gad," Archer heard Lawrence Lefferts say, "not one of the lot holds the bow as she does"; and Beaufort retorted: "Yes; but that's the only kind of target she'll ever hit."

Archer felt irrationally angry. His host's contemptuous tribute to May's "niceness" was just what a husband should have wished to hear said of his wife. The fact that a coarseminded man found her lacking in attraction was simply another proof of her quality; yet the words sent a faint shiver through his heart. What if "niceness" carried to that supreme degree were only a negation, the curtain dropped before an emptiness? As he looked at May, returning flushed and calm from her final bull's-eye, he had the feeling that he had never yet lifted that curtain.

She took the congratulations of her rivals and of the rest of the company with the simplicity that was her crowning grace. No one could ever be jealous of her triumphs because she managed to give the feeling that she would have been just as serene if she had missed them. But when her eyes met her husband's her face glowed with the pleasure she saw in his.

Mrs. Welland's basket-work pony-carriage was waiting for them, and they drove off among the dispersing carriages, May handling the reins and Archer sitting at her side.

The afternoon sunlight still lingered upon the bright lawns and shrubberies, and up and down Bellevue Avenue rolled a double line of victorias, dog-carts, landaus and "vis-a-vis," carrying well-dressed ladies and gentlemen away from the Beaufort garden-party, or homeward from their daily afternoon turn along the Ocean Drive.

"Shall we go to see Granny?" May suddenly proposed. "I should like to tell her myself that I've won the prize. There's lots of time before dinner."

Archer acquiesced, and she turned the ponies down Narragansett Avenue, crossed Spring Street and drove out toward the rocky moorland beyond. In this unfashionable region Catherine the Great, always indifferent to precedent and thrifty of purse, had built herself in her youth a many-peaked and cross-beamed cottage-orne on a bit of cheap land overlooking the bay. Here, in a thicket of stunted oaks, her verandahs spread themselves above the island-dotted waters. A winding drive led up between iron stags and blue glass balls embedded in mounds of geraniums to a front door of highly-varnished walnut under a striped verandah-roof; and behind it ran a narrow hall with a black and yellow star-patterned parquet floor, upon which opened four small square rooms with heavy flock-papers under ceilings on which an Italian house-painter had lavished all the divinities of Olympus. One of these rooms had been turned into a bedroom by Mrs. Mingott when the burden of flesh descended on her, and in the adjoining one she spent her days, enthroned in a large armchair between the open door and window, and perpetually waving a palm-leaf fan which the prodigious projection of her bosom kept so far from the rest of her person that the air it set in motion stirred only the fringe of the anti-macassars on the chair-arms.

Since she had been the means of hastening his marriage old Catherine had shown to Archer the cordiality which a service rendered excites toward the person served. She was persuaded that irrepressible passion was the cause of his impatience; and being an ardent admirer of impulsiveness (when it did not lead to the spending of money) she always received him with a genial twinkle of complicity and a play of allusion to which May seemed fortunately impervious.

She examined and appraised with much interest the diamond-tipped arrow which had been pinned on May's bosom at the conclusion of the match, remarking that in her day a filigree brooch would have been thought enough, but that there was no denying that Beaufort did things handsomely.

"Quite an heirloom, in fact, my dear," the old lady chuckled. "You must leave it in fee to your eldest girl." She pinched May's white arm and watched the colour flood her face. "Well, well, what have I said to make you shake out the red flag? Ain't there going to be any daughters—only boys, eh? Good gracious, look at her blushing again all over her blushes! What—can't I say that either? Mercy me—when my children beg me to have all those gods and goddesses painted out overhead I always say I'm too thankful to have somebody about me that *nothing* can shock!"

Archer burst into a laugh, and May echoed it, crimson to the eyes.

"Well, now tell me all about the party, please, my dears, for I shall never get a straight word about it out of that silly Medora," the ancestress continued; and, as May exclaimed: "Cousin Medora? But I thought she was going back to Portsmouth?" she answered placidly: "So she is—but she's got to come here first to pick up Ellen. Ah—you didn't know Ellen had come to spend the day with me? Such fol-de-rol, her not coming for the summer; but I gave up arguing with young people about fifty years ago. Ellen—*Ellen*!" she cried in her shrill old voice, trying to bend forward far enough to catch a glimpse of the lawn beyond the verandah.

There was no answer, and Mrs. Mingott rapped impatiently with her stick on the shiny floor. A mulatto maid-servant in a bright turban, replying to the summons, informed her mistress that she had seen "Miss Ellen" going down the path to the shore; and Mrs. Mingott turned to Archer.

"Run down and fetch her, like a good grandson; this pretty lady will describe the party to me," she said; and Archer stood up as if in a dream.

He had heard the Countess Olenska's name pronounced often enough during the year and a half since they had last met, and was even familiar with the main incidents of her life in the interval. He knew that she had spent the previous summer at Newport, where she appeared to have gone a great deal into society, but that in the autumn she had suddenly sub-let the "perfect house" which Beaufort had been at such pains to find for her, and decided to establish herself in Washington. There, during the winter, he had heard of her (as one always heard of pretty women in Washington) as shining in the "brilliant diplomatic society" that was supposed to make up for the social short-comings of the Administration. He had listened to these accounts, and to various contradictory reports on her appearance, her conversation, her point of view and her choice of friends, with the detachment with which one listens to reminiscences of some one long since dead; not till Medora suddenly spoke her name at the archery match had Ellen Olenska become a living presence to him again. The Marchioness's foolish lisp had called up a vision of the little fire-lit drawing-room and the sound of the carriage-wheels returning down the deserted street. He thought of a story he had read, of some peasant children in Tuscany lighting a bunch of straw in a wayside cavern, and revealing old silent images in their painted tomb ...

The way to the shore descended from the bank on which the house was perched to a walk above the water planted with weeping willows. Through their veil Archer caught the glint of the Lime Rock, with its white-washed turret and the tiny house in which the heroic light-house keeper, Ida Lewis, was living her last venerable years. Beyond it lay the flat reaches and ugly government chimneys of Goat Island, the bay spreading northward in a shimmer of gold to Prudence Island with its low growth of oaks, and the shores of Conanicut faint in the sunset haze.

From the willow walk projected a slight wooden pier ending in a sort of pagoda-like summer-house; and in the pagoda a lady stood, leaning against the rail, her back to the shore. Archer stopped at the sight as if he had waked from sleep. That vision of the past was a dream, and the reality was what awaited him in the house on the bank overhead: was Mrs. Welland's pony-carriage circling around and around the oval at the door, was May sitting under the shameless Olympians and glowing with secret hopes, was the Welland villa at the far end of Bellevue Avenue, and Mr. Welland, already dressed for dinner, and pacing the drawing-room floor, watch in hand, with dyspeptic impatience—for it was one of the houses in which one always knew exactly what is happening at a given hour.

"What am I? A son-in-law —" Archer thought.

The figure at the end of the pier had not moved. For a long moment the young man stood half way down the bank, gazing at the bay furrowed with the coming and going of sailboats, yacht-launches, fishing-craft and the trailing black coal-barges hauled by noisy tugs. The lady in the summer-house seemed to be held by the same sight. Beyond the grey bastions of Fort Adams a long-drawn sunset was splintering up into a thousand fires, and the radiance caught the sail of a catboat as it beat out through the channel between the Lime Rock and the shore. Archer, as he watched, remembered the scene in the Shaughraun, and Montague lifting Ada Dyas's ribbon to his lips without her knowing that he was in the room.

"She doesn't know—she hasn't guessed. Shouldn't I know if she came up behind me, I wonder?" he mused; and suddenly he said to himself: "If she doesn't turn before that sail crosses the Lime Rock light I'll go back."

The boat was gliding out on the receding tide. It slid before the Lime Rock, blotted out Ida Lewis's little house, and passed across the turret in which the light was hung. Archer waited till a wide space of water sparkled between the last reef of the island and the stern of the boat; but still the figure in the summer-house did not move.

He turned and walked up the hill.

"I'm sorry you didn't find Ellen—I should have liked to see her again," May said as they drove home through the dusk. "But perhaps she wouldn't have cared—she seems so changed."

"Changed?" echoed her husband in a colourless voice, his eyes fixed on the ponies' twitching ears.

"So indifferent to her friends, I mean; giving up New York and her house, and spending her time with such queer people. Fancy how hideously uncomfortable she must be at the Blenkers'! She says she does it to keep cousin Medora out of mischief: to prevent her marrying dreadful people. But I sometimes think we've always bored her."

Archer made no answer, and she continued, with a tinge of hardness that he had never before noticed in her frank fresh voice: "After all, I wonder if she wouldn't be happier with her husband."

He burst into a laugh. "Sancta simplicitas!" he exclaimed; and as she turned a puzzled frown on him he added: "I don't think I ever heard you say a cruel thing before."

"Cruel?"

"Well—watching the contortions of the damned is supposed to be a favourite sport of the angels; but I believe even they don't think people happier in hell."

"It's a pity she ever married abroad then," said May, in the placid tone with which her mother met Mr. Welland's vagaries; and Archer felt himself gently relegated to the category of unreasonable husbands.

They drove down Bellevue Avenue and turned in between the chamfered wooden gate-posts surmounted by cast-iron lamps which marked the approach to the Welland villa. Lights were already shining through its windows, and Archer, as the carriage stopped, caught a glimpse of his father-in-law, exactly as he had pictured him, pacing the drawing-room, watch in hand and wearing the pained expression that he had long since found to be much more efficacious than anger.

The young man, as he followed his wife into the hall, was conscious of a curious reversal of mood. There was something about the luxury of the Welland house and the density of the Welland atmosphere, so charged with minute observances and exactions, that always stole into his system like a narcotic. The heavy carpets, the watchful servants, the perpetually reminding tick of disciplined clocks, the perpetually renewed stack of cards and invitations on the hall table, the whole chain of tyrannical trifles binding one hour to the next, and each member of the household to all the others, made any less systematised and affluent existence seem unreal and precarious. But now it was the Welland house, and the life he was expected to lead in it, that had become unreal and irrelevant, and the brief scene on the shore, when he had stood irresolute, halfway down the bank, was as close to him as the blood in his veins.

All night he lay awake in the big chintz bedroom at May's side, watching the moonlight slant along the carpet, and thinking of Ellen Olenska driving home across the gleaming beaches behind Beaufort's trotters.

## XXII.

"A party for the Blenkers—the Blenkers?"

Mr. Welland laid down his knife and fork and looked anxiously and incredulously across the luncheon-table at his wife, who, adjusting her gold eye-glasses, read aloud, in the tone of high comedy:

"Professor and Mrs. Emerson Sillerton request the pleasure of Mr. and Mrs. Welland's company at the meeting of the Wednesday Afternoon Club on August 25th at 3 o'clock punctually. To meet Mrs. and the Misses Blenker.

"Red Gables, Catherine Street. R. S. V. P."

"Good gracious —" Mr. Welland gasped, as if a second reading had been necessary to bring the monstrous absurdity of the thing home to him.

"Poor Amy Sillerton—you never can tell what her husband will do next," Mrs. Welland sighed. "I suppose he's just discovered the Blenkers."

Professor Emerson Sillerton was a thorn in the side of Newport society; and a thorn that could not be plucked out, for it grew on a venerable and venerated family tree. He was, as people said, a man who had had "every advantage." His father was Sillerton Jackson's uncle, his mother a Pennilow of Boston; on each side there was wealth and position, and mutual suitability. Nothing—as Mrs. Welland had often remarked—nothing on earth obliged Emerson Sillerton to be an archaeologist, or indeed a Professor of any sort, or to live in Newport in winter, or do any of the other revolutionary things that he did. But at least, if he was going to break with tradition and flout society in the face, he need not have married poor Amy Dagonet, who had a right to expect "something different," and money enough to keep her own carriage.

No one in the Mingott set could understand why Amy Sillerton had submitted so tamely to the eccentricities of a husband who filled the house with long-haired men and short-haired women, and, when he travelled, took her to explore tombs in Yucatan instead of going to Paris or Italy. But there they were, set in their ways, and apparently unaware that they were different from other people; and when they gave one of their dreary annual garden-parties every family on the Cliffs, because of the Sillerton-Pennilow-Dagonet connection, had to draw lots and send an unwilling representative.

"It's a wonder," Mrs. Welland remarked, "that they didn't choose the Cup Race day! Do you remember, two years ago, their giving a party for a black man on the day of Julia Mingott's the dansant? Luckily this time there's nothing else going on that I know of—for of course some of us will have to go."

Mr. Welland sighed nervously. "'Some of us,' my dear—more than one? Three o'clock is such a very awkward hour. I have to be here at half-past three to take my drops: it's really no use trying to follow Bencomb's new treatment if I don't do it systematically; and if I join you later, of course I shall miss my drive." At the thought he laid down his knife and fork again, and a flush of anxiety rose to his finely-wrinkled cheek.

"There's no reason why you should go at all, my dear," his wife answered with a cheerfulness that had become automatic. "I have some cards to leave at the other end of Bellevue Avenue, and I'll drop in at about half-past three and stay long enough to make poor Amy feel that she hasn't been slighted." She glanced hesitatingly at her daughter. "And if Newland's afternoon is provided for perhaps May can drive you out with the ponies, and try their new russet harness."

It was a principle in the Welland family that people's days and hours should be what Mrs. Welland called "provided for." The melancholy possibility of having to "kill time" (especially for those who did not care for whist or solitaire) was a vision that haunted her as the spectre of the unemployed haunts the philanthropist. Another of her principles was that parents should never (at least visibly) interfere with the plans of their married children; and the difficulty of adjusting this respect for May's independence with the exigency of Mr. Welland's claims could be overcome only by the exercise of an ingenuity which left not a second of Mrs. Welland's own time unprovided for.

"Of course I'll drive with Papa—I'm sure Newland will find something to do," May said, in a tone that gently reminded her husband of his lack of response. It was a cause of constant distress to Mrs. Welland that her son-in-law showed so little foresight in planning his days. Often already, during the fortnight that he had passed under her roof, when she enquired how he meant to spend his afternoon, he had answered paradoxically: "Oh, I think for a change I'll just save it instead of spending it —" and once, when she and May had had to go on a long-postponed round of afternoon calls, he had confessed to having lain all the afternoon under a rock on the beach below the house.

"Newland never seems to look ahead," Mrs. Welland once ventured to complain to her daughter; and May answered serenely: "No; but you see it doesn't matter, because when there's nothing particular to do he reads a book."

"Ah, yes—like his father!" Mrs. Welland agreed, as if allowing for an inherited oddity; and after that the question of Newland's unemployment was tacitly dropped.

Nevertheless, as the day for the Sillerton reception approached, May began to show a natural solicitude for his welfare, and to suggest a tennis match at the Chiverses', or a sail on Julius Beaufort's cutter, as a means of atoning for her temporary desertion. "I shall be back by six, you know, dear: Papa never drives later than that —" and she was not reassured till Archer said that he thought of hiring a run-about and driving up the island to a stud-farm to look at a second horse for her brougham. They had been looking for this horse for some time, and the suggestion was so acceptable that May glanced at her mother as if to say: "You see he knows how to plan out his time as well as any of us."

The idea of the stud-farm and the brougham horse had germinated in Archer's mind on the very day when the Emerson Sillerton invitation had first been mentioned; but he had kept it to himself as if there were something clandestine in the plan, and discovery might prevent its execution. He had, however, taken the precaution to engage in advance a runabout with a pair of old livery-stable trotters that could still do their eighteen miles on level roads; and at two o'clock, hastily deserting the luncheon-table, he sprang into the light carriage and drove off.

The day was perfect. A breeze from the north drove little puffs of white cloud across an ultramarine sky, with a bright sea running under it. Bellevue Avenue was empty at that hour, and after dropping the stable-lad at the corner of Mill Street Archer turned down the Old Beach Road and drove across Eastman's Beach.

He had the feeling of unexplained excitement with which, on half-holidays at school, he used to start off into the unknown. Taking his pair at an easy gait, he counted on reaching the stud-farm, which was not far beyond Paradise Rocks, before three o'clock; so that, after looking over the horse (and trying him if he seemed promising) he would still have four golden hours to dispose of.

As soon as he heard of the Sillerton's party he had said to himself that the Marchioness Manson would certainly come to Newport with the Blenkers, and that Madame Olenska might again take the opportunity of spending the day with her grandmother. At any rate, the Blenker habitation would probably be deserted, and he would be able, without indiscretion, to satisfy a vague curiosity concerning it. He was not sure that he wanted to see the Countess Olenska again; but ever since he had looked at her from the path above the bay he had wanted, irrationally and indescribably, to see the place she was living in, and to follow the movements of her imagined figure as he had watched the real one in the summer-house. The longing was with him day and night, an incessant undefinable craving, like the sudden whim of a sick man for food or drink once tasted and long since forgotten. He could not see beyond the craving, or picture what it might lead to, for he was not conscious of any wish to speak to Madame Olenska or to hear her voice. He simply felt that if he could carry away the vision of the spot of earth she walked on, and the way the sky and sea enclosed it, the rest of the world might seem less empty.

When he reached the stud-farm a glance showed him that the horse was not what he wanted; nevertheless he took a turn behind it in order to prove to himself that he was not in a hurry. But at three o'clock he shook out the reins over the trotters and turned into the by-roads leading to Portsmouth. The wind had dropped and a faint haze on the horizon showed that a fog was waiting to steal up the Saconnet on the turn of the tide; but all about him fields and woods were steeped in golden light.

He drove past grey-shingled farm-houses in orchards, past hay-fields and groves of oak, past villages with white steeples rising sharply into the fading sky; and at last, after stopping to ask the way of some men at work in a field, he turned down a lane between high banks of goldenrod and brambles. At the end of the lane was the blue glimmer of the river; to the left, standing in front of a clump of oaks and maples, he saw a long tumble-down house with white paint peeling from its clapboards.

On the road-side facing the gateway stood one of the open sheds in which the New Englander shelters his farming implements and visitors "hitch" their "teams." Archer, jumping down, led his pair into the shed, and after tying them to a post turned toward the house. The patch of lawn before it had relapsed into a hay-field; but to the left an overgrown box-garden full of dahlias and rusty rose-bushes encircled a ghostly summer-house of trellis-work that had once been white, surmounted by a wooden Cupid who had lost his bow and arrow but continued to take ineffectual aim.

Archer leaned for a while against the gate. No one was in sight, and not a sound came from the open windows of the house: a grizzled Newfoundland dozing before the door seemed as ineffectual a guardian as the arrowless Cupid. It was strange to think that this place of silence and decay was the home of the turbulent Blenkers; yet Archer was sure that he was not mistaken.

For a long time he stood there, content to take in the scene, and gradually falling under its drowsy spell; but at length he roused himself to the sense of the passing time. Should he look his fill and then drive away? He stood irresolute, wishing suddenly to see the inside of the house, so that he might picture the room that Madame Olenska sat in. There was nothing to prevent his walking up to the door and ringing the bell; if, as he supposed, she was away with the rest of the party, he could easily give his name, and ask permission to go into the sitting-room to write a message.

But instead, he crossed the lawn and turned toward the box-garden. As he entered it he caught sight of something bright-coloured in the summer-house, and presently made it out to be a pink parasol. The parasol drew him like a magnet: he was sure it was hers. He went into the summer-house, and sitting down on the rickety seat picked up the silken thing and looked at its carved handle, which was made of some rare wood that gave out an aromatic scent. Archer lifted the handle to his lips.

He heard a rustle of skirts against the box, and sat motionless, leaning on the parasol handle with clasped hands, and letting the rustle come nearer without lifting his eyes. He had always known that this must happen ...

"Oh, Mr. Archer!" exclaimed a loud young voice; and looking up he saw before him the youngest and largest of the Blenker girls, blonde and blowsy, in bedraggled muslin. A red blotch on one of her cheeks seemed to show that it had recently been pressed against a pillow, and her half-awakened eyes stared at him hospitably but confusedly.

"Gracious—where did you drop from? I must have been sound asleep in the hammock. Everybody else has gone to Newport. Did you ring?" she incoherently enquired.

Archer's confusion was greater than hers. "I—no—that is, I was just going to. I had to come up the island to see about a horse, and I drove over on a chance of finding Mrs. Blenker and your visitors. But the house seemed empty—so I sat down to wait."

Miss Blenker, shaking off the fumes of sleep, looked at him with increasing interest. "The house IS empty. Mother's not here, or the Marchioness—or anybody but me." Her glance became faintly reproachful. "Didn't you know that Professor and Mrs. Sillerton are giving a garden-party for mother and all of us this afternoon? It was too unlucky that I couldn't go; but I've had a sore throat, and mother was afraid of the drive home this evening. Did you ever know anything so disappointing? Of course," she added gaily, "I shouldn't have minded half as much if I'd known you were coming."

Symptoms of a lumbering coquetry became visible in her, and Archer found the strength to break in: "But Madame Olenska—has she gone to Newport too?"

Miss Blenker looked at him with surprise. "Madame Olenska—didn't you know she'd been called away?"

"Called away?—"

"Oh, my best parasol! I lent it to that goose of a Katie, because it matched her ribbons, and the careless thing must have dropped it here. We Blenkers are all like that ... real Bohemians!" Recovering the sunshade with a powerful hand she unfurled it and suspended its rosy dome above her head. "Yes, Ellen was called away yesterday: she lets us call her Ellen, you know. A telegram came from Boston: she said she might be gone for two days. I do LOVE the way she does her hair, don't you?" Miss Blenker rambled on.

Archer continued to stare through her as though she had been transparent. All he saw was the trumpery parasol that arched its pinkness above her giggling head.

After a moment he ventured: "You don't happen to know why Madame Olenska went to Boston? I hope it was not on account of bad news?"

Miss Blenker took this with a cheerful incredulity. "Oh, I don't believe so. She didn't tell us what was in the telegram. I think she didn't want the Marchioness to know. She's so romantic-looking, isn't she? Doesn't she remind you of Mrs. Scott-Siddons when she reads 'Lady Geraldine's Courtship'? Did you never hear her?"

Archer was dealing hurriedly with crowding thoughts. His whole future seemed suddenly to be unrolled before him; and passing down its endless emptiness he saw the dwindling figure of a man to whom nothing was ever to happen. He glanced about him at the unpruned garden, the tumble-down house, and the oak-grove under which the dusk was gathering. It had seemed so exactly the place in which he ought to have found Madame Olenska; and she was far away, and even the pink sunshade was not hers ...

He frowned and hesitated. "You don't know, I suppose—I shall be in Boston tomorrow. If I could manage to see her —"

He felt that Miss Blenker was losing interest in him, though her smile persisted. "Oh, of course; how lovely of you! She's staying at the Parker House; it must be horrible there in this weather."

After that Archer was but intermittently aware of the remarks they exchanged. He could only remember stoutly resisting her entreaty that he should await the returning family and have high tea with them before he drove home. At length, with his hostess still at his side, he passed out of range of the wooden Cupid, unfastened his horses and drove off. At the turn of the lane he saw Miss Blenker standing at the gate and waving the pink parasol.

## XXIII.

The next morning, when Archer got out of the Fall River train, he emerged upon a steaming midsummer Boston. The streets near the station were full of the smell of beer and coffee and decaying fruit and a shirt-sleeved populace moved through them with the intimate abandon of boarders going down the passage to the bathroom.

Archer found a cab and drove to the Somerset Club for breakfast. Even the fashionable quarters had the air of untidy domesticity to which no excess of heat ever degrades the European cities. Care-takers in calico lounged on the door-steps of the wealthy, and the Common looked like a pleasure-ground on the morrow of a Masonic picnic. If Archer had tried to imagine Ellen Olenska in improbable scenes he could not have called up any into which it was more difficult to fit her than this heat-prostrated and deserted Boston.

He breakfasted with appetite and method, beginning with a slice of melon, and studying a morning paper while he waited for his toast and scrambled eggs. A new sense of energy and activity had possessed him ever since he had announced to May the night before that he had business in Boston, and should take the Fall River boat that night and go on to New York the following evening. It had always been understood that he would return to town early in the week, and when he got back from his expedition to Portsmouth a letter from the office, which fate had conspicuously placed on a corner of the hall table, sufficed to justify his sudden change of plan. He was even ashamed of the ease with which the whole thing had been done: it reminded him, for an uncomfortable moment, of Lawrence Lefferts's masterly contrivances for securing his freedom. But this did not long trouble him, for he was not in an analytic mood.

After breakfast he smoked a cigarette and glanced over the Commercial Advertiser. While he was thus engaged two or three men he knew came in, and the usual greetings were exchanged: it was the same world after all, though he had such a queer sense of having slipped through the meshes of time and space.

He looked at his watch, and finding that it was half-past nine got up and went into the writing-room. There he wrote a few lines, and ordered a messenger to take a cab to the Parker House and wait for the answer. He then sat down behind another newspaper and tried to calculate how long it would take a cab to get to the Parker House.

"The lady was out, sir," he suddenly heard a waiter's voice at his elbow; and he stammered: "Out?—" as if it were a word in a strange language.

He got up and went into the hall. It must be a mistake: she could not be out at that hour. He flushed with anger at his own stupidity: why had he not sent the note as soon as he arrived?

He found his hat and stick and went forth into the street. The city had suddenly become as strange and vast and empty as if he were a traveller from distant lands. For a moment he stood on the door-step hesitating; then he decided to go to the Parker House. What if the messenger had been misinformed, and she were still there?

He started to walk across the Common; and on the first bench, under a tree, he saw her sitting. She had a grey silk sunshade over her head—how could he ever have imagined her with a pink one? As he approached he was struck by her listless attitude: she sat there as if she had nothing else to do. He saw her drooping profile, and the knot of hair fastened low in the neck under her dark hat, and the long wrinkled glove on the hand that held the sunshade. He came a step or two nearer, and she turned and looked at him.

"Oh"—she said; and for the first time he noticed a startled look on her face; but in another moment it gave way to a slow smile of wonder and contentment.

"Oh"—she murmured again, on a different note, as he stood looking down at her; and without rising she made a place for him on the bench.

"I'm here on business—just got here," Archer explained; and, without knowing why, he suddenly began to feign astonishment at seeing her. "But what on earth are you doing in this wilderness?" He had really no idea what he was saying: he felt as if he were shouting at her across endless distances, and she might vanish again before he could overtake her.

"I? Oh, I'm here on business too," she answered, turning her head toward him so that they were face to face. The words hardly reached him: he was aware only of her voice, and of the startling fact that not an echo of it had remained in his memory. He had not even remembered that it was low-pitched, with a faint roughness on the consonants.

"You do your hair differently," he said, his heart beating as if he had uttered something irrevocable.

"Differently? No—it's only that I do it as best I can when I'm without Nastasia."

"Nastasia; but isn't she with you?"

"No; I'm alone. For two days it was not worth while to bring her."

"You're alone—at the Parker House?"

She looked at him with a flash of her old malice. "Does it strike you as dangerous?"

"No; not dangerous —"

"But unconventional? I see; I suppose it is." She considered a moment. "I hadn't thought of it, because I've just done something so much more unconventional." The faint tinge of irony lingered in her eyes. "I've just refused to take back a sum of money—that belonged to me."

Archer sprang up and moved a step or two away. She had furled her parasol and sat absently drawing patterns on the gravel. Presently he came back and stood before her.

"Some one—has come here to meet you?"

"Yes."

"With this offer?"

She nodded.

"And you refused—because of the conditions?"

"I refused," she said after a moment.

He sat down by her again. "What were the conditions?"

"Oh, they were not onerous: just to sit at the head of his table now and then."

There was another interval of silence. Archer's heart had slammed itself shut in the queer way it had, and he sat vainly groping for a word.

"He wants you back—at any price?"

"Well—a considerable price. At least the sum is considerable for me."

He paused again, beating about the question he felt he must put.

"It was to meet him here that you came?"

She stared, and then burst into a laugh. "Meet him—my husband? *Here*? At this season he's always at Cowes or Baden."

"He sent some one?"

"Yes."

"With a letter?"

She shook her head. "No; just a message. He never writes. I don't think I've had more than one letter from him." The allusion brought the colour to her cheek, and it reflected itself in Archer's vivid blush.

"Why does he never write?"

"Why should he? What does one have secretaries for?"

The young man's blush deepened. She had pronounced the word as if it had no more significance than any other in her vocabulary. For a moment it was on the tip of his tongue to ask: "Did he send his secretary, then?" But the remembrance of Count Olenski's only letter to his wife was too present to him. He paused again, and then took another plunge.

"And the person?"—

"The emissary? The emissary," Madame Olenska rejoined, still smiling, "might, for all I care, have left already; but he has insisted on waiting till this evening ... in case ... on the chance ..."

"And you came out here to think the chance over?"

"I came out to get a breath of air. The hotel's too stifling. I'm taking the afternoon train back to Portsmouth."

They sat silent, not looking at each other, but straight ahead at the people passing along the path. Finally she turned her eyes again to his face and said: "You're not changed."

He felt like answering: "I was, till I saw you again;" but instead he stood up abruptly and glanced about him at the untidy sweltering park.

"This is horrible. Why shouldn't we go out a little on the bay? There's a breeze, and it will be cooler. We might take the steamboat down to Point Arley." She glanced up at him hesitatingly and he went on: "On a Monday morning there won't be anybody on the boat. My train doesn't leave till evening: I'm going back to New York. Why shouldn't we?" he insisted, looking down at her; and suddenly he broke out: "Haven't we done all we could?"

"Oh"—she murmured again. She stood up and reopened her sunshade, glancing about her as if to take counsel of the scene, and assure herself of the impossibility of remaining in it. Then her eyes returned to his face. "You mustn't say things like that to me," she said.

"I'll say anything you like; or nothing. I won't open my mouth unless you tell me to. What harm can it do to anybody? All I want is to listen to you," he stammered.

She drew out a little gold-faced watch on an enamelled chain. "Oh, don't calculate," he broke out; "give me the day! I want to get you away from that man. At what time was he coming?"

Her colour rose again. "At eleven."

"Then you must come at once."

"You needn't be afraid—if I don't come."

"Nor you either—if you do. I swear I only want to hear about you, to know what you've been doing. It's a hundred years since we've met—it may be another hundred before we meet again."

She still wavered, her anxious eyes on his face. "Why didn't you come down to the beach to fetch me, the day I was at Granny's?" she asked.

"Because you didn't look round—because you didn't know I was there. I swore I wouldn't unless you looked round." He laughed as the childishness of the confession struck him.

"But I didn't look round on purpose."

"On purpose?"

"I knew you were there; when you drove in I recognised the ponies. So I went down to the beach."

"To get away from me as far as you could?"

She repeated in a low voice: "To get away from you as far as I could."

He laughed out again, this time in boyish satisfaction. "Well, you see it's no use. I may as well tell you," he added, "that the business I came here for was just to find you. But, look here, we must start or we shall miss our boat."

"Our boat?" She frowned perplexedly, and then smiled. "Oh, but I must go back to the hotel first: I must leave a note —"

"As many notes as you please. You can write here." He drew out a note-case and one of the new stylographic pens. "I've even got an envelope—you see how everything's predestined! There—steady the thing on your knee, and I'll get the pen going in a second. They have to be humoured; wait —" He banged the hand that held the pen against the back of the bench. "It's like jerking down the mercury in a thermometer: just a trick. Now try —"

She laughed, and bending over the sheet of paper which he had laid on his note-case, began to write. Archer walked away a few steps, staring with radiant unseeing eyes at the passersby, who, in their turn, paused to stare at the unwonted sight of a fashionably-dressed lady writing a note on her knee on a bench in the Common.

Madame Olenska slipped the sheet into the envelope, wrote a name on it, and put it into her pocket. Then she too stood up.

They walked back toward Beacon Street, and near the club Archer caught sight of the plush-lined "herdic" which had carried his note to the Parker House, and whose driver was reposing from this effort by bathing his brow at the corner hydrant.

"I told you everything was predestined! Here's a cab for us. You see!" They laughed, astonished at the miracle of picking up a public conveyance at that hour, and in that unlikely spot, in a city where cab-stands were still a "foreign" novelty.

Archer, looking at his watch, saw that there was time to drive to the Parker House before going to the steamboat landing. They rattled through the hot streets and drew up at the door of the hotel.

Archer held out his hand for the letter. "Shall I take it in?" he asked; but Madame Olenska, shaking her head, sprang out and disappeared through the glazed doors. It was barely half-past ten; but what if the emissary, impatient for her reply, and not knowing how else to employ his time, were already seated among the travellers with cooling drinks at their elbows of whom Archer had caught a glimpse as she went in?

He waited, pacing up and down before the herdic. A Sicilian youth with eyes like Nastasia's offered to shine his boots, and an Irish matron to sell him peaches; and every few moments the doors opened to let out hot men with straw hats tilted far back, who glanced at him as they went by. He marvelled that the door should open so often, and that all the people it let out should look so like each other, and so like all the other hot men who, at that hour, through the length and breadth of the land, were passing continuously in and out of the swinging doors of hotels.

And then, suddenly, came a face that he could not relate to the other faces. He caught but a flash of it, for his pacings had carried him to the farthest point of his beat, and it was in turning back to the hotel that he saw, in a group of typical countenances—the lank and weary, the round and surprised, the lantern-jawed and mild—this other face that was so many more things at once, and things so different. It was that of a young man, pale too, and half-extinguished by the heat, or worry, or both, but somehow, quicker, vivider, more conscious; or perhaps seeming so because he was so different. Archer hung a moment on a thin thread of memory, but it snapped and floated off with the disappearing face—apparently that of some foreign business man, looking doubly foreign in such a setting. He vanished in the stream of passersby, and Archer resumed his patrol.

He did not care to be seen watch in hand within view of the hotel, and his unaided reckoning of the lapse of time led him to conclude that, if Madame Olenska was so long in reappearing, it could only be because she had met the emissary and been waylaid by him. At the thought Archer's apprehension rose to anguish.

"If she doesn't come soon I'll go in and find her," he said.

The doors swung open again and she was at his side. They got into the herdic, and as it drove off he took out his watch and saw that she had been absent just three minutes. In the clatter of loose windows that made talk impossible they bumped over the disjointed cobblestones to the wharf.

Seated side by side on a bench of the half-empty boat they found that they had hardly anything to say to each other, or rather that what they had to say communicated itself best in the blessed silence of their release and their isolation.

As the paddle-wheels began to turn, and wharves and shipping to recede through the veil of heat, it seemed to Archer that everything in the old familiar world of habit was receding also. He longed to ask Madame Olenska if she did not have the same feeling: the feeling that they were starting on some long voyage from which they might never return. But he was afraid to say it, or anything else that might disturb the delicate balance of her trust in him. In reality he had no wish to betray that trust. There had been days and nights when the memory of their kiss had burned and burned on his lips; the day before even, on the drive to Portsmouth, the thought of her had run through him like fire; but now that she was beside him, and they were drifting forth into this unknown world, they seemed to have reached the kind of deeper nearness that a touch may sunder.

As the boat left the harbour and turned seaward a breeze stirred about them and the bay broke up into long oily undulations, then into ripples tipped with spray. The fog of sultriness still hung over the city, but ahead lay a fresh world of ruffled waters, and distant promontories with light-houses in the sun. Madame Olenska, leaning back against the boat-rail, drank in the coolness between parted lips. She had wound a long veil about her hat, but it left her face uncovered, and Archer was struck by the tranquil gaiety of her expression. She seemed to take their adventure as a matter of course, and to be neither in fear of unexpected encounters, nor (what was worse) unduly elated by their possibility.

In the bare dining-room of the inn, which he had hoped they would have to themselves, they found a strident party of innocent-looking young men and women—school-teachers on a holiday, the landlord told them—and Archer's heart sank at the idea of having to talk through their noise.

"This is hopeless—I'll ask for a private room," he said; and Madame Olenska, without offering any objection, waited while he went in search of it. The room opened on a long wooden verandah, with the sea coming in at the windows. It was bare and cool, with a table covered with a coarse checkered cloth and adorned by a bottle of pickles and a blueberry pie under a cage. No more guileless-looking cabinet particulier ever offered its shelter to a clandestine couple: Archer fancied he saw the sense of its reassurance in the faintly amused smile with which Madame Olenska sat down opposite to him. A woman who had run away from her husband—and reputedly with another man—was likely to have mastered the art of taking things for granted; but something in the quality of her composure took the edge from his irony. By being so quiet, so unsurprised and so simple she had managed to brush away the conventions and make him feel that to seek to be alone was the natural thing for two old friends who had so much to say to each other....

## XXIV.

They lunched slowly and meditatively, with mute intervals between rushes of talk; for, the spell once broken, they had much to say, and yet moments when saying became the mere accompaniment to long duologues of silence. Archer kept the talk from his own affairs, not with conscious intention but because he did not want to miss a word of her history; and leaning on the table, her chin resting on her clasped hands, she talked to him of the year and a half since they had met.

She had grown tired of what people called "society"; New York was kind, it was almost oppressively hospitable; she should never forget the way in which it had welcomed her back; but after the first flush of novelty she had found herself, as she phrased it, too "different" to care for the things it cared about—and so she had decided to try Washington, where one was supposed to meet more varieties of people and of opinion. And on the whole she should probably settle down in Washington, and make a home there for poor Medora, who had worn out the patience of all her other relations just at the time when she most needed looking after and protecting from matrimonial perils.

"But Dr. Carver—aren't you afraid of Dr. Carver? I hear he's been staying with you at the Blenkers'."

She smiled. "Oh, the Carver danger is over. Dr. Carver is a very clever man. He wants a rich wife to finance his plans, and Medora is simply a good advertisement as a convert."

"A convert to what?"

"To all sorts of new and crazy social schemes. But, do you know, they interest me more than the blind conformity to tradition—somebody else's tradition—that I see among our own friends. It seems stupid to have discovered America only to make it into a copy of another country." She smiled across the table. "Do you suppose Christopher Columbus would have taken all that trouble just to go to the Opera with the Selfridge Merrys?"

Archer changed colour. "And Beaufort—do you say these things to Beaufort?" he asked abruptly.

"I haven't seen him for a long time. But I used to; and he understands."

"Ah, it's what I've always told you; you don't like us. And you like Beaufort because he's so unlike us." He looked about the bare room and out at the bare beach and the row of stark white village houses strung along the shore. "We're damnably dull. We've no character, no colour, no variety.—I wonder," he broke out, "why you don't go back?"

Her eyes darkened, and he expected an indignant rejoinder. But she sat silent, as if thinking over what he had said, and he grew frightened lest she should answer that she wondered too.

At length she said: "I believe it's because of you."

It was impossible to make the confession more dispassionately, or in a tone less encouraging to the vanity of the person addressed. Archer reddened to the temples, but dared not move or speak: it was as if her words had been some rare butterfly that the least motion might drive off on startled wings, but that might gather a flock about it if it were left undisturbed.

"At least," she continued, "it was you who made me understand that under the dullness there are things so fine and sensitive and delicate that even those I most cared for in my other life look cheap in comparison. I don't know how to explain myself"—she drew together her troubled brows—"but it seems as if I'd never before understood with how much that is hard and shabby and base the most exquisite pleasures may be paid."

"Exquisite pleasures—it's something to have had them!" he felt like retorting; but the appeal in her eyes kept him silent.

"I want," she went on, "to be perfectly honest with you—and with myself. For a long time I've hoped this chance would come: that I might tell you how you've helped me, what you've made of me —"

Archer sat staring beneath frowning brows. He interrupted her with a laugh. "And what do you make out that you've made of me?"

She paled a little. "Of you?"

"Yes: for I'm of your making much more than you ever were of mine. I'm the man who married one woman because another one told him to."

Her paleness turned to a fugitive flush. "I thought—you promised—you were not to say such things today."

"Ah—how like a woman! None of you will ever see a bad business through!"

She lowered her voice. "IS it a bad business—for May?"

He stood in the window, drumming against the raised sash, and feeling in every fibre the wistful tenderness with which she had spoken her cousin's name.

"For that's the thing we've always got to think of—haven't we—by your own showing?" she insisted.

"My own showing?" he echoed, his blank eyes still on the sea.

"Or if not," she continued, pursuing her own thought with a painful application, "if it's not worth while to have given up, to have missed things, so that others may be saved from disillusionment and misery—then everything I came home for, everything that made my other life seem by contrast so bare and so poor because no one there took account of them—all these things are a sham or a dream —"

He turned around without moving from his place. "And in that case there's no reason on earth why you shouldn't go back?" he concluded for her.

Her eyes were clinging to him desperately. "Oh, IS there no reason?"

"Not if you staked your all on the success of my marriage. My marriage," he said savagely, "isn't going to be a sight to keep you here." She made no answer, and he went on: "What's the use? You gave me my first glimpse of a real life, and at the same moment you asked me to go on with a sham one. It's beyond human enduring—that's all."

"Oh, don't say that; when I'm enduring it!" she burst out, her eyes filling.

Her arms had dropped along the table, and she sat with her face abandoned to his gaze as if in the recklessness of a desperate peril. The face exposed her as much as if it had been her whole person, with the soul behind it: Archer stood dumb, overwhelmed by what it suddenly told him.

"You too—oh, all this time, you too?"

For answer, she let the tears on her lids overflow and run slowly downward.

Half the width of the room was still between them, and neither made any show of moving. Archer was conscious of a curious indifference to her bodily presence: he would hardly have been aware of it if one of the hands she had flung out on the table had not drawn his gaze as on the occasion when, in the little Twenty-third Street house, he had kept his eye on it in order not to look at her face. Now his imagination spun about the hand as about the edge of a vortex; but still he made no effort to draw nearer. He had known the love that is fed on caresses and feeds them; but this passion that was closer than his bones was not to be superficially satisfied. His one terror was to do anything which might efface the sound and impression of her words; his one thought, that he should never again feel quite alone.

But after a moment the sense of waste and ruin overcame him. There they were, close together and safe and shut in; yet so chained to their separate destinies that they might as well have been half the world apart.

"What's the use—when you will go back?" he broke out, a great hopeless *How on Earth can I keep you?* crying out to her beneath his words.

She sat motionless, with lowered lids. "Oh—I shan't go yet!"

"Not yet? Some time, then? Some time that you already foresee?"

At that she raised her clearest eyes. "I promise you: not as long as you hold out. Not as long as we can look straight at each other like this."

He dropped into his chair. What her answer really said was: "If you lift a finger you'll drive me back: back to all the abominations you know of, and all the temptations you half guess." He understood it as clearly as if she had uttered the words, and the thought kept him anchored to his side of the table in a kind of moved and sacred submission.

"What a life for you!—" he groaned.

"Oh—as long as it's a part of yours."

"And mine a part of yours?"

She nodded.

"And that's to be all—for either of us?"

"Well; it IS all, isn't it?"

At that he sprang up, forgetting everything but the sweetness of her face. She rose too, not as if to meet him or to flee from him, but quietly, as though the worst of the task were done and she had only to wait; so quietly that, as he came close, her outstretched hands acted not as a check but as a guide to him. They fell into his, while her arms, extended but not rigid, kept him far enough off to let her surrendered face say the rest.

They may have stood in that way for a long time, or only for a few moments; but it was long enough for her silence to communicate all she had to say, and for him to feel that only one thing mattered. He must do nothing to make this meeting their last; he must leave their future in her care, asking only that she should keep fast hold of it.

"Don't—don't be unhappy," she said, with a break in her voice, as she drew her hands away; and he answered: "You won't go back—you won't go back?" as if it were the one possibility he could not bear.

"I won't go back," she said; and turning away she opened the door and led the way into the public dining-room.

The strident school-teachers were gathering up their possessions preparatory to a straggling flight to the wharf; across the beach lay the white steam-boat at the pier; and over the sunlit waters Boston loomed in a line of haze.

## XXV.

Once more on the boat, and in the presence of others, Archer felt a tranquillity of spirit that surprised as much as it sustained him.

The day, according to any current valuation, had been a rather ridiculous failure; he had not so much as touched Madame Olenska's hand with his lips, or extracted one word from her that gave promise of farther opportunities. Nevertheless, for a man sick with unsatisfied love, and parting for an indefinite period from the object of his passion, he felt himself almost humiliatingly calm and comforted. It was the perfect balance she had held between their loyalty to others and their honesty to themselves that had so stirred and yet tranquillized him; a balance not artfully calculated, as her tears and her falterings showed, but resulting naturally from her unabashed sincerity. It filled him with a tender awe, now the danger was over, and made him thank the fates that no personal vanity, no sense of playing a part before sophisticated witnesses, had tempted him to tempt her. Even after they had clasped hands for good-bye at the Fall River station, and he had turned away alone, the conviction remained with him of having saved out of their meeting much more than he had sacrificed.

He wandered back to the club, and went and sat alone in the deserted library, turning and turning over in his thoughts every separate second of their hours together. It was clear to him, and it grew more clear under closer scrutiny, that if she should finally decide on returning to Europe—returning to her husband—it would not be because her old life tempted her, even on the new terms offered. No: she would go only if she felt herself becoming a temptation to Archer, a temptation to fall away from the standard they had both set up. Her choice would be to stay near him as long as he did not ask her to come nearer; and it depended on himself to keep her just there, safe but secluded.

In the train these thoughts were still with him. They enclosed him in a kind of golden haze, through which the faces about him looked remote and indistinct: he had a feeling that if he spoke to his fellow-travellers they would not understand what he was saying. In this state of abstraction he found himself, the following morning, waking to the reality of a stifling September day in New York. The heat-withered faces in the long train streamed past him, and he continued to stare at them through the same golden blur; but suddenly, as he left the station, one of the faces detached itself, came closer and forced itself upon his consciousness. It was, as he instantly recalled, the face of the young man he had seen, the day before, passing out of the Parker House, and had noted as not conforming to type, as not having an American hotel face.

The same thing struck him now; and again he became aware of a dim stir of former associations. The young man stood looking about him with the dazed air of the foreigner flung upon the harsh mercies of American travel; then he advanced toward Archer, lifted his hat, and said in English: "Surely, Monsieur, we met in London?"

"Ah, to be sure: in London!" Archer grasped his hand with curiosity and sympathy. "So you *did* get here, after all?" he exclaimed, casting a wondering eye on the astute and haggard little countenance of young Carfry's French tutor.

"Oh, I got here—yes," M. Riviere smiled with drawn lips. "But not for long; I return the day after tomorrow." He stood grasping his light valise in one neatly gloved hand, and gazing anxiously, perplexedly, almost appealingly, into Archer's face.

"I wonder, Monsieur, since I've had the good luck to run across you, if I might —"

"I was just going to suggest it: come to luncheon, won't you? Down town, I mean: if you'll look me up in my office I'll take you to a very decent restaurant in that quarter."

M. Riviere was visibly touched and surprised. "You're too kind. But I was only going to ask if you would tell me how to reach some sort of conveyance. There are no porters, and no one here seems to listen —"

"I know: our American stations must surprise you. When you ask for a porter they give you chewing-gum. But if you'll come along I'll extricate you; and you must really lunch with me, you know."

The young man, after a just perceptible hesitation, replied, with profuse thanks, and in a tone that did not carry complete conviction, that he was already engaged; but when they had reached the comparative reassurance of the street he asked if he might call that afternoon.

Archer, at ease in the midsummer leisure of the office, fixed an hour and scribbled his address, which the Frenchman pocketed with reiterated thanks and a wide flourish of his hat. A horse-car received him, and Archer walked away.

Punctually at the hour M. Riviere appeared, shaved, smoothed-out, but still unmistakably drawn and serious. Archer was alone in his office, and the young man, before accepting the seat he proffered, began abruptly: "I believe I saw you, sir, yesterday in Boston."

The statement was insignificant enough, and Archer was about to frame an assent when his words were checked by something mysterious yet illuminating in his visitor's insistent gaze.

"It is extraordinary, very extraordinary," M. Riviere continued, "that we should have met in the circumstances in which I find myself."

"What circumstances?" Archer asked, wondering a little crudely if he needed money.

M. Riviere continued to study him with tentative eyes. "I have come, not to look for employment, as I spoke of doing when we last met, but on a special mission —"

"Ah—!" Archer exclaimed. In a flash the two meetings had connected themselves in his mind. He paused to take in the situation thus suddenly lighted up for him, and M. Riviere also remained silent, as if aware that what he had said was enough.

"A special mission," Archer at length repeated.

The young Frenchman, opening his palms, raised them slightly, and the two men continued to look at each other across the office-desk till Archer roused himself to say: "Do sit down"; whereupon M. Riviere bowed, took a distant chair, and again waited.

"It was about this mission that you wanted to consult me?" Archer finally asked.

M. Riviere bent his head. "Not in my own behalf: on that score I—I have fully dealt with myself. I should like—if I may—to speak to you about the Countess Olenska."

Archer had known for the last few minutes that the words were coming; but when they came they sent the blood rushing to his temples as if he had been caught by a bent-back branch in a thicket.

"And on whose behalf," he said, "do you wish to do this?"

M. Riviere met the question sturdily. "Well—I might say *hers*, if it did not sound like a liberty. Shall I say instead: on behalf of abstract justice?"

Archer considered him ironically. "In other words: you are Count Olenski's messenger?"

He saw his blush more darkly reflected in M. Riviere's sallow countenance. "Not to *you*, Monsieur. If I come to you, it is on quite other grounds."

"What right have you, in the circumstances, to *be* on any other ground?" Archer retorted. "If you're an emissary you're an emissary."

The young man considered. "My mission is over: as far as the Countess Olenska goes, it has failed."

"I can't help that," Archer rejoined on the same note of irony.

"No: but you can help —" M. Riviere paused, turned his hat about in his still carefully gloved hands, looked into its lining and then back at Archer's face. "You can help, Monsieur, I am convinced, to make it equally a failure with her family."

Archer pushed back his chair and stood up. "Well—and by God I will!" he exclaimed. He stood with his hands in his pockets, staring down wrathfully at the little Frenchman, whose face, though he too had risen, was still an inch or two below the line of Archer's eyes.

M. Riviere paled to his normal hue: paler than that his complexion could hardly turn.

"Why the devil," Archer explosively continued, "should you have thought—since I suppose you're appealing to me on the ground of my relationship to Madame Olenska—that I should take a view contrary to the rest of her family?"

The change of expression in M. Riviere's face was for a time his only answer. His look passed from timidity to absolute distress: for a young man of his usually resourceful mien it would have been difficult to appear more disarmed and defenceless. "Oh, Monsieur —"

"I can't imagine," Archer continued, "why you should have come to me when there are others so much nearer to the Countess; still less why you thought I should be more accessible to the arguments I suppose you were sent over with."

M. Riviere took this onslaught with a disconcerting humility. "The arguments I want to present to you, Monsieur, are my own and not those I was sent over with."

"Then I see still less reason for listening to them."

M. Riviere again looked into his hat, as if considering whether these last words were not a sufficiently broad hint to put it on and be gone. Then he spoke with sudden decision. "Monsieur—will you tell me one thing? Is it my right to be here that you question? Or do you perhaps believe the whole matter to be already closed?"

His quiet insistence made Archer feel the clumsiness of his own bluster. M. Riviere had succeeded in imposing himself: Archer, reddening slightly, dropped into his chair again, and signed to the young man to be seated.

"I beg your pardon: but why isn't the matter closed?"

M. Riviere gazed back at him with anguish. "You do, then, agree with the rest of the family that, in face of the new proposals I have brought, it is hardly possible for Madame Olenska not to return to her husband?"

"Good God!" Archer exclaimed; and his visitor gave out a low murmur of confirmation.

"Before seeing her, I saw—at Count Olenski's request—Mr. Lovell Mingott, with whom I had several talks before going to Boston. I understand that he represents his mother's view; and that Mrs. Manson Mingott's influence is great throughout her family."

Archer sat silent, with the sense of clinging to the edge of a sliding precipice. The discovery that he had been excluded from a share in these negotiations, and even from the knowledge that they were on foot, caused him a surprise hardly dulled by the acuter wonder of what he was learning. He saw in a flash that if the family had ceased to consult him it was because some deep tribal instinct warned them that he was no longer on their side; and he recalled, with a start of comprehension, a remark of May's during their drive home from Mrs. Manson Mingott's on the day of the Archery Meeting: "Perhaps, after all, Ellen would be happier with her husband."

Even in the tumult of new discoveries Archer remembered his indignant exclamation, and the fact that since then his wife had never named Madame Olenska to him. Her careless allusion had no doubt been the straw held up to see which way the wind blew; the result had been reported to the family, and thereafter Archer had been tacitly omitted from their counsels. He admired the tribal discipline which made May bow to this decision. She would not have done so, he knew, had her conscience protested; but she probably shared the family view that Madame Olenska would be better off as an unhappy wife than as a separated one, and that there was no use in discussing the case with Newland, who had an awkward way of suddenly not seeming to take the most fundamental things for granted.

Archer looked up and met his visitor's anxious gaze. "Don't you know, Monsieur—is it possible you don't know—that the family begin to doubt if they have the right to advise the Countess to refuse her husband's last proposals?"

"The proposals you brought?"

"The proposals I brought."

It was on Archer's lips to exclaim that whatever he knew or did not know was no concern of M. Riviere's; but something in the humble and yet courageous tenacity of M. Riviere's gaze made him reject this conclusion, and he met the young man's question with another. "What is your object in speaking to me of this?"

He had not to wait a moment for the answer. "To beg you, Monsieur—to beg you with all the force I'm capable of—not to let her go back.—Oh, don't let her!" M. Riviere exclaimed.

Archer looked at him with increasing astonishment. There was no mistaking the sincerity of his distress or the strength of his determination: he had evidently resolved to let everything go by the board but the supreme need of thus putting himself on record. Archer considered.

"May I ask," he said at length, "if this is the line you took with the Countess Olenska?"

M. Riviere reddened, but his eyes did not falter. "No, Monsieur: I accepted my mission in good faith. I really believed—for reasons I need not trouble you with—that it would be better for Madame Olenska to recover her situation, her fortune, the social consideration that her husband's standing gives her."

"So I supposed: you could hardly have accepted such a mission otherwise."

"I should not have accepted it."

"Well, then—?" Archer paused again, and their eyes met in another protracted scrutiny.

"Ah, Monsieur, after I had seen her, after I had listened to her, I knew she was better off here."

"You knew—?"

"Monsieur, I discharged my mission faithfully: I put the Count's arguments, I stated his offers, without adding any comment of my own. The Countess was good enough to listen patiently; she carried her goodness so far as to see me twice; she considered impartially all I had come to say. And it was in the course of these two talks that I changed my mind, that I came to see things differently."

"May I ask what led to this change?"

"Simply seeing the change in *her*," M. Riviere replied.

"The change in her? Then you knew her before?"

The young man's colour again rose. "I used to see her in her husband's house. I have known Count Olenski for many years. You can imagine that he would not have sent a stranger on such a mission."

Archer's gaze, wandering away to the blank walls of the office, rested on a hanging calendar surmounted by the rugged features of the President of the United States. That such a conversation should be going on anywhere within the millions of square miles subject to his rule seemed as strange as anything that the imagination could invent.

"The change—what sort of a change?"

"Ah, Monsieur, if I could tell you!" M. Riviere paused. "Tenez—the discovery, I suppose, of what I'd never thought of before: that she's an American. And that if you're an American of *her* kind—of your kind—things that are accepted in certain other societies, or at least put up with as part of a general convenient give-and-take—become unthinkable, simply unthinkable. If Madame Olenska's relations understood what these things were, their opposition to her returning would no doubt be as unconditional as her own; but they seem to regard her husband's wish to have her back as proof of an irresistible longing for domestic life." M. Riviere paused, and then added: "Whereas it's far from being as simple as that."

Archer looked back to the President of the United States, and then down at his desk and at the papers scattered on it. For a second or two he could not trust himself to speak. During this interval he heard M. Riviere's chair pushed back, and was aware that the young man had risen. When he glanced up again he saw that his visitor was as moved as himself.

"Thank you," Archer said simply.

"There's nothing to thank me for, Monsieur: it is I, rather —" M. Riviere broke off, as if speech for him too were difficult. "I should like, though," he continued in a firmer voice, "to add one thing. You asked me if I was in Count Olenski's employ. I am at this moment: I returned to him, a few months ago, for reasons of private necessity such as may happen to any one who has persons, ill and older persons, dependent on him. But from the moment that I have taken the step of coming here to say these things to you I consider myself discharged, and I shall tell him so on my return, and give him the reasons. That's all, Monsieur."

M. Riviere bowed and drew back a step.

"Thank you," Archer said again, as their hands met.

## XXVI.

Every year on the fifteenth of October Fifth Avenue opened its shutters, unrolled its carpets and hung up its triple layer of window-curtains.

By the first of November this household ritual was over, and society had begun to look about and take stock of itself. By the fifteenth the season was in full blast, Opera and theatres were putting forth their new attractions, dinner-engagements were accumulating, and dates for dances being fixed. And punctually at about this time Mrs. Archer always said that New York was very much changed.

Observing it from the lofty stand-point of a non-participant, she was able, with the help of Mr. Sillerton Jackson and Miss Sophy, to trace each new crack in its surface, and all the strange weeds pushing up between the ordered rows of social vegetables. It had been one of the amusements of Archer's youth to wait for this annual pronouncement of his mother's, and to hear her enumerate the minute signs of disintegration that his careless gaze had overlooked. For New York, to Mrs. Archer's mind, never changed without changing for the worse; and in this view Miss Sophy Jackson heartily concurred.

Mr. Sillerton Jackson, as became a man of the world, suspended his judgment and listened with an amused impartiality to the lamentations of the ladies. But even he never denied that New York had changed; and Newland

Archer, in the winter of the second year of his marriage, was himself obliged to admit that if it had not actually changed it was certainly changing.

These points had been raised, as usual, at Mrs. Archer's Thanksgiving dinner. At the date when she was officially enjoined to give thanks for the blessings of the year it was her habit to take a mournful though not embittered stock of her world, and wonder what there was to be thankful for. At any rate, not the state of society; society, if it could be said to exist, was rather a spectacle on which to call down Biblical imprecations—and in fact, every one knew what the Reverend Dr. Ashmore meant when he chose a text from Jeremiah (chap. ii., verse 25) for his Thanksgiving sermon. Dr. Ashmore, the new Rector of St. Matthew's, had been chosen because he was very "advanced": his sermons were considered bold in thought and novel in language. When he fulminated against fashionable society he always spoke of its "trend"; and to Mrs. Archer it was terrifying and yet fascinating to feel herself part of a community that was trending.

"There's no doubt that Dr. Ashmore is right: there IS a marked trend," she said, as if it were something visible and measurable, like a crack in a house.

"It was odd, though, to preach about it on Thanksgiving," Miss Jackson opined; and her hostess drily rejoined: "Oh, he means us to give thanks for what's left."

Archer had been wont to smile at these annual vaticinations of his mother's; but this year even he was obliged to acknowledge, as he listened to an enumeration of the changes, that the "trend" was visible.

"The extravagance in dress—" Miss Jackson began. "Sillerton took me to the first night of the Opera, and I can only tell you that Jane Merry's dress was the only one I recognised from last year; and even that had had the front panel changed. Yet I know she got it out from Worth only two years ago, because my seamstress always goes in to make over her Paris dresses before she wears them."

"Ah, Jane Merry is one of *us*," said Mrs. Archer sighing, as if it were not such an enviable thing to be in an age when ladies were beginning to flaunt abroad their Paris dresses as soon as they were out of the Custom House, instead of letting them mellow under lock and key, in the manner of Mrs. Archer's contemporaries.

"Yes; she's one of the few. In my youth," Miss Jackson rejoined, "it was considered vulgar to dress in the newest fashions; and Amy Sillerton has always told me that in Boston the rule was to put away one's Paris dresses for two years. Old Mrs. Baxter Pennilow, who did everything handsomely, used to import twelve a year, two velvet, two satin, two silk, and the other six of poplin and the finest cashmere. It was a standing order, and as she was ill for two years before she died they found forty-eight Worth dresses that had never been taken out of tissue paper; and when the girls left off their mourning they were able to wear the first lot at the Symphony concerts without looking in advance of the fashion."

"Ah, well, Boston is more conservative than New York; but I always think it's a safe rule for a lady to lay aside her French dresses for one season," Mrs. Archer conceded.

"It was Beaufort who started the new fashion by making his wife clap her new clothes on her back as soon as they arrived: I must say at times it takes all Regina's distinction not to look like ... like ..." Miss Jackson glanced around the table, caught Janey's bulging gaze, and took refuge in an unintelligible murmur.

"Like her rivals," said Mr. Sillerton Jackson, with the air of producing an epigram.

"Oh,—" the ladies murmured; and Mrs. Archer added, partly to distract her daughter's attention from forbidden topics: "Poor Regina! Her Thanksgiving hasn't been a very cheerful one, I'm afraid. Have you heard the rumours about Beaufort's speculations, Sillerton?"

Mr. Jackson nodded carelessly. Every one had heard the rumours in question, and he scorned to confirm a tale that was already common property.

A gloomy silence fell upon the party. No one really liked Beaufort, and it was not wholly unpleasant to think the worst of his private life; but the idea of his having brought financial dishonour on his wife's family was too shocking to be enjoyed even by his enemies. Archer's New York tolerated hypocrisy in private relations; but in business matters it exacted a limpid and impeccable honesty. It was a long time since any well-known banker had failed discreditably; but every one remembered the social extinction visited on the heads of the firm when the last event of the kind had happened. It would be the same with the Beauforts, in spite of his power and her popularity; not all the leagued strength of the Dallas connection would save poor Regina if there were any truth in the reports of her husband's unlawful speculations.

The talk took refuge in less ominous topics; but everything they touched on seemed to confirm Mrs. Archer's sense of an accelerated trend.

"Of course, Newland, I know you let dear May go to Mrs. Struthers's Sunday evenings —" she began; and May interposed gaily: "Oh, you know, everybody goes to Mrs. Struthers's now; and she was invited to Granny's last reception."

It was thus, Archer reflected, that New York managed its transitions: conspiring to ignore them till they were well over, and then, in all good faith, imagining that they had taken place in a preceding age. There was always a traitor in the citadel; and after he (or generally she) had surrendered the keys, what was the use of pretending that it was impregnable? Once people had tasted of Mrs. Struthers's easy Sunday hospitality they were not likely to sit at home remembering that her champagne was transmuted Shoe-Polish.

"I know, dear, I know," Mrs. Archer sighed. "Such things have to be, I suppose, as long as *amusement* is what people go out for; but I've never quite forgiven your cousin Madame Olenska for being the first person to countenance Mrs. Struthers."

A sudden blush rose to young Mrs. Archer's face; it surprised her husband as much as the other guests about the table. "Oh, *Ellen* —" she murmured, much in the same accusing and yet deprecating tone in which her parents might have said: "Oh, *the blenkers*—."

It was the note which the family had taken to sounding on the mention of the Countess Olenska's name, since she had surprised and inconvenienced them by remaining obdurate to her husband's advances; but on May's lips it gave food for thought, and Archer looked at her with the sense of strangeness that sometimes came over him when she was most in the tone of her environment.

His mother, with less than her usual sensitiveness to atmosphere, still insisted: "I've always thought that people like the Countess Olenska, who have lived in aristocratic societies, ought to help us to keep up our social distinctions, instead of ignoring them."

May's blush remained permanently vivid: it seemed to have a significance beyond that implied by the recognition of Madame Olenska's social bad faith.

"I've no doubt we all seem alike to foreigners," said Miss Jackson tartly.

"I don't think Ellen cares for society; but nobody knows exactly what she does care for," May continued, as if she had been groping for something noncommittal.

"Ah, well —" Mrs. Archer sighed again.

Everybody knew that the Countess Olenska was no longer in the good graces of her family. Even her devoted champion, old Mrs. Manson Mingott, had been unable to defend her refusal to return to her husband. The Mingotts had not proclaimed their disapproval aloud: their sense of solidarity was too strong. They had simply, as Mrs. Welland said, "let poor Ellen find her own level"—and that, mortifyingly and incomprehensibly, was in the dim depths where the Blenkers prevailed, and "people who wrote" celebrated their untidy rites. It was incredible, but it was a fact, that Ellen, in spite of all her opportunities and her privileges, had become simply "Bohemian." The fact enforced the contention that she had made a fatal mistake in not returning to Count Olenski. After all, a young woman's place was under her husband's roof, especially when she had left it in circumstances that ... well ... if one had cared to look into them ...

"Madame Olenska is a great favourite with the gentlemen," said Miss Sophy, with her air of wishing to put forth something conciliatory when she knew that she was planting a dart.

"Ah, that's the danger that a young woman like Madame Olenska is always exposed to," Mrs. Archer mournfully agreed; and the ladies, on this conclusion, gathered up their trains to seek the carcel globes of the drawing-room, while Archer and Mr. Sillerton Jackson withdrew to the Gothic library.

Once established before the grate, and consoling himself for the inadequacy of the dinner by the perfection of his cigar, Mr. Jackson became portentous and communicable.

"If the Beaufort smash comes," he announced, "there are going to be disclosures."

Archer raised his head quickly: he could never hear the name without the sharp vision of Beaufort's heavy figure, opulently furred and shod, advancing through the snow at Skuytercliff.

"There's bound to be," Mr. Jackson continued, "the nastiest kind of a cleaning up. He hasn't spent all his money on Regina."

"Oh, well—that's discounted, isn't it? My belief is he'll pull out yet," said the young man, wanting to change the subject.

"Perhaps—perhaps. I know he was to see some of the influential people today. Of course," Mr. Jackson reluctantly conceded, "it's to be hoped they can tide him over—this time anyhow. I shouldn't like to think of poor Regina's spending the rest of her life in some shabby foreign watering-place for bankrupts."

Archer said nothing. It seemed to him so natural—however tragic—that money ill-gotten should be cruelly expiated, that his mind, hardly lingering over Mrs. Beaufort's doom, wandered back to closer questions. What was the meaning of May's blush when the Countess Olenska had been mentioned?

Four months had passed since the midsummer day that he and Madame Olenska had spent together; and since then he had not seen her. He knew that she had returned to Washington, to the little house which she and Medora Manson had taken there: he had written to her once—a few words, asking when they were to meet again—and she had even more briefly replied: "Not yet."

Since then there had been no farther communication between them, and he had built up within himself a kind of sanctuary in which she throned among his secret thoughts and longings. Little by little it became the scene of his real life, of his only rational activities; thither he brought the books he read, the ideas and feelings which nourished him, his judgments and his visions. Outside it, in the scene of his actual life, he moved with a growing sense of unreality and insufficiency, blundering against familiar prejudices and traditional points of view as an absent-minded man goes on bumping into the furniture of his own room. Absent—that was what he was: so absent from everything most densely real and near to those about him that it sometimes startled him to find they still imagined he was there.

He became aware that Mr. Jackson was clearing his throat preparatory to farther revelations.

"I don't know, of course, how far your wife's family are aware of what people say about—well, about Madame Olenska's refusal to accept her husband's latest offer."

Archer was silent, and Mr. Jackson obliquely continued: "It's a pity—it's certainly a pity—that she refused it."

"A pity? In God's name, why?"

Mr. Jackson looked down his leg to the unwrinkled sock that joined it to a glossy pump.

"Well—to put it on the lowest ground—what's she going to live on now?"

"Now—?"

"If Beaufort —"

Archer sprang up, his fist banging down on the black walnut-edge of the writing-table. The wells of the brass double-inkstand danced in their sockets.

"What the devil do you mean, sir?"

Mr. Jackson, shifting himself slightly in his chair, turned a tranquil gaze on the young man's burning face.

"Well—I have it on pretty good authority—in fact, on old Catherine's herself—that the family reduced Countess Olenska's allowance considerably when she definitely refused to go back to her husband; and as, by this refusal, she also forfeits the money settled on her when she married—which Olenski was ready to make over to her if she returned—why, what the devil do YOU mean, my dear boy, by asking me what I mean?" Mr. Jackson good-humouredly retorted.

Archer moved toward the mantelpiece and bent over to knock his ashes into the grate.

"I don't know anything of Madame Olenska's private affairs; but I don't need to, to be certain that what you insinuate —"

"Oh, I don't: it's Lefferts, for one," Mr. Jackson interposed.

"Lefferts—who made love to her and got snubbed for it!" Archer broke out contemptuously.

"Ah—*did* he?" snapped the other, as if this were exactly the fact he had been laying a trap for. He still sat sideways from the fire, so that his hard old gaze held Archer's face as if in a spring of steel.

"Well, well: it's a pity she didn't go back before Beaufort's cropper," he repeated. "If she goes *now*, and if he fails, it will only confirm the general impression: which isn't by any means peculiar to Lefferts, by the way."

"Oh, she won't go back now: less than ever!" Archer had no sooner said it than he had once more the feeling that it was exactly what Mr. Jackson had been waiting for.

The old gentleman considered him attentively. "That's your opinion, eh? Well, no doubt you know. But everybody will tell you that the few pennies Medora Manson has left are all in Beaufort's hands; and how the two women are to keep their heads above water unless he does, I can't imagine. Of course, Madame Olenska may still soften old Catherine, who's been the most inexorably opposed to her staying; and old Catherine could make her any allowance she chooses. But we all know that she hates parting with good money; and the rest of the family have no particular interest in keeping Madame Olenska here."

Archer was burning with unavailing wrath: he was exactly in the state when a man is sure to do something stupid, knowing all the while that he is doing it.

He saw that Mr. Jackson had been instantly struck by the fact that Madame Olenska's differences with her grandmother and her other relations were not known to him, and that the old gentleman had drawn his own conclusions as to the reasons for Archer's exclusion from the family councils. This fact warned Archer to go warily; but the insinuations about Beaufort made him reckless. He was mindful, however, if not of his own danger, at least of the fact that Mr. Jackson was under his mother's roof, and consequently his guest. Old New York scrupulously observed the etiquette of hospitality, and no discussion with a guest was ever allowed to degenerate into a disagreement.

"Shall we go up and join my mother?" he suggested curtly, as Mr. Jackson's last cone of ashes dropped into the brass ashtray at his elbow.

On the drive homeward May remained oddly silent; through the darkness, he still felt her enveloped in her menacing blush. What its menace meant he could not guess: but he was sufficiently warned by the fact that Madame Olenska's name had evoked it.

They went upstairs, and he turned into the library. She usually followed him; but he heard her passing down the passage to her bedroom.

"May!" he called out impatiently; and she came back, with a slight glance of surprise at his tone.

"This lamp is smoking again; I should think the servants might see that it's kept properly trimmed," he grumbled nervously.

"I'm so sorry: it shan't happen again," she answered, in the firm bright tone she had learned from her mother; and it exasperated Archer to feel that she was already beginning to humour him like a younger Mr. Welland. She bent over to lower the wick, and as the light struck up on her white shoulders and the clear curves of her face he thought: "How young she is! For what endless years this life will have to go on!"

He felt, with a kind of horror, his own strong youth and the bounding blood in his veins. "Look here," he said suddenly, "I may have to go to Washington for a few days—soon; next week perhaps."

Her hand remained on the key of the lamp as she turned to him slowly. The heat from its flame had brought back a glow to her face, but it paled as she looked up.

"On business?" she asked, in a tone which implied that there could be no other conceivable reason, and that she had put the question automatically, as if merely to finish his own sentence.

"On business, naturally. There's a patent case coming up before the Supreme Court —" He gave the name of the inventor, and went on furnishing details with all Lawrence Lefferts's practised glibness, while she listened attentively, saying at intervals: "Yes, I see."

"The change will do you good," she said simply, when he had finished; "and you must be sure to go and see Ellen," she added, looking him straight in the eyes with her cloudless smile, and speaking in the tone she might have employed in urging him not to neglect some irksome family duty.

It was the only word that passed between them on the subject; but in the code in which they had both been trained it meant: "Of course you understand that I know all that people have been saying about Ellen, and heartily sympathise with my family in their effort to get her to return to her husband. I also know that, for some reason you have not chosen to tell me, you have advised her against this course, which all the older men of the family, as well as our grandmother, agree in approving; and that it is owing to your encouragement that Ellen defies us all, and exposes herself to the kind of criticism of which Mr. Sillerton Jackson probably gave you, this evening, the hint that has made you so irritable.... Hints have indeed not been wanting; but since you appear unwilling to take them from others, I offer you this one myself, in the only form in which well-bred people of our kind can communicate unpleasant things to each other: by letting you understand that I know you mean to see Ellen when you are in Washington, and are perhaps going there expressly for that purpose; and that, since you are sure to see her, I wish you to do so with my full and explicit approval—and to take the opportunity of letting her know what the course of conduct you have encouraged her in is likely to lead to."

Her hand was still on the key of the lamp when the last word of this mute message reached him. She turned the wick down, lifted off the globe, and breathed on the sulky flame.

"They smell less if one blows them out," she explained, with her bright housekeeping air. On the threshold she turned and paused for his kiss.

## XXVII.

Wall Street, the next day, had more reassuring reports of Beaufort's situation. They were not definite, but they were hopeful. It was generally understood that he could call on powerful influences in case of emergency, and that he had done so with success; and that evening, when Mrs. Beaufort appeared at the Opera wearing her old smile and a new emerald necklace, society drew a breath of relief.

New York was inexorable in its condemnation of business irregularities. So far there had been no exception to its tacit rule that those who broke the law of probity must pay; and every one was aware that even Beaufort and Beaufort's wife would be offered up unflinchingly to this principle. But to be obliged to offer them up would be not only painful but inconvenient. The disappearance of the Beauforts would leave a considerable void in their compact little circle; and those who were too ignorant or too careless to shudder at the moral catastrophe bewailed in advance the loss of the best ball-room in New York.

Archer had definitely made up his mind to go to Washington. He was waiting only for the opening of the law-suit of which he had spoken to May, so that its date might coincide with that of his visit; but on the following Tuesday he learned from Mr. Letterblair that the case might be postponed for several weeks. Nevertheless, he went home that afternoon determined in any event to leave the next evening. The chances were that May, who knew nothing of his professional life, and had never shown any interest in it, would not learn of the postponement, should it take place, nor remember the names of the litigants if they were mentioned before her; and at any rate he could no longer put off seeing Madame Olenska. There were too many things that he must say to her.

On the Wednesday morning, when he reached his office, Mr. Letterblair met him with a troubled face. Beaufort, after all, had not managed to "tide over"; but by setting afloat the rumour that he had done so he had reassured his depositors, and heavy payments had poured into the bank till the previous evening, when disturbing reports again began to predominate. In consequence, a run on the bank had begun, and its doors were likely to close before the day was over. The ugliest things were being said of Beaufort's dastardly manoeuvre, and his failure promised to be one of the most discreditable in the history of Wall Street.

The extent of the calamity left Mr. Letterblair white and incapacitated. "I've seen bad things in my time; but nothing as bad as this. Everybody we know will be hit, one way or another. And what will be done about Mrs. Beaufort? What *can* be done about her? I pity Mrs. Manson Mingott as much as anybody: coming at her age, there's no knowing what effect this affair may have on her. She always believed in Beaufort—she made a friend of him! And there's the whole Dallas connection: poor Mrs. Beaufort is related to every one of you. Her only chance would be to leave her husband—yet how can any one tell her so? Her duty is at his side; and luckily she seems always to have been blind to his private weaknesses."

There was a knock, and Mr. Letterblair turned his head sharply. "What is it? I can't be disturbed."

A clerk brought in a letter for Archer and withdrew. Recognising his wife's hand, the young man opened the envelope and read: "Won't you please come up town as early as you can? Granny had a slight stroke last night. In some mysterious way she found out before any one else this awful news about the bank. Uncle Lovell is away shooting, and the idea of the disgrace has made poor Papa so nervous that he has a temperature and can't leave his room. Mamma needs you dreadfully, and I do hope you can get away at once and go straight to Granny's."

Archer handed the note to his senior partner, and a few minutes later was crawling northward in a crowded horse-car, which he exchanged at Fourteenth Street for one of the high staggering omnibuses of the Fifth Avenue line. It was after twelve o'clock when this laborious vehicle dropped him at old Catherine's. The sitting-room window on the ground floor, where she usually throned, was tenanted by the inadequate figure of her daughter, Mrs. Welland, who signed a haggard welcome as she caught sight of Archer; and at the door he was met by May. The hall wore the unnatural appearance peculiar to well-kept houses suddenly invaded by illness: wraps and furs lay in heaps on the chairs, a doctor's bag and overcoat were on the table, and beside them letters and cards had already piled up unheeded.

May looked pale but smiling: Dr. Bencomb, who had just come for the second time, took a more hopeful view, and Mrs. Mingott's dauntless determination to live and get well was already having an effect on her family. May led Archer into the old lady's sitting-room, where the sliding doors opening into the bedroom had been drawn shut, and the heavy yellow damask portieres dropped over them; and here Mrs. Welland communicated to him in horrified undertones the details of the catastrophe. It appeared that the evening before something dreadful and mysterious had happened. At about eight o'clock, just after Mrs. Mingott had finished the game of solitaire that she always played after dinner, the door-bell had rung, and a lady so thickly veiled that the servants did not immediately recognise her had asked to be received.

The butler, hearing a familiar voice, had thrown open the sitting-room door, announcing: "Mrs. Julius Beaufort"—and had then closed it again on the two ladies. They must have been together, he thought, about an hour. When Mrs. Mingott's bell rang Mrs. Beaufort had already slipped away unseen, and the old lady, white and vast and terrible, sat alone in her great chair, and signed to the butler to help her into her room. She seemed, at that time, though obviously distressed, in complete control of her body and brain. The mulatto maid put her to bed, brought her a cup of tea as usual, laid everything straight in the room, and went away; but at three in the morning the bell rang again, and the two servants, hastening in at this unwonted summons (for old Catherine usually slept like a baby), had found their mistress sitting up against her pillows with a crooked smile on her face and one little hand hanging limp from its huge arm.

The stroke had clearly been a slight one, for she was able to articulate and to make her wishes known; and soon after the doctor's first visit she had begun to regain control of her facial muscles. But the alarm had been great; and proportionately great was the indignation when it was gathered from Mrs. Mingott's fragmentary phrases that Regina Beaufort had come to ask her—incredible effrontery!—to back up her husband, see them through—not to "desert" them, as she called it—in fact to induce the whole family to cover and condone their monstrous dishonour.

"I said to her: 'Honour's always been honour, and honesty honesty, in Manson Mingott's house, and will be till I'm carried out of it feet first,'" the old woman had stammered into her daughter's ear, in the thick voice of the partly paralysed. "And when she said: 'But my name, Auntie—my name's Regina Dallas,' I said: 'It was Beaufort when he covered you with jewels, and it's got to stay Beaufort now that he's covered you with shame.'"

So much, with tears and gasps of horror, Mrs. Welland imparted, blanched and demolished by the unwonted obligation of having at last to fix her eyes on the unpleasant and the discreditable. "If only I could keep it from your father-in-law: he always says: 'Augusta, for pity's sake, don't destroy my last illusions'—and how am I to prevent his knowing these horrors?" the poor lady wailed.

"After all, Mamma, he won't have *seen* them," her daughter suggested; and Mrs. Welland sighed: "Ah, no; thank heaven he's safe in bed. And Dr. Bencomb has promised to keep him there till poor Mamma is better, and Regina has been got away somewhere."

Archer had seated himself near the window and was gazing out blankly at the deserted thoroughfare. It was evident that he had been summoned rather for the moral support of the stricken ladies than because of any specific aid that he could render. Mr. Lovell Mingott had been telegraphed for, and messages were being despatched by hand to the members of the family living in New York; and meanwhile there was nothing to do but to discuss in hushed tones the consequences of Beaufort's dishonour and of his wife's unjustifiable action.

Mrs. Lovell Mingott, who had been in another room writing notes, presently reappeared, and added her voice to the discussion. In *their* day, the elder ladies agreed, the wife of a man who had done anything disgraceful in business had only one idea: to efface herself, to disappear with him. "There was the case of poor Grandmamma Spicer; your great-grandmother, May. Of course," Mrs. Welland hastened to add, "your great-grandfather's money difficulties were private—losses at cards, or signing a note for somebody—I never quite knew, because Mamma would never speak of it. But she was brought up in the country because her mother had to leave New York after the disgrace, whatever it was: they lived up the Hudson alone, winter and summer, till Mamma was sixteen. It would never have occurred to Grandmamma Spicer to ask the family to 'countenance' her, as I understand

Regina calls it; though a private disgrace is nothing compared to the scandal of ruining hundreds of innocent people."

"Yes, it would be more becoming in Regina to hide her own countenance than to talk about other people's," Mrs. Lovell Mingott agreed. "I understand that the emerald necklace she wore at the Opera last Friday had been sent on approval from Ball and Black's in the afternoon. I wonder if they'll ever get it back?"

Archer listened unmoved to the relentless chorus. The idea of absolute financial probity as the first law of a gentleman's code was too deeply ingrained in him for sentimental considerations to weaken it. An adventurer like Lemuel Struthers might build up the millions of his Shoe Polish on any number of shady dealings; but unblemished honesty was the noblesse oblige of old financial New York. Nor did Mrs. Beaufort's fate greatly move Archer. He felt, no doubt, more sorry for her than her indignant relatives; but it seemed to him that the tie between husband and wife, even if breakable in prosperity, should be indissoluble in misfortune. As Mr. Letterblair had said, a wife's place was at her husband's side when he was in trouble; but society's place was not at his side, and Mrs. Beaufort's cool assumption that it was seemed almost to make her his accomplice. The mere idea of a woman's appealing to her family to screen her husband's business dishonour was inadmissible, since it was the one thing that the Family, as an institution, could not do.

The mulatto maid called Mrs. Lovell Mingott into the hall, and the latter came back in a moment with a frowning brow.

"She wants me to telegraph for Ellen Olenska. I had written to Ellen, of course, and to Medora; but now it seems that's not enough. I'm to telegraph to her immediately, and to tell her that she's to come alone."

The announcement was received in silence. Mrs. Welland sighed resignedly, and May rose from her seat and went to gather up some newspapers that had been scattered on the floor.

"I suppose it must be done," Mrs. Lovell Mingott continued, as if hoping to be contradicted; and May turned back toward the middle of the room.

"Of course it must be done," she said. "Granny knows what she wants, and we must carry out all her wishes. Shall I write the telegram for you, Auntie? If it goes at once Ellen can probably catch tomorrow morning's train." She pronounced the syllables of the name with a peculiar clearness, as if she had tapped on two silver bells.

"Well, it can't go at once. Jasper and the pantry-boy are both out with notes and telegrams."

May turned to her husband with a smile. "But here's Newland, ready to do anything. Will you take the telegram, Newland? There'll be just time before luncheon."

Archer rose with a murmur of readiness, and she seated herself at old Catherine's rosewood "Bonheur du Jour," and wrote out the message in her large immature hand. When it was written she blotted it neatly and handed it to Archer.

"What a pity," she said, "that you and Ellen will cross each other on the way!—Newland," she added, turning to her mother and aunt, "is obliged to go to Washington about a patent law-suit that is coming up before the Supreme Court. I suppose Uncle Lovell will be back by tomorrow night, and with Granny improving so much it doesn't seem right to ask Newland to give up an important engagement for the firm—does it?"

She paused, as if for an answer, and Mrs. Welland hastily declared: "Oh, of course not, darling. Your Granny would be the last person to wish it." As Archer left the room with the telegram, he heard his mother-in-law add, presumably to Mrs. Lovell Mingott: "But why on earth she should make you telegraph for Ellen Olenska —" and May's clear voice rejoin: "Perhaps it's to urge on her again that after all her duty is with her husband."

The outer door closed on Archer and he walked hastily away toward the telegraph office.

## XXVIII.

"Ol-ol—howjer spell it, anyhow?" asked the tart young lady to whom Archer had pushed his wife's telegram across the brass ledge of the Western Union office.

"Olenska—O-len-ska," he repeated, drawing back the message in order to print out the foreign syllables above May's rambling script.

"It's an unlikely name for a New York telegraph office; at least in this quarter," an unexpected voice observed; and turning around Archer saw

Lawrence Lefferts at his elbow, pulling an imperturbable moustache and affecting not to glance at the message.

"Hallo, Newland: thought I'd catch you here. I've just heard of old Mrs. Mingott's stroke; and as I was on my way to the house I saw you turning down this street and nipped after you. I suppose you've come from there?"

Archer nodded, and pushed his telegram under the lattice.

"Very bad, eh?" Lefferts continued. "Wiring to the family, I suppose. I gather it IS bad, if you're including Countess Olenska."

Archer's lips stiffened; he felt a savage impulse to dash his fist into the long vain handsome face at his side.

"Why?" he questioned.

Lefferts, who was known to shrink from discussion, raised his eye-brows with an ironic grimace that warned the other of the watching damsel behind the lattice. Nothing could be worse "form" the look reminded Archer, than any display of temper in a public place.

Archer had never been more indifferent to the requirements of form; but his impulse to do Lawrence Lefferts a physical injury was only momentary. The idea of bandying Ellen Olenska's name with him at such a time, and on whatsoever provocation, was unthinkable. He paid for his telegram, and the two young men went out together into the street. There Archer, having regained his self-control, went on: "Mrs. Mingott is much better: the doctor feels no anxiety whatever"; and Lefferts, with profuse expressions of relief, asked him if he had heard that there were beastly bad rumours again about Beaufort....

That afternoon the announcement of the Beaufort failure was in all the papers. It overshadowed the report of Mrs. Manson Mingott's stroke, and only the few who had heard of the mysterious connection between the two events thought of ascribing old Catherine's illness to anything but the accumulation of flesh and years.

The whole of New York was darkened by the tale of Beaufort's dishonour. There had never, as Mr. Letterblair said, been a worse case in his memory, nor, for that matter, in the memory of the far-off Letterblair who had given his name to the firm. The bank had continued to take in money for a whole day after its failure was inevitable; and as many of its clients belonged to one or another of the ruling clans, Beaufort's duplicity seemed doubly cynical. If Mrs. Beaufort had not taken the tone that such misfortunes (the word was her own) were "the test of friendship," compassion for her might have tempered the general indignation against her husband. As it was—and especially after the object of her nocturnal visit to Mrs. Manson Mingott had become known—her cynicism was held to exceed his; and she had not the excuse—nor her detractors the satisfaction—of pleading that she was "a foreigner." It was some comfort (to those whose securities were not in jeopardy) to be able to remind themselves that Beaufort *was*; but, after all, if a Dallas of South Carolina took his view of the case, and glibly talked of his soon being "on his feet again," the argument lost its edge, and there was nothing to do but to accept this awful evidence of the indissolubility of marriage. Society must manage to get on without the Beauforts, and there was an end of it—except indeed for such hapless victims of the disaster as Medora Manson, the poor old Miss Lannings, and certain other misguided ladies of good family who, if only they had listened to Mr. Henry van der Luyden ...

"The best thing the Beauforts can do," said Mrs. Archer, summing it up as if she were pronouncing a diagnosis and prescribing a course of treatment, "is to go and live at Regina's little place in North Carolina. Beaufort has always kept a racing stable, and he had better breed trotting horses. I should say he had all the qualities of a successful horsedealer." Every one agreed with her, but no one condescended to enquire what the Beauforts really meant to do.

The next day Mrs. Manson Mingott was much better: she recovered her voice sufficiently to give orders that no one should mention the Beauforts to her again, and asked—when Dr. Bencomb appeared—what in the world her family meant by making such a fuss about her health.

"If people of my age *will* eat chicken-salad in the evening what are they to expect?" she enquired; and, the doctor having opportunely modified her dietary, the stroke was transformed into an attack of indigestion. But in spite of her firm tone old Catherine did not wholly recover her former attitude toward life. The growing remoteness of old age, though it had not diminished her curiosity about her neighbours, had blunted her never very lively compassion for their troubles; and she seemed to have no difficulty in putting the Beaufort disaster out of her mind. But for the first time she became absorbed in her own symptoms, and began to take a sentimental interest in certain members of her family to whom she had hitherto been contemptuously indifferent.

Mr. Welland, in particular, had the privilege of attracting her notice. Of her sons-in-law he was the one she had most consistently ignored; and all his wife's efforts to represent him as a man of forceful character and marked intellectual ability (if he had only "chosen") had been met with a derisive chuckle. But his eminence as a valetudinarian now made him an object of engrossing interest, and Mrs. Mingott issued an imperial summons to him to come and compare diets as soon as his temperature permitted; for old Catherine was now the first to recognise that one could not be too careful about temperatures.

Twenty-four hours after Madame Olenska's summons a telegram announced that she would arrive from Washington on the evening of the following day. At the Wellands', where the Newland Archers chanced to be lunching, the question as to who should meet her at Jersey City was immediately raised; and the material difficulties amid which the Welland household struggled as if it had been a frontier outpost, lent animation to the debate. It was agreed that Mrs. Welland could not possibly go to Jersey City because she was to accompany her husband to old Catherine's that afternoon, and the brougham could not be spared, since, if Mr. Welland were "upset" by seeing his mother-in-law for the first time after her attack, he might have to be taken home at a moment's notice. The Welland sons would of course be "down town," Mr. Lovell Mingott would be just hurrying back from his shooting, and the Mingott carriage engaged in meeting him; and one could not ask May, at the close of a winter afternoon, to go alone across the ferry to Jersey City, even in her own carriage. Nevertheless, it might appear inhospitable—and contrary to old Catherine's express wishes—if Madame Olenska were allowed to arrive without any of the family being at the station to receive her. It was just like Ellen, Mrs. Welland's tired voice implied, to place the family in such a dilemma. "It's always one thing after another," the poor lady grieved, in one of her rare revolts against fate; "the only thing that makes me think Mamma must be less well than Dr. Bencomb will admit is this morbid desire to have Ellen come at once, however inconvenient it is to meet her."

The words had been thoughtless, as the utterances of impatience often are; and Mr. Welland was upon them with a pounce.

"Augusta," he said, turning pale and laying down his fork, "have you any other reason for thinking that Bencomb is less to be relied on than he was?

Have you noticed that he has been less conscientious than usual in following up my case or your mother's?"

It was Mrs. Welland's turn to grow pale as the endless consequences of her blunder unrolled themselves before her; but she managed to laugh, and take a second helping of scalloped oysters, before she said, struggling back into her old armour of cheerfulness: "My dear, how could you imagine such a thing? I only meant that, after the decided stand Mamma took about its being Ellen's duty to go back to her husband, it seems strange that she should be seized with this sudden whim to see her, when there are half a dozen other grandchildren that she might have asked for. But we must never forget that Mamma, in spite of her wonderful vitality, is a very old woman."

Mr. Welland's brow remained clouded, and it was evident that his perturbed imagination had fastened at once on this last remark. "Yes: your mother's a very old woman; and for all we know Bencomb may not be as successful with very old people. As you say, my dear, it's always one thing after another; and in another ten or fifteen years I suppose I shall have the pleasing duty of looking about for a new doctor. It's always better to make such a change before it's absolutely necessary." And having arrived at this Spartan decision Mr. Welland firmly took up his fork.

"But all the while," Mrs. Welland began again, as she rose from the luncheon-table, and led the way into the wilderness of purple satin and malachite known as the back drawing-room, "I don't see how Ellen's to be got here tomorrow evening; and I do like to have things settled for at least twenty-four hours ahead."

Archer turned from the fascinated contemplation of a small painting representing two Cardinals carousing, in an octagonal ebony frame set with medallions of onyx.

"Shall I fetch her?" he proposed. "I can easily get away from the office in time to meet the brougham at the ferry, if May will send it there." His heart was beating excitedly as he spoke.

Mrs. Welland heaved a sigh of gratitude, and May, who had moved away to the window, turned to shed on him a beam of approval. "So you see, Mamma, everything *will* be settled twenty-four hours in advance," she said, stooping over to kiss her mother's troubled forehead.

May's brougham awaited her at the door, and she was to drive Archer to Union Square, where he could pick up a Broadway car to carry him to the office. As she settled herself in her corner she said: "I didn't want to worry Mamma by raising fresh obstacles; but how can you meet Ellen tomorrow, and bring her back to New York, when you're going to Washington?"

"Oh, I'm not going," Archer answered.

"Not going? Why, what's happened?" Her voice was as clear as a bell, and full of wifely solicitude.

"The case is off—postponed."

"Postponed? How odd! I saw a note this morning from Mr. Letterblair to Mamma saying that he was going to Washington tomorrow for the big patent case that he was to argue before the Supreme Court. You said it was a patent case, didn't you?"

"Well—that's it: the whole office can't go. Letterblair decided to go this morning."

"Then it's *not* postponed?" she continued, with an insistence so unlike her that he felt the blood rising to his face, as if he were blushing for her unwonted lapse from all the traditional delicacies.

"No: but my going is," he answered, cursing the unnecessary explanations that he had given when he had announced his intention of going to Washington, and wondering where he had read that clever liars give details, but that the cleverest do not. It did not hurt him half as much to tell May an untruth as to see her trying to pretend that she had not detected him.

"I'm not going till later on: luckily for the convenience of your family," he continued, taking base refuge in sarcasm. As he spoke he felt that she was looking at him, and he turned his eyes to hers in order not to appear to be avoiding them. Their glances met for a second, and perhaps let them into each other's meanings more deeply than either cared to go.

"Yes; it IS awfully convenient," May brightly agreed, "that you should be able to meet Ellen after all; you saw how much Mamma appreciated your offering to do it."

"Oh, I'm delighted to do it." The carriage stopped, and as he jumped out she leaned to him and laid her hand on his. "Good-bye, dearest," she said, her eyes so blue that he wondered afterward if they had shone on him through tears.

He turned away and hurried across Union Square, repeating to himself, in a sort of inward chant: "It's all of two hours from Jersey City to old Catherine's. It's all of two hours—and it may be more."

## XXIX.

His wife's dark blue brougham (with the wedding varnish still on it) met Archer at the ferry, and conveyed him luxuriously to the Pennsylvania terminus in Jersey City.

It was a sombre snowy afternoon, and the gas-lamps were lit in the big reverberating station. As he paced the platform, waiting for the Washington express, he remembered that there were people who thought there would one day be a tunnel under the Hudson through which the trains of the Pennsylvania railway would run straight into New York. They were of the brotherhood of visionaries who likewise predicted the building of ships that would cross the Atlantic in five days, the invention of a flying machine, lighting by electricity, telephonic communication without wires, and other Arabian Night marvels.

"I don't care which of their visions comes true," Archer mused, "as long as the tunnel isn't built yet." In his senseless school-boy happiness he pictured Madame Olenska's descent from the train, his discovery of her a long way off, among the throngs of meaningless faces, her clinging to his arm as he guided her to the carriage, their slow approach to the wharf among slipping horses, laden carts, vociferating teamsters, and then the startling quiet of the ferry-boat, where they would sit side by side under the snow, in the motionless carriage, while the earth seemed to glide away under them, rolling to the other side of the sun. It was incredible, the number of things he had to say to her, and in what eloquent order they were forming themselves on his lips ...

The clanging and groaning of the train came nearer, and it staggered slowly into the station like a prey-laden monster into its lair. Archer pushed forward, elbowing through the crowd, and staring blindly into window after window of the high-hung carriages. And then, suddenly, he saw Madame Olenska's pale and surprised face close at hand, and had again the mortified sensation of having forgotten what she looked like.

They reached each other, their hands met, and he drew her arm through his. "This way—I have the carriage," he said.

After that it all happened as he had dreamed. He helped her into the brougham with her bags, and had afterward the vague recollection of having properly reassured her about her grandmother and given her a summary of the Beaufort situation (he was struck by the softness of her: "Poor Regina!").

Meanwhile the carriage had worked its way out of the coil about the station, and they were crawling down the slippery incline to the wharf, menaced by swaying coal-carts, bewildered horses, dishevelled express-wagons, and an empty hearse—ah, that hearse! She shut her eyes as it passed, and clutched at Archer's hand.

"If only it doesn't mean—poor Granny!"

"Oh, no, no—she's much better—she's all right, really. There—we've passed it!" he exclaimed, as if that made all the difference. Her hand remained in his, and as the carriage lurched across the gang-plank onto the ferry he bent over, unbuttoned her tight brown glove, and kissed her palm as if he had kissed a relic. She disengaged herself with a faint smile, and he said: "You didn't expect me today?"

"Oh, no."

"I meant to go to Washington to see you. I'd made all my arrangements—I very nearly crossed you in the train."

"Oh —" she exclaimed, as if terrified by the narrowness of their escape.

"Do you know—I hardly remembered you?"

"Hardly remembered me?"

"I mean: how shall I explain? I—it's always so. *Each time you happen to me all over again.*"

"Oh, yes: I know! I know!"

"Does it—do I too: to you?" he insisted.

She nodded, looking out of the window.

"Ellen—Ellen—Ellen!"

She made no answer, and he sat in silence, watching her profile grow indistinct against the snow-streaked dusk beyond the window. What had she been doing in all those four long months, he wondered? How little they knew of each other, after all! The precious moments were slipping away, but he had forgotten everything that he had meant to say to her and could only helplessly brood on the mystery of their remoteness and their proximity, which seemed to be symbolised by the fact of their sitting so close to each other, and yet being unable to see each other's faces.

"What a pretty carriage! Is it May's?" she asked, suddenly turning her face from the window.

"Yes."

"It was May who sent you to fetch me, then? How kind of her!"

He made no answer for a moment; then he said explosively: "Your husband's secretary came to see me the day after we met in Boston."

In his brief letter to her he had made no allusion to M. Riviere's visit, and his intention had been to bury the incident in his bosom. But her reminder that they were in his wife's carriage provoked him to an impulse of retaliation. He would see if she liked his reference to Riviere any better than he liked hers to May! As on certain other occasions when he had expected to shake her out of her usual composure, she betrayed no sign of surprise: and at once he concluded: "He writes to her, then."

"M. Riviere went to see you?"

"Yes: didn't you know?"

"No," she answered simply.

"And you're not surprised?"

She hesitated. "Why should I be? He told me in Boston that he knew you; that he'd met you in England I think."

"Ellen—I must ask you one thing."

"Yes."

"I wanted to ask it after I saw him, but I couldn't put it in a letter. It was Riviere who helped you to get away—when you left your husband?"

His heart was beating suffocatingly. Would she meet this question with the same composure?

"Yes: I owe him a great debt," she answered, without the least tremor in her quiet voice.

Her tone was so natural, so almost indifferent, that Archer's turmoil subsided. Once more she had managed, by her sheer simplicity, to make him feel stupidly conventional just when he thought he was flinging convention to the winds.

"I think you're the most honest woman I ever met!" he exclaimed.

"Oh, no—but probably one of the least fussy," she answered, a smile in her voice.

"Call it what you like: you look at things as they are."

"Ah—I've had to. I've had to look at the Gorgon."

"Well—it hasn't blinded you! You've seen that she's just an old bogey like all the others."

"She doesn't blind one; but she dries up one's tears."

The answer checked the pleading on Archer's lips: it seemed to come from depths of experience beyond his reach. The slow advance of the ferry-boat had ceased, and her bows bumped against the piles of the slip with a violence that made the brougham stagger, and flung Archer and Madame Olenska against each other. The young man, trembling, felt the pressure of her shoulder, and passed his arm about her.

"If you're not blind, then, you must see that this can't last."

"What can't?"

"Our being together—and not together."

"No. You ought not to have come today," she said in an altered voice; and suddenly she turned, flung her arms about him and pressed her lips to his. At the same moment the carriage began to move, and a gas-lamp at the head of the slip flashed its light into the window. She drew away, and they sat silent and motionless while the brougham struggled through the congestion of carriages about the ferry-landing. As they gained the street Archer began to speak hurriedly.

"Don't be afraid of me: you needn't squeeze yourself back into your corner like that. A stolen kiss isn't what I want. Look: I'm not even trying to touch the sleeve of your jacket. Don't suppose that I don't understand your reasons for not wanting to let this feeling between us dwindle into an ordinary hole-and-corner love-affair. I couldn't have spoken like this yesterday, because when we've been apart, and I'm looking forward to seeing you, every thought is burnt up in a great flame. But then you come; and you're so much more than I remembered, and what I want of you is so much more than an hour or two every now and then, with wastes of thirsty waiting between, that I can sit perfectly still beside you, like this, with that other vision in my mind, just quietly trusting to it to come true."

For a moment she made no reply; then she asked, hardly above a whisper: "What do you mean by trusting to it to come true?"

"Why—you know it will, don't you?"

"Your vision of you and me together?" She burst into a sudden hard laugh. "You choose your place well to put it to me!"

"Do you mean because we're in my wife's brougham? Shall we get out and walk, then? I don't suppose you mind a little snow?"

She laughed again, more gently. "No; I shan't get out and walk, because my business is to get to Granny's as quickly as I can. And you'll sit beside me, and we'll look, not at visions, but at realities."

"I don't know what you mean by realities. The only reality to me is this."

She met the words with a long silence, during which the carriage rolled down an obscure side-street and then turned into the searching illumination of Fifth Avenue.

"Is it your idea, then, that I should live with you as your mistress—since I can't be your wife?" she asked.

The crudeness of the question startled him: the word was one that women of his class fought shy of, even when their talk flitted closest about the topic. He noticed that Madame Olenska pronounced it as if it had a recognised place in her vocabulary, and he wondered if it had been used familiarly in her presence in the horrible life she had fled from. Her question pulled him up with a jerk, and he floundered.

"I want—I want somehow to get away with you into a world where words like that—categories like that—won't exist. Where we shall be simply two human beings who love each other, who are the whole of life to each other; and nothing else on earth will matter."

She drew a deep sigh that ended in another laugh. "Oh, my dear—where is that country? Have you ever been there?" she asked; and as he remained sullenly dumb she went on: "I know so many who've tried to find it; and, believe me, they all got out by mistake at wayside stations: at places like Boulogne, or Pisa, or Monte Carlo—and it wasn't at all different from the old world they'd left, but only rather smaller and dingier and more promiscuous."

He had never heard her speak in such a tone, and he remembered the phrase she had used a little while before.

"Yes, the Gorgon *has* dried your tears," he said.

"Well, she opened my eyes too; it's a delusion to say that she blinds people. What she does is just the contrary—she fastens their eyelids open, so that they're never again in the blessed darkness. Isn't there a Chinese torture like that? There ought to be. Ah, believe me, it's a miserable little country!"

The carriage had crossed Forty-second Street: May's sturdy brougham-horse was carrying them northward as if he had been a Kentucky trotter. Archer choked with the sense of wasted minutes and vain words.

"Then what, exactly, is your plan for us?" he asked.

"For *us?* But there's no *us* in that sense! We're near each other only if we stay far from each other. Then we can be ourselves. Otherwise we're only Newland Archer, the husband of Ellen Olenska's cousin, and Ellen Olenska, the cousin of Newland Archer's wife, trying to be happy behind the backs of the people who trust them."

"Ah, I'm beyond that," he groaned.

"No, you're not! You've never been beyond. And I have," she said, in a strange voice, "and I know what it looks like there."

He sat silent, dazed with inarticulate pain. Then he groped in the darkness of the carriage for the little bell that signalled orders to the coachman. He remembered that May rang twice when she wished to stop. He pressed the bell, and the carriage drew up beside the curbstone.

"Why are we stopping? This is not Granny's," Madame Olenska exclaimed.

"No: I shall get out here," he stammered, opening the door and jumping to the pavement. By the light of a street-lamp he saw her startled face, and the instinctive motion she made to detain him. He closed the door, and leaned for a moment in the window.

"You're right: I ought not to have come today," he said, lowering his voice so that the coachman should not hear. She bent forward, and seemed about to speak; but he had already called out the order to drive on, and the carriage rolled away while he stood on the corner. The snow was over, and a tingling wind had sprung up, that lashed his face as he stood gazing. Suddenly he felt something stiff and cold on his lashes, and perceived that he had been crying, and that the wind had frozen his tears.

He thrust his hands in his pockets, and walked at a sharp pace down Fifth Avenue to his own house.

## XXX.

That evening when Archer came down before dinner he found the drawing-room empty.

He and May were dining alone, all the family engagements having been postponed since Mrs. Manson Mingott's illness; and as May was the more punctual of the two he was surprised that she had not preceded him. He knew that she was at home, for while he dressed he had heard her moving about in her room; and he wondered what had delayed her.

He had fallen into the way of dwelling on such conjectures as a means of tying his thoughts fast to reality. Sometimes he felt as if he had found the clue to his father-in-law's absorption in trifles; perhaps even Mr. Welland, long ago, had had escapes and visions, and had conjured up all the hosts of domesticity to defend himself against them.

When May appeared he thought she looked tired. She had put on the low-necked and tightly-laced dinner-dress which the Mingott ceremonial exacted on the most informal occasions, and had built her fair hair into its usual accumulated coils; and her face, in contrast, was wan and almost faded. But she shone on him with her usual tenderness, and her eyes had kept the blue dazzle of the day before.

"What became of you, dear?" she asked. "I was waiting at Granny's, and Ellen came alone, and said she had dropped you on the way because you had to rush off on business. There's nothing wrong?"

"Only some letters I'd forgotten, and wanted to get off before dinner."

"Ah —" she said; and a moment afterward: "I'm sorry you didn't come to Granny's—unless the letters were urgent."

"They were," he rejoined, surprised at her insistence. "Besides, I don't see why I should have gone to your grandmother's. I didn't know you were there."

She turned and moved to the looking-glass above the mantel-piece. As she stood there, lifting her long arm to fasten a puff that had slipped from its place in her intricate hair, Archer was struck by something languid and inelastic in her attitude, and wondered if the deadly monotony of their lives had laid its weight on her also. Then he remembered that, as he had left the house that morning, she had called over the stairs that she would meet him at her grandmother's so that they might drive home together. He had called back a cheery "Yes!" and then, absorbed in other visions, had forgotten his promise. Now he was smitten with compunction, yet irritated that so trifling an omission should be stored up against him after nearly two years of marriage. He was weary of living in a perpetual tepid honeymoon, without the temperature of passion yet with all its exactions. If May had spoken out her grievances (he suspected her of many) he might have laughed them away; but she was trained to conceal imaginary wounds under a Spartan smile.

To disguise his own annoyance he asked how her grandmother was, and she answered that Mrs. Mingott was still improving, but had been rather disturbed by the last news about the Beauforts.

"What news?"

"It seems they're going to stay in New York. I believe he's going into an insurance business, or something. They're looking about for a small house."

The preposterousness of the case was beyond discussion, and they went in to dinner. During dinner their talk moved in its usual limited circle; but Archer noticed that his wife made no allusion to Madame Olenska, nor to old Catherine's reception of her. He was thankful for the fact, yet felt it to be vaguely ominous.

They went up to the library for coffee, and Archer lit a cigar and took down a volume of Michelet. He had taken to history in the evenings since May had shown a tendency to ask him to read aloud whenever she saw him with a volume of poetry: not that he disliked the sound of his own voice, but because he could always foresee her comments on what he read. In the days of their engagement she had simply (as he now perceived) echoed what he told her; but since he had ceased to provide her with opinions she had begun to hazard her own, with results destructive to his enjoyment of the works commented on.

Seeing that he had chosen history she fetched her workbasket, drew up an arm-chair to the green-shaded student lamp, and uncovered a cushion she was embroidering for his sofa. She was not a clever needle-woman; her large capable hands were made for riding, rowing and open-air activities; but since other wives embroidered cushions for their husbands she did not wish to omit this last link in her devotion.

She was so placed that Archer, by merely raising his eyes, could see her bent above her work-frame, her ruffled elbow-sleeves slipping back from her firm round arms, the betrothal sapphire shining on her left hand above her broad gold wedding-ring, and the right hand slowly and laboriously stabbing the canvas. As she sat thus, the lamplight full on her clear brow, he said to himself with a secret dismay that he would always know the thoughts behind it, that never, in all the years to come, would she surprise him by an unexpected mood, by a new idea, a weakness, a cruelty or an emotion. She had spent her poetry and romance on their short courting: the function was exhausted because the need was past. Now she was simply ripening into a copy of her mother, and mysteriously, by the very process, trying to turn him into a Mr. Welland. He laid down his book and stood up impatiently; and at once she raised her head.

"What's the matter?"

"The room is stifling: I want a little air."

He had insisted that the library curtains should draw backward and forward on a rod, so that they might be closed in the evening, instead of remaining nailed to a gilt cornice, and immovably looped up over layers of lace, as in the drawing-room; and he pulled them back and pushed up the sash, leaning out into the icy night. The mere fact of not looking at May, seated beside his table, under his lamp, the fact of seeing other houses, roofs, chimneys, of getting the sense of other lives outside his own, other cities beyond New York, and a whole world beyond his world, cleared his brain and made it easier to breathe.

After he had leaned out into the darkness for a few minutes he heard her say: "Newland! Do shut the window. You'll catch your death."

He pulled the sash down and turned back. "Catch my death!" he echoed; and he felt like adding: "But I've caught it already. I *am* dead—I've been dead for months and months."

And suddenly the play of the word flashed up a wild suggestion. What if it were *she* who was dead! If she were going to die—to die soon—and leave him free! The sensation of standing there, in that warm familiar room, and looking at her, and wishing her dead, was so strange, so fascinating and overmastering, that its enormity did not immediately strike him. He simply felt that chance had given him a new possibility to which his sick soul might cling. Yes, May might die—people did: young people, healthy people like herself: she might die, and set him suddenly free.

She glanced up, and he saw by her widening eyes that there must be something strange in his own.

"Newland! Are you ill?"

He shook his head and turned toward his arm-chair. She bent over her work-frame, and as he passed he laid his hand on her hair. "Poor May!" he said.

"Poor? Why poor?" she echoed with a strained laugh.

"Because I shall never be able to open a window without worrying you," he rejoined, laughing also.

For a moment she was silent; then she said very low, her head bowed over her work: "I shall never worry if you're happy."

"Ah, my dear; and I shall never be happy unless I can open the windows!"

"In *this* weather?" she remonstrated; and with a sigh he buried his head in his book.

Six or seven days passed. Archer heard nothing from Madame Olenska, and became aware that her name would not be mentioned in his presence by any member of the family. He did not try to see her; to do so while she was at old Catherine's guarded bedside would have been almost impossible. In the uncertainty of the situation he let himself drift, conscious, somewhere below the surface of his thoughts, of a resolve which had come to him when he had leaned out from his library window into the icy night. The strength of that resolve made it easy to wait and make no sign.

Then one day May told him that Mrs. Manson Mingott had asked to see him. There was nothing surprising in the request, for the old lady was steadily recovering, and she had always openly declared that she preferred Archer to any of her other grandsons-in-law. May gave the message with evident pleasure: she was proud of old Catherine's appreciation of her husband.

There was a moment's pause, and then Archer felt it incumbent on him to say: "All right. Shall we go together this afternoon?"

His wife's face brightened, but she instantly answered: "Oh, you'd much better go alone. It bores Granny to see the same people too often."

Archer's heart was beating violently when he rang old Mrs. Mingott's bell. He had wanted above all things to go alone, for he felt sure the visit would give him the chance of saying a word in private to the Countess Olenska. He had determined to wait till the chance presented itself naturally; and here it was, and here he was on the doorstep. Behind the door, behind the curtains of the yellow damask room next to the hall, she was surely awaiting him; in another moment he should see her, and be able to speak to her before she led him to the sick-room.

He wanted only to put one question: after that his course would be clear. What he wished to ask was simply the date of her return to Washington; and that question she could hardly refuse to answer.

But in the yellow sitting-room it was the mulatto maid who waited. Her white teeth shining like a keyboard, she pushed back the sliding doors and ushered him into old Catherine's presence.

The old woman sat in a vast throne-like arm-chair near her bed. Beside her was a mahogany stand bearing a cast bronze lamp with an engraved globe, over which a green paper shade had been balanced. There was not a book or a newspaper in reach, nor any evidence of feminine employment: conversation had always been Mrs. Mingott's sole pursuit, and she would have scorned to feign an interest in fancywork.

Archer saw no trace of the slight distortion left by her stroke. She merely looked paler, with darker shadows in the folds and recesses of her obesity; and, in the fluted mob-cap tied by a starched bow between her first two chins, and the muslin kerchief crossed over her billowing purple dressing-gown, she seemed like some shrewd and kindly ancestress of her own who might have yielded too freely to the pleasures of the table.

She held out one of the little hands that nestled in a hollow of her huge lap like pet animals, and called to the maid: "Don't let in any one else. If my daughters call, say I'm asleep."

The maid disappeared, and the old lady turned to her grandson.

"My dear, am I perfectly hideous?" she asked gaily, launching out one hand in search of the folds of muslin on her inaccessible bosom. "My daughters tell me it doesn't matter at my age—as if hideousness didn't matter all the more the harder it gets to conceal!"

"My dear, you're handsomer than ever!" Archer rejoined in the same tone; and she threw back her head and laughed.

"Ah, but not as handsome as Ellen!" she jerked out, twinkling at him maliciously; and before he could answer she added: "Was she so awfully handsome the day you drove her up from the ferry?"

He laughed, and she continued: "Was it because you told her so that she had to put you out on the way? In my youth young men didn't desert pretty women unless they were made to!" She gave another chuckle, and interrupted it to say almost querulously: "It's a pity she didn't marry you; I always told her so. It would have spared me all this worry. But who ever thought of sparing their grandmother worry?"

Archer wondered if her illness had blurred her faculties; but suddenly she broke out: "Well, it's settled, anyhow: she's going to stay with me, whatever the rest of the family say! She hadn't been here five minutes before I'd have gone down on my knees to keep her—if only, for the last twenty years, I'd been able to see where the floor was!"

Archer listened in silence, and she went on: "They'd talked me over, as no doubt you know: persuaded me, Lovell, and Letterblair, and Augusta Welland, and all the rest of them, that I must hold out and cut off her allowance, till she was made to see that it was her duty to go back to Olenski. They thought they'd convinced me when the secretary, or whatever he was, came out with the last proposals: handsome proposals I confess they were. After all, marriage is marriage, and money's money—both useful things in their way ... and I didn't know what to answer —" She broke off and drew a long breath, as if speaking had become an effort. "But the minute I laid eyes on her, I said: 'You sweet bird, you! Shut you up in that cage again? Never!' And now it's settled that she's to stay here and nurse her Granny as long as there's a Granny to nurse. It's not a gay prospect, but she doesn't mind; and of course I've told Letterblair that she's to be given her proper allowance."

The young man heard her with veins aglow; but in his confusion of mind he hardly knew whether her news brought joy or pain. He had so definitely decided on the course he meant to pursue that for the moment he could not readjust his thoughts. But gradually there stole over him the delicious sense of difficulties deferred and opportunities miraculously provided. If Ellen had consented to come and live with her grandmother it must surely be because she had recognised the impossibility of giving him up. This was her answer to his final appeal of the other day: if she would not take the extreme step he had urged, she had at last yielded to half-measures. He sank back into the thought with the involuntary relief of a man who has been ready to risk everything, and suddenly tastes the dangerous sweetness of security.

"She couldn't have gone back—it was impossible!" he exclaimed.

"Ah, my dear, I always knew you were on her side; and that's why I sent for you today, and why I said to your pretty wife, when she proposed to come with you: 'No, my dear, I'm pining to see Newland, and I don't want anybody to share our transports.' For you see, my dear —" she drew her head back as far as its tethering chins permitted, and looked him full in the eyes—"you see, we shall have a fight yet. The family don't want her here, and they'll say it's because I've been ill, because I'm a weak old woman, that she's persuaded me. I'm not well enough yet to fight them one by one, and you've got to do it for me."

"I?" he stammered.

"You. Why not?" she jerked back at him, her round eyes suddenly as sharp as pen-knives. Her hand fluttered from its chair-arm and lit on his with a clutch of little pale nails like bird-claws. "Why not?" she searchingly repeated.

Archer, under the exposure of her gaze, had recovered his self-possession.

"Oh, I don't count—I'm too insignificant."

"Well, you're Letterblair's partner, ain't you? You've got to get at them through Letterblair. Unless you've got a reason," she insisted.

"Oh, my dear, I back you to hold your own against them all without my help; but you shall have it if you need it," he reassured her.

"Then we're safe!" she sighed; and smiling on him with all her ancient cunning she added, as she settled her head among the cushions: "I always knew you'd back us up, because they never quote you when they talk about its being her duty to go home."

He winced a little at her terrifying perspicacity, and longed to ask: "And May—do they quote her?" But he judged it safer to turn the question.

"And Madame Olenska? When am I to see her?" he said.

The old lady chuckled, crumpled her lids, and went through the pantomime of archness. "Not today. One at a time, please. Madame Olenska's gone out."

He flushed with disappointment, and she went on: "She's gone out, my child: gone in my carriage to see Regina Beaufort."

She paused for this announcement to produce its effect. "That's what she's reduced me to already. The day after she got here she put on her best bonnet, and told me, as cool as a cucumber, that she was going to call on Regina Beaufort. 'I don't know her; who is she?' says I. 'She's your grand-niece, and a most unhappy woman,' she says. 'She's the wife of a scoundrel,' I answered. 'Well,' she says, 'and so am I, and yet all my family want me to go back to him.' Well, that floored me, and I let her go; and finally one day she said it was raining too hard to go out on foot, and she wanted me to lend her my carriage. 'What for?' I asked her; and she said: 'To go and see cousin Regina'—*cousin*! Now, my dear, I looked out of the window, and saw it wasn't raining a drop; but I understood her, and I let her have the carriage.... After all, Regina's a brave woman, and so is she; and I've always liked courage above everything."

Archer bent down and pressed his lips on the little hand that still lay on his.

"Eh—eh—eh! Whose hand did you think you were kissing, young man—your wife's, I hope?" the old lady snapped out with her mocking cackle; and as he rose to go she called out after him: "Give her her Granny's love; but you'd better not say anything about our talk."

## XXXI.

Archer had been stunned by old Catherine's news. It was only natural that Madame Olenska should have hastened from Washington in response to her grandmother's summons; but that she should have decided to remain under her roof—especially now that Mrs. Mingott had almost regained her health—was less easy to explain.

Archer was sure that Madame Olenska's decision had not been influenced by the change in her financial situation. He knew the exact figure of the small income which her husband had allowed her at their separation. Without the addition of her grandmother's allowance it was hardly enough to live on, in any sense known to the Mingott vocabulary; and now that Medora Manson, who shared her life, had been ruined, such a pittance would barely keep the two women clothed and fed. Yet Archer was convinced that Madame Olenska had not accepted her grandmother's offer from interested motives.

She had the heedless generosity and the spasmodic extravagance of persons used to large fortunes, and indifferent to money; but she could go without many things which her relations considered indispensable, and Mrs. Lovell Mingott and Mrs. Welland had often been heard to deplore that any one who had enjoyed the cosmopolitan luxuries of Count Olenski's establishments should care so little about "how things were done." Moreover, as Archer knew, several months had passed since her allowance had been cut off; yet in the interval she had made no effort to regain her grandmother's favour. Therefore if she had changed her course it must be for a different reason.

He did not have far to seek for that reason. On the way from the ferry she had told him that he and she must remain apart; but she had said it with her head on his breast. He knew that there was no calculated coquetry in her words; she was fighting her fate as he had fought his, and clinging desperately to her resolve that they should not break faith with the people who trusted them. But during the ten days which had elapsed since her return to New York she had perhaps guessed from his silence, and from the fact of his making no attempt to see her, that he was meditating a decisive step, a step from which there was no turning back. At the thought, a sudden fear of her own weakness might have seized her, and she might have felt that, after all, it was better to accept the compromise usual in such cases, and follow the line of least resistance.

An hour earlier, when he had rung Mrs. Mingott's bell, Archer had fancied that his path was clear before him. He had meant to have a word alone with Madame Olenska, and failing that, to learn from her grandmother on what day, and by which train, she was returning to Washington. In that train he intended to join her, and travel with her to Washington, or as much farther as she was willing to go. His own fancy inclined to Japan. At any rate she would understand at once that, wherever she went, he was going. He meant to leave a note for May that should cut off any other alternative.

He had fancied himself not only nerved for this plunge but eager to take it; yet his first feeling on hearing that the course of events was changed had been one of relief. Now, however, as he walked home from Mrs. Mingott's, he was conscious of a growing distaste for what lay before him. There was nothing unknown or unfamiliar in the path he was presumably to tread; but when he had trodden it before it was as a free man, who was accountable to no one for his actions, and could lend himself with an amused detachment to the game of precautions and prevarications, concealments and compliances, that the part required. This procedure was called "protecting a woman's honour"; and the best fiction, combined with the after-dinner talk of his elders, had long since initiated him into every detail of its code.

Now he saw the matter in a new light, and his part in it seemed singularly diminished. It was, in fact, that which, with a secret fatuity, he had watched Mrs. Thorley Rushworth play toward a fond and unperceiving husband: a smiling, bantering, humouring, watchful and incessant lie. A lie by day, a lie by night, a lie in every touch and every look; a lie in every caress and every quarrel; a lie in every word and in every silence.

It was easier, and less dastardly on the whole, for a wife to play such a part toward her husband. A woman's standard of truthfulness was tacitly held to be lower: she was the subject creature, and versed in the arts of the enslaved. Then she could always plead moods and nerves, and the right not to be held too strictly to account; and even in the most strait-laced societies the laugh was always against the husband.

But in Archer's little world no one laughed at a wife deceived, and a certain measure of contempt was attached to men who continued their philandering after marriage. In the rotation of crops there was a recognised season for wild oats; but they were not to be sown more than once.

Archer had always shared this view: in his heart he thought Lefferts despicable. But to love Ellen Olenska was not to become a man like Lefferts: for the first time Archer found himself face to face with the dread argument of the individual case. Ellen Olenska was like no other woman, he was like no other man: their situation, therefore, resembled no one else's, and they were answerable to no tribunal but that of their own judgment.

Yes, but in ten minutes more he would be mounting his own doorstep; and there were May, and habit, and honour, and all the old decencies that he and his people had always believed in ...

At his corner he hesitated, and then walked on down Fifth Avenue.

Ahead of him, in the winter night, loomed a big unlit house. As he drew near he thought how often he had seen it blazing with lights, its steps awninged and carpeted, and carriages waiting in double line to draw up at the curbstone. It was in the conservatory that stretched its dead-black bulk down the side street that he had taken his first kiss from May; it was under the myriad candles of the ball-room that he had seen her appear, tall and silver-shining as a young Diana.

Now the house was as dark as the grave, except for a faint flare of gas in the basement, and a light in one upstairs room where the blind had not been lowered. As Archer reached the corner he saw that the carriage standing at the door was Mrs. Manson Mingott's. What an opportunity for Sillerton Jackson, if he should chance to pass! Archer had been greatly moved by old Catherine's account of Madame Olenska's attitude toward Mrs. Beaufort; it made the righteous reprobation of New York seem like a passing by on the other side. But he knew well enough what construction the clubs and drawing-rooms would put on Ellen Olenska's visits to her cousin.

He paused and looked up at the lighted window. No doubt the two women were sitting together in that room: Beaufort had probably sought consolation elsewhere. There were even rumours that he had left New York with Fanny Ring; but Mrs. Beaufort's attitude made the report seem improbable.

Archer had the nocturnal perspective of Fifth Avenue almost to himself. At that hour most people were indoors, dressing for dinner; and he was secretly glad that Ellen's exit was likely to be unobserved. As the thought passed through his mind the door opened, and she came out. Behind her was a faint light, such as might have been carried down the stairs to show her the way. She turned to say a word to some one; then the door closed, and she came down the steps.

"Ellen," he said in a low voice, as she reached the pavement.

She stopped with a slight start, and just then he saw two young men of fashionable cut approaching. There was a familiar air about their overcoats and the way their smart silk mufflers were folded over their white ties; and he wondered how youths of their quality happened to be dining out so early. Then he remembered that the Reggie Chiverses, whose house was a few doors above, were taking a large party that evening to see Adelaide Neilson in Romeo and Juliet, and guessed that the two were of the number. They passed under a lamp, and he recognised Lawrence Lefferts and a young Chivers.

A mean desire not to have Madame Olenska seen at the Beauforts' door vanished as he felt the penetrating warmth of her hand.

"I shall see you now—we shall be together," he broke out, hardly knowing what he said.

"Ah," she answered, "Granny has told you?"

While he watched her he was aware that Lefferts and Chivers, on reaching the farther side of the street corner, had discreetly struck away across Fifth Avenue. It was the kind of masculine solidarity that he himself often practised; now he sickened at their connivance. Did she really imagine that he and she could live like this? And if not, what else did she imagine?

"Tomorrow I must see you—somewhere where we can be alone," he said, in a voice that sounded almost angry to his own ears.

She wavered, and moved toward the carriage.

"But I shall be at Granny's—for the present that is," she added, as if conscious that her change of plans required some explanation.

"Somewhere where we can be alone," he insisted.

She gave a faint laugh that grated on him.

"In New York? But there are no churches ... no monuments."

"There's the Art Museum—in the Park," he explained, as she looked puzzled. "At half-past two. I shall be at the door ..."

She turned away without answering and got quickly into the carriage. As it drove off she leaned forward, and he thought she waved her hand in the obscurity. He stared after her in a turmoil of contradictory feelings. It seemed to him that he had been speaking not to the woman he loved but to another, a woman he was indebted to for pleasures already wearied of: it was hateful to find himself the prisoner of this hackneyed vocabulary.

"She'll come!" he said to himself, almost contemptuously.

Avoiding the popular "Wolfe collection," whose anecdotic canvases filled one of the main galleries of the queer wilderness of cast-iron and encaustic tiles known as the Metropolitan Museum, they had wandered down a passage to the room where the "Cesnola antiquities" mouldered in unvisited loneliness.

They had this melancholy retreat to themselves, and seated on the divan enclosing the central steam-radiator, they were staring silently at the glass cabinets mounted in ebonised wood which contained the recovered fragments of Ilium.

"It's odd," Madame Olenska said, "I never came here before."

"Ah, well—. Some day, I suppose, it will be a great Museum."

"Yes," she assented absently.

She stood up and wandered across the room. Archer, remaining seated, watched the light movements of her figure, so girlish even under its heavy furs, the cleverly planted heron wing in her fur cap, and the way a dark curl lay like a flattened vine spiral on each cheek above the ear. His mind, as always when they first met, was wholly absorbed in the delicious details that made her herself and no other. Presently he rose and approached the case before which she stood. Its glass shelves were crowded with small broken objects—hardly recognisable domestic utensils, ornaments and personal trifles—made of glass, of clay, of discoloured bronze and other time-blurred substances.

"It seems cruel," she said, "that after a while nothing matters ... any more than these little things, that used to be necessary and important to forgotten people, and now have to be guessed at under a magnifying glass and labelled: 'Use unknown.'"

"Yes; but meanwhile —"

"Ah, meanwhile —"

As she stood there, in her long sealskin coat, her hands thrust in a small round muff, her veil drawn down like a transparent mask to the tip of her nose, and the bunch of violets he had brought her stirring with her quickly-taken breath, it seemed incredible that this pure harmony of line and colour should ever suffer the stupid law of change.

"Meanwhile everything matters—that concerns you," he said.

She looked at him thoughtfully, and turned back to the divan. He sat down beside her and waited; but suddenly he heard a step echoing far off down the empty rooms, and felt the pressure of the minutes.

"What is it you wanted to tell me?" she asked, as if she had received the same warning.

"What I wanted to tell you?" he rejoined. "Why, that I believe you came to New York because you were afraid."

"Afraid?"

"Of my coming to Washington."

She looked down at her muff, and he saw her hands stir in it uneasily.

"Well—?"

"Well—yes," she said.

"You *were* afraid? You knew—?"

"Yes: I knew ..."

"Well, then?" he insisted.

"Well, then: this is better, isn't it?" she returned with a long questioning sigh.

"Better—?"

"We shall hurt others less. Isn't it, after all, what you always wanted?"

"To have you here, you mean—in reach and yet out of reach? To meet you in this way, on the sly? It's the very reverse of what I want. I told you the other day what I wanted."

She hesitated. "And you still think this—worse?"

"A thousand times!" He paused. "It would be easy to lie to you; but the truth is I think it detestable."

"Oh, so do I!" she cried with a deep breath of relief.

He sprang up impatiently. "Well, then—it's my turn to ask: what is it, in God's name, that you think better?"

She hung her head and continued to clasp and unclasp her hands in her muff. The step drew nearer, and a guardian in a braided cap walked listlessly through the room like a ghost stalking through a necropolis. They fixed their eyes simultaneously on the case opposite them, and when the official figure had vanished down a vista of mummies and sarcophagi Archer spoke again.

"What do you think better?"

Instead of answering she murmured: "I promised Granny to stay with her because it seemed to me that here I should be safer."

"From me?"

She bent her head slightly, without looking at him.

"Safer from loving me?"

Her profile did not stir, but he saw a tear overflow on her lashes and hang in a mesh of her veil.

"Safer from doing irreparable harm. Don't let us be like all the others!" she protested.

"What others? I don't profess to be different from my kind. I'm consumed by the same wants and the same longings."

She glanced at him with a kind of terror, and he saw a faint colour steal into her cheeks.

"Shall I—once come to you; and then go home?" she suddenly hazarded in a low clear voice.

The blood rushed to the young man's forehead. "Dearest!" he said, without moving. It seemed as if he held his heart in his hands, like a full cup that the least motion might overbrim.

Then her last phrase struck his ear and his face clouded. "Go home? What do you mean by going home?"

"Home to my husband."

"And you expect me to say yes to that?"

She raised her troubled eyes to his. "What else is there? I can't stay here and lie to the people who've been good to me."

"But that's the very reason why I ask you to come away!"

"And destroy their lives, when they've helped me to remake mine?"

Archer sprang to his feet and stood looking down on her in inarticulate despair. It would have been easy to say: "Yes, come; come once." He knew the power she would put in his hands if she consented; there would be no difficulty then in persuading her not to go back to her husband.

But something silenced the word on his lips. A sort of passionate honesty in her made it inconceivable that he should try to draw her into that familiar trap. "If I were to let her come," he said to himself, "I should have to let her go again." And that was not to be imagined.

But he saw the shadow of the lashes on her wet cheek, and wavered.

"After all," he began again, "we have lives of our own.... There's no use attempting the impossible. You're so unprejudiced about some things, so used, as you say, to looking at the Gorgon, that I don't know why you're afraid to face our case, and see it as it really is—unless you think the sacrifice is not worth making."

She stood up also, her lips tightening under a rapid frown.

"Call it that, then—I must go," she said, drawing her little watch from her bosom.

She turned away, and he followed and caught her by the wrist. "Well, then: come to me once," he said, his head turning suddenly at the thought of losing her; and for a second or two they looked at each other almost like enemies.

"When?" he insisted. "Tomorrow?"

She hesitated. "The day after."

"Dearest—!" he said again.

She had disengaged her wrist; but for a moment they continued to hold each other's eyes, and he saw that her face, which had grown very pale, was flooded with a deep inner radiance. His heart beat with awe: he felt that he had never before beheld love visible.

"Oh, I shall be late—good-bye. No, don't come any farther than this," she cried, walking hurriedly away down the long room, as if the reflected radiance in his eyes had frightened her. When she reached the door she turned for a moment to wave a quick farewell.

Archer walked home alone. Darkness was falling when he let himself into his house, and he looked about at the familiar objects in the hall as if he viewed them from the other side of the grave.

The parlour-maid, hearing his step, ran up the stairs to light the gas on the upper landing.

"Is Mrs. Archer in?"

"No, sir; Mrs. Archer went out in the carriage after luncheon, and hasn't come back."

With a sense of relief he entered the library and flung himself down in his armchair. The parlour-maid followed, bringing the student lamp and shaking some coals onto the dying fire. When she left he continued to sit motionless, his elbows on his knees, his chin on his clasped hands, his eyes fixed on the red grate.

He sat there without conscious thoughts, without sense of the lapse of time, in a deep and grave amazement that seemed to suspend life rather than quicken it. "This was what had to be, then ... this was what had to be," he kept repeating to himself, as if he hung in the clutch of doom. What he had dreamed of had been so different that there was a mortal chill in his rapture.

The door opened and May came in.

"I'm dreadfully late—you weren't worried, were you?" she asked, laying her hand on his shoulder with one of her rare caresses.

He looked up astonished. "Is it late?"

"After seven. I believe you've been asleep!" She laughed, and drawing out her hat pins tossed her velvet hat on the sofa. She looked paler than usual, but sparkling with an unwonted animation.

"I went to see Granny, and just as I was going away Ellen came in from a walk; so I stayed and had a long talk with her. It was ages since we'd had a real talk...." She had dropped into her usual armchair, facing his, and was running her fingers through her rumpled hair. He fancied she expected him to speak.

"A really good talk," she went on, smiling with what seemed to Archer an unnatural vividness. "She was so dear—just like the old Ellen. I'm afraid I haven't been fair to her lately. I've sometimes thought —"

Archer stood up and leaned against the mantelpiece, out of the radius of the lamp.

"Yes, you've thought—?" he echoed as she paused.

"Well, perhaps I haven't judged her fairly. She's so different—at least on the surface. She takes up such odd people—she seems to like to make herself conspicuous. I suppose it's the life she's led in that fast European society; no doubt we seem dreadfully dull to her. But I don't want to judge her unfairly."

She paused again, a little breathless with the unwonted length of her speech, and sat with her lips slightly parted and a deep blush on her cheeks.

Archer, as he looked at her, was reminded of the glow which had suffused her face in the Mission Garden at St. Augustine. He became aware of the same obscure effort in her, the same reaching out toward something beyond the usual range of her vision.

"She hates Ellen," he thought, "and she's trying to overcome the feeling, and to get me to help her to overcome it."

The thought moved him, and for a moment he was on the point of breaking the silence between them, and throwing himself on her mercy.

"You understand, don't you," she went on, "why the family have sometimes been annoyed? We all did what we could for her at first; but she never seemed to understand. And now this idea of going to see Mrs. Beaufort, of going there in Granny's carriage! I'm afraid she's quite alienated the van der Luydens ..."

"Ah," said Archer with an impatient laugh. The open door had closed between them again.

"It's time to dress; we're dining out, aren't we?" he asked, moving from the fire.

She rose also, but lingered near the hearth. As he walked past her she moved forward impulsively, as though to detain him: their eyes met, and he saw that hers were of the same swimming blue as when he had left her to drive to Jersey City.

She flung her arms about his neck and pressed her cheek to his.

"You haven't kissed me today," she said in a whisper; and he felt her tremble in his arms.

## XXXII.

"At the court of the Tuileries," said Mr. Sillerton Jackson with his reminiscent smile, "such things were pretty openly tolerated."

The scene was the van der Luydens' black walnut dining-room in Madison Avenue, and the time the evening after Newland Archer's visit to the Museum of Art. Mr. and Mrs. van der Luyden had come to town for a few days from Skuytercliff, whither they had precipitately fled at the announcement of Beaufort's failure. It had been represented to them that the disarray into which society had been thrown by this deplorable affair made their presence in town more necessary than ever. It was one of the occasions when, as Mrs. Archer put it, they "owed it to society" to show themselves at the Opera, and even to open their own doors.

"It will never do, my dear Louisa, to let people like Mrs. Lemuel Struthers think they can step into Regina's shoes. It is just at such times that new people push in and get a footing. It was owing to the epidemic of chicken-pox in New York the winter Mrs. Struthers first appeared that the married men slipped away to her house while their wives were in the nursery. You and dear Henry, Louisa, must stand in the breach as you always have."

Mr. and Mrs. van der Luyden could not remain deaf to such a call, and reluctantly but heroically they had come to town, unmuffled the house, and sent out invitations for two dinners and an evening reception.

On this particular evening they had invited Sillerton Jackson, Mrs. Archer and Newland and his wife to go with them to the Opera, where Faust was being sung for the first time that winter. Nothing was done without ceremony under the van der Luyden roof, and though there were but four guests the repast had begun at seven punctually, so that the proper sequence of courses might be served without haste before the gentlemen settled down to their cigars.

Archer had not seen his wife since the evening before. He had left early for the office, where he had plunged into an accumulation of unimportant business. In the afternoon one of the senior partners had made an unexpected call on his time; and he had reached home so late that May had preceded him to the van der Luydens', and sent back the carriage.

Now, across the Skuytercliff carnations and the massive plate, she struck him as pale and languid; but her eyes shone, and she talked with exaggerated animation.

The subject which had called forth Mr. Sillerton Jackson's favourite allusion had been brought up (Archer fancied not without intention) by their hostess. The Beaufort failure, or rather the Beaufort attitude since the failure, was still a fruitful theme for the drawing-room moralist; and after it had been thoroughly examined and condemned Mrs. van der Luyden had turned her scrupulous eyes on May Archer.

"Is it possible, dear, that what I hear is true? I was told your grandmother Mingott's carriage was seen standing at Mrs. Beaufort's door." It was noticeable that she no longer called the offending lady by her Christian name.

May's colour rose, and Mrs. Archer put in hastily: "If it was, I'm convinced it was there without Mrs. Mingott's knowledge."

"Ah, you think—?" Mrs. van der Luyden paused, sighed, and glanced at her husband.

"I'm afraid," Mr. van der Luyden said, "that Madame Olenska's kind heart may have led her into the imprudence of calling on Mrs. Beaufort."

"Or her taste for peculiar people," put in Mrs. Archer in a dry tone, while her eyes dwelt innocently on her son's.

"I'm sorry to think it of Madame Olenska," said Mrs. van der Luyden; and Mrs. Archer murmured: "Ah, my dear—and after you'd had her twice at Skuytercliff!"

It was at this point that Mr. Jackson seized the chance to place his favourite allusion.

"At the Tuileries," he repeated, seeing the eyes of the company expectantly turned on him, "the standard was excessively lax in some respects; and if you'd asked where Morny's money came from—! Or who paid the debts of some of the Court beauties ..."

"I hope, dear Sillerton," said Mrs. Archer, "you are not suggesting that we should adopt such standards?"

"I never suggest," returned Mr. Jackson imperturbably. "But Madame Olenska's foreign bringing-up may make her less particular —"

"Ah," the two elder ladies sighed.

"Still, to have kept her grandmother's carriage at a defaulter's door!" Mr. van der Luyden protested; and Archer guessed that he was remembering, and resenting, the hampers of carnations he had sent to the little house in Twenty-third Street.

"Of course I've always said that she looks at things quite differently," Mrs. Archer summed up.

A flush rose to May's forehead. She looked across the table at her husband, and said precipitately: "I'm sure Ellen meant it kindly."

"Imprudent people are often kind," said Mrs. Archer, as if the fact were scarcely an extenuation; and Mrs. van der Luyden murmured: "If only she had consulted some one —"

"Ah, that she never did!" Mrs. Archer rejoined.

At this point Mr. van der Luyden glanced at his wife, who bent her head slightly in the direction of Mrs. Archer; and the glimmering trains of the three ladies swept out of the door while the gentlemen settled down to their cigars. Mr. van der Luyden supplied short ones on Opera nights; but they were so good that they made his guests deplore his inexorable punctuality.

Archer, after the first act, had detached himself from the party and made his way to the back of the club box. From there he watched, over various Chivers, Mingott and Rushworth shoulders, the same scene that he had looked at, two years previously, on the night of his first meeting with Ellen Olenska. He had half-expected her to appear again in old Mrs. Mingott's box, but it remained empty; and he sat motionless, his eyes fastened on it, till suddenly Madame Nilsson's pure soprano broke out into "M'ama, non m'ama ..."

Archer turned to the stage, where, in the familiar setting of giant roses and pen-wiper pansies, the same large blonde victim was succumbing to the same small brown seducer.

From the stage his eyes wandered to the point of the horseshoe where May sat between two older ladies, just as, on that former evening, she had sat between Mrs. Lovell Mingott and her newly-arrived "foreign" cousin. As on that evening, she was all in white; and Archer, who had not noticed what she wore, recognised the blue-white satin and old lace of her wedding dress.

It was the custom, in old New York, for brides to appear in this costly garment during the first year or two of marriage: his mother, he knew, kept hers in tissue paper in the hope that Janey might some day wear it, though poor Janey was reaching the age when pearl grey poplin and no bridesmaids would be thought more "appropriate."

It struck Archer that May, since their return from Europe, had seldom worn her bridal satin, and the surprise of seeing her in it made him compare her appearance with that of the young girl he had watched with such blissful anticipations two years earlier.

Though May's outline was slightly heavier, as her goddesslike build had foretold, her athletic erectness of carriage, and the girlish transparency of her expression, remained unchanged: but for the slight languor that Archer had lately noticed in her she would have been the exact image of the girl playing with the bouquet of lilies-of-the-valley on her betrothal evening. The fact seemed an additional appeal to his pity: such innocence was as moving as the trustful clasp of a child. Then he remembered the passionate generosity latent under that incurious calm. He recalled her glance of understanding when he had urged that their engagement should be announced at the Beaufort ball; he heard the voice in which she had said, in the Mission garden: "I couldn't have my happiness made out of a wrong—a wrong to some one else;" and an uncontrollable longing seized him to tell her the truth, to throw himself on her generosity, and ask for the freedom he had once refused.

Newland Archer was a quiet and self-controlled young man. Conformity to the discipline of a small society had become almost his second nature. It was deeply distasteful to him to do anything melodramatic and conspicuous, anything Mr. van der Luyden would have deprecated and the club box condemned as bad form. But he had become suddenly unconscious of the club box, of Mr. van der Luyden, of all that had so long enclosed him in the warm shelter of habit. He walked along the semi-circular passage at the back of the house, and opened the door of Mrs. van der Luyden's box as if it had been a gate into the unknown.

"M'ama!" thrilled out the triumphant Marguerite; and the occupants of the box looked up in surprise at Archer's entrance. He had already broken one of the rules of his world, which forbade the entering of a box during a solo.

Slipping between Mr. van der Luyden and Sillerton Jackson, he leaned over his wife.

"I've got a beastly headache; don't tell any one, but come home, won't you?" he whispered.

May gave him a glance of comprehension, and he saw her whisper to his mother, who nodded sympathetically; then she murmured an excuse to Mrs. van der Luyden, and rose from her seat just as Marguerite fell into Faust's arms. Archer, while he helped her on with her Opera cloak, noticed the exchange of a significant smile between the older ladies.

As they drove away May laid her hand shyly on his. "I'm so sorry you don't feel well. I'm afraid they've been overworking you again at the office."

"No—it's not that: do you mind if I open the window?" he returned confusedly, letting down the pane on his side. He sat staring out into the street, feeling his wife beside him as a silent watchful interrogation, and keeping his eyes steadily fixed on the passing houses. At their door she caught her skirt in the step of the carriage, and fell against him.

"Did you hurt yourself?" he asked, steadying her with his arm.

"No; but my poor dress—see how I've torn it!" she exclaimed. She bent to gather up a mud-stained breadth, and followed him up the steps into the hall. The servants had not expected them so early, and there was only a glimmer of gas on the upper landing.

Archer mounted the stairs, turned up the light, and put a match to the brackets on each side of the library mantelpiece. The curtains were drawn, and the warm friendly aspect of the room smote him like that of a familiar face met during an unavowable errand.

He noticed that his wife was very pale, and asked if he should get her some brandy.

"Oh, no," she exclaimed with a momentary flush, as she took off her cloak. "But hadn't you better go to bed at once?" she added, as he opened a silver box on the table and took out a cigarette.

Archer threw down the cigarette and walked to his usual place by the fire.

"No; my head is not as bad as that." He paused. "And there's something I want to say; something important—that I must tell you at once."

She had dropped into an armchair, and raised her head as he spoke. "Yes, dear?" she rejoined, so gently that he wondered at the lack of wonder with which she received this preamble.

"May —" he began, standing a few feet from her chair, and looking over at her as if the slight distance between them were an unbridgeable abyss. The sound of his voice echoed uncannily through the homelike hush, and he repeated: "There is something I've got to tell you ... about myself ..."

She sat silent, without a movement or a tremor of her lashes. She was still extremely pale, but her face had a curious tranquillity of expression that seemed drawn from some secret inner source.

Archer checked the conventional phrases of self-accusal that were crowding to his lips. He was determined to put the case baldly, without vain recrimination or excuse.

"Madame Olenska —" he said; but at the name his wife raised her hand as if to silence him. As she did so the gaslight struck on the gold of her wedding-ring.

"Oh, why should we talk about Ellen tonight?" she asked, with a slight pout of impatience.

"Because I ought to have spoken before."

Her face remained calm. "Is it really worth while, dear? I know I've been unfair to her at times—perhaps we all have. You've understood her, no doubt, better than we did: you've always been kind to her. But what does it matter, now it's all over?"

Archer looked at her blankly. Could it be possible that the sense of unreality in which he felt himself imprisoned had communicated itself to his wife?

"All over—what do you mean?" he asked in an indistinct stammer.

May still looked at him with transparent eyes. "Why—since she's going back to Europe so soon; since Granny approves and understands, and has arranged to make her independent of her husband —"

She broke off, and Archer, grasping the corner of the mantelpiece in one convulsed hand, and steadying himself against it, made a vain effort to extend the same control to his reeling thoughts.

"I supposed," he heard his wife's even voice go on, "that you had been kept at the office this evening about the business arrangements. It was settled this morning, I believe." She lowered her eyes under his unseeing stare, and another fugitive flush passed over her face.

He understood that his own eyes must be unbearable, and turning away, rested his elbows on the mantel-shelf and covered his face. Something drummed and clanged furiously in his ears; he could not tell if it were the blood in his veins, or the tick of the clock on the mantel.

May sat without moving or speaking while the clock slowly measured out five minutes. A lump of coal fell forward in the grate, and hearing her rise to push it back, Archer at length turned and faced her.

"It's impossible," he exclaimed.

"Impossible—?"

"How do you know—what you've just told me?"

"I saw Ellen yesterday—I told you I'd seen her at Granny's."

"It wasn't then that she told you?"

"No; I had a note from her this afternoon.—Do you want to see it?"

He could not find his voice, and she went out of the room, and came back almost immediately.

"I thought you knew," she said simply.

She laid a sheet of paper on the table, and Archer put out his hand and took it up. The letter contained only a few lines.

"May dear, I have at last made Granny understand that my visit to her could be no more than a visit; and she has been as kind and generous as ever. She sees now that if I return to Europe I must live by myself, or rather with poor Aunt Medora, who is coming with me. I am hurrying back to Washington to pack up, and we sail next week. You must be very good to Granny when I'm gone—as good as you've always been to me. Ellen.

"If any of my friends wish to urge me to change my mind, please tell them it would be utterly useless."

Archer read the letter over two or three times; then he flung it down and burst out laughing.

The sound of his laugh startled him. It recalled Janey's midnight fright when she had caught him rocking with incomprehensible mirth over May's telegram announcing that the date of their marriage had been advanced.

"Why did she write this?" he asked, checking his laugh with a supreme effort.

May met the question with her unshaken candour. "I suppose because we talked things over yesterday —"

"What things?"

"I told her I was afraid I hadn't been fair to her—hadn't always understood how hard it must have been for her here, alone among so many people who were relations and yet strangers; who felt the right to criticise, and yet didn't always know the circumstances." She paused. "I knew you'd been the one friend she could always count on; and I wanted her to know that you and I were the same—in all our feelings."

She hesitated, as if waiting for him to speak, and then added slowly: "She understood my wishing to tell her this. I think she understands everything."

She went up to Archer, and taking one of his cold hands pressed it quickly against her cheek.

"My head aches too; good-night, dear," she said, and turned to the door, her torn and muddy wedding-dress dragging after her across the room.

## XXXIII.

It was, as Mrs. Archer smilingly said to Mrs. Welland, a great event for a young couple to give their first big dinner.

The Newland Archers, since they had set up their household, had received a good deal of company in an informal way. Archer was fond of having three or four friends to dine, and May welcomed them with the beaming readiness of which her mother had set her the example in conjugal affairs. Her husband questioned whether, if left to herself, she would ever have asked any one to the house; but he had long given up trying to disengage her real self from the shape into which tradition and training had moulded her. It was expected that well-off young couples in New York should do a good deal of informal entertaining, and a Welland married to an Archer was doubly pledged to the tradition.

But a big dinner, with a hired chef and two borrowed footmen, with Roman punch, roses from Henderson's, and menus on gilt-edged cards, was a different affair, and not to be lightly undertaken. As Mrs. Archer remarked, the Roman punch made all the difference; not in itself but by its manifold implications—since it signified either canvas-backs or terrapin, two soups, a hot and a cold sweet, full decolletage with short sleeves, and guests of a proportionate importance.

It was always an interesting occasion when a young pair launched their first invitations in the third person, and their summons was seldom refused even by the seasoned and sought-after. Still, it was admittedly a triumph that the van der Luydens, at May's request, should have stayed over in order to be present at her farewell dinner for the Countess Olenska.

The two mothers-in-law sat in May's drawing-room on the afternoon of the great day, Mrs. Archer writing out the menus on Tiffany's thickest gilt-edged bristol, while Mrs. Welland superintended the placing of the palms and standard lamps.

Archer, arriving late from his office, found them still there. Mrs. Archer had turned her attention to the name-cards for the table, and Mrs. Welland was considering the effect of bringing forward the large gilt sofa, so that another "corner" might be created between the piano and the window.

May, they told him, was in the dining-room inspecting the mound of Jacqueminot roses and maidenhair in the centre of the long table, and the placing of the Maillard bonbons in openwork silver baskets between the candelabra. On the piano stood a large basket of orchids which Mr. van der Luyden had had sent from Skuytercliff. Everything was, in short, as it should be on the approach of so considerable an event.

Mrs. Archer ran thoughtfully over the list, checking off each name with her sharp gold pen.

"Henry van der Luyden—Louisa—the Lovell Mingotts—the Reggie Chiverses—Lawrence Lefferts and Gertrude—(yes, I suppose May was right to have them)—the Selfridge Merrys, Sillerton Jackson, Van Newland and his wife. (How time passes! It seems only yesterday that he was your best man, Newland)—and Countess Olenska—yes, I think that's all...."

Mrs. Welland surveyed her son-in-law affectionately. "No one can say, Newland, that you and May are not giving Ellen a handsome send-off."

"Ah, well," said Mrs. Archer, "I understand May's wanting her cousin to tell people abroad that we're not quite barbarians."

"I'm sure Ellen will appreciate it. She was to arrive this morning, I believe. It will make a most charming last impression. The evening before sailing is usually so dreary," Mrs. Welland cheerfully continued.

Archer turned toward the door, and his mother-in-law called to him: "Do go in and have a peep at the table. And don't let May tire herself too much." But he affected not to hear, and sprang up the stairs to his library. The room looked at him like an alien countenance composed into a polite grimace; and he perceived that it had been ruthlessly "tidied," and prepared, by a judicious distribution of ash-trays and cedar-wood boxes, for the gentlemen to smoke in.

"Ah, well," he thought, "it's not for long —" and he went on to his dressing-room.

Ten days had passed since Madame Olenska's departure from New York. During those ten days Archer had had no sign from her but that conveyed by the return of a key wrapped in tissue paper, and sent to his office in a sealed envelope addressed in her hand. This retort to his last appeal might have been interpreted as a classic move in a familiar game; but the young man chose to give it a different meaning. She was still fighting against her fate; but she was going to Europe, and she was not returning to her husband. Nothing, therefore, was to prevent his following her; and once he had taken the irrevocable step, and had proved to her that it was irrevocable, he believed she would not send him away.

This confidence in the future had steadied him to play his part in the present. It had kept him from writing to her, or betraying, by any sign or act, his misery and mortification. It seemed to him that in the deadly silent game between them the trumps were still in his hands; and he waited.

There had been, nevertheless, moments sufficiently difficult to pass; as when Mr. Letterblair, the day after Madame Olenska's departure, had sent for him to go over the details of the trust which Mrs. Manson Mingott wished to create for her granddaughter. For a couple of hours Archer had examined the terms of the deed with his senior, all the while obscurely feeling that if he had been consulted it was for some reason other than the obvious one of his cousinship; and that the close of the conference would reveal it.

"Well, the lady can't deny that it's a handsome arrangement," Mr. Letterblair had summed up, after mumbling over a summary of the settlement. "In fact I'm bound to say she's been treated pretty handsomely all round."

"All round?" Archer echoed with a touch of derision. "Do you refer to her husband's proposal to give her back her own money?"

Mr. Letterblair's bushy eyebrows went up a fraction of an inch. "My dear sir, the law's the law; and your wife's cousin was married under the French law. It's to be presumed she knew what that meant."

"Even if she did, what happened subsequently—." But Archer paused. Mr. Letterblair had laid his pen-handle against his big corrugated nose, and was looking down it with the expression assumed by virtuous elderly gentlemen when they wish their youngers to understand that virtue is not synonymous with ignorance.

"My dear sir, I've no wish to extenuate the Count's transgressions; but—but on the other side ... I wouldn't put my hand in the fire ... well, that there hadn't been tit for tat ... with the young champion...." Mr. Letterblair unlocked a drawer and pushed a folded paper toward Archer. "This report, the result of discreet enquiries ..." And then, as Archer made no effort to glance at the paper or to repudiate the suggestion, the lawyer somewhat flatly continued: "I don't say it's conclusive, you observe; far from it. But straws show ... and on the whole it's eminently satisfactory for all parties that this dignified solution has been reached."

"Oh, eminently," Archer assented, pushing back the paper.

A day or two later, on responding to a summons from Mrs. Manson Mingott, his soul had been more deeply tried.

He had found the old lady depressed and querulous.

"You know she's deserted me?" she began at once; and without waiting for his reply: "Oh, don't ask me why! She gave so many reasons that I've forgotten them all. My private belief is that she couldn't face the boredom. At any rate that's what Augusta and my daughters-in-law think. And I don't know that I altogether blame her. Olenski's a finished scoundrel; but life with him must have been a good deal gayer than it is in Fifth Avenue. Not that the family would admit that: they think Fifth Avenue is Heaven with the rue de la Paix thrown in. And poor Ellen, of course, has no idea of going back to her husband. She held out as firmly as ever against that. So she's to settle down in Paris with that fool Medora.... Well, Paris is Paris; and you can keep a carriage there on next to nothing. But she was as gay as a bird, and I shall miss her." Two tears, the parched tears of the old, rolled down her puffy cheeks and vanished in the abysses of her bosom.

"All I ask is," she concluded, "that they shouldn't bother me any more. I must really be allowed to digest my gruel...." And she twinkled a little wistfully at Archer.

It was that evening, on his return home, that May announced her intention of giving a farewell dinner to her cousin. Madame Olenska's name had not been pronounced between them since the night of her flight to Washington; and Archer looked at his wife with surprise.

"A dinner—why?" he interrogated.

Her colour rose. "But you like Ellen—I thought you'd be pleased."

"It's awfully nice—your putting it in that way. But I really don't see —"

"I mean to do it, Newland," she said, quietly rising and going to her desk. "Here are the invitations all written. Mother helped me—she agrees that we ought to." She paused, embarrassed and yet smiling, and Archer suddenly saw before him the embodied image of the Family.

"Oh, all right," he said, staring with unseeing eyes at the list of guests that she had put in his hand.

When he entered the drawing-room before dinner May was stooping over the fire and trying to coax the logs to burn in their unaccustomed setting of immaculate tiles.

The tall lamps were all lit, and Mr. van der Luyden's orchids had been conspicuously disposed in various receptacles of modern porcelain and knobby silver. Mrs. Newland Archer's drawing-room was generally thought a great success. A gilt bamboo jardiniere, in which the primulas and cinerarias were punctually renewed, blocked the access to the bay window (where the old-fashioned would have preferred a bronze reduction of the Venus of Milo); the sofas and arm-chairs of pale brocade were cleverly grouped about little plush tables densely covered with silver toys, porcelain animals and efflorescent photograph frames; and tall rosy-shaded lamps shot up like tropical flowers among the palms.

"I don't think Ellen has ever seen this room lighted up," said May, rising flushed from her struggle, and sending about her a glance of pardonable pride.

The brass tongs which she had propped against the side of the chimney fell with a crash that drowned her husband's answer; and before he could restore them Mr. and Mrs. van der Luyden were announced.

The other guests quickly followed, for it was known that the van der Luydens liked to dine punctually. The room was nearly full, and Archer was engaged in showing to Mrs. Selfridge Merry a small highly-varnished Verbeckhoven "Study of Sheep," which Mr. Welland had given May for Christmas, when he found Madame Olenska at his side.

She was excessively pale, and her pallor made her dark hair seem denser and heavier than ever. Perhaps that, or the fact that she had wound several rows of amber beads about her neck, reminded him suddenly of the little Ellen Mingott he had danced with at children's parties, when Medora Manson had first brought her to New York.

The amber beads were trying to her complexion, or her dress was perhaps unbecoming: her face looked lustreless and almost ugly, and he had never loved it as he did at that minute. Their hands met, and he thought he heard her say: "Yes, we're sailing tomorrow in the Russia —"; then there was an unmeaning noise of opening doors, and after an interval May's voice: "Newland! Dinner's been announced. Won't you please take Ellen in?"

Madame Olenska put her hand on his arm, and he noticed that the hand was ungloved, and remembered how he had kept his eyes fixed on it the evening that he had sat with her in the little Twenty-third Street drawing-room. All the beauty that had forsaken her face seemed to have taken refuge in the long pale fingers and faintly dimpled knuckles on his sleeve, and he said to himself: "If it were only to see her hand again I should have to follow her—."

It was only at an entertainment ostensibly offered to a "foreign visitor" that Mrs. van der Luyden could suffer the diminution of being placed on her host's left. The fact of Madame Olenska's "foreignness" could hardly have been more adroitly emphasised than by this farewell tribute; and Mrs. van der Luyden accepted her displacement with an affability which left no doubt as to her approval. There were certain things that had to be done, and if done at all, done handsomely and thoroughly; and one of these, in the old New York code, was the tribal rally around a kinswoman about to be eliminated from the tribe. There was nothing on earth that the Wellands and Mingotts would not have done to proclaim their unalterable affection for the Countess

Olenska now that her passage for Europe was engaged; and Archer, at the head of his table, sat marvelling at the silent untiring activity with which her popularity had been retrieved, grievances against her silenced, her past countenanced, and her present irradiated by the family approval. Mrs. van der Luyden shone on her with the dim benevolence which was her nearest approach to cordiality, and Mr. van der Luyden, from his seat at May's right, cast down the table glances plainly intended to justify all the carnations he had sent from Skuytercliff.

Archer, who seemed to be assisting at the scene in a state of odd imponderability, as if he floated somewhere between chandelier and ceiling, wondered at nothing so much as his own share in the proceedings. As his glance travelled from one placid well-fed face to another he saw all the harmless-looking people engaged upon May's canvas-backs as a band of dumb conspirators, and himself and the pale woman on his right as the centre of their conspiracy. And then it came over him, in a vast flash made up of many broken gleams, that to all of them he and Madame Olenska were lovers, lovers in the extreme sense peculiar to "foreign" vocabularies. He guessed himself to have been, for months, the centre of countless silently observing eyes and patiently listening ears; he understood that, by means as yet unknown to him, the separation between himself and the partner of his guilt had been achieved, and that now the whole tribe had rallied about his wife on the tacit assumption that nobody knew anything, or had ever imagined anything, and that the occasion of the entertainment was simply May Archer's natural desire to take an affectionate leave of her friend and cousin.

It was the old New York way of taking life "without effusion of blood": the way of people who dreaded scandal more than disease, who placed decency above courage, and who considered that nothing was more ill-bred than "scenes," except the behaviour of those who gave rise to them.

As these thoughts succeeded each other in his mind Archer felt like a prisoner in the centre of an armed camp. He looked about the table, and guessed at the inexorableness of his captors from the tone in which, over the asparagus from Florida, they were dealing with Beaufort and his wife. "It's to show me," he thought, "what would happen to *me* —" and a deathly sense of the superiority of implication and analogy over direct action, and of silence over rash words, closed in on him like the doors of the family vault.

He laughed, and met Mrs. van der Luyden's startled eyes.

"You think it laughable?" she said with a pinched smile. "Of course poor Regina's idea of remaining in New York has its ridiculous side, I suppose;" and Archer muttered: "Of course."

At this point, he became conscious that Madame Olenska's other neighbour had been engaged for some time with the lady on his right. At the same moment he saw that May, serenely enthroned between Mr. van der Luyden and Mr. Selfridge Merry, had cast a quick glance down the table. It was evident that the host and the lady on his right could not sit through the whole meal in silence. He turned to Madame Olenska, and her pale smile met him. "Oh, do let's see it through," it seemed to say.

"Did you find the journey tiring?" he asked in a voice that surprised him by its naturalness; and she answered that, on the contrary, she had seldom travelled with fewer discomforts.

"Except, you know, the dreadful heat in the train," she added; and he remarked that she would not suffer from that particular hardship in the country she was going to.

"I never," he declared with intensity, "was more nearly frozen than once, in April, in the train between Calais and Paris."

She said she did not wonder, but remarked that, after all, one could always carry an extra rug, and that every form of travel had its hardships; to which he abruptly returned that he thought them all of no account compared with the blessedness of getting away. She changed colour, and he added, his voice suddenly rising in pitch: "I mean to do a lot of travelling myself before long." A tremor crossed her face, and leaning over to Reggie Chivers, he cried out: "I say, Reggie, what do you say to a trip round the world: now, next month, I mean? I'm game if you are —" at which Mrs. Reggie piped up that she could not think of letting Reggie go till after the Martha Washington Ball she was getting up for the Blind Asylum in Easter week; and her husband placidly observed that by that time he would have to be practising for the International Polo match.

But Mr. Selfridge Merry had caught the phrase "round the world," and having once circled the globe in his steam-yacht, he seized the opportunity to send down the table several striking items concerning the shallowness of the Mediterranean ports. Though, after all, he added, it didn't matter; for when you'd seen Athens and Smyrna and Constantinople, what else was there?

And Mrs. Merry said she could never be too grateful to Dr. Bencomb for having made them promise not to go to Naples on account of the fever.

"But you must have three weeks to do India properly," her husband conceded, anxious to have it understood that he was no frivolous globe-trotter.

And at this point the ladies went up to the drawing-room.

In the library, in spite of weightier presences, Lawrence Lefferts predominated.

The talk, as usual, had veered around to the Beauforts, and even Mr. van der Luyden and Mr. Selfridge Merry, installed in the honorary arm-chairs tacitly reserved for them, paused to listen to the younger man's philippic.

Never had Lefferts so abounded in the sentiments that adorn Christian manhood and exalt the sanctity of the home. Indignation lent him a scathing eloquence, and it was clear that if others had followed his example, and acted as he talked, society would never have been weak enough to receive a foreign upstart like Beaufort—no, sir, not even if he'd married a van der Luyden or a Lanning instead of a Dallas. And what chance would there have been, Lefferts wrathfully questioned, of his marrying into such a family as the Dallases, if he had not already wormed his way into certain houses, as people like Mrs. Lemuel Struthers had managed to worm theirs in his wake? If society chose to open its doors to vulgar women the harm was not great, though the gain was doubtful; but once it got in the way of tolerating men of obscure origin and tainted wealth the end was total disintegration—and at no distant date.

"If things go on at this pace," Lefferts thundered, looking like a young prophet dressed by Poole, and who had not yet been stoned, "we shall see our children fighting for invitations to swindlers' houses, and marrying Beaufort's bastards."

"Oh, I say—draw it mild!" Reggie Chivers and young Newland protested, while Mr. Selfridge Merry looked genuinely alarmed, and an expression of pain and disgust settled on Mr. van der Luyden's sensitive face.

"Has he got any?" cried Mr. Sillerton Jackson, pricking up his ears; and while Lefferts tried to turn the question with a laugh, the old gentleman twittered into Archer's ear: "Queer, those fellows who are always wanting to set things right. The people who have the worst cooks are always telling you they're poisoned when they dine out. But I hear there are pressing reasons for our friend Lawrence's diatribe:—typewriter this time, I understand...."

The talk swept past Archer like some senseless river running and running because it did not know enough to stop. He saw, on the faces about him, expressions of interest, amusement and even mirth. He listened to the younger men's laughter, and to the praise of the Archer Madeira, which Mr. van der Luyden and Mr. Merry were thoughtfully celebrating. Through it all he was dimly aware of a general attitude of friendliness toward himself, as if the guard of the prisoner he felt himself to be were trying to soften his captivity; and the perception increased his passionate determination to be free.

In the drawing-room, where they presently joined the ladies, he met May's triumphant eyes, and read in them the conviction that everything had "gone off" beautifully. She rose from Madame Olenska's side, and immediately Mrs. van der Luyden beckoned the latter to a seat on the gilt sofa where she throned. Mrs. Selfridge Merry bore across the room to join them, and it became clear to Archer that here also a conspiracy of rehabilitation and obliteration was going on. The silent organisation which held his little world together was determined to put itself on record as never for a moment having questioned the propriety of Madame Olenska's conduct, or the completeness of Archer's domestic felicity. All these amiable and inexorable persons were resolutely engaged in pretending to each other that they had never heard of, suspected, or even conceived possible, the least hint to the contrary; and from this tissue of elaborate mutual dissimulation Archer once more disengaged the fact that New York believed him to be Madame Olenska's lover. He caught the glitter of victory in his wife's eyes, and for the first time understood that she shared the belief. The discovery roused a laughter of inner devils that reverberated through all his efforts to discuss the Martha Washington ball with Mrs. Reggie Chivers and little Mrs. Newland; and so the evening swept on, running and running like a senseless river that did not know how to stop.

At length he saw that Madame Olenska had risen and was saying good-bye. He understood that in a moment she would be gone, and tried to remember what he had said to her at dinner; but he could not recall a single word they had exchanged.

She went up to May, the rest of the company making a circle about her as she advanced. The two young women clasped hands; then May bent forward and kissed her cousin.

"Certainly our hostess is much the handsomer of the two," Archer heard Reggie Chivers say in an undertone to young Mrs. Newland; and he remembered Beaufort's coarse sneer at May's ineffectual beauty.

A moment later he was in the hall, putting Madame Olenska's cloak about her shoulders.

Through all his confusion of mind he had held fast to the resolve to say nothing that might startle or disturb her. Convinced that no power could now turn him from his purpose he had found strength to let events shape themselves as they would. But as he followed Madame Olenska into the hall he thought with a sudden hunger of being for a moment alone with her at the door of her carriage.

"Is your carriage here?" he asked; and at that moment Mrs. van der Luyden, who was being majestically inserted into her sables, said gently: "We are driving dear Ellen home."

Archer's heart gave a jerk, and Madame Olenska, clasping her cloak and fan with one hand, held out the other to him. "Good-bye," she said.

"Good-bye—but I shall see you soon in Paris," he answered aloud—it seemed to him that he had shouted it.

"Oh," she murmured, "if you and May could come—!"

Mr. van der Luyden advanced to give her his arm, and Archer turned to Mrs. van der Luyden. For a moment, in the billowy darkness inside the big landau, he caught the dim oval of a face, eyes shining steadily—and she was gone.

As he went up the steps he crossed Lawrence Lefferts coming down with his wife. Lefferts caught his host by the sleeve, drawing back to let Gertrude pass.

"I say, old chap: do you mind just letting it be understood that I'm dining with you at the club tomorrow night? Thanks so much, you old brick! Good-night."

"It *did* go off beautifully, didn't it?" May questioned from the threshold of the library.

Archer roused himself with a start. As soon as the last carriage had driven away, he had come up to the library and shut himself in, with the hope that his wife, who still lingered below, would go straight to her room. But there she stood, pale and drawn, yet radiating the factitious energy of one who has passed beyond fatigue.

"May I come and talk it over?" she asked.

"Of course, if you like. But you must be awfully sleepy —"

"No, I'm not sleepy. I should like to sit with you a little."

"Very well," he said, pushing her chair near the fire.

She sat down and he resumed his seat; but neither spoke for a long time. At length Archer began abruptly: "Since you're not tired, and want to talk, there's something I must tell you. I tried to the other night—."

She looked at him quickly. "Yes, dear. Something about yourself?"

"About myself. You say you're not tired: well, I am. Horribly tired ..."

In an instant she was all tender anxiety. "Oh, I've seen it coming on, Newland! You've been so wickedly overworked —"

"Perhaps it's that. Anyhow, I want to make a break —"

"A break? To give up the law?"

"To go away, at any rate—at once. On a long trip, ever so far off—away from everything —"

He paused, conscious that he had failed in his attempt to speak with the indifference of a man who longs for a change, and is yet too weary to welcome it. Do what he would, the chord of eagerness vibrated. "Away from everything —" he repeated.

"Ever so far? Where, for instance?" she asked.

"Oh, I don't know. India—or Japan."

She stood up, and as he sat with bent head, his chin propped on his hands, he felt her warmly and fragrantly hovering over him.

"As far as that? But I'm afraid you can't, dear ..." she said in an unsteady voice. "Not unless you'll take me with you." And then, as he was silent, she went on, in tones so clear and evenly-pitched that each separate syllable tapped like a little hammer on his brain: "That is, if the doctors will let me go ... but I'm afraid they won't. For you see, Newland, I've been sure since this morning of something I've been so longing and hoping for —"

He looked up at her with a sick stare, and she sank down, all dew and roses, and hid her face against his knee.

"Oh, my dear," he said, holding her to him while his cold hand stroked her hair.

There was a long pause, which the inner devils filled with strident laughter; then May freed herself from his arms and stood up.

"You didn't guess—?"

"Yes—I; no. That is, of course I hoped —"

They looked at each other for an instant and again fell silent; then, turning his eyes from hers, he asked abruptly: "Have you told any one else?"

"Only Mamma and your mother." She paused, and then added hurriedly, the blood flushing up to her forehead: "That is—and Ellen. You know I told you we'd had a long talk one afternoon—and how dear she was to me."

"Ah —" said Archer, his heart stopping.

He felt that his wife was watching him intently. "Did you MIND my telling her first, Newland?"

"Mind? Why should I?" He made a last effort to collect himself. "But that was a fortnight ago, wasn't it? I thought you said you weren't sure till today."

Her colour burned deeper, but she held his gaze. "No; I wasn't sure then—but I told her I was. And you see I was right!" she exclaimed, her blue eyes wet with victory.

## XXXIV.

Newland Archer sat at the writing-table in his library in East Thirty-ninth Street.

He had just got back from a big official reception for the inauguration of the new galleries at the Metropolitan Museum, and the spectacle of those great spaces crowded with the spoils of the ages, where the throng of fashion circulated through a series of scientifically catalogued treasures, had suddenly pressed on a rusted spring of memory.

"Why, this used to be one of the old Cesnola rooms," he heard some one say; and instantly everything about him vanished, and he was sitting alone on a hard leather divan against a radiator, while a slight figure in a long sealskin cloak moved away down the meagrely-fitted vista of the old Museum.

The vision had roused a host of other associations, and he sat looking with new eyes at the library which, for over thirty years, had been the scene of his solitary musings and of all the family confabulations.

It was the room in which most of the real things of his life had happened. There his wife, nearly twenty-six years ago, had broken to him, with a blushing circumlocution that would have caused the young women of the new generation to smile, the news that she was to have a child; and there their eldest boy, Dallas, too delicate to be taken to church in midwinter, had been christened by their old friend the Bishop of New York, the ample magnificent irreplaceable Bishop, so long the pride and ornament of his diocese. There Dallas had first staggered across the floor shouting "Dad," while May and the nurse laughed behind the door; there their second child, Mary (who was so like her mother), had announced her engagement to the dullest and most reliable of Reggie Chivers's many sons; and there Archer had kissed her through her wedding veil before they went down to the motor which was to carry them to Grace Church—for in a world where all else had reeled on its foundations the "Grace Church wedding" remained an unchanged institution.

It was in the library that he and May had always discussed the future of the children: the studies of Dallas and his young brother Bill, Mary's incurable indifference to "accomplishments," and passion for sport and philanthropy, and the vague leanings toward "art" which had finally landed the restless and curious Dallas in the office of a rising New York architect.

The young men nowadays were emancipating themselves from the law and business and taking up all sorts of new things. If they were not absorbed in state politics or municipal reform, the chances were that they were going in for Central American archaeology, for architecture or landscape-engineering; taking a keen and learned interest in the prerevolutionary buildings of their own country, studying and adapting Georgian types, and protesting at the meaningless use of the word "Colonial." Nobody nowadays had "Colonial" houses except the millionaire grocers of the suburbs.

But above all—sometimes Archer put it above all—it was in that library that the Governor of New York, coming down from Albany one evening to dine and spend the night, had turned to his host, and said, banging his clenched fist on the table and gnashing his eye-glasses: "Hang the professional politician! You're the kind of man the country wants, Archer. If the stable's ever to be cleaned out, men like you have got to lend a hand in the cleaning."

"Men like you —" how Archer had glowed at the phrase! How eagerly he had risen up at the call! It was an echo of Ned Winsett's old appeal to roll his sleeves up and get down into the muck; but spoken by a man who set the example of the gesture, and whose summons to follow him was irresistible.

Archer, as he looked back, was not sure that men like himself WERE what his country needed, at least in the active service to which Theodore Roosevelt had pointed; in fact, there was reason to think it did not, for after a year in the State Assembly he had not been re-elected, and had dropped back thankfully into obscure if useful municipal work, and from that again to the writing of occasional articles in one of the reforming weeklies that were trying to shake the country out of its apathy. It was little enough to look back on; but when he remembered to what the young men of his generation and his set had looked forward—the narrow groove of money-making, sport and society to which their vision had been limited—even his small contribution to the new state of things seemed to count, as each brick counts in a well-built wall. He had done little in public life; he would always be by nature a contemplative and a dilettante; but he had had high things to contemplate, great things to delight in; and one great man's friendship to be his strength and pride.

He had been, in short, what people were beginning to call "a good citizen." In New York, for many years past, every new movement, philanthropic, municipal or artistic, had taken account of his opinion and wanted his name. People said: "Ask Archer" when there was a question of starting the first school for crippled children, reorganising the Museum of Art, founding the Grolier Club, inaugurating the new Library, or getting up a new society of chamber music. His days were full, and they were filled decently. He supposed it was all a man ought to ask.

Something he knew he had missed: the flower of life. But he thought of it now as a thing so unattainable and improbable that to have repined would have been like despairing because one had not drawn the first prize in a lottery. There were a hundred million tickets in HIS lottery, and there was only one prize; the chances had been too decidedly against him. When he thought of Ellen Olenska it was abstractly, serenely, as one might think of some imaginary beloved in a book or a picture: she had become the composite vision of all that he had missed. That vision, faint and tenuous as it was, had kept him from thinking of other women. He had been what was called a faithful husband; and when May had suddenly died—carried off by the infectious pneumonia through which she had nursed their youngest child—he had honestly mourned her. Their long years together had shown him that it did not so much matter if marriage was a dull duty, as long as it kept the dignity of a duty: lapsing from that, it became a mere battle of ugly appetites. Looking about him, he honoured his own past, and mourned for it. After all, there was good in the old ways.

His eyes, making the round of the room—done over by Dallas with English mezzotints, Chippendale cabinets, bits of chosen blue-and-white and pleasantly shaded electric lamps—came back to the old Eastlake writing-table that he had never been willing to banish, and to his first photograph of May, which still kept its place beside his inkstand.

There she was, tall, round-bosomed and willowy, in her starched muslin and flapping Leghorn, as he had seen her under the orange-trees in the Mission garden. And as he had seen her that day, so she had remained; never quite at the same height, yet never far below it: generous, faithful, unwearied; but so lacking in imagination, so incapable of growth, that the world of her youth had fallen into pieces and rebuilt itself without her ever being conscious of the change. This hard bright blindness had kept her immediate horizon apparently unaltered. Her incapacity to recognise change made her children conceal their views from her as Archer concealed his; there had been, from the first, a joint pretence of sameness, a kind of innocent family hypocrisy, in which father and children had unconsciously collaborated. And she had died thinking the world a good place, full of loving and harmonious households like her own, and resigned to leave it because she was convinced that, whatever happened, Newland would continue to inculcate in Dallas the same principles and prejudices which had shaped his parents' lives, and that Dallas in turn (when Newland followed her) would transmit the sacred trust to little Bill. And of Mary she was sure as of her own self. So, having snatched little Bill from the grave, and given her life in the effort, she went contentedly to her place in the Archer vault in St. Mark's, where Mrs. Archer already lay safe from the terrifying "trend" which her daughter-in-law had never even become aware of.

Opposite May's portrait stood one of her daughter. Mary Chivers was as tall and fair as her mother, but large-waisted, flat-chested and slightly slouching, as the altered fashion required. Mary Chivers's mighty feats of athleticism could not have been performed with the twenty-inch waist that May Archer's azure sash so easily spanned. And the difference seemed symbolic; the mother's life had been as closely girt as her figure. Mary, who was no less conventional, and no more intelligent, yet led a larger life and held more tolerant views. There was good in the new order too.

The telephone clicked, and Archer, turning from the photographs, unhooked the transmitter at his elbow. How far they were from the days when the legs of the brass-buttoned messenger boy had been New York's only means of quick communication!

"Chicago wants you."

Ah—it must be a long-distance from Dallas, who had been sent to Chicago by his firm to talk over the plan of the Lakeside palace they were to build for a young millionaire with ideas. The firm always sent Dallas on such errands.

"Hallo, Dad—Yes: Dallas. I say—how do you feel about sailing on Wednesday? Mauretania: Yes, next Wednesday as ever is. Our client wants me to look at some Italian gardens before we settle anything, and has asked me to nip over on the next boat. I've got to be back on the first of June —" the voice broke into a joyful conscious laugh—"so we must look alive. I say, Dad, I want your help: do come."

Dallas seemed to be speaking in the room: the voice was as near by and natural as if he had been lounging in his favourite arm-chair by the fire. The fact would not ordinarily have surprised Archer, for long-distance telephoning had become as much a matter of course as electric lighting and five-day Atlantic voyages. But the laugh did startle him; it still seemed wonderful that across all those miles and miles of country—forest, river, mountain, prairie, roaring cities and busy indifferent millions—Dallas's laugh should be able to say: "Of course, whatever happens, I must get back on the first, because Fanny Beaufort and I are to be married on the fifth."

The voice began again: "Think it over? No, sir: not a minute. You've got to say yes now. Why not, I'd like to know? If you can allege a single reason—No; I knew it. Then it's a go, eh? Because I count on you to ring up the Cunard office first thing tomorrow; and you'd better book a return on a boat from Marseilles. I say, Dad; it'll be our last time together, in this kind of way—. Oh, good! I knew you would."

Chicago rang off, and Archer rose and began to pace up and down the room.

It would be their last time together in this kind of way: the boy was right. They would have lots of other "times" after Dallas's marriage, his father was sure; for the two were born comrades, and Fanny Beaufort, whatever one might think of her, did not seem likely to interfere with their intimacy. On the contrary, from what he had seen of her, he thought she would be naturally included in it. Still, change was change, and differences were differences, and much as he felt himself drawn toward his future daughter-in-law, it was tempting to seize this last chance of being alone with his boy.

There was no reason why he should not seize it, except the profound one that he had lost the habit of travel. May had disliked to move except for valid reasons, such as taking the children to the sea or in the mountains: she could imagine no other motive for leaving the house in Thirty-ninth Street or their comfortable quarters at the Wellands' in Newport. After Dallas had taken his degree she had thought it her duty to travel for six months; and the whole family had made the old-fashioned tour through England, Switzerland and Italy. Their time being limited (no one knew why) they had omitted France. Archer remembered Dallas's wrath at being asked to contemplate Mont Blanc instead of Rheims and Chartres. But Mary and Bill wanted mountain-climbing, and had already yawned their way in Dallas's wake through the English cathedrals; and May, always fair to her children, had insisted on holding the balance evenly between their athletic and artistic proclivities. She had indeed proposed that her husband should go to Paris for a fortnight, and join them on the Italian lakes after they had "done" Switzerland; but Archer had declined. "We'll stick together," he said; and May's face had brightened at his setting such a good example to Dallas.

Since her death, nearly two years before, there had been no reason for his continuing in the same routine. His children had urged him to travel: Mary Chivers had felt sure it would do him good to go abroad and "see the galleries." The very mysteriousness of such a cure made her the more confident of its efficacy. But Archer had found himself held fast by habit, by memories, by a sudden startled shrinking from new things.

Now, as he reviewed his past, he saw into what a deep rut he had sunk. The worst of doing one's duty was that it apparently unfitted one for doing anything else. At least that was the view that the men of his generation had taken. The trenchant divisions between right and wrong, honest and dishonest, respectable and the reverse, had left so little scope for the unforeseen. There are moments when a man's imagination, so easily subdued to what it lives in, suddenly rises above its daily level, and surveys the long windings of destiny. Archer hung there and wondered....

What was left of the little world he had grown up in, and whose standards had bent and bound him? He remembered a sneering prophecy of poor Lawrence Lefferts's, uttered years ago in that very room: "If things go on at this rate, our children will be marrying Beaufort's bastards."

It was just what Archer's eldest son, the pride of his life, was doing; and nobody wondered or reproved. Even the boy's Aunt Janey, who still looked so exactly as she used to in her elderly youth, had taken her mother's emeralds and seed-pearls out of their pink cotton-wool, and carried them with her own twitching hands to the future bride; and Fanny Beaufort, instead of looking disappointed at not receiving a "set" from a Paris jeweller, had exclaimed at their old-fashioned beauty, and declared that when she wore them she should feel like an Isabey miniature.

Fanny Beaufort, who had appeared in New York at eighteen, after the death of her parents, had won its heart much as Madame Olenska had won it thirty years earlier; only instead of being distrustful and afraid of her, society took her joyfully for granted. She was pretty, amusing and accomplished: what more did any one want? Nobody was narrow-minded enough to rake up against her the half-forgotten facts of her father's past and her own origin. Only the older people remembered so obscure an incident in the business life of New York as Beaufort's failure, or the fact that after his wife's death he had been quietly married to the notorious Fanny Ring, and had left the country with his new wife, and a little girl who inherited her beauty. He was subsequently heard of in Constantinople, then in Russia; and a dozen years later American travellers were handsomely entertained by him in Buenos Ayres, where he represented a large insurance agency. He and his wife died there in the odour of prosperity; and one day their orphaned daughter had appeared in New York in charge of May Archer's sister-in-law, Mrs. Jack Welland, whose husband had been appointed the girl's guardian. The fact threw her into almost cousinly relationship with Newland Archer's children, and nobody was surprised when Dallas's engagement was announced.

Nothing could more dearly give the measure of the distance that the world had travelled. People nowadays were too busy—busy with reforms and "movements," with fads and fetishes and frivolities—to bother much about their neighbours. And of what account was anybody's past, in the huge kaleidoscope where all the social atoms spun around on the same plane?

Newland Archer, looking out of his hotel window at the stately gaiety of the Paris streets, felt his heart beating with the confusion and eagerness of youth.

It was long since it had thus plunged and reared under his widening waistcoat, leaving him, the next minute, with an empty breast and hot temples. He wondered if it was thus that his son's conducted itself in the presence of Miss Fanny Beaufort—and decided that it was not. "It functions as actively, no doubt, but the rhythm is different," he reflected, recalling the cool composure with which the young man had announced his engagement, and taken for granted that his family would approve.

"The difference is that these young people take it for granted that they're going to get whatever they want, and that we almost always took it for granted that we shouldn't. Only, I wonder—the thing one's so certain of in advance: can it ever make one's heart beat as wildly?"

It was the day after their arrival in Paris, and the spring sunshine held Archer in his open window, above the wide silvery prospect of the Place Vendome. One of the things he had stipulated—almost the only one—when he had agreed to come abroad with Dallas, was that, in Paris, he shouldn't be made to go to one of the newfangled "palaces."

"Oh, all right—of course," Dallas good-naturedly agreed. "I'll take you to some jolly old-fashioned place—the Bristol say —" leaving his father speechless at hearing that the century-long home of kings and emperors was now spoken of as an old-fashioned inn, where one went for its quaint inconveniences and lingering local colour.

Archer had pictured often enough, in the first impatient years, the scene of his return to Paris; then the personal vision had faded, and he had simply tried to see the city as the setting of Madame Olenska's life. Sitting alone at night in his library, after the household had gone to bed, he had evoked the radiant outbreak of spring down the avenues of horse-chestnuts, the flowers and statues in the public gardens, the whiff of lilacs from the flower-carts, the majestic roll of the river under the great bridges, and the life of art and study and pleasure that filled each mighty artery to bursting. Now the spectacle was before him in its glory, and as he looked out on it he felt shy, old-fashioned, inadequate: a mere grey speck of a man compared with the ruthless magnificent fellow he had dreamed of being....

Dallas's hand came down cheerily on his shoulder. "Hullo, father: this is something like, isn't it?" They stood for a while looking out in silence, and then the young man continued: "By the way, I've got a message for you: the Countess Olenska expects us both at half-past five."

He said it lightly, carelessly, as he might have imparted any casual item of information, such as the hour at which their train was to leave for Florence the next evening. Archer looked at him, and thought he saw in his gay young eyes a gleam of his great-grandmother Mingott's malice.

"Oh, didn't I tell you?" Dallas pursued. "Fanny made me swear to do three things while I was in Paris: get her the score of the last Debussy songs, go to the Grand-Guignol and see Madame Olenska. You know she was awfully good to Fanny when Mr. Beaufort sent her over from Buenos Ayres to the Assomption. Fanny hadn't any friends in Paris, and Madame Olenska used to be kind to her and trot her about on holidays. I believe she was a great friend of the first Mrs. Beaufort's. And she's our cousin, of course. So I rang her up this morning, before I went out, and told her you and I were here for two days and wanted to see her."

Archer continued to stare at him. "You told her I was here?"

"Of course—why not?" Dallas's eye brows went up whimsically. Then, getting no answer, he slipped his arm through his father's with a confidential pressure.

"I say, father: what was she like?"

Archer felt his colour rise under his son's unabashed gaze. "Come, own up: you and she were great pals, weren't you? Wasn't she most awfully lovely?"

"Lovely? I don't know. She was different."

"Ah—there you have it! That's what it always comes to, doesn't it? When she comes, *she's different*—and one doesn't know why. It's exactly what I feel about Fanny."

His father drew back a step, releasing his arm. "About Fanny? But, my dear fellow—I should hope so! Only I don't see —"

"Dash it, Dad, don't be prehistoric! Wasn't she—once—your Fanny?"

Dallas belonged body and soul to the new generation. He was the first-born of Newland and May Archer, yet it had never been possible to inculcate in him even the rudiments of reserve. "What's the use of making mysteries? It only makes people want to nose 'em out," he always objected when enjoined to discretion. But Archer, meeting his eyes, saw the filial light under their banter.

"My Fanny?"

"Well, the woman you'd have chucked everything for: only you didn't," continued his surprising son.

"I didn't," echoed Archer with a kind of solemnity.

"No: you date, you see, dear old boy. But mother said —"

"Your mother?"

"Yes: the day before she died. It was when she sent for me alone—you remember? She said she knew we were safe with you, and always would be, because once, when she asked you to, you'd given up the thing you most wanted."

Archer received this strange communication in silence. His eyes remained unseeingly fixed on the thronged sunlit square below the window. At length he said in a low voice: "She never asked me."

"No. I forgot. You never did ask each other anything, did you? And you never told each other anything. You just sat and watched each other, and guessed at what was going on underneath. A deaf-and-dumb asylum, in fact! Well, I back your generation for knowing more about each other's private thoughts than we ever have time to find out about our own.—I say, Dad," Dallas broke off, "you're not angry with me? If you are, let's make it up and go and lunch at Henri's. I've got to rush out to Versailles afterward."

Archer did not accompany his son to Versailles. He preferred to spend the afternoon in solitary roamings through Paris. He had to deal all at once with the packed regrets and stifled memories of an inarticulate lifetime.

After a little while he did not regret Dallas's indiscretion. It seemed to take an iron band from his heart to know that, after all, some one had guessed and pitied.... And that it should have been his wife moved him indescribably. Dallas, for all his affectionate insight, would not have understood that. To the boy, no doubt, the episode was only a pathetic instance of vain frustration, of wasted forces. But was it really no more? For a long time Archer sat on a bench in the Champs Elysees and wondered, while the stream of life rolled by....

A few streets away, a few hours away, Ellen Olenska waited. She had never gone back to her husband, and when he had died, some years before, she had made no change in her way of living. There was nothing now to keep her and Archer apart—and that afternoon he was to see her.

He got up and walked across the Place de la Concorde and the Tuileries gardens to the Louvre. She had once told him that she often went there, and he had a fancy to spend the intervening time in a place where he could think of her as perhaps having lately been. For an hour or more he wandered from gallery to gallery through the dazzle of afternoon light, and one by one the pictures burst on him in their half-forgotten splendour, filling his soul with the long echoes of beauty. After all, his life had been too starved....

Suddenly, before an effulgent Titian, he found himself saying: "But I'm only fifty-seven —" and then he turned away. For such summer dreams it was too late; but surely not for a quiet harvest of friendship, of comradeship, in the blessed hush of her nearness.

He went back to the hotel, where he and Dallas were to meet; and together they walked again across the Place de la Concorde and over the bridge that leads to the Chamber of Deputies.

Dallas, unconscious of what was going on in his father's mind, was talking excitedly and abundantly of Versailles. He had had but one previous glimpse of it, during a holiday trip in which he had tried to pack all the sights he had been deprived of when he had had to go with the family to Switzerland; and tumultuous enthusiasm and cock-sure criticism tripped each other up on his lips.

As Archer listened, his sense of inadequacy and inexpressiveness increased. The boy was not insensitive, he knew; but he had the facility and self-confidence that came of looking at fate not as a master but as an equal. "That's it: they feel equal to things—they know their way about," he mused, thinking of his son as the spokesman of the new generation which had swept away all the old landmarks, and with them the sign-posts and the danger-signal.

Suddenly Dallas stopped short, grasping his father's arm. "Oh, by Jove," he exclaimed.

They had come out into the great tree-planted space before the Invalides. The dome of Mansart floated ethereally above the budding trees and the long grey front of the building: drawing up into itself all the rays of afternoon light, it hung there like the visible symbol of the race's glory.

Archer knew that Madame Olenska lived in a square near one of the avenues radiating from the Invalides; and he had pictured the quarter as quiet and almost obscure, forgetting the central splendour that lit it up. Now, by some queer process of association, that golden light became for him the pervading illumination in which she lived. For nearly thirty years, her life—of which he knew so strangely little—had been spent in this rich atmosphere that he already felt to be too dense and yet too stimulating for his lungs. He thought of the theatres she must have been to, the pictures she must have looked at, the sober and splendid old houses she must have frequented, the people she must have talked with, the incessant stir of ideas, curiosities, images and associations thrown out by an intensely social race in a setting of immemorial manners; and suddenly he remembered the young Frenchman who had once said to him: "Ah, good conversation—there is nothing like it, is there?"

Archer had not seen M. Riviere, or heard of him, for nearly thirty years; and that fact gave the measure of his ignorance of Madame Olenska's existence. More than half a lifetime divided them, and she had spent the long interval among people he did not know, in a society he but faintly guessed at, in conditions he would never wholly understand. During that time he had been living with his youthful memory of her; but she had doubtless had other and more tangible companionship. Perhaps she too had kept her memory of him as something apart; but if she had, it must have been like a relic in a small dim chapel, where there was not time to pray every day....

They had crossed the Place des Invalides, and were walking down one of the thoroughfares flanking the building. It was a quiet quarter, after all, in spite of its splendour and its history; and the fact gave one an idea of the riches Paris had to draw on, since such scenes as this were left to the few and the indifferent.

The day was fading into a soft sun-shot haze, pricked here and there by a yellow electric light, and passers were rare in the little square into which they had turned. Dallas stopped again, and looked up.

"It must be here," he said, slipping his arm through his father's with a movement from which Archer's shyness did not shrink; and they stood together looking up at the house.

It was a modern building, without distinctive character, but many-windowed, and pleasantly balconied up its wide cream-coloured front.

On one of the upper balconies, which hung well above the rounded tops of the horse-chestnuts in the square, the awnings were still lowered, as though the sun had just left it.

"I wonder which floor—?" Dallas conjectured; and moving toward the porte-cochere he put his head into the porter's lodge, and came back to say: "The fifth. It must be the one with the awnings."

Archer remained motionless, gazing at the upper windows as if the end of their pilgrimage had been attained.

"I say, you know, it's nearly six," his son at length reminded him.

The father glanced away at an empty bench under the trees.

"I believe I'll sit there a moment," he said.

"Why—aren't you well?" his son exclaimed.

"Oh, perfectly. But I should like you, please, to go up without me."

Dallas paused before him, visibly bewildered. "But, I say, Dad: do you mean you won't come up at all?"

"I don't know," said Archer slowly.

"If you don't she won't understand."

"Go, my boy; perhaps I shall follow you."

Dallas gave him a long look through the twilight.

"But what on earth shall I say?"

"My dear fellow, don't you always know what to say?" his father rejoined with a smile.

"Very well. I shall say you're old-fashioned, and prefer walking up the five flights because you don't like lifts."

His father smiled again. "Say I'm old-fashioned: that's enough."

Dallas looked at him again, and then, with an incredulous gesture, passed out of sight under the vaulted doorway.

Archer sat down on the bench and continued to gaze at the awninged balcony. He calculated the time it would take his son to be carried up in the lift to the fifth floor, to ring the bell, and be admitted to the hall, and then ushered into the drawing-room. He pictured Dallas entering that room with his quick assured step and his delightful smile, and wondered if the people were right who said that his boy "took after him."

Then he tried to see the persons already in the room—for probably at that sociable hour there would be more than one—and among them a dark lady, pale and dark, who would look up quickly, half rise, and hold out a long thin hand with three rings on it.... He thought she would be sitting in a sofa-corner near the fire, with azaleas banked behind her on a table.

"It's more real to me here than if I went up," he suddenly heard himself say; and the fear lest that last shadow of reality should lose its edge kept him rooted to his seat as the minutes succeeded each other.

He sat for a long time on the bench in the thickening dusk, his eyes never turning from the balcony. At length a light shone through the windows, and a moment later a man-servant came out on the balcony, drew up the awnings, and closed the shutters.

At that, as if it had been the signal he waited for, Newland Archer got up slowly and walked back alone to his hotel.